Praise for

DARK AGE

"[Pierce] Brown's plots are like a depth charge of nitromethane dropped in a bucket of gasoline. His pacing is 100 percent him standing over it all with a lit match and a smile, waiting for us to dare him to drop it."

—NPR

"An epic story of rebellion, social unrest, and sacrifice."

—*Orlando Sentinel*

"*Dark Age* proves that Brown has truly become a master. . . . Pierce Brown's ability to craft a riveting story with amazing character development [has] grown far beyond the original Red Rising trilogy. . . . With *Dark Age* he graduates to a whole new level, and let's just say that I'm both excited and scared to see some of these threads come together."

—*The Geekiary*

"Much like A Song of Ice and Fire's George R. R. Martin, Brown is an author who is interested in exploring the consequences of his protagonist's actions. Revolution doesn't come without a price and no one can stay a hero forever. . . . *Dark Age* continues the trend of compelling characters, fast plotting, action, and the feeling that no one is truly safe and no one is who you think they are."

—*The Mary Sue*

Praise for

IRON GOLD

"Complex, layered . . . mature science fiction existing within the frame of blazing space opera . . . done in a style [that] borders on Shakespearean."

—NPR

"A thoughtful blend of action, intrigue, and prosaic human drama."

—*Publishers Weekly* (starred review)

"The gritty action and emotional punches will thrill fans eagerly awaiting more from [Pierce] Brown."

—*Library Journal*

"This is one you absolutely will have to read."

—*The BiblioSanctum*

"It's not a Red Rising book unless you feel your very existence is being threatened while reading it. *Iron Gold* certainly fits that bill, so Howlers: brace yourselves and pray for your faves."

—*Read at Midnight*

"The mix of political intrigue, action and thematic journeys elevate this book from a simple sci-fi adventure into something more thought-provoking and rewarding."

—*Flickering Myth*

"Pierce Brown's *Iron Gold* ends up being perhaps his best effort since *Red Rising,* and for a book that expands a trilogy, that's an impressive feat."

—*Culturess*

Praise for

GOLDEN SON

"Gripping . . . On virtually every level, this is a sequel that hates sequels—a perfect fit for a hero who already defies the tropes. [Grade:] A"

—*Entertainment Weekly*

"[Pierce] Brown writes layered, flawed characters . . . but plot is his most breathtaking strength. . . . Every action seems to flow into the next."

—NPR

"In a word, *Golden Son* is stunning. Among science-fiction fans, it should be a shoo-in for book of the year."

—Tor.com

"The stakes are even higher than they were in *Red Rising,* and the twists and turns of the story are every bit as exciting. The jaw-dropper of an ending will leave readers hungry for the conclusion to Brown's wholly original, completely thrilling saga."

—*Booklist* (starred review)

"Stirring . . . Comparisons to *The Hunger Games* and *Game of Thrones* series are inevitable, for this tale has elements of both."

—*Kirkus Reviews*

Praise for

RED RISING

"[A] spectacular adventure . . . one heart-pounding ride . . . Pierce Brown's dizzyingly good debut novel evokes *The Hunger Games, Lord of the Flies,* and *Ender's Game.* . . . [*Red Rising*] has everything it needs to become meteoric."

—*Entertainment Weekly*

"[A] top-notch debut novel . . . *Red Rising* ascends above a crowded dystopian field."

—*USA Today*

"Reminiscent of . . . Suzanne Collins's *The Hunger Games* . . . [*Red Rising*] will captivate readers and leave them wanting more."

—*Library Journal* (starred review)

"A story of vengeance, warfare and the quest for power . . . reminiscent of *The Hunger Games* and *Game of Thrones.*"

—*Kirkus Reviews*

"Fast-paced, gripping, well-written—the sort of book you cannot put down. I am already on the lookout for the next one."

—TERRY BROOKS, *New York Times* bestselling author of *The Sword of Shannara*

"[A] great debut . . . The author gathers a spread of elements together in much the same way George R. R. Martin does."

—Tor.com

"Ender, Katniss, and now Darrow: Pierce Brown's empire-crushing debut is a sprawling vision."

—SCOTT SIGLER, *New York Times* bestselling author of *Pandemic*

BY PIERCE BROWN

Red Rising

Golden Son

Morning Star

Iron Gold

Dark Age

DARK AGE

DARK AGE

PIERCE BROWN

DEL REY
NEW YORK

2020 Del Rey Trade Paperback Edition

Published in the United States by Del Rey, an imprint of Random House, a division of Penguin Random House LLC, New York.

Del Rey and the House colophon are registered trademarks of Penguin Random House LLC.

Originally published in hardcover in the United States by Del Rey, an imprint of Random House, a division of Penguin Random House LLC, in 2019.

ISBN 9780425285961
Ebook ISBN 970425285954

Printed in the United States of America on acid-free paper

randomhousebooks.com

2 4 6 8 9 7 5 3

Book design by Caroline Cunningham

For Lily

THE PLΛΠET MERCURY
CONTIΠEΠT OF HELIOS

In the eleventh year of the Solar War

Commissioned by Sovereign Virginia au
Augustus, 754 PCE

O - - CITIES   ✳ - - BΛSES

BΛY OF
SIREΠS

CALIBΛΠ
SEΛ

SYCORAX SEA
KAIKOS
PRIAPOS
PAN
PETASOS PENINSULA
"THE CHILDREN"
ARABOS
KYDON
PLAINS OF
CADUCEUS
TYCHE
RED REACH
ANGELIA
WASTE OF
LADON
EREBOS
ELEUSIS
HESPERIDES
MOUNTAINS
KERYX
HELIOPOLIS
POLYBOS

DRAMATIS PERSONAE

THE SOLAR REPUBLIC

DARROW OF LYKOS/THE REAPER   Former ArchImperator of the Solar Republic, husband to Virginia, a Red

VIRGINIA AU AUGUSTUS/MUSTANG   Reigning Sovereign of the Solar Republic, wife to Darrow, Primus of House Augustus, sister to the Jackal of Mars, a Gold

PAX   Son of Darrow and Virginia, a Gold

KIERAN OF LYKOS   Brother to Darrow, Howler, a Red

RHONNA   Niece of Darrow, daughter of Kieran, lancer, Pup Two, a Red

DEANNA   Mother to Darrow, a Red

SEVRO AU BARCA/THE GOBLIN   Imperator of the Republic, husband to Victra, Howler, a Gold

VICTRA AU BARCA   Wife to Sevro, neé Victra au Julii, a Gold

ELECTRA AU BARCA   Daughter of Sevro and Victra, a Gold

DANCER/SENATOR O'FARAN   Senator, former Sons of Ares lieutenant, Tribune of the Red bloc, a Red

KAVAX AU TELEMANUS   Primus of House Telemanus, client of House Augustus, a Gold

NIOBE AU TELEMANUS   Wife to Kavax, client of House Augustus, a Gold

DAXO AU TELEMANUS   Heir of House Telemanus, son of Kavax and Niobe, senator, Tribune of the Gold bloc, a Gold

THRAXA AU TELEMANUS   Praetor of the Free Legions, daughter of Kavax and Niobe, Howler, a Gold

ALEXANDAR AU ARCOS   Eldest grandson of Lorn au Arcos, heir to House Arcos, allied to House Augustus, lancer, Pup One, a Gold

CADUS HARNASSUS   Imperator of the Republic, second in command of the Free Legions, an Orange

ORION XE AQUARII   Navarch of the Republic, Imperator of the White Fleet, a Blue

COLLOWAY XE CHAR   A pilot, reigning kill-leader of the Republic Navy, Howler, a Blue

GLIRASTES THE MASTER MAKER   Architect and inventor, an Orange

HOLIDAY TI NAKAMURA   Dux of Virginia's Lionguard, sister to Trigg, client of House Augustus, Centurion of the Pegasus Legion, a Gray

QUICKSILVER/REGULUS AG SUN   Richest man in the Republic, head of Sun Industries, a Silver

PUBLIUS CU CARAVAL   Tribune of the Copper bloc, senator, a Copper

THEODORA   Leader of the Splinter operatives, client of House Augustus, a Rose Pink

ZAN   ArchImperator of the Republic following Darrow's removal, commander of Luna's defense fleet, a Blue

CLOWN   Howler, client of House Barca, a Gold

PEBBLE   Howler, client of House Barca, a Gold

MIN-MIN   Howler, sniper and munitions expert, client of House Barca, a Red

SCREWFACE   Howler, client of House Augustus, a Gold

MARBLES   Howler, hacker, a Green

TONGUELESS   Former prisoner at Deepgrave, an Obsidian

FELIX AU DAAN   Bodyguard to Darrow, client of House Augustus, a Gold

THE SOCIETY

ATALANTIA AU GRIMMUS Dictator of the Society, daughter of the Ash Lord Magnus au Grimmus, sister to Aja and Moira, former client of House Lune, a Gold

LYSANDER AU LUNE Grandson of former Sovereign Octavia, heir to House Lune, former patron of House Grimmus, a Gold

ATLAS AU RAA/THE FEAR KNIGHT Brother to Romulus au Raa, Legate of the Zero Legion ("the Gorgons"), former ward of House Lune, client of House Grimmus, a Gold

AJAX/THE STORM KNIGHT Son of Aja au Grimmus and Atlas au Raa, heir of House Grimmus, Legate of the Iron Leopards, a Gold

KALINDORA AU SAN/THE LOVE KNIGHT Olympic Knight, aunt to Alexandar au Arcos, client of House Grimmus, a Gold

JULIA AU BELLONA Cassius's estranged mother and Darrow's enemy, Primus of the House Bellona remnant, a Gold

SCORPIO AU VOTUM Primus of House Votum (the metal mining magnates and builders of Mercury), a Gold

CICERO AU VOTUM Heir to House Votum, son of Scorpio, Legate of the Scorpion Legion, a Gold

ASMODEUS AU CARTHII Primus of House Carthii (the shipbuilders of Venus), a Gold

RHONE TI FLAVINIUS Lunese subPraetor, former second officer of the XIII Dracones Praetorian Guard under Aja, a Gray

SENECA AU CERN Dux of Ajax, Centurion of the Iron Leopards, a Gold

MAGNUS AU GRIMMUS/THE ASH LORD Former ArchImperator to Octavia au Lune, the Burner of Rhea, a Gold, killed by the Howlers and Apollonius au Valii-Rath

OCTAVIA AU LUNE Former Sovereign of the Society, grandmother to Lysander, a Gold, killed by Darrow

AJA AU GRIMMUS   Daughter of Ash Lord Magnus au Grimmus, a Gold, killed by Sevro

MOIRA AU GRIMMUS   Daughter of Ash Lord Magnus au Grimmus, a Gold, killed by Darrow

THE RIM DOMINION

DIDO AU RAA   Co-consul of the Rim Dominion, wife to former Sovereign of the Rim Dominion Romulus au Raa, née Dido au Saud, a Gold

DIOMEDES AU RAA/THE STORM KNIGHT   Son of Romulus and Dido, Taxiarchos of the Lightning Phalanx, a Gold

SERAPHINA AU RAA   Daughter of Romulus and Dido, Lochagos of the Eleventh Dust Walkers, a Gold

HELIOS AU LUX   Co-consul of the Rim Dominion, with Dido, a Gold

ROMULUS AU RAA/THE LORD OF THE DUST   Former Primus of House Raa, former Sovereign of the Rim Dominion, a Gold, killed by ceremonial suicide

THE OBSIDIAN

SEFI THE QUIET   Queen of the Obsidian, leader of the Valkyrie, sister to Ragnar Volarus, an Obsidian

VALDIR THE UNSHORN   Warlord and royal concubine of Sefi, an Obsidian

OZGARD   Shaman of the Firebones, an Obsidian

FREIHILD   Skuggi spirit warrior, an Obsidian

GUDKIND   Skuggi spirit warrior, an Obsidian

XENOPHON   Advisor to Sefi, a White *logos*

RAGNAR VOLARUS   Former leader of the Obsidian, Howler, an Obsidian, killed by Aja

OTHER CHARACTERS

EPHRAIM TI HORN Freelancer, former member of the Sons of Ares, husband to Trigg ti Nakamura, a Gray

VOLGA FJORGAN Freelancer, colleague of Ephraim, an Obsidian

APOLLONIUS AU VALII-RATH/THE MINOTAUR Heir to House Valii-Rath, verbose, a Gold

THE DUKE OF HANDS Syndicate operative, master thief, a Rose Pink

LYRIA OF LAGALOS Gamma from Mars, client of House Telemanus, a Red

LIAM Nephew of Lyria, client of House Telemanus, a Red

HARMONY Leader of the Red Hand, former Sons of Ares lieutenant, a Red

PYTHA Pilot, companion to Cassius and Lysander, a Blue

FIGMENT Freelancer, a Brown

FITCHNER AU BARCA/ARES Former leader of the Sons of Ares, a Gold, killed by Cassius au Bellona

THE SOVEREIGN

"CITIZENS OF THE SOLAR REPUBLIC, this is your Sovereign."
I stare half blind into a firing squad of fly-eyed cameras. Out the viewport behind my stage, battle stations and ships of war float beyond the upper atmosphere of Luna.

Eight billion eyes watch me.

"On Friday evening last, the third day of the Mensis Martius, I received a brief indicating that a large-scale Society military operation was under way in the orbit of Mercury. The largest in materiel and manpower since the Battle of Mars, five long years ago.

"We are responsible for this crisis. Lured by the false promises of an enemy plenipotentiary, we allowed our resolve to weaken. We allowed ourselves to believe in the better virtues of our enemy, and that peace was possible with tyrants.

"That lie, seductive though it was, has been exposed as a cruel machination of statecraft designed, perpetrated, and executed by the newly appointed Dictator of the Society remnant, Atalantia au Grimmus—daughter of the Ash Lord. Under her spell, we compromised with the agents of tyranny. We turned on our greatest general, the sword who broke the chains of bondage, and demanded he accept a peace he knew to be a lie.

"When he did not, we cried *Traitor! Tyrant! Warmonger!* In fear of him, we recalled the Home Guard elements of the White Fleet from Mercury back to Luna. We left Imperator Aquarii at half strength, exposed, vulnerable. Now, her fleet, the fleet which freed all our homes, floats in ruins. Two hundred of *your* ships of war destroyed. Thousands of *your* sailors killed. Millions of *your* brothers and sisters marooned upon a hostile sphere. Quadrillions of *your* wealth squandered. Not by virtue of enemy arms, but by the squabbling of *your* Senate.

"I have heard it said in these last months, in the halls of the New Forum, on the streets of Hyperion, on the news channels across our Republic, that we should abandon these sons and daughters of liberty, these Free Legions. I have heard them called, in public, without shame, 'the Lost Legions.' Written off by you, despite the courage they have summoned, the endurance they have shown, the horrors they have suffered *for you*. Written off because we fear to part with our ships will invite invasion of our homeworlds. Because we fear to once again see Society iron over our skies. Because we fear to risk the comforts and freedoms the men and women of the Free Legions purchased for us with their blood . . .

"I will tell you what I fear. I fear time has diluted our dream! I fear that in our comfort, we believe liberty to be self-fulfilling!" I lean forward. "I fear that the meekness of our resolve, the bickering and backbiting on which we have so decadently glutted ourselves, will rob us of the unity of will that moved the world forward to a fairer place, where respect for justice and freedom has found a foothold for the first time in a millennium.

"I fear that in this disunity we will sink back into the hideous epoch from which we escaped, and that the new dark age will be crueler, more sinister, and more protracted by the malice which we have awoken in our enemies.

"I call upon you, the People of the Republic, to stand united. To beseech your senators to reject fear. To reject this torpor of self-interest. To not quiver in primal trepidation at the thought of invasion, to not let your senators hoard *your* wealth for themselves and hide behind *your* ships of war, but to summon the more wrathful angels of their spirits and send forth the might of the Republic to scourge the engines of tyranny and oppression from the Mercurian sky and rescue our Free Legions."

At that moment, three hundred eighty-four thousand kilometers from my heart, in orbit one thousand kilometers above the wayward continent of South Pacifica, projectiles skinned with Sun Industries stealth polymer race into the void at 320,000 kilometers per hour toward Mercury, ferrying not death, but supplies, radiation medicine, machines of war, and, if my husband is alive, a message of hope.

You have not been abandoned. I will come for you.

Until then, endure, my love. Endure.

PROLOGUE

DARROW

Blood Red

A GRAVEYARD OF REPUBLIC WARSHIPS floats in the shadow of Mercury.

Of the triumphant White Fleet that liberated Luna, Earth, and Mars, nothing remains but twisted shards and blackened hollows. Shattered by the might of the Ash Armada, the broken ships spin in orbit around the planet they liberated only months before. No longer filled with Martian sailors and legionnaires loyal to Eo's dream, their cold halls are naked to vacuum and populated only by the dead.

This is the last laugh of the Ash Lord, and the debut of his heir.

While I burned the old warlord to death in his bed on Venus with Apollonius and Sevro, his daughter Atalantia stepped out from his shadow to take up his office of Dictator. She slipped the greater part of their armada away from Venus and used the sun's sensor-distorting radiation to ambush the White Fleet in orbit over Mercury.

Orion, my fleet's commander and the greatest naval tactician in the Republic, never saw them coming. It was a massacre, and I was three weeks too late to stop it. The frantic Mayday calls of my friends tortured me as I crossed the void, slipping farther and farther away from my son and wife toward bedlam.

The White Fleet may be gone, but the Free Legions they ferried to

Mercury are not dead yet. Soon I will join them on the surface of Mercury, but first I have work to do.

It would be easier with Sevro. Everything violent is.

My breath rasps in my vacuum-proof suit as I traverse the graveyard. My magnetic boots land silently along the broken spine of a Republic dreadnought, and I peer into a great fissure in the hull to check on the progress of my lancer. The wound in the hull is thirty decks deep. Jetsam floats in the darkness—bits of metal, mattresses, coffeepots, frozen globes of machine fluid, and severed limbs. No sign of Alexandar.

The rigid corpse of a sailor in a mechanic's kit drifts upward feet-first. His legs have been congealed into a single crooked stump from the heat of a particle blast. His mouth is locked in a silent scream, as if to ask, "Where were you when the enemy came? Where was the Reaper I swore to follow?"

He was deceived by his enemies, by his allies, by himself.

While the Republic Senate fooled itself into believing peace could be made with fascist warlords, I pretended killing the Ash Lord would end war in our time. That I held the key to unlocking a future where I could put down the slingBlade and return to my child and wife to be a father and a husband. My desperation let me believe that lie. The Senate's naïveté let them believe Atalantia's. But I know the truth now.

War *is* our time. Sevro thought he could escape it. I thought I could end it. But our enemy is like the Hydra. Cut off one head, two more sprout. They will not sue for peace. They will not surrender. Their heart must be excised, their will to fight ground to the finest dust.

Only then will there be peace.

Lights flicker in the chasm beneath my feet. Several minutes later, a Gold in an EVA suit drifts upward to set down with me on the hull. For fear of enemy sensors, he puts his faceplate to mine to give his sound waves a medium.

"Reactor is primed and ready for necromancy."

"Well done, Alexandar."

He nods stoically.

The young soldier is no longer the callow, insecure youth who entered my service as a lancer four years ago. After war, most men shrink. Some from the rending of flesh. Some from the loss of fellows. Some from the loss of autonomy. But most in shame at discovering their own impotence. Confronted with horror, their dreams of destiny crumple. Only a cursed few relish the dark thrill in discovering they are natural-born killers.

Alexandar is a killer. He has proven himself the worthy heir to the legacy of his grandfather Lorn au Arcos. And I have begun to wonder if he will inherit my burden. He alone held back the tide atop the Ash Lord's spire when Thraxa, Sevro, and I had been knocked to our knees. It woke the hunger in him. Now, he craves revenge on Atalantia for the murder of our fleet.

I miss that purity of purpose.

What was it that Lorn said again? "The old rage in colder ways, for they alone decide how to spend the young."

How many more must I spend? What is Alexandar's life worth? What is mine worth? As if to find the answer, I glance to my right. Past the hull of the drifting dreadnought, the eastern rim of Mercury throbs like a molten scythe.

The planet is barely larger than Luna, but this close it seems a giant. The shadows of a Society minesweeper pass over its face. It searches for the atomic mines Orion left in orbit to cover our army's frantic retreat after Atalantia's ambush. Few mines remain. When they are gone, only the tropospheric shields that cover the prized continent of Helios will forestall the wrath of the Ash Armada. The black ships prowl beyond the graveyard, safely out of reach of Republic ground cannons, waiting to launch an Iron Rain against my marooned army.

When the shields fall, so will the planet.

Ten million of my brothers and sisters will face annihilation.

That is why Atalantia has come. To crush the White Fleet. To kill the Free Legions. To take back Mercury and with its metals and factories, feed the Gold war machine on Venus to prepare for a single, irresistible thrust toward the heart of the Republic.

A tiny laser flickers against the hull between Alexandar's feet. I put my helmet to his again. "They're moving her," I say. His eyes harden. "Time to go."

Together, we push off the hull to float back into the graveyard. We cross through seas of frozen corpses and shattered ripWings to land two kilometers from the dreadnought on the broken fuselage of a dead torchShip. We skip along its surface until we reach a dark hangar bay.

Inside, a prototype black shuttle waits—the *Necromancer,* the personal deepspace shuttle of the Ash Lord, which I stole from his fortress and rode from Venus to Mercury. Today I will make it earn its name.

"Anteater to Dark Tango, do you register?" The Fear Knight's voice is cold and intelligent as it echoes over the speakers in the *Necromancer's* ready bay. The voice matches the man. Atlas au Raa, Atalantia's most effective field commander, is a far cry from his honorable brother, Romulus. Implanted on the surface with his Zero Legion guerrillas, Atlas sows chaos behind our lines and is responsible for my delayed reunion with my army. They don't even know I am here. But neither does the enemy.

The planet was blockaded by the Ash Armada when I arrived to Mercury three weeks ago. Fortunately, the *Necromancer's* stealth capabilities are the most advanced in the Society armada, and the debris field hid our approach.

Hiding in the graveyard, I have used the decryption software on the *Necromancer* to eavesdrop on the Fear Knight's correspondence. He reports his horrors, his impalements, his mutilations, with the detachment of a doctor administering medicine to a patient. Today, he discusses a different matter.

"Dark Tango registers, go for Anteater." A thin Copper voice answers for Atalantia. Some sinister blackops administrator on the *Annihilo*.

"Slave Two is packaged and prepped for delivery," Atlas drawls. *"Blood Medusa primed. Dance floor's looking crowded, confirm escort landfall and chaperone overwatch."*

"Landfall confirmed. Escorts: Love, Death, and Storm delivered to chalk, minus twenty. ETA to handshake forty minutes. Chaperone overwatch primed. Request escort handshake confirmation. Delivery active pending your go."

"Registers. Will confirm handshake. Anteater out."

The audio clicks off.

Slave Two they call my friend. Since the day Sevro and I hijacked Orion's ship in our escape over Luna, the Blue has been my confidante, my stalwart ally, my saving grace against the incredible sophistication of Gold naval Praetors. Now she is their captive.

Slave Two. Those motherfuckers.

Before we arrived, Orion was kidnapped by the Fear Knight from her headquarters in Mercury's capital of Tyche. Her personal guard slaughtered. Her fingers left on her bed to mock the Free Legions.

Unable to extract her to orbit, the Fear Knight managed to stay a step ahead of the trackers my commanders sent in pursuit. I listened to the bastard's reports as he skinned some of them alive and tortured Orion in his hidden mountain bases. Today, he attempts to ferry her to orbit to face Atalantia's arcane psychotechs. It will be a neural extraction—a science in which only my wife is Atalantia's equal. Orion may have resisted torture, but when Atalantia peels through the layers of her mind, the planetary defense architecture of the Republic will be laid bare.

I cannot permit that to happen.

"Fascist assholes," my niece, Rhonna, mutters and tightens her synaptic gloves in Alexandar's direction.

"It was the baked Red peasants who gave up Orion. Not Golds," Alexandar says as he scalps a warhawk onto the giant head of Thraxa au Telemanus with his razor. It matches my own. Thraxa admires it in the reflection of her notched warhammer: Wee Lass.

"The whole planet is an asshole," Rhonna replies. "You should think of buying a villa, Princess."

He blows her a kiss in reply.

"Atalantia's got some flair, at least," Colloway drawls. Never one for wasted effort, the best fighter pilot in the Republic lies on a crate of pulseArmor smoking a burner. His slim limbs splay every direction while pale blue eyes gaze dreamily at the curling smoke. "Remember Dreadhammer and Lightbane? Jove, was the Ash Lord on the nose. If he called it a nose. Probably called it Airdevourer or Consumer of Lifegas—"

Thraxa's Wee Lass thumps the deck, leaving two big divots.

Everyone shuts up.

My apex killer is horny for battle. Thraxa's face is painted orange. Her thigh-thick neck bent forward like a sunblood stallion at the Hippodrome starting block. While I regret my fondness for violence out of a Red sense of guilt, the old-blood Gold bathes in its furor. Not the glory Cassius loved, or the noble fight Alexandar chases, or the cathartic revenge Sevro needs, but the primal essence of battle itself. Never is Thraxa more alive than after thirty days in the field, crusted with saddle sores and sweat, hunting men who have never been prey.

"I like to kill people I don't like," she once said when Pax asked why she follows me. "And your daddy brings 'em like flies."

I survey the rest of my meager force. All save Colloway wear the warhawk Sevro made famous. Alexandar, Colloway, and Thraxa are ready. Are Rhonna and Tongueless? The old Obsidian sits cross-legged on the floor.

From prison guard to prisoner to an unlikely asset, Tongueless proved his worth on the Ash Lord's island. He is a true patriot for the Republic, but I fear he may not be ready for what's coming. I fear we're not. Without Sefi's mate, Valdir, and his Obsidians, without Sevro, Victra, Pebble, Clown, and Holiday the company feels smaller than it should. I am missing my best weapons, and friends.

"The enemy is in motion," I say. "The Fear Knight will attempt to deliver Orion to the *Annihilo* within the hour. If we can rescue her, we will. If we cannot, we terminate. They will not get that intel." I look them each in the eye to measure their will. "You know the plan. You each have kill clearance. Remember why we are here. Our mission is not to save ourselves. It is to protect the Republic, at any cost."

They nod, but I wonder if they understand the extent to which I expect them to honor that principle. There will be those whose consciences will deceive them into holding higher other principles.

I need a core I can depend upon.

"Intel suggests we will encounter at least three Olympic Knights and Gorgon operators." The Gorgons comprise the Fear Knight's blackops legion. Their ranks consist of Shamed Golds from the Institutes, and Grays and Obsidians with antisocial tendencies deemed corrosive to the fighting spirit of the regular legions. "No one is to engage an Olympic unless you're with me."

"Will Fear be there himself?" Thraxa asks.

"His name is Atlas," I reply. "It's possible, but I doubt Atalantia will give up her best ground operator before her Rain. But she is sending Ajax."

Alexandar and Thraxa tense.

"Do we have confirmation from Screwface?" Rhonna asks.

"Screwface is still silent," I say. She looks down, fearing the man is dead. It is likely, since our only mole on the *Annihilo* failed to warn us of Atalantia's ambush. "Any more questions?" None. Refreshing change of scenery. "Good. To your slots. Let's get our girl back."

Rhonna scoops up her vacuum sack, fist-bumps Char and Tongueless, and slides down the ladder to the starShell bay. I feel a pang of guilt. I told my brother I'd keep her safe. If I wasn't so short-staffed, I could concoct a reason to keep her on the *Necromancer*. But for Orion, even my niece is worth risking, especially considering her role today may be more important even than my own.

I grab Alexandar's arm as the rest head out and gesture to Thraxa's paint stamp. I ask him to do the honors. "I know you were close to Kalindora," I say as he picks up the contraption. He nods at the mention of the Love Knight, his mother's younger sister.

He toggles through the options on the paint stamp. "She spent every summer with us in Elysium, always begging Grandfather to train her. But she was best friends with Atalantia and Anastasia. He didn't want to give Octavia another weapon." Alexandar looks up. "When he took the house to Europa, she chose her Sovereign over her family. She is no blood of mine." He points the paint gun at my face. "What'll it be? Goblin black, Valkyrie blue, Minotaur purple, Julii jade . . ."

"Blood Red."

In the spitTube again.

Waiting for the kill.

I hate this part.

A moving mind is always fed. At rest, mine eats itself.

How many times have I been here? Sealed in a womb of metal, not for birth but to eat the living? The confines afflict me with dread. Dread not of what lies beyond—you can never prepare for that game—but that this will be my eternal tomb.

Cursed to live to kill. Is this who I will always be?

Is this the life I crave? To rise before the sun? To smile at the cock and fart jokes of killers as they grow younger and I grow older? To sleep under tanks, in the ruins of cities, amongst the corpses?

I no longer believe in the Vale. I am the walking dead.

Woe to those who cross my shadow.

I miss the promise of life. The smell of rain. The murmur of waves on a shore. The sound of a full house. It is a life I have rented, but never owned.

My wife and son are real. Not ghosts in my head. They are out there breathing right now. Where are you, Pax? Is it bright where you walk? Are you afraid? Has your mother found you? Your uncle? Do you wonder if your father will come? Do you hate him for having left? Will you ever understand?

I have stolen pieces of him and his mother, which I hold for ransom, promising to one day return. I know that is a lie. Mercury will be my end.

I reach for his key, forgetting I set it in my luggage three weeks ago. My thoughts drift to his mother. Unlike Sevro, Virginia did not accuse me of parental malfeasance. She knows the shearing forces at work on my heart. How can I be a father to Pax if I abandon the millions who chose to follow me to Luna? The responsibility to many outweighs the responsibility to one, even though it breaks something inside me. I feel alone knowing Sevro would not make the sacrifice. Am I alone in my conviction, or have I gone mad?

My wife and I corresponded during my passage from Venus to Mercury before I had to go dark as I approached the planet. Now it is too dangerous. I play the last words of her final correspondence. Her voice echoes through my helmet. *"Trust your wife to find our son. Trust your Sovereign to bring the armada. Trust in me enough to stay alive."*

I trust my wife. I do not trust my Sovereign.

She will find Pax with Victra and Sevro. But no rescue fleet will come for my marooned army. Most have forgotten the slingBlade of my people was not made to kill pitvipers. It was made for hacking off limbs of trapped miners. My old mentor, Dancer, has not forgotten. Now the leading senator of the Vox Populi movement, he will amputate us to save the Republic.

Atalantia expects this. If she breaks the Free Legions here, if she feeds Mercury's resources into her war machine, who can match her in space and Atlas and the Ash Legion commanders on the ground when they sail on my mother, my brother, my sister, my son, my wife, my friends, my home?

I will not survive Mercury, I know that. The Free Legions will not survive Mercury. But we can make Atalantia pay so dearly for our deaths, that we break the back of the Gold military and secure a chance for our families, for our Republic and its fragile dream.

I put away my wife's face as I put away the key my son gave me for his gravBike when I sailed for Mercury, and stare at the red light until the enemy com crackles.

"Anteater to Dark Tango. Escort handshake confirmed. We are go in three, two . . ."

. . .

Fury begins upon the planet with a spark. A lone frigate rises from a hangar hidden in the desert mountains. An escort of six Gorgon ripWings follows, burning low across the desert toward the Sycorax Sea where the ground shields do not reach. In orbit above the planet, five dreadnoughts, led by Atalantia's *Annihilo*, plunge toward the western hemisphere.

Free Legion contrails form over the sea in response. Atalantia's strike force of dreadnoughts bombards an unshielded sliver of the planet. Ground cannons reply as Republic squadrons close in on the escaping corvette. Society ripWings descend from the *Annihilo*. It will be a hell of a party over the western hemisphere.

We won't be attending. And neither will the Olympic Knights.

As the battle plays in the background, I follow Colloway's scrutiny of the Waste of Ladon. *"Getting a ghost in the eastern Ladon. That's our bird. Hermes-class corvette."*

"Wait for it to get into the debris field." Sure enough, the corvette has no interest in the scrum over the western hemisphere. It pierces orbit over the eastern hemisphere and sprints for the debris belt. "Char, sick 'em."

"Boom goes the ion."

A thousand tons of high-grade engines and weaponry come alive in the hollow of the dead destroyer. Inertial dampeners throb as the *Necromancer* explodes out of its hiding place.

"Chin to collar." I remind my Howlers as Colloway weaves through the graveyard toward our quarry. They haven't spotted us yet in the debris. "I am the tip of the spear. Move at my pace. Kill all hostiles. Momentum is everything. We stop, we die." There's a shudder as our ship hits debris. I see an open line between Alex and Rhonna. I click in.

"Here's hoping this one's worth a wolfcloak," Alexandar says.

"Bah, he'll make us die puppies," Rhonna replies. *"Stay sharp, Princess."*

"And you, Ruster."

I click out.

"Eyes on target," Colloway drones. *"Pricks and slits, guard your tenders, spit pending."* The ship rumbles as its cannons fire. They've spotted us. It's a race now through the debris field toward their waiting armada. We spin like a top. Ordnance glancing off as the *Blood Medusa* returns fire. The seconds thicken. Each a test of patience. Three weeks I have waited. Three weeks in darkness. Three weeks in torment. Three weeks for this kill.

A magnetic charge builds behind me.

The lights go green.

Yellow.

Red.

Gravity says hello.

I launch from the spitTube.

Momentum and sunlight and spinning metal. Our quarry barrel-rolls through the shards of a torchShip, exchanging fire with the *Necromancer*. Colloway sticks to its tail like a wicked shadow.

The Howler signatures are lost in the debris. I take over my suit's side thrusters and lock on to the corvette, trusting my team to follow. Five hundred meters out. Debris careens past. Globules of frozen blood and water from ship stores become blurs. The heartbeat monitors of my Howlers are jackhammering as they try to keep up.

"Match me," I say. "Match me."

In its desperation to escape the *Necromancer*, the *Medusa* nearly collides with the engine block of a destroyer. It hammers its starboard thrusters and turns at a right angle. Damn fine pilot. But the men inside will be slammed into walls if they're not secure.

I seize the opportunity.

"Breach," I say as I goose my gravBoots and leap forward. The *Medusa*'s hull grows larger. I aim for its centerline, directing Colloway to the breach point.

Systemic rage builds as I prepare for contact.

Atalantia thought she could steal my Imperator.

That her Fear Knight could keep my friend as a toy for torture.

That I would simply run back to Luna and let my men die.

That she could steal my son and there would be no consequences.

Well, here I am, you deviant bitch. Here I *bloody* am.

The motherfucking consequence.

"Five seconds to breach."

The hull of the corvette rips open as Colloway sends a miracle shot home. His warhead sprays out molecular crash webbing.

Two seconds.

One.

Breach.

I pierce the molten hole. The black blur of the molecular crash webbing expands like glossy, replicating fungus.

I smash into the webbing. My teeth bite through my mouthguard. My internal organs throb. The webbing absorbed my crash, but quickly becomes a liability, as Alexandar warned. It seals the breach and traps me upside down in its embrace. I can't reach the dispersal agent on my pulseArmor's thigh.

As the webbing expands, I see only blackness. Masked enemies in tattered desert gear crawl through it. A moment before, the Gorgons were being pushed out the breach into space. Now they are as trapped as I am. I can't reach the razor on my wrist. Not half a meter away, a sunburnt Obsidian with chromed-out desert eyes points a pistol at my head. I push the barrel away and, slowed by the webbing, thrust my left hand into his stomach until the flesh gives. He screams as I reach under his ribcage and squeeze his liver.

"Sound off," I bark.

"Howler Three," Thraxa says. *"Enemy contact, releasing counter-agent."*

"Pup Two. Landfall," Rhonna says. *"Drilling on your go."*

"Pup One? Tongueless?" Only static replies.

The crash webbing bubbles. Thraxa's released the counter-agent. It dissolves into a black soup that hisses against the deck. Sheets of steam roll up. Released, my armor clunks to the floor, my hand still inside the screaming slaveknight. I pull out my razor and bury it in his face.

Others move in the steam as he twitches. Six enemies, all coming for me. I struggle to stand. Then, one by one, the six shapes divide into twelve. A lean figure glides through them all like a Lykos dancer.

"Pup One, reporting."

Alexandar, fresh from bisecting a half-dozen of the Fear Knight's best men, slams to a knee in front of me. He wipes the blood from his family blade and helps me to my feet.

The hole Colloway shot in the ship goes three decks deep. Sparks from broken instruments crackle. Molecular armor on the hull clatters as it seals the breach behind us, locking us in.

Tongueless clicks over the com and appears from two decks below. He boosts up and assembles the ripWing cannon he and Rhonna harvested from the graveyard, hooking the man-sized gun to his armor's homemade exoskeleton. Thraxa pulls herself from a mangled wall. Her fox warhelm is dented. A sharp piece of metal sticks through her lower guts and out the back of her armor. She bends the points of the metal shard down and looks toward the sound of enemies coming up from the lower decks and down the main corridor.

I toss a grenade down to the lower decks. White light flares and a concussion thunders. I peek out into the main corridor.

Masked men in tactical gear move like a hunched organism down the hall. I dip my head back just as bullets chew into the wall and it starts to melt.

"Tongueless, give 'em a lick."

Tongueless levers the ripWing cannon forward on its hydraulic arm while Thraxa braces him from behind. The cannon is meant for ships. Not men. It screams toroids of energy down the hall, bucking the Obsidian into Thraxa. The frame rate of the world stutters. Behind Tongueless, Thraxa pulls her warhammer from its magnetic holster. Alexandar salutes me with his blade and turns to the main corridor.

Kaleidoscopic carnage unfolds before us.

"Pup Two, go for drill," I say to Rhonna.

"Copy."

"Invert," I order. All except Tongueless rotate boots to ceiling. "One hundred meters to the Package. Push."

We charge into the wake of Tongueless's maelstrom. Everything is upside down. The very air ripples with heat. Body parts steam all over the floor. Half-melted doorways tilt. The main corridor runs the spine of the ship. It is the most direct route to the prison cells. But it means we will be flanked in seconds. We must punch through, or it's all on Rhonna.

There's a blur at the far end of the corridor. Drones scream for us, spitting munitions. Three of us open up with our pulseFists. Shrapnel pings everywhere. Then the Gorgons come to play.

Dozens of elite guerrillas fire around corners, but we roll down the ceiling like an upside-down wrecking ball made of energy, razors, and hammers.

I fire point-blank into a Gorgon's chest, killing the armored man behind him as well. The third bends impossibly and squeezes three shots at my head. But I'm already past him and firing my fist at an Obsidian.

A homing grenade clatters against my right thigh. I cut it off with my razor and Alexandar kicks it. It detonates ten meters in front of us, lifting us backward.

"Push."

I was a killer at sixteen. A warlord by twenty. But the younger me wasn't this. He was still tender and new to war. If he was the Helldiver, I am the clawDrill.

I carve through hardcore veterans of the Zero Legion as if they were made of pastry. Still, they pour from every hall. Existence is smoke and fire. My armor pings. Internal warnings scream. I flicker my pulseShields on and off, letting them cool so I don't cook. The Gorgons will not die easy, and there are too many.

We're pinned. Flanked on three sides and can't push forward. Tongueless fires back down the main corridor, sweeping it clear. Something hits him from his right. A hole smokes in his armor. He stumbles as I fire at his assailant and overlap my shields to guard him as he recovers.

"Slide."

Alexandar seamlessly takes point and fires down the hall. Thraxa rotates to take his position. Tongueless recovers and takes hers. Alexandar flickers down the hall like a possessed flame, lashing out his razor in abject slaughter, inverting gravity better than any man I've ever seen save maybe Sevro. He tries to break through the crack fireteam barring our path.

"Hull penetration," Rhonna intones. *"Breaching."*

The Gorgon fireteam perform a perfect Flavinian armorkill on Alexandar. Three nail him with electrical rounds before he reaches them, lowering his pulseShield. Two deliver mass slugs that stun him senseless. He teeters there like a drunk. Their centurion delivers the coup de grâce. His muzzle flashes. Three armor-penetrating digger rounds scream toward Alexandar's head.

Thraxa bolts forward and the rounds sizzle as they ricochet off her intact pulseShield. One penetrates and rips a hole through her left shoulder, spinning her sideways.

"Slide!"

I rotate into her place, rocketing into that damn fireteam on my gravBoots to kill the entire lot. As their bodies drip off my armor and my friends fight behind me, I look down the smoke-filled corridor to see a red heart burning in the gloom. A white skull joins it.

Two silhouettes bar our path to the prisons. The razors of the Olympic Knights glimmer like teeth. The heart and skull emblems of their office glow on their breastplates. The Love Knight and the Death Knight.

Where is the Storm Knight?

Where is Aja's only son?

I pray to a silent god he is not with Orion.

I look left, Gorgons. Right, Gorgons. Then behind us to see three hundred and fifty pounds of apex predator crouched in the corridor, his black and gray leopard warhelm lowered for the hunt.

Ajax.

"Pup Two, we've got the Olympics. You're clear. *On me,*" I bark.

We launch away from Ajax for Love and Death. Each side in grav-Boots and inverting gravity at will. Metal rings as we crash together. Death and I slam into the wall, the ceiling, the floor, smashing Gorgons still in their desert gear. We fire our pulseFists at the same time and melt each other's into oblivion. The force sends us reeling into the Love Knight and Alexandar, who engage in a far more graceful duel of blades. Alexandar turns Love to Thraxa, who is just completing a huge swing of her hammer. Then Death bowls into Thraxa from the side, guarding his wingman's back.

Behind them, Tongueless unloads his cannon on Ajax. I've never seen one close so fast as Aja's boy. He ricochets along the ceiling toward Tongueless, and then slashes down to slide sparking across the floor, flat on his back. Because the recoil of the cannon pulls its barrel upward, Tongueless is slow to angle it back down.

Ajax counted on it.

He slides past Tongueless. His wrist flicks. His slide stops and he pivots to the Root Cutter stance of the Willow Way. One of the last and most complicated forms his mother would have taught him before my friends and I killed her.

Tongueless falls into four pieces, dead before he even hits the floor.

"Thraxa! Hold for me!" I shout as she charges Ajax. She is fast, impossibly strong, tough as nails. But Ajax was born of the unholy genetic union of two apex bloodlines: Raa and Grimmus. He is her superior in every martial way except experience, and in that he's gaining.

He swims past her hammer and scores two strikes to her armor. She reels back, shocked by his speed. I rush to help, but Alexandar is pinned back by Death and Love. They block my way. Ajax has Thraxa on the ground. He bats her hammer to the side.

I go Blood Red.

The razor blows shiver up my arm as I give the Death Knight my undivided attention. He does well to last seven seconds. The opening is small and inelegant. He meets a crashing overhead, and tries to deflect it instead of absorb the blow. He forgets the curve. My blade doesn't turn and my full weight jars his own blade into his armor. Before he can pull it out, I pivot and chop Death's head off.

I wheel around. Ajax was fifteen meters down the hall when I last saw him. He almost takes my head off as he passes above. I deflect his blade at the last millisecond, but the salvo we share would make his mother's eyes gleam.

A very good killer can string together a set of three moves in an onset—a one-second set of preprogrammed, carefully cultivated strikes. Everyone has their signature. As one of the top fifty with a blade in the Core, Cassius could do five. I once saw Lorn do eight. Ajax does eight. It isn't to say he's as good as Lorn, but he is as fast; and fighting him is like being plunged into cold water.

Pure shock.

I don't really see the moves at this point. Even Gold eyes can't track blades this fast. By the time he flips down to bar my way to the prison block, I'm nicked three times. But so is he. He swishes his blade like a walking stick as the Love Knight takes the opportunity to pair up with him and form the Hydra fighting stance. Alexandar limps to my side. Thraxa groans from behind us as she stumbles to join us.

The two parties stare each other down in the narrow corridor. Everyone bleeds. *Come on, Rhonna. I don't want to pay this toll yet.*

"I hoped it would be like this," Ajax says from behind his helmet. His voice is almost as deep as his grandfather's. "First you. Then I work my way down the food chain. Your wife. Your shadow. Your Bellona."

As much as I want to cut off Atalantia's left and right hands by killing her best two knights, as much as I want to end Ajax before he becomes something I can't handle, dying here doesn't end the war.

I hail Rhonna. "Pup Two, status?" I say without taking my eyes off Ajax.

"Package is wrapped. Present deposited. Attaching cord now. Char, any-time, please."

"Coming in hot. Getting frisky out here. Two destroyers and four torches inbound."

"Popping off. Three, two, one."

I turn from Ajax and wrap Alexandar and Thraxa in a hug. I had hoped my presence would draw the Olympic Knights. They all want to be the one who takes me down. I thought I could still punch through. But with the knights the Core has these days, you always buy insurance.

While I drew their eyes, Rhonna's starShell landed on the hull beyond the prison block and welded through to steal Orion from behind their backs.

Duuuuuuuuuuuuuuuuum

The aft section of the ship vaporizes behind Ajax and the Love Knight as Rhonna's bomb detonates. A maw to space opens and the pressure of the ship rips them out into vacuum. We tumble with them into the debris field. Everything's spinning, and all we can do is hold on to one another. I see flashes of the oncoming enemy ships. RipWings slip through the darkness, and the *Necromancer* races toward us. Just when I think it will hit us, it tips on its nose, inverts, and inhales us into its back-facing garage. The doors seal instantly and we ricochet like marbles. Rhonna's mech is locked magnetically to the floor with arms around a bag as if it were a baby.

I grip a rung to pull myself to the viewport just as the reactors Alexandar and I retrofitted activate. A dozen dead ships glow with sudden light. Their hulks begin to crumple from the inside, and then the reactors overload in a wash of blinding light.

The two onrushing destroyers and torchShips ripple as the energy waves wash across the graveyard. The corpses of my dead starships animate into frantic contortions. I howl with Alexandar and Thraxa as the derelict hulks splinter apart to cover our retreat, sending hundred-meter shards flailing into the enemy ships Atalantia sent into the graveyard.

From the other side of the graveyard, her fleet watches their kilometer-long destroyers burn as we roar for Mercury. Colloway hails all Republic craft that the Reaper is inbound. We need cover fire.

Dripping with sweat, I jump down to the floor. Alexandar helps pull Rhonna from her mech. Thraxa winces as she pulls the vacuum bag free of the mech's embrace. We set it gently on the floor. I close my eyes before I open the seal. Tongueless died for this. Though I knew him less well than he deserved, he will have saved more lives today than he'll ever know.

I unzip the bag.

Inside is a shriveled woman in a prisoner jumpsuit. An oxygen globe sealed over her head. I remove it. Her skin is ashen. Her face is half gone. It looks as if it has been eaten. But her eyes are as blue as I remember. They fill with tears as Orion reaches to touch my face with the stumps of her fingers. Through tattered lips, she sneers, "Hail Reaper."

PART I

MISCHIEF

Of iron is the last,

In no part good and tractable as former ages past.

For when that of this wicked age once open'd was the vein,

Therein all mischief rushed forth, then faith and truth were fain,

and honest shame to hide their heads; for whom stept stoutly in,

Craft, treason, violence, envy, pride, and wicked lust to win.

—OVID, *METAMORPHOSES*, 1.129–34

1

DARROW

Till the Vale

I STAND AMIDST THE BLIND. Cloudy eyes set in sun-ravaged faces stare up at the sun, at the stone obelisks, at the meager cubes of protein cupped in their blistered hands, at their leader who brought them to this cursed place, and see nothing but darkness. Their retinas have been fried by the ordnance of our enemies.

They reach to touch my red cloak as if it will heal them. They are Reds, Grays, Browns, Coppers, and the few Obsidians who chose not to heed their queen's call to return to Earth. The legionnaires survived the Fear Knight's ambush in the Western Ladon, only to become 2,301 casualties that we must continue to feed, supply with medical aid, and protect. Why would Atlas au Raa kill when maiming pays dividends? My men look on the living casualties with despair. Others turn their heads away, as if looking at them might invite the same fate upon themselves.

Drop by drop he blackens the pigment of our souls.

I bend in front of a Gray with two cauterized stumps for legs. "You look like you got between a Telemanus and a pint of whiskey, legionnaire."

"Fear so, sir. I'd be back in the fight, had we the gear."

If he were a Gold or Obsidian, he'd be back in the fight by month's end, but we can't spend our near-extinguished supply of prosthetics on regular infantry. Bad investment. I once thought the greatest sin of war was violence. It isn't. The greatest sin is it requires good men to become practical.

"I still see it, sir. Like a ghost tail." The Gray rubs his eyes, remembering the Fear Knight's firebrand. "Bright as day. Can't sleep a wink."

"You and me both. But next time you open your eyes, it'll be Mars you see. You're from Hippolyte, yes?"

"Born and bred in the jade city, sir."

"Then we'll share oysters and cigars there soon. I promise." I pat him on the shoulder, murmur something inconsequential, and move on. I stop before an old Red man with a thin quilt about his shoulders despite the heat. Bald but for a crescent of thin gray hair, he rolls a burner with practiced ease. His eyes flick back and forth as he realizes I am there. He takes in a sharp breath. "Is it you?" He holds out a hand. I take it in mine. His burner begins to shake from nerves. I set my hand on his and motion a woman to toss me her ring lighter. The end of the burner curls with smoke as I give the old Red a light and toss the lighter back.

"Looks like you've had a day," I say.

He takes a deep drag. His hand steadies. "I'm Red, sir. Been blind most of me life. I'll get on fine-like. If there's other mouths need feedin', don't worry about me. I don't die."

His accent . . .

"What mine are you from, legionnaire?"

He grins. "Yours, as it happens."

"Lykos?" I search his face. The crow's feet around his eyes are peppered with blood-fly bites. "What's your name?"

"Don't ya recognize me, sir?" He takes another drag from his burner. It glows, burning hot and fast. His hand holds it the same way it did the day Eo died, between his ring and pinky fingers. I feel the movement of the deepmine winds. The smell of rust and swill. An echo of Eo's laughter. It's been a long time.

"Dago," I whisper. "Dago of Gamma." Could it really be the Helldiver I worshipped and loathed as a child? The man who taught me the meaning of defeat? Who won thirty-two laurels? Now here, on Mercury, in *my* army. Fifteen years later. For him it looks like it's been forty. His age makes me feel the years.

"In the bloodydamn flesh, sir." He shivers from his wound but manages that slash of a smile. Few teeth remain.

"What are— How long have you been—"

"Since Mars, sir. Five years."

"And you never thought to find me."

"Man ain't shit if he slags with a Helldiver that's got his eye on the laurel." His laugh becomes a cough. "But you got it now, sir. Damn well you do."

"Sir." Felix, a pristine Gold of my bodyguard, appears behind me. Hailing from a minor house pledged to House Augustus, he is a dour cynic of a man. Just past forty, he has little love of the lowColors. But he is loyal to my wife, and he is Martian. These days there is no more trustworthy a breed. Two dozen more Gold bodyguards tower clean and strong as gods at the edge of the sea of the blind. The zenith and dregs of humanity. I feel guilt that I choose the zenith instead of my own people for protection. Practicality, again. "Your shuttle is ready to depart. Your . . . fellow traveler is growing restless."

I want to stay, ask a thousand things of Dago, but I can't. I barely have time to visit the men as it is. Time was you could walk among the wounded and find Sevro sprawled in drink with them playing Karachi, poorly. His absence is felt everywhere, not just in the field. So many gaps for me to fill.

"Reaper . . ." Dago motions to me. I crouch back down. He pulls open his thighpack. Two cannisters sit inside. One filled with Martian soil. The other empty for his own ash. Most Martian soldiers fear dying on an alien sphere. How many corpses have I seen shriveled after bombardments, their hands clutched around home soil? How many cans of ash have I sent back to Mars to be spread in the sea? Dago offers me his home soil. It even smells of Mars, that faint hint of iron.

"I can't take that," I say.

"Where's your can then, eh?"

"Left it on Luna. This vacation was unexpected."

He takes a handful of the soil and reaches out to me. "It's from Lykos." He coughs blood into his quilt. "Yours as much as mine. Bring it back and we'll share a dram and some gob, eh?" He reaches for my hand, and flattens it so he can give me half of his dust. "Mars is with you, till the Vale." Others hear his words and begin to thump their chests over their hearts in the Fading Dirge, except it is an inversion. Not the fast beating to a slow stop as in death, but a slow pace quickening to a racing beat. I'm about to say something to Dago, when he lights another burner and blows the smoke in my face like old times.

"No time for words, sir. You got killin' to do."

I clench my fist around the dirt. "Till the Vale."

With Lykos soil in a secure pouch, I depart the desert, spoiling for a fight.

My shuttle bears north over the desert chalk. Behind, Heliopolis trembles in the warped horizon. A great shield wall, a kilometer high and fifteen long, blocks the mouth of two converging mountain ranges. House Votum crafted the wall to shield Heliopolis from the desert storms that come when spring cyclones descend from the Sycorax Sea in the far north to tear south through the Waste of Ladon down onto Heliopolis. Sparks shiver along the wall's crest as engineers weld guns from broken ships into place.

I lament the waste of firepower. The guns are only there to satisfy the demands of Heliopolis's inhabitants and the Master Maker Glirastes, not to counter an invasion. Heliopolis is the second-wealthiest city of Mercury, rich with architecture, famous for its chariot races, and the gateway to the coastal mines, but it is strategically insignificant for my aims. To the north is where I will break the enemy.

Heliopolis is a thorn in my boot. A hotbed of loyalist insurrection, plots, and back-alley murders. Behind its wall, the haughty city of limestone slouches south toward the Bay of Sirens and then the Caliban Sea. Refugees and soldiers boil through the dusty streets and stuff the city with a ripe summer stink. But there is another scent there in that desert city. Not gull shit or fish markets or the exhaust of war machines, but something else, something creeping that clings to the root of the brain.

Fear.

Fear in the eyes of my legions as they look up to orbit where Atalantia fine-tunes her invasion plans, or to the shadowed mountains where the Fear Knight and his guerrillas sharpen their impaling stakes, or to the streets filled with Mercurians, any of whom could be a spy or an assassin.

If the death of the fleet was an amputation, this siege is death by exsanguination. Bit by bit, frontline exposure to the perversions of the Fear Knight's guerrillas and waiting for the Rain deteriorates their psyches. My loyal Martians patrol deserts and mountains and erect war machines and battleworks, waiting to be shot by snipers or hear the bug scream—that dread keening which signals a spider mine's activation.

Each a better fate than being captured by the Gorgons, the Fear Knight's veteran impalers of Zero Legion.

Fear robs my men of their dignity, their nobility of purpose, their belief in our cause. Who can believe in the intangible with a garrote around their neck? They wait to die, slowly strangled by Atalantia and Atlas.

Some hold out hope that the Republic will send a fleet. There is a small chance, but if I hunker down and wait for my wife to move the gears of democracy, there will be nothing left of us when the enemy strikes. We will die like flies, and fear will spread as the shadows of Atalantia's fleet creep across the steps of the New Forum and their titanium boots tread the shores of my home.

So that makes it all very simple.

I must kill it before it kills us.

Our flight path takes us over the Waste of Ladon, the sunbelt that chokes the center of Mercury's main continent, Helios. Half buried in its sands lie the remains of the three armies the Waste has swallowed in its time. Soon I will feed it a fourth.

Somewhere in the Waste's axeblade central mountains, my Howlers herd the Fear Knight toward the tripwire of my trap—the mining city of Eleusis. Sevro should have been leading them. Four commanders on two planets I've sent against Atlas. Four have been returned impaled hole to hole. Only Sevro and I can match the brutality of the Fear Knight. But I have too much weight to bear alone. So I have dispatched my best remaining small-group commander, Thraxa, to lead, and my best sword, Alexandar in case it comes to blows.

To the south, past Heliopolis, commandos install missile systems, mines, and anti-infantry microwave cannons in the tropic archipelagos and deep jungles that sprawl into the Caliban Sea. To the northeast along the Petasos Peninsula are the rising elevations and temperate climes of a tiara of heavily populated cities called the Children.

The capital of the planet, and headquarters for my army, remains Tyche. We have made the treasured seaside home of the Votum into a fortress. Even as we pass over crop latifundia far to its east, you can catch the glint of its spires, and the soothing sight of its guardian mountain: the *Morning Star*.

Due to Orion's free-fall maneuver, the flagship of my fleet survived Atalantia's ambush—what the troops are calling the Battle of Caliban, for all the ships that fell through atmosphere into the sea—and now keeps watch over Tyche as her systems undergo repairs with hopes of one day returning her to the stars.

Tyche is crucial not just as a fallback citadel, but for the gravLoop that runs south under the Hesperides Mountains connecting Tyche to Heliopolis. Safe from bombardment, it will be the single artery for reinforcements if the fight reaches Tyche, *and* it will serve as our escape route to Heliopolis if Tyche falls. The only other path is across the Waste of Ladon, and I'd rather have dinner with the Fear Knight than dare cross that devourer of armies.

I busy myself with reports in the *Necromancer*'s warroom as the shuttle flies north. Beacons from submerged torchShips blink on the command display as we reach the northern extremity of the Sycorax Sea. Across the warroom's data display, a Silver aide drones on about shortages of anti-radiation meds in the south. Most are being hoarded in Tyche for the inevitable fallout.

"Soon we'll have a surplus," I say.

"Have you discovered a new supply, sir?"

"No."

His eyes flutter as he understands.

I feel stuffy. My spirit aches to be released from this endless stream of supply logistics and construction delays. I need fresh air.

I find Rhonna outside the entrance to the garage bay. Orion must be inside. My niece issues a crisp salute. Since her part in Orion's rescue, her popularity with the army has increased, especially with the Blue and Orange sailors and officers. So far, it hasn't gone to her head. Credit her father, Kieran, for that. "How's she looking?" I ask.

"Quiet, sir," Rhonna replies. "Eats alone, when she eats. Spends more time in the shower than the mess. Like she can't get clean. Avoids the men when she can. Night terrors make her dope up to sleep. Never dozes in quarters. New spot every night. Guard detail can barely keep tabs on her."

"Atlas did take her from her quarters," I say. "I wouldn't be able to use a bed either. Have you told anyone about your orders?"

"No, sir. I know you told Imperator Harnassus she passed her psych evaluation. Quiet's the game."

"Good. Good. Has she spotted you?"

"Did you spot me yesterday when you were listening to Aunt V's hologram instead of sleeping like the medici ordered, sir?"

I frown. "Window?"

"Topiaries."

I rub my eyes. "Shit. I'm getting old."

"Or I'm getting quieter."

I suppose it was only a matter of time before everyone started catching up. I consider how young she looks, and how old I must be in her eyes. "Did you know I'm older than my father was when he died? Still think of him as an old man." I chuckle. "He'd be closer to your age, I reckon."

She glances down the corridor and chews her lip.

"Permission to speak like we're blood, sir."

"Don't like me discussing mortality?" She waits for my answer. "Granted."

"I didn't get you until we came back here. You were dead to us till I was near on nine. Everyone ran their gobs about you in Tinos. But I didn't get it. I didn't get that." She points at the slingBlade asleep like a pale snake around my arm. "You were just my uncle. Then we came down with Orion. And I could see it. Every bloody soul was waiting to give Mercury their carbon. Then they saw you jump out this ship." The hairs on her forearms stand on end at the memory. "You ain't old. You just need to let others haul their freight. Even the Reaper needs sleep, sir. Especially if he's gonna get us all home."

She still believes I can work miracles. But my exhaustion isn't made by these last days. A life of war is catching up with me. She doesn't know the weight I carry. How much I relied on Sevro to help carry it. How damaged our legions really are. How tactically sophisticated even the most basic Gray infantry centurion of the enemy is compared with ours, not to mention their Golds. We just don't have the same distribution of brainpower. Or firepower.

"Thank you for the concern, lancer. But I'd caution you against spying on me again." I move toward the door.

"Sir."

I turn, growing annoyed. She stands at attention again.

"When the Rain falls, I request permission to ride with my cohort."

"No. I need you at my side."

"Because it's safer there?" She watches me with the same hard scrutiny my mother wields. Aside from Victra, Lykos women are the most stubborn breed. "You need your men to do their jobs. That's why you let Alexandar tail you onto the *Medusa*. It's why you sent him off with Thraxa. To do his job. You can't protect us from this."

"You're not Alexandar."

"Yet you put me in a starShell and sent me at the *Medusa*." She leans forward. "And now you feel guilt for that. For letting me come to Mercury at all."

She hits the mark. She knows the promise I made her father.

"Sir, at your side I'm a one-point-two-meter, forty-kilogram liability with quiet feet and a dirty gob. In a starShell, I'm decent. In a Drachenjäger, I'm a full-metal god." Blood flushes her cheeks. "I know you're worried about my pa. But it was my choice to join you when Sevro bailed. My choice to be here. My choice to fight." Her voice hardens. "And if they get through us, it'll be iron over my pa's head, over Dio's head, my brothers' and sisters' heads. So fuck your guilt. And let me do my job."

I didn't have a choice but to use her to rescue Orion. I have a choice now.

"My pulseFist's recoil stabilizer is still touchy," I say. "See if you can calibrate it, lancer." I couldn't protect my son. So as long as I have the power to protect my brother's daughter, I will. When the Rain comes, she'll be sent to Heliopolis to wait out the storm.

I leave Rhonna steaming mad to find Orion sitting alone in the back of the cargo hold. Always stout, now stick-thin, the Blue woman is darker than the gloom outside. Her bare feet dangle out the open door.

Orion hears me enter and looks back. Her face is mottled with the resFlesh that has replaced the chunks Atlas took out. New metal fingers extend from her knuckles. "Trouble?" she asks.

"Pushy relations."

Without a smile, she turns back to watch the polar sky. Beyond the atmosphere of the planet, Atalantia's warships rove, waiting for us to just nip our heads outside the great shield chains so they can drop mass drivers down and make craters of us.

"Cold back here," I say over the whistling wind. Our ship passes over the edge of an ice shelf. "Why don't you head to mess? Colloway says it's bad to sync on an empty stomach."

"I like the cold," she replies distantly. "And my autonomy."

"Fair enough." I settle in beside her to dangle my legs. I didn't lie to Harnassus and my high command. She did pass her first psych evaluation, but I have the suspicion Colloway helped her cheat. For five days after her rescue, she spoke only in brittle, pixelated sentences, preferring the company of her protégé, Colloway, to any other. Then she asked to return to duty. I thought it would bring her back to herself. It hasn't. Her duties may be completed on schedule, but she remains the same as all who survive the Fear Knight . . . altered.

I squint at mathematical notations written in the frost on the ship's hull.

"Reminds me of home when they would turn off the heating," Orion murmurs. "They liked to find new reasons to do that. First calculus I learned was on hull-frost. Fingers so numb I could barely hold the stylus."

"Calculus. Poor lass. I only needed algebra," I say, trying to draw her out of her daze. I wish I could say it was solely for her benefit. "Do it in marker on the side of the clawDrill cockpit with one hand." I make a motion of digging with the other. "Can't stop the drill, you see. Stop too long and you're jammed."

"You would need calculus to properly operate a clawDrill apparatus," she replies.

"Yeah, well, Pa said the rest is all instinct. Disagree, maybe you and I can have a duel back on Mars. There'll be new bunkers that need excavating."

She ignores the challenge and watches a herd of pale seahorses crossing an archipelago of ice. They shake their manes and angle their fins as their stunted legs launch them off the ice back into the water. "Fathers are important," she says. "My kind think the notion perverse." She goes to chew her fingernails only to bite the metal of her prosthetics. She looks at the digits as if seeing them for the first time. "Still, they call me Mother, don't they?"

"That's the civil half of the name."

She shrugs. "Children are disgusting. I would never have them. I cannot abide selfishness."

There is no way, Gold or Red, to understand the empathetic connection minds make in the synaptic drift. Orion's communication with her pilots in battle is nonverbal. Instead it is formed of a web where the electric currents in her brain bond and interact with those of the others. To have one side cut short is the cruelest of amputations. The ghosts of the dead linger in her synapses.

I wonder if she thinks of the sailors she lost in the ambush. If she felt like a mother when she saw the *Annihilo* break the *Dream of Eo* in half. If it is selfishness she cannot stand in children or if it is the fear of losing them.

"The Senate recalled too many ships. Even if you saw Atalantia coming, she would have held the orbit. The Senate lost that battle, not you."

Her head snaps in my direction. "Harnassus lost that battle when he didn't spit on the Senate's orders, and sent half *my* fleet to Luna. Your wife lost the battle, when she did not override the Senate."

"She will not break the New Compact—"

"And you think that a quality? Her precious morality for the price of my sailors? Or is it fear of becoming her father?" She shakes her head. "Harnassus and Virginia bear the guilt. I feel none."

"I do. Often. For the Sons on the Rim. For the Dockyards of Ganymede."

"Then you squander neurons."

Her hard shell has always existed. But not to this extreme. It is easy to forget Orion's roots. From an unsanctioned birth, then childhood, in the dim frost of Phobos's Hive city, destined to pilot garbage haulers and take a government stipend till death, to the commander of the most successful fleet since Silenius's Iron Armada. Amongst my own people, I had a home. Orion was never accepted by hers, until she climbed over their backs to the top, and looked down to see them all pretending to have lifted her up. Of all the soldiers left in my army, I trust her the most, because she alone has never let me down. Any other astral commander, including me, would have lost the *Morning Star,* the surviving ships, and the army itself.

"Rail against my wife all you like, she's what keeps the Republic together," I reply. "And Harnassus kept this army together when I wasn't here, and you were captured."

"Harnassus. Please. Oranges are pedantic apes with opposable thumbs used for two ventures: to spin wrenches and climb union ladders. He did what is in his nature." She runs her hands along her head as if feeling for cracks in the skull.

"And what is your nature?"

"The same as yours. To kill the enemy." As her eyes go distant, her voice softens. "Can you think in space?"

"Depends on who you ask."

"I can't think on the ground. Too much weight. Too many disgusting people and their refuse." She wipes her calculus off the hull. "I know you think Atlas broke me."

"If I thought you were broken, you'd be in the sick bay. I think you're dented."

She likes that. "He is an effective operator, to be certain. He presented me with a hideous desert rodent and said my pain would last only as long as the rat ate. It gnawed the flesh off my calves, nose, and cheeks before it split its stomach and died. It was effective. It horrified. It de-graded."

She looks over at me. "Don't you see?"

I frown and shake my head.

"Together you and I . . . we've broken worlds. Who can do what we have done? What our men have done? Yet we put ourselves at the mercy of rats. We free them. Protect them. Die for them. And when we turn our backs, they unveil their little teeth and gnaw at us one bite at a time. And when we turn to face them, they cheer, and we pretend their gnaw-ing hasn't made us weaker. Rats cannot even govern their own appetite. How can they govern themselves?"

"You sound like one of them," I say so low it's almost a growl.

"Is a doctor wrong when he tells you what you don't want to hear? We don't have a monopoly on truth just because our aims are pretty, young man. If I were wrong, this planet would embrace us. Instead it gnaws at us. If I were wrong, the Republic's fleet would already be here." She looks to the sky. "Where is it, Darrow? Where is our *demokracy*?"

My hand drifts to the holodrop in my pocket. The small teardrop of metal holds the face of my wife. I ache to watch her messages again, to drink in her last words to me, her face, the lines that web around her eyes, to somehow evoke the warmth of her skin and breath. But I fear to do so all the same. Sixty-five million kilometers of space separate Luna and Mercury at current orbit. An even wider gulf divides me from her. I do not doubt *her*. But I doubt she will do what must be done. Orion hit the truth of it. She fears too much to see her father and brother in the mirror to dissolve the Senate. I know she thinks her virtue is contagious. But I fear it merely emboldens the covetous nature in mortals of weaker substance.

"My wife promised that she would wrangle the senators," I say without conviction. "That she would bring the armada."

"Then why did you design Operations Voyager Cloak and Tartarus? Why not just wait for salvation?"

I take my hand off the holodrop. "Because hope is an opiate, not a plan."

"Agreed. So how much longer can you hope, absent any evidence, that the *people* of the Republic are good? That they will finally start pulling their own weight?"

When I do not answer, she stands, putting a hand on my shoulder in empathy. As Sevro became softer, I found solace in Orion. We have always been alike, particularly in our growing suspicions of democracy. But it was always said in a grumble over a bottle of whiskey. Never in a screed like this. Her doubt troubles me, and I don't know how to ease it when the same doubts echo unspoken inside me.

"How long will it take to sync your Blues?" I ask.

"About ninety minutes for full fidelity."

"I'll handle Harnassus today." Her lips curl at his name. "You know his opinions on Tartarus. Last thing I need is you two clawing each other's eyes out. You just sync up and get back to quarters. You need rest." She walks away like a petulant child. I stand. "*Imperator*. Your commanding officer is speaking."

She stops and turns. "According to *our* Senate, you're not my commanding officer. You're a traitor."

There's only one thing to do with doubt. Stomp on it.

"Imperator, I don't need your opinions. I don't care about your feelings. I don't care if you doubt the Republic. I don't care if you hate its people. For this army, this is an extinction event. My only care is that my best weapon is sharp before zero hour. Will you be sharp, Imperator?"

She snaps to attention. "As a rat's teeth, sir."

2

LYSANDER

Annihilo

A FAMED OLD BEHEMOTH FLOATS above the mottled planet. It waits to swallow the corvette that ferried us from Io to Mercury.

At just under four kilometers in length, the behemoth is shaped like an atavistic spear. Her battered hull is sable, like the seashells I used to collect with my father on the shores of Luna's Sea of Serenity. Unlike those glossy shells, she reflects no light.

Her name is *Annihilo.*

I annihilate.

I hope that annihilation is not the total extent of Atalantia's designs.

"Big beast," the man beside me says as if discussing the weather. "That killed Rhea?" I turn, wishing he were Cassius, but Cassius died trying to prevent this very moment.

The Rim has come to make peace with the profligate Core.

Instead of my old friend, mentor, and guardian, it is the eldest son of Romulus au Raa who stands beside me on the bridge of the Ionian corvette. Of all the Golds of the Rim, only Diomedes was deemed fit to serve as ambassador for this dire mission. I believe the choice well made. The man has gravitas. He wears a look of wary bemusement. His dark gold hair is streaked with black and tamed by a knot. His scarred, blunt face is not handsome according to Palatine tastes, but like his slumped shoulders and brutish hands, it belies a quiet, terrible potential.

From the brief flicker of swordsmanship he demonstrated on Io, and the reverence paid to his skills by his fellows, I judge Diomedes to be the only Rim Knight equal to Cassius in the ways of the blade. Yet he alone refused to fight my friend—even at cost to his own family.

For that, Diomedes will always have my respect.

"The *Annihilo* was the flagship of the armada that burned Rhea. Others contributed," I reply.

"It is hideous. Of course, it *does* come from Venus."

"My godfather never cared much about how something looked. Only if it worked." He chuckles at that.

When first I saw Diomedes, I thought he was yet another brute, like so many of the Core duelists with more testosterone than brain. I was wrong. The man is an enigma somewhere between monk and barroom brawler. He shares meals with his Grays and Obsidians. He is never the first to speak or last to laugh. When he tells jokes, they usually come as blunt, elliptical rejoinders. He can be endearing, unnerving, and brutal.

Yet when news reached us that Darrow, Sevro, and Apollonius au Valii-Rath immolated my godfather in his sickbed, Diomedes did not rejoice as did his sister and many of his compatriots. Instead he came to offer his respects.

They were a peculiar comfort.

I loved my godfather, despite his deeds. Whether that is evidence of a personal failing or a moral imperative to love those who were kind to one as a child, I may never know.

"At the Battle of Ceres, the *Annihilo* was broken nearly in half by Darrow's flagship," I continue. "Still she managed to destroy two new Republic destroyers and hold off his fleet until Carthii reinforcements arrived. She is durable."

He leans forward gamely. "It would be interesting to board her."

"How would you do it?"

His eyes trace her instruments of death. "Quickly."

There's that Moonie dry wit. I have grown fond of the man and his taciturn demeanor, but worry his blunt form of honesty will prove a poor fit for the games of the Core. As Grandmother said: "A courtier without a Dancing Mask is as vulnerable as a Praetor without armor." Still, Atalantia would be unwise to underestimate the razormaster of the Rim. Not two months ago, he watched his father walk to his own death as a matter of honor. I would not cross him lightly.

"When Atalantia asks how long the journey took, you will tell her three months," Diomedes says.

"You don't want her to know how fast your ships are."

"Strength always fears speed." His heavy eyes search mine. "You profess a desire to make Gold whole. We are not fools. We know Atalantia will turn on us when she has the upper hand. Helios and the council believe you may be able to convince her against . . . rash action."

"And what does Dido think?" He ignores that. "I will do all in my power. You have my word."

"My mother believes this is a ploy for you to seize the throne. But remember: we will have no part in kingmaking."

"You have my word on that as well."

I mean it, and I think Diomedes believes me.

Damn my inheritance. All that matters is that we still the turmoil that wracks the worlds. Gold remains the only viable peacemaker. But not while Gold is itself divided. To defeat Darrow, we must heal the wounds between the Rim and the Core. For that, I sacrificed Cassius. For that, I would sacrifice myself. But would Atalantia sacrifice herself for anything?

I doubt it.

"His word," a low voice drawls. His sister Seraphina joins us from the main compartment. "We've seen how mercurial that is firsthand. *Salve,* Accipiter Vega."

She leans past me to pat the pilot's shoulder with affection. Our pilot, Vega, is a child with ancient eyes. On the Rim, they believe the best pilots start at age ten and end at twenty. Vega is not yet twelve years standard.

My own pilot, Pytha, is superstitious of Rim Blues and has not yet lost her terror of the Moonies after their Krypteia secret police tortured her. Understandable. So for the duration of the journey, she has secluded herself in my quarters watching fifty-year-old Venusian holofilms and eating meditation mushrooms gifted to her by Diomedes's grandmother, Gaia.

The sound of Gaia's piano echoes in my memory. Perhaps Atalantia will know if I played it as a child, and how I could have forgotten. There are chasms inside that I cannot explore. Hidden truths, or lies, or evils my brain has hidden in shadow to protect myself. What lies beneath the shadow? If it is a construct of my grandmother's, Atalantia will know.

"We should trust him as little as we trust that Core slut," Seraphina says to her brother. Her eyes dress me down. "Less, even. At least she has soldier's blood, not a politician's."

"And soldiers are more noble by default?" I ask.

She blinks and turns to Diomedes. "If I have to share air with this Corespawn any longer, I'll castrate him." She looks between my legs and raises a notched eyebrow. "If anatomically possible."

At the end of our journey together, I find myself unusually embarrassed by my initial attraction to the vicious woman. Upon close-quarters inspection, I have discovered she has few of the virtues I respect—patience, prudence, grace, humility, compassion. What virtues she does have—honesty, loyalty, courage—are contorted by her natural disposition: diabolical hunger.

But my attraction still persists. Credit ten years' separation from my own species, I suppose. Either that or I've discovered a latent predisposition for wild things, and shall be doomed for life by my taste in precocious women.

"If you can't share air, hold your breath," Diomedes mutters to his sister.

"We should not be here," she presses. "We're not ambassadors. I should be with the forward commandos and you at Lux's side leading the legions. Not glad-handing sybarites."

Diomedes kneads the joints of his jaw.

"We are what our leaders ask us to be," he replies.

"And if they told you to clean latrines again?"

"Then I would be beloved by all Browns. And pray the mess cooks don't serve Venusian food too often for supper."

She snorts at that.

"This isn't a dishonor, Sera. I was chosen by the council to represent the Rim. You were chosen by a consul. It is an honor. It is *the* honor."

"Even though you don't believe in this war?" Her eyebrows crawl upward. "Well, don't worry, brother. I doubt you'll see much of it. Damn Lux's honor. Sending Raa when a Copper would have sufficed. We're going to be hostages, even if this Core tramp decides she wants to ally with us before she sticks a razor in our backs."

"I rather think it would be poison," Diomedes replies.

Seraphina pats her brother's cheek. "Either way, you'll be a fine hostage. So good at following orders."

She stalks back to join the escort soldiers.

"The Core isn't like the Rim," I say after she has gone, choosing my words carefully. Diomedes despises only one thing more than gossip. "Blood bubbles from spilled wine."

"You worry that Seraphina will provoke someone into a duel."

"Everyone, actually."

"She is violent, not stupid. She demurs to me."

"And if Dido gave her directives that contradict your own?"

He ignores my comment, but I know it strikes home. While Diomedes represents the Moon Council, his sister has only one master: her mother. And Dido is anything but conciliatory to the gens Grimmus. After all, along with the Jackal of Mars, they organized the affair at Darrow's first Triumph, where Dido's eldest daughter and her father-in-law were butchered.

Dido has not forgotten, nor has Diomedes.

He stares at the *Annihilo*. "My father once said anyone interesting is at war with themselves, and can thus be described in just two words. What are Atalantia's?"

"*Velvet buzzsaw.*" He says nothing in reply. "Atalantia has a savage brain and immensely contagious charisma. She is hindered by neither guilt nor doubt. She knows no half measures. She is a social strategist, a herpetologist, a sculptor, a laughing, masterful woman in love with the sound of her own voice, and convinced that *beauty* is the pinnacle of existence—in any form." I do not speak of her vices. It would be improper for him to ask, so he does not.

He lets the silence stretch and then looks over at me. "Do you know what I learned from my father's death?"

I wait for him to tell me.

"Not to ramble."

Exposed to the harsh elements of Io, Romulus wasted precious air on his last proclamations, and fell short of reaching the tomb of his ancestor, Akari.

I swallow my reply.

Lost in thought, Diomedes looks back at Atalantia's ship. After a time of consideration, he speaks. "You are the legal heir of House Lune, and stand to inherit whatever remains of its possessions." He means ships, legions, oaths that have no doubt passed to House Grimmus. Any inheritance I am due will cost Atalantia dearly. "Will she see you as ally or rival?"

I do not know.

I embarked upon this course believing I could reason with my godfather. He was always rational, but now he is dead. Atalantia as Dictator is far more unpredictable.

Ten years changed me. Did it change her?

Though Atalantia detested children on general principle, she made an exception for her nephew, Ajax, and for me, the son of her best friend and heir of her mentor. I was Atalantia's favorite because, unlike Ajax, I won the affection of the only midColor Atalantia has ever respected—Glirastes of Heliopolis. A hybrid architect-physicist, Glirastes was the greatest Master Maker in centuries, and the tastemaker of an age. And because Grandmother chose me to be the sole inheritor of the Mind's Eye, the secrets to which Atalantia always coveted.

Despite that affection, nothing from my childhood with Atalantia—not our nights at the Hyperion Opera, not our hand-in-hand critiques of Violet exhibitions, nor even our mutual affection for equestrian husbandry—could disabuse me of the suspicion that I was little more than a doll for her to dress up and parade around.

I'm ashamed to admit I let her. With my parents dead and Aja often away, I found myself willing to go to great lengths for a kind word.

And Atalantia gave so many, Grandmother so few.

Yet one of Octavia's axioms haunts me: "Fear those who seek your company for their own vanity. As soon as you eclipse them in the mirror, it won't be the mirror they break."

I have no designs for rule. But convincing Atalantia of that is another matter entirely.

"I cannot say how she will react," I reply at last. "But so long as there is no scar on my face, I cannot inherit anything." I chew the inside of my cheek. "Are you frightened?"

"To meet Atalantia? Conditionally." He pauses. "To see my uncle again? Certainly."

I am a little worried to meet the Fear Knight as well.

3

DARROW

Storm God

Owing to its traumatic rebirth, Mercury is a temperamental planet of moods and stark climate zones. Deeming it easier to change a planet than human nature, Gold worldmakers employed mass-drivers on Mercury to alter her rotational period to match Earth's. Such heavy-handed terraforming is sometimes necessary, but it leaves visible seams.

At the seam where the Sycorax Sea meets the polar ice, steam seeps from the wide mouth Harnassus's blacksmiths cut into the façade of a glacier. Landing lights invite us into the glacier where a makeshift industrial world bustles around an excavation site. As we land, the sprawling barracks and engineering garages and mess halls on the floor look like toy blocks compared to the mass of metal being dug out of the ice. The ancient engine looks like an upside-down turtle shell pierced with a trident.

Imperator Cadus Harnassus, the Terran hero of Old Tokyo, meets me on the sand-strewn tarmac. He is a geode of a man. Slump-shouldered, slow-walking, with umber skin and a bulbous drinker's nose set in a face that looks increasingly like an angry puppy's the deeper he plunges into his fifties—all of which belies the intricate intelligence of a starShell engineer who became the hero of his caste.

For eight years, he's kept his cherished Terran Second Legion Blacksmiths intact. In this war Gold may hold a monopoly on supersoldiers and military doctrine, but we have one on creativity. Wary as I am to admit it, much of that is thanks to Harnassus.

I've had brilliant commanders, stupid commanders, and bloody commanders, but finding a steady commander is as rare as an honest man in a Silver guildhouse. If only this steady commander didn't have ambitions of one day sitting in my wife's chair.

Formally speaking, he is the ArchImperator of this army, and I am an outlaw.

It was Harnassus whom the Senate formerly anointed my successor when I went rogue. Orion, they knew, was far too loyal to me. And it was Harnassus who, either for political gain or out of pedantic obedience to the law, overruled Orion and sent nearly half the fleet back to Luna, setting the stage for Atalantia's attack on the remnant. Gone are the days when he could sit at any table and chew the fat with the infantry. The men, like Orion, blame him for this.

But in the end it wasn't Harnassus who chose to invade Mercury. That's on me.

"Look at that. The Myth and his puppy." Harnassus's Orange eyes dance over Rhonna and me as if he knows a private joke. "Have you come to join me in my northern banishment?"

"You're behind schedule, Imperator," I say with a salute.

He returns a half-hearted one and spits out a stream of tobacco juice. It freezes in his tangled beard.

"Then the schedule's wrong." He scratches his head and pulls out a hair. Not that he can spare many. "My lads are worked to the bone for this damn insanity you and the airhead cooked up."

I jerk my head to the engineers that disembark from the steaming shuttles. "That's why I brought more. The Seventeenth is all yours. Their storm engine in the Waste is primed and ready. Orion has had four of hers in the Sycorax burning two klicks deep for a week."

He frowns. "There's five others? You might have told me."

"There are six others. Operational security is paramount."

"Fancy way of saying you don't trust me."

"I trusted you with this one, didn't I?"

"So much you came yourself. Seven all told then." His mind goes to work. "How hot's that witch's cauldron? Forty, forty-one?"

"Forty-three Celsius," Orion says as she comes off the Pale behind me. Her six storm pilots flank her. I hide my irritation. She was supposed to wait. Harnassus eyes her. Privately, he expressed his doubts of her mental readiness for duty. Publicly, he salutes his equal rank.

"I was rounding," he says.

"Well, your kind can afford to round. Not you who does the dying."

"Surprised to see you in the field, Imperator Aquarii." Harnassus wheels those slumped shoulders toward me. "Why is she here?"

"I'll tell you in the briefing."

"Right. Operational security. Well, their meteorologists will have caught that spike, Aquarii. Might be evil little brainwashed warlocks, but they ain't fools like the two of you. Flying in the same shuttle. Shit. What if the Fear Knight got both of you?"

"Then your dreams would come true," Orion says. "And you'd lead the army. My engines are along the volcanic range. Your . . . *warlocks* will think it's hydrothermal vents. They'll never suspect it could creep to fifty Celsius."

"Then what the hell do you need this one for?"

"Total control," Orion says.

"Total control?" Harnassus's suspicions of being kept in the dark are confirmed. He glowers back at the engine. "Didn't you two read the stories? Pandora doesn't like it when you play with her box."

Orion regards him with as much respect as Sevro would a particularly small turd. "Pandora was a fiction written by men to blame the miseries of the world on women. I am not a fiction. So, can we see the merchandise? Or do you want to stand here bickering semantics and freezing our dicks off as I pretend a hundred thousand of my sailors didn't die for your political wet dreams?"

The two unmovable objects glare at each other.

"You two done?" I ask. "Yeah, you're done. I want that machine in the air. *Now.*"

The ice is the color of cold lips as the men and women of the famed Second swarm over the metal hull of an unearthed colossus. Imprisoned for centuries in the ice, the curvature of the machine's top hull, nearly a kilometer in diameter, is warped and rife with fissures. Harnassus roves the perimeter of the dig site bellowing gearslang. He's been in a state of agitation since Orion and her Blues entered the machine more than two hours ago.

The Master Maker Glirastes stands wrapped in the fur of a polar bear. Lean, bald, and as cruel looking as a vulture, the most famous artificer in the Society wrinkles his nose and sniffs a line of demon dust from a dispenser. Orange like Harnassus, he is of an entirely different class. One that rubbed shoulders with Gold autarchs and sculpted libraries and arcane devices for their pleasure from Mercury to Luna. He is not of the Rising, though his cooperation was vital for my Rain on the planet.

"You've worked a miracle," I say to him.

"A miracle he says." The Master Maker snorts in derision and to claim the last of the narcotics from the right nostril of his hooked nose. "When you took this planet, you said in one year's time I would weep in joy at the fruits a single year of liberty would bring. Peer upon this visage, young warlord, is it one in thrall to joy?"

"Year's not up yet," I say.

"These machines are of a primordial power not in concert with human affairs," he says, turning to me with that withering, pinched gaze. "Considering my labors, I trust your promise holds." Before my legions took the planet, I made a promise to Glirastes to avoid bombardment of population centers. Because of that promise, hundreds of thousands of my men died in our Rain, but millions of civilians were kept from the crossfire. That I honored the promise despite its dire cost is the only reason he trusts me enough to help restart the arcane tech within the engines. That and his fear of what Atalantia will do to collaborators, especially ones as famous as Glirastes the Master Maker of Mercury.

The promise I made him then has extended to the Storm Gods.

"It holds," I say. "We won't exceed primary horizon."

"I will not be party to genocide. You know what will happen if . . ."

"Believe it or not, Mercury is as valuable to my cause as its people are to your sterling heart." He senses my sarcasm and scowls.

"Gods know why Octavia kept these infernal beasts enchained," he says, turning back to the engine with a gaze that is equal parts adoration, envy, and fear. "Even the Votum did not know what lay beneath the surface of their planet. Even I did not know."

I hope that means Atalantia does not know.

"Why does a Gold do anything?" I ask him. "For control."

The Storm Gods are leftover weather-shapers from the terraforming of the planet. They worked in lockstep with the Lovelock engines to make Mercury habitable. It took my wife four years and the labor of two hundred Greens to crack Octavia's Crescent Vault in the Citadel. The secret treasures we found inside were worth a fleet of starships. I'm betting ten million lives that Octavia was too paranoid to let anyone but blood in on her family secrets.

Glirastes stares at the Storm God as if waiting for its colossal mass to whisper a secret to him, then he crosses his arms and recedes into the depths of his mental labyrinth. The Maker is a temperamental genius, but he cares about the people of this planet. Thank the Vale for that.

At the wail of a siren, the Blacksmiths begin evacuation of the pit via gravLifts. Above, the last of the clawDrills drift through the air, ferried by heavy-duty cargo haulers bound south, to be stored at our supply depot in Heliopolis. Orion and her Blues are the last to depart the engine. The engineers watch territorially as they float back to me on a gravSled. Glirastes sips the coffee his slave brings.

"Hardware is installed and operational," Orion says. "So much for Harnassus's whinging. Worked to the bone indeed. His Blacksmiths did fine work, for greasers."

"They're doped out of their minds," Glirastes adds.

He's right. If I were younger, I'd think valiant rage or purpose kept them steady. But I'm not the only one light on sleep. My army is a band of marionettes held up by strings called nazopran, dolomine, and zoladone.

"Will it work?" I ask Glirastes.

"I ran five million simulations, only two million of which ended in the engines imploding, killing all aboard," Glirastes says. "So in theory, yes."

"Comforting," I mutter.

Harnassus trudges over, trying to catch our conversation. "Will you do the honors, Imperator?" I ask.

"This is your monster. You wake it up." He tosses the control pad to me.

Annoyed, I activate the flight protocol. Harnassus doesn't even watch to see the gravity engines flare underneath the ancient machine. For a dreadful moment, nothing happens. I stare down. *Rise, you bastard. Rise.*

"I told you it was a mistake including Harnassus," Orion whispers. "He thought this was the only engine. He sabotaged it."

"He's an ass, not a traitor," I say.

Then the Storm God lets loose a terrible groan as it feels the force of Sun Industries gravity engines urging it to waken from its slumber. Except for Harnassus, all the aides and commanders beside me step back.

With a shriek of metal, the machine begins to rise, climbing up and up until it hangs a hundred meters above, blocking the roof of the man-made cavern. Until its gravity engines create a languid field of low gravity beneath it, suspending blocks of ice. Soon the engine will be ready to join its brethren in the sea.

I smile in satisfaction.

4

LYSANDER

Ajax, Son of Aja

U PON LANDING ON THE *Annihilo*, Diomedes and I lead the Rim
deputation down a corridor of Ash Guard. Instead of the ceremonial armor appropriate for the reception of enemy dignitaries, Atalantia's
elite wear field armor. Perhaps that is because they do not formally recognize the Rim's independence. The beetle-black metal of the field armor
is dented and scuffed from war on four spheres. But the pearl House
Grimmus skulls upon their breastplates are polished to a gleam.

The slight was not meant to go unnoticed, nor does it.

This is not the welcome for a prodigal son or an old ally.

This is a presentation of force to blood traitors.

As we pass the rows of hostile Grays, I wonder how many of them
Atalantia pillaged from my Praetorians and my family legions. I search,
but find no Praetorians. No Rhone ti Flavinius, no Exter ti Kaan, nor
even Fausta ti Hu standing as officers before the ranks.

At the end of the corridor of Ash Guard, ten calamitously large Obsidian Stained stomp their axe hafts into the deck to bar our path to the
waiting cadre of Core Golds. The Stained step to the side, and for the
first time in a decade, the two breeds of Aureate measure one another
face-to-face.

The Golds of the Core—battle-scarred and vain—drip in priceless
armor gilded and monstrously shaped by the finest artificers the worlds
have ever seen. Most wear their hair short, in war fashion, and their
eyebrows notched. Their thick-boned frames are fortressed by heavy

muscle grown under strict prenatal observation, esoteric chemical protocols, and tenacious physical competition with their peers.

I would not say they are humanity perfected. They seem more like racing Thoroughbreds jockeying for position.

In comparison, the Golds of the Rim are lean and shabby. Their bodies, like their culture, hardened by privation and self-discipline. They wear their hair long, preferring to comb it before battle in the way of the Peloponnesians. They are clad in simple leather boots and drab robes they sewed themselves. Not one amongst them wears anything that couldn't be bought at a lowColor bazaar for fifty credits, except their kitari short swords and their long razors, which they call hasta.

The silence between the two parties stretches with contempt.

When at last one of the Core Golds speaks, it is a Martian I long thought dead. The winged shoulders of her swan armor are dented, but the flaming heart of her breastplate burns bright in the drab hangar. Her face, smooth as alabaster in memory, is now tough as a miner's heel. But not even war could dim the spark in the eyes of Kalindora au San. The Love Knight.

I remember her as a demure, gentle creature in love not with the glory of war, but the grace of poetry and architecture. When I was a boy, I held only one other woman her age in equal esteem: Virginia au Augustus. The wife of the Reaper, and my grandmother's usurper.

As a man, I behold Kalindora far differently.

Even Diomedes takes a second look. Her lips, though riven by two scars, are full and seem only capable of whispers. Her nose is small and sharp, but her defining characteristic is her eyes. Every gradient of gold that exists spirals toward the pit of her pupils, paling in hue as they approach that darkness so it seems as if one stares at an eclipse.

"Is it him?" Kalindora asks a taller, younger knight in armor the color of a storm cloud. His skin is black, his eyes violent amber. The pelt of a pearl leopard sways from his powerful shoulders as he steps forward to examine me. For a moment, it feels as if we're both looking through a dirty pane of glass, leaning and squinting to see if the apparition on the other side is really a long-lost friend or merely some trick.

I barely recognize the man I once called "brother."

Only the long lashes of his eyes are the same.

In the eleven years since I last saw him, his plump features, often an item of hushed ridicule on the Palatine, have melted away to reveal an

Adonic visage so surly, so passionate, so *manly* even Cassius might, in a drunken moment, declare some minor flaw in the man in hopes of diluting his own utter jealousy.

Octavia was always disappointed in her little genetic experiment. She would not be now. Ajax, son of the loveless genetic union of Aja and Atlas au Raa, is a masculine specimen.

By the phalera that bedeck Ajax's armor, I see he has already fulfilled his childhood dreams. He wears not just his Peerless scar, but insignia signifying the office of Storm Knight, and the rank of a full Legate infantry commander.

With my scarless face and my drab civilian vestments, before the two Olympic Knights, I feel my ten-year absence more acutely than ever.

"You are the man who claims to be Lysander au Lune," Ajax sneers.

"Ajax." Mistaking his tone for banter, I reach to embrace him. The Stained block my path. I actually feel wounded. "Don't you recognize me?"

Ajax's eyes narrow to slits. "Test him with the *Manteío*."

In Greek, it means "oracle." I've played with oracles before. My heart sinks. Then a Pink slave glides forward to present me not with one of Grandmother's pale truth-measuring creatures, but with a black metal orb ringed with serpents. In the center of the orb is an upturned needle.

"A drop of blood, if it please the *dominus*."

Though it may look kinder than my grandmother's oracles, I suffer no delusions. The needle will be coated with a DNA-coded poison. If I prove an imposter, my death will be a misery so profane it could only be designed by the cruelest of Venusian alchemists—the best of which Atalantia has on permanent retainer. Even if I prove my identity, the fate may be the same.

The fact that Atalantia has my DNA at all suggests the depth of her intelligence operations. Owing to two sophisticated poisonings of Sovereigns and one dreadful incident of cloning, my family guards their DNA as if it were life itself.

Why else would we convince the rest of the Aureate to embrace the ritual of shooting the deceased into the sun? Because it looks pretty? Nothing is to be left behind.

I prick a thumb with the needle.

The Core Golds watch as a single drop of blood rolls down the needle to be absorbed into the metal. Whatever poison it contained does not activate. If Atalantia didn't have my DNA before, now she does. The orb ripples with wonderful ingenuity as the serpents carve paths along its exterior until a bust of my preadolescent face stares back at me. The slave returns it to Ajax.

He examines the face.

"DNA profile confirmed," a bald Green adjunct says. His pupils glow from his uplink. *"Security helix processing."* A lengthy pause. Kalindora turns, but Ajax's eyes never leave my face. *"DNA profile authenticated. Forgery probability one in thirteen trillion."*

"I concur," Kalindora says. Her demeanor softens.

The Core Golds stiffen at the news, their competitive brains calculating how my return affects their individual machinations.

Still unconvinced, Ajax tosses the *Manteío* to the slave. "What did my grandfather say to my mother the night he had her execute Flavius au Grecco?"

I don't smile at the memory. "Now that the pig is filleted and eaten, what's for dessert?"

His eyes widen.

"Brother!" He springs through the Obsidians to rattle my bones with a powerful hug that lifts my feet clean off the deck. This is the Ajax I remember. The kind, generous brother who could never bridle either affection or fury. "I'm sorry, we had to be certain. The enemy is devious in his gambits." When he sets me down, he clutches my face between his long-fingered hands and kisses me firmly on the mouth. "Little Lysander. Haha! They said you were dead. But look at you . . ." He dusts off my shoulders. "Corporeal as a cormorant and still a spry dandy of a thing after so long in captivity." He makes a feint at my face. "Not that spry."

Captivity.

Cassius would laugh.

I'm not eager to disabuse Ajax of the notion just yet.

"They said you were your mother's spitting image," I reply. "They didn't say you were taller."

It's an understatement. He's far larger.

Awash with joy, he claps my shoulders and leans his forehead down to press it against mine. He breathes deep. Scent has always been his favorite sense.

"When we received the family code, we thought it was one of the

Slave King's tricks. Then we saw your signifier. The complexity of the code was a symphony upon my heartstrings." He closes his eyes. "Together again."

"Together again, brother," I say. It still seems impossible to me, and I hold back because I know the revelations I must share will be held against me. Only when Ajax hugs me after I have shared those revelations will this reunion be real. "I mourned for your grandfather. He deserved far better."

Ajax pulls away, his face downcast.

"Yes, well, he made his mark, didn't he? Now it is our turn." His eyes break away from our private moment long enough to survey the Raa. His voice becomes truculent. "Unless you have a new family . . ."

Kalindora clears her throat. With apologies, I greet her with less informality than I would like and introduce Diomedes and the Rim deputation. In reply to Diomedes's formal bow, Kalindora merely clicks her tongue.

"When we received Lysander's communiqué, we thought you a mummer's fiction. But here you are, bold as alley cats, and just as dusty."

"On behalf of the Rim Dominion—" Diomedes begins before Kalindora interrupts him.

"Your uncle extends his apologies. Atlas would be here to greet you himself, but war is a . . . consuming affair." Her lovely eyes narrow. "I'm sure you wouldn't know."

Ajax steps territorially between Diomedes and me to measure the Rim Knight. "So *you're* the eldest spawn of Romulus and that Venusian whore. How bold you must be to liberate Lysander from the captivity of the Traitor." So that is what they call Cassius. Not ideal. "I suppose I owe you a debt, *cousin.*"

Odd as it is to hear aloud, they are cousins. Both with the pure Raa blood of the Conquerors in their veins. But, like so many of the dwindling apex genetic lines, they hold little in common except that shared lineage and the layered animosity of ancestral infighting.

Diomedes looks at me, then back to Ajax.

"I hold no man in my debt," he replies.

"I assume the Traitor is dead?" Ajax asks. Diomedes nods. "Did you deliver the killing blow? Did he squeal?" Diomedes does not reply. "I see your aesthetic penury extends to your vocabulary. In the Core, it is polite to answer a question when asked."

Seraphina's jaw muscles work as she watches her brother suffer the insult.

"I take no joy in the demise of an honorable man," Diomedes says to the taller man with princely dignity. "But I fear before he fell, he . . . slew your half-brother, Bellerephon."

Ajax startles Diomedes with a laugh. Despite his admitted dislike for his cousin Bellerephon, seeing amusement at the death of a man he knew all his life fills Diomedes with a sense of disappointed understanding. He is in a different world now where down is up and up is down. One can never really prepare for that.

"Bellerephon?" Ajax laughs. "Never knew the spawn. Our spies say you were barely better than him with the blade. Tell me, who is the most exemplary of the Rim Knights? You?"

"I would be a poor judge. But if you measure the worth of a man by his skill with a blade, then I imagine it is the person least like you."

Seraphina blinks at her brother as if he just grew horns. A slow smile grows.

The Rim is not here to be pushed around.

Kalindora raises an eyebrow at me.

Ajax, on the other hand . . . well, he was mocked as a child, and does not like it any better as a man. He circles Diomedes and succumbs to mock rage when he spies the lightning and clouds on Diomedes's cloak. "It seems you wear *my* crest, goodman."

"It is not your crest any more than it was the crest of the man who came before you. It represents an idea. In our case, humility."

"Humility? And how is that?"

"A man is nothing before the storm."

Ajax stands nose-to-nose with the smaller man. "I am the storm. Take it off."

Oh, Hades is the shared thought of every single person watching, maybe even Ajax. Atalantia certainly doesn't want him killing or getting killed by a Raa in a hangar bay.

Never deny your enemy a chance for retreat. Victory may cost too much.

"Why?" Diomedes replies evenly. "I am the Storm Knight of the Rim Dominion. I make no claim to be that of the Core."

"Yet you are wearing it in the Core, my goodman. How could I bear such a slight to me, and to an office which I hold in such high esteem? To do so would curl my cock with indignity."

It's a clever move by Ajax, and a credit to how bright he is. It allows Diomedes a way out, at a toll. Diomedes recognizes it and pays willingly. He removes his cloak and folds it in his hands.

Ajax spoils his victory and loses the respect of all but sadists by ripping the cloak from Diomedes's hands and pissing on it. Then Ajax seals up his pelvic armor and looks at me.

Do you defend him?

With Ajax, you're either with him or against him. Today, I cannot afford the latter, and recognize the social stratagem he uses now. It is called Requisite Disrespect, a protocol of the Dancing Mask. One of Atalantia's favorite ploys.

"Are you quite done, Ajax?" Kalindora asks with a sigh.

Ajax wipes his hands on Diomedes's homespun tunic. "Quite."

Seraphina has had enough. She steps forward, hand on kitari, stopped only by a quiet click of her brother's tongue. Whatever that click means, she takes it very seriously.

Ten Obsidian Stained make a guttural sound as they lower their axes. But Ajax and the Core Golds simply watch like a row of patient crocodiles. Now they know there is some hot blood in the Rim after all. Whether it is in an hour or five years, they will exploit it, either collectively or individually.

I warned Diomedes.

"By Juno's cunt, your catamite is sensitive, Raa," Ajax purrs, playing it off as a farce instead of a temperament reconnoiter.

"My sister is merely stretching after her long journey," Diomedes replies.

"Sister? *Sister?*" Ajax asks. "But where are the tits? Do you now sear them off like Sefi's winged lesbians?"

"No, but on the Rim, we geld unctuous Obsidians," Seraphina replies. "Step closer, *gahja.* I'll muster a tutorial."

Ajax bows in amusement at the invitation. "Perhaps later, cousin. But for now, I believe Kalindora is at her wit's end with me. Apologies, of course. It is just so *exciting* to have Raa back in the fold. The last ones were too short-lived." With large stepping motions, he mocks how a Julii boot famously stomped Diomedes's and Seraphina's elder sister to death. Then he throws an arm around me and motions the Raa to follow. "Welcome to the Ash Legions."

5

DARROW

Voyager Cloak

"OPERATION VOYAGER CLOAK IS LIVE," I tell the cluster of officers who gather in the mess hall of the construction site. Glirastes has been removed, bound for Heliopolis, where he'll be under guard until the operation is complete. Those who remain are engineering Legates, Blue flight commanders, and cocky sky rangers, all veterans of at least two campaigns. Reliable, in other words. Harnassus sits in stony silence. "You have been laboring in darkness. The details of Voyager Cloak have been compartmentalized for security reasons. Allow me to paint the full picture.

"What you know: Atalantia is meticulous. After our little dance in the graveyard, she has cleared the debris field and the mines. Mercury is fully blockaded. She has tactical and numerical superiority—likely two to one on the ground. From her position she can destroy any ship that attempts to breach orbit, and launch a Rain to reinforce any point on the planet within twenty minutes. Our ability to respond pales in comparison. Effectively, this gives her the ability to flank any of our units at leisure. Our shields are our only advantage. As long as they are up, she has no artillery support and will not risk landing ground elements. If our shield chain falls, we lose. Full stop.

"Once she has destroyed us, she will turn her eyes on the Republic. Some of you believe we should hold tight for reinforcements from Luna." I avoid looking at Harnassus. It isn't time to dress him down. "Let me dispel that notion. *If* reinforcements come, Atalantia will know and launch an invasion on her terms before they can arrive. By that time, the Fear Knight will have already taken steps to weaken our position in ways we cannot counter. They will have the initiative and the sky. Again, we lose.

"We cannot retreat, we cannot surrender, we cannot attack, we cannot wait. Our only option is to define the terms of engagement. We will invite them in." They lean forward.

"The tanks and infantry meant for Mars, Luna, and Earth will die here on Mercury."

I am proud that the officers do not flinch.

Any illusions of rescue that my return might have awoken now dispel. I cannot wave my hands and whisk them back to Mars.

This is no tale of salvation, it is one of sacrifice. This is our Thermopylae.

"What you don't know: Several nights ago, the first stage of Operation Voyager Cloak went into effect when the Fear Knight shot down a blacksparrow east of the Hesperides. On board was a corpse planted by Howler intelligence agents with a dataStack of intelligence information regarding a vulnerability within our shield chain.

"It appears the Fear Knight has taken the bait. As we speak, he is being herded by the Howlers toward Eleusis, which, once destroyed, will lead to a chain-overload of shield generators, creating a small gap south of Pan in the Plains of Caduceus that Atalantia will find impossible to resist.

"The terrain is perfect landfall. It is flat enough for her tanks. Dry enough for her titans. Wide enough to land ten legions at a time. And in perfect position to split our northern forces, overrun our defenses on the Children on the Petasos Peninsula with aerial infantry, and roll tanks westward down the coast to hit Tyche.

"That landfall is our killbox. It is mined with atomics, surrounded by two hidden army groups supported by six of our ten remaining torch-Ships and Red Reach base. When Atalantia's army lands there, it will be annihilated from three sides. She will retreat along the only route available: south into the Waste of Ladon. They say that desert eats armies. I mean to feed it another."

They grin and wait for the reason they've been gathered four hundred klicks north, barred from the field of battle by an entire sea.

"Why then are you here?" I take a moment to look each of them in the eyes. "You are not part of Operation Voyager Cloak. The men and women in this room will form BlueReach Seven, under direct command of Orion from BlueReach One, off the coast of Tyche. If all else fails, you are my insurance policy. You are Operation Tartarus."

After the officers disperse to receive direct orders from Orion, I motion Harnassus to take a walk with me along the excavation site. We have business to finish. And I want witnesses. The engine has settled back into its berth after its test run. Engineers call to one another as they make last-minute adjustments. "So you figured a way to make them sync-compatible," Harnassus says. "And a way to handle the data-load. It will be terabytes per second."

"I know."

"My Blacksmiths saw them installing foreign tech in the control room. If not my men, who designed it?"

"We had to use all available resources on such short notice."

"What resources?"

"The Master Maker Glirastes."

His face goes blank. "Glirastes. He's already tinkered with enough, don't you think?"

"He is the only man on Mercury who studies ancient tech for pleasure," I say. "If you could have done it, I'd have asked you."

"He is a Gold pet."

"I know you disagree with this course—"

"That is an abuse of language." Harnassus's voice doesn't rise a decibel. "When you said we would let them inside our shields, I thought I misheard. When you told me what we were unearthing, I thought I'd gone mad. Now you're telling me there's not one engine but seven, run with the tech of a Gold pet. I haven't gone mad." He jabs a finger up into my chest and calmly says, "You have."

I look down at his puny finger.

"Control yourself, Imperator. We set the tone. Tartarus is merely—"

"Insurance, yeah. I heard."

"You don't think we can match them on the ground."

"No."

"Need I remind you this is still the army that freed both our homes?"

"Except no Sefi, no Sevro, no Seventh." The crossed wrenches on his uniform glint as the Terran folds his thick forearms over each other.

"The enemy is freshly provisioned from Venus, her legions replenished, her machines serviced. These aren't softfoot Pixies. These are the full Ash Legions. That means Legios XX Fulminata, XIII Dracones, X Purdus. On our best day, any of those would test our mettle. But she's brought all of them. And this isn't our best day. Just a week ago, my men were melting down scrap metal so we could fill the Twenty-third's magazines. Scrap metal. Not depleted uranium. *Scrap metal.* Darrow, you know I am no Cassandra. But the moment the first Peerless boot touches Mercurian soil, we've lost the planet. This isn't Thermopylae. This is Cannae. We will die in the Ladon."

I ignore the appeal to the classical obsession I share with the Golds.

"Harnassus, we lost the planet the moment you sent half the fleet home."

He appraises me coolly. "So there it is. You want to flog me for it? You want an apology? Fuck you. There's your apology. I obeyed my oath. The sword of the people should never silence its voice. And the voice of the people is the Senate. Not you."

"And what does the Senate tell you now?" I cup my ear. "The voice isn't speaking. So the sword will."

"You know why I prefer Sevro to you? He might burn hot. But you go cold. There's no talking to you when you're like this. You're inhuman. You're a god emperor."

His Blacksmiths have noticed the tenor of our conversation if not its content. Thraxa worried over my choice of theater for this game, surrounded by Harnassus's men. But you don't get the wolf by the tongue without reaching through its teeth.

He steps close to me. "You didn't come back to save us. You came back to kill them." He suppresses a shudder of anger. "You're rolling dice in the dark. Reinforcements may already be en route. At least try to run their blockade. Get a signal out. Contact the Senate. Learn their intentions. You have a solemn duty to keep the men alive as long as possible. And if you use those engines, we're as bad as the enemy."

"Harnassus. Look around. Does today look like a day where I am inclined to entertain anyone's moral protestations? I am going forward. Are you with me, Imperator?"

"And if I'm not?"

"My left hand can't have a mind of its own."

At my command, ten black-clad Howlers file out of the *Necromancer.* The chameleon properties of their pulseArmor ripple to match the pale ice. Felix tilts his buzzed head.

Harnassus's face falls. "You would use Howlers . . . on me?"

"That choice is yours."

The most terrifying Golds, Obsidians, and Grays in the legions stare him down. Each one would kill him for me, or slam cuffs on his wrists and throw him in the brig. Harnassus glances at his Blacksmiths, wondering if they would do the same. He comes to the correct conclusion and lowers his voice. "If you are forced to choose between saving our army and killing theirs, I need your word you will choose us."

"We are an expeditionary force. Our mission is to find and destroy the enemy." I grin. "Well, we've found 'em. Your answer, Imperator."

He stares at the ground, hands quivering at his sides. He lost the army as soon as I returned. I understand him well enough to know he once harbored thoughts of stepping in if I took us to the edge. Now he knows that was never an option. "Damn you," he says and looks up. "Damn you." Though the anger never leaves his eyes, he delivers his salute with a precision few would think his slumped body could manage. He holds it far too long for my tastes. "Hail Reaper."

"Sir . . ." Rhonna says from behind. "It's Pup One."

In the *Necromancer's* communications bay, a meter-tall hologram of Alexandar warps in and out, eroded by the jamming tech from Atalantia's fleet. Harnassus and Orion crowd in behind me.

"Lost . . . Fear . . . in the . . . Ladon."

"Does that mean Fear's going after Eleusis?" I ask. "Did he take the bait?"

". . . bait . . . no . . . from . . . Ang . . ." Harnassus crosses his arms and strains to hear Alexandar. *"Distress . . . from . . . No . . . cation."*

"Repeat. Pup One. Repeat."

"Did not take bait. No movement on Eleusis. . . . received a distress call from Angelia. Communication from . . . Angelia . . . since 06 . . ."

"Angelia . . ." I murmur. Angelia is a small city in the mid-eastern Ladon, one we used for civilian evacuation from the cities surrounding our killbox. It's under the Northern Shield Chain, but not a generator nexus like Eleusis. Atlas was supposed to attack Eleusis. I left it wide open for him, practically begging to be assaulted.

Perhaps it begged too much.

Harnassus's jaw muscles work overtime.

"The bastard knows. He guessed your plan."

"Specious assumption," Orion replies. "Angelia doesn't have a generator like Eleusis. It's under the shadow of Kydon's."

"Then what does he want there?" Harnassus asks. "What does it have? Darrow?"

I can't wait for further intel. A decision must be made. But if I play my hand too soon, it all falls apart. *Dammit. What went wrong?* "Harnassus, you're done here. I want you back in Heliopolis."

"Away from the fight with the civilians and rear echelon?" he asks.

"The fight will be at Tyche. When we lose the air, we'll need you to continue to supply us reinforcements via the gravLoop. And we need to protect the integrity of the command chain. If I fall in the desert and Orion falls with the engines, the army must have a commander."

That's the thing about Harnassus. Whatever our differences, when the enemy comes, he's got my back. He snaps a salute. As he turns, he glares at Orion. I watch her as he departs. One by one, my bodyguards slide down the passage into the garage below. They know what's coming. *Here we go again.* The thought fills me with exhaustion.

"I need you at BlueReach One," I tell Orion. "Take any of the shuttles, get the rest of the pilots to their engines." I grab her arm as she moves to the passage. "We do not raise the Storm Gods above primary horizon. Swear to me."

"On my life."

I bring her forehead to mine. "From *Vanguard* till Vale, sister."

She smiles in remembrance of that old ship where we met. "*Vanguard* till Vale, brother." She departs and takes something of me with her. You never know anymore when you will see a friend again. Or if. Of all the people I know, Orion has never said what she would do after the war. I feel a need to know now, but she's already calling to her storm pilots and shoving them toward shuttles.

"You think she's all there?" Rhonna says from the disembarkation plank. "If she goes Blood Red . . ."

"I have an insurance plan."

"'Course you do."

I turn to her. About to tell her to go with Harnassus, when I see she understands what I mean . . . what *exactly* I mean by insurance plan on Orion. Fuck. She sees right through me.

"Where is it?" she asks. "Just in case . . ."

In case I lie dead on the battlefield, she means.

When I asked Glirastes to build the sync hardware for the Storm Gods, I had him construct a safety valve so that the Blues running it couldn't decide the fate of the planet without me. I pull the master switch from my coat and brandish it at Rhonna.

"And in armor?" she asks.

"Second thigh box. Right leg."

And like that, she ensures her place at my side. *I'm sorry, brother.*

I send a message to the Howlers: "Alexandar, tell Thraxa to reconnoiter Angelia. Do not engage the Fear Knight. I'm on my way."

6

LYSANDER

Carnivores

"LYSANDER AU LUNE. HOW vital you look, for a ghost." Atalantia lifts me from my knees to embrace me in her meditation chamber. "Look, Hypatia, our old friend," she croons. The tamed black vasta serpent that coils about Atalantia's throat like a necklace eyes me with reptilian indifference. "Go on, my dear, give dear Lysander a kiss."

I'd forgotten how terrifying it is to feel the cold scales of Venus's most venomous creature against your lips. As I pull back from the kiss, I watch the snake's chameleon scales wash pale to match my skin tone, and then darken as it coils back around Atalantia's neck. "She remembers you!" Atalantia croons.

Her meditation chamber is more pleasant than her jewelry. Unlike Grandmother, Atalantia enjoys a little chaos. Her chamber is a garden with some of the most esoteric vegetation I have ever seen. Under a dome of stars, helix trees with violet leaves wend like DNA strands. Birds sing. And even a monkey or two swings in the trees. Were it not for Mercury turning outside the viewport, I would not know I was on a battleship.

My favorite touch is the carnivorous orchids perched upon babbling cupid fountains. Their tongues reach for me as I look at Atalantia.

Like Ajax, Atalantia has changed in my absence. Now in her late forties, the youngest Grimmus sister is lean and hungry-looking. She looks not a day over twenty-five except in the eyes. But where once reclined the whimsical heartbreaker of the Palatine now stands a soldier.

Gone are the gowns and the jewels and the hair swaying in braids down past her lower back. Gone are the diamond nails and spiced champagne flutes and the halls filled with muscled Pink paramours. The gowns have been replaced by a dramatic black uniform with rows of golden spikes and a death's-head on each shoulder, and the paramours by a ship full of the intrepid killers from my generation, the ice-eyed veterans of her own, and the remaining legends of the one before.

Atalantia's hair is faded on the sides, in short braids on the top. One could almost mistake her for one of those humorless martial Martians she used to mock.

Seeing her again is like touching a fragment of home. More even than seeing Ajax or Kalindora. She was close with my parents. While I have always feared Atlas, my father's best friend, I have never feared my mother's. In many ways, Atalantia was as much a protector to me as Aja was.

We are joined by Ajax, Kalindora, and, via hologram, an endangered species—the Primuses of the remaining houses of the Conquering. They are Carthii, the rich and licentious shipbuilders of Venus; the purity-obsessed Falthe, nomadic after their lands on Earth fell; and Votum, the poetic, yet ultimately practical metal-mining magnates and builders of Mercury, recently evicted, of course.

Absent are the upstart families who have risen through war still deemed petty by this lot. And, most notably, the ancient Saud, the infantry purveyors of Venus. Dido's family are the chief rivals of the Carthii, Atalantia's strongest allies. Their absence speaks volumes.

So this is still a den of carnivores. It will prove a difficult audience. At least I am spared from telling Julia au Bellona of Cassius's fate at the hands of the Rim. She is not here.

"I grieved to hear of your father's death," I say to Atalantia according to court protocol. "Long was his toil. Great were his deeds. May he rest unburdened in the Void."

Beneath heavy lids, her eyes flash like matchheads. They search my face, the room, for more fuel to burn. They fall on my vestments and dance with fire. "Dear child, I do say, your fashion seems to have become rather bleak . . ."

"Your father—"

"Did I teach you nothing? Sweet Lysander! Idleness is no reason to discount the hoof maintenance of your steed, just as war is no excuse for poor tailoring. We will have to amend your sins at once. It is a matter of self-respect. I have three of the premiere tailors in all Venus aboard. One week with them, and you will look like a *king*."

That is a dangerous word in this company.

It is better I say nothing.

She sighs and looks up at the stars. I spare a glance for the giant mural that dominates the far wall. It is the one Octavia commissioned of our family, and our closest allies, the gens Grimmus. Ajax, Atlas, and Aja stare out, but of the dead, nothing can be seen of their faces.

Atalantia has painted them out.

Including mine.

"Father always thought it would be Lorn who would do him in, one way or another," she says, noting my interest in the painting and looking at her father, whose death shroud is freshly painted. "He wouldn't have minded that, or even Nero. But a cur, a half-breed, and a slave?" She makes a faint sibilant sound. "What an indecorous age we inhabit, dear boy. No one gets the death they deserve. It is most uncouth."

"What sort of farce is this, Atalantia?" mutters Scorpio au Votum's hologram. He has always been a pedantic, mathematical creature. He has also just eclipsed one hundred years of age, and is on his sixteenth paramour. *"We hardly have the time for this . . . sideshow. There are logistics to discuss."*

Atalantia rolls her eyes to me. As if saying "Look what I must bear," but there's still a gulf between us. She is wary of my intentions, as is only natural.

"Farce?" Ajax hisses, coming to my defense. "And what is farcical about Lysander returning from the grave, Scorpio?"

"At this late hour, a lost boy stumbles to us from the fringes of civilization on an enemy ship?" Scorpio scoffs. *"Pardon my incredulity, but it seems devious engines are at work."*

"How I love the mausoleum of conspiracies in your mind, Scorpio. Such a delight. But I wonder, do you intend to accuse *me* of devious engineering?" Atalantia asks.

"I was suggesting the lupine variety." He wasn't. *"But, since you ask, I would remind you that Mercury belongs to my family, not the gens Grimmus, not the gens Lune, not this confederacy of Two Hundred we have cobbled together to include even the most diluted blood. We built Mercury. We tamed its orbit."*

"Silenius and his heirs did pay for it. . . ." Kalindora adds.

In the mind of the Votum Primus, the youth of Kalindora and her pitiful bloodline, one a scant three hundred years old, is of little concern. He rails on. *"Pray tell, Atalantia, do you truly believe the support of the heir will make us forget our deed to this planet? No. No. Precocious as you are, you are not the only one with an army. You are first amongst equals, but that does not make you our Sovereign. Nor will it ever."*

Atalantia smiles at him. "If I mistook that for a threat, Scorpio, I might insist you have Atlas over for a midnight tea. I know, you can invite your lovely children: Cicero, Porcia, Ovidius, Horatia. Why not just invite the whole lot?"

Atlas's name has a chilling effect on the room. But it goes deeper than their fear of just that man. In an era in which these Primuses have witnessed the extinction of genetic lines as old as their own, threats to family do not just endanger the heart, but the survival of their ancient names.

"Of course, I am no Sovereign," Atalantia says, sharp as a tack now. "What need have I of groveling sycophants? Or the burden of planetary management? My province is war, my goodman. Only war. In it I have proven myself your superior, and enjoy your confidence in its prosecution." None disagree, not even Falthe, and he's seen as many battles as the Reaper himself. *"This* pertains to war. And I say *this* is Lysander. And *this* is the first time I have seen him in ten long years. Yet I am generous enough to share him with you. Why? Because I value your opinions. But if it is accusations you seek to levy at *me* . . . well . . . *that* would be disappointing."

Silence. Ajax looms behind Atalantia like an unshaken fist. Atlas, like an unseen one. Yet for all that menace, the Golds know Atalantia could only kill them at gravest cost to herself. And it is not in the nature of those who rule planets to tuck their tails, nor do they. However, Scorpio's reply is markedly more judicious.

"Lysander au Lune was in the Dragonmaw when it fell. Since he is here, one wonders how he survived. How do we know he is not an agent of the Rising? He may not even know himself. I know I need not remind you of the ruthlessness of our enemy. Or that you no longer hold the monopoly on certain . . . technologies."

"I am willing to accept that he is Lysander," purrs Asmodeus au Carthii. *"Scorpio is just a paranoid arachnid."* As Atalantia's strongest ally, Asmodeus will seek to support her, at my cost. He looks the same since I saw

him last, drunk in the gardens of the Palatine with drugged young Pinks on each arm. Though well over one hundred, the eerie creature has the tanned, unnatural face of a forty-year-old, the blue veins of age rejuvenation no doubt covered by concealer. The Carthii, while always dear to Atalantia, are the very worst of the Core. I let him spill his poison, but remember to look out for the more dire variety.

"We all know that Bellona just barely escaped Gorgo and his assassins on Ceres not three years ago," Asmodeus says. *"The beast reported a sprightly catamite nipping at Bellona's heels."* The famous letch gazes at me in the same hungry way he did when I was a boy. *"I believe we now know the identity of that catamite."*

Kalindora laughs and slaps her armored thigh. "You old pervert. You sure that wasn't a dream of yours?" Ajax snorts a surprised laugh. Asmodeus looks irritated, but does not interrupt the soldier. "Neither Lysander nor the Traitor would so debase themselves." She gives me a wink. "But maybe we should ask the man himself. I suppose he may have some information on the subject, no?"

When I was a boy, Kalindora served on my protection unit before rising to the rank of Olympic Knight. I see she's not lost her touch.

"Honored Primuses," I say loud and clear. "I apologize for my tardiness to the war. But I fear I must clarify my absence. I was not kept prisoner of the Republic nor was I Cassius's catamite. After the murders of Aja and Octavia, Darrow gave me to Cassius as a ward after he killed my grandmother. It was with him that I have spent these last ten years in the Belt."

It was not exactly the reply Kalindora had in mind. Instead of defusing the Golds, it sends them into amazed laughter. Atalantia's eyes widen slightly, while Ajax turns very slowly to face me. "Ward?"

"Yes."

He goes silent, knowing better than to air our dirty laundry before the others. So he's learned discretion. Perhaps I should have tried that instead of honesty, but it all would have come out eventually. Diomedes may be honorable, but if his duty required him to drop this bomb to gain leverage in the negotiations, he'd do it without flinching. Seraphina might tell them just for fun. The arch traitor of my people raised me just as long as our dead Sovereign did. While they might spit at me, it has a corrosive effect on their condescension. Bellona's blood was as old as theirs, and he was a very dangerous man. What did he help raise?

"Well, that is truly abhorrent," Atalantia says with a whistle. "But from what your communiqué relayed, we are to believe Cassius is dead."

"Yes."

She and Ajax share an intense look. "Good. We will take custody of the body so that his mother may honor it with sundeath, if she so chooses."

"I do not have the body."

Atalantia's eyebrows float upward, and around her neck Hypatia begins to slither counterclockwise in agitation. "Why not?"

"The body was stolen and desecrated by familiars of Bellerephon au Raa, whom Cassius killed."

"Desecrated in what manner?"

"I do not—"

Asmodeus hijacks the conversation with a cackle. His jewel rings sparkle as he plays with his smooth chin. *"Gone for a decade, ward to Bellona, no care to return. But now that you see a vacuum in power, you rush back like an eager little piglet to claim your throne. We have our leader, foul boy. Her name is Atalantia."*

"I did not return to claim anything," I say. "I have no scar, no inheritance, no right. I have come only to heal the divide that created the Rising." I look to Atalantia. "If I may?"

She nods. "This will be fun."

The doors open and Diomedes and Seraphina are ushered through. Animosity floods the room. I step back, allowing Diomedes the floor. Seraphina broods at his side.

"By Jove . . ." Atalantia mutters. "Dour as a cloud. Pale as a corpse. Is that a Raa, or the spirit of Akari himself?"

"He's far less talkative," Ajax says.

"*Salve,* Aureate." Diomedes dips his head in respect. "I stand Diomedes au Raa, son of Romulus and Dido, Storm Knight of the Rim Dominion, Taxiarchos of the Lightning Phalanx."

"Ooo, what's that?" Atalantia asks.

Diomedes is caught off guard. "A specialized mobile legion."

"Aren't all legions mobile? Or do you have new flight hardware?"

He blinks at the pivot, then clears his throat. "This is my sister Seraphina, Lochagos of the . . . Eleventh Dustwalkers." He waits for another interruption.

"Go on," Atalantia encourages. "You're doing splendidly, young man."

"It is our duty to bring you the tidings of the Moon Council and the Consuls Dido au Raa and Helios au Lux. They have given us the Dominion Seal." He lifts his fist to show a huge iron gauntlet implanted with rotating stones. "I am authorized to engage in parley with intent to find an agreeable and lasting truce between the Rim Dominion and the Society remnant in order to counter the disease of demokracy."

There's stunned silence.

"I'll be damned," Scorpio mutters. *"It is true."*

Asmodeus cackles in disbelief. *"Dido au Saud a consul? Impossible. Those heathens despise civilized company! Prithee, has Romulus gone mad?"* Secretly he is worried. Dido betrayed her family by marrying a Raa. If she were to ally the Rim with Saud . . . oh dear. His predominancy on Venus may be threatened. Kalindora seems to enjoy Asmodeus's vexation.

"Asmodeus, please desist," Atalantia says. She turns back to Diomedes. "Well, you certainly have your father's . . . presence. But tell me, why is Romulus *the Bold* no longer Sovereign? Did he grow weary of pontificating? Atlas won't believe it."

"Our father is dead," Seraphina replies.

I did not include that in my communiqué.

No one speaks until Atalantia raises a hand like a pupil. "Dead?"

Diomedes nods. "Under an oath of truth, he revealed that he knew the destruction of the Ganymede Dockyards was perpetrated by Darrow of Lykos and Victra au Julii, not Roque au Fabii."

"Darrow did that?" Atalantia laughs and claps her hands together. Hypatia's tongue licks outward at her mistress's delight. "Father was right. I knew it wasn't Fabii. *Darrow. Darrow. Darrow.* That mischievous little cockroach! I'm almost proud of him. One trick too far, it seems. Well, we've all been there. But Romulus dead. Dead? I did not think Romulus *could* die. Tell me, how did he go? Civil war? Assassination? Or did your mother finally eat him right up?"

"After admitting his deceit and his slaughter of White Arbiters, there was only one way to reclaim his honor," Diomedes explains. "He walked Akari's Path to the Dragon Tomb and succumbed to the elements."

They stare at him like he's gone raving mad.

"Did he reach it?" Ajax asks.

Diomedes swallows. "No."

Then, as one, they begin to laugh.

It fills me with loathing to see their disrespect for the man I admired nearly as much as I admired Cassius. Seraphina looks like she would draw her razor if she had one.

Only Diomedes stands unmoved. He's learned from his little talk with Ajax, and he's learning what to expect from the rest of them.

My respect for the man grows. As does Kalindora's, it seems.

"There is your monster in the shadows waiting to strike at Venus, Asmodeus!" Atalantia laughs. "All that fretting over a delusional suicide. Why, I daresay we shan't ever need bring the fight to the Rim. If we can just get them to all lie to one another, their honor will take care of the rest!"

"Romulus was an Iron Gold," I say. "Honorable by any measure."

"Several steps short, it seems," Ajax corrects.

"He deserves your respect," I snap. "Or at the very least the courtesy of not laughing before his progeny."

The militant Falthe finally breaks his silence. *"I will not be lectured about honor by a scarless boy, no matter his name. I was at Ilium, young man. Romulus slew my sister. He drew his blade across her belly until her spine cut down the middle. Until you have fought these . . . woebegone ruminants in a corridor, you know nothing."*

"You ask us to respect Romulus, Lysander?" Atalantia asks. "Respect for a man whose honor outweighed the common good? Respect for the fool whose very rebellion allowed for the Reaper to rise? Respect for the traitor who fought side by side with the slave hordes at Ilium? Who forsook his duty so terribly that even his own brother could not stand at his side?" She wags a slender finger at me. "I think you're still lost, Lysander. Or are you as mad as them? What do you think, nephew?"

Ajax tongues his teeth in contemplation. "He doesn't look mad."

"So you're not mad," Atalantia says. She comes nose-to-nose with me, her tone warm and confiding. "Then what are you? Confused? Did they torture you?" Her eyes flick to Diomedes and Seraphina. "Was it the brute? Or the dusty little mouse? We'll peel them apart if you like. Put them on one of Atlas's poles."

"You need an ally to tip the scales."

She frowns. "No. All I needed was *imperium*. For years, Father kept me on a leash as he waged his conventional retreat. Apologies, *war*. For a hybrid foe, you need a hybrid warrior. *I* have turned the tide, Lysander.

My agents spread poison in the enemy's citadel. Atlas spreads it to the cradle of their birth. Soon the rabble will slaughter one another. We need no traitors here. We are upon the cusp of victory."

I search their faces and find nothing but arrogant isolation. Each is barricaded behind their own power and prejudice. It is warranted. Some recall relatives lost in the Rim's two rebellions. Many believe in the cultural superiority of the Core. But all remember the taxes the Rim's rebellions cost them.

They cannot stand to admit the Rim would be helpful. So they must be humbled first. It would be far easier had I battles to my name. Legions at my call. A scar on my face. But the tools I do possess are not exactly toothless.

"Perhaps you are right. Perhaps you do not need the Rim. But . . ." Atalantia turns on me with a warning look. ". . . if you have all you need, then why are there so many ships still damaged by the Battle of Caliban?" I ask. "Orion did not go down without a fight. Why not send the crippled ships back to the Dockyards of Venus for retrofit?" I look around innocently. No one answers. "Unless there is some reason you cannot? Perhaps the Minotaur did more than kill Magnus after he was freed by Darrow. Did he, by chance, take the dockyards while he was on Venus?"

"You little scheming weasel!" Asmodeus cries. *"How could he possibly know that?"*

"How many ships did the Minotaur take?" I press. "All that were in dock? Clearly this play against the Free Legions is a trap to lure the Republic fleets. Draw their main might and sneak around to raze their planets. But without support from Venus, you can't sail on Mars *or* Luna. The jaws of the trap are set, but your foot is in it too."

"Lysander, please. Enough showing off," Atalantia says.

"After the Minotaur's capture, many of his men must have gone over to you, Atalantia. How many swell to his banner now? How many ships have slipped away? Apollonius was a popular man. And it would make a curious mind wonder why he would be so eager to kill Magnus. Perhaps he was betrayed. Given over to the enemy."

They look at me as if I've suddenly grown fangs.

I may not know the rules of the Rim. But I know the Core. And I was right. Apollonius *was* betrayed. Likely *because* of his popularity.

I feel a sense of loneliness. These are the people who Cassius thought would send assassins for him. The ones he judged so much worse than the Rising that he gave his life to ensure they never won this war. If they do not even agree to entertain the idea of allying with the Rim, then he died for nothing.

"My goodmen, you are mid-stride into a campaign. One which I assume was intended to be an unrelenting advance. But without lifting a finger, Darrow has cut off your back foot. Without your docks and reinforcements, you are unable to go forward or backward. I offer you an ally ten years fresh. One with no claim nor desire nor manpower to rule your spheres. They have been spit upon, and they have come for satisfaction. Refuse them if you must. It is your choice to make, not mine."

The crickets by the fountain carry the conversation.

Ajax is the first to speak. "If we destroy the Free Legions as they strike the Belt bastions and the Dockyards of Phobos, the trauma to the Republic would be absolute. Lysander's argument is not without virtue. Nor does it detract from our imminent endeavor."

"I know his argument has virtue," Atalantia snaps. "It's obvious to a genital wart it has virtue. *I. Just. Hate. Moonies.*" Her fingers trace Hypatia's scales as she thinks. "I will be terribly honest, young Diomedes. I don't think it wise to dance with venomous creatures I didn't nurture as pups. But you did not kill my father, did you? Nor Octavia for that matter. Nor Aja nor Moira. Murdering you would be to court quagmire. And there are so many others you can help me kill.

"Answer me this. Your docks were destroyed, yet somehow you found a way to build new ships like that curious corvette in my hangar. No, I will not dissect it, because it will likely detonate if I do, yes?" Diomedes shrugs. "Clearly you have an energy source to make war feasible, even though the termites have made Mars an impregnable bastion. How? Are you using foil caraval to skim helium from the Gas Giants?" She bares her teeth. "I know Atlas would know if you dared mine the Kuiper . . ." Diomedes remains motionless as Atalantia's queries multiply. "How many warships does the Rim possess? How many legions? These are things I need to know."

Diomedes is amused she thinks he would ever tell her. "In the event of an alliance, any tasks given to the Rim necessary to the agreed-upon strategy will be fulfilled. That is all I will say."

"Oh, to be young and think you know how things are done," she says to the Primuses. "These are not injurious queries, Diomedes. If I don't know how strong you are, why would I choose you for a dancing partner, young man?"

"Because all others are taken, and the song creeps upon crescendo."

Atalantia watches him with a growing smile. "Wait till Atlas sees you!" She sighs. "There you have it, goodmen. The ugly truth. To the boudoir we go again with our ugly cousins." Carthii tries to interrupt. "I am Dictator, Asmodeus. My war powers are absolute. To protect our predominance tomorrow, we must make concessions to pragmatism today."

Only after Atalantia assures the Primuses they will have a hand in crafting the treaty after their *imminent endeavor* do their holograms disappear one by one. It is not done. There will be weeks of negotiations. Neither side will budge. And eventually they will both leave feeling cheated. But the alliance will happen. What's more, I believe Atalantia wanted it to happen as soon as she heard it was a possibility. She does not celebrate, but in her mind she has just won this war, and now has an angle on the next.

First the Rising. Then the Rim.

I feel suddenly very heavy wondering how I will manage to convince her not to turn on the Raa as soon as she sees profit in it.

One of Atalantia's muscular male slaves brings her a piece of bread on a platter. She breaks several pieces to share with the Raa. Once they have eaten, they are formally her guests and under gens Grimmus protection. Whoever means them harm is her enemy. It is a formality that actually bears weight as it did for our ancestors; Atalantia can hardly accommodate another enemy at this stage.

"We will begin discussion tomorrow atop the Water Colossus of Tyche," Atalantia says. The Raa look at each other then at the planet below. "Today, however, I require a demonstration of good faith."

She snaps her fingers and a hologram of Mercury three stories tall fills the star globe. It is stained with markers for known enemy strongholds and legions, and wrapped with thousands of dropship and starShell trajectories.

I knew something was afoot by the battle readiness within the *Annihilo*, but I did not expect this.

So it will be an Iron Rain.

It is a risky and declarative gamble that could prove very expensive. So either Atalantia is swollen with confidence, or she thinks her window is closing. I suspect I know where Atlas is now.

Diomedes takes in the battle plan and frowns. "Our instruments suggested the planet was shielded by a fortified landchain of shield generators."

"All suitable landfalls, yes," Atalantia says. "For now."

"How will you . . ."

She smiles. "Do you think Atlas returned from his Kuiper sojourn just to tan in the desert? We have over nine million Martian slaves trapped. I broke Darrow's armada. I broke Darrow's heart. Now I break his back. If we kill him and destroy the legions here, we shatter the alliance between Mars and Luna. Virginia will see her little rebellion split right down the center."

"And you need the tank factories of Heliopolis and your dockyards need Mercury's metal to further your campaign," Diomedes adds.

"It has been a long war," she allows. "You say you wish to fight with us at the end, Raa?" Here it comes: the proverbial snakebite. "Prove it. Fall with us in an Iron Rain. Shed blood at my side and I will know I have a *true* ally."

The silence grows as Diomedes considers. "I am sorry. But I cannot."

"Of course not," Ajax says with a laugh. "The Sword of Io is best in its sheath."

"I was trusted to be a voice, not a sword. It is impossible."

Atalantia raises her eyebrows, dangling the bait. "A pity. I saw such promise in our union. But how can I trust an ally tomorrow who will not fight with me today? Ajax, please escort them to their ship and send them back to their dust bowl."

I watch Kalindora as Seraphina thinks. Is Kalindora like the rest of these predators? Enjoying the hunt, watching for the takedown? Her face remains the same, but her eyes search the shadows cast by Atalantia's braziers as Seraphina steps forward.

"I will do it." Her brother wheels on her, overestimating yet again the patience of the women in his family. "You are the voice of the Rim, Diomedes. I am here only to assist you in your mission. If I die, what of it?" She holds one hand over the other hand in her family's private way of saying "shadows and dust." "You desire a quota of blood, Grimmus? You may have all of mine. Does that satisfy?"

Atalantia smiles. "It satisfies."

As Diomedes realizes his sister will fall amidst an army of men who would proudly mount the head of his father above their mantels, he grows very still. I feel for him, but after seeing Seraphina amongst the Ascomanni, if anyone can survive their first Rain, it is her.

Diomedes gives me a dark look as he and his sister are ushered toward the door by Ash Guards. Atalantia nods for Kalindora to leave. I am left alone with her and Ajax to watch the door close. Atalantia drifts to the viewport to stare down at the planet. She will be wondering what machinations move in Darrow's mind. I wonder the same.

"Ward?" Ajax says suddenly. I expected his anger, but that did not diminish my dread of it.

"I—"

He moves with the sort of staggering velocity that is impossible in the low gravity of the Rim. His fist cracks against my jaw so fast only the Willow Way's instinct to go with the blow saves me from having my jaw shattered and my neck fractured. I slam into the ground nonetheless.

"Ward?" he roars.

Atalantia doesn't even watch the reflection of the violence in the viewport. I lift a hand toward Ajax. Lovely as he was as a child, his moods could switch at the drop of a pin. It's far more noticeable now.

"Ajax . . ."

"That Bellona cunt killed my mother," he growls, stepping on my groin. "She was more a mother to you than your own, you cockless cur."

"Yes, she was," I wheeze.

"And yet you tagged at Bellona's heels for ten years? Ten fucking years."

"I had few . . . alternatives."

"You could have returned to *us*. To *me. Brother.*"

"I am sorry, Ajax. I . . . should have. But . . ." He pushes down harder, causing nausea to cascade up my belly and my lower back to ache. "I was afraid."

He's horrified by the admission, and almost takes his boot off me completely. "Of what? Us?"

"Not you, Ajax. Never you. Of court. Of Gold eating Gold." I try to stand but he pushes me back down, more gently this time. "You think I enjoyed seeing Aja cut to ribbons? You think it meant nothing seeing Octavia hewn from groin to sternum? You think I did not see how *we* did the Rising to *ourselves*? The Jackal, Fitchner, Cassius, the Martian Feud—all symptoms of the same disease. I wanted no part of it."

That, he understands.

As children, we mocked all the scheming snakes of the court. Only Atalantia ever made it look good anyway, and she did it for laughs. Moira was pure in her obsession for truth. Aja pure in her duty to Grandmother. Lorn pure in his honor. Even Darrow was pure in his then-inexplicable lust to win.

Those were the people we admired. Not the snakes.

"Then why return now?" Atalantia asks. She senses but cannot identify the private understanding Ajax and I share. Is she jealous of it? Or suspicious? Either way, she turns from the viewport.

"Because I believe it can be different," I say. "The Rising has shown itself incapable of rule. While there were injustices in Octavia's time, there were not two hundred million dead."

"Two fifty," Atalantia says. "We hid a famine on Venus."

That the death of so many could be unknown staggers me. "It may not have been perfect, but it wasn't this," I say. "I believe if we quell the Rising, we have a chance to fix what was broken not just by them. But by *us*."

"Gods," Ajax mutters. "He hasn't changed a damn bit."

"Told you," Atalantia replies.

Ajax hauls me up by my jacket. "Still wants to be Marcus Aurelius, I suppose." He leans close, his voice confiding. "The fact is, my mother *spoke* for Cassius. You remember. When Octavia questioned his loyalty, my mother begged her to give him a chance. She saw Lorn in his heart, I wager. And he showed his gratitude by feeding her to the wolves. I know you rationalized it away, because you think your emotions are secondary programs or something. But look at what I am. What I have become." He gestures to the kill marks. His dented armor. The double-thick gray razor on his hip. "Do you think I became this for pleasure?"

"We understand the war inside you, Lysander. We always have," Atalantia says. "But that does not change that this is not the return you should have had. Not for you, not for us, not with *them*. You squandered yourself. You could have come back a *god*. Think how I could have used that. Think how your high-minded dream could have benefited from that."

She sighs and lifts her hand like an opera singer.

"Of course, the legions will rejoice at your return. If used properly, *the return of the Heir of Silenius* could still inspire the worlds. I hear the songs even now.

"*But* you have much to prove. People will wonder—not me, but *others*—if you are not a lackey of the Rim." She flings her hands about. "Is he perhaps the Traitor's trained monkey? Perhaps even the Slave King's puppet? They will wonder: Is Lysander *really* an Iron Gold?"

Ajax takes offense on my behalf. "He may be an egregiously pretentious quisby, but he's no puppet of the Slave—"

She cuts him off with a look.

"Until the answers are incontrovertible, I fear I cannot allow your return to become known, Lysander." She makes it seem like it's for my own good, and succeeds, almost. I go very quiet inside, recognizing Silenius's Stiletto when I see it. My path will grow very narrow very quickly, and it will certainly cut my feet.

There is only one way forward.

I did not come back to be her rival, and so long as I do not have a scar, I could never be. But if I survive what she asks, by the traditions that have guided my people since Silenius, I will earn a scar, and my inheritance, at great cost to her own strength.

The other Gold families will choose a side if they see but the tiniest crack of daylight between us. She knows that. This is a sign of trust. She could do with my support.

Or it is a trap.

I cannot believe that. I will not. Atalantia was there the day I was born. She was the first to set me upon a horse. What she offers is an opportunity to shepherd the alliance and take back the mantle of justice from the Rising, but to do that, I must take the leap.

I bend again on my knee.

I was a fool declaring myself an Iron Gold to Dido. And I feel a fool now. "Dictator, I ask your leave for House Lune to fall in the Iron Rain."

"Oh, he's going to pop his cherry!" Ajax purrs.

Atalantia's smile is incandescent. "Granted, son of Luna." She pulls me to my feet and kisses me softly on the mouth. Ice, guilty excitement, and bewilderment race through my veins as she lingers there, her mouth open, lips wrapped around mine longer than appropriate even by Venusian standards.

When she pulls back, she stares at me in pride.

"*My* little Lysander. Today, you will earn your scar. I have no doubts."

Ajax has grown quiet. "With whom will he fall?"

Still a little bewildered, I nod to him. "With you, brother. If you will have me."

He considers for a moment, suddenly very internal, and then nods. "About gory time. With a good scar, maybe you will look less like a Pink harlot."

With a melancholy smile, Atalantia takes our hands and guides us to the family mural. It is oddly stirring to stand before what we considered our family. I remember the day we all posed for Glirastes. Atalantia had six Pinks fanning her with peacock feathers. My father teased her mercilessly and apparently farted in her general direction. Atlas even cracked a smile. I see him up there, a wan man leaning on the far end of the frame beside Aja and chubby little Ajax. He's smiling at my father, likely because of the fart. I cannot see my mother. Her face is hidden behind a veil of gray paint.

"Octavia, Aja, Moira, Anastasia, Brutus, my father . . . all gone," Atalantia whispers. She grips our hands as if she never wanted to let them go. "Only we and Atlas remain. But where there were three there are now four. Let the slaves tremble." She pauses. Then she rips her hands away from ours as if we were the ones who pulled us all together. "Right! Well, off to war now, boys. I'll meet you in Tyche." She smiles at Ajax. "Or somewhere a bit . . . warmer."

7

DARROW

The Calm

THE SUN HANGS LOW and swollen over the desert as I roar out the garage ramp. More engines whine behind me as Rhonna and twenty bodyguards follow. Guided by Colloway, fist-sized drones careen through the sky to feed data into my helmet. They sight gravBike signatures winding through the sand like rectilinear snake tracks. In their troughs are small depressions. Telltale sign of Gorgon skipper boots.

"Skip trace," I say. "Stick tight."

We abandon the tracks and push toward a string of axeblade mountains. Following Alexandar's coordinates, we ditch the bikes at the base of the mountains and use our gravBoots to scale the escarpments, careful to not fly too high for fear of ground-to-air missiles.

In short order, we find Alexandar sitting with his helmet off in the shadows of an arroyo. He wears lizardSkin light armor, thinner and more sustainable long-term in the desert than my pulseArmor. His looks to be held together more by field patches and dirt than nanofiber. Only his iron lancer badge—a sword against a flying pegasus—is clean.

Four weeks tracking the Fear Knight with Thraxa seem to have worn him down to his essential elements. He is even thinner, and taller, than his grandfather. His sunburnt skin is drawn tight and flakes around patrician cheekbones. On his neck a wretched scab weeps puss. His warhawk is smashed flat and dark with helmet sweat.

He looks up as we scramble down. I recall my helmet into its catch and wince at the heat, squinting hard until I step into the shadows where it is fifty degrees cooler. Alexandar bolts to his feet. Beneath his chrome desert contacts, his eyes are haunted.

"Bloodyhell, just sprawled out Fury-may-care," Rhonna says, her multiRifle on her shoulder. Her eyes scan the rocks. "Fear Knight's gonna gut you while you have your picnic, Princess."

His face is too haunted to feign a smile. "We have pathfinders."

She half-lowers her rifle. "You look a ghost. You prime?"

Not long ago he would have bitten her head clean off with a classist retort. Now he stares at her as if trying to remember who she is. *What has he seen out here?*

"Thraxa is this way, sir."

I find Thraxa lying belly-down on a ridge overlooking a plain stretching from the mountains to Angelia. She props herself up on her elbows. One is made of flesh. The other is unpolished asteroid metal, etched with Obsidian runes by Valdir Unshorn, Sefi's mate, after Thraxa saved his life in the running skirmishes over the Bay of Bengal.

The mountain ridge is littered with boulders and spiked ephedra, but empty of Howlers. I toggle my right ocular implant. Throbbing red embers from the quantum ID dots in their skulls fleck the ridgeline. Sevro's little monsters. They don't feel whole without him. The army may miss its mascot, but the pack misses its big brother. I've been too much a distant father of late.

"Reap." The large Telemanus acknowledges me without looking. Her wolfcloak has taken on the color of the desert, thanks to its chameleon properties. The two Obsidian pathfinders move for me, and I crawl even with her as my own cloak turns brown. Thraxa squints through a pair of optics. Freckles form a mask over her face. She hands me her optics set.

Knowing what I'll see, I put the optics to my eyes. An all-too-familiar forest has been erected in front of the city. I feel nothing, but then again I don't smell it yet.

"He did this while you slept?" I ask. "He would have needed hours."

"I shit the pot," Thraxa mutters. I lower the optics. "We lost him in the Buonides Range when he left the shield shadow to cross a death valley." She means the narrow gaps exposed to Atalantia's guns between our shield chain.

"I told you not to let him out of your sight."

"The valley was too exposed. We had drones, and I sent a man. By the time we found his trail, he'd abandoned his course for Eleusis and had already reached Angelia." The wrong city.

She swats pointlessly at a scrill on her neck. More of the two-headed bloodsuckers make homes in her wolfcloak.

"And your man lost them. Which?"

"Alexandar."

I can't hide my surprise. "How?"

"He crashed his bike into a hoodoo. Fell asleep at the stick."

"One is none. Two is one, Thraxa . . ."

"We were a hundred forty hours without sleep. Even with the nazopran, the lows were hallucinating—had to rest 'em in the cargo bins as we rode, even the Grays. Golds were barely upright. Had to run solo. Alex's the best soldier I've ever seen at his age, including you. Still . . ." She spits in the dirt. "We're all blood and bone."

I pushed them too hard. I thought Alex invulnerable. We all did. But even with the proper gear, this desert eats men. "Where is Atlas now?"

"Gone. Tracks lead north, bearing for Angelia." She nods to the Fear Knight's display before the city. "Should I call medships?"

"No. He came here for a reason, and it wasn't to torture. Get 'em ready. We're pushing in." She rallies the Howlers as I raise my helmet and hail Orion. She's only just made it back to BlueReach One.

"*Trouble?*" she asks.

"Is there a way to spool up the Storm Gods without showing our hand?"

"*The blackslag you think these things are? They aren't a grunt's hair trigger. We can't cool as fast as we can heat. Once we ramp up it's a runaway to primary horizon.*"

"What's the lag on cloud coverage?"

"*I'm told soon as the pressure systems activate, an hour. Electrical in two. What happened?*"

"Unclear."

"*Orders?*"

I hesitate. If it's activated too early, Atalantia will notice the unnatural nature of the storm and call off the invasion. Activated too late, the storm won't matter. "*Watch how a pitviper strikes, my son,*" Father said once as he clutched my wrist and made me play his game. "*Watch it coil upward and upward till it reaches its crest. Don't move before then. Don't strike out with your slingBlade. If you do, then it'll get you. Move just when it's coming down. . . ."*

I look down at the city the Fear Knight killed.

"Initiate Operation Tartarus. Give me a storm."

8

LYSANDER

The Machine

"Y OU'RE GOING TO DIE," Pytha says.
It is easy to believe her. To be ingested by the military machine is to see the last hidden gear of the world. All is loud yet lonely, chaos yet order, functional yet dirty, fast yet slow.

All is big. Except you.

I am thrust into an assembly line of muscled predators. There is little jocularity amongst the lines of Golds as they are given injections for Mercurian diseases, chemical weapons, and flight sickness followed by conditioning enhancement cocktails. Then comes implantation of coms and overwatch. Mission debriefing and caloric ingestion. Measurements for gear. Fitting for gear.

Without my name, I am no one. *There goes another fresh-faced sacrifice,* the veterans think. No. They don't even see me. Their eyes are focused two hours from now. I do not matter. I am chaff.

Atlas's countdown has begun.

"You're going to perish. Die in a ball of fire," Pytha says as one of the four Orange techs seals the greaves of the pulseArmor around my shins. On either side, hundreds of Golds iron up in fitting bays. I didn't even see this many Peerless Scarred assemble for the defense of Luna against the Rising. It was seen as somewhat of a farce. They don't underestimate the Reaper any longer. But it makes me wonder: If the Golds are this scary, how bad has Darrow become?

"Are you always this familiar with your superiors, pilot?" Kalindora says from the wall. Atalantia has sent her to watch over me in the Rain.

"No, *domina*."

Kalindora does not buy the formality. "I recommend reminding your retainer of her place, and yours." She glances at the techs. "This is not the Belt. Now, if you will excuse me, I must tend to a pressing matter. If you lose your way to the tubes, just follow the stench of big humans."

I'm sorry to see her go. Yet I'm pleased to have a moment alone with Pytha.

"Bloody terrifying woman," Pytha mutters after her.

"I think she is sad, rather. Wasn't always . . ." Pytha watches me with unease. "It will probably be safer for you to stay in my quarters while I'm away," I suggest. The lowColors on the *Annihilo* are like drones. The mids, barely better. There's a hierarchical terror in the very air, one that never existed in the Citadel.

"Can't believe she's making you do this," Pytha mutters.

"I volunteered."

"You little shit!"

"Hold," I say to the Oranges crawling over me. They don't know who I am, but my caste and Kalindora's presence are enough for them to stop as if controlled by a remote, and stand at the edge of the bay adjusting their tools. I glance at the grizzled Golds fitting up to either side of me. "Lower your voice, Pytha."

"You little shit," she whispers. "If we were on the *Archi,* I would slap you. What do you even know about Iron Rains?"

"My studies weren't isolated to political theory." It's an understatement.

"It's not like a simulator." Her voice has softened.

"And you glean this from your own extensive experience?" I say as I flex my leg to test the fit of the greaves.

"I've been in a Rain."

I look up in confusion. "I thought you were expelled from the Academy."

"Snakeshit. Before I was a pirate, I was an equites." Her chin lifts in pride. "First Decurion, Twelfth Squadron of the Bellona light-destroyer *Dignitas.*"

"Cassius said—"

"Cassius didn't want you to know only warriors." She sighs. "This isn't what he would have wanted for you. Ever since he died, something's woken up in you. A machine in your brain. It's not you. This isn't you. Or have you just always been desperate to be an Iron Gold?"

I nod slowly. "I won't lie and say that's not a small part of it. But that's not why I must do this. Gold hasn't changed. If anything, the sickness has metastasized. They uphold the wrong virtues." I lean forward and lower my voice. "If Seraphina dies down there . . . if Atalantia betrays the Raa . . . if Darrow wins . . . mankind will disintegrate."

"So what? That's not your burden."

"Look around, Pytha. We teeter upon oblivion. Everything humanity has built. All the sacrifices, the hierarchy, the wars . . . for what? If Gold loses, the Republic will fracture into kingdoms. The kingdoms to fiefdoms. The fiefdoms to tribes. It will become a dark age of fractured planets and war for three hundred years."

"Three hundred years?"

I nod. "According to precedents, longer, but I've run the simulation as many times and ways as I know how." She knows I don't say that lightly. "You think this is about me. It isn't. Darrow thinks this is about good and evil. It isn't. This is about order and chaos. I have chosen my side. But to have a voice, I must have a scar."

"And you think Cassius was arrogant." She looks at the ground, shaking her head at some unspoken thought. Eventually she looks up. "Fear."

"I beg your pardon?"

"You think if you gain respect, you'll be able to change them? Nah. It's about fear. You pretend Lorn au Arcos was the picture of an Iron Gold because he was wise and *honorable*." She jams a thin thumb into her sternum. "*We* know the truth. He boarded *our* ship. Arcos in a corridor was death incarnate. You want to play the big game? Fine. But you play to win. You make them fear you."

"I am not that man."

"Then you're for the worms, *dominus,* and I'm out my last friend."

I kneel amongst killers. Seraphina to my left, Kalindora to my right. All is silent but for the children as they perform the Blood Benediction that has been carried down the generations from Silenius to us.

The voices of children drift through the air.

"My son, my daughter, now that you bleed, you shall know no fear."

A dozen virgin girls with hair and eyes of milky white walk barefoot through the kneeling legions. Iron daggers are clutched in their hands.

"No defeat. Only victory."

Blood drips from my hand as a girl drags the blade across it.

"Your cowardice seeps from you."

Ajax's eyes are fixed on the floor. His bleeding hand clutched in a fist. Clustered about him are his hungry young friends and the grizzled Gold and Gray officers of the double-strong Tenth Expeditionary Legion, the Terran-born Iron Leopards.

"Your rage burns bright."

I feel every tremor of my muscles, every kilogram of my armor. But I do not feel the words.

"Rise, children of Gold, warriors of Earth, and take with you your ancestors' might."

A chill spreads through me as one hundred thousand legionnaires from the Grimmus lands of Africa and the Americas come to their feet. Not a man or woman amongst them has seen their home in over five years. They do not know when they will see Earth again. But they know their path home goes through the Free Legions.

Kalindora moans as Ajax activates his gravBoots and articulates himself into the air. "Here he goes again."

In his storm armor, with its thunderhead shoulders, Ajax looks like Jupiter reborn with snowy teeth and inky skin. He bathes in the roars of his men as can only a man who thinks himself entitled to worship, yet earned it anyway.

Beside me, I see envy creep over Seraphina's face.

I feel the human flaw in myself, but I resist its dark waters, and allow myself to bathe in my friend's risen stature.

He is young wrath manifest.

"My brothers! My sisters! My Iron Leopards! The battle today is to decide the fate of our Society. Whether we cave to the tide of anarchy, the despoiling mob!" He points his arm. "Or whether we carve our own destiny and build a second Age of Order upon the bodies of the slave horde. We have shattered their fleet! But soon more ships will come from their infernal, restless factories to rescue the Slave King and his horde. When they come, what will they find?"

"Ash," the legion booms.

The skin on Seraphina's neck prickles with goosebumps.

"Sevro au Barca, Orion xe Aquarii, Cadus Harnassus, Thraxa au Telemanus, Alexandar au Arcos, Felix au Daan, Colloway xe Char, Darrow of Lykos!" Kalindora fingers the flame-etched hilt of her razor. "These are wanted lives! Bring them to me! Bring them to me! *Bring them to me!*"

The legions roar and Ajax's dark face splits into a death's-head smile.

A golem of a Gold man takes over. He sighs his simian shoulders back and stomps before the cadres of elite Gold knights, smiling like a bulldog chewing a hornet.

"We are Legio X Pardus! We are the vanguard! Ours is a place of honor! *Ante mortem!*" he bellows to the Golds.

"Gloria!" they roar.

He wheels on the Grays. *"Ante mortem!"*

"Gloria!"

He turns to the Obsidians. *"Ante mortem!"*

"GLORIA!"

Ajax lands beside the golem. With the man at his hip, he sways over to his clustering officers. They are a crusty, tight-knit breed. Seraphina and I are total outsiders. Kalindora conditionally so. They give us no room near the front, except for Kalindora. She declines and stays at my side.

"You all know our objective. We're to lend rear-guard support to the Votum as they press for Tyche from the east. I'm here to tell you that's all bullshit. Scorpio can fuck off to Tyche on his own." Through armored shoulders, I see Ajax grin. "We're going to take Heliopolis, my goodmen."

There are murmurs of excitement. But not from me. Instead I feel a sinking disappointment. Scorpio au Votum was right. Atalantia does want his planet. Or parts of it. Seraphina glances my way with a sneer.

"So this is how Atalantia treats her allies."

"Heliopolis is their lone fallback bastion in the south. We take it, they're trapped in the desert." And Atalantia gets the coveted factories and the mines of the south. "Now, the Yellows are squawking about weather, but it's Mercury, and our timetable is set in stone. So it may get choppy. Any questions?"

Kalindora raises her voice. "Atalantia promised Scorpio—"

"When Atalantia has Heliopolis, she won't need to promise Scorpio anything," Ajax says. "Since you are sworn to her, you should welcome that future, Love Knight."

Kalindora stares gloomily ahead.

Meanwhile the monstrous man beside Ajax glares over at me through slitted eyes. "Who the fuck are you?" Three of his front teeth are missing. That is the least of the cosmetic damage. "That's expensive armor for a Pixie wastrel."

"Olympic Knight business," Kalindora replies.

The big man wheels on Seraphina. "Who the fuck is she?"

"Olympic Knight business, Seneca," Kalindora says.

He does not look like a Seneca. He looks like a human boar. He winks at Kalindora. "Oy, Love. Figure Reaper will be anything but atoms before we get down there?"

"To avoid you, Seneca, I believe he just might."

The beast chuckles and Ajax returns to his brief.

"Seneca au Cern, Ajax's Dux," Kalindora whispers after I quietly inquire about the man. His right hand of authority, then. Probably started as a bodyguard. They often do. "Unremarkable, except when he goes Blood Red." The term is unfamiliar. "Radio code for a Red suicide wave." She looks back to Ajax. "It's really not like anything you've ever seen."

Ajax concludes his brief. "To your shells, goodmen. We have termites to kill."

As Ajax and I walk to the starShell ladders with Kalindora shadowing from behind, he glances at her in irritation, then clasps my shoulder.

"This is what you've been missing, little brother. The greatest show ever staged. But you look like you're about to fall asleep. Not nervous, are you?" He leans forward. "Or are you already in that Brain's Hole?"

"The Mind's Eye," I correct. He knows what it's called. "And no, not yet."

He laughs. "Stick close down there. If we get separated, try to link up. If you hear wolves, find me. It's no jest. Only a legion accompanying the Slave King is permitted the howl. If you hear it, he's coming. I've seen that man carve through a platoon of Ash Guard like a shark through tuna. You'll want me there."

"Will he be in Heliopolis?"

"No," he says in disappointment. "But fate is not without a sense of humor. Where the din of battle is the loudest, he will come. And today I plan on making such noise." He steps close to me. "We will avenge our family together, then sort the rest of this shit out. Hear?"

"Thank you," I say. "For letting me—"

He smacks my head. "You're not forgiven yet, Pixie. But what you do today will make them forget all the rest. Let's have you return properly." He puts his head to mine, as we did as children before walking the Line. "The blood of giants fills our veins: honor the valiant dead with your deeds."

"Honor the living with your might," I recite.

He departs.

Seraphina stands at the foot of her own ladder, eclipsed by her Grimmus-painted starShell. Techs mill around its feet making last-minute adjustments. She spits on the death's-head sigil and examines the traction claws on the starShell.

"Good fortune down there," I say to her.

She checks the hydraulics in the knees. "Keep your fortune. Every scar I have earned has led me here. This war is my destiny." She turns. "Cheer up, *gahja*. The courage of a soldier is heightened by her knowledge of her profession." She looks me up and down. "Go do your duty."

I suspected it before, but I feel it now as I see the excitement on her face as she turns back to the war machine.

She didn't betray her father because she loves her mother. There was another, hidden reason, which was the source of the guilt I saw in her eyes as she watched Romulus walk to his death. It is the source of the anger she feels toward him, toward me. Anger that should be for herself, because deep down she knows that it wasn't loyalty to the Rim or her mother that incited her to ferry evidence of Darrow's crimes against the Rim back to the council.

It was her hunger for war.

Now, after weeks of starvation, she is about to be fed.

9

DARROW

Angelia

T HE FEAR KNIGHT IS a sadist.
   Unlike the vain Golds of the Core, he appreciates guerrilla warfare and its effect on armies. Though I met him only once in my days of
service to Nero, I saw enough in him to know he put no stock in glory.
When I squeezed his hand, eager to impress my strength on what then
would have been a superior of stratospheric heights, he let his go limp.
It embarrassed me. Little did I know then that the wan, plain-dressed
man would someday skin, melt, castrate, rape, blind, and mutilate my
legionnaires by the thousands.

   Atlas's reputation was meager before the start of the Solar War. He
was known primarily for three things: His patronage of the Great Library of Delphi. His inglorious position as a ward of the Sovereign. And
his abrupt disappearance, one that was clarified when he returned after
the fall of Earth from nearly a decade of banishment fighting threats at
the edge of the system.

   Born after the failed First Moon Lord's Rebellion, he was raised on Io
with his more famous brother, Romulus. When he turned ten, his parents said their farewells and sent him to Luna to live in the court of the
Sovereign as yet another noble hostage to ensure the Rim's obedience.

   Amongst the Core Golds he was privileged and educated, yet derided
for being the spawn of a traitor. It was there he met Atalantia, and there
that Octavia made him an extension of her will, turning him against
his traitor family and planting the seeds that would make him into

the man behind the Pale Mask. Of all my enemies, I loathe him the most.

We stand before his newest forest of corpses.

Bodies hang impaled on vertical poles. There are more than two hundred. Each with the Fear brand on their bare chests—a fleshy wound in the shape of a child's face ringed with hair of serpents.

A grisly promenade strewn with Republic flags leads through the impaled bodies to Angelia. The white fabric of the flags is tattered and fouled with boot prints and blood. It will be booby-trapped.

I look at the bodies, at their faces. This is why I left Luna. Those glossy peacocks in the Senate read our reports. But the further you are away from it, the more war reads like arithmetic, and past that it reads like fiction, past that it's just an annoying video on your info stream. How could they possibly imagine the anguish on the faces of the dead? How could the mob in the street demanding handouts ever know on a sensory level that when a human rots, it isn't just the skin that stinks, but the intestines, the stomach, the liver?

How could they know that weird tremble of the soul when you realize there is no civilization? There's just a lock on a box. And inside the box is this. Virginia wanted me to reason with the senators. What common language would we speak, I wonder, when they have not seen inside the box and I am its lock?

It drives me fucking mad that they refuse to understand how sick and dogged and obsessed with our destruction our enemies are. Yet they live in a fantasy built on the bodies of my friends.

The chatter of the carrion birds serrates the air, along with the cries of the dying. Of the impaled soldiers, many still live, writhing like worms on a hook. Our four Obsidians stare up at the bodies and make a sign to their gods.

The horror reaches deepest into the heart of Alexandar and pulls him forward. "Arcos, heels down," I bark.

He stops but turns to me, face ghostly vacant. "They are still alive . . ."

"And they're all booby-trapped," I say, though he knows it. Rhonna swallows as she watches Alexandar blink at the result of his error. Fall asleep in the Ladon, you wake up to this.

I walk up to him. "We all carry weight. I need you to carry this. Can you?"

The eyes of his grandfather blink back at me as the impaled cry for help. "Yes, sir."

"Goodman."

I turn back to the Howlers. They stand in a ragged line. Colloway brings the *Necromancer* in for fire support. "It's theatrics. He's buying time to distract us from his objective," I tell them. "We can't help them. Go to air. Packs of three. Use your thermals and sensors to scan for traps. Walk fast but soft. And for Jove's sake keep your chrome in. I need your eyes."

I designate the teams to search potential targets. Dust billows as nearly two score of Howlers jolt upward over their writhing comrades to disperse through the city.

I wait behind with Thraxa and Felix. I raise my voice so the impaled can hear me.

"How many of you saw Gorgons around your feet? Raise your right hand." A sea of right hands. Some lie and keep theirs down. Could be a false positive. Atlas might have booby-trapped none of them. Or all of them. "You may be booby-trapped," I say. "Medships are on the way. Hold out for them, and soon it'll be six weeks of pretty medici and ice frizeé. We'll be back."

I cast a dour look to Thraxa and Felix and we lift off for the city's communications center. I shoot a hole in the bronze dome with my pulse-Fist, scan, and drop through to the marble floor.

As sunlight washes in through the open door, we see them. Bodies strewn on the floor. Ripped apart and chewed up. Heads caved in with all manner of improvised weapons. Bodies chewed upon as if by animals. Atlas didn't do this. They butchered one another. The features of the dead are mottled and monstrously warped by some pathogen.

Gods, what did Atalantia's warlocks cook up now?

They were collaborator civilians we relocated to Angelia, far from any military facility. *Put them out of harm's way,* I said. If Sevro had been there, he would have laughed. "Where do you put a chickenshit officer if you need him to expire?" he once asked me. "Out of harm's way!"

Pax was out of harm's way too.

"You ever seen anything like this?" I ask Thraxa.

She shakes her head. "Maybe he was testing a new bioweapon."

"There are easier ways." I bark at my medici to take a sample and evac to *Necromancer* for transmission. Central Command needs to know. I start to laugh as I realize the game. "It's all to buy time. Puzzles and pain." I look around. The facts don't add up. What is he buying time for? We could get an airdrop and catch up to him, so it wasn't to extend his lead. Eleusis was ripe for the picking. How does this side trip change the board? Thunder peels to the north. My storm is slowly forming.

"Howler One," Alexandar says in my ear com. *"We've got something at the ore refinery."*

Alexandar, Rhonna, and several Howlers are gathered in the control room of the city's ore refinery when Thraxa and I join them. Disabled spidermines and microwave bombs lie on a table.

Marbles, our Green slicer, and Clown's best friend, is jacked into the central computer's input port. A worn black hardwire runs from the computer's port to a small port on his right temple. His eyes roll back in his head as he travels through a virtual landscape. His fingers tap on the plastic chair. After a moment, he sighs. His dry lips smack together and he reverts.

"Sumn nastyfoul darkpart," he says in staccato silicon slang, skipping past the words that make sentences intelligible to us carbon bodies so that it sounds like his mouth is full of marbles. "Rickety roads, slipped package uranium dense, destinations easy as 01100001 01100010 01100011." He stutters the numbers out like a garment needle.

"Alexandar, translate."

Quick with low and mid tongues, Alexandar steps forward.

"No," Marbles says, holding up a bony finger. The dark circles under his eyes war with his sunburn. "I do this time. See, boss, like this. Angelia dustyass worktown. Systems all in a web, redundancy protocol to keep hard grip. We cut web in Rain. Didn't cut shadow web."

"There are latent systems?" Alexandar asks, first to understand. "Old hardlines?"

"Hardlines." Thraxa looks amused. "What dullard missed—"

"Quiet," I snap. "Marbles, you telling me the mining cities are still connected?"

"Only some. Old system. Someone slagged it good, missed shadow somehow. Stupid analog, mostlike. Hardlines under the pan."

"So he sent a command to other mining cities via this console," I clarify.

"Yah."

"What did he send?" Thraxa asks.

"Nulls. Dunno. Mad encryption. Got slicers with Gorgons, right? Slick pricks." He taps his head. "Give this silicon a week, plus three clicks for sleep, and I got your answer."

There is only one message worth sending to the other cities. My gut sinks. Rhonna pieces it together. "Could they send signals to the other reactors?"

"Give me diagnostics on the mine's reactor," Thraxa says. Marbles turns to the computer just as I jerk the hardwire away from him. As soon as he checked the reactor, I've no doubt a neurological attack would fry his brain to jelly. Trap after trap after trap.

"He's going to overload this reactor and any connected by hardwire," I explain, and head for the door. "It's going thermal." Angelia doesn't matter, but the cities it's hardwired to will. Those reactors are what fuel our shield chain. I open my general frequency. *All Howlers, evacuate the city. Buddy flights if you don't got boots. Colloway, bring the* Necro *for air hook.*"

By the time I make it out the door of the refinery, half the Howlers are already airborne. Those with gravBoots lock the magnetic buddy belts around their waists to the Howlers without them. They take off. Rhonna and Thraxa are the last pair away. Alexandar waits for me. I turn around so he can link the metal coupling at his waist to the one at my tailbone. The magnets snap together. He wraps his arms around my shoulders and pats my chest.

I lift off hard from the ground, my gut wrenching as the boots thrust us up till we're free of the city. Overhead, Colloway is scooping Howlers into his shuttle's open garage. Alexandar and I land smoothly and de-couple. I look down at the city and shout for Colloway to get us clear.

The logic is sinister.

That forest of bodies and biological weapons were meant to bring medical and science teams. To slow us down as we patched our wounded and scratched our heads, focusing on the small game instead of the grand stage.

The first explosion at Angelia's nuclear power plant, caused by the meltdown of its reactor, is not like that of an atomic warhead. It stutters outward from the domed building, first as steam, then as fire, lifting the roof of the complex and engulfing the city in a rolling wave. Those impaled soldiers disappear in a cloud, their flesh melted from their bones by the steam, and the rest consumed by the slow rippling tide of fire.

I will see you in the Vale, brothers.

I patch in to Central Command in Tyche. Panic creeps into the professional clip of officers as they report multiple reactor explosions around the Waste of Ladon, stretching all the way to the Petasos Peninsula and the whole of the Plains of Caduceus. Six cities have lost power. More will follow in a chain reaction. Without power, the whole northern shield chain will fall. I wanted a window, but Atlas just kicked in the sky.

Atalantia is coming.

"Someone betrayed us," Thraxa growls.

Or Atalantia is smarter than her father.

"How many generators will fall?" I ask Thraxa. She stares at Marbles's information readout and makes a mental calculation. Too slow. I toss it to Alex. He barely blinks before he has an answer.

"It'll be everything north of Erebos, except Red Reach and Tyche. Their domes are locally powered. They'll hold."

Heliopolis is safe, then. Still protected south of Erebos. Which means the escape route through Tyche is viable if Tyche holds. But six million men will be cut off from the city by bombardment. How do I get them back?

"By the Vale itself . . ." someone whispers.

The Howlers watch in despair out the back of the shuttle as the translucent shield that protected us from the might of the Gold Armada flickers and then disappears one panel at a time until the whole northern sky is naked to the armada above.

My com pings with incoming transmissions. Rhonna fields a call. "Harnassus requests orders of retreat."

Thraxa steps between me and the other aides fielding calls. "Let him think."

In her shadow, I watch the sky. Flashes in orbit. Friction trails scar the blue horizon. The first bombs begin to fall.

The vanguard legions will come soon after. Bloody Peerless cohorts in fast boots and starShells, dropships packed with veteran Gray shock troops, Obsidian slaveknights stoked to mind-melting bloodfrenzy by the drugs of their masters, tanks, titans, esoteric war machines, the full might of a militarized empire out for revenge.

We are out of position. Our mobility will be frozen by bombardment. Legions and static defenses erased by atomics. Those who don't die will be hopelessly shattered and fragmented. Then Atalantia's forces will flank and encircle the marooned remains of my army before we can attempt a breakout.

There is only one option, and it isn't retreat.

"Thraxa." She steps up to me. "We must take the punch."

"Can we?"

"Yes. Atalantia needs Mercury. She won't nuke the Children cities. Red Reach and Tyche are independent of the shield chain. Their domes will hold. And soon we'll have the storm—"

"It will take hours for the—"

"I started the engines two hours ago."

She blinks in surprise. "And the First Army? They won't make it to the cover of Red Reach."

It comes out in a cold rattling of sentences. "Then I'll bring them a shield. Atalantia will likely land south of Pan with at least a third of their army. She'll bottle up the Children and take the cities one by one, trapping our garrisons. If we abandon the cities and mass the garrisons from the Children at Kydon, we can sally to Pan and make an oblique front. It won't hold, but if we hit them from behind with the Second Army out of Red Reach and drive them toward the sea, we can hurt her while the First Army clears a route to Tyche from the north." I grip her shoulder. "Take all six starShells. Go to Kydon and lead the tank legions."

"You need the starShells."

"You need them more. I'll find a skyhook." I look at the darkening sky. "You'll have cover soon. Hold, and I'll gut them from the southwest, then we haul ass to Tyche together. A double atomic burst will signal my coming. Go."

Stalwart Thraxa, spine of the infantry, favorite of her father, knows I send her into the teeth of the enemy. She smiles at me nonetheless. "Hail Reaper."

"Hail Telemanus."

She rushes for the starShell spitTube, taking five of her Golds.

"Sevro, call Harnassus . . ." I turn and find Rhonna at my shoulder instead of my trusted shadow. She looks like I've slapped her. "Rhonna, tell him to send reinforcements to Tyche via the loop. I want every single reserve ripper in the air and bound for the plains. Interdiction protocol.

If they don't take out some of those missiles, we're done. Go." It will leave Heliopolis naked, but she isn't their target.

"Alex—" He doesn't respond. His eyes are fixed on the bombs that already race down through the atmosphere. *This is my fault,* he will think. I actually do slap him.

His eyes light up in anger.

"Contact Feranis. Tell her to expect heavy mechanized assault from the northwest from landfall on the Talarian Peninsula. She'll have to hold Tyche without the *Morning Star.* I need *Star* and the Drachenjäger cohorts at . . ." I glance at the map.

He intuits my purpose. "Sector Seventeen."

I nod. "And call your cousin, tell him to meet us at Skyhook Eleven. I'll ride with the Arcosians today." He rushes to the communications room as I hail Orion. Her bright eyes are glazed. She's in the synaptic drift with the storm.

"How are your storm pilots holding up?"

"Handling . . . the flow. There have been spikes, but . . . within range."

"How long till electronic interference?"

"Ten minutes."

"Can you slow it to twenty?"

"We will try. Must concentrate now."

I click out. The rest of the Howlers haven't moved. They watch the friction trails, a sense of doom upon them.

"You waiting for a formal invitation from the Fury? Asses to the armory. Iron up." Finally, they move. I shout up the corridor to my pilot. "Colloway! Get me to my army."

The ship accelerates, nearly knocking me from my feet. Steadying myself, I take the com off the wall and patch my signal into the powerful transmitters on Tyche to speak to my army while I still can.

"This is Reaper. Broken Sky. Repeat, Broken Sky. The enemy has breached the northern shields. Missiles are already en route. Expect heavy bombardment of north Helios and coms blackout presently. Operation Voyager Cloak is canceled. All officers, open your blackpacks. Keyword: *hazard bedlam.*"

Across Helios, thousands of low-ranking officers, from infantry centurions to ripWing squadron captains, will be opening metal canisters to receive briefings on Operation Tartarus and the conditions they will soon face.

"Operation Tartarus is now live. Second Army, abandon your positions and rally at Red Reach. First Army and all other Cloak units, rally at Sector Seventeen. Cover is inbound. Third Army hold in the Children until the Rain comes, then rally to Kydon. Legate Telemanus is on her way."

About to bark out a curt farewell, I pause, seeing that none of my Howlers have moved. The roughest veterans of a generation stare at me, knowing all is lost. Eight million more are out there in the desert, mountains, coastal jungles, without shields. They need more than orders.

I rasp into the com.

"Brothers, sisters. Atalantia has come for our lives. She thinks we wait looking at the sky for rescue, that fear has made a home in our hearts. She thinks we have forgotten ourselves. But I have not forgotten what we are. We fought in the ruins of Luna. On the plains and oceans of Earth. In the mountains and the tunnels of Mars. Whatever soil we have stood upon, we have freed. We are not marooned refugees waiting for rescue. We are not prisoners waiting for chains. We are the Free Legions. And today we become the rock they break upon. All legions, prepare for Rain."

Then the horizon stutters with white light, and the mushrooms grow.

10

LYSANDER

The Ash Rain

"*L*ET FALL THE RAIN."
      The disembodied voice of Atalantia comes through the communications nodes secured on my auditory canals. Like a conductor's baton, it sweeps the music into motion.

Thumpthumpthumpthumpthump, go the spitTubes.

My world turns and my starShell is ingested into the honeycomb of the wall. Outside the shell's facial shield, the throat of the spitTube pulses with red light.

Thumpthumpthumpthumpthump. Another hundred men.

When falls the Rain, be brave. Be brave, my grandfather said.

I do not feel brave. I am not the center of this symphony. No one even cares I'm here.

Where is the immortal majesty the poets promised me? Where is the stern will my ancestors preached to their children?

It was just an illusion conjured by fools who never left their libraries, or by agents of necessity.

This is the Noble Lie.

Every frayed nerve, every quaking cell, screams in horror, urging me to crawl out of the tube, to escape this insanity. Is a man a coward if he realizes that bravery is just a myth the old tell the young so they line up for the meatgrinder?

My first toy was a wooden sword.

Adults think it adorable.

"Better dead than a coward," Aja would say when a member of the Palatine would fall in combat on some far-off sphere. Better rotting meat for worms than the butt of a passing joke or an embarrassment to the beloved dead. What hilarious things we do for people who will never know we did them.

I have not used the Mind's Eye since the Rim. It makes me feel like my grandmother's puppet. But in my fear, I have nothing else on which to rely.

"Fear is the torrent," I whisper. "Fear is the torrent. Fear is the torrent."

I am not here. I am no physical being.

Electricity tethered to carbon. I am a pattern.

And so is the world.

With that acceptance, I release a measured breath, and sink molecule by molecule into the Mind's Eye.

I see Octavia as if she were before me.

She sits in her Ocular Sphere. The glass walls of the room are open and the city laid out beneath her. Her eyes look down at the Oracle on my wrist, its stinger waving.

"Do not let fear touch you," she whispers. The intricate creases in her face are like the spiderweb in the high corner of the room. "Fear is the torrent. The raging river. To fight it is to break and drown. But to stand astride it is to see it, feel it, and use its course for your own whims. Now, Lysander, I want you to lie to me, if you can. . . ."

The memory sputters, invaded by another.

Curtains waver like guttering candle flames. I'm walking down a hall toward a black door etched with a single phrase. Music tinkles behind the door. There is laughter. But as I reach forward with my little hand to push it open, I am swallowed by shadows.

The spiderweb emerges from the shadows. A fly struggles to escape, but with each strain entangles himself further.

"Fear is the torrent," I rasp with Octavia. "Fear is the torrent."

Her face is bathed green.

I surge forward.

Urine streams into the catheter. My stomach drops to my heels. My vision flickers; a ball of vomit catches halfway up my esophagus as blackness crawls at the corner of my sight. By the time I remember to breathe, the *Annihilo* is already twenty kilometers behind me. My gut swirls again and I cough up bile. It sprays, murky brown, into a plastic catch over my mouth.

Around me, my suit whirs and flashes with the nonverbal communication between Blue pilots and Gold flight leaders. Clipped commands crisscross over the com. I narrow my mind's pupil to constrict the influx of information and collate in the background as I slip into the flight flow etched into me by Midnight School aviators.

My mind runs through a collection of instruction sequences, eyes siphoning and collecting data till I've assured myself and Overwatch, the maintenance support brigade on the *Annihilo,* that my systems are nominal.

Only then do I look up and gape at the grandeur.

The invasion sweeps along in its silent song.

Ahead, the silhouette of Ajax's starShell is dark against the nightside of the onrushing planet. It flickers like white phosphorus as the particle cannons of the *Annihilo* and her gunships lance diagonally across the horizon and toward the breach.

The energy beams illuminate streams of starShells all around me. Hundreds of men in metal. And yet they form little more than a tributary of the great flooding river gushing from the fleets of the Two Hundred lesser houses, and giants Grimmus, Falthe, Carthii, and Votum.

The vanguard of our force falls, uncontested.

The ships become fainter than needles in the darkness behind. The planet grows. Its night face is black, the continents laid out like tatters of a death shroud trimmed in gold by city lights along the coasts. Its North Pole wears a mutating crown of electric green aurora.

As we pass into the mesosphere, we cross the planet's meridian, from night to day. A golden bow of sunlight blazes around the planet as if it were Apollo's own, and we the children of Hyperion, racing our chariots home. For a moment, it makes me miss that far-off city and the home I haven't seen for half a life.

The day face of the world reveals itself.

Beneath the faint shimmer of Darrow's shifting tropospheric shields are small, icy poles, strings of mountain ranges. Temperate alpine elevations characterize the north, jungles stretch to the south. Between them lies a mountain-studded equatorial desert.

The infamous Ladon. Eater of armies.

The infant typhoon detailed in the mission data report does not look too menacing. It forms a thin spiral cloud layer over the Sycorax Sea.

There is time enough to be lost in the majesty, and to remember nature did not provide this with her careless hand. *My* race of mortals carved this paradise from irradiated rock and violent gas by channeling the greatest virtues of all men in common cause.

A patriotic pride that I did not know I possessed fills me. The same blood flows through my veins as the man who sent the last of the Lovelock engines and Storm Gods here. But this zeal evaporates as soon as I realize I do not belong to the age of giants who made this, but to a smaller, meaner age where men think war the height of human endeavor.

I laugh at the cosmic joke. Only humanity could grasp the stars and then let them slip through its fingers for the pettiness in its heart.

But I feel hope. That pettiness defined my grandmother's age. It may yet not define ours.

"Fine launch, goodmen. I trust everyone kept breakfasts down dinners up," Ajax says convivially. There's a chorus of laughter, and highLingo rebarbs. Do they really love this? What creatures could be so at ease here and now? Am I even the same species?

"Heliopolis will still be covered by the southern shield chain. We must penetrate via the breach and fly south. Passing coordinates." The trajectory data appears on my display. His voice becomes solemn as he delivers the Grimmus creed. *"Should the Void take you, celebrate, my friends. For before death, there was glory. Prepare for atmospheric entry."*

I wait for him to hail my private channel. But when the light blinks, it's Kalindora, not Ajax.

"Don't burn your main thrusters till we go horizontal. Let gravity do the work, not your generator. Simulators underrepresent drag. And don't activate your pulseShield till breach. No telling when we'll get a recharge. Last thing you want is your suit dying in a firefight."

Friction heat glows ahead of me as the first starShells begin their descent. I see Atalantia's Ash Legion descending to our left.

The planet resists my entry. The starShell bucks as it enters with enough kinetic energy to compress the air in front of me and turn it into a furnace. A brittle layer of thermal soak tiles in the entry carapace absorbs the heat and sheds away. All around, scores of starShells burst from carapaces winnowed by friction to scream like wrathful locusts down into the blue sky.

Wind and engines roar outside my shell as I join them.

We do not come under fire. The Republic's shields that protect them from orbital bombardment also prevent them from contesting our descent. They shimmer fifty kilometers below, only eight kilometers above the planet's surface. Atalantia parts from us, heading to the northernmost part of the breach as we head to the southernmost.

"Time to breach, twenty seconds," Ajax intones as we pass over a mountain range toward the Ladon.

The horizon toward which we fly is a holocaust of artillery. The concentrated firepower of the Ash Armada bludgeons the thousand-kilometer-wide breach.

Particle beams divide reality. Mushrooms bloom on the surface.

In all the war, no one has used more atomics than this. I am horrified. The atomics drop on depopulated zones, but the fallout will kill thousands before it is scrubbed and meds distributed. Maybe more.

Impossibly, the Republic fires back. Particle beams lance up from the breach at strafing orbital torchShips and high-altitude corvette gunships. Guided missiles chase bombers and send them spiraling down to crash into the southern shields like skipping stones. Atomics flash pale white in the troposphere. A beam connects with a Bellona corvette. Light ripples as the shield overloads and a second beam carves through the helm of the ship.

Thirty million life threads interweave, some carrying on, others clipped short.

It is so horrible.

"Be a giant," Ajax said.

How, in all this?

Strategists, I understand. But warriors . . . I thought I did until now. The insidious arithmetic becomes apparent of how overwhelmingly visionary warriors like Darrow, the Minotaur, and Atlas must be to be able to shift the face of a battle once it's already begun.

"TOB ten."

We're over the desert now, skimming the shield dome.

A gap in the artillery barrage opens as orbital ships redirect their guns to create a hellmouth—a corridor of protective fire. A second later, the first century of starShells from a Carthii destroyer enters the hellmouth and disappears into the breach. RipWings follow. The century after them disintegrates as a particle beam slashes up from the mountains.

"Breach," Ajax says.

Our century streams into a hellmouth.

My senses overload.

Munitions blaze around us, blinding flashes, metal colliding and vaporizing. But we outrace the sounds of the explosions we see, only to cross into the rippling sound waves of prior explosions. I lose Ajax in the mayhem. Airburst shells keen and explode to disperse harpies—fist-sized drones packed with EMP or explosive charges. I fire my left shoulder cannon at a swarm of them. A dozen slam into a ripWing. The engines die and it careens out of the hellmouth into a friendly artillery shell.

Then I'm through.

"Fracture," Ajax orders. The legion's centuries splinter into hundreds of decades. I struggle to match their precision, nearly clipping Ajax's heels as I follow him. Kalindora and Seraphina fall in behind me as we dive toward the jagged Hesperides range. *"Clear your peaks. Leave the air to the rippers."* The com clicks as he switches channels to our decade. *"Decade One, we're on our own. Head north by—"*

Seraphina's voice cuts him off. *"E spike. Shatter."*

My instruments register the electrical spike of railguns charging. Out of the corner of my eye, a pinprick of purple light flashes on a mountain ridge.

I fire my left shoulder thruster and shoot out of formation as a blur of dense metal whips through now-empty air. Four hundred slugs follow the first in three seconds. A starShell disappears in a shower of debris. I can't tell whose. Then Seraphina's rockets slam into the gun installation and bloom over shielding as it continues to fire, unaffected.

I activate my targeting laser, but before I can light the installation up, Kalindora's illuminates it. An orbital strike falls. A beam of white light that would flashblind the naked eye cleaves the mountain peak like a hunk of cheese.

"Good spot, for a Moonie. Compliments on the lighting, Annihilo,*"* Ajax says. *"Decade One, cluster on me. We've a mountain range to clear."* He lights up my personal channel. *"How's the war, little brother?"*

I struggle to reply. "Fast."

He laughs. *"Tune down your inertial dampeners. It'll help you feel the maneuvers. You're flying that masterpiece like it's a cosmosHauler. You quite nearly clipped my heels. Twice."*

"Apologies. It's touchier than the sims."

"Touchier than the sims. Ha! We'll make a Peerless out of you yet. Now, belly down, goodman. Welcome party of aerial termites inbound."

11

DARROW

Red Reach

M Y ARMY DIES. THE world has become a garden for mushrooms. They bloom on the bruised horizon, swelling two hundred kilometers high, dwarfing the mountains. Shockwave after shockwave, diffused by distance, rack the *Necromancer* as we streak north to get me back to Red Reach base and the heart of my northern armies.

With the shields down, we will be encircled. We must prepare to break out in the thin slip of time between bombardment and landfall. If we survive the bombardment.

Desert sand streams underneath the shuttle. Fortified mining cities disappear in flashes of white light. Great desert gun emplacements with enough firepower to take down a torchShip stream fury into the sky, only to be turned into glass by pillars of light hotter than the sun.

Colloway is silent and still wearing his synaptic halo. The ovular pilot's chair bathes the dark man in blue light, making the fighter ace look an elfin boy half his age. Untethered from his body, he is the ship and the ship is him.

"Come on, Midnight," I whisper.

"Almighty, give me space," the ship replies dreamily. *"This party makes Ilium look like a Thermic sailing race. Oh my. Incoming slags. I count . . . Can't be right. Instruments are frazzed."* A pause. *"Never mind. It is six hundred."*

"Kilometers?"

"RipWings."

Shit.

In the wake of the first atomic barrage, the first river of enemy rip-Wings descend. Fifty squadrons stream down against the backdrop of a mushroom cloud like a school of piranha. Missiles stream from their bellies, cascading down on gun batteries and tank formations. Three squadrons peel off to engage us.

"I hope everyone relished their breakfast. You'll see it again soon."

My boots lock to the deck. My gut jerks as we spin in a never-ending corkscrew. I am helpless behind Colloway, despite my blood-red pulse-Armor and all its armaments. Only the storm can stop what comes from the sky, and it is still in its infancy.

You could run a war from the *Necromancer,* survive almost any magnitude of EMP, outrace even a torchShip. But in atmosphere, she's a big boat, and the ripWings gain on us fast.

I hail Harnassus for LongMalice support and give him coordinates. Over the static, I can barely hear his affirmative. In the Hesperides range, hundreds of klicks to the southwest, under the cover of our intact southern shield chain, fifty-meter guns will swivel on their gyroscopes. Colloway thumbs-up to show he heard me.

My body leans sideways as he puts us into a steep climb, straight at the enemy squadrons. As missiles leap from the ripWings, Colloway barrel-rolls sideways and slams us into a nosedive. The missiles blink behind us, some slithering off to follow our countermeasure drones. The rest scream after, undistracted. The desert pan races up to meet us. A thousand meters. Five hundred. One hundred. At fifty, Colloway activates the launch thrusters and the ship ricochets parallel to the ground like a skipped stone. My head jerks forward, chin slamming into the metal of my breastplate. I see stars and hear the concussion through the ship as the missiles plow into the ground. Those that follow are mowed down by Colloway's rear railguns.

There are no cheers from the garage.

Colloway redirects toward Harnassus's firing solution. Harnassus sends us a countdown. At three, we slip past the killzone. The enemy squadrons scream behind, spewing railgun fire. Our shields buckle and fall. I throw my bulk in front of Colloway. A hundred slugs the size of fists tear through the ship. One hits my shoulder instead of the back of his chair, overloading the shield, buckling the armor as I twist and redirect it into the ceiling. Half my body goes numb. Auto-response needles in the suit inject adrenaline into my bloodstream. My world pulses.

"And . . . boom."

Through the sieve of slug holes, I glimpse the sky out the back of the ship just in time to see the LongMalice rounds arch down and detonate, releasing clouds of smaller munitions. RipWings disintegrate.

Our tail free, Colloway accelerates in a straight line. We're out of the Ladon. The sky is blackening to the north. Faint traces of lightning slither through the firmament. The green grass of the Plains of Caduceus unfolds in front of us. It is bedlam.

In the shadow of mushroom clouds, lines of burning tanks and armored personnel carriers spread across the ground like frayed rope. Hundreds of thousands of men run on foot. GravBikes carrying four or five men apiece stutter toward Red Reach base.

"The shield is still up," Colloway murmurs from his sync as the field headquarters comes into view. I barely believe him. Gigajoules of kinetic energy from particle beams turn its dome shield a bloody crimson. But sure enough, Red Reach has not fallen. Thank the Vale it wasn't hardlined to Angelia. Dozens of legions swarm under its protective shelter, forming a logjam of tanks and war machines, which overflow from her acres of guns, barracks, and defensive works.

My Second Army is intact.

Above the shield dome swirls a dogfight of thousands. RipWings churn through the vapor of cumulonimbus clouds that bloom to the north, in from the sea. More dogfights flash all the way up to the stratosphere, buying time for my squadrons to intercept atomic ordnance. As it has before, the grudge between the airheads and dustbacks vanishes. A Blue shield of sacrifice protects their brothers on the ground. They disappear by the dozens, careless of enemy fighters, hunting nothing but the falling missiles. In a way, it is beautiful. In every other way it is horrible to watch.

I must make their sacrifice count. It's hard to see how. Pillars of white particle beams flare down from orbit, piercing clouds, vaporizing men and metal as they rake canyons in the ground. We are outmatched. There is no conventional answer to Atalantia's orbital guns. But if Red Reach can just last . . .

To the south of Red Reach, in the mountains that overlook the northern plains, several ground-to-orbit batteries continue to fire upward. Colloway takes us through a mountain valley, aiming for one of the several dozen skyhooks I scattered across Helios. Of the five in our flight path, it is the only one that remains airborne, docked as it is under a leaning cleft of a mountain that also shelters a Drachenjäger garage. Thousands of starShell rigs await their pilots on the skyhook's tarmac.

"Skyhook Eleven, Necromancer *coming in hot. Thirteen elves, five giants, ten dwarfs, and one Reaper need heavy iron. Prep pitcrews for emergency gearup."*

"Copy. Bay two clear. Pitcrew on standby."

We make an emergency landing on the floating supply platform. Pitcrews swarm its surface, shuttling munitions between the mountain supply depot and the skyhook. They load errant packs of aerial infantry into starShells, and send them into the fray. The purple and silver banners of the Arcosian Knights waver in the air as they land in gravBoots on the far side. There are few actual Arcoses amongst them, but all hail from client houses loyal to the widows of Lorn's sons. I'll need my best men with me.

As Colloway takes stock of damage done to *Necromancer,* I barrel out with the Howlers. A pitboss directs us to a rank of the armored starShells lying on their backs just beneath the garage's vertical door. Inside the garage, the armored Fifteenth Legion Helldivers will be syncing with their Drachenjägers. The forty-meter-tall machines are made to dominate battlefields. They are shaped like boxy humans wearing spiked backpacks, except there is no head or neck, simply a hunched pilot cockpit set low between the shoulders. They have six jointed arms, multiple cannons at the elbows, and huge ion cleavers.

I check to make sure the master storm switch is still in the second right thigh box of my pulseArmor and lie down in one of the starShells, a four-meter-tall mechanized suit capable of flight meant to make men mobile tanks. In concert with Drachenjägers they make regular infantry nearly obsolete, but they are expensive, bulky, and eat fuel like mad.

A crew of twelve Oranges and Reds go to work around me, jacking data-links from the starShell into my pulseArmor, attaching a double magazine, calibrating the gear, priming the fusion sword, and sealing on an extra battery. Ten seconds flat is all they need. They clear off and move to the next. A hydraulic lift punches the back of the starShell. I lever to my feet flanked by nearly thirty armored Howlers. Two Reds hang on to the front of the four-meter starShell, securing the canopy over me. Through their working arms, I see the enemy aircraft making a coordinated mass maneuver away from Red Reach. We call it a nuke flower.

"Atomic brace!" I shout, and look frantically for Rhonna. I spot her rushing a wounded Howler to the skyhook's medBay, too far to make it back to the *Necromancer* or in under the supply depot's closing blast doors.

A siren screams. Hundreds of pitmen scramble for cover or to get off the exposed skyhook to the safety of the mountain garage doors. Rhonna won't make it there. "Alexandar!"

He's already moving, swinging the long arms of his starShell as he rushes to scoop her up and jump back to us. Colloway zips away on the *Necromancer* to hide behind the mountain.

One of the Reds atop me seals my canopy, catching the other's arm in the sealing teeth. The Red jerks at his arm, unable to get down. His hand flails inside the canopy, not far from my face. Blood trickles down his forearm. His fellow abandons him. He can't be more than twenty years old. An iron haemanthus pendant hangs from his neck. His eyes are wild with fear as they meet mine. He's jammed the canopy. I can't open it. I try to cover him with my arms. Alexandar curls his starShell around Rhonna like a cocoon. The huge blast doors close behind us. Pitmen hammer at the doors from the outside. Poor bastards.

"Brace!" I shout. Felix and an Obsidian pathfinder kneel in their starShells with me, forming a wedge with me at the point, sheltering Alexandar and Rhonna. Scores of other wedges form. Pitmen rush to take shelter behind them. The Red outside my canopy screams. Even if I free him, he cannot be helped. He isn't in pulseArmor like Rhonna.

My amplified optics see it now over his shoulder. A lone dagger-shaped speck trailing vapor as it falls toward Red Reach base. Two rip-Wing pilots chase after it, spraying fire. They overload its shield, pierce its casing. And then orbital artillery wipes them away. The bomb falls uncontested.

I patch into Red Reach's Central Command.

A warroom fills my view. Three dozen Martian officers, representing eight colors, stand like ghosts in the pale light of the battlemap watching the atomic fall.

"An omega-atomic will impact in thirty seconds," I say quietly. The Red outside my cockpit is listening too, his face pressed to the glass just two hand spans away from my own. "Your fight is behind you. Remember now your beloved. Your wife, your husband, your father, your mother, your daughter, your son." I meet his eyes. They look so much like my mother's. "Remember the sea, the highland forests, Agea at dawn, Olympia at twilight, Attica in spring, Thessalonica in harvest." As I speak, they close their eyes and unscrew the canisters of Martian soil to clench in their hands. Gold and Red, Blue and Orange, Gray and Obsidian. My heart breaks in half. "Remember home. Remember Mars. You go there now to rest under the shade of her—"

They disappear in a wash of static.

Stillness, as if the sky inhaled sound and time. I close my eyes and hold the Red as tight as I dare.

Primordial light. Intense, tiny, like the pupil of a god followed by a second expanding flash so brilliant and vast it makes my eyelids transparent and reveals every bone, joint, and blood vessel in the Red pitman stuck outside my canopy. I see the X-rayed bones of a dozen others through their flesh. A curled engineer makes a silhouette, transparent like the image of a fetus asleep in the womb.

The flash contracts to reveal a mutinous fireball at the hypocenter of the blast. Air, grass, rock, metal, and men vaporize as their matter heats to match the heart of a sun.

A wall of thermal energy washes outward. A ghost of fire walks through me. The Red's eyes that look like my mother's begin to bubble and then they melt with the rest of him. In the wake of the heat, a colossal wave of pressure races toward us at the speed of sound. The skyhook rocks backward against the face of the mountain. The bones of the Red shatter and blow away in the wind. His severed hand falls off inside the canopy. My boots spark on the flattop surface as the shockwave pushes me back. I stagger, supported by the Howlers. Pitmen who took shelter behind mechs in front of us look like autumn leaves as their tattered bodies are hurled off the floating platform down into the mountains. Others are lifted from their feet and slam into starShells, turning to pulp. Clothing is torn away. Blues and Oranges with weaker bones are pulverized on the spot to become liquid bags held together by bubbling flesh.

Then the debris.

Charcoal birds fall from the sky and crumble to pieces on the concrete. RipWing detritus hails down. A flattened tank cartwheels past, thrown dozens of kilometers from the plains, to crash into a mountain façade above our base. A great grumbling fills the mountain range as hundreds of avalanches roll down the sheer granite cliffs. I swear I even see the planet ripple. I look up, and up, and up, through my starShell canopy; the fireball articulates skyward, with a vortex of debris and smoke swirling around a molten heart of fire where once there was my Second Army.

A million men, tanks, and arms to ash.

The hollow abyss of despair calls to me. The voice that found me in the Jackal's prison tomb. *Reaper, Reaper, Reaper. Look what you have done. Look what you are. In your shadow, nothing can survive.*

Somewhere above, Atalantia will be smiling.

Alexandar's mech steps to my side. I search desperately for Rhonna. She staggers to her feet, her pulseArmor fried, but she is alive. Relief floods me.

"Your order, sir?" Alexandar asks.

The mushroom is reflected in his canopy.

Orders? What orders can be given in this madness? Our long-range coms are down. I cannot adjust my plan. Thraxa is unsupported. About to be cut off. I would pray if I knew any gods were listening. Let the First Army have survived the blast. Let the *Morning Star* have arrived in time for them to shelter under her shields. Let there be life in all this ash. No god listens. There are only men. And what one does, another may undo. That is my only religion. That of the hand and the lever.

"Midnight, are you out there?"

"Barely. EMP nearly fried me. Ship is falling to pieces." Even at short range I can barely hear him.

"The storm is coming in earnest. Can you make it to Kydon?"

"If I have to flap the wings myself."

"When you get there, tell Thraxa to break off and make for Tyche. The Second can't reinforce her. The First is coming to help her retreat to Tyche."

"Where are you going?"

"To make sure Tyche is still ours when you get there."

He says nothing for a moment. *"Happy travels, sir. Midnight out."*

His engines flare and he lurches away. Only my starShells remain on the platform. I give them orders to abandon the stuttering skyhook and gather inside the opening blast doors of the garage. "Rhonna." She whirls to face me. "The Helldivers are inside. See if they got a spare rig. I need a full-metal god."

"Yessir."

Five minutes later, I float over the starShells and the huge Drachenjägers behind them. They stretch into the mountain, rank upon metal rank. Helldiver Legion, the Armored Fifteenth. Martians all, my first and best Drachenjäger legion. I rode with them to end the Siege of Olympia to chase the Minotaur out of Cassius's former home, and then again at Agea against Atlas and the Ash Lord.

"Helldiver Legion! Enemy iron is inbound. Our coms are down. Soon the storm will claim theirs. The First Army will hit them at the Children and then retreat to Tyche. The city will soon come under siege by at least one full army group.

"Legate Telemanus believes the Second Army is now streaming to Tyche to relieve that siege and clear her path of retreat. Of the Second Army, we are all that remains. If Tyche falls, our brothers are lost. Will Tyche fall?" In reply, five thousand pairs of Drachenjäger boots hammer the floor of the cavern with a seismic *booom.* "Atalantia thinks the Second Army is ash. Are we ash?" *Booom. Booom.* "Are we afraid?" *Boom. Boom. Boom.* "What are we!"

"HELLDIVERS!"

"Form columns!"

The air warps with the thermal distortion of five thousand drachen engines growling to life. I see Rhonna slide into a black rig at the rear. Its arms pump as the bolts that stud her body sync with the Drachenjäger. My Howlers rise around me. The Arcosian Knights form columns in their starShells. At the vanguard, I turn to face the darkening world.

Enemy iron streams down to the western and eastern horizons. Little more than gnats in the shadow of the atomics. Obelisks of radioactive smoke and debris grow upon the Plains of Caduceus. High above their stalks, the bulbous heads of the mushroom clouds disappear into the thickening storm cover. Black clouds ride. Lightning shatters the sky. Atalantia has shattered our jaw with her first punch. Now it's our turn. I lift my slingBlade.

"For the Republic! For Mars!"

"Ride hell!"

12

LYSANDER

White Golems

TWELVE RIPPLING RIVERS OF shadow move across a desert of white chalk. The shadows are cast by six thousand starShells flying in twelve iron columns.

It is two hours since breach and I do not feel sane.

My life has disintegrated into a series of fragmented moments of extreme fear and unreal violence. It is defined by new sensations. The crunching of ice under clawed titanium foot. The slip of snow. The scrape of rock. The whistling of air. The tangy chlorine smell of ozone from my railgun. The ever-present tension that a benign ridge will suddenly come alive with anti-aircraft fire.

I no longer trust stillness.

Stillness is the enemy taking careful aim.

After clearing the briar-patch of mountain gun installations, our legion linked with our launch partners, the Terran-born XX Fulminata, the Thunderbolt Legion, to swell our numbers and drive north to make a secure landfall for the first wave of one hundred fifty thousand, and then the two million that will follow in the second and third waves to take Heliopolis.

Sooty smoke rises from the ruins of Republic scout craft and gun batteries cleared by Fulminata. I am relieved to be out of the mountains. Amongst the icy peaks, Ajax took us headlong at any threat like some possessed Homeric hero. I barely managed to keep pace, but my blade is well blooded from the bunker hunts. Kalindora shadowed me through it all, muttering about young pups wanting glory. Seraphina is keen for glory too, but not keen enough to override her discipline.

She is a better soldier than she was a traveling companion. Twice she guarded my flank. Once in the ruins of a mountain bunker when an Obsidian charged from the rubble with an axe. Once in the air when I didn't spot an anti-aircraft battery.

By midday, the first signs of civilization appear on the blasted landscape. A hotel for the wealthy beside a high mesa lake. Water farms, ore refineries, and a mining town with gold pyramids painted on their roofs to ward off bombardment. Small-arms fire flashes feebly at us from a rooftop.

"Leopard Eleven engaging sniper," I intone. I have three rockets left. "Thermal readings indicate multiple civilians in adjacent basements. Red and Brown genus. Switching to guns." Kalindora shadows me as I bank to make a precision shot at the two men on the roof.

A pillar of blinding light divides the horizon.

I break off to avoid the rippling shockwave.

When the orbital strike clears, the town is a molten crater. *"Too slow on the draw,"* Ajax drawls as I reel. *"You'll have to be quicker than a cat to steal my kills."*

"They were civilians . . ."

"Sympathizers. Don't worry, you get half a notch. Used your targeting solution, didn't I?"

"Only counts as one," Seneca adds. *"Hive mind."*

Laughter.

Kalindora hails my private frequency, but I reject the request.

Soon we are at the edge of the sky still protected by the Rising's southern shield chain. This deep in the Ladon, there is no sign of the enemy. Heliopolis is still a hundred klicks south.

When we set down in a shallow playa west of a reservoir city, I am filled with contempt. I pop the starShell's top, desperate for fresh air. But the desert heat hits like an anvil. An ache fills my lungs. Already, I feel the sun burning my ship-pale skin. I suck water from my suit's caches and step away from the commotion of the landing legions. Ajax calls to me, but I ignore him.

I count the thermal signatures from my mental picture. Three hundred and eleven. Some too small to be anything other than children.

I knew war wouldn't be clean. But he used my targeting data on *children*.

The sense of certainty and purpose that brought me here is fading. I feel like a boy from the crowd who thought he could tame lions by stepping in the cage with them.

Seraphina is fine in the cage. She stalks past with an excited glimmer in her eye. Ajax might hold the highest killcount, but she is not far behind. All will be recorded in holographic glory by their helmet cams, and tallied by administrators on the *Annihilo.* "War conforming to your expectations?" I ask.

"Beautifully so," she says between gulps of water. "Beautifully so."

As she walks away, I look out at the alien landscape. Between the Aigle Mountains and Hesperides is a flat belly of desert pavement broken only by dunes of white chalk, mushroom-shaped limestone hoodoos, and pale white cacti the size of houses. Mountains saw the horizon in half. Above them, the sun squats malevolently. White golems trudge through this bleakness like the mechanized overseers of Dante's hell. Pale with desert chalk, the Golds spike beacons into the hard clay of the playa. Elsewhere, scouts in light armor and optics helmets set drones loose as if they were pet falcons. Everyone's a hunter here.

Seneca, Ajax's bodyguard, winks at me as his drones soar north.

There's a crash to my right as Kalindora's starShell lands in a cloud of dust. "Don't waste the peace, Lysander. This grime will kill your shell sure as a railgun." She bends her knees and uses her elbows to cushion her suit as it falls to a sitting position. I join her and we crawl out of our starShells to clean the outsides. I spare glances at Ajax conversing with the Fulminata Legate. I know I should suck down my rising disgust, shadow him, learn from him and make myself useful, but something about him out here makes me feel unwelcome.

I have the sneaking suspicion that the orbital strike was more a message for me than a necessary military action. Could he really discount lives so flippantly?

"What's your core status?" Kalindora asks.

"Sixty-six percent."

"So he still listens." She nods in disgust at the Iron Leopards. "Most of those whelps are walking around sub-fifty because they didn't hold their burn. They'll depend on recharge."

"That was a war crime," I say. "It was only small-arms fire."

"Only a crime if there's a court. Eat." Kalindora tosses me a protein bar. "You move well," she says. At any other time, I'd bask in her compliments as I did as a boy. "Superb instincts. But you're clumsy in takeoff and need to expand your field of vision. You act like you want to use your razor instead of your gun. This isn't asteroid corridor fighting or whatever the blazes Bellona had you at. You did prime work on that aerial infantry though. I saw you put down four. Not your first kills, it seems."

"No."

She sees me staring at the ground. Her voice approaches anger. "What did you expect?"

"I don't know."

"Why did you come back?" she asks.

When I don't answer, she turns her back and crawls into her mech. "Your sensors picked up some people." She levers to her feet as I climb into my cockpit. "Did your sensors tell you they didn't have weapons? No. Did they tell you they weren't saboteurs or snipers? No. Or even Howlers? No. So how can mercy exist when anyone could carry an atomic rocket, and you don't know? That's the problem with this war. Cruelty is necessary. Yet cruelty is a thermal runaway."

The first wave of transports descends from the sky by the time I've sealed myself back in my starShell. Those ships with thrusters kick clouds of debris into the air. The ones with gravity engines form floating cloaks of chalk. GravBikes roar out of pens. Gray legionnaires skinned in desert armor and visor-bearing helmets pour out of personnel carriers. Dozens of humanoid titans, hoverTanks, and spiderTanks decouple from their transports and land on the dirt with a sound like hammers striking on wood.

Then come the engineers.

With a hundred fifty thousand men and women landed, the engineers rapidly begin securing and fortifying the landfall for the primary wave.

I look past the disembarking troops to the north.

There are shouts. Portable railguns swivel on their gyroscopes.

"Signatures inbound!" Seraphina shouts from the perimeter. She bursts back.

"Friendlies!" someone confirms.

A swarm of starShells descend perpendicular to the main landing. They make landfall in a pyramid in front of Kalindora, nearly a thousand in armor of a dozen disparate houses. Not one amongst them is Gold.

Only the best and most loyal of Grays are given license for starShells.

Their leader clomps forward. His starShell viewport and the pulseArmor helmet beneath retract and the face of a young-gunslinger-turned-old-centurion stares at me as if he's seen a man come back from the Void. One thousand mech-suited Praetorians fall to their knees.

"SubLegate Rhone ti Flavinius and the First Cohort Praetorian Guard reporting for duty, my liege." His cheeks are covered with more black and gold teardrops than when he served as my shooting instructor in the Citadel. I didn't think there was any more room.

The Gold knights surrounding us look back and forth between the most famous Gray alive, a thousand ex-Praetorians, and a scarless Pixie in borrowed armor with the Love Knight at his side.

They need no further explanation.

"Rhone ti Flavinius?" I say. "Hades didn't reclaim you yet?"

"And lose his best recruiter? Perish the thought, my liege." His accent is pure Lunese stock. Last in a long line of Praetorians, from birth he was sponsored by my family, and excelled in the *ludus* until he proved himself in battlefields across a dozen spheres under the command of Aja and Lorn. He rose so high as to become second officer under Aja of the XIII Dracones. There is no more famous a Praetorian, save perhaps his treasonous understudies: the Nakamuras.

On the day my grandmother died, he was in orbit preparing to face Virginia.

He would have thought the Line ended that day.

I wave him to his feet and tell him to rise.

"I cannot, my liege. On behalf of the First Cohort of the thirteenth and the scattered Guard, it falls upon me to issue our grievous apologies for abandoning the search, and presuming you dead. Our oath was till the extinguishment of the Blood. If there's punishment due, it is my duty to bear it for my men, in place of decimation, and an honor that my last order come from the Heir of Silenius."

The dragoon commander produces a Praetorian dagger and puts it to the dragon tattoos that circle his neck.

"The fault lies not with you, but with your patron. I was the one who was lost. Now, on your feet, Praetorian."

He stands. In his forties, he's no longer the arrogant lurcher I remember winning the Legion Pyramid at the summer martial games. War has aged him past his years, but the boyish glimmer remains in the sharpshooter's pale eyes. "Exter? Fausta?" I ask, searching behind him.

"Dead. Exter by the Goblin on Luna. Fausta from an orbital strike on Mars." A shame. They were always kind to me, particularly Fausta. "Kruger is still shooting the wings off flies. He's my decurion."

"How did you know I returned?" I ask. He looks at Kalindora. I turn on her in surprise.

"Atalantia cares for Atalantia," she says. "But there are many of us who would not see the heir die on the hour of his return. These men are sworn to you. As am I, my liege. Old oaths outweigh the new."

"Am I to take this to mean Atalantia means me harm?"

"Of course not," she replies. "She wept when she received your communiqué, but you are a Lune, and scar or not, you have no right to prevent these men from honoring their oaths."

This is not what I had in mind when I set out to prove my loyalty to Atalantia. It is a disaster. The Praetorians are not simply men sworn to my house. They are as much a symbol of the Sovereigncy as the Morning Chair itself. I search for Ajax but cannot find him in the mill of his landing legions. Seraphina has wandered over. She recognizes Rhone and takes a step closer.

"I apologize I could not bring more men, and for the accoutrement," he says, frowning at the blue and silver armor he wears. "We believed you dead. The most shameless have gone mercenary. Some have found work with the other houses. Most went to Atalantia. These here were with Julia au Bellona. Her house isn't what it was, but she doesn't spend men as quickly as the rest. She's terminated our contract as a gesture of fidelity to you."

I feel a pang of guilt. My own family glowers at me with suspicion, and Cassius's mother sends me an olive branch. More. A backing of my claim. I know enough of the woman to know she's playing her own little game, but now she's beginning to interrupt mine.

"The Lady Bellona knows I've returned, then," I say to Rhone.

"Little escapes Julia au Bellona." He smiles. "It was a long-range communiqué. But she says she will be joining you shortly. More of the Guard will come from the other houses as soon as they hear of your return." He clears his throat, suddenly very serious. "It will be as it was, *my Sovereign*."

I look past the man to see Ajax watching us.

His eyes are filled with so much wrath you would think I had just arranged for the Morning Chair to be delivered straight to the desert.

"So much for your word to my brother," Seraphina says. Her Rim eyes are chromed out for the desert light and unreadable, but her look of disdain is total.

"Lower your voice, man. I am not the Sovereign," I tell Rhone. "Nor do I intend to be. Purge it from your thoughts lest you wish to see me dead." I wheel on Kalindora. "How dare you presume—"

"Am I to be scolded like a child by a child?" she asks. "How odd this world is."

"Don't mock me. You know how this looks."

"Yes," she says. "Yes, I do."

Dammit all to Hades. I stomp away from her and the Praetorian, hoping to get a word with Ajax, but he is clustered in a thick knot of his officers. They sit on the edges of their cockpits. Seneca has produced a metal canteen from a thigh storage pouch. Another Gold supplies small tin cups, which Ajax fills. "To life and landfall," he says, and they tip the whiskey. "We'll finish the rest in Heliopolis. Sorry, little brother. Lost you in the sea of Praetorians. You should wear a crown so we can find you." No whiskey is poured for me. A woman gives me her own cup too eagerly. I'm wearing my suit, so I can't take it.

The first suitor makes their bid, poorly.

Ajax notices.

"May we have a moment, Ajax?"

He ignores me to address his men. "The intel and sensors didn't lie. We're five hundred kilometers from their nearest deployed force. We are in a slow tango with Heliopolis. They never thought we'd sneak a hand up the back of their skirt."

Atalantia's gambit is bold. While the bulk of the army focuses on the battle with the Republic in the north, she looks beyond the battle. The capital, Tyche, is the emotional victory for Votum. But Heliopolis is the prize—control it, control the south and her thousands of iron mines. Grimmus troops will occupy the Sun City, and they will stay for generations. The poor Votum have no idea what they're paying for her to take their planet back.

It is shameful. And none of them care. As *cliens,* or clients of House Grimmus, Atalantia, their *patronus* owes them protection and sponsorship. She will be sure to richly reward their loyalty and service in arms.

"It will be an assault," Ajax says. "Soon as the ground iron and infantry land, we push west in force. Seneca, take a century. Harass their *vedette* and drones. If it breathes or beeps, it dies. I want them blind as we—"

Ajax is interrupted as a signal comes over the general officer channel. The Golds slide in unison back into their starShells and latch up as the message crackles.

"All officers . . . is Fury Command. Have . . . situation developing. Stand . . . for update."

"THIS . . . ARCHIMMUNES UMBERTO'S FANT . . . FIVE HYPERCANES . . . FORMED OVER . . . SYCORAX. . . . ANOMALOUS PRESSURE CENTERS . . . EIGHTY KILO . . . PASCALS. THE LARGEST . . . WINDSPEEDS OF EIGHT HUNDRED KILOMETERS PER . . . MOVING SOUTH" The signal cuts out and reestablishes. *"WILL MAKE LANDFALL ON . . . HELION COAST IN TWENTY . . . EXPECT CLOUD COVER TO THIRTY KILOMETERS. HEAVY . . . FALL, TURBULENCE, ELECTRICAL . . . INTERFERENCE AND STORM SURGES . . . SECONDARY STORM FORMING OVER . . . WASTE OF LADON . . ."*

Confused glances are exchanged. "Hypercane?" Seneca frowns through his open cockpit.

"Those aren't possible except in the Rim," Seraphina says, coming up from behind with Kalindora.

But I alone know that they very much are. *Grandmother, you left landmines everywhere.*

"Perhaps we should delay landing," I offer neutrally. The officers glare as if I've spit in their eyes.

"Delay landing?" Ajax asks, incredulous. "And let a bit of weather steal our glory? I think your time amongst Moonies has made you superstitious, goodman."

"If there are five hypercanes over the Sycorax . . ."

"That's a thousand kilometers from here."

"A storm with eighty kilopascals has the capacity to cover all of Helios—much less five of them." I do the math. "Eight-hundred-kilometer-per-hour winds will pull down a ripWing. Electrical will slag any orbital relay. The Immunes mentioned a secondary storm. If there are pressure anomalies in the desert, we should suspend the land—"

"Lysander, enough," Ajax says.

It's the first time he's used my name in front of them, though they all know who I am by now. I pull it back. There's no way out of this. No way to avoid alienating him except by playing dumb, but then men die.

Ajax continues. "Thank you. Seneca, I told you to take your men—"

"Ajax," Seneca interrupts, "the northern drones have gone down."

Ajax bares his teeth. "What do you mean, gone down? Did they report enemy contact?"

"They're not responding to commands and their feeds are static. They were picking up some sort of pressure anomaly."

"A pressure anomaly?" Ajax glances at me as if I did this. "Hail the scouts."

"They're not responding either. Something is interfering with their coms."

"Quiet," Seraphina says. She lifts her hand to touch the wind. "Don't you feel it?"

"What?" Kalindora says.

"The storm."

A stone clatters against Ajax's starShell. He looks down with a frown. Rocks bounce against my boots. Then all along the landfall, men shout and point at something to the northwest. Ajax's eyes click upward to look past our semicircle of officers and then widen. *"By Jove . . . "*

Out there, amongst the chalk, coming down the desert flats between the mountain ranges, is a storm like those I've seen only in terraforming holos. A wall of sand rages across the desert. My feet root me to the ground as a great convulsive sigh of horror goes through the vanguard and the first wave.

Seraphina turns on Ajax. "Take cover."

"Helmets up! Prepare for elements!" Ajax shouts. "Land those ships! I want those tanks on the ground!"

The army breaks into frantic contortions.

I see the missing scouts as I shout to the Praetorians to take shelter. The scouts race ahead of the storm, burning their boots for all they're worth. Little dots chased by a great brown tide. One disappears into the darkness. Ajax shouts commands to the transport pilots, but they're caught in landing protocol. Some try to land ahead of the storm, only to make a logjam. Others peel off, but the winds knock them off course and they clash together in the sky as the roaring of the sand wall encroaches.

It is the end of the world.

The sand hits us like a sweeping broom. I watch as three engineers setting up a communications array sprint back to their ship. The sand, traveling at hundreds of kilometers an hour, shreds their uniforms and bodies down to the bone with the thoroughness of a decay time-lapse. Kalindora is with me. We brace ourselves and the wall hits us. I'm kicked sideways, spinning on the ground end over end, unable to stand or orient myself. Finally, after colliding with its door hatch, I manage to crawl behind a heavy tank. Hidden from the wind, I watch as the wall hits the stream of transports.

Decimation.

Hundreds of spaceships with reinforced hulls, state-of-the-art ion propulsion engines, and the battle scars of a dozen engagements meet the force of the Mercurian desert. It clubs them to death with the carelessness of a gargantuan child. It throws a squadron of ripWings into the mountainside. Whips a hundred-meter tank carrier into a death spiral, smashing it into the ground where it crushes half a legion of Grays sheltering inside a ground transport. And, all at once, the mission that took a month to plan and half a year to prepare, one that was to be executed by men and women who've made a vocation of war, comes apart with no explanation except that the Reaper is sharing our planet, and that my family is a line of paranoid tyrants.

A dark shape stumbles out of the storm to join me behind the tank.

It's Ajax's starShell.

He crashes down and sits unmoving, unspeaking.

Lightning flashes in the storm-obscured sky, illuminating his terrified face. His lips tremble. His eyes are wide and white and boyish. I've seen him like this only once before, frozen in place out there on the West Line, a kilometer-high communications hardline we used to dare each other to walk as children. The first time we tried, he froze only a quarter of the way across. What began so confidently ended with his knuckles turning white as he gripped the edge and stared down at the thousand-meter drop. I walked out to him and set a hand on his shoulder, and told him only he could walk himself to safety. A quarter kilometer back, or three-quarters forward and across. Which way he walked was up to him.

He walked back.

It was one of the defining moments of our childhood, when we both discovered the substance of his courage.

I put a hand on his shoulder now. Our eyes meet, and I know he's back on the West Line with me. Slowly, the fear leaves him, and we share a moment of wordless comfort. Forgotten are the Praetorians, my absence, all of it. I have his back. He just has to go forward.

With effort, Ajax manages to gather many of his officers in the garage bay of an infantry transport. The storm has raged for thirty minutes and shows no signs of abating. The hull creaks as we cluster together in the dim light.

Seneca grumbles his way through his report. "Sixty transports destroyed in the first minute. There's no accounting for the rest. We can't establish communications with the fleet, command, or the transports. I've never seen this much electrical interference from a storm."

"*He* did this . . ." Ajax murmurs. His eyes are fixed on the roof of the transport.

"I'm sorry, sir?" Seneca says.

"Darrow," Kalindora confirms. "He's mad."

"It's just a storm," Seraphina says from the corner in irritation. "Unless the Slave King can summon hypercanes at the drop of a pin, it's a freak occurrence. It will soon pass."

"This is Mercury, not the Rim. We don't have hypercanes. Ever."

"He *can* summon storms," I say.

Ajax snorts. "He's a man, not a nightmare."

"He's using Storm Gods," I say.

"The only Storm Gods left are on Triton and Pluto."

"Look at the patterns of the storm," I say, gesturing to the map. "The killzone Darrow intended to land us in was here. The storms form a circle. It can't be coincidence. Those temperature fluctuations in the ocean must be manmade. Like this sandstorm."

Their eyes go hard.

"He intended to pin us in, cut us off from the sky, trash our second wave, bar the landing of the third, and hunt us down inside the circle.

But he didn't expect anyone this far south. I bet my life a Storm God is out there somewhere to the northwest. It is likely to be only lightly defended."

"Where did he get a Storm God, Lysander?" Ajax asks quietly.

"Where it was buried, I imagine."

"And why would it be buried?"

"As a safeguard against Votum rebellion." They blink with irritating slowness, as though they are surprised that a Sovereign who would annihilate Rhea would have moral objections to keeping her family's invisible leash on a planet as important as Mercury. "The ocean storms will have a life cycle even if the Storm God is downed. The desert storm will die quicker. We bring the engine down, the sandstorms will abate."

"How quickly?" Seraphina asks. "An hour? Two?"

"More likely several days. Maybe longer."

The officers glower. This will ruin it all. Ajax watches me like he would a stranger. That this secret should be kept from House Grimmus bespeaks suspicion, as if Octavia and the Lunes believed even they could not be trusted. I see my friend wrestling with the pressure of the men looking at him. The pressure of Atalantia's immense expectations. The pressure of Gold society and his own fantasies the child and then the man wove together in the moments before sleep, night after night, until they resembled nothing short of destiny.

This was to be his moment of glory.

Now he looks total annihilation in the eye.

"We were tasked with taking Heliopolis," he says. "I will not disappoint my aunt. If Darrow planned this, *if* he is using a Storm God, then he did it to freeze our movement. We must contradict his intentions with all our vigor."

"Surely you do not mean to attack Heliopolis now," Seraphina says, coming off the wall. "That storm is a monster. It'll pin the shells to the ground. Sweep away the infantry. I've seen it before. You will die. So will your men."

"She's a Moonie, isn't she?" Seneca growls. "Knew her eyes were too big."

"I am Seraphina au Raa," she snaps at the Core officers. For once it is not entirely unwelcome news. "I've trained for Io's storms. And if you attack Heliopolis in this wind, you'll all be corpses. You must wait for it to pass, or find a way to kill it."

"I concur with the Rim on this one," Kalindora says. "StarShells can't fly in this. It'll be chaos. And Heliopolis's storm wall is no mere palisade."

"Do you think I'm some vainglorious dullard?" Ajax snaps at the women. "They know where we landed. The Reaper would not let sand stop him from moving. He might have thermal grids in the desert by which to navigate. But he will expect the storm to stop us. He has the initiative. We must take it back. So when the sand's veil falls, we will not be here. We will be at the walls of Heliopolis. We will land whatever transports remain en masse, and then assault the city when the storm dies." He looks around. "I will need a commander to lead a cohort to destroy the Storm God while the rest of us push south with the titans."

His eyes settle on me, and I feel the urgency behind them. Hostility has been replaced by desperate faith. Here is the chance to prove myself to Ajax and Atalantia. "Lysander, will you and your Praetorians do this for me? For our family?"

Kalindora shakes her head at me.

"It would be our honor," I say.

"I will go with him," Seraphina mutters. "This isn't my first storm crossing. *Gahja* might get lost."

"Two children leading the Praetorians?" Kalindora laughs. "Of all the jumped-up arrogance. I'll lead the party."

"No. I will need you here, Kalindora," Ajax says.

"The Storm God will have a garrison," she says. "My oath to Octavia still stands. I will defend the heir with my life. And I'm going to kill a storm engine, Ajax. Got a problem with that?"

13

DARROW

Plains of Caduceus

THE DOOR OF MY TRAP slams closed.
The storm is here.
Day has become night. Black thunderheads race off the sea to blind their armada. Lightning shatters the sky, disrupting communications between their landing parties, drones, and orbit support. Winds swirl and clash from multiple storm eyes. They toss ripWings and landing craft like toys. Their first wave is trapped beneath the storm. Their second is murdered within it. Their third dare not descend.

Orion has given me my lever.

I'm putting my full weight on it.

Five thousand Drachenjägers pound for Tyche with half again as many starShells riding upon their backs. More survivors found us, swelling our ranks. We cut through the famed flower latifundia of Mercury. Our titanium feet stomping orderly rows of sunblossoms. The flower pollen paints the clawed metal feet gold. From my perch on Rhonna's mech, I spot ships struggling in the high winds.

My columns hurdle the highway in a single bound and split up to form into wedges. This is not their first shockwave.

The enemy lies ahead. An entire division—four legions—has made landfall between Tyche and the Plains of Caduceus. In the gloom thousands of ships bearing the golden hammers of Votum unload men and war machines onto rolling fields of lavender. They intended to mop up whatever remains of my legions. But their landing has been thrown into chaos by the storm. The customary Gold landfall fortifications aren't complete. Tank wedges are only half formed. War machines barely unloaded. Infantry sheltering from the wind behind grounded transports. They don't expect us yet. And they don't see us coming.

We fall upon them with malice.

A Gold in a starShell with officer markings stands with his officers around a communications array in the shelter of a hill. One of his men points. He turns just as lightning flashes, illuminating our tide of onrushing metal. Rhonna bounds forward and lands forty meters of war machine on the officers. I watch on her shoulder as the starShells crumple.

The first column of Drachenjägers fires four alpha-omegas. The nukes detonate in the center and opposite flank of their landfall, just above their two groups of titans. Daylight. Their heaviest armor—which would more than match ours—vaporizes. A rolling tide of devastation. The drachen wedges fire their particle cannons in tiers, targeting heavy armor. Five minutes before each can fire again. It makes no matter.

Bedlam follows as the wedges hew through the enemy along a four-kilometer front like one hundred spears into paper. The quad railguns fire into the confused mass of enemy. Infantry simply disappears. GravBikes are cut in half. Transports peel away, only to clash against one another as the wind disrupts their flight paths.

The Drachenjägers pull their ion swords. Five thousand blue-white cleavers go to work. When the carnage itself slows the charge's momentum, and we founder on the debris from the nukes, the starShells release. Alexandar and I spin sideways together.

I rip off the door of an infantry transport. A hundred Grays in wargear stare at me in green light. Alexandar opens fire with his railgun. Thunder booms overhead. Felix has fallen to a group of Grays with uranium rifles. We send them scattering and haul him to his feet. Another second and he'd be dead. The Golds are rallying to their legion standard.

The standard rises from the spine of a giant blue titan. The titan is sixty meters tall, four legs, and three main cannons, with disk-shaped alien cockpit. The standard is five meters tall and made of three emblems—the god Helios, a Society pyramid, and a giant pair of golden hammers. A Votum is with us. Please let it be Scorpio himself. Two Drachenjägers plunge toward the standard. As the titan arrests their charge with its gravity gun, Golds in starShell swarm over the Drachenjägers like a pack of velociraptors taking down a tyrannosaurus.

They jump onto the rightmost's back and hew through the spine armor to cut the power lines connecting the stomach generator to the cockpit. The titan's third arm pulls the top half off the cockpit. A Gold in a starShell reaches in and pulls the Orange pilot in half with his armored hands and throws her body into the wind.

Gods, can they kill.

And I thank the Vale that it is the Arcosian Knights with me. Not a Red I know could survive this outside a Drachenjäger. I search for Rhonna, but can't find her rig in the fray.

I gather Alexandar and a hundred of his kin and we drive toward the rallying Golds from the flank. Rhonna appears to the left and her wedge draws their attention. By the time they see us coming to their right, we're amongst them, firing point-blank and drenching our blades.

With Alexandar, I mount the sixty-meter crest of the titan, and kill the two Golds defending the height. Alexandar carves the pilot out and holds him in the air. The Gold man wears an incredible suit of armor that appears nearly translucent. He slashes at Alexandar with his razor. Alexandar bats the lightning-fast blade away and pins it in his starShell's hand. With his other hand, he squeezes the pulseHelm of the Gold until it shears off. That's quality, there. "The Primus himself!" Alexandar shouts above the wind. "Hiding in a titan. What a Pixie."

The veins in the forehead of the old tyrant pulse as he glares up, at the mercy of a man a quarter his age. "Blood traitor!" he snarls. Then he sees my curved blade.

"Scorpio au Votum," I warble out my speakers. Through the rain and spattered blood on my canopy, his vain eyes meet mine, and I drink in his fear. Blood leaks down his face. "For a hundred and one years of rape, genocide, and enslavement of your fellow man, I sentence you to the mud." There atop his titan, I cut him in half at the waist and Alexandar hurls him off the height.

"The blood of the Conquerors thins," Alexandar drawls through the coms. He cuts the standard off the titan and hands it to me. "One more for your collection, goodman."

I shove it back into his hands. "Build your own."

With a grin, he holds it up against the crackling sky and leaps off to land on Rhonna, who trudges to pick us up. He stabs it down into the thick shoulders of her Drachenjäger, sharing the bounty.

"To Tyche!" I bellow. My men pick up the call and we push through the shattered remains of the division to leave it thrashing in the mud. More landfalls lie ahead. More enemy to kill. More. More. More.

A laughing zeal fills me.

By the time we leave the flower fields two hours later, only five hundred drachens have fallen, and the standards of fourteen legions decorate the shoulders of my rolling columns. Alexandar has taken four with his own hand. I trail with three. His second cousin Elander has two, along with the captain of the Drachenjägers, and Rhonna herself. We scalp the cores and battery shards from the dead for our own starShells, rearm when the winds abate, and push for the coastal highlands where Tyche and Atalantia await.

I'm coming, Atalantia. I'm coming for your head.

14

LYSANDER

Into the Storm

O NE THOUSAND PRAETORIANS, the Love Knight, and the daughter of Romulus follow me west to seek the eye of the desert storm.
It makes us a thousand and three worlds of misery. Seraphina and
Kalindora flank me. Each man, each woman, alone in the darkness of
their suits, imprisoned by the wind and sand.

Left foot. Right foot. Left foot.

Courtesy of Seraphina's storm experience, we employ a Rim trick.
Towing wire holds us together like grapes so we do not lose one another
in the storm. Periodically, Seraphina and Praetorians with storm experience detach to scout our perimeter.

Still, our progress is slower than desired. Storm winds hit us head-on
and increase to over eight hundred kilometers per hour, with visibility of
scarcely two meters. The storm robs us of the sky and our instruments.
Bit by bit, trespassing against the wind drains our starShells.

After eight hours of this, only the transition of the storm's dimness to
absolute darkness denotes the arrival of night. When the wind lulls, we
jog, tripling our pace by using the thrusters in small bursts. Several lines
snap because of this, and we lose Praetorians in the storm.

There is no going back for them or for us.

The fear that gripped me in the tube of the *Annihilo* is gone. The
sensation of standing on the edge of the cliff was worse than the fall.

Life has winnowed down to a simple task and survival. That simplic-
ity is a comfort. For years I was in a torpor and cowardly in indecision.

Here I have certainty. I will prove myself to Ajax. To Atalantia. I am their family, not their rival.

Forward. Left foot. Right foot. Left foot. Right foot.

"Something is out there," Seraphina says. I peer into the darkness and see nothing. Still, Kalindora gives the order to hunker down. We prime our weapons. *"Holy hells. Contact."*

There's a chorus of hold-fire calls from the scouts.

Dread shapes move in the murk. Only when they come within five meters and they engage their lights can we see they are starShells. Ten of them. Our headlamps illuminate Votum hammer sigils painted on the chassis. Might be hundreds behind them for all we can see. One steps out before the others.

My com crackles and a handsome, sundark face illuminated by starShell interior lights glows in my HUD. *"Ebb of the evening, goodmen. And we thought we were the only civil company for a thousand klicks. Is that not Kalindora herself I gaze upon?"*

"Cicero, you scoundrel. You're supposed to be in the Plains of Caduceus."

"Squeaks the mouse to the rat," he says with light menace. *"Mayhaps Love is lost in the storm, my friends. Didn't you know Heliopolis is just a skip to the south?"*

A beat of silence. *"I go where I am ordered."*

"Like a good knight. The peril of oaths, no? But fear not, my intrepid father noticed a certain lack of Leopards on his flank in the Plains of Caduceus and has sent us to ensure that no skullduggery is afoot at the gates of Heliopolis." His voice lowers. *"The city belongs to my father, Scorpio, and House Votum. And we are weary of Grimmus henchmen skulking in the dark."*

"Prepare to fire," Kalindora says over the private channel.

"I have them flanked," Seraphina intones. *"I count four hundred. Could be more."*

"Belay that," I snap. "No Praetorian will fire on allies. Nor will you, Seraphina."

"Yes, dominus," Rhone says and gives the order for all Praetorians to stand down. Kalindora goes into a stony silence.

"Private communications, eh, Kalindora? I don't need to crack your code to know what you said," Cicero says. *"Not enough that that Lunese bitch tries to steal our city. She'll spill old blood like there's so much of it left."*

"*Salve*, Cicero," I say, taking over from Kalindora.

"*And who's that?*" he asks. I share my face via hologram. I knew Cicero as a child. Not well, but on the occasions when his family visited Luna, Grandmother insisted I entertain the voluble heir of House Votum. To be honest, I found it tiresome, if not a little entertaining. He is ten years older, and thus his condescension is limitless, and hilarious. Yet unlike Ajax, he recognizes me immediately.

"*Hades on high,*" he says without an ounce of surprise. "*Is that Lysander au Lune in the pinkish flesh?*" So his father told him.

"You never do forget a face, Cicero."

"*Not the pretty ones, at least. Father didn't lie—not dead after all. My, my. Atalantia has roped you into her schemes? How the beast now leads the master.*"

"We are en route to destroy the Storm God," I say.

"*There aren't any Storm Gods on our planet.*"

"There are. Explanations can wait. You want your city back, I won't stop you. But you won't get there if those engines are still running. I imagine your cores are as depleted as ours." He does not reply. "We have a pickup scheduled." That gets his attention. "What say you lend us a hand, and we ride for Heliopolis together in the morning?"

He laughs as if he were on a beach. "*For such a dramatic union, I'll play earnest, so long as you support our claim to Heliopolis when we find Ajax, that mischievous little tart.*"

Kalindora reminds me that it would put me in direct conflict with Atalantia. But she's already done that by summoning the Praetorians.

"Heliopolis was built by House Votum, with House Votum it should remain," I say.

"*Splendid. Then the Scorpion Legion is at your service, my goodman. Or is it my liege? I suppose Father will decide. If he survives the north. Calamity, goodman.*" His mind darkens. "*Calamity.*"

I cannot divine the strength of the Scorpion Legion as they add their numbers to ours. Though Cicero continues to babble in my ear, I'm soon lost in the now-familiar grind.

Left. Right. Left.

I'm deep in the drudgery when a hand grips my armored shoulder. I blink out of my daze to see that it is three in the morning. Landfall plus seventeen. I look back to see the Praetorians arrayed fifty deep to my right. The Scorpions emerge from the dust to my left. They must be several thousand in number.

At dire cost to our energy cores, we have made it to the eye of the storm.

I hadn't even realized.

It is a different world. The eye is fifty kilometers in diameter. The air pacific and clear of sand, as if held in static twilight. A desert deerling watches us with suspicion. A formless beast lurks beneath the mass of a hoodoo, its eyes winking like coins. More beasts of all varieties float within the gravity shadow of the engines. They didn't even bother to diffuse the gravity shadow.

All this is surrounded by a vortex of sand, which swirls around a monolith of gray metal.

The Storm God floats kilometers above the desert.

Wreathing its shoulders and stretching toward the heavens is a swirling marble cloak of clouds veined with lightning. Beneath that, little more than a fringe to that cloak, is the swirling sand. Many of the animals who sought shelter here gather in the grip of its gravity engines.

It breaks something inside me to see an instrument of creation perverted into a weapon. Whatever doubt I held vanishes. Darrow is no longer a good man. Even Atalantia declined to use her atomics on actual cities. But to kill us, Darrow will drown the northern coast of Helios. Tyche, Kaikos, Priapos, Arabos, will all be in the path of tidal waves.

Millions will die.

I do not know if it can be stopped, but he must be.

"This feels like a dream," Seraphina whispers. This war is proving to be all she ever wanted. Cicero eyes the woman with interest and calls something to her.

I can barely hear him for the wind. Our instruments are dazzled with false readings. I fear we will not be able to reach Ajax even in the morning. Which is why he is scheduled to come with pickup at 0600, if we manage to down the engine.

I find Kalindora at my side. Unlike Seraphina, she is not in thrall to the Storm God. Sorrow fills her eyes as she looks up and up. She has seen horror many times before. This is merely its bleakest evolution. "Your thermal runway," I say.

She turns with a grim expression and pulls Rhone to her.

"Prepare to engage in six columns! Double heavy fronts. Prep three wedges for a flank charge!" She summons Cicero. Robbed of our orbital support, we will have to do this the old-fashioned way.

I check my ammunition just as there's a flash from the Storm God. Cicero ducks with me. At the great distance, I cannot distinguish what it is. Before I can pull up my optics, Seraphina tilts her head back at me.

"*Gahja*, don't be such a—"

And then the entire top half of her starShell disappears as a rail slug the size of a man rips Romulus's daughter clean in half. My commands stick in the base of my throat as the legs of the mech teeter and collapse sideways, spilling her intestines out the top.

"Incoming!" Kalindora bellows.

15

DARROW

Tyche

THERE IS NO PLACE in all worlds like Tyche.

Set on an incline between the mountains and the sea on a great strip of lowland connecting it to the Talarian Peninsula, it is the ancestral home of the gens Votum. Though the city is famed for its white sands and coral reefs, there is a reason the Votum family crest is a hammer. They are builders. And they built this city not for greed, but for beauty and symmetry. Her old quarter is carved entirely of local stone and glass. Libraries the size of starships but shaped like bizarre human heads line the mountains behind the city. High, arching bridges link complex systems of archipelagos, some of which migrate into the northern sea in the late summer. Forests and gardens burst from rooftops and flowering plants creep down the narrow, cobbled streets, which then wind in spirals up her twelve great hills.

I remember the Liberation Day, nearly half a year ago now, when I woke in the early morning before the parade and walked alone down to the shore to listen to the gulls. I only wished my wife and son could have been with me to see that sunrise. For once, I did not glare at the sea and wonder how many of my men it claimed. I did not resent the world because it was made by slaves. I saw only a multitude of splendors. I think that's what Sevro called it. On that day, Tyche was the second most beautiful city I had ever seen. I wanted to share it with Pax and Virginia.

Now I am in time to see the city die.

As we pushed through the reeling legions, the storm mutated from friend to wild, convulsing savage. Lunging in from the sea, giant waves crash over the north coast of Helios. As we neared Tyche, a wall of water nearly a half kilometer high forced us to run to higher ground lest it smash us as it does the Gold landing parties on the shore.

Boats float in the center of fields. A shark snaps for air in a tree. Our starShells can no longer attempt the sky. Trees, rocks, and signposts flung at hundreds of kilometers an hour damage our suits, killing two of my precious Obsidian pathfinders.

This is not the storm I was promised.

Orion has either disobeyed me or lost control.

Now, with dread in my belly, I rise unsteadily through the howling wind to the crest of a hill where the Arcosian Knights look down at a city drowning.

From Tyche's southern wharf to the northern business district, a third of the city is underwater. The storm surge from the hypercane spreads east and shows no signs of stopping short of the mountains. Within hours, the entire city will be gone, with only the tallest towers peeking above the sea. The western reach of the city, where the lowlands connect with the Talarian Peninsula, is aflame and shattered by siege. Twisted wrecks of tanks and Drachenjägers litter the ground between huge breaches in the defensive wall where Feranis's legion made its doomed last stand against an army thirty times its size—though only a small part was used to besiege the city. The rest assembles deeper inland on the peninsula highgrounds. Huge, shadowy forms descend in the storm, their eldritch contours suggested by spasms of lightning. Not the gilded might of the Venusian Carthii—which we smashed—but the Ash Legions of Luna and Earth. The heart of Atalantia's loyalist army.

Her forward legions, which took the city, now choke on their victory. A sizable portion of their force has penetrated deep into the city, pressing for the mountains, but they are cut off from the main host. Thousands clog the waterlogged lowlands that connect Tyche to the Talarian Peninsula. The spiderTanks and titans that broke the walls sink in the mire. Men pile onto hovercraft and into any airship that dares take flight.

They stand no chance.

As I watch, the sea ripples like a single organism, and from the gray obscurity of the storm comes a wave that would make a Europan stop and stare. The tidal wave is a kilometer tall. It buckles the first twenty blocks of the city's oceanfront and sweeps uphill toward the mountains, to be stopped only by elevation just short of the Harper's Plaza. The greater body of the wave carries on toward the Ash Legions in the lowlands. A row of Gold knights in black armor stands on the peninsula's rocky heights to watch the legions below be swallowed by the sea.

A hundred thousand men gone in a moment. I should rejoice.

But soon Tyche's population will follow. How many millions down there? How many millions along the coast? This will not be isolated mayhem. A chain of tidal waves will devastate northern Helios. My promise to Glirastes was broken, but not on my orders.

I pull out the master switch I built in case it all went wrong. Turning it on is like killing part of myself. I never thought this moment could come. The moment where Orion failed me.

She has no intention of leashing the storm. It was to be *my* lever. She uses it as a hammer, not to punish just Gold, but the planet she hates. With seas churned to madness by the storm generators, a coastline is murdered.

The wind whips around us.

"This is genocide," Alexandar roars into my ear. I push him off.

Orion, what have you done? What did I let you do?

I focus a coms laser out into the gloom to form a direct line on Orion's engine, which hovers twenty kilometers offshore. She appears on my screen. She is breathing heavily. Her skin is covered in sweat. She kneels in the center of her circular syncNest from where she guided the hive mind. Of the six hologram Blues who should surround her, only one is not dead. He shivers on his knees, blood sheeting out his nose and ears from a cerebral hemorrhage. The blast doors of the nest are sealed. She's locked out my security teams.

"Orion?" I say. "Orion, can you hear me? If you can hear me, stick out your right thumb." Slowly the thumb extends. "I need to speak with you, Orion. Can you slip from the sync?" I wait. Nothing happens. Suddenly her eyes open. Her voice is a faint whisper.

"The dataflow was . . . too much."

"Orion, we're on second horizon, going straight for three. You swore we wouldn't pass primary. What happened?"

"Four . . . is desired." Her eyes close to slits. *"Four will teach them."*

Four is terraforming level. The complete annihilation of the planet's surface by storm. Her eyes are nearly closed. She can't devote attention to anything beyond the drift much longer. "Orion, it is Darrow. Listen to me. You must turn off the engines. Scale back the storm. Can you do that for me?"

"They can't win with Venus alone. So I will take Mercury."

"Orion, think of the army. Think of the people. There's nearly a billion here."

"Rats are . . . complicit . . . rational transaction."

"I can stop you." Her eyes flutter. "I told you I could. Don't make me do it." She no longer replies to me. She is back in the sync. Without Orion's input the Storm Gods will level-off and avert planetary destruction. But if I sever her connection, her mind will be lost by the sudden schism. I look down at the city, back to the hologram of my friend in the visor. The storm's death will not be instantaneous. But the longer I wait, the worse it will get.

I initiate the override.

For a moment, nothing happens.

Then Orion's body seizes and goes limp.

It happens that fast.

She lies there with her mouth agape. Her bright blue eyes staring at nothing as they twitch in her head. Her metal finger scrapes against the floor and then goes still. I swallow a knot in my throat. For ten years no Gold alive, not their science teams, not the crème of their astral academies, not their assassins, could kill this woman. She was a myth. And I turned her off with the flick of a switch. She was not ready for this. I felt it, but I could not believe it. Now Mercury pays.

Numb and quiet inside, I turn off the hologram, and use the override to reduce the Storm Gods' output to zero. Then I am back in the storm.

The sound of the wind and thunder is tremendous. More knights have run up to watch the city drown. Alexandar shouts at his cousin Elandar. The two young Golds point down at people flooding toward the gravLoop and the Ash Legions stomping through them to get there themselves.

I try to make sense of the mayhem, and ask myself how we can help those still trapped in the city. I find myself without an answer. No transport ships could fly in this. We can't carry them. We can't even stay aloft ourselves. Alexandar jogs to me. "I've spoken with Elandar." Just over two hundred Golds with the purple griffin stamped on their chests wait behind him, helmets down. "We request permission to enter the city to lend aid."

"Permission denied."

"Sir . . ."

"There's nothing you can do down there. Tyche is lost."

"But its people needn't be," he snaps. I turn to Alexandar, furious that he would contradict me now. "They're swarming for the gravLoop—many can still escape under the mountains. But the Ash Legions in the city know it's the only way out. If they reach it, they will mow through the civilians and use it to evacuate their men, right into Heliopolis. Again, the knights of House Arcos request permission to deter them."

"No."

"Sir!" I turn to see Rhonna running up the hill in her Drachenjäger. It kneels so we can speak. She squints into the wind as her cockpit pops open. Sweat pours down her face.

"What now?" I ask in exhaustion. She sees the master switch in my hands. She knows Orion is dead and doesn't flinch. So far that makes two who know she's dead. The army can't find out, not now. It will break them.

"Boys caught an enemy scout. Fulminata by the looks of him."

One of Octavia's own?

"Bring him to me."

I peer out over the submerged isthmus to the greater host of Atalantia's legions. Those Gold knights are still on the ridge. I amplify magnification on two figures standing in the foreground. Atalantia's face peers back at me. She wears her own optics. She makes a masturbating motion, then flings the load off into the wind, shaking her head at me. I retreat behind the bluff for fear of snipers. If anyone can shoot straight in this, it's her Gray dragoons.

My Arcosian Knights throw a man down at my feet. He's in Fulminata armor, all right. Here's hoping . . .

I pull him up by the hair to find the handsome, lean face of a Gold male in his thirties. Eyes that could have belonged to the purest of Gold stock—and once did, before Screwface got ahold of him and gave them to Mickey—stare back at me.

I pull the man into a hug, careful not to crush him with my starShell. The Arcosian Knights look more than a little confused, but only Sevro, my wife, Theodora, and Mickey knew the details of how we carved the man a new visage and sent him amongst our enemy as a mole nearly three years ago. Though I will need to know why he didn't warn us of

Atalantia's ambush on Orion's fleet, I am happy to see him. I feel safer all of a sudden.

"Screwface, you old psycho," I say, leaning into him. Alexandar stiffens at the presence of an original Howler. Rhonna grins. She loves Screwface almost as much as she loves Freihild, Sefi's personal assassin.

"The name is Horatius au Savag, you fool. As for 'old.'" Screw gives a little sniffle. "I'm nigh on thirty-five. Savvy, my goodman?" He cocks out a nasty smile. "Figured you'd be near Tyche."

If he burned cover, something bad is on its way. "What's happened?"

"Bad news, boss. Heliopolis is under assault."

I feel a cold inevitability creeping upon me. "What?"

"Twenty legions of the second wave made landfall. Twenty crashed or had to abort. The storm has delayed those on the ground, but he'll likely send a strike force for the storm engine."

More than a million men and tanks. "Whose legions?"

"Leopards are at the vanguard."

"Ajax."

"I know."

After Apollonius was captured on Luna, there was a vacuum in Gold ground command. I wondered who would rise to fill the Minotaur's place as their preeminent Legate. Falthe seemed poised, but Ajax has been making his bid. As violent as his mother, but twice as ambitious, he will assault the city till it falls, heedless of casualties. The man's a raging beast with the unfortunate danger of also having a brain.

"Darrow . . ." Screwface says, stepping close. "What's wrong?"

"Orion is dead."

He looks stunned. For men like him, like me, who have fought this war since the beginning, there are so few who inspire us. Orion was that. We are lesser in her absence.

I can't afford to mourn.

With Tyche drowned and Heliopolis fallen, my army will have nowhere to retreat. We will be surrounded, bombarded, and destroyed.

The moment Harnassus predicted has finally come. I must choose between saving my army and destroying theirs. I stare across the drowning city at the Ash Legions safe inland on the Talarian Peninsula. Atalantia is there. Trapped by the storm. I can find a way to cross, I'm sure.

If Thraxa survives, if the *Morning Star* made it to her, if the First Legion still exists, they will give me the power to destroy Atalantia and her entire Ash Legion, the hard Lunese core of her army.

It would be the greatest victory of the war.

But it will cost me Heliopolis, and in the end, my army.

The Republic could recover. Gold will not.

Us for them would be the rational transaction.

Orion deemed it worth the price.

Hearing the words of the Ash Lord on my friend's own lips haunts me. *A rational transaction.* I look at the drowning population of Tyche, who welcomed us even when Heliopolis spat on us and yet still fell on the wrong side of one human being's moral arithmetic. And I see a spiraling spiritual darkness. Ensnaring not just me, not just the friends whose cruelty I have emboldened, but Eo's darkening dream. Did this all begin with betraying the Sons of Ares in the Rim? With the destruction of the Ganymede Dockyards? With my Rain over Mercury? So many concessions in the name of necessity. So many horrors in the name of liberty. Where is the beauty I saw when Ragnar reached for Sefi's hand instead of his blade as he died? Where has our humanity gone? Is this why Sevro left? He felt the creep of doom and sought to cling to light?

I let fear drive my hope away. I let war become me, and my men followed.

Atalantia's army isn't worth mine.

If I die, it should not be taking her life. It should be saving theirs.

"Rhonna, I need you." Those three words make her ten meters taller. "You can move in this bloodydamn wind. Take the fastest two drachens and find the *Morning Star.* Find Thraxa. Tell them Tyche is lost. Heliopolis is under assault. They must cross the Ladon to relieve Heliopolis."

Her mouth hangs open. "You said . . ."

"I know what I said."

The Ladon has eaten three of the greatest armies the worlds have known. Is the fourth I will feed it my own?

"How will they cross the Ladon in this?" Screwface asks.

"The *Morning Star* will be their stormbreaker. Captain Pelus is more than capable of the maneuver. If he's not, Char may be with them. Tell Thraxa to follow in its shadow. I'll take the armor through the mountains along the Kylor Pass and meet them at Heliopolis. Go."

Rhonna spares a look to Alexandar, something passes between them, and she stands to forty meters. "Nice seein' you, kid!" Screw calls after her as she thunders away.

Now this part.

I take a steady breath and reluctantly turn to face Alexandar. His eyes still watch Tyche in sorrow.

"Does your request stand?" I ask.

He stiffens in surprise. "Yes, sir."

"There will be no rescue. The sea will come in."

"Well, I haven't had a bath in weeks."

"Why are you doing this?" I ask, searching the strong bones of his face. "They're just baked peasants."

"Even peasants don't float, sir."

No amount of arrogance can hide the pain in his eyes. He blames himself for Angelia, perhaps even for this, but it also tears at him to see the suffering in the city. I feared he wanted to do this for me, to find favor in my eyes. All this time I held a mild disdain for him, because I thought my approval was all that mattered to the man. But he believes in the Rising. I see it now, just as I saw this moment coming. The moment I must choose to spend his life. But he has surprised me by choosing to spend it himself. I could not be prouder of the man.

He has become what Lorn should have been. And though the thought of losing him and Orion in the same hour nearly drives me to my knees, I nod.

"Very well. Take your knights."

"Thank you, sir. If you could do me a kindness . . ." His bright eyes quest after Rhonna. She's already disappeared inland. "Tell her to stop biting her nails. It's vile." He pauses. "And that she was wrong about me."

On impulse, I pull out my razor and I am about to deliver him the Peerless scar when he stops my hand. "I know what I am."

"Do you?" I reach back to unclasp my wolfcloak from the ring on my left shoulder. Nearly losing it to the wind, I snap the clasps onto Alexandar's mech. He falls to a knee, looking at it as if it were made all of diamonds. I lift him up. "Howlers never kneel."

For once, he has no retort. Especially not when Screwface steps up to spit in his face to give him a proper welcome. The wind jams the spit back down his own mouth. "Bucket and box will have to wait, kid." Screw shakes his hand and breaks the wind for us.

"Hold Atalantia as long as you can, then take the last tram and blow the tunnel behind you. Failing that, blow the tunnel and make for the mountains." I strip off my extra batteries. Alex pushes them back.

"You must reach Heliopolis, sir."

He is right, so I keep them. "Then your armor will be spent before morning, but if you can get to the Kylor Pass, you can follow it due south and make Heliopolis in two weeks. I forbid you to die, Howler. I want my cloak back. Sevro will never let me hear the end of it."

"Yes, sir." Resolution makes a thin line of his mouth. "Hail Reaper."

I salute him and the knights behind. "Hail Arcos."

He bows slightly in Screwface's direction. "An honor, sir. Big fan."

I watch from the hill with Screw as Alexandar and his Martian kin depart. Beset by rain and storm, the famous knights of Elysium trot down the hill in purple and silver armor to plunge toward the drowning city. They look like the last lords and ladies of a doomed age. Two hundred and three against an army and the sea.

I turn with a heavy heart and head back to my men to lead them south toward the battle in the desert that will decide the fate of us all.

16

LYSANDER

Rider of the Storm

I WAKE IN DARKNESS TO the sound of my starShell's low-oxygen warning. Seraphina is dead. Her prowess in battle far outstripped mine, yet I am alive, and she is not.

It feels so unfair. That should not have been the end of her story.

Just like Cassius's end.

From a distance, death seems the end of a story. But when you are near, when you can smell the burning skin, see the entrails, you see death for what it is. A traumatic cauterization of a life thread. No purpose. No conclusion. Just *snip*.

I knew war was dreadful, but I did not expect to fear it.

How can anyone not, when death is just a blind giant with scissors?

This will not end well. Dido will sense a devious hand at work, because she did not see her daughter become a smear of organs. But Romulus knew. He dreaded this. He gave his life to stop this, and he failed.

I do not look forward to telling Diomedes. If I even get the chance.

The last thing I remember is existence breaking in two. At least that is the sound the sky made when the Storm God fell to the desert floor.

It was not Kalindora or Rhone or Cicero whose payload destroyed the engine. Bitterly contested by the garrison, my Praetorians made three charges against the teeth of the enemy railguns. Only on the last did I manage to dispose my final missile into the gravity engines. It was not a conscious choice to forge ahead alone. An enemy munition simply destroyed my radio transmitter, so I did not know my wingmen were dead. Hours later I still do not know their names.

I feel that is immoral.

I run a diagnostic. My railgun ammunition is depleted. Little charge remains in the energy core that feeds the pulseFist, engines, and life support. The starShell is already sapping power from my pulseArmor to continue to function. I will have to disconnect soon.

It takes the better part of five minutes to free myself from the sand. When I do, I lower my canopy and gasp for air. The morning smells of petrichor and ozone. It is already seventy degrees Celsius.

The sun hides behind irradiated clouds. Lightning dances in the black north. Though I am in a pocket of peace, the sandstorm still roils in the deep desert. In all directions, veils of dust shimmy across the landscape like tattered skirts. Mounds of sand shiver around me as Praetorians and Scorpions climb their way out of the sand.

It is 0630.

Ajax should be here by now.

Did the storm take him?

What fate has befallen the invasion to the north? Is all lost to the sea?

As I move to help the Praetorians, my starShell rattles in protest and freezes as hydraulic fluid pours from the pelvis. I release the inner latch and climb out. I barely recognize the war rig I rode down to the planet. Only my pulseArmor is undented. I check to make sure my Bellona razor is still in its leg holster. Then I ping Seraphina's tracking node. There are no results.

The Ladon has taken the daughter of Romulus.

A bloodfly as thick as my thumb pesters my face. I barely move as it bites and drinks from my neck. I push it against my skin until it pops.

More buzz nearby. Hundreds.

I follow their current until they make a cloud over something on the ground. A dying horse. It is a wild sunblood mare, the most cherished of Mercury's carved wonders. Its legs are beyond mangled, and its skin is gone. Only its orange mane remains untouched by the feasting flies. Rhone kneels beside it, his starShell discarded in a dune.

Freed of his own starShell, Cicero saunters over, rubbing his jaw with his pulseArmor gauntlet. "Oh, pity. A sunblood."

Before all else, Praetorians are equestrians. Before they learn to shoot, they shovel stable stalls. Each is given a young horse to train while at the *ludus*. At the end of their training, they are given a gun and told to kill the horse. The mindless killers that do are bound for the blackops legions. Only those that prove themselves loyal to their comrades, be they beast or man, are trusted to guard the Blood.

Rhone has likely not seen a horse in many years.

"Did you know there were once fifty thousand griffin on Mars?" he asks as he strokes the mare's forehead. "Poachers sell their talons and feathers to new money on Luna. Now there are less than five hundred." The horse jerks as Rhone's pulseKnife sinks into her brain. *"Nothing beautiful survives the mob."*

The flies continue their feast as he stands.

They will have found Seraphina by now.

Who will they find next?

By the look in Rhone's flinty eyes, I know I am not the only witness to the horror. "It's just a wild mare. There're thousands out here," Cicero says. "My stallion, Blood of Empire, makes that one look like a pony."

I turn to him until he leaves, muttering about the Lunese. I look back at the horse, seeing Seraphina in its place for some reason.

"Did you know her well, the Raa?" Rhone asks.

"Not as well as she deserved, I believe. She thought little of me, truth be told."

Kalindora marches up. She looks at the sky. "Ajax is late. Praetorian, report."

By Rhone's count, our casualties were ninety-four. Thirty dead, the rest missing or injured. Of the nine hundred Praetorians left, only thirty starShells are still operational. Cicero's force is slightly larger, but bore more of the casualties.

"Shell cannibalized the pulseArmor power," Rhone continues as I walk with him amongst the Praetorians. "Over seventeen hours of sustained engagement, and that wind." He shakes his head. "Only thirty-three have juice for boot liftoff. It'll be a hike." The Gray Praetorian squints south. Few features interrupt the arid playa. "We can make it."

Cicero laughs from the nearby dune. He slides down it like a child to come to a sitting posture in front of us.

"My goodman, loath though I am to contradict a soldier of your stature, this is my desert. Any man whose boots are dead will die here unless the shuttles come. Without cooling, your pulseArmor will become an oven. How much is left in your water reserves? A third? We are kitted for heavy combat in the north, not the fucking Ladon." He sighs. "But do you really suspect something they call the Eater of Armies is to be anything less than an eater of fucking armies?" He glares at me and stands. "Where the hell is that reprobate Ajax anyhow?" Manmade thunder rumbles to the south. "Ah, so he's begun without us. That muscled, walking penis."

I ask Rhone if the coms are still down.

He nods. "Orbit's no go." He gestures to a group of Praetorians atop the Storm God. "But we're boosting our signal with a field array. Should be able to reach Iron Leopard command in a few minutes."

"What the devil is she doing over there?" Cicero squints at Kalindora. She stands on a dune to the west, looking out at the dust-veiled deep desert. "Composing poetry?"

I use precious suit energy to join her.

I call her name as I land. She motions me to be quiet and cocks her head to the wind. Dust sprays as Cicero lands as well. "Do you hear that?" she asks.

"No," he says. "Is it the planet asking why House Lune hid the Storm God from their vaunted ally?"

"Shut up, Cicero."

"Only because I'm thirsty."

I join her on a knee and listen. Granules of sand clink against my armor. A lizard's tiny claws crackle as he moves shadow to shadow. Thunder rumbles in the north. Wind whispers around me, whistling through the boulders, through my armor. It carries the sounds of distant machines.

I bolt to my feet.

Someone moves within the storm.

"Those are Drachenjäger footfalls," Kalindora says.

"Oh dear," Cicero says. He backs up. "Time to go."

Searching the waste around us, I don't know how we can. Dunes and the storm to north and east. Flat hardpan to the south. The eastern mountains are the closest cover, but the machines move between us and them. Except for the downed Storm God, there is no refuge for our men on foot. Nor can we bear the weight of all their armor. It would take ten minutes to get everyone out of their suits. Far too long.

We burst back to the Praetorians and land where Rhone has set up his coms tower on the hull of the Storm God.

There's a gargling sound as the signal connects. Ajax's voice is washed in static. His face warps in and out.

"Lysander? I see you seized the moment. I had no doubt you would. Octavia would be proud." His voice mocks me.

"Where's our evac?" I snap. "We have inbound enemy armor. Our shells are dead. Our mobility—"

"It doesn't seem long ago that we were last in New Sparta, does it?"

"Ajax, we need evac, do you register?"

"I looked forward to those winters on Grandfather's estate more than anything. Believe me when I say that. You were less serious there, away from the old crone. There was no one to impress. Not until Grandfather took us hunting and left us in the bush. He told us to race back." His eyes narrow. *"You remember. Of course you do. You remember everything."*

Kalindora's face falls as she understands. Cicero's face becomes a mask of utter contempt. I hold out hope that it is not what it seems.

"You remember how I begged you not to leave me behind because I sprained my ankle. Didn't really. I was just afraid of being left alone, because you were always so sure where you were going. If it was just us, you would have helped me. But you had to win, didn't you? You had to show them that you were worthy of being the Heir of Silenius.*"* His lips curl back from his teeth. *"You left me behind. It took me three days to find my way back. And when I did, Grandfather wouldn't even let me join the dinner table because I was . . . unwashed. You found me crying behind the stables. You'd brought me your own food and you sat with me and do you remember what you said?"*

"Ajax . . ."

"'You really must learn your navigations, Ajax.'"

"I see." The silence between us is cold and final and mutually understood. "Is this your choice or Atalantia's?"

"Mine. I will mourn for you, little brother, but I will not step aside. This is my time. Give Kalindora my apologies, but she chose poorly." He pauses, no mockery in his voice. *"Should the Void take you, celebrate, my brother. For before death, there was glory."*

The link drops.

I stand rooted to the spot. I thought if betrayal came, it would come from Atalantia. Not Ajax. I saw the signs, but I chose to believe in a friend. What a pity for us both. For all those memories to come to this.

Is this how Cassius felt?

"I am to die for a brotherly feud," Cicero spits. "This is utterly . . . Venusian."

Rhone speaks in a tight whisper. "My liege, we can evacuate you south via air."

"And how many men could we take?" I ask.

"Less than a third."

I search the Praetorians on the ground beneath as they attempt to leech energy from downed starShells. They came for me. To save my life, I would have to abandon six hundred of them.

I search for some alternative, and find only one. "I would know the names of my wingmen on the third charge."

"Flavius ti Vessia and Charon ti Occipiter."

I repeat the names as the sound of the enemy machines grows louder. "What would Octavia do?" I ask.

Rhone says nothing.

"She would run," Kalindora replies with a blank expression.

"A fine idea," Cicero says. "Let's."

I stare into the dust. "If that is the measure of our loyalty to our men, perhaps we deserve to die."

Kalindora tilts her head at me.

"Are you mad?" Cicero's narrow eyes go wide.

Rhone steps forward. "My liege, you are—"

"Not a Sovereign. Not anything really." I grimace. "But I will not live while men sworn to me die. I know the risk they took in coming here." Kalindora gives me a nod of surprised approval. "Rhone, prepare the Praetorians as you see fit. The enemy won't be long."

This is not how Rhone thought it would be, but he holds his salute for an extra second before hopping down to his men. "I will not die *here*," Cicero says. "Your boots have juice, you fool. Enough to get you to Heliopolis!"

"Go if you must, Cicero. I abandoned the Praetorians before. I will not do so again."

He comes within an inch of my face. "They say a strain of madness runs through the gens Lune. Oh, how right they are. Farewell, ye infected victims of the martial disease." Cicero takes to the air without a word of apology to his men who cannot follow. Two dozen fly with him. More than twelve hundred watch their leader go and look down at their depleted armor.

I remain with Kalindora atop the Storm God as the enemy machines groan and rattle within the dust. I close my eyes, seeking my mother's face. Even now in the darkness, I cannot find her.

I feel so alone. Then I hear Kalindora draw her razor. "Lysander."

When I open my eyes, a single figure emerges from the dust less than a kilometer away. A desiccated rag flaps from his shoulder. He spots us on the Storm God and thrusts his hand up into the profane crux.

Only a few of his words reach us. ". . . heart beats like a drum . . ."

The scout disappears and a moment later the sound that has plagued my dreams from the Palatine to the Belt finds me in the desert waste. The sound could only come from a legion escorting the Reaper.

The howling of wolves.

Ahhhrooooooooooooooooooo

Kalindora goes still.

He should be in the north, pinned in by Atalantia's legions. Not a thousand kilometers south. Not here. How could they still have power? How could they cross so much distance when we barely made it a hundred kilometers into the hypercane's headwinds before draining our suits?

Kalindora's awed voice answers the unspoken question.

"He rode the storm."

The wait for Darrow is not long, but it is horrid. My eyes sting from the heat. It radiates up from the metal hull we perch upon. My nose fills with the fumes of machines, the dry lifelessness of the desert, and smoke.

The enemy emerges from the dust like a line of mechanized Mongols. A depleted legion of filthy metal Drachenjägers carried by the winds of the storm trudges over the crest. They are not so numerous as they sounded. I glance over at Rhone. A grin spreads on his face. With the high ground and an entrenched position, we might yet survive this.

Kalindora thinks otherwise.

My tongue tastes the chalky roof of my mouth and feels the contours of my teeth. I tense my hand around my razor. It feels small in the pulse-Armor gauntlet. I raise my helm.

Ahhhrooooooooooooooooooo

"Stay with the heir," Kalindora says to Rhone. Thirty-three Praetorians with life yet in their starShell cores cluster tight around me atop the downed Storm God's highest perch. Nearly two thousand Scorpions and Praetorians shelter in firing lines along the rim of the broken engine below.

It begins in silence, and then comes the terrific clamor of four wedges of Drachenjägers thundering across the desert. Their armored legs, each twice as tall as a starShell, eat up the distance. Guided antipersonnel missiles slither toward us. Interceptors race to challenge them. Depleted uranium rounds hammer through the wreckage around our position like it's cheesecloth. Praetorians fire back from prone positions all along the rim of the Storm God. There are no better sharpshooters in all the legions. A drachen teeters sideways and explodes. Another runs off at an oblique angle as its pilot is shot through the cockpit.

With a heavy anti-tank rifle, Rhone fires down at the plain.

I scan the charging Drachenjägers. Darrow won't be in one of those rigs. He likes mobility. Where is he? I turn around to search our flanks for Darrow. As a boy, I watched him become a leader. I've studied him more than any other man. I know his trade, but that knowledge seems so useless here in the chaos of battle. There are only four directions, but Darrow has used so many tactics over the years, I freeze. It feels like he could come from anywhere.

I spot shadows moving in the dust cloud kicked up by the Drachenjägers' charge. "He's using them to obscure his movements," I say to Kalindora. "Like at the Battle of Gibraltar. With a frontal sally we can hit him when he swings to a flank."

"I concur. Prepare to charge," Kalindora tells the Praetorians. StarShell pulseFists whine as my men shunt their remaining core power to their weapons and their boots. The heat of the desert invades my suit.

On Kalindora's signal, we break from our position, bursting upward into the sky and ricocheting forward, headlong toward the shadows over the charging Drachenjägers. Then something ripples above in the sky.

A Praetorian's body comes apart beside me, bisected cleanly at the waist. I lift my razor just in time. Something clangs against it, knocking me downward. The air contorts above as men in ghostCloaks shear down through the center of my charging Praetorians. I shoot point-blank at a blur and see the light bend as the railgun round goes through a man's chest. He spins downward, his wolfcloak rippling.

I see the play too late to stop it. Darrow baited us with the shadows, and flanked our aerial charge by sending a small group around to hit us as we forsook our position. They cleave through us.

I pivot in the air to witness slaughter behind me.

The world slows as I see him amidst my men. The camouflage withering away to reveal a hurricane in battered crimson pulseArmor, a white razor sparking as it carves through a Praetorian's starShell to sever half his neck.

I burst toward the Reaper and am smashed sideways as I collide with another body. Kalindora shields me from an armored man's pulsefire. Rhone mows him down. I try to rally the left wing of my men, but it is a slaughter. And at the center of it swirls a god of death. The fighter's helmet flashes. Around his body whirls that famous Gold-killing blade.

As violence reaches for him, Darrow does not flinch like a man; he reaches like a covetous river. He pulls violence to him, drinks it into his current, and leaps around the battlefield with a seemingly mindless capriciousness. Which, when inspected, illuminates the genius of his violence. He herds us together, making sure we are tight and compact so that our options constrict and his men's expand.

It is something you can only understand when you feel dread sinking into you when you realize you're between the claws of a trap, and they're about to close. You feel surprised that it was so easy to trick you. Surprised that this is how it happens. All those years of preparing, reviewing battles, correcting others. It doesn't feel like we fell into a trap. It feels almost accidental, yet still inevitable. I feel small and stupid.

"Kill the Reaper!" I shout as I plunge for him, Kalindora at my right, Rhone and three others at my left. We cut through two Rising knights and then, as if smelling the murder on our minds, Darrow, without even looking, jolts backward toward us at a surprising angle.

A Praetorian's head splits in half. Rhone is knocked from the sky. Kalindora's left arm spins from her body. My own razor arcs forward toward Darrow's turned head and finds only air as he performs some aerial alchemy and bends, floating upward, only to shoot back down.

His razor slashes at me as he flies past. I parry, but the force is incredible. I feel a blazing pain in my arm. I'm struck again as he backhands me like a child with his blade. The razor cuts through my gravBoots and I plummet from the sky.

I slam down onto the hardpan, but do not lose consciousness. I stare up in my broken armor. Metal men dance against the crackling clouds.

Bodies fall like dying metal birds, leaking blood and machine fluid. The Reaper is already passing on, leaving the leftovers for his men.

A starShell crashes down atop me, pinning me down. Another slams into the sand. I feel heat on my right cheek and turn just enough to see a downed shell's broken boot thruster sputtering flame against my helmet. I panic and shove in vain. Heat grows as it melts through the armor from the side. I shout and scramble, but I go nowhere as the heat intensifies and a hole opens in the right side of my helmet. My skin begins to itch. I flail, overcome with dread. The itch becomes agony. My right eyebrow curls as it burns. The epidermis begins to bubble and peel away. Fire reaches down to the dermis, shrinking it and splitting it open as fat leaks out and feeds the flames.

The wolf howls fade in the distance. The flames eat my eye.

Only then do I begin to scream.

17

DARROW

Heliopolis

W E BRUSH AWAY LIGHT resistance at the downed Storm God. Without bothering to complete the kills, we head for Heliopolis. Behind us, we leave the enemy grounded or dying. Radioactive dust drifts south to dim the sun. Soon another sandstorm swallows the daylight entirely.

Visibility shrinks, masking but not slowing our approach on Heliopolis. When we emerge on Ajax's rear, will it be to a conquered city? Will we be alone against ten legions? Will our own guns be turned to be used against us? Or will the *Morning Star* have somehow shepherded my army through the Waste?

I can only hope, just as I hope Alexandar is not drowned beneath the sea.

Forward. Forward. One foot after the other.

Our Drachenjägers have barely an hour of charge left. My starShell is dead in the desert. Half the others managed to save energy by riding the drachen through the storm. All trudge on their own now. We hold on to sanity by a thread. Our water ran out in the night. Our ammunition is low. Stims power our senses and keep us from succumbing to the side effects of either the anti-rads or the radiation itself, but they have hollowed our cores. Twenty-four hours engaged with the enemy. How many days awake does that make it for me now? Six? Seven?

I could not sleep in the passage despite my perch on the Drachenjäger.

The night was hell and howling wind and avalanches so frequent we had to abandon the pass and risk the desert. Blackness was our master. Static and sand and gargling radiometers narrated our endless nightmare. Orion's storm no longer escalates, but it has run wild without her focusing its wrath.

Two sandstorms swallowed a third of our number. The rest, including myself, face cellular decay from fallout. I puke again into my cockpit. The catch is full. The vomit laced with blood. It leaks down into the cracks to trickle over my armored legs. My head pounds. Eyeballs aching at their roots. My symptoms are minor compared with the Grays, Blues, and our remaining Obsidians. Some have already succumbed to delirium as their DNA unwinds. Only the Reds and Golds hold strong.

I just want rest. I just want water. And to sleep.

Forward. Forward. Forward.

The morning is the color of bronze when we come upon the Graveyard of Tyrants. Harnassus dumped the monoliths the Golds built to honor seven centuries of Sovereigns in the desert. The giant statues lie on their backs as sand swirls around them. A skirmish was fought amidst them. Waves of sand lap at the half-submerged and smoldering carcasses of war machines.

The debris field thickens. Phantoms move through the dust. Lone infantrymen without clothes and covered in blood walk past us. We cannot tell their tribe. Blackened husks sit cross-legged in the sand. A desert hyenadile gnaws at a dead man, looks at us, fans the threat-wings on its neck, and flees as an artillery shell detonates nearby. War machines scream and groan in the distance. Their shadows flit through the gloom, growing more substantial with every step.

It is like emerging from one dream into another.

I draw what remains of my force up on a hill with a view of the storm wall of Heliopolis. Our flanks secured by a sheer mountain façade, I survey the siege with Screwface. My heart sinks.

Heliopolis has fallen.

With the desert Storm God down, the storm has lost its direction. It sweeps eastward. Ajax's army fights in the sunshine.

Acrid smoke rises from huge gashes in the storm wall. Iron Leopard and Fulminata shock troops claw through gaps three hundred meters from the ground. Tanks roll into canyons bored through the durosteel by particle cannons. A firefight rages on the ramparts of the wall, where a thin gap exists between the wall and shield. Her great guns are silent. Harnassus may already be dead.

If they take the city, if they take down her shield generators, the Ash armada can reinforce them, and lower torchShips and *Annihilo* herself across the south. My army will come out of the desert after surviving the storm and be met with oblivion.

Screwface understands. "I'll scout forward and see where we should hit." He jumps off the ledge to cross the boulder field below in small bursts.

I turn back to my men.

They can hear the battle if not see it. Less than a third of the force that set out for Tyche joins me on the hill. Many lie dead in the Plains of Caduceus, or were swept away by water or wind on our path to Tyche. Alexandar is gone. Rhonna and Colloway sent into the storm. It has been nearly twenty-four hours since I've seen Thraxa. Only Felix is left amongst my Gold Howlers.

I feel the despair.

"Where is the *Morning Star*?" a Green pilot asks. His hair has already started to fall out. His mech is smoothed by sand like a river stone. Does his gun even work?

"It is on its way," I say. "We must buy Harnassus time. One last charge of metal. I will—"

The Green's head disappears. Screaming munitions slam into my men from above with pinpoint accuracy. A depleted uranium round gouges a hole through my armor and punches through the meat of my right hamstring. I go down hard.

Spitting dust from my mouth, I watch as shrouded figures in billowing desert cloaks fall from a cliff hundreds of meters above. Bursts of air come from their skipBoots, cushioning them as they land on my Drachenjägers' open cockpits to drive razors through the top of my pilots' skulls, or land behind them to scalp off their faces or claim their heads. I can't tell if Felix goes down.

In less than ten seconds, I am the only one alive except for a pilot they pull from his cockpit to vivisect on the shoulder of his own mech.

Rough hands cut me from my starShell and drag me out. Men with masks of child's faces tear off my gravBoots. The pilot screams above me. A boot stands on my throat as the man in the Pale Mask treads the sand to squat in front of me. They pour engine solvent on my face to clean off the blood. A hunched Obsidian with giant sunburnt arms looms with a blowtorch.

"It's him," a heavy Obsidian voice confirms.

"Gratitude, Falthgar." The Fear Knight takes off his gloves and puts them in a pocket of his scorosuit. It is a simple radiation-resistant and water reclamation suit. No armor for this impaler of men. No vestments of rank or gaudy embellishments. His cloak is tattered and eaten by the desert. His forearms cracked and baked brown. His gloveless hands pallid and thin as spider legs. He leaves his mask on. It is the face of a sexless child ringed with hair of serpents. No matter which way he turns his head, the child's eyes stay focused on me. The Pale Mask.

"You asked me a question long ago," the mask warbles. *"It was on Mars before we lost her. You asked, what do I fear? I fear a man who believes in good. For he can excuse any evil."* He holds up a hand to feel the wind. *"What have you done?"*

I try to spit on him, but there is no moisture in my mouth.

"Show me your face!"

"Fear has no face." His head tilts. *"You still don't understand. No matter. Falthgar, Ravan, Kestril, Thorhand, Kaffa. You have the cameras for his wife?"* Five of his hunting beasts step forward. *"Prime. Castrate him. Fuck him bloody in the ravine."* He pauses. *"Before you slit his throat, feed him his cock."*

"Yes, *dominus.*"

Animalistic fear. I struggle in vain against the huge Obsidians. They lift me as if I were a Red again and drag me toward the ravine behind my slaughtered men. The Fear Knight sits in the sand to watch them rape me as Heliopolis falls.

Not like this. Not like this.

The slaveknights toss me to the ground and shove my face in the sand as the rest watch. A boot pins my head down. I can barely breathe as they discuss how to cut off my armor, and then who will go first. A scorosuit buckle tinkles as it is unclasped behind me. A growing nausea and terror and . . . lightness. The hand that pushes on my head loses its strength. I twist my head. Grains of sand trickle upward. The Obsidian's white hair floats in a corona. A shadow creeps across the sand. They try to push me down, only to float upward themselves. A horrible laugh bubbles out of me as a voice filled with static sings over my open com.

"If your heart beats like a drum, and your leg's a little wet, it's 'cause Midnight's come to collect a little debt."

"You pricklicks," I hiss through the sand. "You forgot Colloway xe Char."

With all my might, I shove off the ground. Combined, they weigh more than a ton in their gear, but in the gravity shadow of the moonBreaker, there is no weight. We launch upward. The sudden reversal confuses their equilibrium. They held me down with boots and pressure but had no clean grip. They try to invert themselves to grab at me, but only turn themselves into a spin. I float cleanly away, waiting till a boot spins past my head. I seize it and jerk down, levering the top of my skull into the bottom of a jaw. It shatters. I pin the larger man to myself and headbutt his face until I feel it cave in. Dizzy, I strip his long knife and ride his body to the ground, where I launch up to the next. Blood in my eyes, I can barely see. He tries to orient himself. But I've played more in zero-G. I pass him without touching, drawing the long knife along his body and opening his torso from groin to throat. Two of the others fire at me, and suffer the consequences of recoil. They become minor threats. The last, five meters away, pulls his gun, but the movement itself sends his body spinning backward. I throw the knife and suffer the spin.

I crash upside down into a rock wall. My armor crunches and I hold on backward. I try to orientate myself. The Fear Knight saw me kill his men from only fifteen paces away, but only just escaped the clutter of his floating men. He uses his boots to burst toward me, sliding sideways through the air, his long rifle aiming for my head through the floating mechs. He fires. Then gravity returns. A falling mech intercepts his shot. His men slam downward as the *Morning Star* bursts out of the shroud of dust that hangs over the desert. It boosts upward and roars past toward Heliopolis. I nearly lose purchase on the rock and fall to my death as blinding light explodes from the battered moonBreaker to wipe away an entire cohort of enemy tanks.

A wall of iron churns over the desert to the northeast, appearing out of the shadow of the *Morning Star* and its own shroud of dust.

The First Army has come to Heliopolis.

It passed through the Waste of Ladon in the night, through a path paved in the storm by the *Morning Star*. Most of her cannons have been mangled by the storm, but ripWings pour out of the moonBreaker, followed by starShells, transports, and barges of infantry. A great howling fills the air. A magnificent dusty figure in a streaming wolfcloak and bearing a warhammer falls from the sky.

The Fear Knight looks up at Thraxa au Telemanus in full-charged wargear, looks at me, takes aim, and then disappears in a missile strike. Thraxa catches me before my fingers give out on the rock face. She floats me down to the ground, kissing my face with her fox helmet.

"You beautiful bastard. Rhonna found us. The *Star* paved our way. You beautiful genius. You sick, twisted god."

A quaking of fear enters my chest, and then warps into fury as I think of how they nuked my men, cut their throats, pushed my face in the dirt. *Feed me my cock, will they?*

I push Thraxa off. "I need boots. StarShell. Ammo."

"And this, sir," a voice says. Rhonna skims toward us with my sling-Blade. Her mech is gone. "Found it in the sand." I catch it in the air. Thraxa pats her hammer with a smile.

"Shall we?"

The battle tips with the coming of the *Morning Star*, but with most of her cannons damaged, it does not end. She diffuses her gravity shadow, and hangs over the battle to serve as a support platform. The bulk of the killing lasts well into the mid-afternoon. Temperatures swell to 190 degrees Fahrenheit, where resting a naked hand on metal will blister the skin in half a second. The bloodiest of the fighting takes place at this miserable hour, and it is then that the Iron Leopards' armored line finally breaks. With the mighty main corps finding nowhere to retreat, the infantry is pressed against the broken walls of Heliopolis and butchered.

The bodies stack five meters high. Infantry choke the giant fissures in the wall. Tanks roll over them in the smoke and their desperation to escape. Many suffocate in the press or drown in mud made of blood, urine, and coolant fluid mixing with the dust.

Those who manage to escape the First Army leak into the city, where they are hunted down by Harnassus's enraged defenders, the sky rangers, and the aerial infantry dropping from the *Morning Star*.

I cannot stop the bloodshed. Nor do I stop my own.

Wild and driven mad by the atomic bombardment, the storm, and the desert crossing, my men descend the moral ladder to become demons, severed of any creed they once possessed. The butchery is staggering. Those of the enemy unlucky enough to be cornered can do little but add their corpses to the bulwarks of the dead.

Still they refuse to surrender.

I have never seen such valor. If it is not that, it must be madness.

The Terran legions refuse to yield. They retreat, rally, retreat, rally. Ajax stokes them to a fevered mania. He roams the lines, always just out of my reach. Always sallying forth. Time and again they leak through our assault so that I feel like a man rushing between cracks in a dam trying to hold back a flood with his bare fingers.

I range across the thirty-kilometer front, everywhere and nowhere. I blunt a tank breakout on the western flank, exchange starShells at the foothills of the Hesperides after taking a round to the chest. I chase Gray riflemen into the jagged hoodoos of the Aigle Mountains to the east. I fight two Obsidian berserkers until they crawl legless toward me still swinging their axes. I stifle a counterattack of Gray heavy infantry and take respite and water in the shade cast by a crashed torchShip before abandoning my fourth starShell of the day. Few remain operational. Those that do drain their energy cores before the sun begins to set— a full thirty-eight hours after the battle began.

When Ajax is left alone with a cadre of his personal guard after attempting a breakout, he finds himself cut off. When he sees me coming, he finally takes flight with a fifty-strong core of Peerless. A cry of mockery goes through my legions. I set off in pursuit, but my boots have little energy left. Thraxa likewise only makes it five klicks before doubling back to see me exchanging my gravity boots. She sits down in the shade of the tank beside me and sifts through a stack of battery spikes, inserting one at a time to rebuild her pulseArmor's charge.

"Fuckin' snakeshit," she growls in disappointment. "I wanted that Grimmus head."

A munition slams into the top of the tank above our heads, and skitters into the sky to detonate. We barely look.

"Atalantia might demand it from him after this," I say.

I wait for her to finish off the last bat spike. She picks up her gore-spattered hammer. "Ready?"

"Was waiting on you."

None keep up with me the entire battle, not even Thraxa or Screwface. I rotate bodyguards by the hour, surviving off stims injected into the neck or snorted from smashed cartridges or chewed with my cracked molars. The world is thin and two-dimensional, color leached like a faded mural in the ruins of a child's bedroom. My body is lead. The cells leeched of energy. Stims doing nothing but thinning my patience. The restraint that keeps me from sobbing or laughing maniacally is only as substantial as porcelain.

As the sun begins to set, I hitch a ride on a transport missing its back half to the top of the storm wall.

There I watch the spasms of the desert storm. Waves of sands blanket the fallen. The ranks of the dead stretch farther than the eye can see. My hysterical mind wanders. For a delusional moment I believe the planet knows how far those boys and girls are from home and thinks they are asleep, so it sends them blankets of sand to tuck them in for the night.

A tight pain squeezes my chest. The breath goes out of me. Flanked by exhausted bodyguards, I hunch there on the shriveled husk of a broken gun. Harnassus arrives on the wall with a dozen lieutenants in tow. He stares at me as if I were inside out. "Here you bloody are! I've crossed the entire front," he barks. "They must have released psychotropic gas. Every single man I spoke to swears on his mother that he saw you. Where have you been?"

"Everywhere," Screwface growls from my side.

Harnassus looks confused. He looks ragged. A nasty gash on his forehead leaks blood.

"Report," I rasp. His eyes narrow.

"Darrow, your hand."

I look down at my naked left hand. My gauntlet broke, it seems. My skin is bubbling against the sun-heated metal. I pull it away and watch the blisters contract. *Ah, there's the pain.*

Harnassus babbles something about the enemy rallying at the Hippodrome, and a force of enemy tanks lost in the storm now approaching. I try to reply, but my raw vocal chords finally surrender to the abuse of the day.

Harnassus blinks. Something frightens him. As if he saw a spider on my face. I look down at my arms and legs. A second skin of clay made from blood and dust and irradiated ash coats me. My armor is holed and melted into the cauterized wounds. Joints failing to respond to my depleted battery. The tightness will not let go of my chest.

"By Jove, man, are you having a heart attack?" Harnassus calls for a medicus. The Howlers rush to support me as I nearly tip over. I fail to push them off. Rhonna comes to my aid, understanding my distress.

"Not in front of the legions," she says. "What do you need, Uncle?"

"Stims," I mumble.

"How many pops has he had?"

"Thigh pack's empty. At least six."

"Got four marks on his neck."

"Ten? That would kill a bloodydamn horse."

"*Stims,*" I mutter again, feeling dizzy.

"You'll die, you dumb bastard." Harnassus looks about to fall over himself.

"Men trapped in . . . desert . . ." I look out over the battlements. I still have work to do. I look down to see Harnassus trying to push me back.

"Darrow. Stop." Harnassus reaches high to grab my face between his hands. "You've done enough. Let us carry the rest."

I stare through the wisps of his hair to the bodies melted into the steel of the wide parapet. They look like gargoyles with the faces of teenagers. The wind licks the dust from them. They are teenagers.

The full weight of exhaustion settles on me.

"Who has a boot battery?" Rhonna calls. "Come on. You, hey, shit-head. Gimme." She takes the batteries from one of Harnassus's body-guards and switches mine out. "Uncle, you need to fly now. Do you understand me? For your men."

"He can't even stand," Harnassus says. "He needs a medicus and an airlift."

"Back off," Screwface says.

"Who are you?"

"Screwface."

"Bullshit."

"He is," Rhonna says. "Mickey."

"Oh. Well, I am in command now, Gold," Harnassus says. "Darrow needs—"

"Unless you got a cloak, he ain't your pack. He's been mine since I was sixteen. You've got a battle to finish, sir."

Harnassus walks up to him and sticks a finger in his face. "Get him inside somewhere and keep that man alive."

"Man?" Screwface laughs. "*Hic est Lupus,* motherfucker."

Harnassus departs.

"Use my arm, Uncle." I feel Rhonna take my weight. She can't handle all of it. Screwface comes to my other side.

"Got you, boss. Nice and easy. Just a little drama and you're done, yeah?"

With my surviving Howlers around me, we take to the air. The ragged army pouring into the city roars in a weary wave as they see our tattered wolfcloaks soaring toward the Mound of Votum. When we reach the Mound, the Howlers set me down near the top of the sand-covered steps. Armed men swarm the plaza below, bringing the wounded to the triage stations. Titan cannons boom near the spaceport.

I cannot walk under my own power, but my Howlers cluster around me so tight it appears as if I am unwounded. Dying men call my name. I stop when I can, but soon Screwface and Rhonna haul me away to the Votum family's reception chamber. It alone provides privacy. Under defaced Gold statues, I collapse on the stone stairs, too tired and wounded for my Howlers to dare strip off my armor. A medicus visits. I don't know him. I threaten his life if he tries to make me sleep. Screwface threatens his balls if I die. Rhonna pats his shoulder. The medicine the man administers eases the tension in my chest. I am numb with exhaustion, but I watch through the triangular hole in the ceiling as night falls. Screams and gunshots and wailing machines leak in from the darkness.

In the early hours of the night, there is a commotion in the hall outside. Screwface goes to check on it. Rhonna sits on the steps below me, not speaking, a gun in her lap even though Howlers keep watch all around the building. Blood clots on the right side of her head. The great double doors swing inward and Harnassus and Colloway enter. Thraxa au Telemanus stomps in behind them, brown with dust and blood, her armor holed like cheesecloth. She throws a bundle of Gold standards on the floor. Dozens more legionnaires file in behind her, each hauling an armful of enemy standards, some with Gold gauntlets still gripping their poles. They pile them until the stack is even taller than Thraxa herself. She slams her heels together, raises her burned fist, and declares, "Victory."

PART II

CRAFT

It is easier to find men who will volunteer to
die, than to find those who are willing to
endure pain with patience.

—Julius Caesar

18

VIRGINIA

Sovereign

I STARE HALF BLIND INTO a firing squad of fly-eyed cameras. Out the viewport behind me, battle stations and ships of war float beyond the upper atmosphere of Luna.

Eight billion eyes watch me.

"Citizens of the Republic, this is your Sovereign. I come to you with dire news from aboard the SRN dreadnought *Echo of Ares*. On Friday evening last, the third day of the Mensis Martius, I received a brief from the brave men and women of the Republic Reconnaissance Division. This brief, gleaned from our human and mechanical network of sensors, telescopes, scout ships, and informants throughout the Core, indicated that a large-scale Society military operation was under way in the orbit of Mercury. The largest in materiel and manpower since the Battle of Mars, five long years ago. I considered it in the public interest that this information be kept secret until a resolution was found.

"The darker heart of me feared it would be my part to announce the greatest military disaster in our short but storied history. I thought—and many studied minds, civilian and military alike, agreed—that the whole of the Republic Expeditionary Force would be shattered by orbital bombardment, fractured into isolated centuries, and decimated by artillery, disease, starvation, and thirst. That the Free Legions, the beating heart of this great human enterprise, which has broken the chains on Luna, Earth, and Mars, and around which we were to build future legions of liberty, would perish under an Iron Rain in the deserts and mountains of Mercury.

"Now I stand before you with that precious word on my lips. *Victory*. Attacked from all sides, bombarded from the sky, unsupported by warships or satellites, outnumbered by the enemy air force ten to one, the Free Legions shattered the pride of the enemy host, encircled and destroyed most of their vanguard against the walls of Heliopolis, and, in the face of overwhelming odds, survived. That is victory—resounding, but not eternal.

"Now is not the time to congratulate ourselves, or claim we are responsible for this miracle. We are responsible only for this crisis. Lured by the false promises of an enemy plenipotentiary, we allowed our resolve to weaken. We allowed ourselves to believe in the better virtues of our enemy, and that peace was possible with tyrants.

"That lie, seductive though it was, has been exposed as a cruel machination of statecraft created by the newly appointed Dictator of the Society remnant, Atalantia au Grimmus. Under her spell, we compromised with the agents of tyranny. We turned on our greatest general, the sword who broke the chains of bondage, and demanded he accept a peace he knew to be a lie.

"When he did not, we cried, *Traitor! Tyrant! Warmonger!* In fear of him, we recalled the Home Guard elements of the White Fleet from Mercury back to Luna. With the *Echo of Ares* and her battle group undergoing repairs on Phobos, this left Imperator Aquarii with barely half her fleet to fight the duplicitous Dictator. Now, her fleet, the fleet which freed all of our homes floats in ruins. Two hundred of *your* ships of war destroyed. Thousands of *your* sailors killed. Millions of *your* brothers and sisters marooned. Quadrillions of *your* wealth squandered. Not by virtue of enemy arms, but by the squabbling of *your* Senate."

I gesture to the forty-five Blue captains of the *Ares's* battle group and twenty-eight wrathful centurions of my husband's Seventh Legion standing behind me. While their brothers die in the Ladon, the legion agonizes on Luna, trapped after being summoned to walk in the Triumph honoring Mercury's liberation, of all things. A Triumph the Senate commissioned. They are not pleased with the irony. And I am not pleased Sevro would rather play avenging father than stand with them. I wave my hand at the noble soldiers.

"The *Echo of Ares,* her battle group, and the Seventh sail for Mercury in four days' time. The Senate says they will sail alone. Against the Ash

Armada, they will most certainly perish. But they sail nonetheless, because they do not abandon their own.

"Were it within my power, I would send the entire might of our planetary defense fleets to aid them in this venture. But it is not within my power. That power lies with your Senate. From the inception of this crisis, I have urged them to use it. To bolster this rescue fleet with ships from Earth and Luna's Home Guard or Mars's Ecliptic Guard. Again and again my efforts have been rebuffed by the demagogues of the Vox Populi. They refuse to act. And they are not without support from you.

"I have heard it said in these last months, in the halls of the Senate, on the streets of Hyperion, on the news channels across our Republic, that we should abandon these sons and daughters of liberty, these Free Legions. I have heard them called, in public, without shame, 'the Lost Legions.' Written off by you, despite the courage they have summoned, the endurance they have shown, the horrors they have suffered *for you*. Written off because we fear that to part with our ships will invite invasion. Because we fear to once again see Society iron over our skies. Because we fear to risk the comforts and freedoms the men and women of the Free Legions purchased for us with their blood . . .

"I will tell you what I fear. I fear time has diluted our dream! I fear that in our comfort, we believe liberty to be self-fulfilling!" I lean forward. "I fear that the meekness of our resolve, the bickering and backbiting on which we have so decadently glutted ourselves, will rob us of the unity of will that moved the world forward to a fairer place, where respect for justice and freedom has found a foothold for the first time in a millennium.

"We have let our union erode to tribalism. We hoard our wealth. We abandon our votes for violence. We summon tantrums instead of gritting our teeth in common purpose." I pause and make sure this stands apart, knowing that the Syndicate Queen, wherever she is, will understand my declaration of war. "We aid our enemy. Even now terrorist organizations like the Luna-based Syndicate and its franchises eat at our foundation like termites by funneling helium-3 into the bellies of Society war machines and the ships of Ascomanni raiders."

Reporters murmur from the shadows beneath their camera drones.

"I fear that in this disunity we will sink back into the hideous epoch from which we escaped, and that the new dark age will be crueler, more sinister, and more protracted by the malice which we have awoken in our enemies.

"I believe this truth manifest: the Free Legions are *not* lost." My fist hammers my lectern. "While we abandoned them, they did not abandon us. They did not cave to despair. In the cold of our neglect, in the shadow of atomic clouds, they triumphed. Yet. Despite this victory, their time is short. They have blunted Atalantia's blade, but not her will. Pushed back to the city of Heliopolis and its attendant lands, millions of free men and women dig in to face the onslaught of enemy armor. Their supplies run low. They are surrounded. They are outnumbered. They have risked all to protect you. Now it is your turn to risk *something* for them.

"I call upon you, the People of the Republic, to stand united. To beseech your senators to reject fear. To reject this torpor of self-interest. To not quiver in primal trepidation at the thought of invasion, to not let your senators hoard your wealth for themselves and hide behind *your* ships of war, but to summon the more wrathful angels of their spirits and send forth the might of the Republic to scourge the engines of tyranny and oppression from the Mercurian sky and rescue our Free Legions."

I let the silence stretch to the hearts of the free, and into my own. There was a moment before this doom. One I cradle close, like the last candle on a dark day. A moment of peace, where Darrow was not yet my husband, and we sat in the sands of Earth watching Sevro and Victra swim out to see the eagle nests amongst the sea stacks. Darrow cradled Pax in his arms. They had only just met. But he loved him because he was my boy, and bit by bit he realized he was his boy, our boy that we made together.

He put his ear to Pax's chest to listen to his heartbeat. He told me then what he felt when he declared this war within the Hives of Phobos. How he was not close enough to hear the fading beat of his father's heart, or Eo's. But how, in that moment, he could feel the hearts of his people beating across the darkness. How in the heartbeat of our son, he could hear them all again.

I have never equaled my husband's spirit. For so many years, I led for guilt, for duty, seldom for love, all while fearing the coldness in my ancient blood would forever rob me of the passion to hear the pulse of the people.

But I hear it now. I hear it as free hearts beat behind me. As they beat in their bunks on the torchShips that patrol the edges of free space. As they beat in the shadowed veins of asteroid mines, in the smoky dens of hinterland trade depots, in ore caravans, deepspace waystations, in the rattling assembly lines of Phobos that make the ships which protect our liberty. I hear it in the megalopolises of Mars, the broken streets of fallen Olympia, the tempestuous wine bazaars of Thessalonica, the quiet shadow of the Agean Citadel from which my father once gripped the throat of a planet and now there towers a monument to the rebel girl he hanged and made immortal. I hear them in the jungle sprawl of Echo City. In the glittering spires of Old Tokyo. In the martial training grounds of New Sparta.

Yet I sense them fading in the assimilation camps, the overflowing prisons, the broken cities, the tenement houses filled with laborers who have lost their purpose to progress, in the chanting Vox hordes who clog the streets of Luna, and in the halls of power where senators whisper how much they charge.

Soon those fading hearts will join the ashes of New Thebes in their silence. They will join the mining townships made into necropolises by the Rat War, the lingering rubble the Block War left strewn west of Hyperion, and the irradiated stormland of the Helios. I fear that my subjects will return to their private concerns after this speech. It is always the same. The eyes wander away and vapid glitter again rules the feed.

"Brothers and sisters." My voice nearly falters as I feel more than ever the absence of my husband's hand on my shoulder. My son will not be waiting on my shuttle to critique my speech. "Brothers and sisters . . . there will dawn a day when these hostile hours, these days of hatred and violence, seem the faintest of memories, but dark and steep and long is the road up out of hell. So do not tire, do not despair, do not abandon your brethren, and do not forget that through this darkness we and we alone carry the light of freedom. We must defend it with every cell in our bodies. If not now, when? If not us, who?" I make my hand a fist and raise it in salute. "Hail libertas."

In the back of the room, beyond the jaded circus, an old Red janitor forgets himself and bellows with all his tiny might: "Hail Reaper." More join him. "Hail Reaper!" More and more until half the room shouts my husband's invocation. But the rest stare in stony silence.

At that moment, three hundred eighty-four thousand kilometers from my heart, in orbit one thousand kilometers above the wayward continent of South Pacifica, a new battery of twin prototype railguns, named the *Twins of South Pacifica* for Earth's favorite son and daughter, set their telescopic sights on a path of empty space ten days ahead of Mercury's orbital path and fire at full power. Projectiles skinned with stealth polymer race into the void at 320,000 kilometers per hour, ferrying not death, but supplies, radiation medicine, machines of war, and, if my husband is alive, a message of hope.

You have not been abandoned. I will come for you.
Until then, endure, my love. Endure.

19

VIRGINIA

Stiletto

L UNA IS A DREAM, a noise, a blaze of light, a soup, a swagger, a
mother, a vampire, an addiction, a beggar, a lament, a suburb of
Hyperion, and a memory of the future we thought we wanted. A dozen
fleets waver through the gutter puddles of her rain-soaked streets, only
to be shattered by the calf-high boots worn by the children of four planets and thirty moons. They swarm to her to climb her jigsaw bedlam of
human and metal ladders. They are geniuses, architects, idiots, swindlers, warlords, the lost, the found, the indifferent. And indifferently she
waits, throbs, beats, swarms, suffocates, promises, and robs.

They call her the City of Light, but no one calls her home.

"What does Luna mean to you, Centurion?" I ask from inside my
private office aboard *Pride One* as we descend. Holiday ti Nakamura was
raised along the sunny shores of South Pacifica, where there was not a
building taller than a grain silo for a hundred klicks. I have named her
Dux of my Lionguard—the elite bodyguard unit drawn from my house
legions. Of the one thousand Martians, she is the lone Terran. That not
a single man questions her appointment is proof enough of her reputation. They call her Six, meaning she's always got your back.

"Quicksand," she replies in regards to the moon.

The reply mirrors the cold-rolled spirit of the woman. Of all my husband's instruments, it is Nakamura I've envied the most. Reputation,
but little ego. Flexible, but unbreakable. Brutal, but not cruel. Over
these last weeks, she has led the investigation into my son's abduction
with grace. When their shuttle went down during Ephraim ti Horn's

failed rescue attempt, it was as if the moon had swallowed Pax and Electra. I fought every instinct to tear apart the city to find them, knowing a stampede of Republic Intelligence would disturb the breadcrumbs. Holiday was the scalpel I needed.

"And you, ma'am?" she asks, folding her datapad back into its arm sheath.

What does Luna mean to me? How to answer that. A thousand things.

"Renewal." I catch her smirk in the window. Like Daxo, she doesn't suffer hollow sentiments. "Maybe one day that'll be true. My mother loved Luna, in fact. Before she decided throwing herself off a cliff and abandoning us was preferable to a single day more of matrimony with my father, she told me Luna was a place of magic. For it was the one place even Nero au Augustus had to bow. Of course, she meant he had to bow to Octavia. Reductive thinking, really."

Holiday waits for me to explain. I treasure her more than she knows. Especially over these last days. The unspoken peril of power is the receipt of unending, exhaustive peacocking. Unlike most, Holiday is not waiting for her turn to flash her feathers. She listens because she's heard enough noise to know that truth, if it ever appears, creeps in on quiet little feet.

I step closer to the window.

"There's something here," I say. "Something . . . else that gnawed at Octavia. You know that feeling, Centurion." I look back at her. The diamond teeth of skyscrapers reflect in her eyes as we pass Quicksilver's Zenith Spire. "This moon hungers."

She makes a small sound of agreement as we pierce the cloud layer.

Beneath it, Hyperion seethes in existential mania. For fear of Gold ships over her skies, protesters fill the streets. Violence has broken out between Optimate and Vox street factions. Watchmen sirens bathe the sky in green and silver. Strikes have shut down the public trams and now only the aerial arteries flow.

"Have you ever heard of Silenius's Stiletto?" I ask.

"After the Conquest of Earth, the powerful houses engaged in a land grab," Holiday replies. "Silenius was faced with a dilemma. To his left, anarchy. To his right, tyranny. Instead, he found the narrow path between. Barely wide enough for the edge of a stiletto."

"Well, well. Look who found time to read *Meditations*."

"If Virginia au Augustus gives someone something to read and they do not read it, they don't deserve the faculty, ma'am."

I raise an eyebrow at her. "You talk to your husband with that Copper tongue?"

She grins. "Then they're a fuckin' idiot, ma'am."

I smile. Raw compliments are the best kind. "Whatever you think of his politics, Silenius was wise. He knew patience is the heart of cunning. Theodora has discovered Senator Basilus has been taking bribes from Sun Industries. I am allowing him to retire to his home in Echo City next month. I will need a replacement for him before the year is out."

She blinks when she understands my intent. "I don't know if a toga would fit me, ma'am."

"How many senators were Praetorian dragoons who can also quote Silenius's *Meditations*? Not one, I'd say. Aside from Rhone ti Flavinius, you're the most famous Gray alive. And Earth loves you." I set a hand on the shorter woman's shoulders. She's really built like a pit bull, isn't she? No neck. "We need symbols, Nakamura. The old ones are fraying with use. Tell me you'll think on it."

She nods dutifully but, like all true soldiers, doubts she'll survive long enough to have to make the decision. As much as I value her at my six, I wish she were with my husband on Mercury. Sevro too for that matter. My husband needs a conscience on his shoulder. Thraxa and Orion aren't exactly a pacifying influence. As for Harnassus, well, dogs and cats.

My datapad flickers with an incoming call. Nakamura heads to the door to give me privacy. "Wait." I gesture to one of the ranadium chairs before my desk. "I'll want your opinion afterward."

As she sits, I open the call on the desk's projector. Dancer appears from the waist up. He's in a shuttle. A dark red jacket with a high collar substitutes for his loathed toga. The aging Red doesn't look like he's slept in weeks. Pressured by me for the vote, and with his radical left solidifying around ArchImperator Zan, the Blue commander of Luna's defense fleet, how could he? As my father said: "Never trust the man who sleeps under siege. He's either lazy or disloyal."

"If it isn't the loyal opposition," I say with a smile.

"My Sovereign." He says the word as if it carried no more weight than "coffee" or "peanut." "Must say, for a kilo of gilded Palatine snakeshit, that was some damn fine oratory. Churchill?"

"Humans haven't changed, why should the speeches?"

Despite the liver spots and heavy lines on his face, he is still as handsome a Red as I've ever seen. He grimaces. "I must say, it is odd. I've been called a traitor before. By Daxo, Quicksilver, Orion. Never suspected it'd feel so raw coming from you."

"I didn't quite—"

"Virginia."

"I suppose I did." I brush invisible lint from my jacket cuff and sigh. "A rhetorical ploy only, I assure you." He's no traitor. He's just afraid, but if I accuse a Red man of *that,* he'll bite down and hold on like a tick. "It doesn't have to be this way, you know. You and I flourish when we cooperate."

"We have had our moments."

"But."

"Here she goes . . ."

"But our system isn't working as it should. The division of military command is a flaw we saw coming, yet kicked down the lane because we thought we were all going the same direction. Irresponsible of us, but understandable. Facts: our enemy can respond with greater urgency and secrecy than we can, and not all senators prize prosecution of the war over the continued habitation of their togas. I need to be able to run this war efficiently."

He knows I admire respectful dialogue, and speaks in a neutral, even tone. "Virginia, the Senate was intended to be inconvenient. A check on despotism. You know as well as I: whatever the executive gets, it keeps. Forever. You are measured. You are thoughtful. If we give you temporary control over the defense fleets, it may work this time. *May.* But your hamartia is that you think wisdom is contagious. It fuckin' ain't. You won't always be Sovereign. What if it's Daxo next?"

"Or Zan?" I suggest.

"Or Zan." He rubs his lantern jaw. "Only person besides you or me that wouldn't wreck the world is Publius. Self-righteous little twat that he is." Reds do hate their Coppers.

"Publius? Ha. He'd just give speeches all day on civic duty," I say.

"And ladle soup for the poor."

"Long as there are cameras."

"Naturally." We're united in a smirk, then return to our corners as he continues. "Raw talk. You know I love the Free Legions. They're the best of Mars. You know I love Darrow like a son. But he's gone, Virginia. I buried him the moment I heard he landed in Tyche. Abandon this crusade, for the good of us all."

I watched the speech he gave denouncing my first attempts to send a fleet. He looked like he was picking the varnish for his own son's casket. The guilt must be devouring him.

"If he's alive, he's encircled," he continues. "Atalantia will dangle him like bait. This is just another trap. We have more ships, but only if we leave a planet vulnerable. They will lure us out, take us away from our orbit guns, and kill us, or just slip past and kill the planets. We're vulnerable in attack, strong in defense. Who do we have left that can match Atalantia and her Gold Praetors in space? Zan?" He shakes his head. "Atalantia'll eat her alive."

"Kavax, Niobe, and the Arcos matriarchs will lead the fleet."

"Golds against Golds." He hates that he wonders how it always comes to that, because he knows the answer. "Not one of ours under sixty. Atalantia is in her prime. Ajax is a rising terror. And Atlas . . . Fact is, there's five hundred of them that'd make even Nakamura run in a meat straw."

The old soldier likes his colloquialisms. This one is for a close-quarters battle where two sides blow men into either end of a ship corridor till one runs out of breath, or men. It is an infantry term, so it is rather gross.

"More like five thousand," Nakamura murmurs. Not one for bravado, she makes a sniping motion, her only salvation against the apex predators of my breed. I've seen her take down a Peerless in close quarters. I also know the price she paid. Her legs are bionic from the femur down. At least they match her robot eye.

"And then there's Aja's brood," Dancer mutters. "What happens if Ajax boards the *Reynard*? Kavax can barely walk around the garden."

He knows what I know. Darrow was the force of nature we rode to victory after victory. Yet whenever the Gold Legates or Praetors caught our other leaders in the field, they consistently made mincemeat of them. Wanting lowColors to be equal to Peerless in warfare is not the same as them being equal.

Without Darrow, he has no confidence in our arms. But the risk is necessary.

"Dancer, my husband and the Free Legions are our two greatest symbols. If the Republic abandons the Free Legions, Mars will give up on

Luna. Then Luna falls to Atalantia. Atalantia takes Earth. Mars stands alone. And, eventually, Mars falls. Give us an alternative. A compromise. I'll send my own ships, Kavax's, Arcos's, but I need a hundred ships-of-the-line from the defense fleets to stand a chance against Atalantia. That's less than a third of Luna's fleet."

"And if you lose?"

"We won't."

He sits in silence, rubbing his outsized hands together. The movement slows as his resolve forms. I hear the door shutting before he looks up. I missed my opportunity, or perhaps it never really existed. "I cannot risk those atomics coming here," he says. "I may hate this human swamp, but it's filled to capacity."

"Then I wish you good health and ill fortune."

"Wait, Virginia." My hand hovers over the datapad as he leans forward, voice barely above a whisper. "You know this will escalate. If I somehow fall off a balcony or eat an unruly fishbone—"

He hits the nerve.

"Pity. I never confuse you and Harmony. Yet after all this time, you still think I am my father. Or is it my brother?"

"It's not you. It's your people."

"Daxo, you mean."

"And Theodora, the Seventh, the Arcoses."

"I have them under control."

If he knew Sevro was here and out of control, he'd be shitting himself.

"That's either a big fat lie or you're drinking your own swill. You and I both know Darrow and the Reaper are two different things entirely. And the Reaper didn't gnaw through the Society because he was a better military strategist than the Ash Lord. His gift is making men go mad. You've seen it."

I have. Fighter pilots going "Polyphemus" and driving straight into the bridges of enemy torchShips so much the Golds put them in the center of the ships. Unarmored lowColors using their tattered bodies to weigh down armored Golds so their fellows can finish them, like hounds after a cougar, baying my husband's name.

"I didn't stop carrying a rifle because I was old or it was heavy," he says. "I did it to counter the Reaper's weight as I never could in the legions. Some literally think he is a god. If they think he wants it . . . they'll murder cities. They'll murder me."

There is a frail quality in him that goes behind weariness of the flesh. One he has never permitted me to see before. But the frailness is not weakness. It is a cornered spirit too tired for anything except a killing blow. "If I am assassinated . . . the Vox will retaliate."

"I will control my people," I say. "I wish I believed you could control yours. I will see you in three days, Senator. Try to avoid fishbones."

I punch off the datapad. It fizzles with broken circuits. I punch it again. What good is being smarter than everyone if no one listens? Is this how my father felt? My brother? Is evil born of pure frustration?

Holiday watches the blood drip from a gash on my knuckle. It's already coagulating. Even Mickey couldn't match that genetic blessing. "Centurion, if I told you to kill Dancer O'Faran, would you do it?"

"No, ma'am."

"Why not?"

"If Darrow and Orion are dead, you two are the Republic."

We don't know if they are or not. Communication to the planet is down. But I reject the concept of doubt. Darrow and Pax do not die. It is a paradigm of my life that will be true until proven beyond reasonable doubt.

I lick clean the congealing blood. "Good answer." Even Kavax would never have refused my father like that. If Holiday only knew how much her presence restrains my darker urges, she might think it wise to put a few rounds through my skull just to be safe. "Make sure the word goes through the ranks again. If anyone so much as touches a hair on Dancer's head, the last face they'll ever see will be mine as I entomb them in the bowels of Deepgrave, with only lonely Boneriders for company."

"Yes, ma'am. But it's not them you have to worry about." She lowers her voice. "The Seventh is climbing the walls. They think the Senate is filled with traitors. If Sevro goes to them . . ."

"He has thirty thousand elite shock troops within twenty minutes of the Citadel. I'm aware, Nakamura. I am very much aware." I stretch my neck as my ship approaches the Moonhall landing pad. "Silenius walked his stiletto. I've no doubt we'll walk ours."

"What makes you so confident?"

"Well, for starters, we have smaller feet."

20

VIRGINIA

Politicos

*D*ICTAEON *ANTRON*, THE PERSONAL SKYHOOK of my closest confidant, Daxo au Telemanus, and for ten years the informal headquarters of the Vox's nemesis, the Optimate Party, floats over the Citadel. Daxo designed it himself to look like a brain. Viewed from above, it resembles little more than a pair of very engorged testicles. And everyone, excluding perhaps four people, is afraid to say so. For years, I had him park it over the Sea of Serenity to maintain the impartiality of my office. And for aesthetics.

There's little point to either anymore.

Under its conjoined domes, an army has assembled. Instead of armor, these soldiers wear high-collared suits, lion pins instead of phalera of valor, and carry datapads instead of rifles. The politicos of the Optimate Party are ready for war. As is Daxo's floating office.

Inflatable beds fill hallways and offices in anticipation of the seventy-two-hour blitz before the vote. Coffee carts trundle. Medici prepare their stim stations. Commissaries check their food stores. Dozens of senators join us in hologram conference from their homes in Hyperion and offices in the Citadel.

The politicos assemble along the dome's tiered rows of data stations that encircle the gravity shaft down to Daxo's office.

The politicos applaud as I enter, hailing my speech and chanting for Mars in honor of their fellow Martians, which comprise most of the Free Legions.

They know the vote will be momentous. Not just because of its material consequences, but because it represents a tectonic shift in our politics. Years ago, I predicted the natural evolution away from Color tribalism to planetary nationalism. Now it is here and people are shocked, as though interest groups carve themselves out of the ether.

We stand to lose moderate Lunese, who fear invasion. Dancer stands to lose most Martians, possibly all Reds—who often vote against me, but have rediscovered their zealotry for my husband after his victory. As for Earth—it'll be up for grabs. But after all the shifting and shaking, the vote will come down to Copper and Obsidian—who have declared solidarity and plan to vote as blocs. Win one, it's a knife fight. Win both, it's victory. Lose any of our foundation—Silver, Gray, White—and it's bedlam. The problem is, I know Sefi is not in her estate on Earth or on Luna. She smuggled herself to Mars weeks ago to link up with elements already there in Olympia. Bit by bit, she smuggles more Obsidian, and prepares her plans. Whole legions have gone missing. She thinks I don't notice. But how will her senators vote, considering those plans? I haven't the faintest clue.

I ask Flagilus, one of Daxo's premier Pink apprentices, where his master is hiding.

"In a meeting with Senator Caraval."

"A meeting? In his office?"

Flagilus's cadre of politicos chuckle to one another. "Much to our dismay as well. It seems Senator Caraval has more testicular fortitude than his side part would suggest. Senator Telemanus asked for you to do the honors and to join him after."

I feel a minor pang of disappointment. Only Daxo loves this weird game as much as I do. I was not as close with him as a child. In fact, I found his intelligence entirely too much like that of a shark—restless and indefatigably predatory. But it was not Pax or Kavax or their sisters who pumped the water from my lungs when I struck my head on a coral reef as a girl.

He saved my life then, a deed that would soon become a habit. How many days did we sit together composing ridiculous game theories and mock debates after I broke my leg in a fall from my father's prized sunblood?

Without Daxo, this is a lonely endeavor. "They can wait," Holiday says. She's been watching me.

"That obvious?" I ask.

"I never drink tequila without Trigg," she says. "You and the brain have been planning this for weeks. It can wait five minutes."

It's just the excuse I was looking for. I flash her a smile. "Careful of the politicos. They're carnivorous."

"Atlas already tried that. I'm inedible."

"That I do not doubt."

I jump down the shaft and free-fall two hundred meters until the gravity well slows my descent. My feet touch down in the center of an aquarium. Walls of water stand a hundred meters high, held back from the central axis of the office by a stasis field. Smaller bubbles of water, restricted by secondary fields, wander through the office ferrying carnivorous passengers to and fro.

It is a game, you see. The trick for Daxo is never to let one of his seventeen infant gigavok—cartilaginous pale deepsea predators—exist within a sphere or wall of water with another. The species has stunted pituitary glands that limit their size to one meter unless their glands are stimulated via cannibalism. In six years there have been no fatalities within Daxo's office, except the unfortunate case of the Peerless Venusian assassin who thought Daxo was sleeping. Seven gigavok shared her for lunch. It was the most horrible thing I have ever seen in my life. Victra clouted Sevro bloody when she caught him showing it to their daughter Electra late at night up in Lake Silene.

My sister-in-law, for lack of a more accurate word, has a theory that is not altogether mad. "If *Dictaeon Antron* is actually supposed to be a brain, pray tell what is the purpose of giant albino swimmers? They're sperm, Virginia. Giant predatory cannibal sperm, and not even five people have the nerve to say so. Daxo is playing a joke on the world, just to measure who isn't afraid of him. I love that freak."

And I miss that woman, despite her irascible idiocy. She might be the only human alive who can make me lose my temper with a single sigh about how coffee just tasted better when it was picked by slaves.

I follow the sound of Daxo's voice through an amorphous corridor of water. A gigavok stalks me from a water bubble above. I try to ignore the metaphor.

I find Daxo reclining on a fainting couch set on a Turkish rug with the insouciant entitlement of a vacationing heiress, albeit a colossal, bald heiress who is equally at ease coaxing a political concession from a rival as he is smashing Venusian skulls with his personal collection of exotic weaponry.

Sitting across from Daxo in a simple, off-the-rack suit, legs folded, hair parted, unremarkable face passive, is Publius cu Caraval, The Incorruptible, Tribune of the Copper bloc, the media's Voice of Reason, and the most important vote in the Republic.

What a catch. How in Jove's name did Daxo manage to part him from his soup kitchen?

"Come, come, Publius," Daxo purrs, making a small hand gesture to acknowledge my presence. "You know how the game works. Concessions are as detestable, natural, and necessary in politics as flatulence in humans."

"Daxo, please. We both know when it comes to battles of rhetoric, you have me unarmed. I've told you once, I'll tell you again, I cannot in good conscience vote to expand the Sovereign's powers when she continues to let Quicksilver run roughshod over this government and its people." His voice has a surprisingly alluring quality. He's already a fine orator. If he weren't so Pecksniffian, and added a little bombast to make up for his lack of presence, he would be nearly as good as me.

Daxo makes a sound of mild disgust. "Is the fate of the Free Legions worth such moral rectitude?"

"Possibly, yes. He gouges us with prices, threatens the fabric of society with his attacks on unions and the common man. Just last week, his automatons put a million laborers out of work in Endymion. It wasn't enough he stole the Reds' mines through legal skullduggery, he's taking Luna too!"

"It is unreasonable to expect her to give the Silvers nothing, Publius."

"It is immoral to allow private citizens to hold this government hostage," Publius replies. "I am sorry, Daxo, but it is a nonstarter. The military side of your strategy is convincing, not that I could tell a decurion from a centurion. But I cannot vote for the bill if you cede to his demands. It is an issue of principle."

I clear my throat and step out from behind the water wall. Publius jumps to his feet, startled, and sweeps into a bow perfectly attuned to the sizable respect he has for my office.

"Senator Caraval," I say, kissing him on the cheek. "I admit I'm surprised to see you here, of all places."

"Yes, well, desperate times call for sacrifices from us all," he replies. He casts a look around, certainly irked by the gigavok and the ostentatiousness of the office. His own offices are kept in the same nondescript lower Hyperion building where he served as a public defender for lowColors before the Rising. His assigned offices in the Citadel are too grandiose for his tastes. Before the Rising, I couldn't imagine a world where he and Daxo would ever be in the same room, much less speaking as relative equals. Makes me smile a little inside, especially noting Daxo's annoyance.

"I was under the impression you viewed the legions as lost," I say, taking a seat on a Turkish cushion.

The Incorruptible nods and retakes his seat. "A deplorable presumption on my part, I fear. The numbers, you see. While my assessment was based on the data I had at the time, I admit to a certain . . . dimming of faith." He hangs his head. "I am ashamed for that, but not the assessment. I said the same to Daxo here: I judge a case based on its evidence. You know I am loath to flimflam, flip-flop, or whatever they call it these days, but the situation has changed. What your husband did . . . staggering, my Sovereign. Staggering."

"And the moral ramifications?" I ask.

He waves his hand before his face. "Fascism is a scourge. Sometimes we must sacrifice to destroy it."

"So you no longer presume the legions lost."

"No," he says. "Your speech, Daxo's dogged pursuit, the Battle of the Ladon, they have woken the slumbering patriot. If we can bring them back, we make a statement that will ring through time." He steeples his fingers and leans forward. "Yet I am in a bind. I am from this moon. I am expected to vote with the Vox."

"Even as they descend into fits of nonsensical maudlin hysteria stemming from Cassandra Syndrome?" Daxo asks.

Publius levels a look at him. "I disagree with them, but I will not abide intellect-slander." He turns back to me. "My prior vocation taught me to be detailed in assessment and concise in judgment. The Vox fear momentary pain for long-term gain. We must save the legions. But the Silvers know how desperate this vote is. They will bleed you dry. I cannot allow this Republic to become another plutocracy. I will not."

"So you blame them for ransoming their votes, yet you've come to do the same to me. You've learned well."

"I am not proud of it. Politics is an ignoble profession. But as I said, sacrifices. My electorate does not have trillionaires, much less a quadrillionaire benefactor. We are public servants. Ten times the population of Silvers, we have but the same ten senators they have. We must use what leverage we can."

I expected as much. He's a patient man, honest to the point of obnoxious, but worst of all, he knows when he has a strong hand. He knows I have more tricks. He wants me to use them on Silver. Somehow he's found the only way to keep clean hands in this world is to outsource the dirty work.

Lucky for me, I have access to gloves, and a long eye.

"Hypothetically," I begin as if the plan weren't already in motion for weeks now, "what if I told you I could get the Silver vote, maybe not all, but enough, without one concession? And when the Senate temporarily expands my powers, I will annul many past concessions?"

He leans forward. "Then hypothetically, I am intrigued. But I should hear no more, of course."

"Of course."

"I'll take my leave, then." He stands and shakes Daxo's hand, then mine. A servant appears to guide him to a secondary door in the floor. Before he descends, he glances about. "Senator Telemanus. I must admit, the architecture certainly makes a statement. It is a remarkable man who can bare his balls to the world."

Daxo is stunned silent. Publius bows. The door closes. And I burst into a fit of laughter.

Daxo waits for me to recover, entirely ignoring Publius's remark. He taps his chin in thought with a forefinger the size of a steak knife as I sit down. "You want to know how I lured him here?"

"Sure, let's talk about that."

"I told him Darrow sent a communiqué from Mercury telling us to beseech Publius cu Caraval. 'He is the conscience of the Republic, and our last hope.'"

"You are a cretin."

"Yes, aren't I? There is only one thing in which Publius is not forthcoming—his irascible vanity."

"Unique trait."

"Sarcastic ripostes are seldom clever enough to prove that they are little more than the desperate cries for validation of a petty and insecure mind."

"Oh, shut up, Father."

"He did teach us half of what we know."

"The cold, evil half."

"Which has kept us alive amongst predators, my dear. Returning to my thrust—when has a Copper ever been a savior?" He chuckles to himself. "Now all you have to do is wrest the Silvers away from Quick, and victory shall be ours."

"Stop talking in that tone. We already seem evil enough in this aquatic lair of yours. All that's missing is you twirling a mustachio."

He strokes the gold angels embedded on his bald head instead. "Speaking of facial hair . . ."

"Theodora has Sevro under control."

"Does she?"

I sigh. "Daxo . . ."

"It is hardly pedantic to advise my Sovereign to utilize her best assets. Theodora has proven herself capable, but she is not me nor is she you. Nor is she any of the two hundred Peerless on Luna equipped for the task."

He sighs and pets a passing gigavok through a water sphere, almost losing a finger for it. He smiles, not offended. He likes it when things obey their natures.

"I confess. I have always viewed Sevro as a marginal character in our great endeavor. He is ill-tempered, rash, and braggadocious in nature. I don't know if he's ever read a book. Let me loose, and I will subdue the illiterate halfman in short order."

I pretend to consider it.

If one listed all the qualities a tyrant might possess, one might start by describing Daxo au Telemanus. He is cruel, thorough, calculating, cold, arrogant, and, though he does not lack empathy, he is fairly unconvinced of its logical merits. Just as he is entirely unconvinced of democracy. But he is obsessively competitive. And he chose his team long ago.

More than any man I've ever met, Daxo was entirely content being a lonely child. Thank Jove Kavax told me to memorize *Paradise Lost* before I met his firstborn. We might have lost the war if he found me wanting.

"A thought's just occurred to me," I say. "Did you model yourself after Milton's depiction of Lucifer?"

"Finally." A slow, immense smile spreads across his lips; he is as pleased as a lizard on a hot rock. *To be weak is miserable, doing or suffering.*"

"Jove on high," I say. "It took me twenty-seven years to get that."

"You are my only friend to guess."

"Daxo, you only keep one friend."

"At a time. You lasted longer than the rest. There are more private secrets to uncover. Hiding in plain sight."

"The gigavok are metaphors for your virility, and your fear that if you had children, they would eat each other."

"Fuck."

He glares at me.

I lean back. "You see, communication is our salvation. So . . . no, you don't get to play with Sevro. Exponential oddity is a perilous game."

"Very well." He sighs his colossal body from his couch and offers me a hand. The waters part as he escorts me to the gravity well. We look up at the light of the politico chamber. "Are you certain we can't dissolve the Senate?" he asks. "It would just be so much simpler to feed them to my metaphors."

"No."

"Worth a try."

We put our heads together and recite our mantra.

> Matter, how tiny my share
> Time, how brief my allotment
> Fate, how small my roll to play
> Self, all that can be mastered

Then, hand in hand, we ascend.

Hundreds of political adjuncts quiet as we arrive.

"Good morning!" I say to the Optimate army as Daxo looms over my shoulder like an evil Proctor. Silence falls. Their faces turn toward us in excitement. Gods, so many are as young as I was when I served Octavia. "I hope you're all rested. I'll be brief. Most of you have done this before on the Conscription Accords and that sham of a peace treaty. We've learned our lesson from those losses: press to the Forum. And we didn't have momentum then. We've got it now, dammit. Three days from today, we vote to save eight million lives. Until then, cancel your families, cancel your social calendars . . ." They laugh at that fantasy. Daxo has no patience to teach anyone but obsessive-compulsive Martians, and stone-cold political killers. "You have only this . . ."

I toss up a hologram pyramid the size of an assault shuttle, subdivided into empty blocks representing the seventy-one-vote majority needed to give me the power over the defense fleets.

"Fill. This. Pyramid," I say. "Twice we've tried to vote. Twice, the Vox have turned the screws and denied us the eight Tribunes to call a quorum. With his victory, Imperator O'Lykos has given us the Tribunes. With ours, we give him a chance."

They rap their knuckles on their desks.

"For those of you fresh in from Mars, prepare yourselves. Good demokracy on Luna is not like that of Agea. Here, good demokracy is a knife fight. No vote is set in stone. No word eternal. What we gain, we must fight to the bone to keep. The Vox will use every tactic at their disposal. Daxo has given you your assignments. He alone channels my will." They know that already. "From here to the vote, Hyperion will descend into a fit of political hysteria. But we will endure because . . ."

"Hic sunt leones!" they shout, as is their custom. I feel the inner heat building toward that exultant moment. I extend my hand to Daxo, and take from his titanic hands the giant hourglass Mickey grew from Venusian glass coral and gifted me upon the legalization of inter-Color reproduction. I hold it up, cherishing the vibrations before the storm, the fear and nervousness bubbling from my allies, and then slam it down.

"Fill. This. Pyramid!"

Senator holograms blink away. Aides enter their iso pods. In my offices in the Citadel of Light, in the halls of Senate Crescent, all over Hyperion, thousands of soldiers in my political army rotate the great pistons of our demokratic engine. Lobbyists flood restaurants and offices. Trillionaires turn their screws. Organizers activate their armies. Media surrogates prepare for cameras. Senators become the courted, the hunted, the pressured, the wooed, the fooled, the bamboozled, the corrupted, and the purchased.

A thrill of excitement goes up my leg. I do love this.

21

EPHRAIM

Mauler, Brawler, Legacy Hauler

Y OUR MAJESTY, YOU HAVE SUFFERED a catastrophic collision.
Two life forms in critical danger.
A distress signal has been sent to your employer.
A distress signal has been sent to your employer.
*Smoke in the nostrils. Pressure. Shivering. Try to move. Can't. Thumping
blood in the deep of my thigh. Lights stutter and crackle. Bent metal every-
where. Panic creeping.*

*Pinned to the floor by collapsed hull. Right leg trapped. Bullet hole in
chest, no exit wound, resFlesh torn. Probably fatal. Smoke. A boy gasping.
Push myself up. Can't. Why not? Left radius and ulna snapped. Compound
fracture. Pokes out through skin. Looks like a barracks "beef" rib through
blood pudding.*

*Losing blood. Body cold. Hear voices. Threat? Reach for weapon. Can't
find it. Darkness creeping in.*

*Molten square opens hole in hull. Crash of metal. Volga? No. Filthy crea-
tures in tatters. Big boys. Glowing laser eyes. Respirators, radiation gear.
Scavengers. Swat my hand away. Look under my eyelids. On my neck.
Searching for legion ink.*

A distress signal has been sent to your employer.
A distress signal has been sent to your employer.
*Fear. Bickering. A child's body dragged out. Limp. Heavy cutting laser.
Going to help me. Cut the hull away. Free me. Smell roasting meat. Mouth
waters. Feel pressure. Look down. My hip, but no leg. Where is my leg?
Volga. Help me.*

I fall out of the horror back into the shell of my body. Incomprehensible agony radiates from the interior of my right thigh. The rest of me does not move.

"*. . . rejecting the artificial tissue.*"

The words slither through the thick wool of my brain. My ring is gone. I look down at my body, or try to look. The body is naked, pinned to a table like a vivisected frog. My right leg is skinless synthetic meat from the hip down. Green, webby fibers spasm over translucent bone. Artificial vessels worm in fleshy strands. An emaciated human with two hundred glass eyes affixed to his head hunches near my feet, spinning membrane. Someone screams. I think it's me.

"*Massive coronary agitation.*"

"*. . . withdrawal complication.*"

"*Keep him alive,*" a voice rumbles beyond the light. "*Your Queen wills it.*"

"*. . . sedative!*"

I drift into the dark. It is warmer than I expected. There is a boy there, on a raft, his hands behind his head, his skin freckled from the sun. He floats off a shadowy shore watching a big sky, not one collared by metal towers, but dusted with stars and stretching the horizon. All I want is to float there with him. To smell the salt. To lie in that cradle as the sea rocks us to sleep.

The moon pulses in the sky like an atomic dilation. Drawing me up into its gravity. No no no no no nonononono.

> *Chop 'em if they're taller.*
> *Stomp 'em if they're smaller.*
> *Mauler, brawler, legacy hauler . . .*

Chanting in the tunnel to light.

A girl stands over me. Her hatchetface pulled into a sneer. A scalpel glints in her hand. She holds it over my throat. My memories, my life, my guilt, return and I push my throat up into the metal. "Go on, slick. Gimme a nick."

I laugh when she can't. Never comes when you want it to. The laughter won't screw off. I scramble for the Z valve inside. It ain't there. The laughs turn to sobs. Till I'm bawling like a softfoot waking first night in his bunk to find his ass gettin' torn up by a line of leatherneck triarii, fresh in from killing Moonies.

I crank and crank on the Z valve.

Volga'll be dead by now. Dead like the Scarhunters I trained. Rest of my freelance team's toe tags—Cyra, that greedy idiot, Dano, poor pickpocket kid I made into a real operator.

Dead by association.

Fuck me.

Where's *my* fucking ring? Takes me a while to realize I'm shouting it. I thrash against the restraints.

When the tears dry up enough for me to actually see, the girl's gone. The boy's replaced her. So he's alive. Well, that feels . . . good. Got a nasty scar that's gonna take some healing from his right eye to his left jaw. I crack a smile that splits my dry lips. "Hey, kid."

"Tinman." He dangles my engagement ring on the end of a chain. "Been watching out for it."

"Good lad. Give it here."

He doesn't. I spot the med-bank behind him. Look at all that dope. Bottles and canisters and packages. Oh my.

"Where are we?"

"Mars."

"Mars. Huh. So, kid. Need you to do old Tinman a favor. Got some joints need oilin'. Got a *condition,* you know. Hard life and all. Maybe zoladone? Might be some in the med-bank back there." He doesn't move. "Just a little panel to take the edge off. Liquid Z ain't kill-juice. That zombie shit's all *propaganda.* Helps me with my demons." He just watches. "Come on, now. Come onnnn. I ain't goin' nowhere."

"No."

"Little rich shit. Saved your ass from a pillaging. Get some Z. Don't do me like this. I'll eat your fucking heart." He steps back. "Come on. Hey." I try a smile. "Heyyyy. I didn't mean. Was a joke." My laugh comes out as a bark. "Gods, you're tight as Juno's cunt. We made a good *team* back there. But you gotta have my six. It'll calm me down. Had an operation, see? Please. Please, little man?"

"December sixteenth, 737 PCE."

"Huh?"

"Four *turmae necāre* of Legio XIII Dracones, the best of Flavinius's

Praetorians, were given orders by Aja au Grimmus to assassinate reformers in the government in a coordinated purge. One squad visited the Hysperia Gardens, an illegal house of torture. Before insertion, they were given their standard op-cocks. What they did not know was that their customary stimulants had been replaced with zoladone.

"Upon insertion, the killsquad received new orders that even Aja knew her prized dragoons would find . . . difficult. Freed from empathy by the zoladone, the dragoons followed their orders and butchered seventy-five men, women, and children guilty not of sedition, but of enduring a life of sexual torture, and possessing compromising information on loyal members of the ruling regime. Including Atalantia au Grimmus. Afterwards, the dragoons melted their victims with hydraxic acid. Even the children." I know this already. But the judgment of a child is a horrible thing. It was his race that gave the order. Not mine. "When Trigg ti Nakamura came off the zoladone high, Holiday found him with a gun in his mouth. She encouraged him to seek Ares to make up for the blood on his hands. This according to her testimony on . . ."

I thrash forward at him. Things that'd make an ironclad leatherneck with six rain badges turn her head and blink pour out of my mouth. Slides off Pax like he's on the Z himself.

"Do you want to live like a zombie, when they made him one?" He holds up the ring. "This ring belongs to Ephraim ti Horn. When he asks for it back, I'll give it to him."

"—gives you the right?" I snarl. "Spoiled little—"

"You asked for Z before you asked for Volga," he snaps. "But you risked your life for her? You're an addict, Tinman. If you refuse to hold yourself to account, I'll do it for you. Jove knows, you don't have anyone else."

I lie awake screaming at him long after his footsteps echo away. Soon I grow too tired. In the silence, memories of Trigg hunt me down. Volga soon joins. In the cacophony, I revert to all I know, and from my lips seeps the old footfuck creed veterans screamed into my face as we marched until it was drilled into our gray matter to replace human vertebrae with titanium chain links. I whisper as I fall asleep:

Chop 'em if they're taller.
Stomp 'em if they're smaller.
Mauler, brawler, legacy hauler,

smoke that crow, earn this holler.
Mauler, brawler, legacy hauler,
smoke that ant, pay off your collar.
Legio!
Aeterna!
Victrix!

One more time, you fuckin' dogs!

Mauler, brawler, legacy hauler . . .

22

EPHRAIM

Unshorn

I WAKE IN A LARGE four-poster. Light seeps through pale blue curtains. How long have I been out? There's an IV pumping saline into me. My stomach rumbles as I pull it out. The itch of the zoladone hunger has morphed from rabies-infected ragebeast to small dog. It pisses in the corner and squeaks out a bark. I ignore it, for now.

Kid visited, didn't he? Has my ring. Has Trigg's story. That uppity brat. Gods, my head aches.

Right leg itches too, like it's made of Venusian acid ants. I toss off the blankets to reveal my legs. The artificial muscles and sinew are now covered by a new growth of pale skin that mismatches with my darker left leg. It's fancy tech—well muscled already. Puckered pink flesh makes a knot on my mid-torso where Gorgo's rail slug passed through the Duke of Hands and then into me. More pink flesh makes a finger-long ridgeline on my forearm where it broke in the crash. I peek under my medical shorts.

Hello, oldboy. Glad you're still around.

I wiggle the toes. Nerves are already calibrated. No phantom pain, except a weird ache in my chest. Only get work this good if you got the patronage of a rich house. But I ain't rich. I ain't a crusader. So *qui solvente*? Who's paying? Where's Volga? Where am I?

I push open the curtains. The suite is expansive and fit for a brooding but secretly sensitive knight from a holoCan drama. Stone walls and floor. Expensive rugs. A hearth fit to dance in. A pair of fuzzy pink slippers sit by the bedside, along with an arctic bear cloak. Someone thinks they're hilarious.

I slip both on and go to a wooden door punctured by beams of sunlight. I'm blinded as I push it open. A wash of cool air whips in. I wrap the coat tighter and step out onto the terrace. Covered with spots of snow and topiaries, an expanse of stone pushes to a low stone balustrade covered thick with flowering vines of green and silver.

Beyond that is a sight to see.

In the first year of the Battle of Luna, my boys and I were hunting some Gold gladiator impresario when the building adjacent to ours was struck by a termite munition. When the dust cleared, a Gold woman stood in the ruins of her block empire. An arm missing from the elbow down, body fleeced of skin and all the blueprints underneath vivid as traffic arteries. She swayed there, tilting her chin upward at us. As if to say, "Witness my glory, peasants."

She bled out instead of accepting our help.

The ruins of the Martian city of Olympia remind me of that woman. Beautiful, regal, tough as a bare-fisted brawler, and pissed at the world for breaking her perfect nose. I watched on Luna as the Minotaur made his stand here against Sefi, holding out until the Reaper himself came with the bloody Seventh to wreak a path of hell all the way to the old seat of Bellona and send the Minotaur scurrying like a kicked puppy.

What a sight. What a city. But while the war moved on, Olympia didn't.

I know her cloud towers fell to become squatter havens west of the city. I can see their humps in the distance. The rest of the old Bellona capital spills against the northwestern lip of the Olympus Mons, and shimmies toward Loch Esmeralda in an hourglass shape. Each war-battered kilometer reflecting the architecture of six centuries of stately Bellona taste. And it is a fine taste, despite her broken skyline.

Only fascists should make cities. Demokrats never have a salient thesis.

Her air traffic is sparse. Cooking fires twirl from broken buildings. Land traffic congests the northern gates. Markets, overgrown grottoes, and old statue parks are filled with bonfires and vagrant tents. People live here, but not well.

I turn back toward my room and look up in awe. Eagle Rest, citadel of the fallen Bellona, yawns up the tallest mountain in the solar system. Libraries, government buildings, dancing halls, and villas ascend the winter mountain, held up by the wings of a dilapidated stone eagle.

What the hell is going on? Why am I here?

The old senses are triggered, and I feel someone inside my room. He's not trying to hide. I just didn't see him at first. I thought he was a sofa. One of the biggest men I've ever seen lies on a beast skin in front of my fire, roasting walnuts in the coals with his bare hands. If you can call those hands. The right one is huge and twisted like ginger roots.

"Do you see your fate in the bones, Grarnir?" he asks in a low, sibilant voice. He is bald, black-skinned like many tribes of Mars's North Pole, and incredibly fat. His eyes focus on the coals. I glance to the ajar door. "A man may run, but none has escaped his fate. Yet."

"Who are you?" I ask.

His eyes scour the room. "I see *his* fate. A young eagle's nest was this. To plume his feathers, he went away, and met the man around whom all fray. Now he lies in memory's cavern, head a blossom, heart judged by Saturn, on a cold stone floor he found an early autumn." He breaks a piping-hot walnut shell with his fingers and slurps out the meat as if sucking down an oyster. He is a living tattoo. Bright blue runes swirl across his face, down his bare arms in interlocking patterns. Seven ridiculous rings weigh down the fingers of his left hand with rubies and diamonds. There is nothing left of his ears except keloid-rimmed holes in his head. But what he lacks there, he compensates for with arcane eyebrows thick enough for dung beetles to disappear behind. Greased leather bags litter a scarlet scale belt underneath a glossy cloak of raven feathers.

A shaman.

I would see the freaks on occasion in the Block Wars, charging naked and high on God's Bread toward the enemy, with their engorged pricks out like a lance. They were always surrounded by insane spirit warriors called *skuggi*. As important to the warbands as the legionary eagle is for a legion. Maybe more so. After all, Grays don't believe in magic.

If he's here, skuggi will be outside that door. My prey instinct shrieks inside me. In full kit, I'd take the window. But I'm wearing slippers and bear fur, so I sit beside him as he gestures. I'm smaller next to his mass than a nine-year-old Gray is to me.

"Your fate is not in these bones, Grarnir." He gestures toward the coals.

There's bones amongst them. Marrow seeps out of fissures as they heat and crack. Human bones. Is that an eye socket? I swallow. They hiss.

"The men that came for you," he says.

"Syndicate?"

He nods. "Price on your head so big, they lost theirs." He chuckles. "Freihild and the skuggi castrated them and, once they spoke their truths, fed them to the sky queens to make them strong. They had much fun." Marrow bubbles and trickles down what looks like a femur. The shaman leans toward it, so close his eyebrows begin to curl. "I have seen your fate in bones, Grarnir. Sometimes gods speak, but you never know which one. Some play more tricks than others."

"Name's Ephraim, oldboy."

The eyes slide in his huge head to look sideways at me. He chuckles again. "Shhhhh. He comes. He likes fear. Show none. Perhaps his wrath will not come undone."

"Who?"

He submerges his whole left hand in the coals, reaching around as if rummaging through a backpack, and pulls out a steaming walnut. This he rips open and shows me the bronzed meat.

"Unshorn."

I stand up in sudden panic, almost losing my balance on the untested new leg. It's got some thrust. "*Valdir* the Unshorn?"

"Be wise, Grarnir. The Queen's concubine has much power. Little leash."

I look for somewhere to hide. I hear boots. Heavy fucking boots. The candles on the wall shiver. A shadow moves in the hall outside the door. Torc rings make an unholy clatter, each taken and melted from the sigils of a fallen Gold. They don't even bother with Grays.

"Silly man. Your destiny is not out the window," the shaman says without looking up. "But find out for yourself if you must."

I glance down at him. No way he's fast enough to stop me.

"Nice to meet you, Mr. Shaman." I run out the terrace, my gait uneven on the new leg, my fur coat streaming behind me, and hurl myself over the balustrade.

I grab two handfuls of vine and feel them sag under my weight. My feet dangle over a kilometer drop down the snowy cliffs. People always make such drama of heights. Still haven't met one worse than the Unshorn.

I climb down the sheer face of the parapet. High-altitude wind nips at me. My hands are already going numb. The vines are beginning to fray. A thick stone support column upholds this section of the castle. It too is covered with vines. I shimmy to the right and plant both feet on the stone and shove off, trusting the acrobatics that helped me become a legend of the underworld. Ephraim the Reptile. Ephraim the Climber. Ephraim the . . . oh shit.

I fly straight past the column.

My right leg is a freak. When I pushed off, it didn't push. It shot me like a bloody ballista. Three times as strong as the old one ever was. Two-comma tech. Maybe even three. I'm going to sail out into nothing—

I slam into solid stone. Another column! Ah that hurts. Fingers scramble on bare stone for a grip as I bounce off. I snag one as I fall. The vine begins to unravel. I plummet down, breath stuck in my chest until I come to an abrupt halt. Skin tears off the palm, but I hold on to the vine for dear life. My slippers drift off into the expanse below.

O blight my balls.

I've fallen past safe harbor, at the extreme west of the network of support columns. There's nothing beneath but jagged cliffs and twirling snow. My only salvation is to the left, toward the western edge of the foundation of Eagle Rest. It's more than twenty meters away. Not far enough down. I rock myself toward it. The vine sags. *Keep at it. Better than Unshorn.* I swing in a parabolic arc, not close enough yet. The vine begins to fray. *Hold on, vine.* I rock back into nothingness, sagging a little. Rock back toward the eagle wing, reach the zenith of the parabolic arc. And let go the vine. Gravity tugs. I fly feet-forward, body perfectly horizontal, and then jerk my shoulders back, pull my knees up, twirling into a flip. *Stick it, stick it, stick it . . .*

Jarring force shoots from my heels into the knees as I land barefoot on the stone. Haha! Then I slip on a patch of ice and twist sideways just before a fall that would mean certain death. I scramble to safety. Bloodied, freezing, and cackling, I glare at the drop and spit.

Now, time to descend the cliff face, get to the city, get some shoes, a ship, and get out of Dodge. Do I know anyone in Olympia? Hope not, Syndicate will have a price on my head.

Then I hear something in the wind. I look up at the sky. Nothing. I can't even tell which parapet was mine, I'm so far down. No one pursues.

See my fate in your bones now, shaman? Then the wind wails behind me. I turn around to face the city, cupping my eyes against the sun. It winks off the distant loch. Must have been . . .

Oh.

Jove.

On.

High.

Six monsters rise from beneath the edge of the stone eagle wing. Pale blue feathers. Wingspans of twenty meters. Huge birds of prey with bodies of feathered lions, wrapped in rune-laden pulseArmor.

Griffins.

I run, because what else do you do?

A missile of fur, feather, and muscle hits the stone in front of me. I sprawl backward. From amidst a cloud of spitting snow the biggest damn thing I've ever seen uncoils her white mass. I've seen the monster once before as it devoured Euripedes au Votum atop the Dome of Endymion. It is Godeater, the albino steed of the Obsidian Queen. But no one rides in its saddle.

The griffin's razor-scarred beak is the size of me. It opens to scream into my face as a mountain of a man lands in its shadow. My cilia wail. The man's armored boots are big. His tattooed arms like tree saplings, and ringed with gold torcs. His helmet is three times the size of a human head. Made from the skull of an African sand hydra, and plumed with green meter-long poison feathers of a Pacific archipelago jungle dragon. His pulseArmor is battered and white, shoulders set with the skulls of the Peerless warlords he killed with the man-sized greataxe strapped to his back.

The Reaper's greatest armored cavalry commander stomps toward me. The long valor tail of hair from which he gets his name falls down his back to his tailbone, sewn with trophies. I pick myself to my feet.

To his people: he is Big Brother.

To Golds: the Sky Bastard.

To everyone else: Valdir the Unshorn. Warlord and royal concubine of Sefi the Quiet.

"Well, this isn't where I parked my ship," I say up at him. Black eyes within the hollows of the hydra skull flick toward the mountain face and stone columns where I made my passage. "Have you seen it? Shiny, long, two swollen engines at the stern. Plenty of thrust." No reply. "Listen, I was working with the Sovereign. Your ally. Give her a call. I ain't saying I haven't made mistakes, just don't give me to Barca. I ain't earned that."

Now he looks back at me. *"Earned?"* The voice filters through the sonic chamber of the hydra, each decibel contorted.

"Well, I mean, I did go face down the whole Syndicate. Ask the kids. Either of them. I was pretty impressive."

"In the land of my mothers, those who steal children declare ashwar. A holy war against the spirit of tribe. So their covetous juntak are shorn from their bodies and cast into the fire, so their seed may not spread, but crackle pleasantly and share warmth with tribe. Children peck their eyes from their skulls with crow bones, so the nomen shall be at the mercy of the tribe from which they sought to steal. This is what you have earned."

"Crow bones?"

"Crow bones."

"Well, that sounds insidious. Lucky for me, we're in Republic territory. If you would just call the Sov—"

He shoots me point-blank in the chest with a tacNet. It knocks the wind out of me and contracts. He drags the line to Godeater's saddle and barks at the griffin. Riderless, it springs off the stone wing and into the winter air. Valdir flies beside it on gravBoots, keening a savage song. I'm dragged beneath as we climb back to Eagle Rest, pissed beyond all belief.

Last place I wanna die is Mars.

23

EPHRAIM

Queen

V ALDIR'S GOONS DUMP ME unceremoniously onto the gravel. The tacNet retracts, leaving patterns of duress on my skin. Griffins set down and Valkyrie women slip from the saddles. Male braves with red runes on their armor land beside them in steaming gravBoots. One of them kicks my ass until I stand to my bare feet. They ache from my failed escape and the cold. Did I fracture them when I landed? "Anyone got slippers?" I ask. None pay me any mind. "Fine. Socks will do. You got socks?"

"They do not like Grays, Grarnir. Especially the men. The braves were slaveknights in your legions, or gladiators, or worse." I turn toward the voice. Wrapped in his raven cloak, the shaman sits in the lap of a giant headless statue eating walnuts.

"Oh, you again."

He slides down from the statue and wobbles toward me. Valdir barks something in Nagal at him to the effect of "Try not to lose your idiot again, idiot." The shaman flaps his crow cloak at the warlord and covers his earholes.

"You got any more slippers?" I ask him, tightening the fur coat around me for the chill. "Lost the last pair."

"Only a fool gives a gift when the first is valued so little," he says. "I told you your destiny was not out the window. Now you suffer."

"Yeah, well. I'm Hyperionin. We're natural skeptics."

He tilts his big head and laughs. "Maybe next time you are given something, you will value it." He flicks walnut shells at my right leg.

"*You* gave me this?"

"Idea, not money." He touches his chest. "Ozgard." He points at me. "Grarnir. It means—"

"Hold up. *You're* Ozgard?"

He grins. "Ozgard the Mad. Ozgard the Bad. Ozgard the Berryclad." He bows.

"You're not as blue as I expected."

"Berries only for when gods dance," he says, glancing at Valdir.

"When do they dance?" I ask.

He smiles. "When blood spills. Worry not. Today for talking only."

Near Godeater, Valdir has taken off his ridiculous helmet. The champion's face is unusually delicate for an Obsidian. His nose is twice broken, his cheeks gaunt and freckled. But all the savagery can't hide the avian structure of his bones, the motes of silver in his black irises, his full, notched lips, and the haughty grandeur of the only human besides Darrow to have survived a duel with the Minotaur.

Gotta admit. He's damn slick.

Valdir barks at Ozgard, this time motioning with his fingers, and we set off toward a large triumphal arch. The women lead and pay me no mind, but the trailing men catcall me and shove me with their axe hafts when I slow. The path ascends up the spine of the mountain. My raw right foot is yet without calluses and is agony on the stone. "What's this all about?" I ask Ozgard, panting a little for the elevation.

"You will see." He begins ticking off fingers as we walk. When he's reached his twelfth, I curse.

"By Juno's dilapidated tits . . ."

The path opens up to a damn impressive sight. Above Eagle Rest, the stone training squares of the Bellona *ludus* rib the mountainside, the highest disappearing into the clouds. Where once generations of genetically modified fascist knights trained in the arts of subjugation and extermination, now thousands of Obsidian youths practice calisthenics, climbing courses, and weapons training.

We make for a lower training square where a huge crowd of warriors and older students have gathered amongst broken statues. A lone crest of dirty-blond hair moves amongst the white manes. Two trios duel as teams on the training square. Electra, fighting in sync with her trio, is dismantling an Obsidian who must have her by fifty kilos. The lad looks as young as you can look while still having a full beard. It's coated in blood from a nose smashed flat. They wield traditional aurochs' femur practice staves. The opposing group seems to be trying to reach a large skull in the center of the training square while Electra's lot defend.

Valdir holds us up out of respect for the bout. The Obsidians murmur amongst themselves, unable to pass up a wager on bloodsport.

I've seen kids fight before. It's a bit like drunks fighting underwater. Electra's like that except switch out the water and put in an elastic rubber room, a human-sized needle, and flick it. Yet for all her mania, she fights as part of her group, switching opponents, using her own allies to guard her blind spots as she strikes. The instructor calls the fight when the last manboy of the opposing trio stumbles back from a stave to the temple that makes him all soupy. Electra doesn't pursue.

Electra and her wingwomen help the fallen up. All six bare their throats to the instructor, a lithe young Obsidian woman with a topknot and black skuggi runes on her face, and to another in the crowd before jogging to sit with other students around the square. The little demon, Electra, looks right at home. "Children of the tribe are hard," Ozgard murmurs to me. "Sent back to ice to learn our ways. Hunt many days. Fight with axe from six summers to death. Yet Valdir could not put boy and girl with children of tribe. Their spirits are those of wolves."

"Boy's all right. Girl's straight psycho. It's in the blood."

Ozgard makes a small sound of disagreement. "The lesson is called the Three Seasons. Do you know this?" I shake my head. "Three seasons of war exist. Wind, Fire, and Ash. Pride, possession, annihilation. Freihild—"

"The one who cut off all those Syndicate balls?"

"Yes." He gestures to the young instructor. "She gave secret order to attacker, sweep enemy from square, reach skull, or destroy enemy. Girl saw them advance for skull. Girl listened. She became ice, and the enemy wing in the end accepted it was her wing's skull. Ownership was respected. A balance found. This pleases the Queen."

I follow his eyes to a patch of grass spotted with snow. I've never seen Sefi the Quiet in person. She looks almost inanimate as she sits amongst her Valkyrie on the knoll. All legs and arms. No contained, kinetic violence like the Golds—who always seem a hair trigger away from atomic. Only a subdued, sleepy grandeur. Like one of the statues that surround the training square. Her shoulders are broad but bony under a fantastic high-collared white cloak with a blue fur collar. Her right hand is gloved.

A crown of what looks like ice sits on her head. She watches intensely as a new batch takes the square, sparing a long look for Valdir, who tilts his chin upward toward his mate.

Pax is amongst the new batch. I trace the monsters he's supposed to fight. It's not just the size difference that worries me for the more sensitive of the two Gold spawn. It's muscular development. Shy of puberty, Pax isn't yet the man he'll become. Though his bare calves do look more sculpted than's right for a boy, the Obsidians are already giants.

The three opponents take their places in a triangle and receive their order from Freihild. Pax's crew form together around their skull, not yet knowing their enemy's intent. Pax seems uninterested. "That's a trillion-credit skull you're about to let those goons crack," I say.

Ozgard examines me. "You care about boy. Warmth still in your stone heart. This is good."

"It's not a bloody marriage. He's just my meal ticket. But he ain't like the other one."

"No. She is better fighter. He is more dangerous human. I warned Queen. He will refuse lesson this time. Rage festers inside. Watch."

The Obsidians bellow a war challenge, which Ozgard says is a Season of Wind. Their intent is to sweep Pax's crew from the square to show their valor. As Pax's wingmen move to the center, he separates and stands on the very edge of the square. The three enemy don't chase him. They use their numbers to drive his wingmen back and off the square. Then all three come for Pax in a V. As soon as they are in striking range, Pax steps out. The veteran warriors watching howl in condemnation. Pax's enemies declare victory, and spurn his cowardice by turning their backs on him. He steps back into the square. Only Valdir smiles.

What follows is appalling.

Not the violence itself, but its tone of boredom and clinical cruelty. *Crack.* The sound of femur on skull rattles the training square. One of the Obsidians teeters sideways. The other two brutes wheel around to fight Pax. He silently deconstructs them. He's slower than Electra, and almost looks asleep, but every movement is like part of a dance. As if he's seen this all happen before, and must bore himself and mock the Obsidians by going through the motions. He doesn't need to, but he collapses the kneecap of one of the older boys and then cracks his skull with a sweep of the stave. As he spins out of the movement, I see his eyes were closed. The other brings his stave down in a diagonal downward strike at Pax's head. Pax falls flat on his back. The stave strikes the ground and shatters. Pax grabs the Obsidian's ankle, pulls himself between the Obsidian's legs, flips around him, ends up on the Obsidian's back, and brings his hand down on the Obsidian's neck. Somehow he grabbed a shard from the Obsidian's broken stave and buried it two fingers deep in his neck.

"Do not move," Pax says. "The bone is two millimeters from your carotid artery." The Obsidian's eyes widen; he goes very still. Pax slides from his back. The watching warriors are disgusted; not one has moved, not even the instructor. Pax turns to Sefi.

"You mock us?" Sefi asks in a quiet voice. "It was the Season of Wind, not Ash."

"Mock? No, Your Majesty. I understand the purpose is to instruct me in the old ways of the Obsidian." He points at Ozgard, somehow noticing his arrival. "Your shaman teaches the children of the Ice that war is the first language of all peoples, but not every war need be the last. As a child, I am to be impressed with your wisdom. As hostage, I am to be convinced by inclusion in your tribal rites that I am an ally. As ward, I am to impart this lesson upon my own people. To be friend of the Obsidians, who showed me their sacred rituals and treated me with respect. What a pity it is that there will be no Obsidians left."

The braves stand at this insult. Not rising to the insult himself, Valdir watches the reactions of his fellows with careful consideration. So he's a thinking monster. Rather handsome too, if you can get over the batwing ears.

"Gods forbid I insult your pride," Pax crows. "A wonder you have any left. If you still think war is a dialogue, allow me to remind you the Golds of the Core do not believe you are human beings. You are cattle. They created the Seasons of War so the tribes would be locked in eternal strife. They did not want their herd *culled*. They wanted it *honed* to better wage their wars.

"From the crib the children of Peerless Scarred are now raised to know one truth. War is not for pride or for land. War is for extermination. Valdir the Unshorn knows this. He served beside Ragnar's father, Pale Horse, as a slaveknight in the Grimmus Legions, then beside my father and Ragnar, who put the razor in his hand. Many of your bloodbraves have seen this in their service. Never has it been more evident than upon Mercury, where my father faces atomic annihilation."

So the Red prick ended up back on Mercury. Must have been a Gold counterattack. Is he still a fugitive?

"But *you*. You scurrilous lot. You hide from that truth behind tradition. You abdicate oaths to feign wisdom. There is no wisdom in the company of deserters. There is only shame. You left your Morning Star to face your common enemy alone. But do not fret." His grin is the nasty sort I did not know he had in him. "It will be short-lived when the engines of doom kill my father and arrive on Mars to chase even the oathbreakers to their graves. Make no mistake, Sefi, Queen of the Obsidians, this is no war of Wind or Fire." He gestures to the dismantled Obsidian youth around him, with pity to the one holding the bone fragment in his neck. "This is a war of annihilation, and you are outmatched by the darker breed of my kind.

"I am the son of the Morning Star. The flesh and blood of the man who broke your chains. Yet you hold Electra and me as insurance and to bargain for ships and information. So I look upon you with my father's eyes to ask: what do your old ways say of honor?"

He drops the femur and walks out, leaving the Obsidians in stony silence.

"Damn, son." I scratch my leg, remembering what an idiot I was at his age. Electra rushes to catch up to Pax. Sefi watches them go, and signals their guards to follow. But the accusations Pax made remain in his wake. All is not well in the warbands of the Obsidian host. "Talk about a guilt trip."

"Yes, he is . . . precocious," Ozgard murmurs, clearly disagreeing with Pax. Oddly, Valdir does not. His eyes watch Pax with something like sorrow, and when he marches down to meet his Queen, it is as if the weight of ten worlds were on his shoulders. His anxiety evaporates only when he passes by the instructor Freihild. She takes pains not to meet his eyes. She *is* a pretty young thing. Lithe instead of muscular, without the hirsute appearance so common in her people. File that one away for later.

I am led down to Sefi. Despite just being dressed down by a prepubescent plutocrat, she is more impressive than her reputation. And it is a colossal reputation. Warlord, Gold killer, hero of the Rat War, sister of the demigod Ragnar Volarus, Queen of the Obsidians. She is not barbarically handsome like Valdir, or lively like Freihild. Instead she's a cold fusion between worlds. A horizontal iron bar punctures her nose at the bridge, even as a cochlear implant blinks in her ear. Astral runes mark the shaved sides of her head. A datapad is embedded in her left forearm. Her eyes are large black marbles, but in the right light show fibers of optic implants. A second set of blue eyes are tattooed on her eyelids. Fourteen long, heavy-knuckled fingers fold together in her lap, stroking her valor tail.

And then I see the weapon she wears. The inert blade of the razor that punched through Trigg's chest ten years ago is coiled around the long leather glove that reaches up to the elbow. The same blade that killed her brother, Ragnar. I blink like a dumb blacktooth addict. Thought Barca owned Aja's blade.

Valdir kneels before his mate and bares his throat before announcing me and stepping to the side. Sefi raises an eyebrow at my bloody feet and knees. "He is guest, Valdir."

"He dressed himself while falling out a window."

"Climbing gracefully," I correct. *"Njar ga hae, skati,"* I say to Sefi, baring my throat in respect and submission. Valdir is shocked I know any Nagal.

Sefi is not surprised. She accepts my respect with an open palm to show she holds no weapon against me. *"Njar ga hir, grár. Hir ganga ni hallr."* She nods to the White who stands behind her clutch of Valkyrie. "Xenophon said you knew our ways. *Fótr heill?*"

"Sorry? Nagal's a little rusty."

"Limb is healthy?"

"Seems like." I wiggle the appendage. "Surprised you sprung for fleshtech. Not cheap. Suppose I should thank you for that."

"It is a gift." She shrugs. "My court is large from long war. I welcome all. Including you, Scarhunter." She says the title fondly and tilts her head. "Your body wanted death. Your heart is not pure. It became silent three times. Narcotics weakness."

Valdir makes a sound of disgust and lies down on the ground beside his mate to comb his hair. He looks like a bloody Frankish painting.

"Valdir thinks you are stupid to use zoladone."

"He is stupid," Valdir says.

Sefi sets a hand on his shoulder. "He thinks that I am stupid to waste wind on you." She spares a smile for Ozgard. "But I know weakness in your kind does not mean broken. So tell me, why kill passions with zoladone?"

I glance at Aja's razor. "Makes life's flow a bit smoother."

"Poor little man," she mocks. "Life is meant to be felt. Else why live? Valleys make the mountains."

I nod to Ozgard, who has strayed back to the training square to examine the blood on the stone. "That fellow right there's high as a cloud. He seems to be living just fine."

"Fool's comparison. God's Bread fills warrior with heat of gods. Spirit Berry opens mind. Lets one hear Aesir. Zoladone makes warrior cold, narrows mind. Makes machine man. Vile."

"And Fever Cloud?" I ask. "Your berserkers love that."

Her face darkens. "Berserkers are no more. Fever is an evil I do not accept. It makes men savages. We are not savages." The only other Color on the knoll besides Obsidian is a lean White in midnight robes. It's a *logos*. I thought they were all killed by lynch mobs. Bald, childish of face, the White could be thirty or eighty years old. You never can tell. Their skin is the color of raw chicken. Their eyes the color of milk. A large diamond is embedded between the eyes to signify their class. If anyone's on a permanent zoladone high, it's that mammalian computer. I don't point out the hypocrisy.

"With Spirit Berry, Ozgard sees god's hand upon your shoulder," Sefi continues. "He is responsible for the breath you draw. You crashed in a scrapland. Scavengers found you. There were Brothers of the Ice amongst them. They are known to Ozgard and offered you to me."

Well, that's a turn. "And the wee warlords. Must have cost you a fortune to outbid the Sovereign."

"My respect was payment enough to them."

"Syndicate must have loved that."

"They attempted to substantiate their claim," the White says. "The Unshorn disabused them of that notion." Whatever malice Valdir Unshorn feels for Ozgard, he seems to trust the White. He nods to the advisor like an old friend.

"So if the kids are your hostages, and we're here . . ." I murmur.

"Wards," Sefi corrects.

"Sure. Then I take it to mean I'm not on Barca's menu . . ."

"Why would we fix you to kill you? That would waste money. You have not hurt Alltribe."

"I completely agree. But . . . ain't you allies with the Sovereign and

House Barca?" I've never heard of the term "Alltribe" before, but one thing at a time. "Hell, till that kid started talking, I thought you were still the Reaper's heavy air cav." By glancing around at the faces of her warriors, I can tell that's old news, but still raw, particularly for the males. World changes fast. Was it Wulfgar's death? Or something else? If they aren't allies, then my errand for the Sovereign has probably been perceived as a double cross. Which means Volga is likely dead back on Luna. I need zoladone. The ache inside nearly makes the knees buckle.

"So I'm thinking I'm alive for a reason," I say. "It ain't gratitude for this little boon. It ain't fidelity for an old Scarhunter. I've been thoroughly reminded what you lot do to thieves." I glance at Valdir. "So maybe tell me what this is all about."

Sefi surprises me by standing.

"Come, Mr. Horn. There is something I would like to show you."

Sefi leads me from the training *ludus* through hangars that once held Bellona warcraft. Within the stone caverns, a nation of people is set to one industry: knowledge. Obsidian youths labor beside old women, young men, war-tested braves, learning skills that ten years ago were forbidden to them under pain of liquidation. They study under Orange master mechanics, Blue navigators mapping astral trajectories and training in flight simulators. They work with Green coders, Yellow doctors, and Red builders. It is an odd sight.

Sefi says nothing as we walk, and by the time we end our little tour in another garden of broken Bellona statues, my head is full, my eyes are struggling to stay narrowed in contempt, and my bare feet ache like hell. Sefi gestures for me to sit at a long table set for two. Pale faces marked with black runes watch from the shadows of the garden. Skuggi. A chill goes down my spine as I sit. The spirit assassins. Valdir's eyes linger on them before he sits on the rubble of a statue.

The chair is a relief for my leg. A bowl of warm water filled with black flowers is brought for my feet by a stunning Pink servant. I sigh as I dip my feet in and feeling returns to them along with a peculiar tingling that must be from the flowers. Ozgard murmurs there is nightgaze in the water before wandering to the garden.

Night is coming. The sun ebbs in the sky. Battered Olympia sulks beneath Eagle Rest toward Loch Esmeralda like a centurion's wet cape and I sit with the queen.

"You're breaking with the Republic," I say, tightening my fur coat. "That's what you mean by Alltribe." She says nothing. "You already united Obsidians in war, promising them a homeland, didn't you? Looks like you found one." I glance down at Olympia, but Sefi's eyes are on the horizon beyond. That's trouble.

"On the ice, when a limb is sick, it is cut away to save the body. The Republic rots from inside with weakness, like you before we cured you. My people must prosper. This is the burden my brother set upon me. To prosper, we must become one tribe. So I will found a kingdom for my people, for all Obsidians."

"Volkland," her Valkyrie whisper, rattling their torcs at the holy word. I begin to laugh. First the Reds, now the coldbloods.

From his seat at the base of a statue, Valdir pulls his axe.

"He does not mock me, Valdir," Sefi says. "He mocks life. Is that not right, Mr. Horn?"

"Close enough. You're buying yourself another war."

"We know war," Valdir says in dismissal.

"With your old pal the Reaper?" I ask, causing him to stand up. "Ask Gold how fun that is."

"Valdir is a warrior. Honest and proud," Sefi says, waving her mate down. Valdir simmers in discontent, and I don't think it's just aimed at me. "He speaks truth, because he lives true. We know war. But it is not all we know or will know. Seven centuries, they say kill. So we kill. Seven centuries, they say send sons to stars. So we send sons. Republic says we are free. Then Senate says obey. Send sons *and* daughters to stars. Kill for us. Die for us.

"We ask only for homeland, they give rocky islands on Earth. We ask for city, because we are not savages who want to fish all day." She waves at Eagle Rest and Olympia. "They give broken ruins, and say be satisfied. What is there for us on Mercury? We cannot live under weight of sun. We are hated there. So now we say the word Ragnar taught us: *no.* Now we embrace the truth Morning Star taught us: *destiny is not given, destiny is taken.*"

So much for Sefi the Quiet.

I look for Ozgard. I wonder if it was this destiny he saw in the bones of a fire, as he claims to have seen mine. I find him climbing a tree toward an owl's nest. Fitting.

I sigh. "What do you need me to steal? Come on, you don't have to butter me up." Not feeling very masculine with my feet in the little bowl of water, I slap my leg. "Call in your debt."

Sefi remains quiet as the slender Pink now brings a bottle of wine. He shows her the seal to prove it has not been tampered with and pours it into three golden goblets. "Thank you, Amel," Sefi says.

The White *logos* steps forward to sip the wine, swishes it in its mouth, swallows, and nods as it detects no pathogens. Straight eerie *logos* shit. Even Arbiters like Oslo, my Ophion Guild contact, are wary of *logos*. They're null as a doll down below and on a permanent zoladone high. Only the richest Golds could afford them for trophies.

It seems Sefi collects rare creatures. And rare wine. She sniffs the wine in her goblet.

"What do you want me to steal?" I repeat as she takes a sip.

She looks both insulted and mildly amused by my tone. How long since anyone's had the guts to give her lip when she's got men like Valdir by the balls? "Of all the words in Common, do you know my favorite?" she asks.

Jove on high. "Destiny? Voluble? Captive audience?"

She leans forward. "*Practical.* Nagal is the superior language to Common. It conveys the soul better and has more beautiful words. *Weldschmer.* The pain in discovering the world fails to fulfill expectation. *Fenwehr.* The longing to be somewhere else. But we have no word for *practical.* Only honorable or shameful."

Her eyes look through me. "You are this way. I need practical men. As master mechanics teach our lame and weak, as Blues teach our small and bright, *you* will teach my skuggi." She makes a clicking sound, and Freihild, the instructor from the training, steps from the shadows of the garden along with several other skuggi.

They are all young, but none are beautiful like Freihild. Her face, though tattooed with subtle black markings, is unscarred. Her cheekbones are sharp, her eyes slanted and as close to dark blue as Obsidian black. All the skuggi are more slender than Valdir or the brutish Valkyrie, more like deer than elk. Freihild even has the eyelashes of a deer. Valdir notices too, don't you, boy?

"Teach them what exactly?" I ask. "I'm no assassin. They're the best."

"We are not," Freihild says in a slow, mocking voice. "The Howlers and Gorgon are the best. It is truth."

"Good thing you kept one of them as allies, eh?"

Freihild is amused.

"My skuggi are orphans from ruins of shattered tribes," Sefi says. "They promise their spirits to their Queen. Their loyalty is beyond the flesh, so their wombs are stripped, their seed made infertile by my shaman. But do you know why my skuggi are not the best?" She motions for Freihild to step back. "Not because we do not know how to walk with the silent shadow, or bring the long death, but because Howlers and Gorgons are more than assassins. My skuggi are not. They provide one solution: death. *Practical* creatures provide many solutions. For Red Hand death works. Skuggi have hunted them these last weeks. Six thousand they have killed for me. Red Hand flees. The Republic was too soft on them. Soon they will be no more. But I will need my skuggi to beat the Gorgons, to beat the Howlers if necessary. Teach them to be . . . freelancers. To melt into city. To exist behind enemy lines. To gain allies. To sow discord." She points a long finger of her gloved hand at me. "You stole the Sovereign's child. You will give us your knowledge."

If she wants a kingdom, she knows she'll have to play dirty like all the rest.

With a grunt, Valdir bursts to his feet and stalks away. Sefi watches him go with a strange expression. "My mate believes we are mistaken to leave the Reaper. He does not wish us to change or practice shameful arts. But he is just a man. Men are impulsive and blinded by the snake between their legs."

"Won't argue that." Then I say with narrowed eyes, "Skuggi are sacred to your people. Servants of Allmother Death, yes? Valdir won't be the only one pissed. Your braves know it might've been Gold that held the chain, but Gray *was* the chain. You hate us even more than you hate them."

She makes a dismissive motion.

"Your Majesty, I've seen berserkers rape wounded legionnaires on the battlefield as they scalp them. *Your* berserkers. I don't have any loyalty to the legion. But those Grays were my people. Gold might be scariest. You might be biggest. Red might be toughest. Gray . . . we got the longest memory."

The idea of teaching the skuggi to become even more effective makes me nauseous. This is selling my soul in a way I never considered.

"That world is past. Not all of the clans believe as I do. They resist change. But they follow strength. I am strength." Sefi runs a long finger over the rim of her wine cup. "You are cunning. You made fool of Lion-heart and the Fox Lords. I want that cunning. I know how this world works. I am willing to make you a very rich man."

"And if I say no?"

"You are guest. When safe, you will be free." Free to be tossed off a high cliff by Valdir, more like. "But a man on his own is nothing. You will be hunted by Syndicate, Julii, Lion, Republic . . . Goblin. You will be noman. No hearth. No blood. No *aeta*. No hands to carry your cold body to the sky when they find you."

"Cat's got nothing on me." I lean forward with a feline grin. "I got a thousand lives. They can each have one. Anyway, Mars is for suckers. I got business on Luna."

"You speak of your woman." Her eyes glimmer as I flinch. "Volga Fjorgan is on Luna no longer. *Xenophon.*"

The White steps forward. "Six weeks ago, two known members of the Horn Gang were abducted from Augustan property and are currently on Phobos, pending transfer to Mars."

I glance up at the twin moons moving over the city.

"Nah. Citadel is impenetrable. Place is crawling with heavies, tech even I've never seen. The Minotaur got chewed up with a full century of Peerless. Real Peerless . . ." I squint at them. They don't look like they are capable of bluffing. "Who?"

"The Julii," the White says.

"She doesn't have the skill set."

"But she has something better. Money," Sefi replies.

Xenophon explains. "Ignorant of Virginia's deal with you, she employed the freelancer known as the Figment to collect your gang members as leverage against you after frontal confrontation with the Sovereign promised to escalate."

"That psycho?" A chill goes through me, but it makes sense. Birds of a feather, and all that. I squint at Sefi. "You said two. Who's the extra?"

"The Red," Xenophon replies. "Your inside woman."

"Lyria? Lyria of bloodydamn Lagalos?" I can't even laugh. I thought she was a cooked little rabbit. I lean back over the railing, mind whirling like a rubicon wheel. *Get out, oldboy. Save your precious skin while you can.*

But this voice is quieter without the Z. Lyria of Lagalos and Volga Fjorgan, alive after all, and above Mars. What a thing. That settles it, even if I pretend it doesn't. Of course I have to throw a fit first, but I'd have had to agree anyway just to survive the meeting. Now I actually might stick around, till I get what I need.

"How do you know they're alive?" I ask. "If the Julii took them—"

A holo appears in Sefi's long hand. It is of a cell. Inside, Volga rocks back and forth. The poor girl. I see her smiling on race day in Hyperion. Laughing at the bar. Offering me a cocktail. She was just a kid when I pulled her in. I was all she had. But she didn't have me. Not really. I bite my tongue bloody so I don't belt out into tears. Without the Z valve, it's all so much. Her image flickers away.

The cold bitch Queen stares at me. "The Julii does not waste resources. I told her I would pay her for their release. If you pledge fealty to me, they are yours."

Don't do it, oldboy. She's gonna die bad. Dreamers all do. Don't you know?

But some greater, hungrier part of me scrambles after this new flicker of hope. *Volga, I'm gonna save you, Snowball. Treat you like the queen you are.*

"What's the Julii paying you for the kids?" I ask, trying to distract myself and them. "Gotta be a big nut."

"That is not your concern," Sefi says. "Your answer."

Time seems to thicken. I find myself nodding.

"No fealty," I say. "I'm no one's dog, and I'm sure as Hades not dying on Mars. You draw up a contract with Amani Guild specs—"

Xenophon produces a holodocument from a datapad and flicks it to the table. Sefi smiles. She knows who she's doing business with. Clever girl. I glance through it. It's Amani Guild specs all right, not some savage blood oath. Maybe the world is changing.

Sefi sips her wine as I eye the particulars. Three-year sunset clause. Contract void if I take zoladone. What is it with everyone? Recognition of skuggi deathmark on my life if I skip out. That's fun, and probable. I breeze to the remuneration and feel my toes tingle.

The girls in six weeks. A quarter kilo of grade-A diamonds in a Martian month, a ship with the deed, a signing bonus of twenty-five million credits. Fuck me. They're overpaying by a kilometer.

"I want the girls on signature."

"No," Xenophon says predictably. "You are a flight risk."

"Then double the monthly salary. A half kilo plus expenses. Gonna be killing my neutral reputation throwing my lot in with blackops spirit killers, and my girls need retirement money." The White begins to say no, but I cut it off. "Listen, milky. You're the one with the scarcity problem. Fixed my leg up. Spared me from the Howlers. You need me for something you can't do. And I'm betting it ain't just teaching skuggi." None of them react, but that's not saying much for these folk. "You can't move your army from Earth without showing your cards. I get it. But that means something's coming. You'll tell me when I need to know. That's fine. But I'm getting hazard pay, because I'm sure it's gonna be manic."

"You think highly of your talents, Mr. Horn," Sefi says. "Or very little of your life . . ."

"Now it's one kilo. Wanna go for two?"

I put my hand out for the kill.

Sefi's entourage tenses at the insult. Even gibbering blackteeth know Obsidian rules of contact. But then she surprises me. My hand disappears beneath her seven gloved fingers.

"To a fruitful endeavor," she says. "One more task. The Reaper's boy is fond of you. He resists us. Bring him close. We may need insurance."

"Sure, yeah, whatever."

I grin as she releases my hand. *I got you, Snowball. Just hold on and I got you.*

24

EPHRAIM

Skuggi

"**L**ISTEN UP, AND LISTEN GOOD," I say just like my tessarius did
half a life ago.

Two hundred black-eyed assassins watch me inside the empty hangar
with suspicion. Taken from the remnants of tribes shattered by Gold
after Sefi joined the Rising and formed into one of the most feared assassin groups in the war, they are all prime specimens, and not one of
this skuggi band is over thirty.

Some, like their leader, Freihild, are barely taller than I am. Others are
built like tree stumps, others taller even than Ragnar Volarus. Others
spindly and clever-faced. Each wears their bone-white hair in a topknot
and a pale blue sleeveless tunic with the Alltribe's winged crest tattooed
in black on either shoulder. Those will have to go.

"My name is Ephraim ti Horn, and I was once considered the third-
best freelancer in Hyperion, which means I was the third-best freelancer
alive. Two months ago, I became the best. Those rumors you've heard?
They're true. I stole the heir of the Reaper and the Sovereign, and the
hellspawn of the Goblin and Victra au Julii. And I stole them twice,
with nothing but a Red, a Green, and an Obsidian. Oh, and the second
time I did it solo."

They're skeptical. Good. They take their cues from Freihild, who
looks at me as I'd look at Volga trying to teach me how to use a coffee-
maker. I glance at Ozgard, who stands beside me nodding along as if I
spoke the greatest wisdom ever known. Since my fateful meeting with

Sefi, he's shadowed me like a somnolent ghost, eating walnuts, sleeping outside my door and sometimes in my room with absolutely zero understanding of personal space, private property, or hygiene. Somewhere in that time, he claims to be teaching Pax and Electra the ways of the Obsidian, but frankly I doubt it. I know drug addicts, and he smacks of one.

"Now, you lot have done some killing. You know that business. You've fallen in Rains, stormed breaches, killed Golds and a whole lot of people that looked just like me. You know asymmetrical warfare, direct action, and reconnaissance like the top of your bleached pubes. But your natural talents are not enough. Your Queen is of a mind that the world is changing, and you must change with it."

Freihild yawns. I jab a finger at her. "You. What's the best way to take out a killsquad of fully armored Gold?"

"When they stop to piss," she answers. There's laughter.

"Wrong. With a high-powered neodymium magnet."

"That would not kill them," she says.

"Killing ain't your mission anymore. Your queen wants a kingdom, so she needs operators focused on the mission, not the kill."

"EMP would be better," Freihild says.

"Wrong, moron!" I say, irritating her savage sensibilities. "Unless it's nuclear powered, you ain't gonna do shit to that new armor. You're two years late. If you're not reading mechanical specs, you're not doing your job. When was the last time you read a spec report, skuggi?"

Freihild doesn't answer.

"Thought so. *I* will teach you unconventional domestic warfare: Soc Legion spycraft, surveillance, countersurveillance, how to dance a laser grid, subvert security systems, foster insurrection on enemy soil, groom assets of every Color without beating them to a pulp, talk about anything for ten minutes, use neodymium magnets, hot-wire anything with an engine, manipulate anything with a prick or gash, and how to do it all without anyone knowing you were ever there. You will become ghost soldiers of the city jungle. You will not just become part of the underworld. You will own it. And I will make you appreciate the works of the Spanish Surrealists. Because they are the best artists the world ever conspired to create, and they are unappreciated by modern society. Are there any questions?"

They stare back blankly.

Ozgard clears his throat. "Ephraim."

"Yes, Ozgard?"

"Forgot to mention. Only half speak Common."

I close my eyes. "I hate you."

25

VIRGINIA

Oligarchs

"——Aɴᴅ ɪᴍᴍᴇᴅɪᴀᴛᴇ ᴄᴇssᴀᴛɪᴏɴ ᴏғ federal tax-shelter provisions for unionized labor, guilds, and other collectives deleterious to the will of the free market. This brings us to proposal six point three . . ."

Senator Britannia ag Krieg has period marks for eyes, and a widow's peak that could chip ice for my nightly bourbon. Chief negotiator for the Zenith Ring, the Silvers' common interest federation, Krieg stands in the center hollow of their halo table located within Sun Industries' Zenith Spire. Stained by city lights, the clouds form a carpet far beneath the spire. At fifteen unnecessary kilometers in height, it is the tallest building in all Hyperion, dwarfing the memory of the old Society military headquarters. Another apt metaphor for its creator as well as our time.

There are no senators present, save Britannia. The kept pets are sequestered downstairs, awaiting the orders of their true masters. Thirty-three Silver trillionaires of the Zenith Ring sip tea from Ionian porcelain in smug satisfaction that they don't visit the Sovereign, she visits them. Heralding from asteroids, planets, moons, and deepspace trade stations, they share only four common virtues: their Color, their religious conviction in their definition of the free market—not that they mind the government being their chief customer—their obsession with individual autonomy, and their determination to act, at all times, like complete assholes.

Not one of the oligarchs, save Quicksilver, was rich before the war. Now they represent the machine of war—Drachenjäger factories, shipyards, textiles, pharmaceuticals, rubber plants, shipping interests, silicon products. Without their companies, which I admit they *did* build against intense competition, we'd fight with sticks and stones.

Quicksilver, the lone quadrillionaire, doesn't bother sitting at a place of prestige. He's off to the far right of the asteroid-diamond table, sandwiched between a munitions supplier and the asteroid-mining magnate who donated the table and deducted it from his taxes.

The slump-shouldered, ham-fisted titan of industry doesn't look like the man who, along with Fitchner, engineered the destruction of the Society. He is more concerned with the sugar in his tea than Senator Krieg's outrageous demands. He knows he'll get what he wants, because I don't want to fight with sticks and stones, because I need their Silver votes, because without his helium, the ships he builds us will sputter and die.

Even the eerie silver orb robot that floats ever-present over his shoulder couldn't make him aware of my promise to Publius. If he knew, he'd be beating me in private with verbal uppercuts and haymakers. He has been an enigma of late. His demands increasingly peculiar and opaque. Which leads me to consider the possibility that he knows something I don't.

I interrupt Krieg's soliloquy to gesture behind her. "What the devil is that?" The artwork beyond the ring table is a fifteen-meter-tall vanity of unrefined metal morphed into a shape roughly mimicking a winged heel.

Britannia looks back at it in irritation. "That is the *Dawn of Hermes*. Sculpted from fused Oort Cloud dust by the Master Maker Glirastes of Mercury. The honorable Regulus ag Sun acquired it two years ago at an Ophion Guild auction for a record purchase price of ninety-four billion credits."

Roughly the cost of two destroyers, or enough food to feed the Cimmerian assimilation camps for forty-six and a half months.

The industrialists clatter their teaspoons on their teacups in salute.

Krieg continues her ransom demands. It is not the first time I've wished for her to be infected by the agonizing intrusion of a parasitic organism. I should have introduced her to my brother when I had the chance. By the sound of Nakamura's shifting armor behind me, I can tell she agrees.

A middling account executive for silicon goods before the Rising,

Senator Krieg made her fortune negotiating buyouts of liberated mines from Red clans for Sun Industries during Quicksilver's mad dash to buy up the majority of the h-3 market. What I released from my family's holdings to Reds, he purchased not two months later.

The Reds were properly represented by the White Guilds and chose gross proceeds instead of a one-time buyout. The contracts were thorough. It was all perfectly legal. But so is murder during wartime. Who possibly could have expected there to be no gross proceeds, because the immensely rich helium mines still, according to the books, operate at a net loss?

Me, namely. But the Reds, like everyone else in our Society, suspected I acted in self-interest and thus paid no heed to my warnings.

". . . resetting automation limits to their former levels, and concluding with an elimination of Senator Caraval's 'flesh and bone' quotas . . ." Her words devolve into a faint buzzing, and I yawn as she progresses to the last demands before finally reaching her denouement.

". . . an oral agreement will suffice for now, but amendments must be placed on the bill before the vote. Not all, naturally. We don't want to kill it, but certain provisions so that we can feel comfortable moving forward in good faith. These are our . . . recommendations."

The teacups tinkle, and the industrialists sit back in smug satisfaction to wait for my usual reluctant agreement. But I've been saving up my chips. I uncross my legs and put my boots up on the table. Quicksilver sees and tilts his head in interest. I extend a hand backward. Nakamura hands me my apple. I strip small pieces away with my bootknife and watch the Silvers as I eat.

Quicksilver chuckles to himself, and waits in good nature for me to conclude the show. They look so smug. And why not? They've always gotten what they want from me, because it was cheaper to agree with them than to teach them. And they are good at what they do—staggeringly efficient, inventive, ambitious, and productive. But ancient Celts didn't invent spurs because horses are obedient.

When the apple is little but core, I toss it on the table. I extend my hand back to Holiday again. She hands me earcaps. I insert them and reach back one last time. Now she hands me her anti-tank railrifle.

"My answer to your proposal."

Spitting an apple seed out of my mouth, I stand, shoulder the gun, take aim over the oligarchs, and fire a round into the *Dawn of Hermes*. They dive to the floor in terror. The magnetically propelled uranium round carves a trail of blue friction flames over their heads, setting the hair of Senator Krieg on fire, and hits the statue with the force of a *pilum* missile.

The oligarchs hold their wailing ears and peek out from behind the table. Smoke twirls through the hole blasted in the back of the room. The statue is in ruins. I admire the gun and toss it back to Nakamura.

I take off my earcaps to dead silence.

"You just bankrupted three insurance companies," Quicksilver says, stirring the dust into his tea before taking a sip.

One of the Silvers clutches his cravat and, ears deafened by the report of the gun, shrieks in angst.

"Apologies, Bartus," Quicksilver says. "I told you, you should have split the liability."

"The forty-nine-year-old human male is temporarily experiencing reduced auditory function of ninety percent," Quicksilver's sentinel robot explains.

"Oh. Remind me to tell him later."

"Yes, master."

Of the thirty-three industrialists, Quicksilver alone did not move. The moment the gun touched my hand, the air distorted around him, bending the flames away. Sound also seems not to have penetrated. Curious technology. Did it come from his Sentinel drone? I can't tell. It drifts above his head like a pendulum, emitting arcane high-pitched frequencies. Interesting. Holiday tracks it like a scout, no doubt wondering how best to kill it, and how many ways it could kill her. She better be using that sensor packet she brought. I like mysteries even less than bad breath.

It is time to address the room. "My goodmen," I repeat four times until I have their attention. "Today is not a day for extortion. Today is the day for patriots. You should ask what you can do for our distressed Republic. Instead you present it with demands. Instead of rallying votes to help your comrades, you jockey for gain." I look at Quicksilver. I asked for a private meeting, and he ambushed me with this, as I knew he would. For too long, he's been distracted, cantankerous, as if his coronation were on the horizon and all this was merely an inconvenience. He's working on something, some project even with all my spies I am unable to identify. We don't have time for pet projects. What hesitation I had is now gone. The deck must be reshuffled. I soften my tone for him. "There was a time when two men stood against tyranny. Fitchner au Barca and you. Where did that man go?"

He doesn't care to answer.

"Give them the recording, so I know they all heard me," I tell Nakamura.

I turn back to Quicksilver. "My answer to your extortion is no. My counteroffer is this: You have five seconds to tell your senators downstairs they will vote with me. Or . . ."

"Or what?" Quicksilver asks, as if I am still the aspiring politico he knew twelve years ago. I am not. She had better legs, but far less menace.

"Or I punish you in proportion to your ransom," I say. "You are being intractable for some inscrutable reason. So you will be spanked."

"Oh dear. How? Will you shoot more of my belongings? Have Sevro drop the ceiling and castrate Daedalus over there?"

A handsome young Silver caught digging in his ear regains his hearing at just the wrong time. He pales and looks at the ceiling. "What did *I* do? I make condensed proteins."

"Grow up, Virginia. These antics of your family have grown tiresome." Quicksilver jabs a finger into the table. "This is how the world works. Quid. Pro. Quo."

I nod to Nakamura.

She starts counting. "Five . . . four . . ."

"Ridiculous theatrics." Quicksilver strokes that Gold eyeball ring of his. "Matteo isn't even this dramatic."

"Three . . . two . . . one."

I walk toward the door.

"Remember, we built this Republic!" Quicksilver calls after me. "Us. Not you." His voice spikes sharply toward anger. "Virginia! Don't be a fool. Come back and be reasonable. You *need* us."

"That's what you fail to understand," I say at the door. "There's no scarcity principle at play here, goodman. You taught me better than anyone, where there's need, a Silver will always appear. Doesn't have to be you." I toss the earcaps across the room. They land in Quicksilver's teacup. "Your votes, goodmen. If not for the Republic, for yourselves."

I leave.

Holiday smiles as we enter my shuttle. "Did you enjoy that, ma'am?" she asks.

"Far too much."

"Will Sefi strike before the vote?"

"I doubt it. We've gained half the Silvers today, but in a month they'll all come begging." I look at my datapad and glower. "To Sunhall. Looks like the Goblin has made a new mess."

26

VIRGINIA

The Goblin's Prey

T HE CHIEF ASSASSIN OF the Syndicate is dead. The Duke of Heads'
cranium has replaced that of a neo-Rococo mermaid who endures
the unwanted attention of a particularly immoral agate satyr. The pool
beneath is brackish with blood. Scarlet frogs hop along the lip of the
fountain. I am thoroughly repulsed.

Bravo, Sevro. You've outdone yourself. Your wrath is *so* legendary.

In my private office off Sunhall in the Citadel, I chew the inside of my
cheek and cycle the hologram. Theodora's investigators sent it from the
North Hyperion mansion not ten minutes ago. With Daxo managing
the vote hunt, I have precious time to spare to search for evidence they
missed, just no time at all for my untouched dinner.

The arch-assassin for the Syndicate was a Gray man with a heavy
mustachio held together at the ends by two platinum bands. He had big
bones. And a strong neck, before it was severed by a razor. Amplifying
the image, I find minor imperfections in the cut. Sevro's razor. He's the
only Howler who uses a serrated blade. Doesn't make much difference
when the edge is so sharp, but he thinks it looks scarier. He's right.

Little else remains of the Duke's body. The carnivorous fish in the
pool below were as thorough as my tax collectors should be. All that
remains is his skeleton, and the hook that lowered him. What a waste of
a chance. If Sevro finds the Duke of Hands before I do and does this,
then I fear we will never find who is truly behind this.

Since he snuck onto this moon, Sevro has brought the horrors he learned on the front lines fighting the Fear Knight to the prime stream of the holoNet. I've managed to cover most of the massacres up, but some slip through.

To make matters worse, he's in lonewolf protocol. No contact until the mission is complete, until the Queen is dead. Damn Victra for setting him to this madness. It has netted him little more than eight hundred Syndicate thorns, seven narcotics-processing facilities, sixteen minor nobles, a duke, and a duchess, but no Queen. It has cost him far more. Three Howlers, three weeks of precious time, the attention of the Republic Warden, and a declaration of war by the Syndicate Queen.

Gruesome details flicker past: appendages nailed to walls, headless bodies sitting around an equally offensive topaz table, corpses in the atrium wearing glossy green armor. Emerald Orphans, by their markings. A freelancer company from Mars, consisting of elite ex-legion Grays. Mercenaries. A predictable but frustrating escalation.

Unable to stop him on her own, the Queen of the Syndicate has turned to the free market to rid herself of Victra's attack dog.

The highest-priced contract in the history of the war hangs over Sevro's head. It is sufficient to draw every bounty hunter, hitman, and freelancer in the Republic to Luna for the greatest private manhunt in a century.

A small economy has spawned from the underworld wagers on who will claim top prize. Sevro will not see it coming. Death will fall from a quiet man atop a skyscraper some kilometers away. A smart-slug or a DNA-seeking hunterkiller drone. And then my husband's best friend is gone.

He should be on Mars with Victra, or Mercury with Darrow, or working with me. Is revenge worth *that* much to you, Victra?

Gods, she pisses me off.

They underestimated the Queen. As did I, at first. She has training. Military-style organization and compartmentalization, safe-houses, heavy arms, an impressive network of spies, even several military-grade attack ships.

Theodora's women were thorough in their forensic investigation of the scene. I give up on finding exotic clues and deactivate the hologram. Here in a vestibule of my private sanctuary, the walls are covered with fragments of paper. Remnants of my childhood that Darrow thinks best burned. I keep them to remember what madness lurks within myself. To stay on the stiletto path, and realize what waits if I am tempted to wander off.

Within the frames on the wall of the vestibule are 311 puzzles, all that remains of those that my brother Adrius would make for me when we were children. I stare at them. Many are mazes, others complicated cryptograms or esoteric experiments. Each I solved. But I cannot solve this puzzle of who threatens my Republic. I gently stroke the leaves of the night lily at the base of the puzzles. Many more of the plants decorate the room. My office, like many of the rooms in the Citadel, contains defense mechanisms. Most are violent in nature. But some, like the escape tube concealed in the walls behind the puzzles, are only meant for retreat. I prefer the flowers, personally. The maids and staff know they are never to be touched, on pain of incarceration. They don't know why. The lily's necrotic needles quiver at my touch, but it was gentle enough to leave them docile. If one seized the plant, the needles would spring forward. The pain is said to be worse than amputation. The poison spreads slowly, but eventually death follows. Dangerous to keep around, but so incongruent with the rest of my personality that it seems a necessary last line of defense.

I cross my arms as I look at the puzzles. They all challenged me. My brother was clever. But once they are solved, they seem so simple.

Will I think the same when I unwind the Queen of the Syndicate?

When I discover why Quicksilver continues to stonewall?

I look around. Am I being played right this very moment?

A fire crackles in the hearth across the room, and I wonder if this isn't the beginning of my tragedy. If Victra fails in her clumsy gambit to retrieve my son, if no ships sail to Mars, will I reign for sixty more years in the shadow of their memories? An old woman in an empty castle?

Boots clack against the metal floor behind me, and I seal the vestibule of puzzles behind a security wall. "I just spit in the eye of my oldest ally, Nakamura. While the godfather of my son decorates my doorstep with corpses. I could really use some good news." I turn to face the centurion at the door. She wears a rare smile along with her black lion assault armor. In her arms is my white box. "She got him?"

"She got him. Lionguard is kitted and ready to roll."

I grab both her shoulders and kiss her straight on the mouth. She gawps at me and then laughs as I rush out the door. "Come, Centurion, the hunt's afoot."

Four stealth shuttles filled with Lionguard elite, a Sovereign, and a former Howler fly west as the blitz presses into its twenty-fourth hour. Beneath, Hyperion boils. Armored, with my precious white box in my lap, I watch the holoDisplays.

Dancer was right. Tempers have escalated.

On the Via Appenia, a human river of Vox march south toward Hero Center, united now with Lunese who fear war returning to their moon. Optimate supporters and my husband's zealots march west along the Via Triumphia. Riot police, energy barriers, and mechanized units descend to keep the peace.

Yet the demagogues keep pouring the fuel.

ArchImperator Zan stokes fear to swell the supporters of the Vox's radical wing. She pounds her pulpit, as enthusiastically as a frigid Blue can stirring up a frenzy of Lunese patriotism, claiming Atalantia will come to Luna and not a ship will be left to protect the moon. Vox Blackchains— lowColor civilian shock troops wearing chained necklaces—terrorize highColor neighborhoods, beat Silver businessmen, break windows, and intimidate local magistrates into begging senators to vote for Luna. Worried midColors flock to Dancer's moderation. He soothes them, his message carrying hope and notions of sacrifice. It is easy for them to feel noble. It isn't the children of Luna who die on Mercury.

Despite Publius the Incorruptible's public support for my cause, we have lost the Silvers and the vote is descending into madness. Back home on Mars, Reds burn effigies of Dancer, and march with slingBlades. The same crowds that sing the Forbidden Song wave lion icons and chant, "Lionheart! Reaper!" ArchGovernor Rollo gives a rousing screed that ends with "Treason might float on Luna, but not on Mars. Any senator that votes to kill the Free Legions and the Reaper of Mars better enjoy that bloodsucking moon, for if they come back, I'll pull their bloodydamn feet!"

Thunderous applause.

To make matters worse, it looks as though the Obsidians will vote against me. Sefi is playing too many games for her own good. Does she not know that every step she has taken since she departed Luna has been part of my design? I thought her wiser than that.

Amidst all this, a ray of light. Theodora has proven herself worthy of the second chance I gave her after she resorted to torturing Lyria of Lagalos against my orders.

We unload on the roof of the blacksite before the shuttles can set down. Leading the Lionguard ops team, Holiday jumps out like a kuon hound, her flinty eyes roving the shadows for signs of danger, her ambirifle packed with all sorts of Sun Industries mayhem. I land in gravBoots with a heavy *clomp*, tuck my white box under my arm, and head toward a door stamped with radiation warnings.

The blacksite is quiet. The lights dim. Behind two high-security doors, several of Theodora's Splinter operatives, deadly Pink assassins in next season's Hyperion couture, lounge incongruously atop mass-produced furniture, smoking burners with a famous Violet soprano of the Hyperion Opera. The soprano bursts to his feet upon my entrance. He's still wearing the costume of a Renaissance courtier: a rapier, a fur-trimmed night cloak, and a carnival mask that dangles from a string around his neck. I applaud as he sweeps up from his low bow.

"My Sovereign."

"Bravo, Basillicus. I heard your performance tonight was one for the ages. Both the aria and the fourth-act seduction. Would that I had seen it all."

"We all play our small part." His voice rings clear and thin. "And what a stage you gave us, my liege. Perhaps you will attend the Orphia again soon, when the days are less dire. Lucreto does so miss your patronage. Of our great benefactors, we see not even the Master Carver these days."

In fact, no one has seen Mickey for a month. I have my theories. Daxo's are hilarious.

"Perhaps," I say to the Splinter. "We all would be better for seeing beauty more often. Your service tonight will not be forgotten."

"Hail Reaper," he replies softly, pulling a small slingBlade necklace from beneath his cravat. He kisses the blade as though it were sacred. "We pray to the Vale and the Old Man who stands astride the Path that he and the Lost Legions will be delivered. We also pray for you."

"Save your prayers to gods and spirits, Basillicus. Humans made this mess. Humans will fix it."

The interrogation room is a soundproof white cube in the center of a dilapidated propaganda factory, the windows of which have been welded over. In the gloom, water slithers down hunched old machines to feed fungus growing on piles of plastic Ajas and toy *Vanguards*.

Two of Theodora's Green psychotechs sit in front of the interrogation cube's transparent data wall illuminated with neurological data from the prisoner inside.

"Theodora," I call as we cross the room. "You beautiful carnivorous flower. I'd kiss you, but it would fluster Nakamura. You're worth ten legions, you gem." My spymaster wears a long black citycloak. Her white hair is coiled atop her delicate head like a nesting albino snake. Eyes cold and lovely as rhodolite garnet sweep over us.

"Only two legions actually, but that was when I was sixteen." The smile of the shorter woman is slow and minor. A musk barely perceptible to even my senses lingers in the air. I feel a little nauseous. Hardly a coincidence.

"Do they know he's missing?" I ask.

"He snuck away for his deprivations. We probably have several hours before they know. But they may have taken precautions."

"And the leak?"

"Dripping."

"Nakamura, what are you doing?" I call.

She's crept closer to the interrogation cube. Theodora steps in her path and puts a delicate hand on her breastplate. "Easy, girl." Holiday pushes her to the side in her eagerness to draw even closer to the Duke of Hands, stopping only when Theodora breaks smelling salts under her nose. Holiday blinks out of her reverie and looks down to see her safety is off on her rifle. She clicks it back on.

"Sorry. I . . . what was that?"

"Pheromonal defense mechanisms," Theodora says.

"PDMs aren't that strong."

"His are." Theodora smears the smelling salt under Holiday's nose. "Should be lucid now. Do tell us if you start getting a little warm down between the thighs, dear."

A flush spreads across Holiday's cheeks. "I'm fuckin' fine."

Theodora turns back to me. "You were right for us to use salts. He's also trained in *psychesonics*. Even my Splinters had to wear earcaps to filter."

I sniff the air. "Smells like roses and poppyseed oil."

Theodora is impressed. "You can actually distinguish it? My, my. Would I love to take your nose on a walk through the forest."

"Yes, well, sewers are interesting. How did Ephraim manage against that man?" I ask. "Those pheromones would knock Darrow on his ass."

"Zoladone," Holiday says. "He was jacked to the gills for a decade."

"Of course. Conclusion on our breed hypothesis?"

"Custom hybrid, Eunomian embryo and either Priapian or Aenean sperm. Whichever it is, it made a Rose of a very dangerous strain." Theodora looks back at the cell with a contempt so gracefully articulated with her lips and eyes that it makes me feel as coordinated as a bow-legged colt. "Rarer even than mine. I believe he came from the Hysperia Gardens breeding tubes."

"Hysperia." Holiday's eyes go sour.

"You've heard of it?" I ask.

She nods. "Trigg and I were sent there on a Dracones kill detail once. We saw the death rooms. It was what made Trigg pull the trigger to seek Ares."

"I believe they were called pruning chambers," Theodora says.

"Atalantia was a patron," I say, examining the man. Could he serve her? Would he still? This whole charade doesn't fit Atlas. But even absent hard evidence linking Atalantia, it's certainly eccentric enough for someone who learned her trade in the silk viper pit that was Octavia's court. I knew Atalantia for a little over a year. She made even Daxo seem tame. "Octavia often worried her erotophonophilia spoke of greater character flaws—not that I can imagine anything worse than deriving sexual pleasure from executions. Aja despised her for it."

"And now the psycho has the Gold war machine." Holiday grunts. "Shame your brother's pet crashed her ship into Hysperia. Trigg and I had a date with the proprietors."

This Duke of Hands will have seen the worst of my kind. I feel no small amount of pity for that. But the two women standing with me are proof anyone can write their own destiny. I open my white box and head to the cube. "I'll conduct the extraction myself."

"You'll want the salts," Theodora says, glancing warily at the cylinders in the box.

"Please. This horse rides for only one man."

. . .

An hour later, pressurized air hisses as the door seals me inside again. The walls, ceiling, and floor are white, but there are no corners and no perceivable curvature. It is as if the slender man sits in a chair at a table suspended in nothingness.

Even with his pink hair lank and a bruise swallowing his left eye, the Duke of Hands is how I imagined Narcissus would look, mythic vanity made supple flesh and angular bone, so physically attractive he could drown himself in his own reflection and not pity his own death. Already his body will be adjusting to me, intuiting my predilections, beginning its assault on my sexual drive. But they didn't call my father a cold fish for nothing. Houses of the Conquering, especially mine, learned long ago the dangers an alluring Pink could pose to the young scions of their line. In reply to this one's pheromonal assault, my neurological defense systems activate. Deep in my medulla my chemoreceptor trigger zone detects the pheromones, interprets them as emetic agents, and relays stimuli to the integrative vomiting center, which nearly triggers emesis. It feels rather like radiation poisoning. Familiar.

Thank you, Father.

Swallowing the nausea, I peek around the table at the Duke's pink feather loafers. "Ridachi?"

He snorts in amusement. "Quite."

"Hummingbird?"

"Griffin."

I wag a finger at him. "The Valkyrie would have your rib cage."

"Oh dear, a pity you've none about. Word streetwise is that they've simply vanished. Like a carnival trick. That must set you on edge . . . my Sovereign."

Not quite. The words are true, verbatim to the ones he spoke when he first saw me an hour ago.

Incredible, the brain's consistency.

I've planned this meeting for some time, and prayed it would happen before Sevro found this chief prize. On the day my son disappeared, the master thief had already vanished into the city when my Lionguard arrived at his Endymion highrise, leaving only his blood behind. It'd been sprayed with an agent to destroy its DNA markers. Seeking him has been like catching smoke.

"When I was a child . . ." I begin.

"Oh Jove, a story."

I smile at the déjà vu. What a peculiar feeling this is. Does he not notice the ache at the back of his skull?

"—my father took me to visit the gens Votum. He was keen on impressing upon me the vagaries of gens Votum diplomacy. But I was a young girl and easily bored. I looked at Mercury and I did not see iron or political intrigue. I saw a strange, violent little planet with a Master Maker who carved desert mountains into wonders, and jungles so deep and dark you'd think you'd lost the sun and ended up on Pluto.

"I begged Father to let me see the jungles. Simply begged. Till at last even he could not do anything but send me off. It was a ridiculous procession. Votum botanists and scientists accompanied me and Lionguard and my father's politico, Pliny, into the heart of the jungle. There were many odd sights there, as you can imagine. But there was one that arrested me. One that reminds me of you.

"It was a scene I witnessed at dusk not far from our camp. I was watching a zebracore drink from the banks of a river when suddenly the jungle moved and a bush hydra struck from the treeline. It choked the zebracore to death and then unhinged its jaw to swallow it whole. I'd never seen anything like it. There it lay, perversely gorged and supine. Right there, on the bank of the river. Couldn't believe my eyes. But it gets better. As it digested its meal, a single sarissa ant discovered it. You know of them, of course. We found them in your highrise. Soon there were two ants. Then ten. Then a million floating like water across the jungle. And, as the hydra lay glutted on the ground, too full to escape, I watched them devour it till all that was left was a skeleton around another skeleton."

He's been excreting pheromones at a phenomenal rate. "Don't you think we'd be better without all those eyes watching us?" he purrs. His eyelashes flutter. "I wither under lights. Wouldn't you like to turn off the cameras?" he asks. "So much stress on those shoulders of yours. Wouldn't you like release?" His tongue wets his upper lip. "I can do that. You'll believe you've ascended into the clouds of Jupiter."

I lean forward, as if drawn to his magnetism, then squeeze his nose and make a farting sound.

His eyes go rancid. "Cold bitch."

"Waste of hair."

He sneers because my insult was better, and leans back. "They all say you're the brightest star in all the heavens, a face to make angels weep and a mind to make a shadow of the sun, but you're just withering meat like all the rest. Aren't you?" He sniffs. "I can smell the decay. Your tits already stretch and sag from childbearing, your mind murmurs of the madness that ate your psychotic brother and wanders to the fate of your marooned husband and your little boy, and slowly you begin to wonder if you're not a tragedy instead of a triumph." He laughs so sweetly you'd think he was massaging my feet. "I suppose those maladies give you allowance to make such opera out of your childhood." He bats his eyes and leans forward, mouth open seductively. "Honestly—"

"Do I look a hydra?" I finish for him. He pauses in confusion as I steal the words right out of his mouth. I keep going with what he's going to say, because he said it just forty minutes ago. Not that he remembers it. "My bones are brittle as porcelain. My nerves tender and tight. Why, with one swat of your hand, you could shatter this frail anatomy. No. I am no hydra. I am the ant, and you are the fat snake who has swallowed what you cannot digest. And we surround you, devouring bite by bite by bite."

He's dumbstruck. Not understanding how I could possibly predict his little soliloquy. "Perhaps," I say in reply to myself. "Perhaps you are right. Time will tell. But insects have short life expectancy. So I guess time kills too. Tough metaphor for you."

He swallows, seeking confidence, some semblance of control. All my life, I've tamed myself to not frighten others. Sometimes it is fun to let the lion out.

"Have we met before?" he asks.

I lean forward. "Wouldn't you remember?"

He considers the question, his mind stumbling over the gaps I made in his memory. He shakes his head. The tweaks I made to the psycho-Spike implanted in the back of his skull have improved results drastically. Octavia was so close to perfection with her Pandemonium Chair. The device was stored in her Crescent Vault. It has the capacity to shift through and edit memories. But while the chair is a blunt-force instrument, my psychoSpikes are scalpels.

"You really look so thin on the holos," the Duke of Hands says, eyes tracing my legs, "but you must have me by fifty kilos for the chair to sag like that. The bone density *is* startling. I would ask if it is hard to swim, but I suppose everything is proportionate. I wonder . . ." His eyes settle on my knuckles. "Could you shatter my skull with one punch?"

"Like a soft-boiled egg."

"It must be . . . intoxicating. Godlike." He admires it. He craves it. He knows he'll never have it. Like my brother with Father's love. I'd feel bad if I didn't know the dangerous pressure that puts on a naturally cruel soul. "But of course you do not notice." He licks his lips, nervously, off his game. He's gotten used to owning the conversation. "What do you think would happen if I were you and you were me? If I was given that warborn body of yours, and you were given this frail vessel of mine? Do you think you would have the courage to do as I have done? To wait behind a door, no older than fifteen, wondering who your master has sold your body to?"

He's said this before, but I let him say it again. No one should steal these words from him. It is immoral.

"And then to see them enter, and look at you like a meal without conscience or soul? Could you stomach it once? Twice? Satiating them. A thousand times watching yourself be devoured, feeling them throbbing inside of your body, violating the only possession you were given in this world until they shudder in ecstasy and at last withdraw and look at you with contempt. Are you that strong?"

"No," I continue his train of thought, now allowed to steal the very words that he said from our earlier conversation. For the speeches to be so similar, he must have rehearsed this meeting many times. "How could you ever sit where I sit now and face you down, never having been the stronger party in a fight? I daresay it would have broken you. But it did not break me. If I were given your body, your life, why, your hardest day would be a mean meal, and I"—I touch my chest—"would be king of all things."

He's given up confusion for horror. "Cat got your tongue?" I say with a toothy smile. "Now is where I offer you a reward for the Queen. You spit in my face. You tell me you need no trinkets, you've gained them yourself. You are not my whore. What you have, you've taken. What you want, you will take. You are a man, not a rat. And a man must have a code. But it seems we are two apes dancing around fire. Shall we poke the blaze? You want to ask about your little boy, don't you?"

His unspoken words from my mouth incite a frenzy in him. But I keep going, torturing him, making him tiny. "He's been raped and fed to dogs," I sneer. "Piece by piece. They started with the legs, and saved the eyes for last. Not even a twitch? Iceheart would have fit better. Don't you care about your son?"

Words have deserted him. He's trapped in a nightmare.

"Of course I care, but you don't have him," I say. "Someone far more dangerous, but far more predictable does." I glance at my datapad. Holiday has given the signal. Finally. The novelty was wearing off. Fidelity is confirmed. I have what I want.

"Bitch . . ." he hisses. "How are you in my head? What is this?"

"In part, this is me measuring the fidelity of your brain patterns and predictive behavior to help me develop an evolving technology. But more to the point, this is me killing time."

His pretty eyes narrow. "For what?"

Finally, the lights go out. "The Goblin of Mars."

27

VIRGINIA

Pack

"YOU HAVE TO PROTECT ME." The Duke strains on his handcuffs. I'll never get used to seeing the fear Sevro wakes in people. Deep down they know Darrow is operating on a framework of logic. No one, not even me, believes that Sevro is completely sane.

"How's the saying go?" I ask the Duke. "That's right. 'The Reaper may go through you, but the Goblin stays for seven courses.' "

"I'm a prisoner. I have rights. You can't let him butcher me. I don't have the little bastards! I'm a prisoner of the Republic. I have rights."

"I'll see if he agrees. Wait, please."

I disappear out the door as the Duke shivers in terror.

With the power cut, the warehouse is dark but for the lights around the small camp outside the interrogation cube. Theodora and Holiday sit at the table sharing tea and quietly debating whether the white sand beaches of South Pacifica or coastal vineyards of Thessalonica are more pleasant. I join them and kick my feet up. "Obviously South Pacifica. Impossible to get the stench of the Valii-Rath out of Thessalonica. Could you please pour me a cup, Centurion?"

"Sugar?"

"No, thank you."

"A little indulgence never hurt anyone," Theodora says. I raise an eyebrow toward the screaming Duke in his cube. "Well, except for him."

I sip the sugarless tea and scan the shadows, wondering if he's already there. "Sevro, stop wanking off in the shadows and come down." No response. "We have tea."

A shadow parts from the darkness amongst the rafters and lands in the center of the floor. The short, plump figure wears light-absorbent tactical gear and a lupine helmet with a snarled snout and feminine ears. It is severely damaged and torn in several places. The helmet slithers back into its catch to reveal a round face with flushed cheeks. Pebble's smile is awkward.

I tip my cup. " 'Lo, Mars."

" 'Lo, Minerva."

"How is Luna treating you these days?"

"Garbage detail, you know. Better than dead horses, I guess."

"Is Sevro joining us for tea or just going to skulk up in the rafters?"

"Boss?" she calls up. "Think it'd be rude at this point not to—"

"I hate tea," a synthesized voice growls from above. *"It's just coffee with piss instead of coffee."*

"He says—"

"He'll like this kind. I brewed it for him."

"She said you'll like this kind. She brewed it for you."

"Ask her what kind of tea it is."

"He wants to know what kind of tea it is."

"Wolfsbane, obviously."

"She says it's wolfsbane tea."

Silence. *"That's fucking hilarious."*

A second shadow parts from the ceiling and falls twenty meters to land with a thump beside Pebble. Covered head to toe in battered scarabSkin and weapons, my son's godfather stands to his full, unimpressive height. He swings his multiRifle around to his back, where it attaches to its magnetic holster. Though his fingers play with the hilt of his father's old razor. Never has trusted me fully.

He stops as he passes Theodora and fixes his helmet's eyes on her citycloak. *"Where's your wand, Merlin?"*

"Where's your wife, savage?" She eyes the scalps hanging from the hook on his utility belt, hardly impressed. "Vile. Have you gone full Ascomanni, my dear?"

"Please. The petty pirates copied me. Like Rollo with that goatee." Sevro raises two fingers twisted together in the crux and slumps into the chair I kick out for him, though he does take a diva's care not to rumple the rancid wolfcloak that hangs from his left shoulder. Holiday pours him a cup from a second thermos.

"You look ridiculous," I say. "Take off the helmet."

"Slag off. This is custom Cyther armor." The weird wolfhead regards the cup with crimson duroglass eyes. *"I drink coffee."*

I squint at the armor. "I knew it. You can't see color in that thing."

He pauses. Then the cracked snout and spiked ears ripple backward into their catch to reveal a pinched, cruel face, pitted by relics of childhood acne, and almost more feral than the helmet itself. His head is shaved but for a short warhawk with a zigzag running down the center of it. He squints at the cup, sniffs, and finds that it is indeed coffee, not tea.

"You think your tricks are so charming," he says. He picks up the cup, pretending he isn't desperate for his private stash of Jamaican Blue Mountain. "If I get even a slight bit dizzy, you get a tranq in the face from Min-Min."

Holiday snorts. "Like that ruster could hit the broad side of a Telemanus's ass." In mockery, she holds up her teacup by its handle. Half the teacup in her hand turns to powder as a silent rail slug passes through it and into the wall behind, striking it like a gong. Unimpressed, Holiday measures the remaining half of the cup and holds up the measurement to wherever Min-Min is as if the Red were a sloppy shot. Guess it gets boring on campaign.

Sevro mutters under his breath and nods to Holiday. "Holi."

"Sir."

He fails to find a wolfcloak on her shoulder. "You look lost."

She actually looks ashamed. For not going with Darrow? For sitting beside me instead of Sevro? I didn't spend time to think of that. Just because she's doing what she thinks is right doesn't mean she likes it. Whatever closeness I feel to Holiday must pale in comparison with the intimacy of the pack. Ten years on four spheres. They're her home, and Sevro is the master of the house. No wonder a toga would sound so horrible. I feel suddenly like a presumptuous interloper.

"I was lost, Sevro. How was Venus?"

"Vacations, you know. Hopped around the islands, visited some old friends, warmed ourselves by a fire, then came home to an empty house. Speakin' of fire. How's the cooch rash?"

"Better than your face."

"Good, so you'll be bringing your kid-stealing ratfuck relation to me in no time. He's got a special reservation." He pats his scalp hook. "Yeah, you can get back to me with that answer, but I'm charging interest." He sips his coffee and glares at me. "So, 'Stang, you found the right bait to make yourself a wolf trap. Clever you."

"Well, you weren't answering my calls."

He barely shrugs.

"Didn't even have the courtesy of telling me you were on Luna. That's hardly the behavior I expected from my son's godfather."

"Was busy eating my way up the food chain." He rolls his head to crack his neck, uncomfortable with the stillness. "You talk with the apex asshole?"

I nod. "Before he made landfall."

"He woke the Storm Gods."

"He saved his army," I correct.

"So Mercurian lives don't count?" he asks.

"More to me than to you I imagine," I reply.

He shrugs. "Pebble always wanted to surf." He glances over his shoulder. "Didn't you, Pebble?"

"That was Thistle, sir."

"Who?"

Thistle was the Howler who betrayed them and joined my brother's Boneriders ten years before. That's how Sevro is. Betray him and you're purged from existence.

"The civilian toll was likely catastrophic," I say, "but go on and make jokes."

"Civilians." He snorts. "You haven't met many Mercurians lately. Mosquitoes, all of 'em. If Darrow wants to die, he couldn't pick a better planet to take with him. Those freaks actually like chains." He yawns. "Surprised. Thought if anyone could get him to come back for his boy, it'd be you."

"Oh, so we're making him a monster so you feel better," I reply. "I said: Pax is in danger, race back and rescue him because I'm not actually the most powerful person in the Republic. I need my husband. Boo hoo. Weak and helpless am I. Pax needs you." I look at Pebble. "And Darrow replied, 'Pax who?'"

Sevro just sits there.

"I didn't ask him to come back, you little diva. I agree with his decision. He's where he should be."

His eyes narrow. "You're a mother, how could—"

"Careful, Sevro. I've never questioned your love for your children. Do you *really* want to question mine?"

"He chose war over his boy. He's gone Iron Gold on us. Doesn't care about anything else," he drawls.

"And you want to pretend that was easy for him. I see. Does that soothe your conscience? It was a long ride back from Venus." He looks away. "Don't tell me you weren't eaten alive with guilt. Electra is one person. *One.* You chose her over ten million who'd die for you. Ten million you inspired. Who chanted your name. Who left their families behind to follow you." It's risky, but he needs this slap in the face. "What about your responsibilities? What about the families of the Free Legions? What about your oath to this Rep—"

"Fuck the Republic."

Behind him, Pebble looks at the floor. I thought so.

"Selfish jackass," Holiday snaps at him.

"Traitorous twat."

"Traitor? That's rich after Wulfgar."

"Accident." He looks at me. "He got in our way." He jerks his head back at Holiday. "Seriously, shut the fuck up. You don't even have a kid. We were your family. We put you back together after Trigg punched the ticket. And you didn't even have the balls to come with us to Venus. So teeth together and look crusty beside your new master, cuz we all know you're wet bread inside."

Theodora really doesn't like that.

"Sevro, dear. You haven't had your balls for ten years. You gave them to Victra as a bridal dowry. And let's not get started on how many times I've seen you cry. Wet bread indeed."

Sevro looks calmly over to me. "They know I hit women, right?"

"We're trying to save Darrow's life," I say. "We are trying to protect the future while you—"

"My girls are my future," he snaps. "They got a lot of life ahead of them. Only way they'll be safe is if I teach the Syndicate a lesson no one will ever forget. If you touch a Barca, you cease to exist."

"You are shortsighted, emotional, and in dereliction of duty, Imperator." I glare at Pebble, and at the shadows on the ceiling. "That goes for all of you." Pebble rocks from foot to foot. "You want me to butter you up? Say I understand? Give you a hug? Get over yourself, Sevro."

"Talk. Talk. Talk." Sevro spits on the table, getting my hand. The coffee does little to hide the halitosis he gets in the field. Gross. "Slag it. My balls are growing a beard." He pulls Tickler, a knife as long as a child's forearm, from his boot and sets it down on the table. "You got a duke that needs castrating. We got history, so I gave you a word. Bored now."

"You won't be castrating anyone," I say.

"Think you can stop me?" A grin slashes his face. "When was the last time you got your hooves bloody in a tussle, horsey? You're gonna need more than those forty rear-echelon Pixies on the roof and old Holi here to stop us. Maybe you got big bitch Daxo hiding in the wings? A horde of Lionguard waiting to pounce? You don't want to go full metal with me, not today."

"Don't insult your own intelligence by insulting mine," I reply. "If I wanted to put you in irons, I'd have activated a containment field and embedded gravity engines in the ground that would subject you to an ungodly quantity of G's that would knock all of you idiots unconscious in your fancy armor, Cyther-made or not. But I didn't because this is a family affair, and I fear further damage to your already questionable gray matter."

He doesn't trust me. "Winkle," he says into his com. "Sky? Still clear?" He grunts at the reply. "Keep an eye out. Daddy's going to carve a steak." He sets his coffee down and stands.

"You're not the only one who lost a child," I say. That makes him pause. "Yet you play this charade, knowing the pain I'm in. Knowing the fear I feel. I would never do this to you."

It's one of the first times I've seen pity in his eyes.

"Pax is safe. We got it under control. . . ."

"You have half the bounty hunters in the Republic after you," I say. "The Wardens are one step behind. You and my husband *killed* Wulfgar. He was their founder. Their war hero. Accident or not, they want blood." I put a hand on the table, minding the spit. "Sevro. Brother. What about this seems in control to you?"

That plays on his guilt and his insecurities. He doubts Victra's plan. His shoulders curve forward into the slump he always wore as a young man. Selfishly, I want him to choose to tell me. I need that choice from him so I don't resent him for the rest of my life.

"Sevro, where is my boy?" I ask one last time. His eyes are starting to go glassy. "I know this isn't your doing. You'd be with your daughters, not carving up my city. But you can choose to tell me." He swallows, looking for some escape. He wants to tell me, but he loves his wife more than his conscience.

"I wasn't here," he mutters. "I had Darrow's back till I had to have Victra's. You're third in line. So don't keep asking. We'll get Pax to you. That's an oath. But I gotta have my wife's back."

"So you won't tell me."

"Maybe I'd tell Mustang. But you ain't her. You're the Sovereign now. I finally get that. V's been telling me that for years. You're the Sovereign. Darrow's the Reaper. Everything else is second. Shit, I ain't even supposed to be talking to you."

"Yet you are."

He nods. "I'll catch hell for it. She thinks you're some sort of mind reader. Or that I'm a dumbass that'll spill the beans. Prolly true."

It hurts to see him like this. I want to be angry with him. In some ways I am. But this isn't his fault. Victra is to blame. Julii have always had cantankerous genes. There is no right or wrong for her, only hers and everyone else. I was hers. It was a warm place to be. But over time I alienated her as Virginia shrank and the Sovereign grew. Perhaps it was inevitable, a faultline between the consciences of our two clans that now has ripped open into a gulf. It may never mend. But Sevro is Sevro. I have to believe that. No matter what he does, he doesn't go cold like Victra and Darrow. This is breaking him apart. The horrid violence, the lowered head, the refusal to communicate—all remnants of his early survival mechanisms. Do we ever leave them behind?

I don't need him to betray Victra. I can't ask him for that. But I can relieve this burden from him, and maybe this gulf between us. Communication is our salvation.

"Sevro, I already know what she's doing."

"Naw." His eyes harden. "She said you'd say that. Try to pick me for intel." He hefts his knife. "Now stay real still. I don't want to poke any of you. But this needs doin'."

"He's never seen the Queen's face, Sevro," I say.

"We'll see about that."

He expects Holiday to rise up and block his path as he walks toward the cube, but she stays seated, as I ordered.

"I know why Victra went to Mars," I call after Sevro. He doesn't stop. "She's going to pay the ransom."

He stops short of the interrogation cube's door.

"Victra wouldn't go to Mars unless our children were there. And you wouldn't dare attack the Syndicate if they still had them. So they don't."

"Nice try. Ain't fallin' for it."

"That leaves us with four possibilities. A third party hired the Syndicate to steal the children and received them as planned. A fourth party intervened and has them, and the Syndicate's original plan and backer are out of luck. Or Ephraim sold the children to another buyer. Or he absconded with the children and is ransoming them."

Holiday emotes nothing.

Sevro turns his head a quarter of the way around.

"The last two are unlikely, judging by the fact we found Ephraim's right leg at the crash site. The first is unlikely because the Syndicate has put out a bounty on Ephraim, and made no ransom demands to me. So that leaves the second possibility. A fourth party has them."

Sevro turns all the way around. I feel a sudden swelling of excitement as I realize he won't betray Victra, but actually wants me to guess it right. He wants to come in from the cold. He doesn't want this division. But at the same time, he's afraid his wife is right. If I guess what they're doing, I'll bring a stop to it.

"Assuming that is correct, and taking into account Victra's actions, they have asked for a ransom from Victra instead of me. Wise. Victra is paying that ransom. It is a ransom she thinks I would not pay, otherwise why cut me out of the loop, considering my assets? She may be spiteful, but children are sacred to her. She'd never hurt me that way to teach me a lesson. She prefers knuckles to jaws.

"So, what do you two have that I don't have, and who is it valuable to? The list is appallingly small. Shipyards, ore haulers, tradeships, and hubs. Taking into consideration the curiously timed pilgrimage Sefi has taken to Earth—and the overabundance of evidence supporting her existence there—I know she is not on Earth. Nor is she with the Obsidian fleet heading opposite Mars's orbit toward the Belt under auspices of chasing Obsidian pirates. She is on Mars or still within the *Heart of Venus,* which she purchased through a shell company, awaiting Victra's ships and possible further aid in stealing Quicksilver's helium mines in Cimmeria." I lean forward. "That's aiding and abetting an attack on Mars."

Sevro has gone very still. His eyes flick to Pebble.

"Look at me," I say. "No one betrayed you. This is simply what I do."

The shame is apparent on his face, but he holds my gaze. "Sefi said she would kill Electra and Pax if we didn't get her the ore ships."

"You believe her?"

"Ragnar was my brother. But Sefi is . . . ice. If you interfere . . ."

"I don't intend to." He cocks his head. "Could we stop them getting the mines? Yes. But not without dire cost to the Ecliptic Guard and the Martian Legions. We will need all we have when Gold comes. Obsidian lost too many at Mercury—a planet they can't even live on. They are done with the offensive war, but if they have a stake on Mars, if they have a homeland . . . they'll defend it against the slavers.

"War has stretched us thin. We haven't had the money to rebuild Cimmeria. They will, from the helium they sell us. Helium we already buy from Quicksilver. We haven't the resources to divert to eliminating the Red Hand. Sefi will, with greater prejudice and focus than I could. Quicksilver has convinced the Zenith Ring they own the Republic. He's in need of a valuable lesson. And what does it cost us? Land and pride. Two things we can spare.

"The public will cry foul, but it will happen after the vote. Soon Atalantia will come. The Silvers will fall in line. Sefi will understand I allowed it when I withdraw all Republic forces as soon as they begin their assault. The first ambassadors she receives will be Darrow's brother, Kieran, and Kavax's wife, Niobe. They will have weight with her. They will offer a defensive military alliance with the Republic and secure a helium contract. Then we turn our eyes on Atalantia."

"Victra said . . . we thought you would never let it happen."

"Victra can be an idiot, and so can you. When can you say the same for me?" I wait. "I am sick and tired of everyone swimming around like drunk piranha because they assume I am toothless. Whether or not we save Darrow, atomic war is coming to the Republic. The time for disunity is over." Finally, I stand up and step toward him. "You are in a democracy, Barca. The people chose *me* as Sovereign. They chose *me* to lead. Until my term or life comes to an end, *I* am in command. If you want to abandon the Republic we built to play with your kids, fine. Slag off and wait for mushroom clouds. But if you want to be a part of it, get your head out of your ass, stop making my life difficult, and report for duty."

Clown falls from the ceiling to land beside his wife. Min-Min comes next. One by one, the Howlers separate from the shadows to join them on the floor until twenty-five of the hardest killers in a demokracy of eight billion stand looking at Sevro. Their demands are clear. Sevro picks his teeth with Tickler, tucks the blade away, and snaps to attention. The Howlers stomp their heels together.

"Imperator Barca and Howler First Cohort reporting for duty, ma'am."

"Good to have you back, Imperator," I say. "Your first order." I motion him forward and wipe salt under his nose, then place my datapad controller to the Duke's psychoSpike in his hands. "There is a terrorist in that interrogation cube. When I tell you, activate this program. Afterward, if he knows what color his eyes are without looking in a mirror, shoot him in the head. Can you perform this task, Imperator?"

Sevro raises an eyebrow at me. He knows I know he wants to torture the Duke for the Queen's location. He wants to express his doubts. But if I don't have his trust after what just went down, I'll never have it. I need to know now.

"Yes, ma'am."

He walks into the cube. I watch with the Howlers from outside. Theodora turns on the sound. The Duke is snorting in thin derision at Sevro.

"—think I'm afraid of you, mongrel? I've seen my Queen make eunuchs with her kuon hounds. I've seen her kill a room full of Endymion heavies with nothing but a hatchet. I've seen her melt babies in acid. I'll never tell you where she is."

Sevro squints at the neurolink and activates the program.

The image of a masked woman in a crown fills the room. It ripples past, replaced by Gorgo, the Queen's right hand. A derelict tank-manufacturing plant blooms. More images of Syndicate facilities whiz past. Sevro goes very still when the face of an old friend appears in the images. Dancer. At first he must think it some mistake. Then more holograms of the man appear in the Duke's memory. Sevro looks at me through the glass with a dead look in his eyes.

"Boyo, I think you already did tell us," Sevro whispers.

The Duke stares in horror at his memories given holographic form. He begins to scream at what he's done, not understanding, not knowing how we have secrets he would have died to protect. Then the program moves to its second phase. The psychoSpike on the back of his skull glows. The Duke goes rigid. His eyes blank. The veins of his neck stand out. In five seconds it is all over. He slumps in the chair, breathing heavily. When he looks up, he is not the same man. Gone is the agony. Gone are the inflections of sexuality. He is purged of himself. Sevro is even taken aback. Theodora smiles over at me.

"What color are your eyes?" Sevro asks. The man who was the Duke of Hands stares at Sevro in confused terror. "What color are your eyes, asshole?" The Duke touches his eyes. For a moment, I think I miscalculated and I've wiped his verbal functions. Then he stammers an answer.

"I . . . I don't know." He looks at Sevro's eyes and gives the logical answer. "Red?"

Sevro looks wide-eyed back at us through the cube. "Whoa." He turns back to the man who was the Duke. "Do you know who I am? What's my name?"

The man shakes his head, terrified of the armored beast in front of him. Who wouldn't be?

"What did you do?" Pebble asks me.

"Octavia was a paranoid autarch. Fearing deception, she employed teams of Violet Carvers and Orange Master Makers to create biological esoterica and machines to divine truth.

"There is one that piqued my interest upon accessing her vault. It was the apogee of her devices, one called the Pandemonium Chair. A battering ram into the mind, so to speak. A crude one which I've been refining as a way of decompressing before bed." I gesture to my white box to show her the three thin spikes no longer than a Red's pinky. "I call them psychoSpikes. Far more elegant than the chair. Far more useful. Whatever was the Duke of Hands—memories, predilections, personality—is now erased. He is tabula rasa."

I hold up a small datachip. "That which was flesh is now silicon."

"By Jove . . ." Pebble whispers. "Is it permanent?"

"We will see."

The Howlers scoot closer to the cube. I tell Holiday to prepare to depart. "Theodora, your new recruit is ready. I advise a restart with the spike before uninstallation. No one should have to look at Sevro the moment they're born."

"I think the Duke of Hands will make a fine Splinter," she says with a smile. "With some tender love and care, he might even become as patriotic as you, my Sovereign."

"I am counting on it."

Inside the cube, the man who was the Duke is shaking like a leaf.

Sevro has his helmet up now to terrify him. Sevro circles and sees the small metal spike embedded at the base of the man's skull. He comes back around and crouches in front of the overwhelmed Pink, cackling with laughter.

"*Boyo, sorry to be the one to tell you this. But I think you just got skull-fucked.*"

He leaves the Duke there and stomps out of the interrogation tube. "How long have you known about Dancer?" he asks me.

"Less than an hour."

"And what does my Sovereign propose to do with the traitor?" he asks.

"Isn't it obvious?" I reply. "Communicate."

28

EPHRAIM

Karachi

THE SKUGGI AND I SQUANDER our first days together on basic language skills, which I off-load to Yellow linguists and datadrops. I rely on a translation insert for my ear so I can understand the coldbloods. They're not babies. Most, like Freihild, served a tour or two in the Free Legions. They know more than they let on. But hundreds of years of Golds culling the clever ones has taught them to hoard information behind masks of stupidity.

They play dumb or angry when they don't trust you.

And they don't trust me a lick.

Thought my deeds would get me some street cred. False hope. As Freihild is only too keen to impart: I violated the sanctity of one of their sacred heroes by filching the Reaper's brood. Pax is literally a godchild to them, Electra not far behind. No amount of Ozgard's support will gain their respect.

While the social element of my improvised training regimen flounders, the Obsidians are natural physical learners. Like Volga, they learn the tricks of my trade as fast as children picking up a new sport. By week's end, they're destabilizing laser grids, dissecting thermal sensors, and picking locks. Some already knew laser grids from the legions, but their methods are outdated and grunt-slop. Still, you only have to show them something once. Telling them something, on the other hand, is like trying to push a whole handful of sand through an ear canal. You lose right about ninety percent of it.

Over the next weeks, my primal terror of being crushed underfoot diminishes and I settle into a comfortable routine. On occasion, Pax stops in from his own lessons to watch. He shakes his head one day when the thirtieth Obsidian in a row is unable to tell a lie to one of Sun Industries' first-generation lie detectors.

"Compared with modern Bloodhounds, this thing's as gullible as a nineteen-year-old farm boy with a concussion," I shout. "Most operatives rely on being inconspicuous. You will never be inconspicuous. You are very conspicuous. So you must be good liars. Next!"

As the next skuggi ambles up to try their hand, I slump over to Pax.

"Go on, I know you want to correct me, halfbreed," I say, plopping down beside him on a low wall. His chin sports a fresh bruise from Valdir's martial lessons. No wonder he's not warming to them.

"Actually I was coming to say thank you," he says.

"For what?"

"Sefi's started letting me use the garage at night. There's an old two-seater gravBike they found in one of the old depots. Looters didn't think it worth stealing. Used to belong to Karnus au Bellona. She's letting me take a crack at fixing it up. Spent all last night taking off the kill-spikes. Thought I had you to thank for it."

"Don't know what you're talking about."

I certainly do. After his brutal protest against Sefi's attempts at instruction and her command that I bring him close, I thought it best to do a little recon to see what thorn was under the little lord's saddle. Seems Sefi's personal Oranges have noted spanners and hyper-crooks missing from their stores. Considering the security in the household complex, there were few possible culprits.

A single night's stakeout provided the answer I suspected. Who was it skulking in the garage in the dead of night? Why, the Reaper's own— he'd slipped away from meditating in the tranquility gardens with Ozgard. When I visited the garden, Ozgard was deep in a trance trying to decipher the message in the veins of a leaf, and Pax was there beside him, a small bulge under his armpit, pretending to decipher the falling snow. I sneezed "bullshit" and went on my merry way. I think I saw him crack a smile. He likes me. Guess I'm a nice and cozy reminder of Hyperion amongst all the deranged giants.

"Sefi says you told her I needed a workplace."

"Can't you see I'm working?"

"Are you?"

"Shut up. Not my fault they're stubborn." I gesture to his chin. "Drop your guard?"

"Valdir might be a great warrior, but he is a bad teacher," he says. "He thinks that being louder makes him clearer. Ozgard, on the other hand, makes his lessons into games."

"Thought you didn't like his lessons either. Aren't they all just purposeless distractions from the oh-so-necessary war?"

He shrugs. "Prepubescent temper tantrum, though the thesis is true."

"So you haven't stabbed anyone lately?"

"No. Electra got territorial." He smiles. "Their complaints may be valid, but I suspect their solution is flawed, the timing dreadful for the Republic, and deleterious to existing internal class tensions regarding the matriarchal hierarchy. But there's little I can do but go along." He doesn't mention his parents, though I know they are always on his mind. "Electra is far more at home here than I am."

"Well, you got more on your mind. And more of a mind than old Hatchetface." Neither of us mentions Mercury. But that we're both thinking it creates some awkward tension. "So what's the curriculum?"

"Actually, everything about Obsidians except violence."

"So drinking, shagging, gambling, and eating." He watches me in amusement. "I miss anything?"

"*Spakr,*" he says. "In Nagal, quiet and wise are the same word. So if I say '*Mann ni spakr,*' it means that man is not quiet, and thus stupid and loud."

"Wait, you're saying it's Sefi the Wise?"

"To them."

"I was about to say, it's the worst moniker ever. All she does is talk about her Alltribe."

"She was silent for more than thirty years. You should try it. You might learn something."

"I liked you better when I was unconscious. Speaking of which, you got it?"

He pulls the thin chain around his neck to show me my engagement ring.

"Some asshole stuff to do to a man in withdrawal. Pretty fucked up, young man."

"I'm not as young as I look. Uncle Sevro used the stuff for a spell. Zoladone, I mean."

"Did he now?"

"The Rat War was hard on everyone. He's not really a Goblin. He's actually very sweet."

"I'll be sure to tell him that if he ever catches up to me."

Pax holds the ring, contemplating if it is time to give it back.

"Hold on to it for me," I say.

He tilts his head.

"Gotta be responsible to someone."

He grins.

"Now get. I gotta earn some liberty for two ladies." I hesitate. "Glad you like the garage."

"He makes his lessons into games!" he calls after me.

I mutter to myself as I walk back to the Obsidians just as a skuggi with a cleft lip tries to convince the Bloodhound that he lived on Pluto before he had pubic hair. The Green supervisors titter to themselves.

"Get out of here. You're worthless," I shout at them. They scurry away, making faces at one another in response to some subliminal communication between their cranial implants. "Anyone have a pack of Karachi cards?" The skuggi do not answer. "Come on, I know you're a bunch of gambling degenerates, even if your spirits are pure as snow. You." I point at Freihild. Today she wears ghastly jade earrings. "Gudkind."

"I am Freihild," she says, knowing I know her name.

"I am Gudkind," the man with the cleft lip says. I think it's a woman, actually. Nope, a man. He's got a beard. Wait, do some Obsidian women have beards?

"Freihild, girl, you look like you got shit out an aurochs." She doesn't. But the best thing that can be said about my new appointment is the vast potential for cursing at skuggi killers without fear of physical dismemberment. "Gimme your cards."

"No cards," she replies, unable to take that devilish gleam from her eye. I thought she'd make a fine liar. Turns out, she can't turn it off. She just always looks smug as a fox in a hen hutch.

"Liar. Fine. Whoever gives me cards first gets a pass on argot homework. And a hundred credits to gamble away down in Olympia."

Ten Obsidians rush forward. Freihild pulls out a pack too. "You sly minx. I knew you were lying. Go to the Bleeding Place and sit in the center for two thousand breaths." I look at the rest of them. "You do not lie to your tessarius, you sorry sacks of offal. Lying to your tessarius is akin to killing a baby." They do not react. Have they killed babies? "Akin to lying to Sefi! Do you understand?" They glower. "Akin to lying to Valdir." There, that's the right comparison. Freihild has not moved. "You deaf, brave?"

Her eyes widen a millimeter. "Gold spirits live in Bleeding Place."

I grin. "So I hear."

"I do not have shaman wards."

"Move. Your. Ass. And no tiny Red breaths. Obsidian breaths."

She slouches away. I grab a pack from another Obsidian and sit on the floor.

"Freihild."

"I am Gudkind." He points to the woman I just sent away. "That was Freihild, which you know. For all know Freihild, because she is deft in all things."

"Right. Fetch me Xenophon. He's in the war hall. Sorry, varHal." Gudkind breaks into a loping sprint. I smile to myself and look around into the 198 frightening faces who watch me as if I'm about to pull a snake out of my boot.

"Who's the best at Karachi here?"

"Freihild, for she is deft in all things, for she learned at the hip of Valdir the ways of the axe, and Screwface in the ways of cards."

So Freihild was Valdir's student. Scandalous.

I stare at the brave, utterly annoyed. "Jove on high. Who else?" I pick five from the ones with packs. "Everyone else, fall in, bear witness to slaughter. Come on, pack in." Unable to crowd together for fear of touching, they align themselves according to height. Stupid Golds and their cultural departments. Must have had a riot thinking that one up.

I shuffle the octagonal cards, throwing in a couple tricks that made Rising coldies croon. I deal them out. "They had a saying in the Free Leg: as easy as taking chit from a coldie." They've heard it before. "Now, I know you lot love your cards. Problem is you're not any good at it. The Whites believe Karachi is their game because they invented it to fit their skill set. That's why half of you are in for a quarter kilo of gold at the gambling dens down in the city. They count the cards in their heads, so they always know their chances and they bet accordingly. All their dealers do it. Simple statistical probability."

Xenophon pushes through the Obsidians, looking disheveled. His voice is flat. "I was in the middle of an audit on the assimilation camp—"

"You play Karachi, right, Xenophon?"

The *logos's* eyes lose their glaze and do a little dance. "It's a little early, no?"

"Education has no schedule."

"Then let yours begin." The *logos* doffs a fine midnight coat, pools their midnight robes, and sits cross-legged. A coin-file appears in their hand and they push the release, spilling gold stamped with stars on the floor. "Deal me in. If you dare."

"So that's how we get your blood moving. Comets are low. No third draw. Five limit." I deal the cards. Forty minutes later, I own Xenophon's coat and coins, seventeen Obsidian warrior torcs, fourteen sets of earrings, and a custom pulseFist carved to look like a dragon's mouth. "Can anyone tell me what just happened?" I ask them.

"Bald robbery," Xenophon says in his customary drone. The *logos* shivers, missing the jacket as wind comes off the mountain. It's the first time I've noticed how thin Xenophon is. Built almost like a salamander.

"I only won two hands of seven," I say. "You won three. Why do I have all the chit?"

"Because you cheated on the last hand. I imagine there is a card-shooter on your wrist." I pull back my sleeves to reveal no card-shooter. "Then an ambideck." The *logos* takes a card in hand and bends it in half. No permutation of pixels in the card surfaces.

"Xenophon played cards. You played Xenophon," Freihild says with an apologetic smile for the *logos.*

I look up at the pretty Obsidian. "The ghosts didn't get you, I see."

I glance at Pax, who watches from a low wall. I saw him follow Freihild. Boy just can't stand staying out of other people's business. Or maybe he's just gathering his own intel. Mother rubbed off on him, I see.

"Freihild."

"*Ja?*"

"You're still a liar. But you're right." Someone starts to say Freihild is deft in all things. "Yeah, yeah, shut up. You nailed it. I played Xenophon. And now you deserve to have your name remembered, Freihild, deft in some things." She looks loftily at the other skuggi. Gudkind gives her a powerful nod, like she just killed a foe. That means a compliment from me is worth something. So maybe I read them wrong. Maybe they don't distrust me down to my very marrow after all.

"Pinks are the best players of Karachi in the worlds, not Whites, not Coppers, not Reds," I say. "The only people that could hold a candle to them were those Gold snakes on the Palatine. Lies were their first musical instrument. But I've seen even the Fury herself lose a hundred billion credits to Quicksilver's Rose on a lone star bluff."

They guffaw. "A cunning foe like Atalantia would not lose to a Pink," Gudkind says, offended.

"She did," Xenophon confirms. "At the Aristotle Club. January eleventh, 732 PCE. Were you robbing the place, Mr. Horn?"

"Security, asshole. Not even I'd rob one of Atalantia's clubs." I look back to Gudkind. "So the Fury lost. How, you ask."

Gudkind blinks. "I did not ask anything."

"Rhetorical," Freihild says.

"Ah." He vaguely remembers the lesson.

"May I continue now?"

"*Ja.*" I wait for Gudkind to correct himself. "Yes."

"Rhetorical again. Mind the sarcasm," Freihild says. "It is all he speaks."

I continue. "Everything you need to know about Karachi can be found in the faces of the other players, in the breathing, the blinking, the talking, the silence, the deviation from any pattern. Obviously don't be a mule's tit and bet the bank on a minor star match, but if you got a lock on your opponent, you're on high street. Now you lot have the most paralyzed faces this side of a Silver's at a slave auction, but your body language gives you away." I jab a finger out. "Hammerhead over there started heaving like a thirty-year-old virgin soon as he got that major star run. Skeleton here got squinty when she tried to bluff with a lone high comet. Even Xenophon has a tic. You lot read the snow as kids, right?"

They nod.

"And the wind and beast droppings and whatever else was on your pole. Reading people is no different, but it is everything. It will tell you if you can bribe a person, intimidate, manipulate, bamboozle, befuddle, seduce. Killing is easier sometimes, but rarely better in the line of work you'll be doing. Killing removes an obstacle. And what are obstacles?"

"Potential assets," Freihild leads half the skuggi in answering.

"Exactly." I beam. "That is how the Sons of Ares toppled the greatest war machine that ever existed. That is how I kidnapped the Reaper's only son. *Hieg?*"

"Hieg," they echo. Some, including Freihild, touch their foreheads at the word *Reaper.*

"Now, the other Colors have practiced lying since birth. Bullshit is the vernacular of cities. Gudkind over there probably thinks whores actually like his Venusian earrings." They make huge guttural sounds. I flinch, thinking they're about to kill me. No. It's just two hundred Obsidian assassins laughing their asses off. A few of them take a knee and wipe their eyes. Right, no sexual mores here.

"Gudkind does love whores," Freihild says. "He is deft in many things, especially whores."

Gudkind nods. "I do. I am. It is no lie. They are such delight for my spirit."

"Well, everyone's got a hobby." I absently pat his arm. They freeze. I swallow and take my hand off him. Gudkind laughs and pats my shoulder.

"Indeed. A hobby! My hobby is whores!"

I manage to press on. "By the time I'm through with you, you'll be such lie detectors you'll never be able to go to another brothel without having an existential crisis." The word doesn't translate. "Without losing your . . . Pax! You still here?"

"Andi," he calls from the wall.

"Without losing your *andi.* Your spirit. Now . . ." I light a match. The wind blows it out. Freihild kneels and cups her hands to shelter the next match from the wind. Making progress here. I light two burners and flip her one, then Gudkind too for equality and all that. "Now . . . I don't wager physical pain will make a tick's prick of difference to you, so we'll put the pain where it counts. Today, we play Karachi until you are all poor as Reds or learn to read people just as well as snow. And to make sure it is real, you will each make real bets, backed by your war hoard. I know you're all bloody millionaires. Or were before you found Jewel Street down in the city. So break into groups of seven, and get started."

It is the fastest they've ever obeyed me. As they form into groups, I sense movement on a balcony in the war-wing of Griffinhold. Valdir stands flanked by his braves watching Freihild laughing as she forms up a group of skuggi for cards. They all seem to be competing for the chance to play against her. The look on Valdir's face is not one of anger, but something far more complicated.

Then his eyes flick to me, and his face betrays him again. He knows I saw how he looked at Freihild. Man might be used to everyone thinking he's a walking death god, but if Sefi saw him looking at the young skuggi like that, I'm not sure how long he'd be walking. Something about the Queen tells me she isn't exactly the sharing kind.

"Careful, Mr. Horn," Xenophon says as Valdir goes back inside. "If I have learned one thing, it is that Obsidians are predators who think they are prey. Never pit them against one another."

"Didn't dream of it."

"Good."

"Valdir seems to like you. Thought he was all about the Old Ways. You ain't exactly that."

Xenophon shivers from the cold. Out of pity, I return the midnight cloak. The *logos* nods in thanks. "I was a slave of Atlas au Raa since my graduation from the Menta. It was Valdir who found me in a . . . pitiable state. I have proven my worth to Sefi many times over, including against Peerless." The word sounds like a curse on those thin lips. "I also advocated she remain with Darrow."

"So whose idea was all this nonsense?" Alltribe and whatnot.

"The shaman's." Xenophon blinks very quickly, the same tic I spotted when they disliked the cards in their hand. "He also advocated for hiring you, against my advice. But I serve the Queen. As do you. And when her mind is made up, the only way is forward. Thank you for the cards. I look forward to analyzing the data." The White bows. "Until our next game."

What begins as an awkward, contrived hilarity soon becomes an actual lesson. As the Obsidians play, they act, guffaw, boast, and lie, not well, but by the end of the day of my poking and prodding, five or six could beat one or two lowlifes I knew on Luna. I partake in several games, and even let Freihild beat me on a hand so deep she wins back all I took during my demonstration. After that, going on 2200, I call it a day, and the braves tilt their chins up to me in respect as they pass.

"It is called skillgift," Freihild drawls to me. She's the last in the courtyard besides Pax. "Much was hidden from us by the Golds. Many of my people have had their war treasure lost to Reds and Grays. It is a dishonor to us. You give us a chance to reclaim honor with this skillgift.

This pleases my brothers and sisters. And me. Even Screwface would lose to you in cards, I believe."

"It's just a tool," I say. "Won't be protecting the Alltribe with a game of cards."

"I know." She lingers for a moment, appraising me. "My brothers and sisters do not trust you."

"Valdir seems to share that opinion."

She watches me, trying to understand what I mean. "I would be careful speaking of Valdir, even in respect. He is Big Brother. Our protector and pride. If he doubts you, it is because he senses weakness. He is protective of our Queen, as am I." She sticks a thumb in her chest. "My tribe was destroyed when Sefi joined the Rising. I had no people. Then Sefi gave me *vjr* again. Purpose. She gave us all purpose. You will not betray her."

"Is that a threat or a prophecy?"

"I do not believe in prophecy." She smiles. "I know it is Old Way. Spirits in Bleeding Place?" She makes a face. "Superstition enslaved my people. I pretend because I must. And because my Queen needs my faith. My tribe needs my faith. Tomorrow we will learn better. The next day, better still. We have much more to do for tribe."

Pax watches Freihild disappear inside the barracks and comes over to me. "She's sleeping with Valdir," he says. I squint at him. He taps his ears. "Their hearts beat faster when they're in the same room." He taps his nose. "And she has his scent today."

I light a burner. "Figured."

"Do you think Sefi has?" he asks.

"Not our war, little man. Where's the she-devil?"

"Probably playing with axes."

He looks lonely. I tousle his hair, surprising him. I do it harder till he swats at me. "You really are a good egg, aren't you?"

He straightens his hair. "Why'd you say that?"

"General comportment. And you haven't asked me to break you out of here."

"Could you?"

His bodyguard of six Valkyrie watches us from a portico. The biggest, Braga, spits toward me. "Rule number one, kid: always have insurance. You think I got you the garage so you could play with bikes?" He perks up. "What do you say we get wild drunk and I show you the schematics for a certain harness we'll be needing if things start to go south . . . You can even tell me some crazy stories about your old man if we have time."

He's wary of me. "I have work to do in the garage. Speeder's got a fuel cell leak."

"Then why'd you hang around here all day? Come on . . ."

He tilts his head. "I suppose I could multitask if you can picnic."

I grin. "Sounds like a plan, little man."

29

VIRGINIA

The Dust of Reverie

A PACHELBEL SINGS MOURNFULLY OUT the window as I sit on the edge of my son's bed in darkness. It smells like him: machine oil and pine nettles. His gizmos form a pile on a dark workbench at the far window, next to a shelf crammed with souvenirs my husband brought from his campaigns: hydra eggshells from Africa, sunpetals from Mercury, coral growth from the Thermic Sea. But no totems of war, as if my husband wanted to pretend he'd gone to explore instead of kill. Pax's clothes still hang in the closet. His shoes line the wall, laces still tied, the backs squished down.

One day he'll wear them again, but hopefully never learn to wear them properly.

Bring my son back to me, and I'll leave Luna, I pray. But who hears a prayer to no one? Not Victra. She believes only in the power of herself. I hope it is enough. It must be enough.

Out the gabled window, water laps against the stone stairs that lead down to the lake. Beyond the shadowed trees, the estate's Lionguard detail patrol, here only to protect Deanna, Darrow's mother. She hates Luna, but lingers here as if knowing Darrow will need her when he comes back. I turn over an enigmatic device I find under Pax's pillow. Something he built from the parts of six others. He had a meeting scheduled with Quicksilver to try to market it for his consumer products division. Was it for this? I activate its trigger and it emits a soft hum. I angle the concave projector toward myself and dip into a stream of opera. I tilt it away and the stream disappears. Elegant.

"He built that for you." I look up and see Deanna at the door. "He thought you could have your guards use it on you in all those meetings of yours."

"Always thinking of others." I set the device down on the bedside table. "It's a fly in amber," I say. "The rooms that remain. When your husband died, what did you do with his possessions?"

She leans against the doorframe. It tires her to stand too much these days. Barely over fifty, she's had a hard life. "Used what we could. Bartered the rest for rations. Darrow liked to eat." She searches my face. "I've spent enough time in the past, love. The dead need no tears. They don't rest easier for our vengeance, or our guilt." She shrugs. "They'd want us to live. And life's about the now and the future, eh? Dale gave me three wee ones to remember him by. I'm lucky at that. And they gave me more wee ones to love. And they're all still breathin', far as I know, so don't start wallowin' now. We got our family to save, hear?"

"I think you might be the only person alive who still scolds me," I say.

"That's because I'm the only one you still need to impress," she says with a grin. "Now off your ass, lass, the man's just landin' and he's gonna be mad as a piter at me."

Laughter comes from outside the house. The front door opens with a creak. An engine powers down. Shuffling footsteps come my way. Dancer limps with Deanna around the kitchen corner. His smile dies as soon as he sees me.

"Well, ain't this the dirtiest of traps," Dancer says. "Since when did you stoop to politics, Deanna?" He turns to leave, but Deanna blocks him.

"Don't be a bloodydamn idiot. Either of you. You've been like two bickering hands. It's embarrassing. Now sit. *Sit,*" she snaps. Grumbling, Dancer takes a seat across from me. Deanna shuffles to the stove and ladles out three bowls of beef stew. "I slaved over this for hours. By the time you're done eating, you will have come to an agreement. Or I'll be back here to paddle the shit out of your ears. Hear? Now I've got pants to patch. Can't have Pax coming back to holes in his knees as well as his family."

When Dancer found out from the media that Pax had gone with Victra on vacation to Mars, he was not pleased at missing a chance to say farewell to my son. He was as much a grandfather to the boy as Kavax was. A cruel ruse, but necessary to dispel his curiosity at Pax's sudden disappearance. We linger in awkward silence. I've always felt very much a slaver in the old Red's eyes. Guilty for my height, my health, and suddenly feeling foolish for the expense of my clothes.

Dressed in a scuffed brown jacket, leather boots, and drab gray pants, the resilient man makes no airs. In fact, he more resembles a Martian agriculturalist than the terrorist captain who became a senator who became a Tribune. He sits down to shovel stew in his mouth to get it over with. I join him. He pauses. "That third bowl isn't for Deanna, is it?" He looks around warily, focusing on the open window and the dark gardens outside. Pachelbel twitter in the trees.

"You're like a desiccated turd, old man." Dancer wheels about as Sevro parts from the shadows near the pantry. "Must be hard holding back a fleet all by your lonesome."

"Sevro. You are one stupid bastard."

"Says the pot to the kettle." Sevro sits on the counter, one leg dangling off.

Dancer glances to the hallway that leads to the front atrium. "I brought a cohort of Wardens. If they saw you here, at the scene of the crime . . ."

"Nah." Sevro draws Tickler from his boot and starts cutting his nails. "Those blue capes hate getting dirty almost as much as the Pixies wearing them."

"They're burning down the city chasing after you."

"Instead of chasing the Syndicate," Sevro replies. "Well done, them."

"In case you've forgotten, Wulfgar founded them. Just as you did the Howlers. This time they'll go for the kill."

"Then don't invite them in," I say, annoyed. "Sevro will behave."

"Virginia, now is not the time for the Sovereign to be sharing stew with fugitives. No matter who they are. Or how untouchable she thinks she is."

"A fugitive leads our best army," I remind him.

"Lass, don't false-equivocate. Mercury ain't Luna. This is supposed to be the heart of law and order. At current tally, that human right there is wanted for sixty-eight counts of homicide and a hundred more capital offenses, half of which are against the state." Sevro just stares at him. "I will not reduce my office to meeting with secret cabals. That is beneath us now. We are not the Sons of Ares. We are legitimate. I will act that way, even if you do not. . . ."

He heads for the door, wanting so hard to be legitimate.

"Pax and Electra didn't go with Victra to Mars. They were kidnapped by the Syndicate," I say. He freezes. "That's why Sevro has been on Luna. That's why he's in this room, amongst other reasons." Dancer blinks, processing, then exhales and slumps back into his seat in pain. I glance at Sevro. He watches Dancer without even a hint of affection.

"When?" Dancer asks.

"After Quicksilver's birthday."

"Sadly, I know the date." His lips make a tight line beneath his beard. "That explains a few . . . irregularities. So you and Darrow would have found out after Venus . . ." Sevro just watches, so I nod. "And he still went to Mercury."

"Apex asshole, right?" Sevro chimes.

"Please stop," I say.

Dancer doesn't let it go either. "Going back to his men is one of the only good and true things he's done in the last year, Sevro. Which is more than I can say for you." Dancer glares and looks down the hall to the sitting room. His eyes linger on the hearth where Deanna knits. It broke my heart, but not my expectations, that some Reds saw my boy as a perversion. Dancer never did, no matter what he thinks of me. He would sit with Pax on his knee by the fire, smoking his pipe as my boy slept. Did it right up to the age where he'd be the one to fall asleep, and Pax would put the pipe out for him, and tuck a blanket under his grizzled chin. Dancer is thinking of the passage of time. How many years ago that was, and wondering where they all went. I know because the same thought monopolizes so many of my own hours.

"So. Tell me. How badly are you compromised?" he asks.

"I'm not the one who is compromised," I say. He frowns as I pull the datadrop from my pocket. "I've long suspected that the Syndicate Queen was working for or in conjunction with another party—possibly one within our government. Thanks to Theodora, and a new method of interrogation, I've uncovered evidence."

"You know who she is?" he asks warily.

"No. Unfortunately, she doesn't even trust her Dukes with that information. But . . . there have been revelations."

"Show him," Sevro says.

I tell the datadrop to play. Sevro scoots forward so he's within the three-dimensional perimeter of the holo. Memories are imperfect. They bleed into each other. We skitter through fragments of his life. The Duke is at the beach one moment, bending to pick something up. Then he is riding in a shuttle, speaking to his Queen; her face is obscured with a mask that writhes with what looks like locusts. It was too much to hope for a perfect look at her face, but I'll get one soon enough. We have her location. But first we will make sure our own house is in order.

Finally, a hotel suite expands around us, faded where the Duke of Hands' peripheral vision ends. The ceiling is the clearest, carved with cupids and forest creatures. Candles float, beneath the ceiling, dripping down wax. Heavy breathing comes from the memory. The sound of sheets clenched as the breath quickens to agonizing climax. Then a perspective distortion that makes the cupids grow larger than the closer candles. Spasmodic psychedelic light pixelates the cupids above, dissolving their bodies. They drift for what must be a minute, before racing back together. Focus pulses out, then in. Breath eases out, and a man's head rises upward, laying kisses on the Duke's chest until Dancer's face fills the memory as he closes his eyes to kiss the Duke on the mouth.

"It seems reveries are imperfect," I say. "Auditory recall is extremely flawed. So are actions. They reflect latent guilt and sometimes alter to seem more heroic. Faces, on the other hand, are almost never forgotten. The colors are often different depending upon the time extract, the mood more magnetic or colder. A brain is not a hardrive. The spaces between—that jump you noticed—are . . . Well, I guess no one has ever called them anything before. Let's name them fissures. The fissures are the time between the memories we retain. I've not had long to make a reconnaissance. Some span minutes, some weeks. Most reveries are laced with fissures. I only found this one because it was entirely intact. He cherished this memory, it seems. Unfortunately, a hologram is a poor means of communicating the memory; prime fidelity occurs from sympathetic shadowing." I tap my head. "Literally experiencing it. I assure you, it is quite strange."

"How?" Dancer asks, his face flushed a deep crimson. His outsized miner hands are squeezing the edge of the table. The wood is starting to splinter as he stares at the reverie.

"I have technology that maybe one, probably two others are familiar with, though not to my degree of sophistication, I don't think. But they're on Mercury."

"I meant how is that any of your bloodydamn business," he growls, looking at me like he's about to lunge forward and rip out my jugular. Sevro slips closer to my side, as surprised as I am by his venomous reaction. "You think you can blackmail me with this for my vote? Ruin me? Drag me in front of the branders like some poetic horror? I don't care if my people spit on me. If they say I should be gelded. If you rob away the only thing that matters to me. Slag you."

Even Sevro is rocked on his heels by the anger in Dancer's eyes.

I made a mistake.

The moment the video started to play, Dancer thought this was a shakedown. He's kept this secret his entire life, because the only people left in mankind to look at homosexuality as an aberration just happen to be his own. While the one that embraces fluidity is the one he's warred against for most of his life. The one that sculpted his culture as they saw fit.

Mine.

He thought I was threatening to expose his inner life.

Knowing he thought me that cruel is a jarring blow. Sevro is there to pick up the slack. "You really ain't got a clue," he mutters. "It ain't about that, boyo."

Dancer looks ready to kill. "Then. What. Is. It. About?"

"Just that the man you were . . . you know . . . playing hide the viper with is third in the line to the throne of the Syndicate. That's all, I swear."

Dancer goes sheet white. Anger vaporized in a snap of the fingers, replaced by sheer bafflement. His mouth opens and closes. *"What?"*

"The Syndicate . . . black coats, prostitution, child slavery, narcotics, hired murder, kidnapping . . . you know the lot. Sort of the worst people on the moon."

"That . . ." He looks at the datadrop. ". . . was the Duke of Hands?" He sits motionless. "Shit." He rocks his head back. "Shiiiiiit."

Sevro and I exchange a glance.

Dancer eases out a breath. "You two thought I knew. That I was his accomplice?"

"She didn't," Sevro says. "I did. Sorry." He backs away to the counter as if distance will erase the memory of Dancer wanting to rip his throat out. Forget malice or anger. All should beware the wrath of an offended soul. "She insisted we talk before . . . you know. So . . ."

"His name is Faustus. Or I thought it was. Found me in the park. You know I can't stand all these buildings. He told me he was a painter. Face like that, you'd believe anything. But I know the games. I don't keep intel at my home. Or talk in my sleep, even for someone like that." He nods to me. "Your father's agents were cruel teachers. We learned to be careful."

"Got sloppy, though, eh?" Sevro says. "He that good in the sack?"

Dancer doesn't speak for a moment. "Guess I thought I deserved something good. Was off and on for a couple months. I told him I wanted it to stay on. Then he disappeared." He plays with his knuckles. "Do you think I put Pax in jeopardy?"

"No," I say. "You didn't have our flight plan. He might not have wanted anything from you," I say. "It might just have been the association. I believe you were the fall man. Steal the children, release this to me. Or to the public."

"Bet your DNA is all over that little love crib," Sevro says. Dancer looks at him in irritation. "Hey, you did the deed. Syndicate probably took video too. All the good angles." We both look at him. "He literally fucked a terrorist. I can say what I want."

"What does the Syndicate want with the children?" Dancer asks.

"They don't have them." I tell him all I know, including how the Obsidian must have reached the downed shuttle before my men did. And Sefi's intended plan. When I have finished, he leans back and rubs his jaw. In the wake of the revelation, he's demure.

"Gods, letting them take the mines is a risk. What if they use blunt force?" he asks. "A storm on Mercury is one thing but warbands of Obsidian on Mars . . ."

"Sefi has seen what insurrections do to militaries. She won't alienate the populace."

"I hope not . . . but you're right about one thing. We need the Obsidian. You want me to convince the Reds of Cimmeria to get on with Sefi, I take it?"

"Not for free," I say. "I need you to convince the Reds to do it in return for Sefi giving them the share of the mine profits Quicksilver stole. It will be a partnership."

"And if I vote to let the Reaper die on Mercury, I won't be able to convince them of anything. The Reds of Mars will think I've become a Lunese."

"Correct."

"Question," Sevro says. "If Dancer's the Red herring then who do you think the Queen's partner is? Who are they trying to protect?"

It could only be one man.

"If Dancer was set up to fall, if Pax was meant to get leverage over me . . ." I say. "*Cui bono?* The most immediate effect is a power vacuum in the Forum. So it must be a senator. With my son out for ransom, I'd be compromised. So the Tribunes would vote for a new—"

"Daxo," Sevro sneers.

"Oh, shut up," I say.

He's put off. "If anyone is an insidious mastermind, it is that obelisk of a human. Octavia did want him alive."

"She's right," Dancer says. "Wouldn't be Daxo. Wouldn't be me if they released this. It'd be compromise. They'd need two-thirds vote. Vox would block Daxo. Optimates would block any Vox. It'd have to be someone both parties would agree on. Someone the public would accept. Someone . . . incorruptible."

"That gasbag?" Sevro says. "No way he's a criminal mastermind."

"Publius is allied with the Queen," I say.

I feel the certainty forming in me. Ten years ago Publius was no one. Just a public defender for lowColors. How did he rise so high so fast with no benefactors? No campaign donors? Is it so impossible to believe that someone came to him years ago and offered him the world if he would only answer the call when it came? Is it so impossible I could have been fooled by someone so close? No. I make mistakes all the time. And thinking of how he left Daxo's office, with that comment on the decor, I realize it wasn't an offhand remark from the mouth of babe. It was a taunt.

All his years of crafting that incorruptible reputation suddenly make sense. He's not going to vote with me. It's a trap. With the Silvers I lost, and no Coppers or followers of Publius, no fleet will sail.

"The vote is tomorrow," I say. "Even if we had evidence on him, it wouldn't matter. He's too popular. We take steps to gather evidence, isolate him. And, if he is indeed a collaborator with the Queen, with Atalantia"—Dancer's aspect darkens at that—"we will bring him down with all the proper and legal might of Moonhall. But for now, we must address the issue. The enemies of our Republic expect us to be divided. They found the faultlines between us, and they jammed a wedge in. We must stand together. Dancer, I need your trust, and I need your votes."

"You think Atalantia did this through the Queen?" he asks.

"Her or Atlas must have coordinated with her in some way. I don't know which, but it is a Gold hand holding the strings. They seek to turn us on one another."

Dancer looks at the datadrop. Before I can react, Sevro smashes it to dust. "Far as we're concerned, boyo."

Dancer stares down at the dust of the reverie. "I believed I was dirt once," he says slowly. "For these." He tilts up his sigils. "And this." He traces shapes through the dust and his voice loses the learned words and the sharpened consonants as he sinks back into the mines. "Was my own clan that did me wrong." His heavy eyes flick up. "Didn't know that, did ya? They burnt off me what makes a man a man. Ares found me bleeding to death in a tunnel.

"He knew what they'd done. He fixed me, in more ways than one. But he did one better. He taught me it was Gold that broke us. Taught me Red could matter. Taught me *I* mattered. Ten years, I never saw his face." He looks up at Sevro. "When he took that helmet off to you, to me, and I saw Gold, I wept worse than when they gelded me. First man who said I wasn't broken was *the master*. The *slaver*.

"Hit me good. Right here." He thumps his chest with a flat hand. "And I saw it hit him. I wasn't his best. I wasn't his favorite. But I was the only one who believed like he did. Was *me* that chose Darrow. Was *me* that had the keys to Tinos." He swallows. "Boy . . . that father of yours never judged me 'cept by what I'd done. Began to understand I owed him the same.

"Made a choice, then. I'd stand before him. Him that freed me. Him that made me different, made me a *force*. And I'd tell him what he told me long before: a man is his actions, not his blood." He looks back at the remains of the datadrop in sorrow that even now he still hides his truth. "The Jackal came before I got that chance. That is the greatest regret of my life. Your pa was my hero then and he is my hero now. I knew I'd never see his like again. I was wrong."

Dancer blows the reverie dust from the table and stands to look up at me. Ares dreamed of individual freedom, because of his son and his Red wife. Darrow dreamed of a world without monsters. Dancer's private dream was more delicate. He believed it was Gold who made his people wicked. And without Gold, they could be good. Bit by bit, he's seen reality wither that dream on the vine. But now that he knows it was still a Golden hand poisoning the soil, making him indict the very object of his faith, doubt the mission of his life, inside that stalwart chest awakens his holy wrath.

There is the warrior.

"Got a lot of hate in me," he says in a low growl. "Got a lot of fear that you won't ever understand. But none of it's for you, Virginia. We'll disagree again soon, I'm damn sure of that. But if our enemies think we'll devour each other . . . Nah. *Today* my Sovereign is the Lionheart, and tomorrow *she* will have my votes. We will rescue the Free Legions."

" 'Bout bloodydamn time," Sevro says.

30

VIRGINIA

Ocular Sphere

T O SEE THEM FROM ABOVE: *the roving herds of beasts, the rivers carving stone, the rituals of man in all their varied panoply, to see the
clouds roil over the patchwork latifundia of Asian plains, to see the mines of
our home, is to remember the patterns of the world, and the majesty and
complication and impermeable obscurity of distant lands. It is to remember
how few people you know. How many do not know you. How many will
soon forget you. How many praise you today to offer contempt tomorrow.
Permanence of fame, power, dominion of the individual, are illusions. All
that will be measured, all that will last, is your mastery of yourself.*

This is what my father told me. It was his warning about power,
though he sought it to his end. I've never understood how a man so wise
could be so undone by himself. Perhaps I never will, and that is what has
always frightened me. Not that I cannot control my own fate—that is
impossible—but that I cannot control myself.

Now I stand without him, wondering if he should be my compass
when he could not even follow his own needle—and the roar of the
distant ocean fills my ears. I watch the Earth turn from the Ocular
Sphere, a glass chamber suspended atop the highest pinnacle of the Citadel of Light. Created by the Master Maker Glirastes, like too many
other wonders, it floats like a teardrop escaping upward to heaven from
the tip of a bronzed sword. Octavia would often come here for her meditation and solitude. Of course, as an outsider I could not insinuate myself upon her here when she would wrap herself in that psycho-mystic
credo she taught lonely Lysander—the Mind's Eye. I would wait for her,

thumbing through intelligence reports in the library below, or discoursing with Moira, or entertaining Atalantia with the newest gossip I'd plucked for her ravenous appetite.

But Octavia is gone, and Lysander swallowed by the great expanse with Cassius. Though my opinions of Cassius are weighted and complex, and not understood completely even by myself, I hope they found happiness out there. There was so little of it for them here.

The Sphere is mine now, as are so many of Octavia's trophies. It is a hollow oddity, that possession. While she lived, these talismans and icons of hers—her Dawn Scepter, Silene Manor, the Sphere, the Pandemonium Chair, the Sovereigncy itself—were wrapped in mystery and portent. As if they held some great secret of life that I was too young, too foolish, to possess. I craved them so much—maybe as much as my father craved for whatever his desire actually was. But now, in possessing them, I see them for what they are; and they all feel lesser for that possession, as does indeed the world itself. The scepter is a hunk of iron. Silene Manor a house. The Sphere a clever device. The Chair a dangerous tool. Cities are measured by cold statistics of consumption and output. Planets by their loyalty and strategic importance.

All that matters is my son, my husband, and those I love and know, and who know me back.

Of all the people that lived in these last seven hundred years, none know the minds of the gens Lune as I do now. None know the weight, the fear, the anger, the ambivalence, the pride, the love, the disgust, the disappointment, the hope, and the utter frustration of ruling over billions of souls.

Octavia lost her husband and daughter. If I lost my son and husband, could I go on?

Or would I grow to be the villain of someone else's story?

Waving my hand at the curved glass wall of the Sphere, I watch the Earth grow until it consumes the entire pane. I fly amongst the peaks of mountains, along the cool fingers of Eurasian rivers running toward the sea. I rotate my hand and find the great mechanical prison, Deepgrave, trundling along beneath the surf. And with a flick of a finger, my sight races to Mercury. Much is white and black, to signify old images. Many telescopes have been destroyed in the war. But through the swirling clouds of the hypercane, I glimpse a Society bastion—a mobile operations command city—upon the desert sands. A jamField covers Heliopolis, where my husband licks his wounds. What hell does he suffer? What greater hell does he prepare for his enemies?

It is torture to see and not to know.

But worse still to know and not be able to affect.

I hope he knows we have not abandoned him.

That I still love his heart, despite its weight and anger and complications.

I love him so much I cannot bear to think of him.

I turn the Sphere to look down at the New Forum, where the Senate is soon to assemble. A grand crowd, a million strong, pours through the great Citadel gates beneath the Silenius Arch to witness the vote. According to the Compact, the Tribunes decide if the public should witness. Despite the fever, they are right to include them. It will be beautiful when Dancer and I unite the Vox and the Optimates in common cause. When Publius's betrayal fails to hijack the vote. It will be a victory for our way of life and our means of governance. In the plaza east of the New Forum, vendors sell sticky sweets and steam swirls up from hot spiced Martian wine. Children hold their parents' hands. Men carry icons of their political religions. The Vox with upside-down pyramids, broken chains. Some broadcast my head with a bloody crown from holoprojectors on their shoulders. The Optimates stand in small clutches with plastic slingBlades or pegasuses or lions projected into the air.

"Don't look too bloodydamn happy," Sevro mutters behind me. "Dancer still has to prove he's not a load of steaming shit."

"And you have a Queen to kill."

I cycle the Sphere until Old Tokyo fills the view. The megacity of Earth sprawls in the night. With the information gleaned from the Duke of Hands' memories, I have found the Syndicate Queen's refuge. Fifty thousand of my house troops along with Darrow's Seventh Legion will move in a coordinated strike against Syndicate operations on Earth, Mars, and Luna, while Sevro and two cohorts pull the chief weed out themselves. They will do it when all eyes are on me and the vote.

"Looking forward to it," Sevro says.

I turn from the central plinth to find him standing behind me in the Sphere with Daxo. Fully armored, wolfcloak on his shoulder, face painted jade green, he is ready for transport. Beside him, Daxo looks the picture of majestic civility in his senatorial toga. His arms are bare beneath the toga, and how mighty those Telemanus limbs look—made for violence, but restrained in favor of words because he trusts me, if not my faith in demokracy. Kavax saunters in to join us. He stands quietly behind his son with a hand on his shoulder and Sophocles threading between his legs.

Next to Daxo and Sevro, both in their prime, he looks pale and old. Even his genes can't hide the ravages of war. His beard has gone white. He still blames himself for Pax's abduction. It has not been an easy road to recovery for him, but he favors me with a smile. "Niobe is off to Mars to rendezvous with our house fleets and the Ecliptic Guard," he says. "She sends her love, and she'll see you through the fires of the *Annihilo*."

"And the bodies," Sevro says. "Never forget the kindling."

"Of course! The bodies," Kavax says. "Sevro, could you fetch my cane? My legs ache."

"Slag off, old man. I'm not a servant. I'm a terrorist war—"

"Now!" Kavax booms. "It's just outside the Crescent Vault. Fetch it or Sophocles will bite you!"

"By myself? That place is creepy shit. *Fine*. Losing your marbles." Muttering to himself, Sevro humors the old man and leaves the Sphere. He appears a moment later. "I'll know if you talk about me." He leaves again.

The two Telemanuses wait for him to reappear. When he doesn't, they join me in the center. "We'll bring Thraxa home," I tell Kavax. "I will keep that promise."

Kavax glances once more at the door to make sure Sevro is gone. "There are things I doubt in this world," he replies in his luxurious private tone. Intelligence radiates from eyes usually misted by his lifelong ruse. "The constitution of Obsidian virtues, the ramifications of universal suffrage, Sevro's personal hygiene, my violence on behalf of your father, my wife's mental perspicacity for selecting me for life"—he adopts his public face—"to join in union a doddering madman! Weird woman! Addled in the wits! Madness! Absolute madness!" His internal cleverness reclaims his face. "But never Virginia au Augustus." He cups my face. "Daxo told me what you did with Dancer. What you did with Sevro. You never get the credit you deserve, my dear. Because people are suspect and frightened of what they do not understand. I've hidden myself for so many years—from Nero, from the world. But you never have. That is a bravery I cannot understand. You are good, my dear. You are patient when it is not in your nature. You are attentive when you are taken for granted. You are kind when the world insists it is convenient to be cruel. You are good. True good. Victra will bring Pax back. I know this. You will save your husband. You deserve this day."

I nod, knowing there's much work left to do.

"No, look at me, child." He turns my chin so that I look deep into the eyes underneath those tangled eyebrows. "It has possessed my thoughts. You deserve this day. You deserve this joy. You deserve this proof that your faith is not just right, but necessary."

I find myself in tears, and I can't reason why. There are things you know, but when revealed to be known by others can make the world shine in a peculiar way. I feel seen, as only my husband has ever seen me. Kavax dabs the tears away. "There, there," he says, bringing me into a hug. I've been too busy to see Kavax. Or maybe just too frightened to see him weak. How dare I presume his strength is in his body. I hug him hard and Sophocles paws my leg in jealousy. Always mindful of his father, Daxo scoops the fox up to give us the moment.

"Will you come today?" I ask, pulling away.

"No," Kavax says. "No, I am tired of all this rancor. I think I will go to the sea with Sophocles. I don't like the Citadel without Niobe." He takes Sophocles back from Daxo. "And I've been promising this one a swim, haven't I, and you know how passive-aggressive the little prince gets. Yes, he does. Yes, he does. Shit in my shoes! In my closet! Everywhere!" He open-mouth kisses the fox, who takes perhaps too much enjoyment from it.

"But we will have dinner tonight at my estate. A family dinner. For my son"—he sets a hand on Daxo's shoulder—"who has done himself proud, resurrected his family's honor, and whom I could not be happier for. Except if he found a wife! I want babies to ride Sophocles! Or a husband!" He covers Sophocles's ears. "Cloning is always an option, remember." He laughs to himself. "And my daughter will come too"—he looks at me—"for she has been the twinkle in my eye since that summer she joined our family." Sevro appears in the door. "The sea!" Kavax booms. "To the sea I go."

"Here's your stupid cane," Sevro says.

"I need no cane! What am I, an invalid? A dullard?" Kavax booms. "I just wanted to see if you'd get it. Now who is the dullard! Ha!"

"Man." Sevro chuckles. "You're so crazy."

After Kavax has sauntered away with his pet, Daxo makes a small noise of distaste. "That was emotional. I hope he's not dying."

"He's not. I just think he's finally realized he's mortal," I say.

"I think we should clone him," Sevro says.

"Jove. The fox is bad enough," I say.

"Yes, but could you imagine a child Kavax with that beard?" Sevro asks. "He'd be a right legend. He could marry Electra!" I make a face. "What? She can't marry Pax. No offense, but he's too smart. And my girl likes being stupid." He scratches his goatee. "Bet Mickey would do it. We'd need to keep it secret. Yes." He chews his lip in thinking over the logistics.

"I could raise him," Daxo says. "I have always wanted a worthy child to shape and mold."

Sevro and I look at each other. "Nah, prolly a bad idea," Sevro says. "You know, clones are creepy and all. Always something wrong with the human ones." Daxo is lost, peering at the ceiling in thought. Behind his back, Sevro makes a big X with arms at the cloning idea.

"Be careful on Earth," I say. "Old Tokyo is Warden territory. Get in. Get out. And bring me that Queen's head."

"Attached?"

"If possible. If not, permission to cauterize. And, would you mind taking the tunnels out, please."

"Done." He lurches forward to slap Daxo's ass and stalks out. The smell of wolf lingers.

"I have thought it over. I think I would be a good father," Daxo says at last. "After all, I have a fine example to follow."

31

VIRGINIA

Day of Red Doves

THE DAY IS CRISP AND CLEAR, and bountiful with the scents of a Luna spring. The sky is the color of young fire. The trees along the promenade that leads from the Palatine Hill through the central Citadel park to the Forum blaze with color and life and pungent floral notes. Soldiers stop to salute as my motorcade rolls past. Administrators rush along park paths toward the Forum to make it there in time to watch the vote from the steps. Gaggles of children from the Citadel schools trot along in small packs, amongst them Lyria's little nephew, Liam, his eyes gazing wide up at the trees and the monkeycats swinging from the branches with fresh sight. Though Victra took the girl, and likely has already disposed of her, Lyria's bravery should be rewarded. I made sure Mickey himself gave the boy his sight months ago.

Lionguard greet me as I arrive at the western entrance to the Forum with Daxo and Holiday. The whole cadre of loyal Optimate senators, Golds, Grays, Whites, and half the Silvers wait with two dozen Martian senators as Daxo and I disembark. Publius the Incorruptible stands beside this group surrounded by dozens of Terran and even a few Lunese senators that I sacrificed my Silver alliance to gain. With Holiday standing watch, I shake the traitor's hand.

"A fine day for a fine moment," Publius says.

"Couldn't agree more."

I take Holiday by the shoulder and step away. "After Dancer gives me the Vox votes, the crowd may get unruly. . . ."

"We have support legions ready to go on the field of Ares, ma'am."

"Good." I sigh. "This is it then."

"Ma'am . . ." I turn back to her. "It must be said: It is in honor to serve a true Sovereign."

I don't think I can adequately explain how much that means from someone like her. I nod and step away from the protection of the Lionguard to that of the blue-cloaked Warden, guardians of the Senate and Republic.

I begin my ascent up the Forum's Western Stairs, Daxo at my right, and the phalanx of Optimates and new allies behind in their flowing togas. At the crest, we enter the grand fifty-meter-high doors, through the stone columns onto the varnished floor. From the Southern Stairs, Vox Populi make their own entrance, Dancer limping along at the head of sixty strong senators of Red, Orange, Brown, the core of the Vox, and their less zealous allies, Blue, Green, and Violet. They carry a standard made of raw wood and ugly iron—an upside-down pyramid unadorned with flourishes. Under the watch of the neutral Wardens, the two opposing factions descend to their seats as the oceanic sounds of the crowd in the East Park lap into the Forum. The Obsidian are already seated, making it clear they stand apart.

If only all knew how far gone they already were.

I do not yet take my Morning Chair down in the center of the Senate pit. I walk around the rim of the pit to the East Door, where several stout Gray Wardens stand guard, and look down the Eastern Stairs, past the line of Wardens and anti-matter pulseShields that stretch between metal pylons at the base of the stairs, to the park below. A sea of humanity fills it, their disparate faces distorted by the shields so that they look like the confetti brushstrokes of a Frankish Impressionist. Roars of approval and condemnation lap against me. I smile. Soon they will witness the vindication of our way of governance.

"Senators of the Republic, you are convened today in common assembly to vote upon a matter of dire urgency," I say from the discomfort of my chair. The senators surround me, looking down from their seats on the tiered marble steps. "Much has been made of the divide between our peoples. Today I hope to see that divide closed. A resolution has been put before you by Senator Telemanus. Senator."

Daxo stands to his imperious height. The Optimates shout acclamation. He looks around with vibrant eyes and that clever, mocking smile.

"Being that the greater strength of our veteran legions are trapped behind enemy lines due, in no small part, to our own befuddled hands, I reintroduce that very same resolution which was voted down one long month ago." The Optimates stamp their approval. "Prior arguments against this resolution disparaged the strength of those Free Legions." The Optimates guffaw. The Vox rumble in discontent. "And contended that they would capitulate to the strength of the enemy before rescue could avail them. That they would fold!" Laughter from the Optimates. "That the Reaper of Mars was but a shadow of his former self."

"No! No!" roar the Optimates.

"While the Reaper has much to answer for"—the Vox murmur agreement—"he has been embraced by the troops as the commander in the field, and it would be folly to discredit their wisdom on this day. The Free Legions live. With their victory, we can see that such . . . pessimism, such defeatism, such . . ." He wants to say "cowardice," but a look to me reminds him to stay his tongue and preach conciliation. "*Caution* was unfounded. And while it is a courageous notion to hold fast our lines, to protect our spheres with all our might, I cannot see a world in which we, my goodmen, my goodladies, can rest our weary heads and look ourselves in the mirror knowing we condemned our brave fellows to death. Therefore! I reintroduce my resolution to grant the Sovereign wartime *imperium* over the defense fleets, so she may, in her wisdom, prosecute this war to its rightful and expedient conclusion!"

As Daxo sits, the Optimates stand with a roar. And outside, the smaller part of the crowd echoes their agreement as they watch the great projection of the Senate that streams above the Forum. But the greater part, the lowColors with their more numerous constituencies, wait for the man who has bound them together and given them a voice as loud as any Gold's in the Society.

Dancer politely waits for the other blocs to speak.

The Silvers sit in silence. I have half their votes, if not their love, votes from those who fear my wrath outweighs their fear of Quicksilver's. The Coppers also sit in silence. I look to Publius and tilt my head. It is his turn to stand. Yet he demurs, passing his time to the next bloc. I try to catch his eye. Something has changed. This should be where the trap springs and he denounces me. Has he made a deal with Zan?

Does he know I have Dancer?

My internal com beeps a priority message from Theodora. Keeping my face blank, I allow it through. *"My Sovereign, Sevro has a priority-one message from Earth."* I instruct her to put it through to Daxo as well.

Dancer eases to his feet.

The rugged man in brilliant white looks at me with a soft smile of reassurance as I wait for Sevro's message.

"It is good today that the weather is fine and bright. That so many of our concerned citizens parted with the rigors of their own lives, and many rigors there are, to attend this assembly, lifts my heart." He tries hard to match Daxo's eloquence, but is more at home with simpler diction. "How far we have come in ten short years from the darkness of Society. How many of you could envision this day? Not as some dream, but as reality? Few. Very few, I wager. Even Fitchner Barca, the father of this revolution, had doubts. As did I." He smiles, perhaps remembering the pain of those long years with the Sons. "My fellows, you are to be congratulated for your part, small as it may seem, in making this grand experiment possible."

He hiccups softly before continuing.

"Our union is based not on our shared past, but on our hopeful future." He frowns in irritation as a Brown senator behind him hiccups loudly into her sleeve. "Yet, even now agents of the enemy seek to divide that . . ."

"Mustang . . ." There's fear in Sevro's voice. He's out of breath. I hear boot steps on metal grating. *"Mustang . . . Boneriders in Old Tokyo . . . trap."* There's an explosion and the feed cuts to static.

Boneriders.

I hear blood in my ears.

I look over to Daxo. Billions are watching on live stream. I can't leave. We need this vote now. Theodora will have to take point. She'll dispatch units to aid Sevro.

Boneriders?

How could it be possible? They should still be imprisoned in Deepgrave. Has the prison been penetrated yet again?

Are they working with the Syndicate?

It makes no sense. It has to be a trick. Sevro must be mistaken.

If Sevro is not mistaken, this is exactly the sort of public venue where the Boneriders would like to make a splash. I look up and search the ceiling as if I'll find a bomb hidden there. The Forum was checked a dozen times by Holiday and the Warden. It has to be clean. If Old Tokyo was a trap, then how did the Syndicate know I was coming? A mole? Did they count on me cracking the duke? I whisper for the Pegasus Legion units I have on standby north of Hyperion to come to the Citadel to join my Lionguard on the Field of Ares. Outside the Forum, Holiday goes on high alert.

Another hiccup escapes Dancer's lips and he reaches up with a hand to scratch his throat. "Our Gold enemy profits when we are divided." He clears his throat roughly. ". . . So today I seek an end to that—"

A great mucus-filled hiccup escapes his lips and his hands wrench into a cramped, infantile movement to paw at his chest. The Red senators beside him rustle in concern. But then another hiccups in their ranks. And another. Using the shoulders of the senators beneath him, Dancer pulls himself upright, his eyes confused and unfocused. "Today I seek to—"

Then comes the horror.

A clump of blood and lung tissue vomits out of Dancer's mouth.

It bathes the togas of the senators beneath him in red pulp. Hands windmilling, he topples over onto their heads. They collapse under the weight and with shouts set him on the ground. Panic swirls around Dancer as he contorts violently on the stone, blood dribbling from his bodily orifices. His eyes bulge from his head and his hands paw the ground. Publius rushes to cradle his head. "Gas!" I shout, holding my breath. But the pathogen detectors do not wail. The room does not seal and vent. And my personal defense-ring around my wrist continues to blink silver, detecting no abnormalities.

I summon the Lionguards waiting underneath the Forum, but none reply on my internal com. None come through the interior doors.

I connect to Holiday. "Evacuation Protocol. The Wardens are likely compromised. Fire if they move to engage."

"Already moving to West Door. Support. Lionguards unresponsive."

Daxo rushes to me along with the Gold and Gray senators, and they form a wall around my person. Through their shoulders, I watch Dancer and his lieutenants die, helpless to stop it.

The Vox Populi shout in anger, in fear, calling for medici as the Yellow senators push through their ranks to come down the stairs. But then one stumbles and grips his chest before heaving his own blood onto the floor.

Amidst Vox Populi, the clutch of Dancer's most stalwart moderate lieutenants reel, beset by the same violent malady. Blood pours from their convulsing bodies as their limbs flail in an atavistic dance and those around them are torn between helping and running, for fear that the pathogen is carried in their blood.

"Wardens, help them!" someone shouts.

But the Wardens above, around the rim of the Senate pit, do not rush to give aid. In their green cloaks, they watch without pity or connection, and then file out the doors. On the floor, Dancer's spasms have subsided. His blood smears Publius's face and hands. He pulls back from the Copper to look up at me with eyes wild and white as a dying horse's. His mouth opens, a bloody, twisted maw. He mouths something to me, but his voice has been robbed from him and no sound comes out.

"He's dead . . ." Publius whispers. "O'Faran is dead!"

The hope in me dies with him.

Then Publius cu Caraval stands in the chaos.

I know, as his lips curl back from his white teeth, as his eyes glimmer bright with long-hidden fervor, and his bloody finger extends in my direction, that he knew Dancer and I had come to terms. *How?*

"Murderer!" the Incorruptible wails. "Tyrant!"

"Tyrant!" the surviving Vox echo, pointing their fingers like blood-drenched scarecrows amidst the field of their dying compatriots. "Tyrant!"

We flee in force. Optimates cluster around me and we ascend the stairs away from the charnel house. My internal com swarms with dread.

"Citadel and Skyhall are under attack. Republic forces . . ."

"Seventh Legion shuttles taking fire . . ."

"Warden forces firing on Lionguard outside Moon . . ."

"Echo of Ares reports their captain has been shot . . ."

"ArchImperator Zan moving on Augustan ships."

". . . Lake Silene has inbound Republic assault craft."

Ships are going for Darrow's mother, Vox legions assaulting ones loyal to me.

It is a coup.

With Daxo pushing me along in the center of a knot of Optimates, I rush up the last of the stairs to the West Door. We make the flats around the senate pit and rush to the exit. At the head of a clutch of heavily armed Lionguard, Holiday exchanges heavy fire outside the Forum with Warden elements. Taking casualties, they press up the stairs outside the forum as aerial soldiers in gravBoots dogfight over the parks.

But as they reach the top stair and make to meet us at the door, a forty-meter-tall Drachenjäger lands at the edge of the park. Its twin railguns train themselves on Holiday. She shouts to take cover. Too late.

I watch in horror as metal slugs moving at three times the speed of sound make my Martian soldiers mist. The slugs shred the marble steps and skip up into the Forum, raining splinters of rock down on us. I'm flattened by Gold and Gray senators, who use their bodies to shield mine. Senator Tiberius ti Han screams as his arm is taken off at the elbow by a ricochet. The next one takes his torso off at the hips.

From under their bodies, I see out the doors. The Drachenjäger is teetering sideways, a huge hole in its cockpit. From amidst the bodies of dead Lionguard, Holiday turns her anti-tank railrifle up the steps at the Wardens blocking our escape. Five Wardens are cut in half. A sixth Warden explodes in a shower of gristle and metal. His cape detaches and slaps wetly against the groaning marble door as it slides to trap us inside the Forum. Daxo reaches the door alone and hauls against it till the veins stand out in his neck and his fingers crack the stone. A shoulder pops from its socket.

"Run, you fools!" he roars at us.

I push the Gold senators off me, but I'm too far from the door and the mechanized hinges cannot be stopped even by a Telemanus.

"Go!" I shout at him. "Daxo, go!"

My heart breaks as Daxo looks at the narrowing sliver of salvation. His face is red from exertion. His lips pull back from his teeth. He could escape, abandon me, but instead a calmness comes over him and he releases his grip on the door. It seals with a loud thump and he turns to me and shrugs.

With my com I open a master channel to my entire security network. "Black Cathedral," I say. "Repeat, Black Cathedral—" But the signal goes down. Daxo puts a hand on my shoulder. His eyes are fixed on something behind me. I turn in time to see a concussion detonate outside the East Door. In the plaza beyond, the colorful crowd has disintegrated into a frenzied mob.

"The shield . . ." Daxo whispers.

Smoke billows. A shield pylon teeters sideways. Sparks shiver out from its sides and, with a blue shimmer, the barrier separating us from the mob disappears. Oh no.

A tide of humanity rolls up the white steps toward the only open door.

Senators scream and scramble to beat against the other doors for escape. The remnants of the Vox Populi, some thirty of their fringe zealots, huddle around Dancer's body down in the Senate pit. Publius is amongst them, his face wild with righteous rage as he shouts for the mob and points toward us as if he were some necromantic conjurer hurling his murderous spirits forward.

"Optimates, to me!" I shout.

Barely half of them hear me. The rest have broken up amongst the Forum to beat on the doors, to hide behind columns, to raise their hands in supplication to the mob that teems toward the open East Door. Their faces sunburnt and pale, wide and narrow, eyes Red and Brown and Orange, mad with communal rage, their arms carrying bent bits of fences, stakes from propaganda signs, hammers, and even blackmarket scorchers, they roil toward us. A dozen in front, a hundred behind, and thousands pushing them forward.

I watch a Blue senator tear herself away from her hiding place amongst the columns and stand bravely at the East Door and face down the mob with an outstretched hand. "No violence!" she declares majestically. "No violence!" she repeats just before a Red man caves her head in with an iron Vox pyramid on the end of a wooden pole. The mob swallows them. They disappear and all I can see is the iron pyramid rising and falling above the swarm. A Pink senator falls. Frail bones shatter as he curls inward like a dying spider. They pull Optimate senators from their hiding places and smash their heads open against the marble.

Senators flee from them, tripping and falling, skinning their knees and prying themselves up to scramble away, their togas white but for the hems that are stained in blood, so that they look like the fluttering wings of red doves in flight.

The Obsidian senators, all women, all former warriors, join our lines with a solemn nod.

"Virginia, stand behind me," Daxo says in a low growl. I step to his side. With a small laugh, he peels the wool of his toga as if it were made of paper. Free of the encumbrance, he stands bare chested, bare limbed, a monster clothed only in undershorts before the mob. His shoulders are broad as a thunderhead. His back muscled like a sunblood stallion's. The angels on his head glorious and golden and dancing down his spine to his lower back. But his huge hands are bare and empty.

"Daxo!" I hand him the Dawn Scepter. He spins it, a meter of solid iron with the fourteen-pointed star of our Republic glittering on the end. "Gold and Obsidian, first rank! Gray second." I shout over the furor as the mob runs around the sides of the Senate pit to reach us. Those soldiers amongst the Optimates, many old and stooped, but sinewy and dogged in the ways of war, rustle forward to stand fifteen abreast in velvet slippers and white togas to defend the cluster of thin-boned senators behind us.

I pull on the metal tab underneath the left pocket of my jacket. My secondary razor slithers out of the spine of my jacket, to form into a meter and a third of rigid metal. I lean toward Daxo.

"On my command: terror."

The mob does not hit us in a wave. The wild vanguard was prepped. Pupils flaring with stims and intoxicants, they sprint headlong at us with homemade weapons—hammers and knives—a few with blackmarket scorchers. A scorcher flares. White light ripples across the Forum and the Obsidian senator to the left of me screams as her stomach ruptures open. She stumbles away, half her torso boiling.

"Now," I tell Daxo.

"LIONHEART!"

. . . and death for four meters.

He cleaves the Red with the scorcher in half with the edge of the Dawn Scepter's star. A man swings at him with a knife. Daxo is already past him, but reaches back to shatter his hand and take the knife. He wheels it down on the head of a Brown in a hammer stroke, flattening the head, and then casually flicks the scepter back into and through the face of another man before bringing it about in a wheeling stroke that shatters three more of the rioters. He kicks a Brown woman in the chest. Her sternum collapses and a bulge from his foot pushes out her back. The last, a young Red man with piercings through the bridge of his nose, stabs at Daxo. Daxo catches the blade in his left hand. It sinks into the palm but bends against the reinforced bone as Daxo pushes back till the man's straightened arm snaps like a twig. Daxo embeds the scepter in the man's chest and grabs the man's other hand. He pulls on both arms, lifting the man in the air so that he is eye to eye with Daxo, his feet kicking half a meter from the ground. With a roar, Daxo pulls off both the man's arms. The body drops to the floor, spitting blood. Daxo rips the scepter out of the man, pulling ribs with it, and beats his own bloody chest with gore-spattered hands. "LIONHEART!!!" He spins the scepter, pointing it at the crowd. "Dogs! Traitors! In the name of your Sovereign, disarm! Disarm!"

The mob behind the massacred men skids to a halt, terrified of the Gold monstrosity. All their lives they've known of Gold power, but war is fast and smoky and small through a screen. They always suspected the myth of our violence overwrought. Now they see what our manners have protected them from. The courage in their numbers withers at the terrible sight of this machine of war unlocked from his civil chains. But the mob is a machine as well, and its engine of courage comes from those at the rear. They push forward, screaming and shouting and firing over the heads of those terrified in the front, and the press breaks forward, dozens amongst them falling to be trampled by the weight of the distant brave.

The mob hits more like mud than water. Seeping around Daxo, fighting to run away, heels skidding over bloody stone. My razor carves through the outstretched arm of a young man holding a scorcher, through the face of a fat woman with a rock, the neck of a screaming, terrified teenager with a mouth blue from cloud candy. Bodies push me back and I chop madly, blindly at arms. They seep through.

I fall back to swing again, but I collide with someone behind me and am pushed forward into the bodies of those I've maimed, who wail and hold bloody stumps and are trampled by those behind them. I wheel and hack and slash against flailing limbs. A hammer hits my collarbone. Bone holds. Man dies. A knife digs into my cheek and breaks a tooth in half. Spit sprays into my eyes. Blood. Teeth bite my leg and metal digs into my calf. Searing pain. I stomp on someone until I feel something give.

Not ten meters away, Daxo kills and maims in a tyrannical whirlwind like the kind Darrow and only few others still living have ever seen in person, much less produced.

I try to cut my way to him, but I don't have the mass. Bodies obscure me. Hands pull at me. Shoulders of screaming men subvert my balance as they hit my knees. The back of a head breaks my nose. I headbutt someone else and feel the weaker bone crumple. Sharp metal scrapes down my back ribs and stabs repeatedly into my flank. I howl, pinched between bodies. My legs are caught by someone's arms and I'm wrestled from the side by a big Red man, his whiskers scraping into my neck. I teeter sideways, pulled down by a mass of bodies. A gun goes off against my thigh. I feel pressure. They pin my sword arm to my side and bite and saw at my hand till the razor slips free.

I crash to the ground under their weight, arms and legs unable to move against their grip as boots stomp on my head and kick my face. Sound goes in and out, my vision stuttering between black and the swarm of feet and legs at the claustrophobic underbelly of the mob. I swallow a tooth and bite the finger off a man.

"Virginia!" I hear beyond the curses and shouts. "Virginia!"

The big Red man atop me twitches. The iron points of a bloody star erupt through his forehead. His eyes roll back into his head and blood sluices onto me as Daxo pulls the Dawn Scepter out of his crushed skull. Another man falls between us. Daxo seizes his belt and hurls him through the air like a doll. I glimpse my friend for a moment, his wild eyes set in that thoughtful face. And despite the horror around us, despite the anger in him, I see the panic of love. He will save me. He will protect me, like he did when he pulled me from the tossing surf as a girl.

And then he is gone, greatness borne down under a human wave that crashes down from all directions.

A boot connects with my temple. My head lolls sideways. Something stabs through my cheek and takes two teeth. Numbly, I feel them tearing at my hair, my clothes, ripping off my boots, cutting my pants with knives and my razor, the blade scraping my skin. Two men rip off my jacket as a woman kicks at my face, and hands paw at my breasts and claw between my thighs. I black out in the darkness, feel hands lifting me up, punching me, jamming into my body.

Then I am free of the mob, the press of bodies above me gone. I open swollen eyes and see through a crack in the darkness. Jeering faces swim beneath me, hands pass me above their heads like a trophy. Sharp objects stick into my buttocks, my thighs.

"Daxo," I murmur through broken teeth, mouth full of blood and mashed lips. "Daxo . . ."

I see him again through the crowd. His huge body is splayed out on the ground, held down by a big Obsidian with gold teeth as four others stand over him guarding a muscular Red woman in a Hyperion sanitation uniform. Tall for a Red, she hacks at Daxo's neck with a hatchet till his head dislodges. She holds it by its spine.

Without looking, she flicks Daxo's head to the mob. He was a man who could have ruled worlds if he had even the smallest ambition for it, who chose to serve the people even though he despised them. He did that for me. And now his head is tossed around like an inflated toy ball. The golden angels dance no more on Daxo's crown. They are drowned in his blood.

The woman turns to look at me. Even set in that face, I recognize her eyes through the Red contacts.

A demon from the past, now undead.

Lilath. My brother's dog of war.

She is alive. She is the Queen of the Syndicate.

How?

Lllath begins to laugh at me.

With a disembodied moan, I tear my eyes away and look up for some escape to the sky. But it is hidden from me behind the painted plaster, where my husband floats golden and glorious, with Sevro at his side, giving his speech to the mob of Phobos, where he heard the heartbeat of humanity and exhorted it to violence, to war, to the taking of lives for liberty.

All that fills my ears is the roar of the human ocean as it sings the song of my husband's first wife.

32

DARROW

In Wake

Heliopolis steams under the early morning sun. Though northern Helios still buckles under Orion's storms, the monsoon clouds that drenched Heliopolis with torrential rain have slunk back to the Caliban Sea, leaving the city gleaming white. It might be lovely but for the fact that the rain was irradiated from nuclear warheads, and the air is so thick with humidity steaming in off the Bay of Sirens that the simple act of walking is like wading through pudding.

My wounds are not yet healed. Everything aches. Nausea from anti-rads grips my belly. Sweat trickles down my back as I stand in a thick cluster of my officers to partake in the Fading Dirge. Before us, a sea of Martians sleep upon a bed of lavender. Spread across the tarmac of the spaceport south of Heliopolis, their faces are green and blue, their bodies distended by the sun so that they look like inflated dolls. There is no Triumph, no victory march for the dead. There is only this meager honor.

Scarcely one hundred thousand of the four million lost to the sea, the sand, and the atomics have been gathered for the Fading Dirge. Ten square kilometers of lavender were cut from the southern latifundia by my corps of engineers to mask the smell of the bodies. It was meant to give some semblance of dignity to the departed as we say farewell to them together.

There is no dignity here. A southerly wind prevails. As we beat our fists against our hearts, the ceremony disintegrates into farce as the dank stench of rotting eggs and used toilets drifts up from the bodies. The infantry maintain their ranks, but support and naval men and women unaccustomed to the degradations of ground combat waver, many upturning their stomachs onto the baking concrete.

The bodies are arrayed to be cremated before our remaining ships of war. The battle-scarred *Morning Star* looms like a mountain, one and a half kilometers tall, nearly eight long. Four torchShips lie in her shadow, and the rickety remains of one destroyer. From atop her hull, welders shade themselves under the guns and pause their labor to watch. How many times has the *Morning Star* saved us? By the looks of her hull and the wounds she sustained from the storm and the battle, I don't think she can do it again.

Some will call the Battle of the Ladon a victory for the Republic. I cannot. With Naran falling the night before, we have lost all the major cities of Helios. Four million of my men are missing or dead. Just over five million survive to huddle beneath the shields of Heliopolis. Supplies dwindle, especially the anti-rads. Most were in Tyche. Barely one-third of my men are fit for duty, even by our elastic standards. Our tank regiments are depleted. RipWings down to two hundred operational craft. Drachenjägers reduced to seven hundred. All that protects us from being bombarded is the shield overhead. All that protects us from being overrun are the storms beyond, and Atalantia's fear of what new horror I'll conjure.

Despite our vulnerability, Atalantia has not opted for another frontal attack on Heliopolis. Instead, with us trapped inside, she extends her grip over the storm-ravaged continent and squeezes with the thoughtful patience of an anaconda. It means no relief fleet is on its way.

But I must have hurt her badly.

By our estimates she lost twice as many as we did, most to the storm on the northern coast of Helios. The military camps of Venus can always provide her fresh bodies, but her precious veterans are irreplaceable— XIII Dracones, Ash Guard, Fulminata, Zero Legion, the Iron Leopards. With the Iron Leopards captured or killed, a third of the Ash Guard drowned in Tyche, Fulminata pounded by Thraxa outside Heliopolis, how many more will she sacrifice for us? None, I wager. They are needed for the Republic. She will wait for reinforcements from Venus, and use the raw recruits as a battering ram. There will be nothing we can do to stop them.

All know it.

Amongst the engineering officers, Harnassus stands like an old sea captain squinting into salt spray. Even though she suffered grievous burns in the battle, Thraxa's shoulders loom over the heads of the Gray, Gold, and Red infantry commanders. But amongst the naval officers, there is an absence. For ten years the Blues orbited around Orion with the fidelity of moons to a planet; now the planet is gone, and the moons drift untethered. They will need a new leader.

But from where? Captain Pelus, a veteran of ten years, might have flown the *Morning Star* through hell, but he is no leader. All my Imperators, save Harnassus, are gone. Half my Praetors. More than two-thirds of my wing commanders. Atalantia gnaws through officers who cannot be replaced. Officers who earned their bars and then their wings under Orion and me. Where will we find more like them? In the fat, filigreed Home Guard? In the jockeying politicians of Skyhall? I can only pillage the Ecliptic Guard so far before it is staffed completely by children.

I turn to my lancers and find no one there. Not Alexandar, not Rhonna, only Screwface. He's taken weight off my shoulders since his return. Elated to be back with his own, he seems the only one with any energy to spare. I envy him that, and gave him Rat Legion to put his counter-espionage skill set to work clearing the city of dissidents and any spies the Fear Knight snuck in. "Where's Rhonna?" I ask him.

"Tunnels again."

"Colloway?"

"He split from the medWard at 0400. Was wings-up by 0430."

"He went out again?"

"With a full squadron. Man won't rest until he finds Orion. I thought you knew."

I look back at the bodies. "I didn't."

If he dies out there, how many heroes will we have left? A murmur goes up amongst the men. I follow the current of hands that rise to shade their eyes. A ripWing smudges smoke across the morning sky. Of the twelve ripWings that went in search of Orion, three stagger back.

Colloway is not in his right mind. Since we took refuge in the city, he has been on the ground a total of ten hours. The time it takes to eat seven meals, receive two blood transfusions, exchange seven crippled ripWings for fresh ones, and be locked in the medBay under guard. Lazy guard apparently.

Early morning condensation turns to vapor as Colloway and his wingmen set their battered ripWings on the concrete before the dead. Colloway's canopy is so mangled with enemy fire it has to be welded off. When he's free, he bypasses the ladder and slides down his wing before coming around to the belly of the ripWing where a bloated body is clutched in its towing claw.

Colloway pries the body from the towing claw and tries to carry it. She is too heavy, even in the light gravity. He stumbles, and I find myself moving from the officers to reach him. Dozens of others join, including Screwface and Thraxa, but not Harnassus. He watches stone-faced from his officers, unable to forgive Orion, or me, for the storm and the millions of civilians it killed.

Seawater is not kind to a dead body, nor are fish. But on Orion's swollen right hand is the trident ring I gave her when I named her Navarch of the Fleet. It rests on my shoulder as we carry her to the field of the dead and lay her amongst the lavender and corpses of fallen ripWing pilots. Colloway falls to his knees there. At first I think it from his exertion. Then he breaks into sobs. I squat behind him, knowing there is nothing to say. I take him by the shoulder to lead him away, but he thrusts my hand off and wheels on me.

"Plus twenty-four, sir," he says. "But they'll just send more. There are no more Orions." He storms away from the funeral, making it halfway across the tarmac before collapsing. Medici rush to him and bear him away toward the city.

"Twenty-four makes 193 kills in six days," Thraxa says with a whistle. "A feat which will never be encroached upon in our time." As others grow numb, she grows callous.

I stare after Colloway.

Despite his natural laziness, there has always been a fever behind his eyes—even back on Luna with a Hyperion sprite splayed across his lap. I suspected it was a fever for kills, chasing some imaginary number where his soul would finally be quenched and deem it enough. Today is the first time I realize the number isn't counting up. It's counting down. How many more can he kill before he goes?

I look back on Orion's body one last time. It is a horrible thing to see someone so full of life, so important in yours and those of others, humbled by death. The corrosion of the sea was cruel. It is no comfort to know this thing is no longer her, just the rotting shell of what held a miracle of a soul. Does she go to Eo and Ragnar and Fitchner? Or is she simply gone? I do not know. Nor do I know how I will go on without her. I feel cold despite the sun, desperate to feel the warmth of my family, my wife, my son. Knowing how short our time in the light is, am I the greatest of fools to not spend every moment by their side?

Thraxa lights a burner. "Here's for you, old girl. How many kills you suppose you got? Bet it was more than a hundred ninety-three."

Fighting the instinct to break Thraxa's jaw, I turn away from her and return to the officers. Soon the warning siren blares. The legionnaires and I turn our heads. Bright white light flares from the *Morning Star*, washing away the meager light of morning, and when we turn back, the men are nothing but ashes. The smell of ozone sanitizes the air, and their comrades walk forward to scrape the ashes of their friends into canisters in hopes of one day giving them back to Mars. Not one of us believes we'll ever see home again, but they sing nonetheless.

Defense barricades and screening facilities have been erected around the mouth of the Tyche-Heliopolis GravLoop Station, which towers at the east end of the Water Plaza. With the power severed in Tyche, the loop's cars stranded many refugees in the tunnel. I stood in silence watching our first convoys ferry the refugees through. I thought it would be a miracle if Alexandar saved a thousand. But the convoys continued to flow for nearly three days—families and children of all Colors. Each sharing the same story of the Griffin Knights who held back an army to give them time to escape the sea.

Whether or not they know we summoned that sea is another matter. Some blame the Society. Some us. Others blame nature herself.

Eventually the flow became a trickle and the trickle became no one at all and the fragment of me that held out hope submitted to reality. Alexandar will not appear staggering behind the last survivors, with a limp, a wry smile, and somehow perfectly coiffed hair. He is drowned in the sea. Sentimentality is no reason to allow this potential enemy highway to continue to exist.

"How long has she been here?" I ask the centurion in charge of the barricade. A Red, he wears a bandage over his eye and a necklace of Red charms around his neck. A rat skull is most prominent. Rat Legion. Toughest of those who fought in the Rat War in the tunnels of Mars. Of course they survived the storm, and labor while the others lick their wounds.

"Going on six hours, sir. She's in the atrium. Do you need an escort?"

"No. We'll be out in a minute. I put Rat Legion on R&R. What are you doing here?"

"Nineteenth lost most of their men to a gravity bomb. Thought they wouldn't mind us picking up the slack, sir."

I nod. After holding Heliopolis against Ajax's army for half a day, if anyone deserves rest, it's Rat Legion. "Prepare the charges." With my bodyguards scanning the surrounding roofs for snipers, I head up the station's main steps.

I find Rhonna sitting against the base of a broken statue inside the atrium. The right side of my niece's head is shaved from where the surgeons repaired the gash a Gray digger bullet made as it tore open her helmet.

"Aren't you supposed to be in the medWard?" I ask.

"Ain't you supposed to be running an army?" She chews her nails as she watches the stairs leading up out of the tunnel.

"Can I sit?" She shrugs and I slide down next to her with a sigh.

"Didn't want to miss the Princess's dramatic entrance," she says.

"If he were coming by tunnel, he'd be here by now."

"I know."

"Then you know we have to collapse the tunnel. It would be difficult to explain to my brother why I did it on his daughter's head."

"Yeah." She swallows, thinks about saying something, then forgets it. We sit in silence watching the stairs. In truth, I've been afraid to see her since we took the city. I'm not so distracted I couldn't see the tension between her and Alexandar was growing into something else. For two people who can't stand each other, they certainly found enough reasons to always be in the same room.

"He may still have taken the Kylor Pass," I say.

"I know what's what. Even if he got through the storm and the Votum, those mountains will be crawling with Gorgon." She looks over at me. "If it had been me instead of Alexandar, would you have let me go?" My first instinct is shame, because I've always resented the sort of Gold Alexandar represented—haughty, entitled, rich. But it wasn't enmity that sent him to Tyche, it was respect.

"Yes."

"You didn't just . . . dispose of him . . ." she asks plaintively.

"Of course not."

That answers something for her. "Such an asshole. Just when he starts being worth a damn . . ." She shakes her head and looks once more at the stairs. "All right. Slag it." She forces herself up. She wobbles, still woozy from the operation. I steady her and we walk out together to join the centurion behind the barricade.

"What's the final refugee count?" I ask the centurion.

"Eighty-three thousand four hundred and twenty-six souls, sir."

"Eighty-three thousand four hundred and twenty-six souls," I say to Rhonna. "Not many are lucky enough to know how much their life is worth."

She gives a small nod of appreciation. I signal the centurion. The engineers go to work and soon two thousand meters of tunnel caves in on itself. Rhonna watches dust billow out from the mouth of the station and then turns to me at attention. "Request permission to return to duty, sir. I'm no good to you in the medBay."

"Granted."

She nods and heads back to my transport. She looks so small against the towering statue of Poseidon. The god of the Water Plaza holds up ninety-nine disks of water, and thousands of thirsty birds. Rhonna disappears inside the shuttle. She's a soldier now. Like me.

I linger to witness the last of the rocks settle. Knowing that Alexandar is dead, that those people he saved will soon forget him or may die yet in the siege, I wish for one small moment that I were a young man again who could charge forward nourished by his own righteousness. That man would damn the danger and search for Alexandar as Colloway searched for Orion. But that man would have died in the desert and taken all his men with him. That man isn't what my army needs. Hell, I don't know what they need except for a miracle. I turn and head back to my transport, dragged forward by the weight of the day.

West of the city, between the Bay of Sirens and the old city, squats the four-century-old Votum government complex known as the Mound. It is a heavy basilica straddled by a half-kilometer-tall statue of the city's patron god, Helios. Each of the fourteen spikes on his sun crown stretch the length of ten men to puncture the blue sky. His left hand holds a scepter, and the right moves according to the path of the sun, so that at sunset he will cup it in his palm as it sinks beyond the horizon. As if any man had such control.

"The rain is radioactive," Harnassus says, dumping a box of dead cats on the table of the old Votum warroom. Thraxa paces along the arched windows, more interested in the bunkers our clawDrills are carving than the inconvenient report. We are all bald by now.

"We eat here, thank you very much for the drama," Thraxa says.

Harnassus grumbles on. ". . . fallout from the atomics used locally. So far the Golds are scrubbing the stratosphere so there's limited risk of permanent global contamination. But we're in trouble. Orion drowned half our anti-rads in Tyche before we could evac them. The Gorgons eliminated another third in that bombing before we rounded them up." Sweat soaks Harnassus's dirty uniform. He looks even more exhausted than I feel. Like me, he put on a brave face for the men at the funeral, but the Gorgons who snuck in before we locked down Heliopolis are giving us hell, and native insurgencies have sprung up faster than Screwface can put them down. "Bottom line: we don't have enough for our men and the civilians."

"Why are you always bringing me bad news?" I ask him. Harnassus's bitterness has increased exponentially since Orion summoned the storms. I sympathize with the man, even if I find him a damn thorn in my side. Hate the storms all he likes, the only reason we have an army at all is because of its cloud and electrical cover.

"Because I'm the only one not sucking your balls."

"Oh, do say it more directly," Thraxa says. "As if it adds gravitas . . ."

I rub my shoulder as I receive an anti-rad shot from the Yellow medicus. The nausea has come in waves over the last days. I thought it would be starvation that ended us, not fallout. On my way to the Mound, I saw men with red-stained handkerchiefs, others sitting in the shade with their heads in their hands as they queued for the latrines.

Harnassus plods on. "Engineering corps believes the symptoms will spike dramatically. We're already experiencing weakness, nausea, and headaches. It will progress to vomiting and diarrhea. Which I've already got. The civilians will soon figure it out. We'll have full-on riots soon as the deaths start."

"There've already been riots," Thraxa says, turning her eyes from the mountains to the refugee-choked streets of Heliopolis. "If we share our supplies, we won't make it two weeks. We're already on half-dose, already denying it to five hundred thousand men too far gone. These people are not our allies."

She's not wrong. We are not wanted here. Tyche was a fine enough home. But of the Mercurian breed, Heliopolitans are the most cantankerous, cruel, and noisy. Save Glirastes, it is hard to remember even one who welcomed us when we took the planet. And with Orion's storm and our waning campaign, the teeth have come out. My soldiers dare not go anywhere alone at night. Mobs have already tried storming the food centers I set up. Even Glirastes has spurned my calls, lurking in his palace above the city after haranguing me about betraying my oath not to raise the storms past primary horizon. He doesn't believe Orion went rogue.

I find myself thinking about Pax, and if I would have sent him into Tyche like Alexandar. Would I spend my boy as I've spent so many others? Didn't I spend him in a way by not returning home? It all seems so transactional, war. Did I spend my boy the day he was born by the virtue of my role in the Rising? I can only hope that my wife has found him by now. That they are together and that the fleet is coming for us. *Hope.* Hope won't bring back Orion or my men. But my wife deserves it. And here, shorn of everything else, I am sustained only by her strength.

"We brought this upon them, Telemanus," Harnassus says, cooling himself with an absurd peacock fan. All power, including that of the climate control, is being conserved for the defense. "First we invade their planet and bring war to their cities. Then we sink a coastline. Now we let them wither as we huddle in their city?"

"Did I create the Mercurians to be of insubstantial fiber?" Thraxa asks. "No. They lack the warrior constitution to fight for their own freedom. Mercurian Reds are anemic compared with ours. Well, if they want to be slaves so badly, let them embrace their own degradation, I say."

"Thank you, Ash Lord. Let me get this proper. Because they do not agree with us, we let their children decay and their families die?" Harnassus sneers. The two have been at each other's throats since we returned to Mercury. The enmity has grown worse in Heliopolis. Harnassus considers Orion's storm a genocide. Thraxa thinks it the noblest of sacrifices.

"The populace is a time bomb," Thraxa says. "You want to keep it ticking. We could just let it fizzle out." She looks to me. "They're going to take up arms against us. We can make sure right here, right now, they can't lift those arms."

"I always suspected you were a demokrat of convenience," Harnassus replies. "At least Orion's villainy can be traced to anger. Yours is just cold blood."

"Cold blood wins wars," Thraxa says. "You should know. You're no snowy virgin yourself. Not after Echo City." Harnassus's jaw clenches. "If the Vox had more cold blood and less envy, the fleet would never have been split and vulnerable to Atalantia, and we'd never be in this quagmire. Your friends are to blame, Harnassus. You are to blame. And now you quibble and pretend like this is all Darrow's fault. The hypocrisy disgusts me."

Harnassus stands to his full unimpressive height. "I will not stand by and watch children decay."

"Then you will lie on your back shitting blood as your men decay," Thraxa says. "While my men do not."

"Enough," I snap. "You're like children. At least try, for me?" The door opens and Screwface prances in.

"Apologies," he says, stripping off his scarlet Heliopolitan scarf and riding gloves. "Two Gorgon were caught in the water filtration plant. Blaggards thought the Reds would be on their heels from rad poisoning. Sturdy Rat Legion is sturdy. I got this place on lock." He flops down in a chair and wrinkles his nose at Harnassus's cats. "What'd I miss?"

"We're just cutting to business," I say, "Harnassus, you've taken stock of the engineer and support legions, Thraxa the armored and heavy infantry, Screw the special ops and navy. What do you perceive our chances of escape to be?"

They grow quiet. Screwface looks at his manicured hands.

"That low? You'd never guess we just won our greatest statistical victory of the war."

"We just don't have the ships to escape," Harnassus says. "Four torch-Ships, one destroyer. The *Morning Star* may never fly again. If we take out all extraneous systems of the other ships, we could just barely fit the men. Doesn't matter anyway. Just two of Atalantia's dreadnoughts will make us atoms, and those torchShips of theirs are faster than the *Star*. If we get to space, they'll hunt us down. But we won't get to space. They have the gravity well. If a single ship made it to orbit, it would be a miracle."

"What if we . . . acquired their ships?" Thraxa asks, looking to Screwface. "Get a team to orbit and try to take one or two of those dreadnoughts."

His eyes go wide and he whistles. "I wouldn't volunteer personally . . . they're blasting anything that comes within a hundred klicks. And the Gorgon have response teams on board. Atalantia's just waiting with a net."

"She knows me too well for that to work this time," I say to Screw's nod of agreement. "If we saw an opening, it would likely be a trap. The noose is tightening. If we move outside the shield, she'll stomp on us like bugs."

I intended to move the ships in the storm cover, under the veil of electronic interference, to prepare some devilry for Atalantia. But the level of storm Orion summoned made that impossible, and even killed four of our torchShips. Now all my cards are used up. They know it. I know it. And I have the sneaking suspicion Atalantia knows it. There are no tricks left to play. "We are in a cage," I say. "All that can deliver us is the Sovereign. And I believe she will."

"You believe?" Thraxa says. "She won't move the Senate. The Vox will sacrifice us. Dancer will let us die to get back at you for the Sons on the Rim. No one is coming."

Sadly, Harnassus agrees. "I know Dancer. He'll wear diamonds before he risks Atalantia's trap, not after that false peace. He's prouder than he thinks. I know neither of you want to hear it, but after that battle we're not an army anymore. We're just bait on a hook. All's left to do is remove the bait."

"Surrender?" Thraxa asks in horror.

Harnassus's lips barely move. "Perhaps."

"If we surrender, they will kill all of us," Thraxa says.

"Worse," Screw says. "I would know. I've watched her play with Howlers." He blinks and covers his unease with a smile for a seagull that lands on the balcony outside.

"They would torture and kill us four," Harnassus agrees. "But they will need labor to rebuild after this. Not all of the men will survive, but some will. Some is better than none." He meets my eyes. "At least tell me you will consider it."

I lean back in my chair as Thraxa and Screwface hold their breath. "Harnassus, in order for me to consider that, I would have to continue to make the same mistake that put us here: doubt my wife. I have done that before, to the detriment of us all." With me taking shortcuts, as Sevro said. "And I would have to make a mistake I have not made in fifteen years: fool myself into believing slavery is better than death. I will not do that."

Thraxa nods. The tension releases from Screw. He's afraid of Atalantia. More afraid than he'll ever admit. Harnassus says nothing. He disagrees.

"I was ready to sacrifice this army to break theirs, because I did not believe the Republic would come. Because I thought killing them would give the Republic the best hope in this war. In that moment of choice, I listened to you, Harnassus. If we save this army, it will be a victory to inspire the worlds.

"We will save this army by having faith in our Republic, in our Sovereign. There will be no surrender, no escape plan that exposes the army so Atalantia can drive a stake through our hearts. My wife said the ships would come. So they *will* come. Until then, we share what we have with the civilians."

"It won't last the week," Thraxa objects.

"We share what we have with the civilians."

A knock comes at the door and Rhonna steps through looking frightened. "Sir, we've received a tightbeam from the *Annihilo*." Screwface's head snaps in her direction. "Atalantia has requested an audience." Her eyes dart to the floor. "She says it concerns your wife."

33

DARROW

The Devil's Deal

"I t's disappointing we didn't get to meet in person," I say to Atalantia. "I had such plans for you."

"Yes, well, I'm not terribly fond of having conversations when I'm on the back foot. And I will admit, you put me there."

"Lady, I fucked you up."

She grimaces. "Indeed, but that is the nature of you and me. Gamblers both. I won the first hand. You won the last. Though I must admit, I am surprised you had the temerity to use those machines. What devious designs freedom requires. One must worry about the strength of a principle when it must compromise itself so often to survive. At least we're consistent, eh?"

I do not tell her it was Orion's decision. More the monster I appear, more hesitant will she be in encroaching upon Heliopolis. Today she is in a playful mood, which worries me. I know I hurt her worse than she's letting on. Her eyes are of warm gold and her mouth sensuous in a way that reminds me of Nidhogg, the serpent of Obsidian myth who gnaws at the root of the world tree. She walks around her absurd gold throne, tracing her nails along its spikes. The snake that she customarily wears around her neck coils around the throne's arms.

She laughs at a private joke, then makes it public. "Don't you find it peculiar? The human conviction that we are the heirs of history instead of paragraphs that are almost over. A survival mechanism, no doubt.

"My father knew otherwise, of course," she continues. "He was even more avid an historian than Atlas with his little library. That's what made them fond of each other, you know. My father could read Sumerian, Akkadian, Eblaite, Hurrian, Hittite, Ugaritic, First Chinese, and thirty-two other dead languages. And all he learned from them was an aversion to risk. He was never fond of betting it all on a roll of the dice, like we do. But one story did stick. He told it to me when as a girl I had it in my mind to brawl with Aja when she rode my favorite sunblood stallion without asking."

She pulls the snake from the arm of her chair and lets it coil around her neck.

"In the years between 280 and 275 BC, a young king dared to resist the expanding Roman Republic." Her finger traces along the snake as it moves. "This king was beloved by his men, shrewd in the ways of battle. Much like you. To the surprise of the known world, he enjoyed initial successes against the legions. Appalling them with fearsome beasts from barbarous lands." The snake lifts its head toward Atalantia's face. "War elephants and the like. But these battles cost the king. He could not call up more men from his lands. And elephants are so few. In contrast, the Romans could draw from an immeasurable well of manpower." The snake's mouth slowly opens before Atalantia. "The king soon realized this and when congratulated for a victory, he cried out, 'If we are victorious in one more battle with the Romans, we shall be utterly ruined.'" Atalantia extends her tongue to take the smallest prick from the right fang of the snake. She shudders as the microdose of poison races through her bloodstream. Her voice creeps toward sensuous as she slinks toward her chair and sinks into its embrace. "I measure you know this king's name?"

"Pyrrhus," I answer. "Don't fret. I didn't waste your tax dollars to get a bad education."

"I presume you know, then, what happened next?"

"Rome consumed Pyrrhus because of his victories. But there is one problem. You are not Rome, are you?" I say.

"We are greater than Rome. You may have wounded my legions, but my fleet would eviscerate the Scepter Armada of ten years ago. With the reserves on Venus, my legions dwarf Octavia's standing army. We were a shadow of ourselves in her time. A tiny fraction of Peerless Scarred holding up the morbid obesity of the Pixies. But you have sharpened our edge. Given me a new generation of soldiers who want nothing more than to be the hand that killed the Reaper. The first is already in the fray. In four years' time, half a million will turn sixteen. You know the breeding protocols my father made law when Luna fell. Six hundred thousand triplets raised with one thing on their mind: subjugation."

"I wasn't talking about the Society, Atalantia. I was talking about you. You are what's lacking." She smiles, welcoming the critique. "Just the least-loved daughter of a butcher. I imagine you have convinced yourself it was because you were misunderstood. A survival mechanism, I imagine. But I knew Magnus. I fought him for almost a decade. We had chats like this, he and I. Though he never babbled like you, and we had a mutual understanding to not atomize every plot of ground we couldn't take.

"You were not misunderstood by your father, Atalantia. You were simply disliked. Aja was his pride. Moira was his joy. You were just . . . *there* with your silk, and your Venusian orgies. Acting out to get attention. And now you're his last resort. The pitiable last sentence of a family saga that is almost over." Her mouth takes on a truculent expression. "Even if you beat us here, the world has changed, and there is no place for you in it."

"No," she snaps. "Your civilization is a clumsy design. Given liberty, each man will seek his own delight. Few indeed are the men whose delight is war. Your civilization, then, does not want war. Our civilization is an efficient engine. It wants what I want. And what do you think I want?"

She smiles. Not because she knows she is right, but because she knows something I don't. For a woman with such a thin reputation before all this began, she has changed. The frivolity is gone. But the capricious cruelty natural to her spirit remains, emboldened now by her training under her father, by her collaboration with Atlas.

"You may have won a victory, but your situation is untenable. You are treading water," she says. "I understand it makes sense, knowing what you know. You believe your wife is coming for you. That she and Sevro will save you as they always have. I have beliefs too. I believe in beauty above all things. And I believe your religion of demokracy to be a disease. A disease that deceives you. That devours itself every time it has infected a civilization—Athens, the American Empire, the Indian. I proposed to my father that exposing this disease would cauterize it far more thoroughly than warfare. He was dubious. A pity he never saw sins of the past come to fruition."

Atalantia claps her hands together and her face disappears to reveal my wife speaking on the floor of the Senate. She looks younger than I remember. Pure and dazzling, when my world has become nothing but so much dust. In fact, everything seems absurdly white and clean—the robes of the senators, the marble, the air itself. Daxo rises to speak, and then my old friend Dancer. I sense something is wrong long before the blood spews from his mouth. And with creeping dread that mutates into abject revulsion, I watch the Senate disintegrate into a horror more appalling than I could ever imagine. The mob devours the Optimates.

They even sing Eo's song as they bear my dying wife upon a sea of bloody hands. I stare at her, at Daxo's head tossed about like a rubber ball through the crowd. I have felt this once before, when Eo swung upon the gallows. As if the foundation of my being were gone, and I glimpsed for one small moment the reality of my existence. There is no life without that woman. There is just a cold world and the ugly creatures who fight for its scraps.

I buried my wife in Lykos.

I took her down from the gallows and placed her remains in the dirt of the garden we found together, knowing it would be my death.

But that was the boy.

The man is broken, but he is not allowed to break. I blink as the Senate hall erodes into a flurry of light particles that coalesce into the face of my enemy.

"Your work?"

She touches her chest. "Subcontractor. For the culprit, I suggest you look a little closer to home. Even I couldn't poison the togas of that many senators. I wonder what they used. Anyway, I call it the Day of Red Doves." She frowns in pity. "Poor little Sisyphus pushing that boulder uphill for so long. It is beautiful in a way to see a man struggle against natural law. To see what human will can accomplish. And then to see your face now." She shudders with pure pleasure. "No betraying inflections. No microexpressions of grief. Simply obduracy, despite the dread clawing at the back of your eyes—a doomed army, a lost child, a dead wife." She wags a finger heavy with rings at me. "*That* is a Peerless Scarred. How much more gravitas he has than all the squabbling rats of demokracy."

"I assume you will be broadcasting this to my army," an empty voice says from my mouth.

She shrugs as if to say it is out of her hands. "I would not dare interrupt the demokratic process. Did not Virginia once say that transparency is the heart of the thing? You poor creature. All these years, you must have felt so trapped. Knowing what needed to be done, but unable to do it because of people weaker than you. If you had just marched your legions into the Senate instead of chasing after my father, you could have won this. Once you had the power, you could have remade the world with your wife at your side however you saw fit, and put your son on the throne. But that is the noble lie of demokracy, isn't it? The belief in humanity, even though humanity is a screaming, selfish mob. I love humans, truly. But humanity . . ." She shivers. "I wanted, I *needed* to see your face as you realized we were right all along. It is true beauty."

Is my wife dead? If not dead, scheduled to die at the hands of maniacs? Who leads them? Publius? It seems impossible for Dancer to be dead. What then of my son? What then am I? A creature so singleminded that he left his wife and child to be torn apart by a mob? I convinced myself my duty was here, and it would be selfish to return to Luna. I deluded myself into believing in the virtues of a Republic that is nothing but a sham. Was that just an excuse for me to carry on my bloody path?

"Virginia is not coming," Atalantia says. Her voice is harsh, done with its play. "Sevro is not coming. No one is coming. Disarm your forces. Assemble your men south of the city. Lower your shields. And submit to your fate with dignity. If you do this, I will behead you and your high command with proper ceremony. The rest of your men will be spared and put to labor according to their nature in rebuilding the planet you have left in tatters. If you commit suicide, this offer for your men is forfeit. If you reject my offer, I will drop atomics on Heliopolis and kill every man, woman, child, and dog for two hundred kilometers. Even the cockroaches won't survive. This is the only mercy you will receive."

"Bluff," I say robotically.

"I beg your pardon?"

"Rhea was one thing. This is Heliopolis."

"Heliopolis, Heliopolis, Heliopolis. It is a sty. A reliquary for the past, no matter how much that traitor Glirastes opines on its virtues. All I need is the metal in those mountains, your life, and those of that Te-lemanus bitch and that ugly Orange bastard." She hesitates. "And that beautiful Colloway of yours on a leash. As for Mercury." She makes a face. "And Mars? Helium can be mined in hell for all I care. As long as my bathwater is warm, I'll never notice."

The horror of an entire generation of Reds slaving in an irradiated wasteland overwhelms me. Mutations. Death by thirty. That cannot be how this ends.

"You are not a Sovereign," I say flatly. "You are just glue. Glue that barely holds together the Two Hundred. If you destroy Heliopolis, the Votum will decry you. How many of those Two Hundred will wonder what you'll do to their cities? How would Julia au Bellona like you atom-izing Olympia? How would the Carthii feel about a mushroom cloud over Harmonia?

"No," I say with rising anger. "If you nuke us, you will be deposed. But you need to leave. Don't you? So desperately you can feel it in your bones. The Republic is in turmoil, you could drive a nail through it if you could just use your ships. Yet they're stuck here guarding me like two-bit tinpots. Is it because I put the Minotaur on Venus? Is it some-thing else? Or maybe it's just that no matter how many strapping young Golds you send after me, all you get back is piles of meat. You need us to surrender, because you're afraid of me, and even more afraid of be-coming Pyrrhus yourself."

"Perhaps," she says. "But it's your bet."

I replay the conversation between Atalantia and myself to the officers of my high command. Screwface straddles the balcony outside, his desert shades hiding his eyes. No aides line the warroom, the coffee is forgotten at a side table. The Day of Red Doves has streamed on every screen in Heliopolis that has power. It is the only signal from beyond our cage. They mock us from orbit. But this conversation is what matters. The image dissolves, leaving darkness on the faces of my commanders. Har-nassus slumps in the chair to my right. Thraxa stares at a fly hovering over a vine by the window. She has not spoken since she learned Daxo has died. The news has rattled her in a way nothing else ever has. What of her mother, her father, her sisters?

"Until now . . ." My voice betrays me. I clear my throat. "Until now our strategy was based upon the belief that the Republic was on its way. I do not believe it . . . practical to continue in this assumption. I have reason to believe that Publius is an agent of Atalantia's. Or that the events that took place in the Senate were the product of her designs. The Vox Populi are compromised. I would caution you against recognizing the authority of any element on Luna." I look at Harnassus, knowing Atalantia will likely beam him a message from Publius and the surviving Senate demanding surrender.

"We have been given an offer with a twenty-four-hour clock. An offer that we have no reason to believe our enemy would honor." I pause, knowing what I am about to say is true, but feeling a coward nonetheless. "I do not believe that I can chart an unbiased course given the situation." I wave a hand as Thraxa and several others rise from their seats in protest. "Just let me get this out." Colloway and Harnassus remain absolutely still. Of the two, I can't tell which looks worse, though the ripper pilot is certainly drunk. I hear Screwface had to pull him from a brothel to get him here. "An army is not a democracy. But given our situation, I do not believe it should be despotism." I try to look around the table, but find it difficult to meet their eyes. I fell into Atalantia's trap. I brought them here. I sowed the seeds of my wife's end, and the end of our Republic. I may not have done it alone, but it hardly matters. "Most of you have been with this army as long as I have. It is your family as much as it is mine. You will decide its fate. I will accept any decision you make. The only plea I offer is that you decide based on what is best for our men, and then the Republic."

With that, I leave Thraxa, Harnassus, Colloway, Screwface, and the rest of the high command in the high warroom to decide my fate and that of the Free Legions. I walk along the lower balconies where night mist beads on the stone walls. The waves crash all around the roots of the building. Both were made by man. Perhaps at first in hope, to give our species a new home to live and to love. But in time, I don't know when, their creation became a vanity of will, and in the shadow of that vanity, man grew lesser for having more. Lesser for mastering the keys of creation, because he mistook himself for god, and cared less for his people, and more that his works endured.

Have I done the same?

With a great sucking sound, the black water pulls back to reveal the work it has done to the roots of the stone after all these years. And then the waves crash back. A cavernous solitude makes a home in my chest, where once there was only purpose that made far too little room for my boy and my wife.

I return to my room and take Pax's key from my luggage. I wrap its chain around my neck and hold it as I stare at the ceiling.

34

LYSANDER

Shadows of War

"ARE YOU AWAKE OR ASLEEP, *Lysander?*"
I'm not in the desert.

I am at Lake Silene.

Snow clings to the evergreens. It makes the stones slippery under my feet. My legs tremble as I haul myself up the stairs that wind up the cliff from the lake to the house. I drop a stone the size of my abdomen atop a cairn. My hands are bloody and shaking. It is the winter after my parents died.

I look up to see the severe face of my grandmother.

I am terrified of her, but desperate for her approval. Even now, knowing what she did, the boy in the memory cannot hate her. He is too afraid to hate.

I thought the week would be just for Aja and me. I never get her to myself. Atalantia had taken Ajax to Echo City to watch the water races. I thought Aja and I would take the horses north, but Grandmother has come back from Hyperion to continue my lessons.

She is inescapable.

"I asked you a question."

"I am awake."

"Are you? How many crows are in the trees that line the steps?"

I look to Aja for help. She watches evenly from her perch on a fallen log.

"Will you look to Aja every time you need saving?"

"I do not know how many crows there are."

"You do not know?" I look down. "Never manifest shame physically. Look

at me." There's no anger in her face. There never is. "How many owls are there? Hawks? Squirrels?"

"I don't know, Grandmother."

"Do you really think you've earned the right to use contractions yet?" She leans forward. "Why do you not know? I will answer, since your tongue is lead. Your mind was asleep. Do you at least know how many steps there are?"

"Four hundred thirty-one."

"How many turns?"

"Seventeen."

"Are you certain?"

"Yes, Grandmother."

"Good. You know something at least. Pick up a rock." I obey. It weighs half as much as my body. "Close your eyes. And run back down the steps."

"Octavia . . ." Aja whispers.

"You have already spoilt your churlish spawn, Aja. Let us not ruin the batch. Is something the matter, Lysander? You said there are four hundred thirty-one steps. How many times have you run them? A thousand? Ten? This should be no difficulty. Begin."

I surge downward, knowing this I can do. I can impress her. My steps are confident, even in the ice, even with the weight. I see the steps burned into the backs of my eyelids. I make it three hundred twenty-one steps before something on the steps starts. There's a flutter of movement that slaps into my face. I lose my balance. The weight of the stone is unforgiving. It pulls me forward.

When I open my eyes, I am at the bottom of the steps. The bone of my right arm is out of the skin. It looks curiously pale. I begin to shudder. Aja is at my side, holding me. My grandmother descends the steps.

"Aja."

"His bones haven't fully—"

"Aja."

Aja lets me go and I lie in the snow staring up at my grandmother.

"Stand up." I struggle to my feet and look her in the eye. "Why did you fall?" I cannot speak for the pain. "Recede into your Mind's Eye. Exist with the pain, then let it draw your inner pupil to tighter focus."

I do as she demands. The pain does not lessen, but it no longer clouds. Its current pulls my mind narrower and constricts my concentration to retrace the memory. Sure enough, I find the outlying variable. A slight crunch as I descended the three hundred sixteenth step. Just before the crows.

"You put feed on the steps for the crows," I whisper.

"Good. But are you not in control of your own body? Why did you let me dictate where you fell? If you were awake you would have sensed the crows were not in the trees any longer. You would have felt the seed underfoot, and adjusted to the fresh variable." She bends down. "You have a brain like mine. That is why you are my heir. That is why I have made you my son. But you must never let your mind sleep. Your Mind's Eye must rove without rest. Even as you speak, eat, move, it is not enough for it to collect data, it must digest it as a subfunction, or you will miss something and become a slave to another."

She kneels to look me eye to eye. "You are known. Another will always seek to bridle you. With fists. With kisses. With tricks." She brushes snow from my shoulders, and pain comes into her eyes. "The tragedy of the gifted is the belief they are entitled to greatness, Lysander. As a human, you are entitled only to death." She stands. "Now, are you awake or asleep?"

"Awake."

"Prove it. Again."

I walk suspended between the past and the hard reality of the desert. There is pain. More than I thought possible. The left half of my face is a ruin of melted meat. It is swollen with fluid that expands the skin to bursting. Pus leaks through the bandage Kalindora helped me attach. My left eye is blind and obliterated. Bits of melted metal have hardened over much of the wound. Unable to see my reflection, I can only imagine the horror.

All I can do is walk.

Foot after foot over the hardpan. There is no more water left to share amongst our ragged band. While I could survive nine days without it in a temperate climate, the desert and my wound conspire to drain every drop.

I will not last long.

I cannot help but feel we are being followed. That something watches from the desert.

It is hard to tell. More bands like ours wander the playa, only to disappear behind veils of dust. It would not be good to congregate with wayward infantry anyway. Supplies dwindle. Weary bands trudge toward their imagined salvation. But we are all just burnt shadows of war.

The killing field was days ago, yet it stalks me like a ghost through the days. Perhaps that is what I feel. The sensation of destiny broken. The dread of the killing field. Two starShells pinning me down. Mutilated men and metal carpeting the ground. The battle had moved on shortly after I woke. Its sound echoed like distant thunder, and all I could do was lie there as night came, listening to the delirium of the dying.

When the sun dipped behind the mountains, the nocturnal predators came to feast on the dead. Their eyes glowed like coins as they fed. I could hear men wailing as they were dragged into the night. Then came the human scavengers down from the bleak mountains to sift through the bodies and harvest electronics and weapons. Heads covered in dust-colored cloth and silver goggles. A boy with a welding torch came for my sigils. There was a firefight, I remember. Then familiar faces.

I think it was Rhone and Kalindora who freed the first of us. The pain consumed me and makes it hard to remember. But I know I was guided by Kalindora away from the slaughter to where survivors exchanged water from their suit caches and bandaged wounds. Rhone said he would come back for us once they freed more Praetorians from their suits.

He never did.

We hid in the foothills, leeched of bravery as Rising soldiers landed in force. We were too weak to contest them. So we watched as they gathered up Rhone and our comrades and herded them onto shuttles at gunpoint. They headed south, to Heliopolis, I imagine.

So Ajax lost.

I can feel no satisfaction in that. How many men died for Atalantia's avarice? For Ajax's glory? For Darrow's victory?

For days we have walked, striking north in hopes of finding Society patrols. We were thirty at the start. Then seventy as elements of Ajax's shattered legions caught up with us before their boots or bikes died. On the second day, Cicero and four of his Golds found us camped in a ravine. They joined us without comment, all but guns and water satchels discarded. Though later we learned that Ajax fled the battle when the tide turned, and few of his men escaped.

The Scorpion Obsidians die first from the heat. Then many of the Grays, including my Praetorians. Only the hardiest amongst them stagger with us now. We have little water to share.

Seven Golds remain, including Kalindora and Cicero. To the west, the mountain peaks ride the waves of the heat-warped horizon. To the east, the waste stretches as if it were all that existed. War machines move beyond the irradiated clouds.

Desiccated tanks from Darrow's surprise retreat across the Ladon stand blackened in the distance, victims of lucky hits by naval guns through the mess of the electrical storm. How Darrow slipped the noose is beyond understanding. Or it would be if the Golds fought as an army instead of as a collective of greedy autarchs.

We did this to ourselves. And our men, my Praetorians, millions of civilians and loyal legionnaires paid the price.

Umbra visit us as we walk. White chalk twisters that spin ninety meters high. They cake us with chalk and coat our lungs with a thin white film that comes out in clumps when we cough.

A fever has gripped me since I was pulled from the killing field. Reveries come and go. I see my father and grandmother often. Sometimes there is a chair. Great and silver and carved with eccentric faces. I have never seen it before. And there is a white door that appears always on the horizon, accompanied by the sound of cicadas and the crashing of waves.

I have seen it before in my dreams.

Sometimes I reach it.

It swings open to reveal nothing but shadow. And then it is on the horizon again.

I stumble often on the unstable sand and chalk, but Kalindora steadies me. She cauterized her left arm just beneath the shoulder where Darrow's blade hacked it off. Still, she is the source of our momentum, the quiet, optimistic heart of our desperate push toward Erebos. We will not make it, I think. With the interference from the storm disrupting our trackers, our best hope is a chance encounter with Society forces. If any still remain.

In late afternoon, we discover the remains of a stork crashed into the sand. We harvest it for supplies, and gather around to see if its coms are working. They are not. But at least we have water and rations. Kalindora declares it our camp for the night. Five Praetorian Grays and seven Golds hunker between the boulders to wait for the sun to depart.

Soon after nightfall we hear ships in the sky.

"They can't see us," Cicero says from the nest he's made in the dirt. Of all the survivors, he seems the only one to retain any of his humor.

"Thirty million soldiers fought in that battle," Kalindora says. "Even if they could, you try picking up all those pieces."

"But we are the scions of ancient houses," Cicero protests. "The very desert should lift us to salvation. I tell you. When I saw the *Morning Star* emerge from the storm, I thought I'd take any form of possible future as grace. But between the heat, the sun, this blasted sand, the nightcrawlers, and Rising hunting parties, I have the sneaking suspicion that we are going to die in the most worthless fashion."

"*Pulvis et umbra sumus,*" I reply.

"That was a Raa, wasn't it?" Cicero asks. "The one who tried to dance with the rail slug?" I nod. "I swear, those fuckers quote themselves almost as much as the Augustans. *Here be lions* indeed. What I'd give for a nice lion hunt right now. Sherry by the fire on the savanna as a nice flank of meat bubbles over the fire."

"You eat lion?" I mumble, though the act of speaking makes my face feel as though it will fall off. "Isn't it—"

"Stringy? Oh indeed, it's more about the aesthetic and political innuendo really. Actually, I have a tale! You lot look like you could use one." He rubs his hands together. He always did love the limelight. "Father let me join when he took old Nero au Augustus himself for a hunt once—my, but that man was mad. Refused to eat anything he didn't kill with a razor. He was fast, though, almost caught a white gazelle at a watering hole. Two more strides and he would have had him in the sprint."

"No one can catch a desert gazelle. I don't care how ancient one's genes are," Kalindora says. "The Augustans were no faster than anyone else."

Cicero pauses, cocking his head toward the desert as if he heard something. With a shake of his curled hair, he returns to his story, frowning when a clump of it falls out. "That's what Father told old Telemanus. But Kavax just told him to watch. You know what Nero did when the gazelle escaped? He kept running, even when it had him by two kilometers. He was gone the whole night. And then he came back with it on his shoulders while the Browns were laying out breakfast the next morning. All covered in cuts and dirt. I'll remember what he said till the day I'm shot into the sun." He takes on a very obnoxious rendition of Augustus's Martian timbre. "Beasts must stop for water. I carry mine."

Kalindora belts out a laugh that startles one of the sleeping Grays. "That's a load of shit."

Cicero looks direly offended. "How dare you impugn my honor. As sure as Heliopolis is the second most beautiful city in the worlds, Tyche being the first, of course."

Kalindora snorts. "More like Elysium. No arguments for Hyperion, Lysander?"

I shrug.

"Elysium is as cold as a *logos*'s groin," Cicero crows. "And he said what he said, 'I carry mine.' What a man, Nero. But that's not the best part. Father doesn't like to be the small man on his own planet. So the next day, he shot himself one of those big Nemean lions and tried serving it up to Augustus at dinner."

"I imagine that went well," Kalindora says.

"Surprising fact about Nero," Cicero says with a wag of the finger. "Vast sense of humor."

"Like you knew him."

"I did. And I watched as he ate without complaint and even asked for seconds. Old Kavax was sitting there all quiet-like, though. You could tell he was nervous. And then a month later, after the trade talks were complete and we all felt a little slutty about making Augustus richer than Jove, he sends this young man. A lancer. One of those Martian war machines. You know the type, Kalindora. The sort that made sure you were no spring flower by the time you got to Luna. Killing in their veins. Huge. Not the biggest man I'd ever seen, mind you, that was Magnus's slaveknight—Pale Horse or whatever his name was—but his anger was like heat off a tank barrel. His manners were flawless, for an upstart, still you could hear that Martian war-drum heart beating along with Nero's silent boast. *Look at my fresh crop. I have more of these.* In his hands, that big killer carried the most delicate, beautiful box. Carved ivory with lions in all sorts of dramatic poses. 'Compliments of Mars,' breathed the man and away he went back to a gorydamn destroyer with helium to burn."

"What was in the box?" Kalindora asks. "A head?"

"Grapes. Only grapes. And a little note. 'Work in progress.' Father went white as the box and didn't sleep for a week. Mother had to buy five new Stained and a whole new fleet of courtesans before Father would even use his harem again."

Kalindora grins down at her ration bar wrapper. "Now, that is cold."

"None colder than old Nero," Cicero replies. "Want to hear the best part? Guess who the lancer was?"

"Darrow," I rasp through my tattered lips.

"That's right," Cicero says with a squint. "We had him here. I think it was sixteen years ago. Just after the Institute. One of his first missions. Seventeen, a lackey to a god, and ticking, ticking, like a time bomb."

Later, after Kalindora has gone to sleep, Cicero slides over to me. "So much for Atalantia's bagwoman." In the darkness, Kalindora looks less like a warrior. Peaceful in a way, as peaceful as a woman with a cauterized stump for a left arm can look while suffering radiation sickness. Maybe it was foolish to meet the Reaper in open battle. But I cannot erase the pride I felt when she nodded to me at my decision to stay. Still, how many Praetorians lie in the dust for that valor? How many men and women drowned in the sea? Cicero eyes the rancid stump where her left arm used to be. "Think she'll die of infection?"

"Not before rad poisoning," I say. "Or thirst."

He eyes the soiled bandage on my face. "How much does it hurt?"

"Enough."

"You knew that story," he says. "How?"

"You mean how did I know about the Storm Gods?" I reply, intuiting his real question. "Nero had his helium. You have your metals. Octavia had her information."

"Information, yes. Speaking of information . . ." His voice lowers. "I've some information an erudite mind like yours has no doubt already deduced. Based on our water requirements, and our likely rate of consumption, we'll run out several days from Erebos. We don't have enough to get all of us there. The Grays will have a trial in this next stretch. It's straight desert for several hundred klicks. If a patrol doesn't find us, or we don't get lucky with civilians . . ."

"No," I say.

"You couldn't stop me. You can barely walk," he says flatly.

"If that's the man you want to be, go on then," I say, with every intention of killing him in the night if I suspect he intends to kill my Grays.

"You think I want to do it for myself? You think I'm that venal? I'm not a Venusian or a Lunese sucking others dry," he says in disgust. "We Votum are builders. You don't know me at all. What I've had to watch." I don't say anything to that. "Darrow might have broken our planet, but Atalantia and her father have been raping it for years to feed their war. It's a lonely feeling when you realize your father, despite his many triumphs, is an invertebrate. I'll tell you that. My brother and sister stood up to Atalantia, but they were at Tyche. And that storm . . ." He looks north and doesn't finish the sentence. "Father can't handle her on his own."

"What do you want from me?" I ask. "Permission to abandon good men? You won't have that."

"You abandoned yours," he says. "Watched them fly right away to Heliopolis. Including Rhone ti Flavinius himself. So who are you angry at, me or yourself?"

He's right, and he knows it. Still, it's the principle. And if I give up that, I'll have nothing left. "I might not be able to stop you. But if you go for the Grays, you'll have to kill me too."

He mutters something to himself as he edges away to find a place amongst the rocks. Soon he is fast asleep. Kalindora opens her eyes. She's been listening.

"I'll take watch," she whispers. "Try and get some sleep."

35

DARROW

Endure

I'M WOKEN IN THE EARLY MORNING by a presence. A lean man moves through my room. He stands by the edge of the bed with his hands hidden. But I no longer sleep in beds, not even here in the center of my army. From the bathroom, upon the thin campaign mattress, I watch with my hand clutched around a pistol. How did he get past the guards? I aim for the base of his skull. A sliver of light from a passing ship illuminates his face as he turns. It is Screwface.

I clear my throat and he turns, jumping a little as he sees the gun.

"What is it?"

"I want to show you something, boss."

I've nearly died that way before. When Cassius took me down to the river to stab me, and Lea led me into Antonia's trap at the Institute.

"Just tell me here," I say.

"Oh, come on. Who do you trust, if you don't trust old Screw?" He has been with me since the beginning. Never asking for anything. Never earning fame like Sevro, or family like Pebble and Clown. He is maybe the most like me. A creature of war. It looks lighter on him. He extends a hand down to help me up. With a weary nod, I take it.

My friend leads me by the pale light of a lamp through the pale stone halls of the Mound. Maritime wind lolls through the open windows, carrying the tang of brine and the murmurs of seagulls. It creeps past the guards of the night watch, stirring their cloaks, to kiss the bald, weary soldiers who cough flecks of blood under the gaze of Votum portraits in the grand ballrooms, libraries, and pillaged galleries of a more decadent age.

We go out the back of the palace. Descending down the switchbacking sea cliff stairs that connect with the ancient seawall. The sky pales to a dull chrome in anticipation of sunrise, but the bay beneath remembers the darkness of night. Its high tide crashes against a coral scarp at the base of the seawall. And with a backrush, the tide reveals a second world of wildlife. Coral crabs and sealarks skitter and dodge the gulls and fire eagles that swoop through the spray to feed.

We pass Red Rat legionnaires sharing coffee at the base of particle cannons. While the rest of the army withers from radiation poisoning, only my Reds soldier on. In the absence of Pegasus Legion, Rat Legion has become the spine of the army. They nod to us and return to their coffee. Soon we pass lines of coughing Mercurians fishing off the side of the seawall, then descend the wall's interior stairs and exit through a gate that leads out beyond the wall to a barrier beach running parallel to the shore.

A congregation of two parts gathers in the gloom. Men and women wet from the sea make the first. They are jubilant. An aching song drifts from them, a Red one I remember hearing as a child. But it is not just Reds who sing it; other Colors are scattered through their ranks. The second and more numerous group by far is a long line of hunched, bitter creatures who wait in silence. One by one they slump out to a man who stands waist-deep in the surf. He whispers something to them. They clutch their fists out before them and shout as they are dunked into the sea. Many are blind. All are already so sick with radiation, they don't fear the seawater.

It seems I have entered a dream, and it cracks as I am seen. The song fades. And they turn warily to watch me. Even the blind know I am here. I feel ashamed to have intruded on this private moment. They are Martians all. The dirt so many of them brought in canisters from home is clutched in their hands. They followed me here, but I do not feel like one of them any longer. These arms and legs that have stripped lives from so many seem all the heavier and more alien here. This height given to me by a mad carver seems like a monstrous feature I wish I could hide and be rid of so that I could stand amongst them, part of them, a man of mines, following someone else.

I salute them and retreat across the sand.

Screwface catches up to me. "What was that?" I snap at him.

"I thought—"

"That I wanted to have a holy communion? You think those men need to see their Imperator begging for forgiveness?"

"Nah, but I thought maybe you needed it."

"What I need is to be left alone."

He doesn't leave me alone, and I don't want to go back to the Mound and face the decision of the high command or be burdened with more endless complaints and problems. I don't want to sit in my room and think about my son and wife. So I strike south along the beach, leaving the penitent behind, wishing I could join them, but knowing a leader cannot.

It would be immoral to rob them of that last bit of confidence they have left in me.

In time, I begin to forget where I am as I walk. Screwface follows behind at a distance. The ocean sighs against the shore. Sand crabs skitter along the waterline, navigating mounds of kelp populated with sea fleas. I walk until we reach a climate seam. Soon, low-altitude Agathis trees sway along the shoreline. Migratory Nymph trees wade in the water on legs of white and pink roots. Jungle archipelagos dapple the horizon, the nearest home to a Free Legion defense gun. Local birds perch atop its metal barrel.

The topography reminds me of South Pacifica, where outside his ancestral estate Daxo taught my son to build a sandcastle. He spent more time with Pax that day than I did, taking him into the woods with the huntmasters, walking through his statue garden to listen to birds and see if he could name them, and back to the beach to see their mighty sandcastle washed away by the night tide. All while I sat inside preparing the invasion of Grimmus-held Africa.

How sad I didn't cherish a moment there with my son.

All moments are like that sandcastle, it seems.

There is no permanent happy future. There is no Vale.

It all washes away.

The shield flickers overhead. I glance back at Screwface with a frown. Barefoot, he jogs up holding his boots. "Friendlies?"

I see them now through the clouds. Streaks of falling fire. The shield ripples back on, killing birds in its energy arc, but now the falling projectiles are inside it. My first thought is that we've been betrayed. But the projectiles slow over the sea. The air around them distorts from gravitational fields. Water floats upward along with fish and a long ebony squid before crashing back down.

Nearly forty six-story obelisks stand end-on-end offshore. The water boils around them as they cool.

"What are they?" Screwface asks.

"That looks like Sun Industries stealth hull," I say.

He gives me a bored look and raises an eyebrow. "What say we do a little reconnaissance, boss?"

"We should wait for reinforcements."

"Some badass you are." He strips off his shirt and pants and runs to the water. "Where's your sense of adventure!" He dives into a wave.

"Ah, shit." I strip off my shirt and follow him in. The sea is warm as bathwater. Flash-cooked fish float around the obelisks, killed when the obelisks transferred their heat into the sea. I dive down and find the bottom of an obelisk thoroughly embedded in the seafloor. By the time I surface, Screwface is already climbing up the slippery hull along a line of rivets. I follow. There seems to be a hatch at the top.

"Ah, the cavalry," Screwface mocks a minute later as a line of shuttles swoop our way from Heliopolis. There's men onshore waving to us from beside their gravBikes. They seem to be celebrating. My fingers ache from supporting my body weight with their tips. Screw shows off by hanging on to the rivets with two fingers and leaning off to wave to the men. He glares at the shuttles.

"Going to let the airheads take your glory?" I ask.

He scoffs and hoists himself up another meter. By the time we make it to the top, a shuttle has sped ahead of the rest. They race us to hover over the hatch of a nearby obelisk. Screwface makes it to the top first. Me a second later, fingers aching like hell.

Screwface beats his chest and howls just before the shuttle makes it to the top of the closest obelisk. Through the viewport, I catch sight of Char giving us the crux.

"Infantry!" Screwface bellows. The men on the shore echo the call and join his howl. He slaps at me to do the same. I turn my attention to the hatch. It is painted with the Republic star.

Soon the deserted patch of coast swarms with engineers. Heavy hauler shuttles drag the obelisks to shore after the bomb squad inspection. I wait with Screwface and hundreds of perimeter guards and dockworkers as they open the first obelisk. It parts down the middle, revealing a superstructure of pods. They crack the first one open. It is filled with thousands of duroglass cylinders.

I stumble forward and fall to my knees before a mound of the cylinders. Each is stamped with a silver winged heel. Each is filled with enough radiation meds to last a man a month, and there are thousands of pods, thirty-eight obelisks. Each cylinder will become a life saved from radiation. I run my fingers over them in a state of grace. Screwface collapses to his haunches beside me; he opens a pod and finds it filled with food, medicine, and materiel. He falls backward onto the sand, rolling around until he looks like a sugar-covered pastry.

I sit in shade as the rest of the boxes are unpacked and ferried back to Heliopolis. Inside one of the obelisks, they found a message for me. I rub the datadrop between my fingers, and activate it.

"'Lo, husband," my wife says with a gentle smile. I pause it. Her face floats in my palms. I hold it there for a minute, cherishing the words on her lips, the absence of any other thought but me on her mind. The wind makes the palm fronds overhead swish like the skirts of Red girls at Laureltide.

Reluctantly, I resume the message, and the strain of the worlds floods my wife's face. I see the weight and worry behind the eyes—for our son, for me, for her Republic. Her battle may be different from mine, but it is battle all the same, and she is tired.

"I must be brief. These pods were launched with the new guns. It wasn't the intended method of delivery, but efforts to send ships have . . . stalled. There are games afoot on Hyperion and beyond. Victra has quit Luna for Mars. Sevro has been chewing his way through the Syndicate here, and meddling with my own designs, as per custom. Sefi has disappeared, with machinations for the mines of Cimmeria. Though I no longer believe she is the Queen of the Syndicate, she has the children. I believe Pax is safe in her custody and will be ransomed back to Victra for her aid in Sefi's acquisition of the mines."

Relief floods through me. Despite the bedlam of Luna, my boy might have escaped it. He is not with enemies. Pax will be safe. Valdir would die before he let Sefi touch a hair on his head.

"An unseen hand moves the pieces, a clever one by any measure—Atalantia? Atlas? I presume so. My theories are attached. I believe I am beginning to divine the pattern, and soon I will make my move. I have included *my files in case they aid your situation. Also included are the intelligence reports of the System's current standing. They will be two weeks old, so use them wisely.*

"I believe your victory has given me the momentum to swing the Senate. Five days from the time this message was recorded, we will have voted and the fleet will either be under way when you receive this or it will not. But no matter what the Senate decides, at midnight on the first of May, I will come to Mercury. If fortune favors, it will be as a Sovereign. If not, it will be as a wife."

She pauses. Her voice softens, and she becomes my wife again.

"I know you are weary. I know you think Mercury will be your grave. That the Republic has abandoned you, and that the weight of what you have done threatens to eat a hole in you. But for me, for your son, I beg you not to despair. Our crusade was not founded on the success of our arms but in the righteousness of our cause, and our belief in our fellow man. So believe in your men. Believe in our Republic." She smiles self-consciously. *"Believe in me and in yourself.*

"You know I believe we all begin equal parts light and dark. I fear you think your strength lies in your darkness. But the measure of a man is not the fear he sows in his enemies. It is the hope he gives his friends. I could no more ask Pax to stop tinkering with my datapad than I could ask you to change who you are. I know that. I only ask that you remember what you mean to me, to your people, to your son. You have not been abandoned. I will come for you. Sevro will come for you. The Republic will come for you. Until then: endure, my love. Endure."

"Do you remember that spring on Earth in Pacifica?" I ask Thraxa as she walks me down the hall to the warroom. The high command has decided on a reply to Atalantia's offer. "Daxo taught my son to build castles in the sand. Pax cried when the waves came in. Your brother sat him on his knee and told him that's all life is. Moments you build only to see washed away. But that doesn't mean it's all for nothing." I stop at the door and tap my temple like Daxo tapped Pax's. "The key is having a long memory for the sweet, and a short one for the bitter. I will miss your brother, Thraxa. But he isn't gone."

She nods but does not smile. "You might be the only person from whom that sentiment doesn't sound cheap. But if they killed Niobe or Kavax, I will personally drown Luna in blood."

She opens the door and goes in.

Harnassus sits at the head of the warroom table in my chair. The rest of the high command fill either side of the table. I stand before them. "Right then, what's what?"

"Darrow, I apologize that it took us so long to come to a decision," Harnassus says. "But given its gravity, we wanted to give it due respect." He turns his attention to the officers. "You all know I am a proud member of the Vox Populi and even prouder to have called Dancer O'Faran my friend. In his name, First Citizen Publius cu Caraval and the Senate have ordered me to seize command of the army, arrest Darrow as an enemy of the people, and surrender to the enemy, using the terms Atalantia and our Senate have agreed upon." The officers sit without expression. "In reflection of this body's consensus, I have sent a reply to Atalantia regarding her terms of surrender: '*Bloodydamn.*'"

"Bloodydamn?" I ask. They begin to smile

A sucking sound comes from the heart of the sky. I rush to the terrace as several panes of the shield chain protecting the peninsula and the city disappear. A half breath later, the world is swallowed in light. There is a great roar. I'm blind for half a minute. When my vision returns, the afterimage ghosts of particle beams throb, and the distant guns on the mountains over the city glow like embers. In orbit, one of Atalantia's dreadnoughts burns.

Her retaliation falls just as the shields go back up.

I walk back inside as the room vibrates with manmade thunder.

"Bloodydamn, and a full barrage from our particle cannons." Harnassus leans back and grins. "I believe it is a well-measured reply that leaves little ambiguity for her deviant brain to conjure."

He turns his eyes to the officers and cracks his knuckles one by one. "It's been a long war. I've seen things that I'll never scour from my memory banks, but never have I seen such a travesty as that *farce* on Luna." He leans forward, true menace in his voice. "My friends, our system of governance has been hijacked. Our heroes murdered. Our Sovereign taken captive." His lips curl back from his teeth. "That will not stand with me. We are in an alien, inhospitable land. We must get home before there is no home left."

He rises from my chair and walks across the room to stand close to me as if in challenge. He points to the chair.

"That is a chair I cannot fill. I will not fill. Every man and woman in this army volunteered to fight with the understanding that they would be led by the Reaper of Mars. Behind him, we liberated our homes. Behind him, we found our way from the desert. He will deliver us from this planet. And he will take us home, where we will fix this madness and string Caraval up by his ears." He tilts his chin upward. "Even if he does not, I would rather follow him to the Vale than abandon him and live to a hundred and fifty."

"Fuck the Vox," Colloway calls from his chair. "Hail Reaper."

The officers echo the call.

I walk to the chair without a word. I pause before it. It is an ornate Votum treasure carved with birds and trees. I did not notice before, when it meant nothing to me. I sit down in it, and the arms of it embrace me. For a moment, I imagine they are the arms of my wife and son. I close my eyes and think of them. I believe they are alive. I believe I will return to them. And if not, on the road to home is where I will die. I grip Pax's key on its chain. When my eyes open, my officers are waiting for a miracle. This is my family too. Colloway, Screwface, Harnassus, Thraxa, Rhonna. We have given Mercury Alexandar, Orion, Tongueless, Felix, Marbles, and so many more. I am done with sacrifice. I will get my family home. I will endure.

"Summon the Master Maker Glirastes."

36

LYRIA

Victim

I LIE ON THE COLD FLOOR, starving myself to death.
When last did I dance? When ever did my brothers spin me between them till I tumbled to the dirt and watched their pale legs move
beneath a horizon of skirts and ribbons? Was the rhythm of life really
once made by dancing drums and shift-calls and boots rattling as
Gamma miners came home to the squealing of kettles?

Or was that all a dream?

They said we were slaves. And we were, I reckon. I ain't so dumb or so
lonely to forget that forty years once marked a man as old, or the radiation tumors that'd make a child's belly swell. But that world at least
made sense, before we were told it didn't.

It had rhythm I felt. It had family I loved. We had purpose I understood. Now that world's gone. Not just for me. For everyone.

But there was no purpose to the assimilation camp, where my family
was hacked to pieces by the Red Hand. There was no family in Hyperion. Save Liam. And no rhythm in this prison chamber where I lie victim to sound and light.

Light spasms in the center of my prison. The light combusts with the
violence of deepmine gas, only to melt into thin red ribbons like the
ones sweethearts would tie on the sleeves of Lagalos gallants for the Laureltide dance.

Noise pumps through the walls to torture me. Not music, but human
screams that morph and stretch and scrape like teeth along ragged rock.
Deafening percussion makes my eardrums crackle. I'd cover them but

then I can't cover my eyes, and even when I cover my eyes, the light flares so bright I can see the bones in my hands. They look like the veins of a leaf.

What I'd do to hear a leaf whisper in the wind again.

Sometimes when all those bodies crammed into my family's shack grated on my nerves, I'd go sit at the edge of the jungle and listen to it speak.

Since that bitch of a Brown plunged the syringe into my neck, I've heard nothing of jungles or the wind. Last thing I remember was the warm water of the shower falling on my tummy. The cold of the stone against my back. When darkness came, I felt I'd slipped back into my mother's womb. I dreamt of her, and my sister. Then I woke to the cold of my chamber, a headache pulsing behind the left eye, and bile crusted on my lips.

How long ago was that again?

A week?

A month?

Five?

Of my family, only Liam survives. I hold out hope for his father, Varon, my sister's husband. And for my brothers: cherished Aengus, and even brooding, angry Dagan. But all three are at the front. Who knows if they have gone on to the Vale, if Liam has.

I wish I could dream of them as I did my mother and sister. But dreams are scarce now. Fragments of sleep crumble through my fingers, shaken away by the noise, the light. Even if I do manage to doze off, the gravity inverts, wrenching my guts as the ceiling becomes the floor and I collide hard enough with the metal to scare me.

The room is cold, glossy black, ten long paces by ten. There is no bed, only nodules that retract to reveal a tube for my piss. You gotta really seal your squat to the floor or the room will stink something fierce. It's worse for shit. If I miss, I gotta scoop it up and push it in with my fingers or find myself falling into it the next time I doze.

I've given up shouting through the food delivery nodule. No one is listening. At first I thought the Julii cow might want something from me. But she doesn't. This is revenge. Took her first and only visit to drive that through my skull.

A rectangle of light carved the darkness and then she was inside the room staring down at me. Time was, I would have thought her a god.

Some warrior maiden pulled from my pa's savage tales. But there's no romance to her, to *them* any longer. Her Gold rage seemed petty. Her glamour vile in the face of the poverty I've seen in my family's assimilation camp on Mars and in Hyperion.

Still, I told her all I knew, thinking she would be rational. All I told the Sovereign. She said nothing, and it was then I knew the deepspine truth: she doesn't care two licks 'bout what I know. Only when I crawled to her on my hands and knees and begged her to let me out to see Liam did she finally part those rich lips.

"I want to be forthright and say I visually enjoy your degradation." The words seemed to boil, as if drawn up from a black cauldron deep in her belly. "I am aware you are not a member of the Red Hand, nor are you a Gorgon operator. However, stupidity is not a crime without victims. Seeing as how you have deprived me of my daughter, my nephew, whom I love like my own bone and blood, it can only be reckoned fair if I deprive you of something: your 'sanity.' Consider it a mercy that I left that blind child out of this. Would that you had the same decency."

I choked on sobs knowing Liam was safe somewhere beyond this room. Pathetically, I thought to beseech her.

"I didn't mean for this . . ."

"I didn't *mean*," she mocked, making her lips quiver like mine. Her eyes flashed as my hand touched her spiked boots. "You carried unauthorized, alien hardware onto a governmental shuttle, despite attending multiple security briefings instructing you against such indiscretion. You are either sinister, careless, or a gibbering idiot. Embrace the consequences of your actions, young lady. In the end, you may not have your freedom, but perhaps you'll find your dignity. A true woman needs little else."

Then the light swallowed the Gold right back up.

I raced for the shrinking door, but it just disappeared into the wall. I beat at it with my fists and screamed till knuckle bone peeked out my skin.

I knew it would never open again.

I wept and curled around my hands and licked my aching knuckles like a sad dog. I hated that woman. I hated her so much, but deep down I knew I'd do anything for her to fill the room again. To see another person once more . . .

When my bladder grew tight, I just pissed where I lay. I no longer even tilted my head to look as the food slot opened. What was the point? Everyone knows there's nothing worse than a Julii scorned.

I decayed. I am decaying.

How long since I've eaten?

Are there really butterflies in the room?

I remember the mad look in Dagan's eyes when Pa found him three days lost in the deepmines. He swore he saw demons. He was never the same again. His kind heart replaced by a sour doppelgänger's.

Am I going mad like he did? I must be.

Demons visit me as my body wastes away, specters made from the light of the place. The scarred woman of the Red Hand who shot my brother's head off. The liar, Ephraim, who saw I was broken, and put me back together only so he could use me. His Obsidian henchwoman who shot Kavax. That Brown bitch with the needle. The lean, sweaty boy-men who cut my family and clan to pieces with curved iron, and gnawed the innocence out of a hundred Gamma girls.

They mock me in the chaos of light.

But they also bring their victims. Those I love, my brothers, my family, little blind Liam, Kavax who took us from the mud and brought us to Luna, who alone could make Liam's face shine when his mother lay in the dirt.

What did I ever do to protect them? What did I ever do to save them?

All I did was run or hide.

As the light spasms above me and my body grows light with exhaustion, I sense a calm clarity that turns my life into a tapestry. A story told by someone else.

Here's little Lyria. She watched herself be freed. She watched herself put in a camp. Others watched her complain. She watched her family die. She watched big bad Hyperion chew her up and spit her out. She watched as she decayed in her cell.

Is that all I am? A watcher? A victim?

Disgust seeps up through the cracks in the bottom of my heart.

How many times did I blame the Reaper? How many times did I roll my eyes when Red legionnaires would visit our camp and spin those yarns of Darrow and the *Vanguard*. Darrow and the undead Goblin. Darrow, the Julii, and Valkyrie at Ilium. Darrow and the Jackal and the Two Hundred Seventy Days our messiah spent in the monster's table.

"The Second Birth, they call it, lass," the young Red legionnaire said, swiveling on the water drum when he saw I wasn't swallowing the hook like my brothers. His hand touched his chest as he looked around, his voice barely a whisper. "From Mars to Mercury, all know that's when he became the Reaper. When the man became something more. I've seen him in the flesh. At Echo City. He's got something in him, I'll tell you that. Something like thunder in a bottle." He waved his hands at the potential recruits, his voice rising. "And that's in all of us. Each clanfolk with Red in their eyes. Lambda to Gamma. We may not be big. No. We may not be rich. But we got what he got. *Wrath*. Seven hundred years of it thundering in our veins."

Forty-five lined up to give their lives to the Free Legions that day, including two of my brothers. They were just a lot of fools worshipping some jumped-up Helldiver with a Gold wife and a Gold spawn. He wasn't one of us any longer. I blamed him for taking my brothers, for leaving us mired in the camp, for all that'd gone wrong. But one person couldn't do all that. He freed us, and then we stayed in the camp and waited for him to do all the rest.

Waiting. Waiting.

Waiting while the tales that made us big began to make us feel small, because we didn't make the choice like those brave boys and girls did.

We didn't choose to fight.

Well, fuck me if I'm gonna wait any longer. Survival is my fight.

When the synth food shoots through the tube some hours later, I make a choice. My body is weak, my pants crusted with my own filth as I crawl. But I make it there and I choke down the tasteless fiber cubes and protein and wash them down with water from the tube. When food comes again, I jam it down. Soon the hallucinations disappear. The dread loneliness grows smaller, dwarfed by the anger at my own eagerness to surrender.

Despair robbed me my mind. With my despair numbed, I find a way to sleep by tearing a strip of cloth from my jumpsuit and tying myself to the vent duct when gravity makes it the floor. Soon as I doze off, the floor becomes the ceiling again, and I hang there like a deepmine bat, bits of jumpsuit shoved in my ears and wearing a blindfold fashioned from my pant leg.

Sleep is the Vale itself. I eat again. I sleep. I eat. I sleep. I grow bored and make the dancing lights my playmate, racing to touch the tips of the light as it morphs and expands. It reacts to my touch, turning crimson or purple. There's pattern to it, a code maybe, but I just can't crack it.

One day or night or afternoon, I fasten myself to the duct to sleep again, and notice a rolled ball of cloth in the vent. Making a little hook with a piece of rubber gnawed off from my prisoner slippers, I hook the cloth and draw it toward me.

The light illuminates brown letters in a blocky, flaking print. It is a message written in blood.

"My name is Volga. I am a prisoner. I do not know for how long. Am I alone?"

I stare down at the piece of cloth as if it were a message from an alien race. A weird numbness prickles across my face. The same numbness I felt when Vanna of Omicron spit in my eye and called my pa a tinsucker when I was eight.

Pure rage.

Volga was the name of Ephraim's Obsidian. The Hyperionin lowlife who shot great Kavax in the chest so that his skin melted from his rib cage. I ball the cloth in my fist.

Yet I do not drop it.

Suddenly, all I can remember of the woman is the hollowness in her eyes as she looked down at me in the back of their aircar. That was a soul ripping itself to pieces. I know because I felt it too, because I wore those eyes when I knew what Ephraim had used me to do.

Was that Volga's truth? Did she feel the same shame I did? Could it be I wasn't the only one used by Ephraim fucking Horn? Maybe . . . or maybe I just want to talk to someone. Maybe I just want to prove I'm alive.

I bite my thumb till it bleeds and tear the edge of a nail away. I dip it in the blood and begin to write on the back of the piece of cloth: *"My name is Lyria. You might remember me . . ."*

37

EPHRAIM

Heart of Venus

COMMUNICATION ON EAGLE REST has been cut off to all but high-ranking Alltribe personnel. Sefi doesn't want information getting out, or possibly in. HoloNet access severed. Several of my skuggi, including Freihild, were called away for service to the Queen before a scheduled run-through of a highrise infiltration down in Olympia, which was summarily canceled and all passes to the city general revoked.

Pax and I gossip audibly in case of listening devices, and arrange the peas on our plates in the code he developed for us. Having recently gone through Xenophon to acquire fiberwire for the skuggi, I set out six peas. Pax, having built the harnesses I requested, sets out two, then seven in query of the ship Sefi promised me. I squash the peas. No ship. Still a flight risk.

The door bursts open. Electra stalks in.

"Hatchetface! We saved you some peas." I gesture to the ones I smashed. At first I think she's jealous of our little suppers, until she throws open the windows and goes out onto the terrace. Pax frowns and we follow. Beyond the pulseBubble encasing my suite, something is happening in Olympia.

Down in the city, candles flicker from broken windows and atop crumbling towers. A sea of them move through the street. The Forbidden Song drifts ominously in the wind.

She looks over at Pax.

Has Mercury fallen?

Before anyone can put words to the fear, the door to my suite opens again. Ozgard comes out onto the terrace. "The Queen has summoned you. All of you."

Instead of being taken to the throne room, we're led through the night to an armored military shuttle. "You got a bead on this?" I ask them as we board. Electra ignores me.

Pax shakes his head. "You?"

"I've got a few ideas."

"Thank Jove for the mercenary and his professional opinion," Electra snaps, but her teeth are dull today. Is it her parents or Pax's that have gone down? Is it Mercury or Luna, or something else?

The military shuttle has no view windows in the bunkrooms or mess we're sequestered within for the three-day voyage, but all of us can feel the calm before the storm. Pax devotes his days to a sort of waking slumber—a meditation practice Ozgard has taught him. Together they recite obscure prayers while Electra drives all mad by pacing the deck like a pissed-off alley cat.

"What kind of Nagal is that?" I ask Pax before we bunk down for the evening. "Didn't sound familiar."

He glances at Ozgard. Finding the shaman sleeping, he explains in a low voice, "It isn't Nagal. It's Tetkjr. Some of the old prayers survived. Ozgard found remnants of them in old temples on Mercury. He's been teaching me. Hasn't been spoken inside the Belt since the Dark Revolt."

The Dark Revolt was a myth in the legions, believed only by conspiracy theorists and drunks. But after the Fall, the Republic published the history that the Society did their best to scrub out of existence. Read like fiction. Five hundred years before the Reds rebelled, the Obsidians nearly toppled the Society, led by a shadowy figure known as King Kuthul. Of course, Pax is only too eager to explain in excruciating detail.

"Gold was seldom generous in victory. The genocide that followed the Battle of Peitho consisted not just of mass culling, but social and cultural reengineering. A domestication of a wild breed into a more . . . sustainable and predictable stock. Technophobia was introduced as well as other paradigm alterations. Allfather became Allmother. Mongol sociological structure became Norse. Patriarchy became matriarchy, an inversion of the division protocol they used on Reds."

My skin begins to crawl. "And now you speak their language. That's gotta be all sorts of bad luck."

He smiles, captivated by the subject. "Some of my mother's more fanciful theorists think that the Ascomanni speak it. Or at least parts."

"Aren't they just assholes from the ice tribes who didn't follow Sefi?"

"Sure, but their correspondences are odd if that's the case. For instance, they allude to a central figure, a *Volsung Fá*—it means 'Volsung the Taker,' sort of like a king." He pauses when Ozgard murmurs something in his sleep, and lowers his voice to a whisper. "You know, not all the warlords of the Dark Revolt were captured."

I moan. "Gods, now you sound like a legion drunk."

"Shh. It's true. Some hid in the Belt. Some were chased to Neptune, where their fleet was smashed. The stragglers were believed to have been hunted and killed to the last warband. But . . . about a hundred years preceding the reign of Octarius au Lune, ships began to go missing in the Kuiper Belt. They would simply vanish. Common consensus was pilot error or environmental degradation on equipment. Then one vessel escaped."

"Go on."

"I thought I sounded like a legion drunk."

"Pax."

"They reported a loss in artificial gravity, followed by light failure, and sounds from outside the hull. Later welding patterns were found outside. Diamond drill marks."

"Creepy."

"It wasn't until Octarius that the first Kuiper Obsidian was spotted, and the name Ascomanni began to circulate. At first, they were of little concern. Further reconnaissance suggested nomadic caravans of ice miners, subterranean dwellings, sparse populations, and fractious tribal dynamics. It seems the Ascomanni even managed to take some carvers with them. Their skin was said to be red, possibly from genetic sculpting with *Deinococcus radiodurans,* an extremophilic bacterium highly resistant to deepspace radiation, vacuum, dehydration, and cold.

"Closer to the reign of Octavia, they became bolder and began to raid at will. After the death of her daughter, around fifteen years ago, Octavia sent the Fear Knight on an expeditionary campaign when terraforming on Pluto was threatened by the raids."

"Why didn't Octavia simply send out the Sword Armada and finish them off?" I ask. "Seems like something she'd enjoy."

"Cost, benefit." He looks annoyed by my vacant expression. "At times, it frightens me how little people care about the tiny corner of the galaxy they inhabit. Earth is one AU from the sun. Neptune is thirty. The Kuiper Belt is fifty. It is twenty times as wide and almost two hundred times as massive as the Inner Belt. Moira's estimates suggested it would take the Sword Armada five thousand years to search half the Kuiper Belt. Octavia had other things on her plate.

"Back to the Fear Knight. One year in, he reported back that the situation was untenable. He'd been ambushed and lost all but two ships. Octavia told him to go radio silent until the operation was complete. It was an execution. But seven years ago, he returned. And at about the same time that deepspace miners began to suggest the Ascomanni had united under a single ruler. An outlander they called *Volsung*—'He Who Walks the Void.' . . . Obviously, our treaty with the Rim makes further inquiry . . . difficult."

"An outlander from where?" Electra asks. She's been listening from her little nest in the top bunk above Ozgard's. The psycho's eyes gleam at the idea of evil, red-skinned, far-flung Obsidian warlords.

Pax shrugs. "Could be someone the Fear Knight helped to power. A translation discrepancy. Or maybe Atlas's ships were damaged and he lost coms for ten years and tucked tail. Whatever the case, if this Volsung Fá exists, it would be highly unlikely Martian or Terran Obsidians who turned raiders would have any interaction with true Ascomanni. They're years away on the ships they have. People just gave the pirates the name because people like legends. But it makes you wonder, what if they have met with their long lost brethren? What if they are coordinating and Volsung Fá rules not just the far Obsidian, but the pirates too?"

Electra leans back in her bunk, no doubt eager to dream of nightmares beyond the void. I lie back in mine, thoroughly disturbed.

"You're shit at bedtime stories," I say.

"Apologies. Next time I'll tell you the tale of Sophocles the clone, a creature so noble and so wise he learned to cheat death." He rolls over to go to sleep. I lie awake for a while, and roll on my side. Ozgard stares at me from his adjacent bunk. His eyes like two black mirrors. He was listening the whole time.

On the fourth day, the vibration of landing gears reverberates through the ship. The shuttle makes contact with a metal hull outside, and I feel the more substantial pull of capital ship gravity.

"We've rendezvoused with their fleet," Electra guesses. Pax shakes his head, but doesn't correct her. I don't know how or when he figured it out, but he alone is not surprised when we step out into the VIP hangar of an old baroque cruise liner.

Thousands of bloodbraves prepare for war in the hangar. I don't recognize these men or women from Olympia, because they aren't from Olympia. These are the frontline veterans, still wearing the deep sunburns of Mercury. Jogging troops carry tattered war standards of the tribes Sefi formed into her forward legions: the Ice Ravens, the River, the Blackhearts. Pax stares at his father's former soldiers. They should be on Mercury, or in the lands the Republic gave them for barracks on Earth. Somehow they're here, and I think I know why.

"Horn!" Freihild calls as we descend the landing ramp. Ten of my skuggi are arrayed beneath a giant coral archway gilded with golden letters reading *Heart of Venus*. I thought the design looked familiar. It's an old luxury cruise ship.

"So this is where you snuck off to," I say as we are herded toward them.

"We've been preparing for your arrival, sir," Freihild says with a crooked smile for Ozgard.

"Where's the rest of the skuggi?" I ask.

Freihild shrugs. "Come. The Queen awaits."

I know this ship all too well. I thought the *Heart* was destroyed in the war. Instead, it is as if the cruise ship has gone schizoid. The halls, long ago looted, are cluttered with refuse. Automated doors to staterooms and spas open and close at random. The lights inside flicker, with climate zones oscillating between freezing and swamplike. And everywhere there are Obsidian bedrolls, meal stations, stacked arms of a bivouacking army, and dust, so much Mercurian dust, from their gear, the engines of their ships, even their boots.

So that's how she smuggled them under the nose of the Republic. They must have left when the Senate recalled half the fleet. Pax and Electra watch them with contempt. Left the Reaper in quite a lurch.

To leave the VIP zone, we take an eccentric gravLift upward. The glass tube rises through an aquarium in the heart of the ship. Once, it treated tourists to a view of the rainbow life beneath the Venusian waves. Now the glass is crusted with barnacles and smeared with algae. Without her caretakers to maintain balance, the ecosystem seems to have been hijacked by predators. They lurk under coral reefs and lumber through unfiltered murk. Ozgard chews his walnuts and watches as an ebony tentacle ripples through the shadows.

He murmurs something reverential in Nagal. Eyes wide and delighted, he points toward the shapes and murmurs to the children: "It is battle of strength. They eat each other. Soon one will remain . . ." He looks out at the water, the word a song on his tongue: ". . . victorious."

I pick the threads of my Alltribe uniform. "Then he'll starve. Or eat himself. King of a kingdom of one." They all stare at me. Ozgard and Electra in annoyance, Freihild in amusement. Pax in agreement.

The mezzanine level fares no better than the aquarium.

The central playground where tourists would throng to restaurants and ballrooms and pleasure palaces has become a parlor of ghosts. As if a fine old party was in full narcotic-fueled bloom, and everyone suddenly vanished, leaving their glasses on the table and their jokes half told. The air is freezing. A thunderstorm rumbles through the halls. Fizzling here and there from dead speakers.

"Trapped in echo," Ozgard explains reverently.

It ain't the only one.

Some decade and a half ago, I vacationed here for the month round-trip to Venus. I walked its seafoam green carpets, martini in one hand, designer burner in the other, pockets weighed down by casino chips purloined from Silver tycoons mystified at how they could lose to a Gray. Karachi has the tendency to humble those used to playing life with a stacked deck.

Cost me half a year's wages to rub shoulders with the highColors here, but Trigg let me pretend. It mattered to me. I was an uppity idiot desperate to prove I could spend money too. He tried his best to make me happy. He really did. That first night we danced to Venusian wave, then bit by bit he withdrew into himself until all he did was sit in his room and watch the news.

I know the Obsidians see what he saw.

How we drank as they froze and killed and sold off their men to gods to eke out another season in the poles. How the Gray phalanxes stood in orderly ranks to form the chain to their collar. Gray. So frail on our own. So impregnable when we lock arms.

Been a long time since that happened.

"What happened here?" I ask.

"War," Freihild says. "Sons of Ares released achlys-9 years ago. Left the ship to drift in the Ink. Scavengers, looters, thieves, all come in seasons. Time passes. Servants of our Queen found and put to purpose for tribe."

"Sounds more like Gorgons than the Sons of Ares," Electra says.

Freihild shrugs. "All trees bear bad seeds, some bloody in bloom."

"The Red Hand," Pax clarifies. "Or its early form. Harmony, one of Ares's more violent agents, composed it from radicalized Sons who believed Ares's Gold origins was my mother's propaganda. They claim her brother killed Ares. And that Ares's true identity was Narol, my father's uncle, instead of Electra's grandfather."

"You have a fucked-up family," I say.

He frowns. "Yes."

I feel half frozen and haunted all the way through by the time we reach the rococo entrance to the *Heart's* Starboard Theater.

We follow Freihild into the dilapidated theater to the sound of a soprano delivering her aria. The impossibly thin Violet—a girl the color of a rainy street with a neck twice the length of mine—sings on a star-backed stage beneath an ivory mermaid. The theater is a sea of mouldering green silk, with a lone island of life near the front row. We draw closer down the aisle. Each step taking me deeper into the dream.

The Queen of the Valkyrie sits watching Wagner.

I would laugh if it all weren't so damn haunting. A dozen Valkyrie veterans lounge in the rows behind their Queen. Valdir lies on the floor, giving an exaggerated yawn to Freihild as she sweeps in with us. She hides a smile. Xenophon sits rigid several rows behind the Valkyrie.

Onstage, the giraffe-necked Isolde now cradles the body of Tristan, her lover. The audio snags. The soprano begins to crackle, distort, and then dissolve.

Holograms.

Amel, Sefi's Pink, sweeps onto the stage, tapping his datapad. "The file is corrupted, Your Majesty." Sefi waves a hand for silence. She greets me with a nod and motions for the children and me to sit beside her.

"Welcome to the *Heart of Venus*," she says. "You are just in time for the show." She gestures to Amel, who looks suddenly confused standing in the center of the stage. "Amel here was a whore of the Aphrodite House, before I killed his owner. He was no more than the well of pleasure he could provide his clients. They would dip into it and sip. But there was always less in the well. Age comes for us all." She glances at Valdir, who frowns, then back to Amel. "The Silvers would call this a well of diminishing returns. Soon he would have no purpose. I offered Amel *aeta*. He receives one hundred thousand credits per year. Less than a whore of his pedigree would earn in a Lunese brothel, but more than ten welders. Do you think that fair, Amel? That you earn less than whore, but more than welder?"

"Yes, Your Majesty." If the Pink is nervous, he doesn't let on. I, on the other hand, notice the shadows moving in the wings of the stage. Skuggi. Freihild seems surprised by their presence.

"Do you miss being a whore?" Sefi asks Amel.

"No, Your Majesty."

"Good. I am happy you are happy, Amel." She smiles at him. "There are some who believe Pinks cannot be trusted. My people believe that the spirit rots when the body is weak." Her eyes are on Valdir, not Amel. "It rots and rots until the rot turns to poison. Do you believe this to be true, Mr. Horn?"

"I know a few who live up to that," I reply carefully.

"What do you believe, children?" she asks, taking her eyes from Valdir.

"Spirits are imaginary constructs derived from human fear of mortality," Pax replies.

Electra shrugs. "You heard him."

"Amel?" Sefi asks. "Are you rotten inside?"

"No, Your Majesty. The rot my Gold master put upon my spirit was cleansed when you bathed his dining table with his blood and set his children to the knife. You are my Deliverer."

Sefi sighs. "Finish the song for me, Amel."

The Pink blinks. "I beg your pardon?"

"Finish the song. I know you can."

Amel flinches as the skuggi step from the shadowed wings of the stage. Gudkind leads them. Freihild glances at Valdir for explanation. Amel's shoulders sag, and slowly he begins to sing. His voice is not that of the Violet's but has a purity of its own. The skuggi slip onto the stage and begin to light a fire in the refuse of the set design. Flames lick over wooden boulders and trees as the Pink's voice breaks from fear.

He glares at Ozgard. "I do not know what the madman has told you, my Queen, but you have cleansed me. I serve only you."

"Amel is loyal," Valdir protests to his mate. "Do not be misled by the madman." He glares at Ozgard as if this were all his doing.

Fear has taken Amel. "I did not betray you, my Queen. On my honor!"

"A man has little, a whore has none," Sefi replies.

He stands there trembling. The soprano hologram sputters back to life, echoing the Pink's song as Gudkind and the skuggi descend on Amel and hack him to pieces with cleavers. I watch in horror as they toss the pieces of the beautiful man into the flames.

Black smoke swirls.

I grow very still inside as the scent of burning flesh hunches through the opera house. I don't know who this was for. A warning for Valdir and Freihild, or for me. And neither do they. Is their secret known? Will they join Amel? Is Sefi proving her skuggi are loyal to her, and not Freihild? The children watch this in dead silence. If Sefi wants them to learn about Obsidian virtues, she's doing a fine job of it.

"My people have a word," Sefi murmurs to me, "*rahgschni*. There is no translation in the Common tongue. As close as can be said is: the sorrow one feels in seeing fresh morning snow, knowing its beauty cannot last." She looks back at the fire. The flames saw her black eyes. "The Sovereign is dead."

I grow cold, realizing why the city of Olympia was lit up with candles and Eagle Rest went on lockdown. Pax does not move. "What?" Electra bolts to her feet.

"She was butchered in the Senate by a mob along with my senators," Sefi says as she stares into the flames. "It was the signal to begin a general coup. The ArchGovernor of Mars was shot in the head by his butler within his sanctum in Agea. Sevro was captured on Earth, Howlers slaughtered. More than a dozen others were killed. Valdir, heat of my heart, you say Amel here was loyal. But he received coded message from deepspace relay station home to Gold intelligence. I was to be assassinated with the rest."

"Amel is loyal," Valdir says.

"I sensed a quavering of his spirit long ago," Ozgard confirms.

"You fat devil!" Valdir bellows. "You will be the death of us all. Maybe you sense a quavering of mine next. I know your game, serpent. I know how you coil close to heat, for the cold blood in your own veins."

"Am I stupid, heat of my heart?" Sefi says to Valdir. "To act only on the senses of shaman? To be guided like puppet? It was Xenophon who brought this to me, not Ozgard." Valdir's anger cools somewhat as he spares a look at the trusted White. "For some time, Amel has been passing information to this relay station, to his Gold overlords. Including my diet, and list of preferred vintages. A poisoned bottle was found in his possession. He served me many years. But was rotten in the end."

Valdir grows quiet. To him, Xenophon's word is worth far more than Ozgard's hunches. Yet he cannot accept it.

By the way Sefi's looking at me, I might just be joining Amel in the fire. She's cleaning house.

She watches me for a moment, her black eyes peering deep into me before flicking away toward Electra, who is still on her feet.

"Who did it?" the girl demands. "How did a mob kill Virginia au Augustus? Is my father alive? Tell us!"

"We do not know," Xenophon answers. "Publius cu Caraval seems to be the instigator and perpetrator of the coup, and allied with Arch-Imperator Zan and Vox elements in the government. We have confirmed this with Niobe au Telemanus, who now leads the Ecliptic Guard to Luna to demand the Sovereign's return. Whether she is dead or alive, we do not know."

"Publius? That dreary little shit?" Electra is stunned. "Naw. He doesn't have the juice, even with Zan."

"He is likely the puppet of Atalantia," Sefi says. At that, Pax loses his ability to listen. He stands, quivers, and bolts from the opera house. Electra glares down at Sefi.

"How long have you known? Three days? You cold bitch."

Sefi nods. "World is hard. He must be too."

"*You* weakened her by leaving," Electra snaps. "You abandoned them. This is your fault. I know it. He knows it. We all fucking know it."

"Your mother weakened her too."

Electra flinches at that and storms after Pax. Sefi jerks her head, and Ozgard pursues. Valdir watches the child go with a deep sense of sadness. He is more complicated than just a warrior. The loyalty he feels to Darrow must be immense, and I wonder if Sefi isn't the villain here after all.

"You didn't have to do it like that," I say.

"I did not bring you here to play nursemaid to children or lecture me, Mr. Horn. You asked me when first we met what Julii would pay for her firstborn. Today, I tell you. She has provided us with information and ore ships on which to transfer my forward legions under nose of Republic fleet."

At Sefi's instruction, Xenophon still steps forward to fling a holo onto the opera stage where Amel's remains still burn. Blueprints unfold from a tiny mote like the tendrils of jellyfish. My eye darts, my brain decrypts, analyzes, reverse engineers the Byzantine mess to see the hundreds of complexes, sophisticated killzones, subterranean bunkers. No. Not bunkers. I feel for my Z dispenser.

"I was right. You want to start another war."

"No. I want to end war. The Republic breaks under its own weight. Obsidian must not. These are schematics for helium mines of Cimmeria. I was hesitant to act when Virginia sat upon Morning Chair. Now, no precautions, no hesitation. We strike." The Queen's smile crawls upward, her devious nature burning hot and bright beneath that ice exterior. "Helium is blood of empires, Mr. Horn. Master it, master destiny. And I will master our destiny. In one week's time, we take mines of Cimmeria, and the continent as our homeland. It is time to test your skuggi."

"They are not ready," Valdir says with a worried glance to Freihild. "My battle plan will get you the—"

Sefi holds up a hand. "You break planets, Valdir. I do not want a broken Mars. That is the last resort. I want a Mars that welcomes me as protector, as Great Mother. Mr. Horn, I need defense grids lowered. Tell me. Are your skuggi ready?"

With the smell of Amel's burning body in my nostrils, I look at Freihild, who gives me an eerie smile.

"Yeah, they'll do your dirty trick. World's burning anyway."

38

LYSANDER

The Horizon

I WAKE FEELING MORE TIRED than before I slept. It is still dark out. The quiet sounds of the soldiers preparing for the day's trek north surround me. I sit up and gag at the pain of my wounded face. It is infected. My dreams were warped by fever and fear. Again the chair, again the door, again the shadows and laughter on the other side. I don't know how I get to my feet.

It is in silence that we set out into the cool dark. Kalindora walks closer to me now, always keeping herself between me and Cicero. Despite her grievous wound, I feel safer in her shadow. She whispers quiet poems to herself as the sun begins to rise.

> *"What think you the dead are? Why, dust and clay,*
> *What should they be? 'Tis the last hour of day.*
> *Look on the west, how beautiful it is*
> *Vaulted with radiant vapours! The deep bliss*
> *of that unutterable light*
> *Perhaps the only comfort which remains*
> *Is the unheeded clanking of my chains,*
> *The which I make, and call it melody."*

The words keep me walking. But temperatures ascend as the sun climbs over the mountains. Just when I believe I can't go another step, I feel Kalindora's hand on my lower back, steadying me. Always it lingers there, and I find I miss it when she takes it back.

We walk and walk until we break for water in the middle of a playa.

"Nobody move," Cicero says. We freeze at the tension in his voice. He gestures slowly to a cactus, beneath which is a hole in the hardpan. "If you value life, slowly, back away."

We put a hundred meters between us and the animal hole. "What was that?" I ask him when we collapse down for water in the shadow of a yellow cactus as tall as five men.

"Hydra burrow," he says. "They hunt sunbloods. We'd be a nice little aperitif for them." He wanders off to inspect a nearby cactus blossom. Kalindora squats in the dirt beside me and stares east. The remains of an unmarked bomber lie several kilometers off. Several of the Grays hack at cacti with utility knives to suck water from the meat. It's barely worth the effort. The storms have thrashed the flora. I take enough water from the canteen to fill my mouth. There will be none left after this break. "Take more," Kalindora says. "That burn is sapping you dry."

She can barely stand herself.

"We don't have enough."

"Take more. There's always a chance we'll find something, maybe in that bomber. But no chance at all if you die now." She tilts the canteen and I swallow another mouthful. She sits down beside me and splays out her long legs. The fabric of her thermaskin, like mine, is caked white with chalk.

"While the lips are calm and the eyes cold, the spirit weeps within."

Kalindora smiles softly as I recite.

"I see you're still fond of Shelley. Does it help take your mind away?"

"No," she replies. "I just don't think anyone should die without hearing poetry one last time." Whether she means me or herself is unclear. "I'm going to have hot tea," she says suddenly.

"What?"

"When we get back. A hot tea and a cold bath. How about you?"

"Fralic juice and vodka," I say.

"Fralic juice and vodka?" She squints at me, finding more meaning in it than I meant. "Why?"

"I don't know. I've never even had it before." That seems to puzzle her. "Octavia said that her greatest mastery of the Mind's Eye came when she could make herself taste a food simply by thinking of it," I say.

"Well, I can do that," she says. "Watch. *Dust.*" She licks her lips.

"Gods, just like the real thing." I am unable to smile from the burn. "What's it like?" she asks. "The Mind's Eye."

"It is difficult to explain." She waits for me to try. "Have you ever had a moment where you couldn't fail? Where everything seemed slow, except you? Like you were the center of all gravity, all time, and your thoughts themselves were second to your actions?"

"Sometimes, in combat."

"Bad comparison," I say. "You were a sailor before, yes?"

She considers. "Sometimes when the wind is strong, you slide like a knife over the water . . . it feels like you're flying."

"Then you have touched it. But imagine you could control that peace, that sense of harmony, and summon it according to your will."

She reconsiders me.

"You can do *that* at will?"

"At times. Octavia could like this." I snap my fingers. "It isn't without flaw. It didn't make her a warrior equal to Aja. But it made her very . . . dangerous. She said it could even stop poison, if mastered."

"All poison?"

I'm about to answer when I see movement to the north. I squint out at bright chalk flats. Amidst a cloud of dust, a herd of pale sunbloods race one another against the horizon. Not one, not ten, but hundreds. I stand up to watch, wondering if it is real or a desert mirage. Either way it is one of the most beautiful things I have ever seen.

Then I realize it is not one another they race.

"Not again," Kalindora whispers.

A dark smudge rolls across the desert behind the stampede.

"Sandstorm!" Cicero shouts. "Damn that man! Damn him! Everyone, to the bomber! That sand will shred us to the bone! Hurry!"

We bolt to our feet and run east toward the wreckage, but the Grays and I are falling behind. Kalindora tries to help me along, but with me weighing her down, she'll never make it.

Uninjured, Cicero and his Golds chew up the kilometers with their rangy legs. They don't even bother looking back for us. The wall of sand is close enough now that it seems to scrape the sky.

It swallows a dozen horses whole. I shove Kalindora away. "Go!" She bats my arms out of the way and lunges to try and pick me up with one arm. I back away from her. "Go!"

She glances at the encroaching wall, then back at me, with real fear in her eyes. For a moment, I think she will stay. Then she turns and sprints away, long strides making her bounce like a jackrabbit in the low gravity. I am left alone.

I face the wall, and grip Cassius's razor as if it will save me. Everything has darkened. Dust obscures the sky. The Grays continue to try to make it to the bomber. They won't. I search for some hiding place. Some boulder or wreckage to shelter behind. There is nothing. *Nothing*.

A cool certainty slides over me.

I race back the way we came and see dirt swirling over the hydra burrow's entrance. It is wide enough for a Red, but not for me. Flattening my thumb against the shape sensor, I form the razor into a wide-mouthed falchion and chop furiously at the ground, expanding the hole's circumference.

The wall is nearly upon me. I dive into the burrow at the last second. My shoulders clear, my hips stick. Ripping skin from my sides, I crawl into the darkness just as the wall hits.

39

LYSANDER

The Mind's Eye

THERE IS A MONSTER sharing the darkness with me. A dread creature I cannot see or hear for the howling darkness of the storm outside. I can sense it moving, judging the creature that has invaded its home.

I have never seen a hydra with my own eyes. Five hundred years ago, the Votum commissioned a sect of Lunese carvers to create them so that they might have something challenging to hunt. Some say the carvers were far too ambitious in their designs.

I lie trembling on my back, with my razor rigid and pointed outward from my belly as the hours creep past. They are the longest hours of my life. Especially when a mass of scales rested against my leg. The Hydra is digesting another meal.

When the storm finally passes, I hear a faint hissing, like dry skin dragged over tin. Very carefully, I slide backward out of the hydra's burrow, keeping my razor pointed downward in case it decides to make a last-minute meal of me.

When I finally see the sun again, I stumble away from the hole and almost vomit from tension. Only when I am far enough away do I fall on my back and start to laugh and cry.

I never knew I'd be so happy to not be a hydra's lunch.

After a half a minute, the sun begins to burn my face. I sit up and squint into the waste.

The playa is cleansed. Cacti sway like leftover shish-kebab sticks. No life stirs. No debris can be seen. The Grays have been swallowed by the desert. I make my way over to the bomber, now just a hump of sand, and call for Kalindora. There is no answer. Nor is there when I call for Cicero.

I dig through the sand and find nothing but two decaying Blue pilots, half-eaten by predators. They wear no insignia but a child's face wreathed in serpents. Gorgons. This was one of Atlas's bombers.

The hold is empty. The magazines have ruptured inward. Unfired missiles lie in the hold. A ration bar wrapper lies on the floor. One of ours. Outside the bomber, I find indentations in the sand, indicating the passage of a shuttle. A spent railgun battery lies on the ground.

Not one of ours. Sun Industries tech.

I squint south and see the shuttle as a dot racing for Heliopolis. Kalindora must be on it. Another captive for the Rising.

I go back inside the bomber and collapse in the hold amongst the unfired missiles. I lie there forlorn until I fall asleep. When I wake, my loneliness in the silence is absolute.

Pytha knew this was coming.

But I believed the myth of war.

Worse, I thought myself special. Immune to the horrors lesser men face.

Diomedes was right. All men are tiny before the storm.

There is nothing but pain from my ruined face and deep, indescribable exhaustion. Seraphina is dead. The alliance may be broken because of it. My Praetorians rotting or captured. The tears sting my wounds as I weep. Why did I betray Cassius? For this? Why did I return to this horrible place?

My hopes of a united Gold, of peace, now seem so laughable.

Not only did I overestimate my own importance. I underestimated the scope of war.

There is no escape from this. It will eat us all.

I could flee this pain, find refuge in the Mind's Eye meditation and slip slowly into the Void as my body fails, but I cannot give Grandmother that honor. She did something to me. Something I cannot understand. I was a child who needed love in the shadow of his parents' deaths. Instead, she beat me into the shape of a cup and poured her lessons into me. I will not let those lessons be my last act in this world.

"Cry not, mortal child," a voice says in the darkness. *"They come on wings of sable, to rend your precious flesh, and send you to the doom which lies beyond this realm of pain."*

I sit up. Am I going mad?

"Lie still and it will end. Lie still and the seed of Silenius will wither to time."

"Who is there?" I ask. A translucent mass squats in the shadows of the downed aircraft. It seems immense. The air warps above the ghostCloak with hornlike projections. If it is a ghostCloak and not the madness of the desert creeping in.

"Dwell not on me, mortal. Nocturnal devils are afoot. Awake, arise, or be forever fallen."

I hear it now. The sound of gravBoots.

I watch through a fissure in the hull as seven armored men land in the night. Seneca's voice drifts from the darkness. "Lysander, oh, Lysander, come out, come out, little boy. Death has come."

So Ajax has sent his boar of a bodyguard to finish the task.

The thought of dying at the hands of some thin-blood brute fills me with irrational fear. I am not fit for this world of rough killers. My hand goes to the side of my neck where I received my mission implant. They tracked it at last. I turn to the man in the darkness.

"Help me," I beg.

"I help no man who does not help himself, and no man do I help who is no boon to me. Six years I have collated knowledge to become the mightiest of mortal vessels. Yet one morsel still eludes my voluminous mind. Hidden in no Fury. No books. Trusted to no digital void. It lingers yet, this knowledge in one sepulchre. Four days I have followed. Four days you have denied me my quest. I must know the Mind's Eye. Show it to me. Or perish."

The air ripples as the man slips out of the ship.

"Lysander," Seneca taunts. "There's nowhere to run. Will the Heir of Silenius die in a rat hole? Have dignity in the end; your *ancient blood* demands it." The thin-bloods chuckle to one another.

I spotted seven of them, all in fresh pulseArmor. I won't stand a chance. But will I die here cowering? Or will I die with dignity? As I stand, my feet disturb the spilled munitions on the floor, and I sense a fresh variable.

Seven Peerless Scarred stand in the darkness as I emerge barefoot.

Their predatory Iron Leopard war helmets watch with no human emotion. As if my left arm were broken, I cradle the internal payload of a firebrand munition wrapped in torn seat lining.

I need those helmets off.

"Ajax couldn't even take out his own trash," I mock. My voice is ragged. "How admirable."

Seneca chuckles. "He would, but Atalantia has him under lock and key, such is her grief at the death of *precious* Lysander. Shall we formalize it?"

Seven razors unfurl. Mine remains on my hip.

"What did he promise you, Seneca?"

"A torchShip each," one of the Golds says.

"That's the price of my life?"

"Draw your iron, boy. Ajax made me promise you'd die well."

"Does any man die well if he cannot look his killer in the eye?" I peer around at the grim visages of the battered warhelms. "Which of you will it be? Which of you will kill the last Heir of Silenius? Don't you want me to know as I lie dying?"

Oh do I know my people.

Their helmets unfurl to reveal their faces.

My name still means something. They want me to see their eyes as they kill me. They want me to comprehend their superiority. And each wants to deliver the blow, and with it declare themselves stronger than my decrepit bloodline. They are the future, not the last blood of Lune who couldn't even survive a week at the front. And they want me to know it.

I take my razor and let it unfurl into the killing blade.

"No bribe? No begging?" Seneca asks. "I expected more whinging from the entitled cur."

"As a human, I am entitled only to death."

"That's the spirit." Seneca smiles with his pack. "Kill the Pixie."

Seven Peerless butchers slip forward. My left hand pulls the activation wire of the firebrand payload, I drop the seat lining, and toss the payload into the air. I bury my face in the sand.

The air stills as the firebrand detonates overhead. It releases no kinetic wash of energy, only spasms of ultraviolet light brighter than that of a nuclear explosion. It makes no sound.

Even with my head in the sand, I go blind.

But so do the bare-faced killers. As they scream from the weapon flash burning their retinas, I search myself for the fear that has stalked me since I landed on this planet. I need not search further than what I felt in the hydra burrow. Fear writhes like a dark, maggoty river from my pelvis to the tip of my spine. Pulsing. Roaring. Not fear of death. Fear of failure. Fear of being a fool. Fear of inconsequence. Fear of being alone. Fear of proving I am nothing more than my grandmother's puppet. Fear that I am weak and meant for the maggots.

But the Mind's Eye waits for me like an old glove.

I am the last of its acolytes.

It is not Grandmother's anymore. It was never an inheritance. *I* earned it by suffering as a boy as she did as a girl. *Fear is the torrent.*

My transition into the folds of harmony is fulfilling.

My eyes may be blind, but my mind sees.

The world rushes through the multi-sensorial pupil of the Mind's Eye. The projection stems from memory. I see the grains of sand as they were before the blast of light. I feel the weight of the men on its surface. Smell the musty sweat of unwashed armor, the bitter roast of coffee, the sweet reek of combat chemicals and the protein cubes they ate before they descended. Blood pumps in their veins. Insulated feet slide in their boots. I feel their skins, knowing where instinct will take them, where training will guide them to my blade like sheep to slaughter. I see them in the blindness, and I take on the Winter Whirlwind stance of the Willow Way.

Are you awake or asleep, Lysander?

I slip forward.

Three die without even swinging their razors.

The pommel of the Bellona razor jolts in my hand as the blade carves through pulseArmor, bone, and flesh of the third man. I feel the heat of blood sluicing down my arm. Hear the puking as it comes out of the man's mouth. I pull the razor upward from his belly, holding his sword hand down, and saw through his breastplate. I stop shy of his heart so that he will continue to scream. I trip him and ride his momentum down to the ground, rolling forward then upward and crouching on a knee.

They shout to one another now. The noise of the dying a bedlam to muddle their ears. GravBoots whine as one takes blindly to the air. I rip the pulseFist off the dying man. With the Mind's Eye, I sort through the soup of sound until I find the whine of the gravBoots and feel the reverberation. I swivel toward it, brace myself on a knee, lead the sound by several meters, and fire five shots in a diagonal line. I hear the snapping sound of a pulseShield absorbing the blast. There he is. I fire thirty shots until I hear the pulseShield collapse with a scream. Metal and man crash down into the sand.

Four down. Three left.

I slide toward the ship as they fire at anything that makes noise. GravBoots whine at my eleven o'clock. I fire a full stream from my cover. The man gets away. Several seconds pass. There is a thump in the desert. My visitor doesn't want any escaping either.

The last two are difficult to locate. My memory is outdated now by a minute, but as I killed I populated the mental image with my victims. I know the second body is approximately nine meters and a half west and has a pulseFist still. I know the fourth body creates a tripping barrier between a broken wing of the downed bomber and the fuselage. And when I hear a *clink,* I know one of the two survivors is checking the pulse of the first corpse two meters behind me.

I swoop to kill him with a backhand flick of the razor. It glances off his risen helmet. I parry his first riposte, knowing it would come as a lower thrust because he was in a crouch and it is the natural transition strike to prepare for a diagonal downward slash. I parry that slash and three more blows of a tight set. He is a clever swordsman, far stronger supplemented with his armor, but he relies upon sustained contact to know where I am. I break off. Wait. And as he probes the darkness with tentative thrusts, I rotate around and slip soundlessly forward. The razor digs the roots. It severs his leg at the thigh. The second strike takes his hand. The third his ankle.

I let him bleed out. His groans give me cover to move.

Seneca calls to his compatriots. None answer but the wounded.

"What the fuck?" he growls. I hear his razor hissing through the air as he swings wildly. His pulseFist roars. "You little prim bastard! How can you see?"

"Rather, how is it you are blind, Seneca?" As I move quietly over the sand, I can hear the heartblood pumping out of the dying men. *Glug. Glug. Glug* into their broken armor. "Is this how you saw your future?"

He fires at the sound of my voice. Unlike the others, he is difficult to find. I think he's stripped off his boots too now. His heart rate is steady. His feet quiet despite his mass. This is a real killer. To guard Ajax's back, he'd have to be.

"Is there even a future past this moment, Seneca?"

He fires again and misses again. He's back near the ship. I weave through the downed bodies and find a pulseFist. I set it back down. It doesn't seem honorable.

"Only an animal does not plan past the moment." I slip sideways as he fires at where I was. "So what does that make you?"

The sand is cold under my bare feet as I stalk closer.

It's a trap. He's hunched forward now, not bothering to speak. He waits for me to make a sound. Obliging, I toss a rock against the hull. He ignores it. But he does not ignore my feet as I push off the sand to jump toward him. He fires as if I were running. Blisters bubble on my feet as the pulseblast warbles just beneath them.

I land a hair too close and swing my razor down. He catches it in his hand. There's a jolt as it splits his gauntlet and divides the radius and ulna bones down the elbow. It sticks there. I sense his razor coming for my belly. I toggle my blade into a whip, and twist to the side, holding on to the razor pommel with my left hand. His blade misses most of me, but bites hard into my hipbone. The pain is excruciating. His left shoulder crashes into my face. I stumble backward, retract the razor out of his arm, and parry his following slash upward. I push away from him as I fall. He pursues. I switch my razor back into a whip and lash it around his ankles as they pass each other mid-stride. Then I transition the razor back to rigid form, and from my knees deliver the coup de grâce of the Willow Way, the Weeping Noose.

The whip encircling his ankles stiffens and retracts into a straight metal line. It goes through armor, flesh, and bone to do so.

With his feet cut off at the ankles, Seneca falls with a crash.

"No!" he roars on the ground, slashing wildly. I gather myself into a crouch and stay out of range. "No! Fucking brat. Fucking child. They said you were a Pixie!"

"It would seem they judge the wrong virtues."

I wait for his riven body to tire. When his protests grow weak, I approach and stand before him. I favor the deep wound in my hip. "Who is your favorite poet?" I ask.

"What?" Seneca barks.

"Your favorite poet, man."

He sighs. "Kipling."

I sort through what comes to mind, and decide upon a passage.

> *"Time hath no tide but must abide*
> *The servant of Thy will;*
> *Tide hath no time, for to Thy rhyme*
> *The ranging stars stand still—*
> *Regent of spheres that lock our fears*
> *Our hopes invisible,*
> *Oh 'twas certes at Thy decrees*
> *We fashioned Heaven and Hell!"*

"Fuck you, you fucking P—"

I decapitate Seneca. As his head rolls to the sand, I let go of the Mind's Eye and the world throbs.

I am spent. Exhaustion falls like a sweaty anvil. There are wounds upon my body that I did not notice until now. Lines of fire race along two deep gashes in my thigh, though the most painful is the last one Seneca gave me because I passed on the pulseFist in favor of the razor. Apparently honor is expensive. Then from behind, a man applauds.

"Apollonius au Valii-Rath, I presume?"

"*Indubitably. So the Mind's Eye is real after all. Atalantia swore it was a myth. But to see it . . . ah, to see it.*"

"Octavia refused to teach her," I say. "Is that what you desire? My grandmother's secrets?"

"*Beggar the whole bounty for this chief prize.*"

"The Eye is not a razor to be wielded by any man," I say, taking a seat on the ground in exhaustion.

"*I am not just any man. Would any man have such demons as I? Ajax, Atalantia, Atlas . . .*"

"They were responsible for your stay in Deepgrave, I gather. But what of the source of all this? What of Darrow?"

"*A kinship bonds all men betrayed, for they alone know the deepest breaking of the soul. In time, he must fall so I might rise. But what savvy butcher would loosen the vise that keeps his demons in thrall before their comeuppance comes due?*"

"Then the answer is no."

"No?" His laugh is beautiful and presumptuous. "Atalantia and Atlas are not my enemies."

"But Ajax is . . . after his betrayal?" How long has he followed me? I do not answer him. He chuckles to himself. *"One is the father, the other the lover. They will choose Ajax. Without my aid, you will die here, seed of Lune. Without my aid, you will die anywhere."*

"I have no quarrel with you, Apollonius, but will not be bridled with a debt to you either."

"Yet you begged me to aid you."

"That was the boy inside. He is dead."

"That was five minutes ago!"

"Are you the same you were then? Is Seneca?" He does not reply as I stand. "You sound hungry, Apollonius." I do not feel stronger now than I did five minutes ago. I am no supreme being with a plan for escape. All I know is that there is more inside me than I knew. If I die, it will not be on my knees.

Menace enters his voice. *"I could kill you now. I am not these men."*

"Yes. You could. But you won't."

The sand sighs as his mass steps forward. *"Are you so sure, little seed?"*

"Reasonably. Though we have never met, I know there is one thing Apollonius au Valii-Rath cannot resist." I stand and cut the mission node from my neck and hold it out for him. Huge metal fingers take the device. "A good show."

Apollonius stands in silence as I forage from the dead. I am far clumsier outside the Mind's Eye, but I fear the toll it would take to sustain it. I may die in the desert, but if I took his offer, it would mean war against Atalantia and Atlas. I would give legitimacy to his faction against theirs. After Atalantia's attempt to take Heliopolis, the Votum might come over to me just to spite her. After Seraphina's death, the Rim might join Apollonius—they know his martial worth—or they might declare war on Atalantia if my testimony is . . . accusatory regarding Seraphina's death.

I could ruin Atalantia if I went with Apollonius.

But what would that do to Gold? She is apparently our best tactician, and despite Ajax's cruelty, despite her capricious vanity, I still love her as family. Ajax's treachery may still be his own. Moreover, Gold cannot afford that divide. Just as the worlds cannot afford a man who wrecks a planet simply to win a battle.

I may not be what I thought I was. This world itself may just be a maze without a center. But I will not wait to die. I will not wait to be bridled by another. I will go forward as I see fit.

I stand waiting for Apollonius to stop me after I've taken all I need from the dead Golds. When he does not, I reach for Seneca's gravBoots. They are gone. Apollonius chuckles.

"You don't get everything you want, little seed." He picks some choice items from my haul for himself. *"A good show, says the hopeful autarch."* He pats my head. *"Even if you survive this walk, you can never best Darrow, if that is your intent. He would climb up your blade to chew upon your jugular. To best a living god, it is not enough to survive, nor to eat of the ambrosia of conquest. Who would follow a churlish princeling over that Slave made War? After all, you have no sense of theater."* He claps me on the shoulder so hard my teeth rattle. *"Enjoy your walk. I will be watching."*

I walk north, blind, but blinded no more.

Uncertain of where I go, but certain of one thing. Ajax abandoned me to the enemy. He tried to kill me, Darrow tried to kill me, Seneca tried to kill me, the desert tried to kill me, but I am still here. Pain the only proof I am not yet dead. Be it one of anguish or joy, my life is mine. I have earned it back.

And I have no intention of wasting it.

40

EPHRAIM

Kjrdakan

T HE BURNER'S ON ITS last legs as I tap it over the railing to see the ash spiral down. I've done my bit and submitted a full tactical brief regarding how the skuggi could neutralize much of Quicksilver's mine security. Now I watch the braves prepare in the gymnasium of the *Heart of Venus* and marinate in the guilt of being complicit to genocide.

I'm an old hand at briefs—in the legions, as an investigator. They sit in digital folders and gather electronic dust until they are deleted to cover the political ass of whatever high-up gave the contrary go. "All analysis supported my decision," is their favorite line.

Valdir is Sefi's *varKjr.* Her warlord. He's used blunt-force trauma to pound a legacy from Mars to Mercury—surviving a decade that sent more than seventy percent of Sefi's commanders to Valhalla. He wants a frontal assault. So a frontal assault it'll be. No niggling brief from a mercenary will dissuade him. It'll work, I'm sure. With the hard-boiled legions the *Heart* is packing, even the Citadel of the Republic might fall. But it will turn so many civilians and backline Republic troops into meat confetti that Mars will loathe them for centuries. The faceless future dead make me think of the sounds my boys made as they were skinned on Luna. It makes my hand shake for Z. That won't be the end of the killing. It'll be the beginning. Only famine is uglier than occupation.

What would Volga say if I told her this was the price of her life?

I rub my temple, trying to ease the vibrations of the hot drill digging into my brain.

I'm just destined to be a footman to devils, I guess.

I light another burner.

It goes down before I know it.

Below, Obsidians study Quicksilver's robots—machines meant to kill blood and bone. I wouldn't face them for anything in the world.

"You've been avoiding me." I look over to see Pax coming from a gravLift.

"Consolation isn't my thing," I reply.

He peers over the railing without expression. He's grown harder since I took him from that Lionguard shuttle. How could he not? Braga and his other bodyguard amble behind him. They watch me without much appreciation. I'm emblematic of their Queen's New Way.

"I guess even a warrior race has to concoct new ways to die," I mutter. "Death by axe has to get tedious after a while." I twirl a new burner.

"You think it's going to be a massacre."

"Either in the taking or the keeping. Don't you?"

He doesn't respond immediately. "I don't know everything. What I do know is that the Obsidians will defend Cimmeria better than Quicksilver ever did, maybe even rebuild it. Might be better for the Reds this way. Sefi knows the danger of letting them boil over. They'll outnumber her people a hundred to one. When Atalantia comes . . . maybe they'll stand together. Even if they don't . . . I don't know. Maybe the Obsidians have earned this day more than anyone."

"Cimmeria is just one continent." I reply. "The richest in helium, sure, but Apollonia is the heart of Mars. Agea will go into a frenzy. This is civil war within a civil war. The death of the Republic. Without helium—"

"No, Obsidian is a land power. They'll have to trade the helium for it to be worth anything. If the Obsidians get Cimmeria and dig in, Agea will negotiate. And even if the Vox have my mother, my tribe is resilient. Victra's still out there. Telemanuses . . . maybe." He goes quiet. "They'll ally with Obsidian to face Atalantia."

"If the Vox don't eat the Republic."

"Yes."

He's written off his father on Mercury then. Without the Sovereign to lead a rescue fleet, they're as good as dead.

"Do you think your mother knew about this?" I ask.

He sighs. "I don't know. Judging by the scale of the operation, I assume she had to. Subtlety isn't Sefi's strength, and she doesn't know all my mother's tools. So the fact that it's reached this point means either Victra clued my mother in, Sevro did, or she just found out because she's her. *Was* her." He rolls his jaw, looking ten times his age. He's been different since he discovered his mother's demise. While Electra has squawked on and on about revenge, he's just gone quiet. Of course Hatchetface thinks life is just a substance to be pushed through. With a brain like Pax's, he's already guessed there's nowhere to push. It's just a hard road to a cliff, with all the good ones falling over it far too quick.

"You want to talk about it?" I ask.

"No." We stand in silence for a while. "Don't," he says when he hears my intake of breath. I lean forward and light another burner and offer him one.

"I'm eleven."

"So, we beat cancer, remember?"

He shrugs and takes the burner, holding it like it's straight black smack. I light it for him. "Mother would kill me."

"Thought your da was the killer."

"He wouldn't notice."

"Come on. Petty doesn't look good on you. Least your da is slick. Mine was just a horny grunt who passed his seed for a ten-K bonus. *Keep the legions strong.*" I snort.

I don't like seeing Pax like this. It depresses me. I should say something interesting, but I can't think of something he wouldn't just shoot down. *All right. Let's get real.*

"Met a man once," I say as Pax becomes a cloud. He doesn't cough. Good on him. Neither did I. "Wasn't much younger than you. It was before the Legion Ward House got ahold of me. Was a lookout for the local tough, when I heard they were selling ice frizeé down by the Light Plaza. You know that mound. Heroes' Plaza or whatever now." He nods. "Anyway. Got caught stealing said frizeé and was gonna get cuffed real bad by the local urbanes, when a man piped up for me. Said I was with him. The urbanes gave him one look, a long salute, and went on their way. He was a Gray. Looked *such* a legend, leaning on the fountain like he owned it. Had a Titan Rain badge on his chest, a shattered Rhea beneath, a shower of golden teardrops on his face, inky in Legio XIII blacks. You weren't around then, but even Golds gave that sort a nod." I roll my burner in my hands. "Smoked that burner like the unimpressed footman of a god. I remember that clear as day. Jove, he looked slick. He gave me my first. Like I'm giving you yours. I asked him if he was a hero, and he looked me dead in the eyes"—Pax looks over—"and he said, 'Fuck heroes, kid. It's all about being slick enough to squeak through. That's the last man standing.' Took that to heart. And here I bloody am."

"And what's that supposed to teach me?" he asks. "Be an asshole?"

"I dunno. Don't be like your folks, I reckon. It ain't on you to save the world. They were some impressive people, all told. I ain't saying you're not. But they was them, and look where they are." I set a hand on his shoulder. "I want you to get old, that's all."

"Why? I'm just a mark to you."

"Everyone's a mark to someone. Bet you a pretty credit, Sefi's someone's mark." I hold the smoke in my lungs until they tighten. "Guess I'm telling you because age doesn't look good on me. But I think it'll look good on you. That's all. That's the pep talk."

He looks back down at the braves. "You're shit at pep talks."

"Yeah, well, maybe that's why I'm alive, and why you're wearing Trigg's ring." He plays with the chain. "He was as good as we get. Just a shish kebab in the end."

"My father wishes he knew him better," Pax murmurs.

"You don't have to pander."

"Truly. Say what you want about my da, but don't ever think he doesn't notice his men. It's the best thing about him. When they go, it breaks him."

"Well, he's the one givin' the orders."

"Someone has to." He looks at the fire of the burner as it works its way through the tobacco. "I don't hate him. I mean I do, but I don't. If that makes sense. I hate him for leaving for Venus, but not for Mercury. At his best, he's how men should be. So maybe that means it's the world that's flawed."

"That's the damn truth."

We lean and smoke in silence. He really is a good egg. I don't give a shit about Sefi's instructions to brown-nose him. If she tells me to use him, I'll pop her between those black eyes.

"Grarnir. It is time." Pax and I jump at the voice. Neither of us noticed Ozgard sneak up behind us. For once he's not in good humor. The shaman's eyes are rimmed with ash. "The *kjr* assemble for the Kjrdakan. As *aefe,* you must join."

I squint at him. "The what for the what as what?"

"You're letting a Gray into the Kjrdakan?" Pax asks in shock. "The Lord Wager," he explains to me. "The Volk's war ritual before important battles. My father was the first person not of the Volk to join one. He was an *aefespakr*—a wise planner. It's an honor."

"Sefi accepted my plan?" I ask Ozgard, dumbfounded. "Not Valdir's?"

He laughs at me. "Grarnir is blind. Still he does not see. Freihild and skuggi are already en route back to Mars. We press for Phobos for transfer to ore haulers." He pauses, black eyes searching mine. "Come. Kjrdakan awaits."

Pax understands the seismic statement Sefi is making choosing the plan of a Gray outsider to that of her most successful warlord. It is a declaration of change, and a choice on her part to pick risk over slaughter. Entirely too civilized to be true. But it is also spitting in her lover's eye while putting me directly in the cross fire between them. Valdir will be pissed.

More than a little worried, I flick my burner away and follow Ozgard. Pax grabs my arm before I get far. "Whatever you do, don't bleed into the rib cage."

"Huh?"

"If the campaign fails and you've given a blood wager, you're killed in ritual homicide."

"Yeah. I'm going to need a few more details. Walk and talk, kid. Walk and talk."

Incense burns from braziers on the stage of the opera house where Amel was butchered. It's so thick my eyes itch back to the retinal nerves. I shift foot-to-foot in my place in the circle of towering war leaders as a giant albino aurochs with twisted horns is led onto the stage by Ozgard's acolytes. Sefi approaches the muscled cow with an axe the size of a tree on her shoulder. I cross my arms and settle in to watch the pagan absurdity.

Sefi tightens the glove on her right hand and crouches to peer into the beast's eyes with the tattoos on her closed eyelids. Apparently it only takes a minute to see the aurochs's "spirit." She whispers some alien sacrament that sounds like a pressure release on a gas rifle, and then rears back with the axe and splits its skull down the center in a tremendous blow. Blood sprays on my boots. The blade is so long it divides the aurochs's neck halfway down the spine. I watch in mild horror as the beast shudders and sways and crashes to the floor, spurting blood everywhere.

Sefi reaches into both sides of the split beast's head and rips out its tongue to show that it has been divided in half. Impossible precision.

The Obsidians rattle approval with the torcs on their left arms as Sefi hands one half of the grisly appendage to her *varKjr,* Valdir. The two eat the tongue raw, staring at each other with feverish enthusiasm that borderlines on erotic. My stomach twists as blood and juice trickle down their chins.

Seems excessive.

But these maniacs are just getting started.

As the dead beast twitches on the floor, Ozgard cavorts around it in some mad, spasmodic dance that would be funny if anyone but an Obsidian did it. The great folds of his skin ripple and flap as he waves his arms and shakes his bare torso. An atavistic song rumbles from the back of his throat. His circuit increases in speed, until the aurochs's hooves no longer scrape the ground. When it is still, Ozgard walks one more circuit. His footprints in the blood have made an intricate, spiraling shield glyph for protection.

Utter nonsense.

Then the *vynKjr*—Valdir's four wind lords—come forward to each take a leg and together roll the aurochs on its back, where Ozgard slices open its belly and butterflies its torso. He takes a black jar full of Jove knows what and fills his mouth before spitting it down on the aurochs's organs. Two hatchets appear in his hands and he smashes them together until their sparks catch on his spittle. A fire mushrooms in the belly of the beast. Its organs crackle. The fat under its hide catches fire and curls the white hair. Soon it is a conflagration. Flames dance over the faces of the Obsidian war leaders as they chant together.

Not even the incense can keep the claws of the burning intestines and liver from scouring the backs of my eyes. Tears stream down my face. At least the Syndicate were a familiar fright.

They chant until the fire subsides and leaves nothing but charred tissue and marrow leaking out of cracked bones. The rib cage of the aurochs curves outward and reaches upward like a pair of fossilized hands.

Ozgard crouches amongst the steaming debris and lifts his arms, shouting some nonsense in Nagal about a prophecy of fortune in the firebones. He then asks for the Kjrdakan. The Lord Wager. It starts with the *vagKjr*—the lowest-ranking wing lords. Two women, dressed in more modern garb, drop strands of hair into the rib cage. Wagering their honor against the battle's success. Their hair will be shorn in failure and they will lose their ranks and become braves who must earn command all over again. A bold wager, and the one Pax recommended I take. Then the third, a man in tribal garb, looks at me, looks at Valdir, then Sefi, and drops a single golden torc. There's silence. Sefi looks like she's about to murder the man. Only Pax's rushed lecture on the way here saves me from turning around in bewilderment. It's the lowest form of wager. A single torc. A fraction of battle honor.

An insult is what it is. Some of them don't believe in this gambit.

As all the male *vagKjr*, then some of the higher-ranking *vynKjr*, give their meager wagers, I realize why. I could give a shit if they don't like Sefi's plan for modernization or her betrayal of the Republic. But the men are protesting me. Calling *my* plan bullshit. With each clattering torc and arrogant giant, I find my insides heating up at the professional insult. Barely off the ice, and already superior to me. These savage idiots.

When Valdir throws in a single torc as well, I nearly leave. He spits on the floor in my direction. Ozgard translates his Nagal for me.

"You are noman," he echoes. "No *aefespakr* for the Volk. You are parasite. You have nothing to teach us but weakness." He looks at Sefi and lifts his chin to expose his throat. "You are my Queen. I stood against Gold with Nakamura, Arkadius, Vesuvian. Noble Grays. But this . . . *dog* belongs in gutter. His scheme will fail. And skuggi will die for nothing." He slaps his arms. "We must show strength, not tricks, if we are to betray our oaths."

His supporters, mostly men, rattle their torcs in agreement.

Sefi does not reply. It is a sort of betrayal I'm not sure I understand completely.

Ozgard gives me a little nudge forward to make my wager. Valdir's protesters laugh in derision as I pull a piece of hair, and they mutter there is no honor for a thief to risk. The anger boils up in me mighty fast. These uppity barbarians. Laughing at *me.* They don't even know what a rhetorical question is.

"You all know what I did," I say, turning and looking at the giants in their obstinate black eyes. "I stole those Gold spawn twice. You just scraped us up like vultures. And you call me a parasite? I was a Son of

Ares when you were still in the dark age, shitheads. I hunted Peerless while you were still serving them or pulling your people off the Poles. But you call me a dog? Fair enough. Spit on my honor. I don't give a damn. But don't you ever! Ever! Insult my work."

I jab my hand against a fragment of rib cage bone. Bright blood leaks out the meat of my palm. I hold it over the rib cage and let it dribble down. The Obsidians are stricken with confusion. Even Valdir looks like he swallowed a turd.

Having seized the greatest claim to valor if today is a victory, I stalk back to my place as the Obsidians murmur, and some put their hands to their foreheads in signs of respect. Ozgard whispers in my ear.

"Your faith inspires me." He's mocking me.

The hangover of regret comes hard and fast. The anger floods out. It wasn't just memories Z protected me from. It was always myself. Always the overcompensating pride of a street dog who can't bear to be laughed at, so he buys nice suits, drains his account on fashionable flats, yaps at monsters, gambles with people who can afford to lose. Well, Volga would be laughing her ass off now.

The Obsidians quiet as Sefi walks to the rib cage. She plays with her long hair, then gives me a sinister smile and very casually draws a dagger to slice a chunk of flesh from her left forearm to toss into the ribs and match my wager. When she speaks, she does so to Valdir in Common. "My way in victory. My head in defeat."

After the Obsidians depart, Sefi stands watching the remains of the bones smolder. "You will not be with your skuggi. They must move faster than you can follow." I nod, happy with that. "You know you will be killed if we fail?"

"Seems we both will."

"Pride blinds," she says. "But sometimes it leads." She sets a heavy hand on my shoulder. "I know our ways are strange to you, but hard ways are necessary to govern wild spirits. If we win, you will be my guest at the Hunt of the Last Light. You will have much treasure. You will be honored. They do not see your worth. But I do, Horn. I see fear in you. Most run from that fear. But you, you spit in its face." She lowers her face to mine. "As do I. As do I."

41

EPHRAIM

Obsidian Rising

WARSHIPS ROVE OVER THE birthplace of the Rising.
"So ends the tale of Ephraim ti Horn. Ritually murdered or atomized by a particle beam." I stick my hands in my pockets. "Lovely."

The greatest heist of the war rumbles slowly into gear and I'm pinned inside a fatass Julii ore hauler heading toward Mars with no escape plan, no intel except what the Obsidians give me, and no weapon, not even a wrench.

To put the olive on top, I'm stone-cold sober.

Far from kicking my Z habit, I must have begged half the shadier-looking braves on the *Heart of Venus* for just the dust of a cut gram. Seems Sefi put the word out. Not even the former berserkers in their ranks will trade me some of their Republic stimpacks.

I stare out the cramped bridge with doom squatting on my spine. The lights are dim. The pilot, a crack ripper Blue from Sefi's allies, the Rho Sect, hunches like a Karachi player in concentration over his controls even though a mentally disenfranchised elephant could fly this tub. Behind him, Ozgard stands there stroking his braided beard and eating walnuts without a care in the world. He's painted in his blue berry juice.

Idiot.

"You will not be ritually murdered or atomized," Ozgard replies. "The breath of the Allmother herself will carry you to Valhalla."

"Pass. I'll take a nomadic island on Venus with limitless Pinks."

He turns. Behind the annoyance in his eyes is a confidence that leaps far past the border of sanity. "Is that the depth of your soul?"

"Just the warm shallows."

He sighs. "You will not die, tinman, because if you die, we have failed, and Sefi too will die. She cannot die."

"Let me guess, you saw her fate in the firebones."

"Be careful not to insult a shaman on the eve of battle." He comes so close I can smell the eggs he had for breakfast in his beard. "You do not know what I have seen."

"No offense, but I find your faith a little disturbing."

"Bah." He reels away. "I find your face disturbing. It is soft. Like goat cheese. But I do not complain. You prepared skuggi. You are good at what you do. So are they. To fret now is seed of angst."

Prepared. Please. Like a few weeks' instruction will ready them for this.

It would be so easy if Sefi didn't want so many mines. We could fly the haulers into the mines' loading docks and pump Obsidians out. An old Reaper favorite. Problem is, to do that, we'd have to land hundreds of haulers at the same time at mines across a thousand-kilometer theater before the mines go into lockdown. Quicksilver's defense computers would quickly see the breach and eviscerate us. So a quarter of the mines will be taken that way. The rest require more creative infiltration by the skuggi. As for the hunterkiller defense robots? Well, there's a reason the Obsidians are in full armor.

If they follow my instructions, the skuggi and Quicksilver-hating Reds will bypass the sensor grids in retired tunnels, infiltrate the exhaust ducts, access the power grid, and disable the anti-aircraft guns. Piece of pie.

But the skuggi aren't even close to ready for this kind of coordinated infiltration. I hear the steady *drip drip drip* of the bloodbath filling up.

The Obsidians think I believe in Sefi enough to risk my life on this gambit for the mines. It's gained me some respect from her bodyguard of Valkyrie, but not from Ozgard. He knows I'm full of shit, because I've long suspected he's full of it too.

Ozgard sets his bag of walnuts on a gear box and leans toward the pilot to whisper something. I pull out my burners to settle my nerves and find the pack empty. I left my stash in Olympia. Damn. I grab one of his walnuts and busy myself trying to open it as I stare out the duro-glass. The moon of Phobos and most of the remaining Republic defense fleet are on the opposite side of the planet now, along with Volga. Ozgard eases back from the pilot and nudges me.

"Have you seen a nightgaze upon the pole with your flesh eyes?" he asks.

"Never been to either pole. Restricted zones. Savage locals."

"Nightgaze are the most tender of the Ice's life. They grow only in darkness, but oh, the light they make of their own ichor . . . They are truly a gift from the gods."

"Gift from the gods." I roll my eyes. "We're flying in a spaceship. Your ancestors were made in test tubes. The nightgaze by a drunk Violet. And you believe in gods? Hell, I get the racket. For a man you've done right fine by yourself with the matriarchs. But stop trying to con a conman."

He shrugs, ignoring the insult.

"Human knowledge is small. Universe vast. Mystery infinite. My gods were true before they were stolen and used against us. They are still true. And will be true long after we are food for the—" He freezes as he sees the walnut shells around my feet. His eyes flare wide and he grabs me, manhandling his fingers down my throat. I fight against him until I sick up all over his chest. I shove him and push too hard with my new leg, flying backward into the wall. I hit my spine on something sharp and hard.

"What the hell!" I gasp.

"You ate from my bag."

"I'll buy you another walnut, asshole." I spit the bile out and wipe it out of my goatee. "Jove on high. Who does that!"

"Walnut?" He squints at me. "What is walnut, jackass? These spirit berries from home. These for shaman only."

I squint. "I thought spirit berries were berries . . ."

"No!"

"Oh, well . . ." I hiccup. "What's spirit berries do?"

"To see spirits and hear gods."

"Literally?" He's threading his hands through his beard in worry. It's some sort of hallucinogen. That's about all I know. I look at my hands. Are they vibrating? The roof of my mouth tastes like chalk and asparagus and ice cream. "Will I die?"

He shrugs. "We will see!"

The walls turn to pulsing jelly as Ozgard leads me through them like a drunk puppy. Sefi's war council was a blurry dream. All the orders fragmented in my head. If I focus on anything longer than a moment, the world pulses between reality and into some peculiar hidden fourth-dimensional plane. *Keep the eyes moving. Stay lucid, oldboy. Stay atop the high.*

You love drugs. You *love* drugs.

We enter the mouth of a beast. No, just a hangar, empty of helium crates and filled with warriors. They vibrate like dark teeth. My head is spinning. Whole body flushed with electricity. I've never liked psychedelics. Too little control.

Ozgard jerks me out of the way as a column of Valdir's Stormbreakers jog past us in gray heavy armor painted with blue runes to load into the assault transports. A goddess with a luminous headdress of white feathers floats before a pack of Valkyrie in sky-blue armor. "Who is that!" I cry.

"Sefi."

"She looks fantastic!"

"Yes."

"She's going down herself? But there are killer robots!" He looks at me and I almost scream. The shaman has become a demon. His face is bright blue and his beard smokes. Fire leaks out his eyes and his mouth rumbles an orchestral thunder that is made of semisolid mutating colors. "What if she dies?" I hear myself weeping. "What happens if Sefi dies?"

"A queen that does not ride at the vanguard is no queen!" he bellows as Valdir stomps past, looking as big as a thunderhead. His hydra skull bubbles cruel laughter. "This is not her death! I have seen the griffin ascend on Red wings!"

"I mean what happens to me!" I cry.

"You are high, my friend! Have courage and ride the tumult!"

His laugh is cruel and mocking, and when he looks at me, lightning flashes in the veins of his black eyes. The whole world goes dark behind him and begins to tremble and distort. I fall down. The hard steel jars me out of the reverie. *It's just turbulence, you fool!* Ozgard picks me up like a toy and wraps my hand around a rung. "Stay and witness the griffin rise!" He bats my arms away and runs off toward Valdir and Sefi.

"Don't leave me!" I moan. "Oh gods. Oh gods." I curl up on the floor as the monsters trample past. *Stay atop the high. Stay atop the high.* I dive for safety into a pack of crates. Armor. I try to strap it on. Too big. Grav-

Boots. I don't want to fall into the ceiling. Lightning crackles there. I strap the boots on. They're huge, but the ankles manage to lock high up on my calves. That'll keep me safe. I grab an insidious weapon from the wall. A rifle of unknown and horrible power.

Oh Jove, what's that?

Iridescent sea creatures from the depths of the ocean swim through my eyes, mingling with the warriors. The creatures disappear inside the metal bodies and entwine their souls with the savages the world thought to tame. A dark torrent streams from their mouths and forms a crackling cloud of lightning and unruly thunder over their snowy heads. The song! The death chant of the Obsidians! I've heard it before in the ruins of Luna, but not like this. Not ever like this.

I don't just hear it.

I *feel* it. The vibrations grip my bones with their terrible beauty.

Before the soldiers of the gods, Ozgard takes a creature from a pouch and lets it bite his tongue before devouring it whole. The chanting thickens. The clouds swirl. Suddenly he throws off his cloak. He is naked beneath, his whole body painted blue, manhood swinging between his legs like a pendulum of power. He roars a horrible creed as he walks through the Obsidians, his arms uplifted, stomping his gravBoots. The Obsidians join him in stomping so that it feels like the heartbeat of a dead world awakening.

"*Baga duna!!!!*" he screams, and throws down his arms.

"*Duna fiel!*" Valdir and Sefi scream at him.

The hangar doors retract. Freezing wind pours in like the breath of a cold god, and Sefi is baptized in moonlight ahead of her bloodguard Valkyrie. Valdir and his worldbreakers slam their heads together. I close my eyes, praying for it to end. Knowing it isn't real. Am I real? Am I real? The darkness seeks to swallow me. "Witness!" It rumbles to me in Ozgard's voice. Terrified, I open my eyes, squinting into the maelstrom of wind.

"*Njar la tagag, syn tjr rjyka!*" Ozgard shouts.

The Obsidians echo him.

He points at Sefi and Valdir and flails his face, summoning the demon from the Queen and her mate.

"*Hyrg la Ragnar!*" they scream, and the Queen of the Valkyrie and Valdir the Unshorn run forward, two dark blades cutting through the light of the moon. Their acolytes follow in a blue and gray tide, jumping out the back of the ship in tight, beautiful martial lines that'd make any Gray proud. The assault shuttles follow.

Boots over the edge of the ship door, Ozgard laughs uncontrollably. Possessed. As if this were all his making, and he were a god overjoyed with the fidelity of his children. He points to me and reels my soul toward him. I clutch my terrible rifle tight and abandon my safety. As his arms wrap around me where the floor ends, I feel my terror flee and the evil in him disappears. My jacket whips in the wind. My pants are pierced with freezing air. But I feel nothing but warmth and love and acceptance from his laughter and from his naked body as we stand together overlooking the face of a living world.

"See!" he roars. "See! Do you see with your spirit eyes?"

Mars is captured in twilight. Her two moons watch us on the horizon. Beneath our metal feet is a great white shield mountain of northern Cimmeria. It seems the head of a giant standing with his feet warmed by the molten core of his world.

The city of Nike sweeps from his northwest shoulder toward the sea like a cape of stardust. Explosions flash in the city near its spaceport. Across the landscape, lumps of metal lit by lights hunch in the gloom like little lonely goblins. Mines. They spit no fire. Only their warning sirens flicker, staining the ground red. Their sky guns are down. It's working! Triumph swells in me. The skuggi did it. Freihild lowered the defense grid. That beautiful maniac. It's working!

I'm not going to be executed!

Ore freighters on the horizon drop assault shuttles and airborne Obsidian over the winter landscape, over the shield mountain, and along the plains, spitting Sefi's children down on the mines my plan and the skuggi prepared for them. The Republic defense fleet won't be able to react. Quicksilver's missiles streak up out of the mountains from hidden installations, but Alltribe ripWings swing down to silence them. All the colors dance in a wild, vivid frenzy. The ground, the sky, the ships, the mines, the air itself, are alive with spiritual fire. This is the domain of the Obsidian. A world within an unseen world.

Beneath the hallucination, I feel the beauty and inevitability of this day.

For ten years, the Obsidians were to the Republic as Volga was to me. Doggedly carrying the weight of all the rest. Only to be denied the fruits of their labor. *Fight,* the little ones said to them. *Kill for us, Valdir. Leave your homeland, but have none of our land, Sefi. Don't shop in our stores, Volga. Don't stand too tall, Volga. Because we are afraid of you.*

Well, a pox on hypocrites one and all. They had their chance, and now the Queen of the Valkyrie has come for their helium mines. I find myself proud of them as I laugh with the mad shaman, because in all this stupid, greedy world, the spirit comes alive when you see someone say, *no more*.

"Do you see!" Ozgard shouts beside me with tears in his eyes. His face is like that of a child, not a monster. "We have come home! Do you see! *This* is our Volkland!"

"Yes!" I proclaim, pumping my dread rifle in the air. "Yes!" He pushes me back and says he must join. "Yes!" I shout. "We must!" He bellows at me, and only after I jump off the edge of the transport ramp do I realize he bellowed at me to stay, that I wear no armor. But I do not care, because the gods protect me. He has seen my fate in the firebones, and I do not die here from the missiles that streak past me. I do not die from the railgun rounds that tear apart the sky. I fly toward a pack of falling Valkyrie, screaming for the glory of the Obsidian people and all their justified vengeance. I fall in amongst them. Armored women and men look at me. They gesture with eyes wide through bone helmets. They are laughing.

"Onward, Valkyrie!" I scream as wind pulls my lips back from my teeth. My gravBoots accelerate with a twist of my toes, and I dive toward the vanguard, streaking past Sefi and Valdir, filled with righteous glory as I tear toward the burning mouth of an open mine, unscathed through tongues of fire, and pierce the crust of the world to land amongst towering behemoths of metal.

They turn their glowing evil red eyes toward me, and I laugh when they do not fire, for I am a spirit warrior and I point my rifle at them, pull the trigger, and shit down my leg, because I am alone amongst a pack of hunterkiller robots and it is no rifle in my hand, it is only a mop.

Then Sefi and Valdir land, and the world goes mad.

PART III

TREASON

During war, the laws are silent.

—Quintus Tullius Cicero

42

LYSANDER

A Chorus upon the Pale

I RUN THROUGH THE WATER I stole from Ajax's assassins in two days. Though heatstroke is unlikely due to my physiology, dehydration plagues me and obscures even the most basic mental and motor functions.

Though my eye was not blinded by the firebrand due to avoiding its core flare, my vision is dreadfully impaired.

Three times I nearly lose my way when the features of the desert mislead me and I lose sight of the mountains. But I keep as straight a path north as I can, knowing I must eventually run into Erebos if I stay along the mountains.

I could not accept Apollonius's help, but I might find some unaffiliated aid in Erebos. If I recover enough, I can decide how to reach Atalantia without chancing Ajax's interference.

I eat the meat of cacti, and suck the water from desert lotus, but I feel myself fading. I find myself wishing I were back on the *Archi,* listening to Cassius and Pytha bicker as I lie reading in my bunk. I wish Kalindora were with me, that she hadn't assumed I died.

I wish Seraphina had simply stepped to the right.

Only my anger at the desert itself keeps me going. Everything seems like a bleached mirage now. The sun is a malevolent fat troll that squats over the desert, burning any uncovered skin in fifteen minutes and punishing me when I dare walk in the day. I sweat and sleep when I can find shade, and walk through the mornings when the playa is barren of grace. On my fourth day, I find the rotting carcass of a glass leviathan somehow swept in from the sea. The translucent flesh of the giant sea creature writhes with clouds of predatory bloodflies and a wake of buzzards thick enough to blot out the sky. I steer well around it.

When the northern storm sweeps rain showers over the desert, I lie down in joy to let it soothe my mangled face and the razor cuts Seneca and his men opened on my thighs and hip.

Mercury is a lovely planet, with temperate coasts, and mountain hotels, and hot springs, and cool valleys, and coral seas, but to have all that, it had to have the hell of the Ladon around its equator.

I curse the bastards that terraformed this planet. I curse the rocks. I curse the sun, the sand, myself for needing so much gorydamn water. And I curse Ajax. But more so, I curse the culture that let him grow wicked.

The Peerless scar was formalized by Silenius to mark a Gold worthy of respect, not worship. Our rigorous Institutes were built to educate us to be shepherds, not cannibals. The world provided Darrow to show us how far we'd lost our way. To fight him, we did not find our path again, we strayed further and further, learning all the wrong lessons.

Gradually, the desert gives way to a semi-arid climate as I make my way to more northern latitudes. The transition is subtle, barely noticeable at first. But even the smallest signs of life give me hope. Torrential rain has eroded hillsides but also seduced weeds and flowers to spring out of the rocky soil. My vision returns enough in my right eye to see green interspersed with brown. The ground is still unforgiving and spartan, but the worst danger is over. Where there is water, anyone can survive. Deerling with spiraling black antlers and birds shaped like faeries feed off the orange berries of gnarled geran shrubs only to zip home to their hivecastles amidst cacti the size of houses. While I haven't the strength to hunt either with my razor, I eat as many berries as I can find amongst the thistles, never minding the cramps the excess fiber causes in my belly. I eat grubs from underneath boulders, and swallow the yolks of bird eggs I find in low shrubs. Tubers and roots make the bulk of my diet, which causes more cramps, until I find a sulfur viper basking in the sun beneath a dead olive tree. I crush its head with a rock and drink its blood, knowing my immune system will likely handle the pathogens it carries. The mild nausea is well worth the valuable vitamins. When I've drained it, I roast its meter-long body over a fire. Its meat is tough and elastic, like langsat flesh, but the calories give me fresh optimism as I make my push toward Erebos.

Pausing on a ridgeline that leads to a fertile valley, I look back at the desert one last time. It waits there in the distance, patient, eternal, the graveyard of armies. But not me.

I turn my back on it, but carry its lessons with me.

The next kilometers are almost pleasant. While the temperature hovers around fifty degrees Celsius in the morning, frequent showers from the roiling clouds keep me cool and soothe the agony of my burn. Birds twitter in orderly citrus groves, which I eat heavily from as I pass.

Following the tracks of an abandoned combine, I find a shed and a small farmhouse that looks to have been abandoned in haste. It has been looted at least once, and I'm unable to find medical supplies. But in the garden, I find an aloe plant, which I'm able to distill into a paste for my burn. It takes the sharp edge off the itching sting, but does little for the deep nerve trauma, and nothing at all for my eye, which throbs down to the very root of the ocular nerve.

The power is out in the farm, but it is nice having a puzzle to solve that doesn't include imminent death. In a few hours I'm able to rig the solar panels of the combine to work with the stove, on which I cook dry-pressed curry from a freshcan. I also manage to power the ancient HC in the living room. The HC won't link with the holoNet, and instead shows only a Society emergency broadcast message, giving instructions for all citizens to evacuate Erebos and the surrounding lands for Naran, a hundred kilometers northeast.

I think of the tight showers on the *Archi* as I draw myself a bath. I slip into the cold water and shudder. It is the most pleasant thing I have experienced since the caldarium with Cassius. My legs are too long for the tub and splay out awkwardly against the fraying wallpaper. It's only then I realize how much weight I've lost. Twenty kilos maybe? My body looks like it belongs to a rust lung victim. It is emaciated, any skin exposed to the sun swollen and peeling. I doze lightly in the bath for hours. After drinking another liter of water, I collapse onto the forma-Fab bed and sleep for an entire day.

I set back out two mornings after arriving at the farm. I have changed the tattered pulseArmor underlining for the farmer's clothing. I look ludicrous, the sleeves barely coming to my elbows, and the pants to my shins.

I look back at the farm, sorry to leave it, and wonder for a moment if I shouldn't just stay there. What am I rushing back to? A future as Atalantia's rival? A duel with Ajax when he must face what he has done? A short life of politics and betrayal? Revenge which I don't want, even after Darrow took half my face? To be with my people? Why? Gold has grown sicker in my absence. But even knowing all that, there is still an undeniable itch to return, as if my spirit were drawn by gravity.

I need to realize the promise I made to Dido, the excuse I gave to Cassius when I betrayed him. I must unite Gold. More than that. I must change it. That is what makes me leave the farmhouse behind. That and the understanding that I must help liberate Kalindora, Rhone, and the Praetorians from Heliopolis. It would be immoral not to help those who risked all for me. By the good repair of Seneca's gear, it seems the Ash Legions weren't broken entirely. An invasion will be coming for Heliopolis. One I doubt my friends will survive.

The walk to Erebos is leisurely compared with the desert. I cut through groves of wild cypress, and orchards redolent with the smell of starheart blossoms. At times I see hovercraft on the horizon, or the occasional Society patrol in the lower atmosphere. Though black clouds brood to the north, the worst of the storm seems to have passed.

I pace myself, stopping frequently to gorge on the food I foraged from the farmhouse and the pack of tangerines pulled from the trees. My route takes me parallel to the Via Gloria, the white frictionless highway that connects the cities that border the Ladon by land. It is broken by bombardment and littered with blackened Republic assault vehicles and desiccated corpses.

I sleep under a grapefruit tree and the next morning come across a family of sunbaked Red natives walking along a country road pushing a cart full of their life's belongings. They watch me approach with unease. I greet them politely and comment on the weather, as Mercurians always do. They look at each other, then up and up at me and my melted face, and then they bow.

"Odd weather, yes, *dominus,*" the man says quietly.

"Devil weather," the woman says with a little more heat, much to her man's distress. "Greedy Martian thought he could break our spirit. Not this spirit, *dominus,*" the woman says. "A little weather won't tame us."

"Darrow you mean?"

"Don't even give him a name, *dominus*," she says bitterly. "His men ransacked our employer's latifundia. Took him away, saying he harbored the Fear Knight—Vale bless the man. Did it all with smiles, of course, but when they were done, what've we got left? Just what they left us. We work for our share. We don't take the pity of Martian marauders." She spits. "Latifundia went to bits. Our headTalk started running the place, but no one ever came for the haul. It's just sitting out there rotting. You with the legions?" she asks. "You look like you've seen Hades itself, *dominus*."

I scan the road behind her. "Only its gatekeepers."

"If there's anythin' you desire . . ." Her eyes dart to my burned face and she waves to her cart, again to her husband's distress. They barely have enough for themselves.

"Just information. Have you seen any Society forces?" I ask.

"Fear Knight's men were through here not too long ago, *dominus*. Never know where you can find them, though. Like Vale spirits they are. Rest of the legions are out to the east last I heard. A bastion's set down. Hear there be Ash Legions in Naran. It's flooding with refugees from Tyche and the coast. Poor souls. Whole city's gone. We're heading east to the riverlands, hear they're hiring folk out there for the cleanup."

"There's no legions in Erebos?" I say in confusion.

"Erebos? It's drowned, *dominus*," the man says.

I frown. The waves couldn't have come this far. "What do you mean, drowned?"

By late morning, I summit a hill that looks down into the Valley of Erebos, and see for myself.

Erebos was a proud library city once, a serene and bucolic vanity created as a gift for my grandmother by the Master Maker Glirastes. The high city, all in thrall to the great library, was hewn from the back of a low mountain just beneath a great dam. The dam protected the city from seasonal floods caused by the melting of mountain snow, a quick affair under Mercury's sun. When I saw it as a child at Glirastes's side, I deemed it a giant turtle with a vine-wrapped city upon its back. He grumbled that it was a tortoise representing the patience and inevitable victory of knowledge.

Now it is a watery necropolis.

The great dam has broken, the pulsefields likely failing during the storm. The rush of water left a path of destruction across the city so thorough it would be a wonder if anyone survived. Carrion birds rule here now. There are no medical teams from either army, only bands of refugees across the flooded valley and plains beyond, trundling north in lines by the thousands. I sit down, finally feeling the exhaustion of the last week in my bones.

Darrow has broken the planet.

A sense of futility rises in me. What could anyone do to fix this?

Resolving to refill my water and connect with one of the refugee trains, I stumble down the foothills, passing through forests entirely scalped by the wind. Not a tree stands. I wade through fields of lavender, where bees still pollinate, and draw to a halt. At the foot of the Via Gloria a peculiar arrangement sprawls around the Arch of Octavia, which leads into the city. Even with my blurry vision, I know what it is.

I walk down the hill.

There beside the great archway, I find a scene of horror. Amongst a sea of lavender, the remains of more than four hundred humans hang upon metal poles blistering and naked but for the wake of buzzards that clothe them in feathers of yellow and scarlet.

The poles that puncture the humans are as thick as my wrists, sharp at the point and tapered. Each has been driven into the anal cavity of the victim to the point of perforating the mid-torso. In death, the legs droop, the back arches, the arms wing out and downward, and the head reclines backward, as if each victim perished in exultation. Sockets picked clean by the birds stare at the sky.

A great hunk of stone stands at the entry to this atrocity bearing the message:

HERE LIE MARTIANS ALL
THRALLS OF THE SLAVE KING
WHO THOUGHT WITH WICKED DELIGHT
TO TAKE YOUR PLANET'S TREASURE
AND BREAK THEIR MASTER'S MIGHT
ALL YE WHO ENTER HERE:
WITNESS THEIR WORK,
AND DESPAIR

The flooded city is their work. And the impalement ours.

Is this what the Society thinks will inspire the people to return to the fold?

Atlas was no monster in the court of my grandmother. He was odd. Always rather cold to me, and quick to leave the room when I entered. He despised children. Though he and Aja made Ajax together, their coupling entailed no relationship from what I understand. In fact, Aja could barely stand the sight of the man. But I cannot believe my father's best friend would be this new monster.

Though he was formally a hostage, my grandmother trusted Atlas without equal. He spurned galas and festivals, and seemed only to stir himself from his library when my grandmother required his unique services. What they were, I never saw until now.

I have always held in respect those Golds who do not relish their station. Atlas never seemed to. Yet he has let his Gorgons loose in ways that demean any claim we have to dignity. So my judgment on him is harsh.

I stumble down the line to see the faces of the dead, thinking obscurely that someone should witness them here. All the families they represent. All the strands of life that are linked to theirs. Cruelty will travel down those lines, ensnaring more and more.

No one has come to take them down. No footprints have even come within a hundred meters. There is a whispering. It comes from a young Red man.

A sound comes from one of the Red bodies. A whispering.

He is alive. Barely more than a boy, a faint bit of hair covers his top lip. His cracked lips part, trying to say something more. I give him the remaining water from my pouches. Most of it spills down his chest. He tries to speak again. I edge closer to hear him. "The . . . Vale. Send me . . ."

It's then I notice perhaps as many as a dozen still wheeze, their burned skin rising and falling with each insidious breath. I do not care if they are enemies. If impaling is an effective tactic. Or even if they deserve this judgment. It is not the jurisdiction of any man to deliver it.

I go closer to the boy. My mouth is so dry I barely manage the words. "Are you certain?" He cannot reply until I spill some of my water into his mouth.

"Send . . . me."

There, so close to him I can see the flecks of copper, brown, and even gold in his Red irises, I feel a terrible sadness. I wish I knew that the eyes of his spirit looked upon his Vale. That his ancestors were waiting for him in their cool highland valley. But I know it is not so, because I know the Vale was created and cultivated by the Board of Quality Control in order to provide an important sociological prerequisite for obedience: a carrot at the end of a hard life. That very same belief that made them able to endure untold hardship in the mines has become a militant faith. He begins to whisper as I draw my razor. *"My love, my love, remember the cries, when winter died . . ."*

He is joined by the others until there is a rasping chorus there upon the pale.

The Bellona razor's leather hilt is warm from the sun. Tension travels down my arm as the blade penetrates his chest and then his heart. "Go to your people," I whisper. He jerks and then is still.

More men and women beg for mercy down the line. I move to the next man. He's an older Red, with a thick beard shot with white and a face like a bulldog's. He begs for mercy, but when I stand in front of him, he and several others begin to laugh. I blink in confusion. Their faces swim in the heat. Why are they laughing?

"Burn with us, ya golden cunt," he manages from a mouth crusted with blood. "Burn with Mars."

Then I understand the trick.

I do not move. I look down, knowing what it must be. I push lavender out of the way and blow down into the dirt. A thin mat of pressure-sensitive material lies under the topsoil. If I move my foot, the mine hidden beneath will make me a shower of meat. Even if I dive away, only two mines of the hundreds this war employs have a blast radius I'd be able to clear.

"I was trying to help you," I say. "I was trying to be decent."

The Red just laughs through teeth shattered to the nerve.

Without a way to apply equal pressure to my weight on the pad, I dig a small tunnel through the dirt adjacent to the pad to reach the mine. Blindly reaching into the hole, I graze the side casing of the munition. It's a Lotus-13, judging by the octagonal top rim. If I can slide my razor between the pressure pad and the mine, I should be able to sever the hardwire connection. With hands shaking from adrenaline, I toggle the razor's edge to the thinnest setting possible, so the blade is narrow as a piece of paper, a hand's width wide. I slide it sideways down into the hole and trip a countermeasure.

Bweeee. Bweeee.

Dirt and shredded lavender explode up into my face. I'm blasted upward. I lose my razor. The air rushes out of me as I land hard on my back. Something constricts around me, ensnaring. I push at it, but it cuts my fingers and the more I push, the more it constricts. A tacNet, I realize in relief, not an explosive.

But the relief is short-lived as I realize my predicament.

I lie there in the morning sun, the only shade cast by the poles, the lavender stalks, and the bees. The meters to my razor and water might as well be a thousand. Every time I try to roll or wiggle closer, the net constricts more until it breaks the skin of my scalp. Soon I am immobilized with blood trickling down my face. For hours I lie there as the sun traces its way across the sky, leeching my body of water as it forms blisters on my exposed skin. I'm the color of a tomato. The lavender sways. The bees buzz. The buzzards chew. I drift in and out of consciousness, woken only when the buzzards engage in a hearty squabble for a choice piece of thigh meat. The Red man is dead. They feed on him and watch me.

If I could laugh, I would.

Heir of Silenius, eaten by birds at the feet of Reds, because he tried to be merciful. Lesson learned.

It was my guilt for the *Vindabona* and the helpless people I left for the Obsidians that distracted me. I should have known about the mines. I see those victims I abandoned now on the hill, lying in tacNets, watching me with smiles, waiting for me to join them in death.

All those lives lost so I could save Seraphina, who ran to her own slaughter with a smile.

"Well, look at this, fresh catch," one of the victims says to me.

"And a blood traitor by the looks of it," says another. *"He killed some of the bait."*

"Scar?"

Heavy desert boots stop in front of me. A child's face bends down from the sky and peers into mine. Something is wrong. It is the color of a dust moth's wings. Oh. It's a mask. Purple works its way into the mask as its wearer crouches near the lavender. *"He's missing half his gorydamn face. Eyeball's all mush."* A gloved hand twists my head. *"No scar. We got ourselves a Pixie, lads."*

They're Gorgons.

"Rising?"

"Who else? We don't send unscarred boys to battle."

"Let's leave him to bubble. This trap's done. Shit to show for it. Stragglers are all herded into Heliopolis for the big hammer."

One of them whistles. "Look at the detailing on his big iron. Sciantus-made, bet my life."

"Slag off. How would you know what a Sciantus blade looks like? You wouldn't even be able to afford the hilt."

"The Minotaur had one. Treated it like a thirsty lady. Always running his fat mouth about it. See the flower petals?"

"Where?"

"Over the wing."

"If you say so. What's a Pixie doing with a piece like that?"

"If it don't fit, it's Howler shit. Search him for trackers and let's ride. Fear'll sort it." The child's face looks down at me again as I try to speak. "Time to take a nap, traitor." The last thing I see is his boot coming down.

43

LYSANDER

The Enemy

THE GORGONS TRAVEL VIA GRAVBIKE. The ride is long and covers several hundred kilometers back the way I walked. Back into the damn desert. In the late afternoon, they make a stop in a high-desert town surrounding a large mine. I watch tied to the back of a gravBike as lowColor townsfolk run out to greet the butchers like heroes. Children run along as we trail out of the town heading toward the snowline of the mountains.

Clouds eddy across the darkening sky as the gravBikes slow to go single file along a mountain track. We come to an abrupt halt. Boots crunch the snow and something hits me again on the head.

When I regain consciousness, I am cold and wet. The floor is stone. I do not open my eyes yet. My hands are chained above me, bracketed into the wall of a cave. Streams run to either side. Hushed voices converse.

"He never asks us any questions. Never any. He just takes something away. I told him all I could think of. I just wanted it to stop." The man sobs.

"Spare us your weeping, Hadrian. It's bad enough already without you bubbling like a Venusian harlot."

"Let him be, Ignacius. We've all told him something, Hadrian. It's prime, brother."

"He made . . . time slow down. Something he gave me. I could feel every molecule as he took . . . as he . . . " The words are lost in the sobs.

"How many guards have you counted, Drusilla?"

"He hoods me every time."

"What's it even matter what we've seen? We know he's listening right now. That's the only reason he'd let us stay together. How many Howlers has he caught? How many have been retrieved? One—and Orion was so mad she fucked a continent. We're dead, goodmen. Go with dignity at least. Soon we'll be upon the pale."

"Sure, dignity with a metal pole up your ass. Sounds like a Tuesday for you, Ignacius."

A beat of silence.

"The boss will come for us," the leader says.

"Faithful to the end, Alex? Your Red god is drowned by now or blasted to bits. The only grace we'll receive is the Void. But that's prime. It's just nothing, after all."

"He's not dead."

"You really did go full lupus. The whole army is dead, because of the Senate Vox. Taking our ships, the tiny bastards. Heliopolis will have fallen in the siege, and the army will have been trapped in the desert under the guns of the Ash Armada. They're probably already nailing Darrow to the bow of the Annihilo to sail on Luna."

"Then why are we still in a cave?"

There are at least five around me. All of them Golds. Martian accents mostly, Elysian with a faint flavor of the Jovian Moons. I listen a little longer. Europan dialect. Howlers, Darrow, Alex, the accents. It leaves little left to guess. There're two others sleeping. How many more, I can't tell because of the sound of the stream. I would guess nine.

"Scarface is awake and listening to us," the one called Ignacius says.

"Are you awake, my goodman?" another asks with more authority. The leader. His accent would be near-cultured but for how he mumbles. "Don't be afraid, we're all fucked here. Eyes open or closed, doesn't much matter." He laughs with thin confidence. I make a show of opening my right eye. There are ten other prisoners chained as I am against the wall. Two are sleeping. Two Gorgons sit about thirty meters off in the throat of a tunnel that is the room's only exit.

"Told you he was awake," Ignacius says. He's a huge, handsome brute.

"I don't see a scar," the woman says. Drusilla.

"Like they weren't wise to that after year one," Ignacius says.

"What's your name?" Drusilla asks. Her face is darker than the rest. Kind eyes watch me from swollen eyelids.

"Easy now, my goodman," Alexandar says. "You've been mauled

rather gruesomely." Even with both his ears missing, and half his face grotesquely swollen, I can tell he is around my own age and that he used to be a handsome man. Staggeringly, I wager. His shoulders are incredibly broad for his frame. Legs meant to eat kilometers are folded under him. The last time I saw him was in a holo Cassius and I watched on the *Archi* as he stood behind Darrow during a speech.

Alexandar au Arcos, Lorn's grandson, my estranged cousin, and Kalindora's nephew on his mother's side.

"What's your name?" he asks. "Take your time. Concussions befuddle the best of us."

I heed Octavia's ministrations and fall back on an identity with long-term upside, which I can defend and they will be unable to verify. Can't be Rising. Can't be Society. I have no scar on my face, and can properly emulate the Mercurian dialect popular in what counts as high society in Erebos. The identity is natural, and a little hilarious. But I'm half mad from dehydration, so I dive in.

"Cato au Vitruvius," I say. The identity I used for security reasons when I would visit Glirastes for studies. It belongs to a fictional son of a real local family of high history and middling future.

"*Salve,* Cato. I'm Alexandar. Drusilla, Ignacius, Crastus, Hadrian." In turn, he nods at the kind-eyed woman, the giant, a pretty man in his thirties, and a squat bull of a Gold male. "The Knights of Elysium at your service, such as we are."

"Oh, now you're a Knight of Elysium," Drusilla mutters.

"Arcosian Knights," one corrects.

"Who are you?" Ignacius demands of me.

"He means how did you end up in this hell?" Alexandar asks. He smiles crimson. Not one of his teeth remains. I'm surprised by the kindness of him, considering. He looked haughtier on camera, and Grandmother's Securitas file said he was incredibly arrogant, intelligent, if not too creative, with a paternal deficit complex after the death of his father. His defensiveness of the Reaper suggests the complex's newest placeholder.

I tell them a nervous story of the dam breaking at Erebos. Ordnance falling on the city accounts for my burns; trying to rescue survivors, for the sunburns; and trying to take the impaled victims down, for the tacNet wounds. Drusilla asks me sly, trick questions about my home, suggesting she's been to Erebos. But so have I, and I trapped it all in amber.

I can still see the silk market, and the bright belts of the citizens, and the gold filigree in every single street sign.

I pass their meager tests.

"You've been here a while, haven't you?" I ask.

"Yut," Alex replies, with another trap.

"Pardon?" I ask, flummoxed.

"You're not a soldier, are you?" Alexandar says.

Another assumption trap. "I don't understand."

"Never mind."

"I hardly know a single mate who's enough money to pull the Institute," I reply. "My parents are . . . were silk merchants, and not grand ones by any judge."

"Then what did you do?" Drusilla asks.

"Drank mostly," I reply. "My father bribed the magistrate to let me stay in Erebos after the Conscription as a civil engineer magistrate. War is such a ghastly affair." I give a little shudder.

"So he's a duty-dodging Pixie. I'm not swallowing this snakeshit," Ignacius says. "He's a plant or, at the very least, a slaver by participation."

"So's every person on Mercury according to you."

"They all act like it. Only thing you get out of hugging a Mercurian is a knife in the back. They're all swindlers and drunks, the sundark lot of them."

"I'm darker than him," Drusilla says.

"Semantics."

"Will you two hens stop pecking?" Alexandar snaps. "Why'd you want to know how long we've been here, Cato?"

"It's just that Heliopolis hasn't fallen," I say. "You said it must have." Even Ignacius listens intently. "I heard from a man who'd been in the Ladon that Darrow led his army across the desert under the cover of the storm. He hit Ajax au Grimmus as he was besieging the city."

"That madness worked?" Alexandar asks. He grins hideously with empty gums at Ignacius. "I told you. The boss has everything under control."

Or he's lost control completely.

44

EPHRAIM

Hunt of the Last Light

Xenophon leads me into the skuggi hangar with a bored expression on that wan face. "Gods, it's quiet," I mutter. Not in the city below, where construction crews work night and day to bring Olympia to its former glory, or in the lands around, which vibrate with the sound of Obsidian flocking to the Volkland, or on the coasts where Alltribe ripWings eye Republic fighters across the Thermic, or in the mines where Reds and Oranges hijack Quicksilver's robots to continue helium operations. It is quiet in Eagle Rest and only Eagle Rest because Sefi and Valdir have taken the children to hunt, my skuggi are off on missions, and I am left like an old man to rattle around an abandoned house.

"Walk faster, please, we mustn't be late to the kill," the *logos* says.

"Maybe we should be heading to the landing pads then, genius."

"We are . . . in a way." We turn the corner and I stop dead in my tracks. One of the most beautiful ships I've ever seen sits beside ugly skuggi tactical ships like a two-comma Pink in a frontline brothel. She is sixty meters long, sleek hulled, equipped with twin-ion engines, two railguns, sensor-resistant hull, and is shaped like a sideways hammerhead shark. She is painted jade green. "Apollo's cock, that's a beauty."

"A gift from Her Majesty," Xenophon says, handing me the slim omnicard.

"Naw."

"It *is* in your contract. A top-tier flier. It was collected from Quicksilver's mansion in Nike. I daresay you'll get more use out of it than he will." I put in the contract because I thought I'd need an escape route out of here. I never expected to *actually* get it just when I'm thinking I may not need it. Still, I snatch the omnicard and practically levitate toward the ship. She's not just a racer, she's a deepspace tigress. Could probably run from Mars to the sun in two weeks flat. Well, maybe not *that* fast. "Keep in mind, tracking measures have been installed. And the children are not allowed within a kilometer of it."

"Uh-huh." I run my hand over the hull. "What's the catch?"

Xenophon smiles as a gaggle of dignitaries comes around the corner. "I fear her maiden voyage will be as a taxi. What will you call her?"

I turn back to grin at the White. *"Snowball."*

"It's green."

"Still a Snowball."

As the South Pole slumps toward the gloom of winter, a wind the Obsidians call Breath of the Underdark moans through the glacial valley. This slow, incessant current will freeze the eyelashes off a man and blacken the skin in twenty minutes. It signals the beginning of darkness for the Pole.

From the warm confines of my thermal gear, two-thirds the way up a young mountain, all I feel is the gentle tug of nature telling me I don't belong. I look around and the crouched braves behind give me a nod and murmur, *"Kalt, Grarnir?"*

"Njr, Grarnir kann njek kalt," another says. *"Fer ragnver en la."* I dust snow off my shoulder.

Cold, Gray Fox?

Nah, Gray Fox can't get cold. God fire burns inside him.

I'm a walking, talking totem of invulnerability. A spirit warrior. Proof of the existence of gods. Only Ozgard knows I was under major psychotropic influence during the mine heist. The Obsidians either don't know or don't care that the hunterkillers didn't fire on me because I had Gray DNA and held a mop. I wasn't touched by the gods. I just wasn't a threat, according to their software. All they know is that when Sefi and Valdir caught up, I stood amongst the enemy howling like an ice-veined banshee.

Sefi and Valdir hit like the hammer of god five seconds after I landed. Can't rid myself of the sight of armored Obsidians hacking at tripod robots, or how their meat smelled as the robot lasers cleaved through five braves at a time.

Thirty-five thousand Obsidian crack troops died cleaning out the hunterkillers in the mines of Cimmeria. And me? Not a bloody scratch. Ozgard got me drunk for three solid days. Pax stood in amused silence when he saw me being carried on the shoulders of Valkyrie. Electra literally almost died laughing when I told them what's what afterward in my rooms in Olympia. I thought she'd be jealous. But she thinks it's the funniest thing she's ever bloody heard, though the mop jokes are rather overdone. Now she actually talks to me without looking like she wants to cut my balls off.

That's all it took?

Freihild and the skuggi are drunk with valor for their part in taking the mines. Several of the females have even been given the honor of taking part in the hunt. The men stand on the ledge with me, Valdir, and the highest-ranking male jarls, tribal leaders. They were no less brave in battle, and they know it. It has always been this way, but that doesn't mean they like it.

Sefi and Pax peer off a ledge not twenty meters away amongst a long pack of Valkyrie hunters. The furs they wear are crusted in a shell of ice from days of tracking. It crackles when they move, and twinkles when light from the shoulder lamps of the mechanized guards catches in the gloom.

For six days the Valkyrie have stalked their prey. While Electra accompanied Freihild on the stalking expedition to the White Shards, Pax accompanied Sefi to find scale-trace at the Sundered Peaks. The know-it-all could tell you the molecular structure of Obsidian arrowheads, but couldn't have cared less the day of their departure. The boy misses his mother.

Apparently Sefi knows something about children. It is difficult to hold on to grief after six days of whiteout conditions, frostbite, saddle sores, and sleeping in seal-hide lean-tos. Pax knows how lucky he is to sit in the saddle behind her. Of the Obsidian braves, not even Valdir ever has mounted a griffin for a hunt. Pax's melancholy has been replaced by intense focus.

His head snaps back when a high-pitched whistle echoes across the glacial valley, several notes higher than the screaming wind. Xenophon, wrapped to his nose in thermal gear, explains to the political guests I ferried on the *Snowball:* Freihild is in motion. The chasers are out. The beast is flushed from its alpine cavern.

The killwing waits. Sefi waits.

The snow settles on her shoulders and bone helmet. She looks like a god of winter, a permanent and unyielding feature of the mountain.

A second whistle trills.

The younger Valkyrie look to her in expectation. The older hunters know the Queen's patience and stay motionless. The guests murmur in excitement.

A third whistle sounds, impatient, urging her forward. Sefi resists. Pax shoots her a glance. Seconds tick past. And then Sefi raises a clenched fist.

"*Sljr,*" she whispers, jumping off the ledge. A horn moans.

"*Sljr. Sljr. Sljr,*" shout the Valkyrie, and fifty women slip over the edge. Pax goes with.

"Hunt," Xenophon parrots.

The Valkyrie disappear and a moment later a series of screams rises from the other side of the ridge. Sefi's pale steed bursts off the ledge beneath. Pax rides in the archer's saddle behind her, not out of place or afraid like I thought he'd be.

A rush of air forces snow into my mouth as several griffin banking overhead dislodge snowdrifts above. Two Red allies stumble into each other, laughing and marveling at the mounted Valkyrie careening down into the valley keening death. Bare-armed in the cold, Valdir steps forward and watches with a practiced eye, and a purity of awe, love, and jealousy. Anyone could see how much he wishes to fly upon the beasts of his people. I don't like the man. He's a closed book. But I feel for him. No longer a slave of Grimmus, but still not quite free.

"Your first hunt?" Xenophon asks me, taking a pause from the narration so the onlookers can collect themselves.

I nod. "Not yours, it seems."

"My third. During the war, Her Majesty would return when she could to honor the sundeath. I believe she feared she would forget who she was if she spent too long away from the Ice. I advised her against this hunt, however."

"Ozgard and Valdir seemed bullish enough."

"They would. It may invigorate the spirit of the shaman and satisfy

Valdir's expectations of a queen, but such considerations are specious for a modern head of state, given the unnecessary exposure to risk. Not to mention the details of state which pile up in her absence. I designed her government to function with a monarch. Without one, it functions at fifty percent efficiency, not that Valdir or the madman would care for such trivialities." Xenophon looks around. "Have you seen the madman?"

"He's probably drunk in a cargo hold somewhere," I say, growing annoyed. I want to watch the hunt.

"It is a high probability." The sexless mammal squints to the west as Valdir points and calls out to the others. "Ah, the drake. Excuse me."

I look west. Scales glint in the gloom, rippling low against the snowy boulders of the valley floor. The glint becomes a blur that becomes a leviathan of the ice. Though I know its ancestors were carved by mad Violets in conjunction with Yellow geneticists, the ice drake seems an ancient creature. Something older than we are.

I realize I've forgotten to breathe.

"This specimen is a black ice drake of the *Níðhöggr* strain—one of the rarest and most revered creatures in Obsidian mythology," Xenophon explains to the guests. "'He Who Strikes with Malice' is said to be the bringer of winter. This one is an old bull, as can be divined by the nine lateral tusks and triple horn, which mark his decades. Of course, the hunting of sows is forbidden, and punishable by the Blood Eagle."

The guests whisper with awe, as if the creature were magical, and not thirty tons of lab-engineered death.

Pursued by Freihild and her chasers, the bull tears through the mountain valley. Even at our distance, I feel a chill. The Obsidian guards watch in appreciation, Valdir in pure love. Few would have ever seen a drake in flight, or slipped into a lair to kill and drink the blood of a hatchling to begin the Way of Stains.

The drake spots Sefi's hunting band ahead and banks right, thinking to escape over the north side of the valley. Thunder crackles from the peaks. Obsidian youths, who summited the mountains with hooks and rope, light sulfur-based charges into their braziers, and launch them into the clouds with slings. Huge claps of sound frighten the dragon back and forth across the valley as it seeks some escape, only to be herded again and again by small explosions from surrounding peaks.

Someone screams as it banks our way. Amidst the guards, skuggi light fuses on the brazier and hurl the clay bombs into the air. They laugh as the pots explode. Gudkind tosses me two. I light them and hurl them skyward. *Boom. Booom.*

The rush of air from the drake's wings nearly knocks me off my feet. It passes a stone's throw from us. Debris and rocks the size of a man's head are crusted in the ice along the wyrm's belly. Attendants scatter, laughing in relief as it pinballs back down into the valley toward the Queen. Valdir rushes to the cliff's edge to lean forward and watch. Scores follow him.

Above a frozen alpine lake, an inverted V of Valkyrie hunters forms around the drake. Sefi waits at the far tip of the V to deliver the killing stroke. But as the first arrows from the Obsidians fly from their flanks, the drake uses an updraft to go into a precarious climb. It knocks two griffins from the air. Their riders flail from the saddles, but their safety ropes snap them back toward their tumbling steeds. One recovers. The other collides with a mountainside below as her griffin is bisected by the razor tips of the drake's wings.

The guests are horrified. Valdir touches his heart. A good death. His eyes search the chasers, young griffin riders with more spirit than experience, looking for Freihild, I reckon. My optics pick her up by the green plumes of her headdress. Electra sits in the archer saddle behind her, priming combustible arrows.

Sefi blows a horn, and the griffin V inverts as the riders kick their griffins into motion. The beasts bank upside down and race beneath the drake as Freihild leads the chasers to follow it to the higher altitude. Huge sounds rattle the valley as they shoot arrows with combustible tips to herd it back down. The sound scares the dragon off its ascent, forcing it back toward Sefi's re-formed V nearer the ground. The first of Sefi's hunters begin to harry the drake, soaring past to hurl spears or shoot arrows into its side.

Only Sefi continues flying away from it, pushing her griffin two hundred meters past the rest before she banks back around. Her wingsisters pull taut ropes connected to the spears and arrows embedded in the creases of the dragon's scales. The first riders are jerked sideways by its mass, but soon more than twenty ropes are secured and together the skyhunters anchor the drake along its path toward their Queen.

"The weakest scale is just beneath the dragon's eyes," Xenophon explains as I switch to long-range optics. "A difficult shot for even the most skilled archer. Skyhunters aid their daughters in crafting their first bow from godtree wood and the gut string of leopard seals. Only when the daughters are strong enough to draw this bow do they begin to practice marksmanship. Two more bows will they make before they fashion their skybow from the horn of a tanngrisnir goat. In her time, Sefi killed six ice drakes with her bow, named in honor of her father Promise of Pale Horse. The same bow which slew two Gold overlords of this province on the Day of Breaking."

Harnessed from the sides, the dragon continues its course toward Sefi, not yet noticing her. Two hundred meters, one hundred. Pax hands her the skybow from her saddle. It is twice as long as a man. She nocks a great arrow. "The drake will be slowing from the marrowfish venom in its veins," Xenophon says, but the drake seems, if anything, even angrier. Sefi stands in her stirrups. The drake is at eighty meters. She draws back on the bow. And then . . . nothing. She seems to freeze. I zoom in with my hood's optics. She draws back on the string again, and again stops halfway, unable to summon enough strength to draw the arrow back to her face, much less her ear.

Xenophon has gone silent. Valdir stands. Something is wrong.

The drake is fifty meters out, and sees only Sefi and Pax atop Godeater blocking his escape. Sefi's given up trying to shoot, and veers Godeater swiftly down and to the left. The drake follows, lashing out with its wings and severing half the ropes, while hurling other skyhunters, including Freihild, through the air. Electra nearly falls from the saddle. Something's gone terribly wrong. The drake closes on Pax and Sefi, extending its neck to impossible length. Its teeth snap off the back of their saddle, almost tearing Pax in half. Godeater slashes futilely against the hard scales. The drake coils its neck for another lunge when Freihild slashes past and buries a spear in its eye, just missing the sweet spot.

She hurls herself from her griffin and lands on the dragon's head, burying two climbing hooks, she is tossed sideways, almost losing her perch. The drake ignores her and bears down again on Sefi and Pax, trapping them against the valley's side. Godeater scrambles along the sheer walls, unable to escape.

I act without thinking. I rush to a stupefied brave and demand his rifle. "The creed forbids it!" a guard growls.

"Fuck your creed." I jerk at the rifle, but in his hardened grip, it goes nowhere.

"Give him the rifle," Valdir orders from behind me.

Grudgingly, the guard surrenders it.

Praying I've not run out of time, I rush past the gawking onlookers and fall prone, steadying the barrel on a divot in the rocks. Its energy pack whines as it charges up. The targeting computer is slow to start. I go analog. Thanks to the guard's delay, I've lost time. The lights from the nearby shuttles reflect against the optic. They disappear. I glance sideways to see Valdir blocking them for me with his body. Not his first time as a spotter. For a moment, I think he won't let me take the shot. I could hit Freihild, but he nods. "Wait for it to turn its head."

I peer back into the optic.

Godeater has gone to ground, trapped by the drake on a rocky scree as the other Valkyrie fruitlessly try to regroup and bypass its razor wings. Only Freihild protects her Queen, stabbing in vain at the thick scales of the drake's head, but her efforts dirty my shot.

I sink into my breathing and try to forget Valdir looming over my shoulder as I settle the crosshairs on Freihild's back. The dragon's head is faced away. She blocks the shot. *Move. MOVE.* My hands shake from nerves. Her arms raise to plunge the spear into the back of the dragon's neck. I wait for it to sink deep. It bites into the meat behind the ear slits. The drake whirs its face around, snapping at her. I aim two hands above her shoulder and squeeze.

A beam of white light divides the gloom.

A city forms around the downed drake on the frozen plain. It is called a *drekinhaugr,* a dragon mound. Tribeswomen and men of the Valkyrie Spires along with a great many of their allied tribes bring huge logs for the bonfire on sleds pulled by aurochs. Lesser shamans ferry vats of hard grog, berry liquor called *azag,* and sweet mead in leather gourds the size of bathtubs. Chanting and drums resound from a train of thousands as they flow into the valley to witness the last harvest of light.

They chant Freihild's name, and mine. Protectors of the Queen. The young skuggi sways over to where I stand with Pax and Xenophon in a great bear cloak and wraps me in a hug. "They sing of us, Garnir! They sing of the glory of our arms! No sound is sweeter."

"Here I thought they'd pin me to a rock and splay open my ribs," I say to Freihild.

"A poacher's gun is not a poacher's heart," she says, then draws close.

"But I would have killed it on my own." She sees me eye the cooked skin of her right shoulder. "Close shot. Close shot!" She saunters away laughing and shouting encouragement to the harvesters.

"Did you know you would hit it?" Xenophon asks.

"I knew I had a chance."

The White considers that. "And if you had killed her while Valdir stood over your shoulder?"

"I doubt we'd be having this conversation."

"True enough. Now I believe I have had enough excitement for the day. I must return to my functions."

"See you at the party. First drink's on me."

"I am not invited." The White looks me up and down. "Your assimilation is not surprising. You display traits any martial culture would value. I, on the other hand, will always be an alien. Enjoy the sundeath. I am told its color composition can be quite moving to the warrior spirit."

The White sways away toward a flier to be taken back to the *Echo of Ragnar,* which Sefi disappeared inside as soon as it set down on a mesa overlooking the valley. The destroyer, more a mobile city of war than a ship, makes even the mountains look small.

"That's one sad human," I say to Pax.

"They're not sad," Pax murmurs, more focused on the harvesting than our blathering. "If anything, they're sad that they're not sad."

I soon forget about Xenophon. The harvest is a sight.

Young braves climb the dragon's flank, wedging climbing hooks between the slippery scales to carve the most flavorful meat from the sides of the spine. Electra races several Obsidian youths up the side, and has them beat by ten meters when a dead scale sheaves off and she plummets back down the flank, hits the elbow of the dragon's broken wing, ricochets, and plunges into a gaping incision made by harvesters. When she emerges covered with gore, the Obsidians whoop with laughter.

Poised on the ridge of the dragon's back, the crews use levers to dislodge the scales and long saws to butterfly the spine. Great hunks of meat are stacked in steaming piles atop a parade of sledges brought in ceremonial fashion by youths as the elders drink and call out capricious instructions.

Pax whispers the destiny of each body part to me. The scales are for ceremonial rites and griffin battle armor. The joint fluid and eyes for poultices and elixirs. The blubber for candles and lamps and to be mixed with berries to make a dish called *atuka*. The liver and brain to be eaten frozen or raw, "obviously cooking would destroy the vitamin C."

"Obviously."

I poke his hip. "You're not wearing your harness."

"We were hunting."

I slap his head. "I told you to always wear your harness." The harness he made himself in his garage. "After all, I got a ship now."

"Which?" he asks.

"The jade one."

He whistles. "Too good for you."

A group of skyhunters with pierced noses and tattered ears stomp over to me to give a sign of respect. The women look at Pax and cover their eyes in shame. He pretends not to care as he examines my ship in the distance.

"Looks like you're the fall man," I say.

"Naturally."

"What happened up there? Why could Sefi not draw her bow?"

He focuses on the harvesting, pretending to not notice the scornful looks passing braves give him. "The cord has an immensely strong molecular composition, but can contract if not protected from the cold. I forgot to keep it in its heat sheath during the stalk."

"Is that true?"

He makes no expression. "Of course. I am a heatlander, and a man. It was expected I would draw the gods' ire by joining the sacred hunt. I forgot my duties to my wingleader."

"When was the last time you forgot anything?"

He looks over with a chiding expression. "Sometimes it's better to let a wheel squeak than break the cart trying to fix it."

The truth sits unspoken between us. Either the bowstring was tampered with, which seems an awkward way to assassinate Sefi. Or something is wrong with Sefi herself. But how wrong?

"Oh shit . . . what is that?" I cry as harvesters pull two brain-sized gelatinous sacks from the drake's belly.

"The testicles, of course. They have intense hallucinogenic properties when dried and ground down. Berserkers used them to summon the winter rage. Now they are forbidden, per Sefi's decree."

I wince as the testicles are tossed onto a fire by a shaman. "No wonder the men never speak up around here."

At a jingle behind us, Pax's face lights up. "'Lo, Ozgard!" he calls as the shaman arrives on a sleigh pulled by two blue-painted aurochs, each with tiny bells hanging from their great ivory horns. The shaman drinks from a hollow tusk and jumps down from a bed of furs to greet us.

"Stupid heatlander," he snaps at Pax, striking at him with his riding crop. "Everyone talks—brave to pup. You forgot string-guard. You embarrass me. You embarrass all men. You nearly killed our Queen." He gesticulates drunkenly. "They think I am stupid. Teach you nothing." He tosses Pax a hooked blade as long as Pax's leg. "Do not sit back in shame. Go harvest. Unless you forgot my instructions. I need two kilos liver, ten kilos lung, one kilo spleen, two-ounce flame ichor, and four gonad veins. Do not embarrass me again, stupid boy."

Without objecting, Pax departs at a jog. Good little soldier.

"Bit late," I say to Ozgard.

"Should have used boots or ship." Ozgard sighs and punches his most muscled aurochs on the flank. "Preparing for my Godspeak in ruins of Spires. Nefelfjar sensed evil sprits within a crag. Became frightened. I gave him grog. And he found his courage." The aurochs sways back and forth, drunker than his shaman. Ozgard squints at Pax joining the harvesters, who make a show of excluding him.

"It is sacrilege to kill a high beast with a firearm," Ozgard says. "Valkyrie nailed two poachers to a rock and had a buzzard eat their liver for just that two weeks past."

"I've been told," I say as another group of skyhunters come to pay their respects to me. "What's wrong with Sefi?" I ask as they depart.

He doesn't hear me. "What was the alien doing during this?"

"What is it with you two?" I mutter. "Xenophon didn't cast a spell. And you know as well as I do that Pax can draw Olympia by memory from a single glance. Kid didn't forget to warm a stupid string. So what's wrong with Sefi?"

He pours himself more grog and pretends not to have heard me. "When the sun dies tonight, I go to read the firebones. It is custom for the drakeslayers to bear the bones. I expect you will observe this custom at least?"

. . .

That night, in the small city that has grown about the remains of the dragon, the Children of the Spires, last of Ragnar's people, throw one hell of a party for the dying sun.

They light a great bonfire of dragon fat and mountain pine. In the flames, great hunks of flesh are roasted on long skewers and served with wild tubers, mountain berries, oysters, and great horns of grog passed out by a stout Obsidian man with no nose.

Freihild and I are given fresh necklaces of dragon's teeth to mark us as the drakeslayers. Mine is given with a degree of comedy, and grumbling from Valdir's conservative cohort, but not Valdir himself.

As the Obsidians feast and laugh, Ozgard leads a troupe of braves wearing masks made from the bones of sacred tribal creatures. They pretend they are ice sprites, dropping little diamonds in cups or tucking thin bars of gold behind ears. The warriors wheel about, trying to catch the sprites, only to snag empty air and roar with laughter. If they are caught, the sprites must drink until their captor is satisfied. I catch three, including poor Gudkind, and send them reeling from grog to pass out by the fire. Sprawled on furs, Electra listens to Obsidian veterans tell stories about their days with the Goblin. Pax bickers back and forth in Nagal with one of Sefi's warchiefs about the strategic necessity of his father using the Storm Gods on Mercury. I sit in comfort, warmed by the fire, light-headed from the grog, and satiated by the meat from the hunt. I've not felt this tranquil in years.

There is a joy here. A sense of eternal family, with no worry of the world that seeks to destroy them. They are home and free.

Is this what it is like to be them?

Mars is not what I expected—neither Olympia nor the Ice. It is simpler here, sure. But my mind is quieter without the peripheral madness of Hyperion. There the current demands you do something to define your own essence, to rise above the human rivers in the street, or be drowned under them.

Here you can simply be.

I wish I could give this to Volga. Poor girl has always feared her own people, what they would think of her birth, but maybe she would find this to be the home she was always looking for.

Hell, part of me wishes Lyria could feel this again, what with her family all gone. I'm in such damn good spirits that I wish even Xenophon could share in the feast. The poor creature is always standing to the side, never included unless Sefi needs information or a task fulfilled. Not that Xenophon seems to mind.

This warm peace is an illusion, I know. My time in it is fleeting. It will not last, not the night, not the celebration, not the hunt, not my friendship with the Obsidians, nor Cimmeria's acceptance of Obsidian rule. They give them jobs, a percentage of the mine profits, chase the Red Hand north, but more and more Obsidians flock to Mars by the day. How long till the Reds resent them? Or Agea feels the power balance shift?

In the morning, the *Echo of Ragnar* will absorb us and lift off. Then back to Olympia we go. Sefi to her government. Valdir to his hunt of the Red Hand. The children to their lessons and grim future.

Me to being me.

Part of me wonders if I can't stay in this moment. Find a place in Olympia with these people who have welcomed me. They have a dark spirit in their nature, sure. We all do. At least here seems a people, seems a leader, intent on finding their better virtues. I play with the dragon's teeth and watch Sefi across the fire for some sign of ailment. There are none except the long glove she always wears. She pulls it up as she watches Freihild hold court from behind her chalice of wine. Sefi's eyes wander to her mate. Valdir is drunk, and worse than ever at hiding his lust for Freihild. It's so obvious why the big man watches her. While Sefi is by nature reserved and seems aged prematurely from the weight of her crown, Freihild brims from life. She fends off long-haired suitors with a stick, swatting them toward the fire before twirling around to lead the braves in song. Sefi is the past, the present, but more and more it seems Freihild is the future.

Dizzy from ale, I use Pax's head to help me stand and excuse myself to take a piss. I wander away from the fires to where their warm light licks at the darkness beyond. It's so cold I pull up my hood and watch through the thermal vision as my piss carves runes in the snow.

I hear the jingle of metal behind me, and pull off my hood. Valdir unbuckles the huge ruby clasp of his belt. I step back in surprise. "Do not fear," the big man rumbles, "I am not here to rape you."

"That is a very odd thing to say."

He drops his pants.

"Oh."

His huge thighs are moon-pale in the gloom, as thick as tree trunks. As he squats to shit, long muscles ripple beneath tattooed skin notched and striated from old wounds. Drunk, he drinks more from a huge horn and nods to my hood. "Does thermal vision make it look bigger?"

"It's not the bark that counts, oldboy. It's the bite. I'll leave you to your defecation."

"What is 'Horn' for?"

"Surname of the seed donor."

"Your father?"

The earthy scent of his shit wafts over to me. "More or less."

"Was he a great man?"

"No."

He wipes his ass with snow and pulls up his trousers. He considers me and nods in approval. "You come from no one. I too come from no one." Then he turns and stumbles back to the fire.

"The Queen knows about you and Freihild," I say.

He wheels back, and with one step closes the distance. I have to step back to look into his eyes.

"It's not my business what you do with your cock. But at least have the decency not to undress Freihild with your eyes like a titanium-hard teenager. Your Queen doesn't seem the forgiving kind. And others notice, even if they're too afraid of you to say it."

I slip past him and leave him to his dung.

45

EPHRAIM

Nightgaze

THE OBSIDIANS ARRANGE THEMSELVES in a crescent and groan a song of farewell to the last sliver of sun as it dips beneath the horizon, not to be seen again until summer. It has a faintly tragic quality, this sendoff. The dark months of winter are a reality the Obsidians have left behind. While Olympia undergoes repairs, they will return to their cities and highrise penthouses and skyhook bars and brothels in the cities of Cimmeria, leaving only the sparse remnants of savage clans to suffer the season.

Sefi gives us a blessing before we go, dipping her finger in blood and pressing it to my forehead, then Ozgard's. When she comes to Freihild, her jaw locks and she presses hard enough with her nail to leave a small gash.

I wave dramatically at Pax as the *Snowball* takes off to the clamor of drums and horns, the skull of the dragon dragging behind on a tow cable. As I fly, Freihild looks joyfully ahead while Ozgard plays with his jeweled rings.

Half an hour's flight finds us beside the ruins of the Valkyrie Spires. We drop the skull by the site Ozgard and his acolytes have prepared for the Godspeak at a rise. We set down south of it and hike up. I raise our thermal tent while Ozgard and Freihild douse the skull and timber with dragon fat and lay out a circle of scales etched with runes.

Soon fire leaps along the skull and the pine beneath. Freihild and I sip heated grog to ward off the chill as Ozgard finishes laying his runes. She looks so young in the firelight I can barely remember thinking her a savage. She catches me watching her finger the small scratch Sefi gave her.

"I saw you and Valdir speaking in the shadow," she says. "He returned haunted. Did you give him some Gray wisdom?"

"Nothing he doesn't already know."

The fire crackles between us. She knows I know.

"I have tried to end it before. It is a war in here." She opens her hand over her heart. "Sefi gave me purpose. Valdir . . . everything else." She looks out at the snow. "She is stubborn. She is the strength in the bond. She must release him. But she will not. I do not know what to do."

"Yeah."

"Yeah," she mocks. "No funny joke? No cruel cuts? Just 'yeah'?"

I rub my hands together trying to soak up the warmth of the fire. "I don't know what you want me to say. It is what it is. Maybe she loves him too. I don't know. But you know it ain't just between you and Sefi and Valdir. How many others have found out?" Her jaw clenches. "Take that number and triple it. Hell, multiply it by ten. Gossip like that . . . exponential echoes." I sigh, knowing I should mind my own business. But I care about this weird assassin, and I guess I care about Sefi. "Seriously, what's Sefi supposed to do? Have you killed?"

"No. That is dishonorable. My Queen is honorable. She would challenge me. Out here, I would win. In a circle, no."

"Lucky for you, she's forbidden challenges, remember? Her New Path? *Alltribe no kill Alltribe.* Anyway, do you want to kill your Queen?"

"*No,*" she snaps. "She is all." Her face goes blank. "Maybe she will find another mate."

"And what does that tell the others? You saw her fail to draw that bow. Others did too. Some'll buy the Pax bit, but not all. Are you trying to be queen?"

She reels back, offended. "No."

"Well, maybe you make that clear to everyone, especially Sefi. Right now, she's being the big girl. You're spitting in her eye. She might have the throne, but you're the only one who can fix this."

She weaves a dragon tooth into her valor tail. "I have never feared the enemy. But speaking to Sefi . . ." Her expression becomes tragic. "Valdir is my heart. I do not want it to be so, but he is. When I wake, when I sleep, he is a warm shadow that goes with me always."

"Well, kid. It's on you. I'd like to say there's another shadow or whatever out there for you, but I found mine and he's stuck with me. . . ."

"But some things are more important," she says.

I stare into the fire. "Maybe."

"Alltribe is more important than me. I know what I must do." She claps my shoulder hard enough to rattle my teeth. "Like I said. Gray wisdom." She grows dour, sinking into the weight of her decision. Restless from all the thinking, she stands up and tells Ozgard she will find the nightgaze, and he can warm his old bones by the fire, and maybe learn something from the Gray.

The old shaman wheezes as he sits down. "What did you say to her?"

"Oh, just being wise. You know. Like a fox."

I tighten my jacket, feeling chilled under the gaze of the hollow towers. They hunch together, lording over the scattered stone and shadow, the many empty doors and windows like so many eye sockets. Once this was home to Sefi the Quiet, Ragnar the god. Now only wind moves in the dead city.

"Do you hear them?" Ozgard cocks his head to the wind. "Not all the people of Alia had heart to follow Sefi to the stars. Those who remained felt the wrath of Gold. Their spirits are trapped in the stone, shamed for all time."

"Poor sods."

He snorts. "If it were true, yes."

"I'll be damned. Is that skepticism I hear from a shaman?" Ozgard shrugs and prods the crumbling pine of the fire with a distant look. His mood is different than amongst his people. Less frivolous. I shift closer to the flames. "So . . . what now?"

"We drink until Freihild returns with nightgaze. The gods must be offered strength of the beast and beauty of the land to speak." He sounds bored.

"Right."

He sighs and looks at the darkness creeping around us. "I confess, I hope she does not hurry. It is good to be alone in the snow."

"Thought you liked Freihild."

He chuckles. "Freihild is clever woman, but she is blind, not like us."

"How's that?"

"The more blessed the creature, the less they question life. She is like

Valdir and his big muscles this way. Blindly forward with purpose. Guided by the trough of expectation." Ozgard plays with his rings. "But us . . . that which is thin to us is thick to others. Dull to us, resplendent to fools. I envy the blind. To accept mystery. To witness a corpse and think Valhalla instead of maggots.

"Did you know I was born to a woman of power? You would not think it. Brood of a great queen. Destined to fight the gods' battles in the stars. But I was cursed for my mother's impiety. So our shaman said."

He brandishes his twisted hand.

"Amniotic band syndrome. Agony. Bred out of the other races, but not ours. My fingers were never formed. My spirit berries dull the pain."

"Why not just get an upgrade?" I pat my new leg.

He turns the twisted hand. "Many of the braves believe it is the root of my power. At four, my mother found me amputating my own hand with a fish knife to stop the pain. They said a dark spirit was within me. Fools. Shaman pressed coals into the soles of my feet, and I was given to the Ice. No Valhalla for a cursed child.

"They now say spirits found me. Raised me with their arts. That I sacrificed my hand to Mimir for a drink from her well of wisdom." He spits into the coals in disgust. "Cruelty is the heart of myth.

"There was no Mimir. I could not walk for the wounds. So I crawled, dragged my child's body with one hand until my fingers blackened. No spirit came. No gods. It was the kindness of a noman that saved me. A shamed man cast out from his own people who lived as a hermit in the mountains. He became my father, my mother. But his life was withering. Hepatocellular carcinoma, I believe. Soon I would be a boy alone on the ice. So he gave me all he could to survive when he left. Omens, prophecies, tricks. He taught me religion is a lever. With a slight force at a clever angle: immense power to shift tides of humanity. When his *andi* returned to the Allmother, I gave his flesh to Sky and bones to Ice, and went to find a people."

He passes me a horn of grog. I take a generous swig, then another, and scoot closer to the fire, intrigued and a little mystified he's letting me see beneath the mask. Risky business, that.

"The first tribe found value in my father's tricks. I was clever, but reckless and cruel. Their shaman had a trick in wooing ice serpents. He would light a fire of bitternettle to make them sleepy. I changed the nettle for a mangroot. I declared him a falsifier. When his snakes killed

him before his Queen, I became their shaman. Soon, they were conquered, and I became shaman to that tribe, and the next. To survive, I
replaced other clever men. I used the lever. I learned to say what queens
want to hear. In time, I learned to say what queens need to hear. And
when I came upon the shaman who put coals to my feet, having left my
mother after her tribe was conquered, I fed his manhood and liver to
him and burned his body on the tundra. But I despaired. I felt no joy.
The river of blood flowed and flowed. Tribe fighting tribe. Queen fighting queen. Shaman unseating shaman. We were cannibals. When Sefi
and Tyr Morga slew our gods, I saw a queen who could tame the darkness inside us."

He grows quiet and watches the stars.

"That's some story."

He glares. "You doubt me?"

"Well, you're not exactly Victra au I-cannot-tell-a-lie."

He grins. "And what can bond sinners but their sins? None of my
people would understand. Secrets are weight."

"I'll drink to that." I take down another gulp and pass the horn.
"Quite a pair, eh? Two con men just trying to stay above water. Was
wondering if you'd ever drop the mask." He laughs and drinks deep.
"Was the Alltribe her idea or yours?"

"Mine. Sowed over years. Too long she listened to Xenophon, thinking Gold wisdom wisest. And to Valdir, guide of her heart, a stonebrain
who worships the Reaper because he is master of violence. Were it not
for the cost of the Mercurian Rain . . ."

"A fool could never have made a kingdom."

"You listen too much to others. I am not a fool."

"Naw, you really aren't, are you? Fair's fair. What are you then?"

He chooses carefully. "Liar. That is what I truly am." The sigh of a
man disappointed in himself eases out of him. "A liar who lied because
he did not want to die. Because he did not want to live in the ice without
a people. Is that a sin?" He sits in penitence and stirs the coals, searching
for something. "I know you laugh at firebones. Others see you fall in
mine victory and think you blessed. But we know how lucky you were
to live. All my life, I looked in firebones and saw nothing. Nothing but
my own spirit growing darker and gods more distant. Not once did they
answer me. My father said they were not real. Only the chains of our
masters." He grasps his chest. "But inside this heart, a coal *burned*.

Wanting them to be real. Something to be real. This world is so cold, you know?"

Freihild knows. It's why she fears to lose Valdir. And I know. I know all too well. He reaches into the fire to take a coal brighter than the rest. The stink of burning skin fills the air.

"I do not know if the gods are real. But something, someone, spoke to me, and the coal long dormant ignited. It was on Mercury. Using the bones of our braves fallen in the Rain, I saw a griffin in the flames. Winged and stained red, red as the eyes of a Helldiver. And the gray smoke that formed above the griffin took the shape of a fox, one old and cunning, but held back by thorns of darkness." He looks up at me, the reflection of the coal burning in his eyes. "Fear became me. After so long . . . so long, my gods had spoken. But I feared knowing their origin. Feared my own doubt. And then I saw you on Luna. And I knew. I knew our path. Your path. And my Queen set sail for Mars. It is our destiny to be here. Yours, mine, Sefi's."

The fire crackles. In the dark, wind whistles through the ruins.

"You want to know what insanity is?" I pull out a gold ten-credit piece. I wave my hand over it, and it disappears. I pull it from behind his ear and feign awe. "Falling for your own con. You weren't seeing the gods, you were high, oldboy."

He takes no offense.

"There *is* a world to be seen through god's breath. It is a real world. Vibrations. Energy. Fear. Exultation. But all that is in serotonin, prefrontal cortex, easily manipulated. Xenophon has told my Queen this many times. But my Queen knows something Xenophon does not . . ." His bones creak as he leans forward. "I took no god's breath that day."

He puts the red-hot coal in his mouth. Then he seizes my hand and spits the coal into my palm. I almost drop it. But he holds my hand closed. The coal is cool as snow. I've never seen that trick before.

"I know tricks. More tricks than you." I turn the coal over in my hands. It glows with light. "What I have seen was no trick. Fire and ash will come. And end of worlds. Serpent will strangle wolf. Lion will battle lion. Darkness will battle light. Sister murder brother. Son murder father. Father murder daughter. This is what the fire told me. All I have seen has come true. As others are consumed, Sefi will rise from the ashes to bind the Obsidians, to become one with Red, to found a kingdom watched over by a gray fox. Watched over by you."

An uncomfortable silence grows between us.

"There's a lot of Grays in the worlds, oldboy. This one's just passing through. I get my girl, and I'm gone."

He shakes his head. "You have your games. I had mine. But a man must someday stand his ground, or he is no man. Soon, when Volga is returned, you will have a choice to abandon us or to stay. I know you will choose to be a man. You are here to watch over Sefi. It is your destiny, and *we* are your tribe."

We finish the rest of the grog in silence. Bored of waiting for Freihild, Ozgard retires to our tent and tells me to wake him when she returns. I remain at the campfire as it dwindles, listening to him snore and creatures howl in the shrouded mountains.

Ozgard is a liar. A fraud. A charlatan running on thin ice. We're too alike to ever trust each other, but also too alike to miss the chance to try. I envy him now. He's found a cause. Where is mine?

Save Volga, then what?

Abandon my contract? Carve out a life on the run? Could I really stay?

Freihild is taking forever, and the fire is doing little to keep me warm. Remembering I have another coat in the ship, I head back. In the darkness, I lose my way, and wind up along a scree of rubble from a fallen tower. My hand light illuminates a rock carved with griffins.

The Gold orbital strikes from a decade ago melted most of the carvings away. It's not right. The wings are unique to each griffin. Someone took care to carve this. And then, with a push of a button, a drone of a human wiped it all away.

A faint silver glint in the rocks distracts me from my melancholy. I climb up and shine my light on it, thinking it might be some relic or a starShell fragment. It's neither. I almost laugh at my dumb fortune. How could Freihild miss this? It stretches in the darkness all the way to the base of a pale tree set against a jagged obelisk.

A few minutes later, I retired to our camp. I stir Ozgard gently from his sleep. He wakes with a snort, clutching a dagger under his furs with his good hand. "You want to see some magic, shaman?"

He grins. "Always."

We retrace my path through the rubble and climb the pillar. The silver light washes Ozgard's face of its creases. As he witnesses the field of nightgaze amongst the ruins, his expression becomes that of a child jumping into a public fountain on a hot day. The flowers are like pools of liquid silver. Ozgard's thick hands stroke the petals with tender care. They curl around his dark fingers. A great laugh escapes him, and he walks in rapture, following the veins of flowers that skin the rubble and leaning towers in mutinous silver light.

He glances back at me. "Thank you for this gift. It will never be forgotten."

I'm about to reply, when a subprogram in my brain flickers a warning. Something has changed. Ozgard senses the tension and frowns as I walk past him to the shattered obelisk I spotted earlier.

"What is wrong?" he whispers.

"There was a tree here . . ."

Ozgard comes to my side and squints at the obelisk. It is a fractured piece of a throne. A broken wing is all that remains of one of the armrests.

"This was the throne of Alia," Ozgard whispers. "Sefi's mother."

He leans to pick something from it. Several dark stones roll in his palm. They are shaped like humans, but wrong. Their phalluses are engorged, their craniums far too large and studded with spikes.

"Ozgard, don't react. We got company." I motion down with my eyes.

In a silvery pool of crushed nightgaze blossoms lies a single bootprint. Next to it my boot looks no larger than a Red child's.

Ozgard drops the dark stones.

I lift my hand as if to scratch my head, brushing off my pistol's safety and activating my ear com. Static washes. We're being jammed. The wind whispers through the dead city. Someone is out there. "Ozgard, I want you to stay on my six. When I give the word, we go as fast as we can back to the ship. Stick together." He nods. "Now."

Fear claws into my chest as we sprint back the way we came. It is unexplainable, total, like the shrieking of cat claws on a windowpane.

We race under the looming towers. Silver pollen sprays around us as our boots turn nightgaze petals to pulp. Then Ozgard stops. I wheel around, hissing at him to keep running. Coated in silver pollen, he looks like a skeleton made of mercury as he stares at something. I rush back to him and find him looking through the open face of a fallen tower. Inside, illuminated by the phosphorescent flowers, a body pierced by three huge arrows hangs off the ground like a fish on a line. A rusted iron hook punctures the neck, loops through the jaw, and protrudes out between shattered teeth. As the body sways on the chain, its face turns to us, lower jaw hanging broken and unhinged.

It is Freihild.

Then I smell the stink of breath, feel heat on the back of my neck. I stick my gun under my left armpit and pull the trigger. The gun explodes in my hand as the barrel is crumpled shut by a huge hand. My index finger twists like kindling as I try to tear it free of the mangled gun.

"Ozgard! Run!"

I try to follow my own advice, but three dark shapes fall to block my path. I fall to a knee in case they fire, then strip a thermal flare from my belt and toss it, hoping they're wearing optics. I roll right, turn a corner, the thermal ignites. A rippling tide of inky black rolls through the night-gaze veins as the delicate petals are exposed to the high-frequency light waves. I turn into a dead end of rubble. There's a soft thump behind me. I turn around and find myself staring eye to eye with two pits of darkness. They are set within the giant head of a pale nightmare, and it is crouching.

When the nightmare uncoils from its crouch, my eyes are no higher than the melted face of an old tattoo obscured behind its white chest hair. The Obsidian is big. Bigger than Valdir. Bigger than any man I have ever seen. Metal mingles with the pale flesh of his arms and pectorals, and ribs his trachea. His huge mouth is a blood-smeared maw. And the language that seeps sluggishly from it is alien to my ears.

"Ginjik kheljheenii nokhoinuud kjhichneen jijig ve."

I try to step back.

A hand as large as my head seizes me and strokes my cheek with its thumb. A metal nail sharp enough to fillet bone traces paths along my cheek, gently, almost affectionately. **"Shhhhh."** The thermal flare goes out. Darkness again. The giant forces my right hand open and puts something heavy and hot in it. Warm fluid drips between my fingers. The iron smell of raw meat. **"Stay."**

The giant flows past me to stand in front of a witless Ozgard, who has been dragged to us by several tall shadows.

"We have heard your prophecy, shaman." The giant laughs at Ozgard's wilted arm. **"Who is a mongrel to speak for the god? The Allfather speaks one truth, and that is might."**

Ozgard comes alive and with a wild screech jerks his knife toward the giant's ribs. The giant catches the hand and squeezes it against the knife hilt until Ozgard shrieks and there's a wet crumpling sound.

"You like prophecies, shaman. Here is my prophecy." The giant presses a metal-nailed thumb into Ozgard's right eye and submerges it to the knuckle. Screams bubble out of Ozgard's mouth as his eyeball collapses and dark fluid leaks down his face. "When next you behold me, you will take the other." The pale giant laughs. "Only blinded do liars finally see."

He tosses Ozgard to the ground as a spoiled child discards an old toy. My friend paws at his mangled eye with his broken hand. My own shake around the warm mass they hold. I've seen war, but never felt this afraid. The Obsidian gestures to my hands as ship lights carve the darkness. It is a heart that has been gnawed upon. Freihild's heart. I feel the bile rising.

"The skuggi was worthy." The giant bares a narrow scratch on his neck. "I have honored her strength. It is a part of me now. Gift her heart to your Liar Queen. Tell her I have heard in the Ink she is Queen of All Volk. I have come to contest her claim. Tell her: she is now prey."

The ship lights silhouette the monster. The shape of a man barbed with metal eclipses me. "Who are you?" I call after him as he walks to his ship.

Laughter corrupts the darkness around us. The giant smiles as the darkness answers for him with a long groan made of a single, distended syllable. "Fáaaaaa."

46

EPHRAIM

Whirlpool

THE ASCOMANNI ARE REAL. And so is their king. It's all I can think about as a whirlpool of carrion eaters churns over the body of Freihild. On the shoulder of the very mountain where she was born, the host of Obsidians watches in silence. Only the light of braziers holds back the winter night. When the last bit of flesh has been stripped away, the great host melts into the gloom back to their ships. They are solemn. Freihild was much loved, and this was a bad death. One by one, the skuggi drop strands of hair onto her bones and whisper something to her they never said to her in life. They invite me to do the same. When it is my turn, I look at the grisly remains and see Volga. I cannot shake the feeling this is my fault instead of that of barbarians from deep space. How ridiculous that sounds. Only hours ago, Freihild was so full of life. So in love with her tribe, her Queen, Valdir. How can I keep Volga from this fate, when horror seems to follow me everywhere I go?

"I wish I could have seen you grow old," I say, and sprinkle several hairs over her bones. "You would have been a sight."

My chest tightens as I leave her to her last mourner. Sefi watches from the distance as Valdir collects her bones to sew them together with the hair given by her mourners. Afterward he will hide her bones away in the high mountain tombs of her kin. The bones clack like wet wood behind me. Then an inhuman shriek comes from the man. I glance back to see his great shoulders convulsing as he saws off his hair, the great valor tail that no Gold could shear, and with it ties together the bones of his lover.

Sefi flies away.

. . .

A feast is thrown in Freihild's honor in Sefi's newly appointed Griffin-hold. It is a dour, ugly little affair held under the stupid faces of griffins carved by Olympian artisans. More than anything, the Obsidians are confused by my tale. They knew the outcast tribes of Mars and Earth were pirates. Like the Republic, they called them Ascomanni after the old legends. But now they must take my word and Ozgard's that the myth is true. That there's another breed out there. That Volsung Fá is as real as a heart attack. It is a tough pill to swallow. Especially to Valdir and his male warriors. They liked Freihild. They don't like me. And they like Ozgard even less. How convenient it is for us to blame her death on myths from deep space.

I sit amongst the skuggi at a low table in silence, nursing a cup of hard liquor. Gudkind is missing. Sefi selected him and several other pathfind-ers to assess the scene and check the story Ozgard and I gave her.

At the high table with Sefi, the children, and the highest-ranking fe-male jarls, the tribal leaders, Valdir drowns his agony in endless horns of *azag*. His rage ferments like the berry liquor that stains his lips purple. Not even the old rough bastards with the long valor tails dare speak to him. He stares across Sefi to Ozgard, the only other man at the high table. The shaman, his eye patched, his hand in a cast, withers under that hard gaze. Neither man listens to the braves who stand one by one to toast Freihild's memory with trite little expressions of respect.

Deft in all things, but not dying, it seems.

Some deaths make all feel terribly mortal.

Xenophon, who stands by the cupbearers of the high table, seems as unimpressed by the funeral toasts as I am. The White spares me a grim nod. Of Sefi's council, the *logos* was not the only one skeptical about the tale of Ascomanni but he was the most vocal. From the far end of the table, Pax watches Valdir with narrowed eyes. Sefi stands and lifts her horn.

"Freihild was born in bondage, but made herself free. Her worth, if weighed, would make a mountain light as air. She drinks now beside Ragnar, and feasts in the halls of Valhalla. I swear on my brother's blood, the creature known as Volsung Fá will hang upon Griffinhold by his entrails. His skin will be fed to mice. His heart to fish. His balls to dogs. He and his Ascomanni are nomen. I declare *ashvar* upon them. Forever-more, they stand enemy of Alltribe."

"*Skol!*" the room grumbles. She sits, and as Xenophon brings her a message, she fails to see the choleric rage corrupting Valdir's face.

"Lies," the champion mouths. He stands, draws his axe, and slams it through the table, breaking it nearly in half. Cups of spirits and plates of meat tumble to the floor. Sefi's jaw flexes as, to the horror of the host, he repeats his accusation. "Lies."

She whispers something to Valdir, and reaches for his shoulder. He rips away from her. "Ascomanni?" He spits on the broken table. "Ascomanni are scavengers. Flea-bitten raiders too weak for our warbands. They have no king. There is no Volsung Fá." He thrusts a finger at Ozgard. "You spun him from rumor. Like you spin all your shit." He flings a hand at Xenophon. "The White does not believe your lie. When has the White been wrong?"

Sefi remains seated, and turns to look out at the host instead of her fuming mate. Maybe she thinks if she ignores him, she can let this insult slide, and that Valdir will not go too far in his accusations.

Big fool just might. "I saw the tracks myself. I saw no hunt signs. No traces of evil Obsidian from the dark. Freihild would never be taken unaware, even by myths. She is not blind." He looks at Sefi, then back to the shaman. "She was shot from the front by a bow at no more than twenty paces. How would Freihild, skuggi, Minetaker, Drakeslayer, be so stupid? How could she die when two weaklings did not?"

"Did I take my own eye?" Ozgard says in protest.

"Odin did. What is an eye to a fool? Your only weapon is your tongue."

"I saw Volsung Fá. A creature from the blackness! From the edge of the Ink itself. He spoke in the lost tongue! He challenged our Queen! Grarnir saw what I saw." *Great. Thanks, oldboy.*

Valdir nearly tips over as he turns to glare at me. "The Gray is a whore, who will do anything for money. Did you pay him to lie, Ozgard? To pretend it was Ascomanni? Or did you, *my Queen?*"

The room goes dead quiet.

If duels were allowed, any brave could call him out for challenging their honor like that. But to challenge the Queen's . . . shit. I don't know. She could probably just kill him here. An insult to her honor is an insult to the tribe. Punishable by death. Still she does not move. Valdir is the heart of the male braves. Their pride, their Big Brother. Gods, I feel for her.

"Sefi the Quiet," Valdir crows, stumbling as he waves his arms about.

"No need to use that cold tongue. Your eyes sang your jealousy. I saw. We all saw. Did you decide to kill her because she took the mines? Or because she killed the drake? Or because she held my heart in her hands? Or because she is young? And you are old?"

"Your cock is yours," Sefi says out to the host. "Fuck a goat for all I care. But your valor is your tribe's. Do not sully it by wagging your tongue like stupid heatlander."

"You feel nothing," he hisses into her face. "It is not you who is quiet. It is your *andi*." He grabs the flagon from his cupbearer and shoves his way out of the room. Pax lifts his eyebrows to me and Electra takes the *azag* from the neighboring jarl and downs the whole horn.

Sefi sighs and eats a grape from a spilled dish. She waves to the open doors, where light snow drifts down. "It is foul weather outside. Much thunder." She admires the high walls and vaulted ceiling. "Stone echoes loudly, but it remains stone. Strong, with no memory." She smiles at her host, her message clear and clever. "Minstrels! Drown out the thunder, please."

Many laugh as the minstrels pour into the hall. But not all. Not Valdir's cadre of male braves. Not the skuggi. Not me.

As the minstrels sing, I feel the need for fresh air. I stand in the archway between the Bellona doors to watch snow fall on Olympia. Even in the night, the construction does not pause. Skyscrapers rise anew.

"Seems your myths have a nasty bite," I say. Familiar soft footsteps approach from the hall. Pax extends a hand out into the snow.

"I told you they weren't myths. I just said they were far away."

"Looks like you don't know everything." I squint over at him. "You believe me, right?"

"I believe you think you saw Ascomanni. But from your description, they seemed to be built the same as our Obsidians. After several hundred years, that would be unlikely."

"I only saw Fá clearly. The others were . . . it was dark and fast." I chew the inside of my cheek. "You think it might have been imposters?"

"I don't know. It doesn't make sense. If it is the real Volsung Fá, how did he get here so fast? How did he make it to the surface? Why did he target Freihild? The Ascomanni raiders in the Belt are resourceful, but none could evade the Republic sensor grid, or the instruments of the *Pandora*."

"Maybe he was already here," I say. "Maybe he knew Sefi was coming here."

"How would he know that?" Pax asks.

I glance back into the hall where Ozgard watches the minstrels from Sefi's side. "That is the question, isn't it? The two servants in Sefi's favor, Ozgard and I, walk away with their lives. The one screwing her concubine hangs on a hook."

"Do you believe Valdir then?" he asks. "That Ozgard is complicit?"

"I don't have a bloody clue. All I know is that Fá is the scariest man I've ever met. And I've met quite a few." In the hall, Sefi departs. Xenophon heads our way.

"One question puzzles me the most," Pax says. "Why would the Ascomanni have any interest in the Alltribe? For five hundred years, the only enemy they knew was themselves and the Moon Lords." He hesitates. "And the Fear Knight."

He's prevented from saying more, and takes on a thoughtful expression as Xenophon arrives.

"The Queen would like a private word. With both of you." Xenophon motions us to follow. I linger behind with Pax.

"You and Hatchetface wearing your harnesses?" I ask.

"Always."

"Good lad."

In her private chamber, Sefi hunches over the fire as I tell her for the third time what I already told her underlings of our night in the ruins. Her gloved finger strokes Aja's razor. Electra slouches by the fire, poking it with her own finger. Pax remains quiet, not yet addressed.

"You know humans well," Sefi says carefully to me. "Did . . . did it seem to you that Ozgard knew this Fá?"

I look between her and Xenophon. "Who is asking?"

"I am," Sefi says.

"I don't think so. He looked scared shitless. But I'm not a Bloodhound."

She purses her lips and looks at Pax. "Do you believe Volsung Fá is real?"

"Yes. The context of the RRD briefs my mother passed to me suggest he is a myth to the pirates, but a real figure in the Kuiper Belt. However, we have intercepted tightbeams with phrases such as 'the Fá orders' or 'send them to the Fá,' followed by instructions. Not just as an epigram."

She mulls this over. "You remember these messages?"

"Verbatim, however it could simply be they've adopted the word Fá as a title."

"You will transcribe the message for Xenophon." The White stands apart from us, keeping record. Pax says he will. "This Fá. Did your mother believe he is from the Far Ink?"

"According to classified Society records, yes. There is a civilization there, as you know. One that has harried the Moon Lords for years. But the transit would take over a year's sail on a destroyer. And the Moon Lord sensors are at least as sophisticated as ours. They hunt down Ascomanni as they do everything—thoroughly."

Sefi frowns in thought. "If he could make the transit, what size of force could he wield?"

"Again, that would be guesswork," Pax says. "Fifty thousand if the raiders in the Inner Belt are his allies. If his real strength is in the Kuiper Belt . . . it would be ridiculous to even posit a guess. But even if it is a large force, the convoy required to ferry them here would have been spotted by the Moon Lords."

"Maybe they sent them," Sefi hazards.

"Romulus would rather die than ally with Obsidians," Pax says.

"He allied with your father."

"Romulus would never ally with Obsidians."

"Men change." She shrugs, probably thinking of Valdir.

If Sefi arranged this to kill Freihild, she's putting on an elaborate show. "I believe it time to consult with your mother, Electra," Sefi says. Electra keeps prodding the fire. "Republic must think we are strong, we cannot ask them. Will she aid us if we need assistance?"

"It'll cost you one of us," Electra says. "She'll ask for me. You'll say no. She'll block your calls until you're attacked. She'll call and ask for me again. You fear you won't have leverage if you give me. So you'll give Pax—with his parents likely dead he means less in the macro. But it's Pax she wants, because she'll put Darrow and Virginia over herself and Da, and because it is moral."

"Well, that was brutally succinct," I mutter.

She just glowers at the fire, stooped and unhappy. The door bursts open. Braga, Pax's chief bodyguard, and one of Sefi's wingsisters, stand with tears in their eyes.

The stone stairs up to the griffins' aerie are covered with feathers and dander. There's sobbing from above. Blind Obsidian stablemasters weep into their hands. When we arrive at the roost, we are greeted with a scene of carnage.

Sefi staggers past pools of blood and half a dozen butchered stable-hands toward the pale mass of her griffin. Godeater lies on the floor, her neck hacked to the bone. Her huge eyes stare wide and terrified at the ceiling as she twitches in agony. The rest of the griffins are gone. I can barely make out their silhouettes against the moonlight over Olympia as they fly toward Loch Esmeralda.

The stablemasters dare not approach Godeater. Her long claws rake against the stone in pain. Only when Sefi approaches with her throat bared does the beast still. Sefi strokes her muzzle and puts her head to its great sternum. Frowning at what she hears, she closes her eyes to look at the griffin's spirit. Pax watches thoughtfully as she drives her razor into Godeater's heart. Sefi breathes in the griffin's death rattle, and wraps her arms around its neck before standing.

Several dozen Valkyrie stand sweating beyond the dead animal. The mangled corpses of three of their sisters lie broken and hacked as if by a mindless monster. Medical teams attend three survivors. The rest part for Sefi. Valdir kneels on the stable floor amidst the straw. He is drenched head to toe in blood and covered with long gashes from the griffin's talons. Burn marks from stun weapons congeal patches of the blood. The axe he murdered Godeater and the Valkyrie with lies on the floor covered with feathers and viscera.

He pants like a dog on a hot day. Muscles twitch from residual electric shock.

"Did you love her so?" Sefi whispers.

"As much as I loved you before you became stone." His voice morphs into a mad growl, making Sefi tilt her head. *"You feared she would become queen instead of your Volga. My pathfinders found skip trace back to the Echo of Ragnar."* At first I thought I misheard him, until Pax and Electra glance at me, just as confused. Valdir's head twitches as he twists it around. His teeth are purple and pulled back in a primal grimace. *"Do you feel anything now, Sefi?"*

Sefi takes the stunFist from Beildi, one of her bodyguards, and shoots him again and again and again until he steams on the floor, flat and laughing. Only when I call her name does Sefi pause, just short of killing him. She drops the stunFist and orders without a trace of emotion, "Bind this creature and throw it in the deep cells."

In one of the stables, Pax crouches by a discarded flagon of *azag*. "Give that here," I say, taking over as Valdir is dragged from the room. I signal Xenophon and several minutes later one of his aides returns with a sample kit. We feed several drops of *azag* in. When the readout comes, Xenophon's hand twitches.

"What is it?" Sefi demands. Xenophon lets the kit go, and I bring it to Sefi. She takes it in her bloody hands and her face grows dark with rage. "Bring me the shaman."

"There is no proof that it was his doing," Xenophon intones. "I caution you against—"

"Obey, servant!"

Twenty long minutes later, I watch Ozgard fall to his knees, begging for Sefi to believe he did not put the fever cloud mushroom into Valdir's *azag*. The Queen watches him from inside her sanctum as snow falls outside. She has not spoken since the Valkyrie dragged him in. Half of Griffinhold writhes in rumor, half in grief.

"All I have done, I have done for you, my Queen," Ozgard begs, and I believe he thinks as much. Valdir was always a threat to him, a skeptic of his prophecies, a man who held sway over Sefi's heart in a way he never could. I know the type. In his story to me on the ice, he seemed tragic and noble in his lies. But now the underbelly of that self-myth reveals the reptile. He finally saw his chance to end a competitor, a man he could never challenge, who mocked him daily. And he took it.

Still he bleats on. When even he runs out of words, Sefi finally looks at him.

"You brought us to Mars, Ozgard. You helped me believe in the All-tribe, and make my brother's dream. For that, I am in your debt. Your prophecy is the *andi* of the tribe now. I will not sully it. But this is the last time I speak to you. For good of tribe, you will live amongst us, but you are a shadow to be seen, never heeded, never heard, never noticed. Begone."

The shaman knows better than to call her bluff. Broken, he looks at me. *Yeah, right, oldboy. You're on your own.* He stands and shuffles toward the door. "Ozgard." He stops and turns to his Queen in hope. "I will find the truth. If this . . . *Fá* is known to you, there will be no mercy."

The Valkyrie shove him out.

Of the four in Sefi's council when first she hired me, only the human calculator remains. This fact almost makes me hold my tongue. Almost.

"Why would Volga be queen?" I ask.

Sefi nods, expecting the question. She gestures to the hearth and calls for the servant to bring wine. I do not join her in sitting. She watches Amel's replacement open the bottle and pour the wine. Xenophon samples it, nods, and returns to his perch behind her shoulder. She drinks heavily and gestures for me to join her.

"I don't think I'll be drinking anything around here anytime soon. Why would Volga be queen? What was Valdir growling about?"

She twirls the wine with her gloved hand. Xenophon pipes up. "Your Majesty knows I was hesitant with regard to the hiring of Mr. Horn. I believe he has contradicted my assessment. More than ever, he is of value to the Alltribe. Show him or you will lose him."

A shadow of herself, Sefi listens to her White. She takes off her coat, then her vest underneath, and rolls up her right sleeve and removes her glove and a thin layer of a medical wrap. The limb smells of rotting meat.

I recoil. "What is that?"

"Yellow death," she replies.

Her skin is sulfur yellow and hideous. Mottled scales climb from her elbow down to her hand. Raw fissures crack the skin and wind through the patches to weep murky pus. Where she would have held her griffin's reins, a strip of raw skin shows where the scales sheaved off. Fresh scales are already pushing their way to the surface. She winces as she moves the hand.

"A gift from Atalantia," she says. "It is a designer poison. It corrupts the DNA itself, I am told. It cannot be contained by removing the arm. If the arm is removed, it moves to find another region of the body." She rolls her hand around to inspect it. "It has not conquered me yet, despite what Valdir thinks. It disgusts him, as it should. That is why I let him lie with Freihild. It is why I grew cold to him. What it touches, it infects."

"And it's why you couldn't draw the bow."

"At times I grow weak until the pain passes. For all the medici and scientists, it is only Xenophon who slows it. But I was foolish. I did not take his medicine on the hunt. Old Creed." She grimaces. "It cannot be stopped by any means we possess, or all our helium can buy."

"When?"

"Several years still," Xenophon says. "Her Majesty is strength."

Sefi grimaces at that and tries to wrap the medical bandage back around, but fumbles. Tenderly, Xenophon kneels and helps her, taking care not to touch the skin. Gently, the White fits her glove back on and rolls down her sleeve. She smiles absently at the loyal servant in gratitude.

"In my time, I did what no one has done. I have united the tribes of all Ice." She snorts. "Most Ice, at least. But they have not forgotten their old feuds or the Old Creed. When I die . . . Valdir would lead them to more of Tyr Morga's wars. Only one thing can bind them, maybe in peace. The blood of Ragnar. I am not the last to carry it. Volga is Ragnar's daughter."

I feel hit by a train. "Naw. She was born on Luna. She was an experiment. A tube baby."

"In a breeding stable run by the family Grimmus, the owners of my brother, my father, his father before him. My father, Vagnar the Pale Horse, was their prized stud. He begat scores of spawn. When he coupled with my mother to make their brood, he had long been in the stars. It was his privilege to return to the ice on the condition he make more slaves. In time, he'd made enough. He took my brother and me hunting one last time before the gods called him back. I never saw him again. When they took Ragnar . . ." She shakes her head. "They found a more practical method. A way to make as many spawn as they desired and keep him at their wars."

"How many?"

"Two hundred from his seed. We thought all died when the Jackal's atomics destroyed the facility. But when the Julii captured Volga, she ran her DNA."

"Who else knows?"

"Valdir, Ozgard, and Xenophon. This is second reason why I push toward modern age. So when I die, Volga will not be seen as abomination Golds made, but Queen. I heeded Xenophon's warnings. Truly, I feared Ozgard's ambition to seize the mines. It is too much to risk to make a kingdom for a prophecy, when I knew it would shatter at my death . . . My DNA is corrupt. It would transfer to any kin. But with a living heir with Ragnar's blood . . ."

"You were going to use her." So much for her benevolence, for giving her back to me. I wasn't earning Volga's freedom. Sefi was going to keep her all along. We're all pieces on a board to her.

"I am going to give her a kingdom. My brother's blood will fulfill our dream for our people."

"And you wanted me to be your spokesman, to vouch for you," I say, backing away from her. "That's why you bought me with a ship, took me on the hunt, had Ozgard pour honey in my ear. Not for *me* but because you needed me to recruit her. To drag her into this . . ." I surprise her with applause. "What a clever lady you are."

"Volga belongs here. With her people. Even if she is . . ."

"An abomination?" I smirk. "You've thought it all out. But you got one problem." I tap my temple. "I know how the rest of this plays, and it's all downhill. Dreamers die bad."

"Mr. Horn. Ephraim, my people deserve a future without war. It cannot be done in my time, but in Volga's it may be. I need her. My people need her—"

Her world is Freihild on a hook. Ozgard scheming and poisoning his way into halls of power. Valdir butchering women and dreaming of the war I ran from. Sefi was crueler from the start than Volga ever could be, and even she drowns in yellow death and deceit. Now we're adding barbarian enemies from the Ink? Fuck that.

"This place would eat Volga like it's eating you. That girl might have your blood, but I'm her people. She deserves more than dying for yours. If you want her as your heir, it'll be over my dead fucking body."

47

LYRIA

They Are Sleeping

I FOLD THE NEWEST LETTER from Volga so that the light can catch the words. Written on a strip of her jumpsuit's legging, it is her longest yet. The penmanship is poor and untidy. The letters awkwardly cramped together. I smile to think of the large woman hunched over a bit of nail trying to cram as much in as possible. Though my handwriting is better, I know fewer words than the thief, and puzzle over the longer ones. It's a right shame Kavax and I never got very far in our lessons. Felt safe in that big man's company, him stooped over my cramped writing, then leaning back with a smile to praise it.

I squint down at the letter.

You are lucky to have had a father, even if he was not so kind all the time. I wish I had a father to tell me ghost stories of Golback the Dark Creeper. It sounds like a legend I once heard in Hyperion from a deepspace trader. Long ago, after the Dark Revolt, the Obsidians who survived the great purge went beyond the moons and there they became less than men. In darkness, they learned to hunt other men. After hundreds of years, a king amongst them rose. They call him Volsung Fá, Volsung the Taker. Eater of men and ships. He is said to be out there now. Waiting for new ships to eat. They say he carries a chain of enemy skulls. It is a ridiculous story but very scary. Ha. Ha.

Your brother Dagan sounds much like Ephraim. Very mean because he fears loss. So he makes himself alone. I like Aengus better. Happy people

*make me happy. But there are so few of them. I hope they are safe on
Mercury. If they are with the Reaper, they will likely come home heroes.
It is good Aengus showed you how to explore the vents. All should explore.
I do not know why they make you girls wear dresses, though. Maybe to
make it hurt more to explore. Who knows. Maybe they made Red women
weaker than Red men on purpose? Ephraim says Obsidian women are
weaker but smarter than Obsidian men. I think we are smarter than all
men. Ha. Ha.*

Smiling, and finding myself unable to decipher only about twenty
percent of the words, I flip the strip of cloth over.

*Like you I did not see the sun until I was grown, when they sent me from
Luna to Earth. My world was small too. There were many doctors. Want to
know something ridiculous about me? My body is backwards. My liver to the
left. My heart to the right. Not even close to center. I don't know why they
did that. Maybe just to see if they could.*

*I remember many needles, and they would watch us sleep, and sometimes
hurt us if we did not obey. A dark woman would come and watch us play. She
had a great skull ring and many beautiful dresses. And a necklace made of a
snake. A snake! One day she gave me a toy ship. I would lie in my bed at
night with that ship and dream of space. I thought one day, I would sail it
and be a pirate like in the stories. Not a bad pirate. But not a good one.
Good is boring. I would be dreadful but fair, and would only steal from bad
people. They deserve it, you know? I would not have a bird like Orion xe
Aquarii, but a gorilla. Have you ever seen a jadeback gorilla? My Jove, they
are scary. Maybe when we leave here, we can be pirates together. You can
have the sword, but only I get the gorilla. Ha. Ha.*

*Tell me about the Sovereign, if you do not mind. I have always wanted to
meet her. Her soldiers were very frightening, but not cruel. That is the sign of
a good ruler. Strength, but decency. Yes?*

—Your friend, Volga.

*And I will have Manchurian steak, rare, with corn and greens when we
escape. Your fresh fruit is boring. Had too much on Earth. Berries are for
Pixies.*

She ends each letter the same. "Your friend."

It seemed a quirk at first, but reads more desperately with each letter, as if she's pleading for me to end my letters the same. I won't. We ain't friends. We're both just desperate to not disappear without a trace. In the real world, she's a killer. I've seen her in action, all kitted up with hardware. She was made in a laboratory anyway. What the Hades do Golds make in a laboratory with Obsidians except weapons?

Still . . . she did fail. They did drop her on Earth to haul freight.

There I go again, trying to make excuses for her. It's damn hard not to. She's adorable, for a killing machine raised by a devious cur.

I carefully tear a strip of cloth from my jumpsuit. The sleeves are already gone, soon both legs will be too. I pick the scab on my finger and dab my nail into the wound. Then the light freezes in the middle of an indigo pattern. For the first time in months the music stops.

Light pours in from a hallway as the door opens.

I stare like an old bat. This cell is mine now. *My* territory.

Two terrifying Grays in heavy combat gear emblazoned with a screaming Julii sun enter. *Fuck,* they look scary. Both are modified with metal facial implants connected to sockets on their thick necks. One's nose is as flat as my chest, and pitted with some weird pattern like he caught the bad end of a chemical attack or something. Sol Guards.

Maybe it's not my cell after all.

Then a woman joins them.

If I weren't hanging from the ceiling by my own legless, sleeveless jumpsuit, I'd probably rush her all manic and get my skull split by one of those Sols.

This woman once stuck a needle in my chest, but she doesn't look like a devil.

If anything, she's got the look of an old, tired owl. Brown, frizzy hair. Lean and small compared with the Grays. But athletic. She stands like a dancer. Her skin is bootleather, her eyes narrow and mean, and she has a nose you could shelter beneath in a downpour.

Yet there's something *off* about her.

She seems like she's in pain. Not emotional, pure and physical.

The woman tidies her expensive silk leisure suit as if she was some highborn Gold. Her only weapon is a slim silver pistol in a lowslung holster. "I see you have adapted," she drawls. "But adaptability is never something Reds have been accused of being short of. Intelligence, on the other hand . . ."

I say nothing.

"Pacified too. Hmm. Scurry down from there, you little monkey. We got business."

I don't.

"Told Julii she'd go mad," she mutters under her breath to the Sol Guards. They don't seem to like her much at all.

"What business?" I ask.

Ignoring me, she bends down to riffle through the small stack of Volga's letters, which I've secured in the crease between the food tube and the floor.

"Don't touch those," I snap.

"I must confess, it was interesting to watch. Transit voyages on warships can be tedious, you understand, even with the HC being so full of drama—so thank you for the entertainment." She begins to read from one of the letters. *"My favorite time of day is the early morning. Before it is really morning, but when it's not quite night. The world is very still. And if you watch closely, you can see it breathe as it wakes up."*

"Those are mine."

"Takers, keepers, darling." She begins to read again. I pull myself up to create some slack, and untie the knot so I can fall to the floor. I manage to land on my feet. "There. Now, that's a predictable monkey."

I extend a hand. She throws the letters at me and watches me as I collect them. "Hardheaded, softhearted. Bad combination. That Obsidian is one dangerous customer, *lass*—"

"I know."

"No. You really don't. And the Syndicate bounty on her . . . Julii's lucky I've a professional code." She whistles. "Wonder what would have happened if you and the beast had to share the same cell and no food. How long before she gobbled up your scrawny little monkey legs? Two days? Four?" She reflects on that a moment. "Probably four. Volga does like to pretend she's warm and cuddly, even to herself."

I don't rush to Volga's defense. The Brown is so odd. Her nails are painted a brilliant shade of orange. She wears two great diamond rings. And her tanned skin is etched with ornate white lines. Almost like a blueprint.

"What kind of Brown are you supposed to be?" I ask, stuffing the letters into my jumpsuit.

"Brown?" She grins. "I'm whatever my employer pays me to be. And I've never quite had anyone pay as well as Madam Barca."

"Mercenary." I spit at her feet.

"Hold her down," she tells the guards. "I want to spit in her eye."

"Do it yourself, scum," one of them says, a Martian from Apollonia by his accent. "You're not our centurion."

"Scum. Mercenary," she hisses in irritation. "Why does no one abide the word *freelancer*?" I blink and she's nose-to-nose with me. Her hand is around my throat. "Call me Fig."

My eyes open in surprise and Fig spits a big hot wad of spit right in the left one. She pushes me as I aim a knee at her cunny. Caught off balance, I trip over her foot behind my left heel and sprawl on my ass.

"Bitch." I fight to get up, but Fig steps back, activating the room's lights. She moves about the room with a speed that seems almost unnatural, tapping a pattern in the contorted shapes. As Fig touches each bit of the light, the room begins to sprout new fixtures. First a sheet of flooring pulls back and a bed with a cozy wooden frame rises from the floor. She touches a few more bits of the light, and a fire springs up. Then a spit of roasting meat, a table, and a cobbled stone on the floor.

And the puzzle is solved. I had suspicions there was a code.

The room then becomes lost in a Europan storm. All the walls are replaced by images of a roaring sea. Monsters move in the ocean. Waves crash at the windows. But in the midst of the storm the fire crackles. A full kitchen of delights awaits. Floating flame globes drift over a case of weapons big enough to hunt prey bigger than men. And an image, just like the famous mural on the Senate ceiling, bleeds into the storm clouds above, a picture of Darrow and a glorious, comely Sevro standing over a beheaded woman. Even I know it's Aja au Grimmus. Lionheart is off to the side preening, and a stooped, ugly, but very tall man in pristine white armor patterned with birds and a sun looks sheepishly at the blood.

"Didn't you realize it was a puzzle?" She's mocking me. "Low intelligence quotient, I suppose." Fig examines me, less than impressed. "At first I thought you were on Eph's crew. But now . . ." She laughs at me. "Just can't understand how you made such a dent on the oldboy. Maybe he's gone senile. Who knows. Quite a turn he's had of late, however."

She sees my confusion. "Don't you know? Eph's a regular hero with the Obsidians. A real *bloodbrave*." Fig snorts. "He's arranged for your exchange. Yours and the big lass. So move your ass."

Did I mishear? "My exchange?"

"I'd pay half my salary to know why. But that man and I don't exactly get along anymore. Strawberry Lacuna, long, hot night in Adonis, the camel." She winces. "Long story. The White is our intermediary, anyhow. But I'll tell you, something's got Sefi all hot and spicy." Her eyes go distant as she considers what it could be. But not in a human way. More like a hyperneedle on a silk loom pausing, then stuttering quickly back into motion. She snaps her fingers at the Grays. "Clean her up, the Alltribe's got a boat inbound." They don't move. "Julii's orders, not mine. Do it."

They grab me and haul me to the door.

"Where are we?" I ask as they pull me into the hall. "This some sort of prison barge?" The Grays laugh to each other. "A prison barge," one cries. "Naw, lass. Welcome to the JBS *Pandora*."

They push me into the light. The room is huge. Not a prison block, but some sort of simulation training deck. Dozens of pilots and infantry queue for the simulators, which form a honeycomb along the crescent wall. Even I know the *Pandora*. A ship synonymous with House Julii. Nearly two hundred years old, a predator of the deep, and veteran of a hundred battles, or something like that.

Then I see Volga.

While only two guards were needed to guide me out to the walkway, ten surround the Obsidian. She's taller than the tallest Gray by at least two hands, though she hunches to seem smaller. Her jumpsuit is destroyed from letter writing, and her frazzled white hair looks one part tragic, one part feral. But those arms . . . those legs . . . They look more like knotted Cimmerian cebola trees than human limbs. They could break me in half with a twist.

Maybe that's why my hands are free and hers are bound behind her back in reinforced cuffs. Her eyes widen as she sees me, and she smiles awkwardly until she sees Fig. Her eyes go rancid. "Figment!"

"You gilded idiots," Fig snaps at the Sol Guards. "I told you to put a slave ring on the bear!"

"She's just—"

Fig slips forward and secures a thin bit of metal around Volga's neck.

"Hands," Fig orders, gesturing in front of Volga. Fig slaps Volga across the face and the slave ring crackles till I smell burning skin. Wincing, Volga brings her hands around. The Grays back away and raise their rifles warily as her cuffs drop to the floor with a *thunk*.

Somehow she unlocked herself.

I grin a little. That's a freelancer all right.

Unfortunately, she ain't the only one. Fig produces a spiderlike contraption from her belt pouch. Fourteen rings constrict around the tips of Volga's fingers, interlocking them as a thin wire snakes around her waist. "Not like last time, big girl. Made this specially for us."

Volga's voice is deep and mocking. "Fig the Pig. I thought I broke your spine in Old Tokyo."

"You did." Figment sniffs Volga. "Gods, you smell ripe as a dead seal. Good to see you again." Volga grunts. "Julii wants you doused in cinnamon before we give you back to the old man. He's probably worried stiff. What's a man like that to do without his bear to kick? Move."

They shove us toward the gravLift.

"It is nice to meet you, Lyria," Volga whispers down to me as we load in. It earns her another jolt from Fig. Volga flinches and turns to look at the woman over the heads of the Grays. She stares at her until the doors open. "I was just being polite."

They take us to a barracks locker room. It's older than the rest of the ship. Some of the lockers look like those in Lagalos. At least two hundred years old, then. There's not a spot of rust here, though. Volga is guided to another block, escorted by Fig. My lone Sol Guard tosses a change of clothing on a bench and gives me a crooked smile from behind his helmet's jaw armor. Doesn't look much older than me. "Pipes tend to rattle in this one." He shows me the spigot handle and the dryer controls. "Name's Paxton. So you're, like, a badass thief or something?"

I laugh, but he doesn't get what's funny.

"You know Ephraim ti Horn?" I ask.

His eyes narrow. "Of him."

"What's he doing with the Obsidian?"

"He's a merc, ain't he? Sefi's got a big purse."

"All Grays are mercs. You're paid to kill for the Julii, ain't you?"

He squares up with me. "Julii's mum paid for my father's house on the Thermic, and my mother's burial when she died forty years out of service. Julii herself has given me a birthday present every birthday of my life." He pats his rifle. "Gave me this on my seventeenth. Where I come from, that's loyalty." His voice lowers. "From what we hear, you worked for the Telemanuses. I know some boys over there. Loud fuckers, but good lot." He looks me up and down, eyes going sinister. "Not like you Vox rats."

"I'm not Vox."

All hundred kilos of man and thirty of armor step forward. "People like you are why Lionheart's dead. Why Reaper's in the pinch. Fuckin' wastes of carbon's what."

I blink at him. "The Sovereign's dead?"

"You happy about that? Not enough just to steal her boy?" His fist balls at his side. "If it weren't the madam that needed you in one piece, I'd teach you a lesson right here." He winks and smiles. "Enjoy your hot shower."

I wait for him to leave and turn on the spigot. Sure enough, the pipes rattle like an old man's knees. I should feel soothed by the hot water. Instead I feel numb. The Sovereign is dead?

I can't imagine that shining woman as a corpse.

How could she be dead?

The guards shout at me to get moving. I wash out the shampoo and reach for the spigot nodule when I hear a thin shriek. But I didn't twist the nodule yet . . .

The sound becomes a high-pitched frequency that makes my ears ache. Then it stops before beginning again. I turn off the shower and creep through the steam toward the noise. Maybe a broken air filter? The sound grows more intense as I reach the far wall.

I lean closer, looking for the source, and a burning sensation makes a thin line down the side of my head. I lurch back as if bitten.

There's nothing there.

Just a metal bulkhead. Something hot drips down my neck. I touch it and my hand comes back wet with blood. I trace the left side of my head and find a razor-thin gash running from skull to earlobe.

What the . . .

I couldn't see it from the straight-on angle, but now I see it from the side—a blade emerging from the wall, so thin it is almost invisible. Viewed from the side, it is as flat as a butcher's cleaver. Small teeth blur as they vibrate on the bottom. The blade disappears back into the wall.

Steam seeps through the thin cuts in the metal. Three cuts, together making a triangle. There's a *clunk* and I barely scramble back to grab hold of the shower station when the triangle in the wall becomes a tunnel four meters long as a section of the bulkhead disappears backward into space.

I brace myself for the decompression.

It never comes. No alarm wail. I turn to look.

Steam swirls into the triangular hole. On the far end of the tunnel a viscous membrane seals the tunnel's exit. When I see it growing on the inner aperture, I backpedal and call for Fig.

She comes around the corner irritated until she stops dead in her tracks, eyes on the hole. The membrane has grown fast, now covering the hole like the head of a drum. Dark red veins slither through the fleshy substance.

Something happens to Fig. A pulse goes through her that makes my hairs stand on end. The white lines on her skin throb and her flesh ripples, and then subdivides to thicken until it looks like the scales of a lizard.

Her slender pistol appears in her hand.

I hear wet thumps behind me and turn to see dark shapes emerge from the membrane. They fall on the floor dripping with viscera like stillborn babies.

But they aren't babies. And they aren't dead.

If anything, they look like they are sleeping.

48

LYRIA

Monsters

S OON THE ROOM IS filled with armored men and heavy weapons as
Fig summons our escort of Sol Guards. Human faces become metal
screaming suns as their helmets slither closed. I only just remember I'm
naked. I shove on the clothes and shoes Paxton set out and let the guards
push me over to Volga. She stands dripping. The guards didn't undo the
cuffs or take her out of her jumpsuit for her shower.

Figment approaches the sleeping intruders as the Sol Guards fan
around them.

"Backup inbound," a Sol Guard growls to Fig.

"Are they dead?" Paxton asks.

"Zilch on thermal except respiratory exhaust. They're barely breathing."

"Obsidian?"

"That one's too small. It's like a baboon. And look at the size of their
heads."

Six long men and one powerfully built, but shorter even than me, lie
on the floor completely naked, with long, pale leather packs strapped
onto their backs.

No, not men.

There's something wrong with them. The dark, earth-red skin that
covers them looks more like hide. White scars make intricate lines over
it. Amphibian-like folds cover their eyes, ears, and nostrils. Their heads
are unnaturally large and shaved except for long black tails of coarse hair.
Grease from the membrane shimmers on their skin.

The small one shows the first signs of movement.

He looks up at us through the steam with a flat human face, though his passive black eyes are as big as eggs. There's a soft crack and he begins to chew. Blood pours out his thin-lipped mouth. Bits of glass tinkle on the floor. He shudders in ecstasy.

"Shoot it if it moves," the lead grunt barks.

Paxton toggles his sights. The light in the room spasms off, then back on. A low whine goes through the ship.

"What was that?" Fig asks the soldiers.

"Electronic surge."

Fig tilts her head at the small creature. "Fuck this." She shoots it in the chest. The creature is kicked back three meters by the blast. It lies with a hole in its guts, as if the skin parted itself for some invisible wedge. There is no burning scent.

Never seen anything like that gun.

It made the light in the room bend. The soldiers glance sideways at the weapon, but Fig's already dialing the big bitch.

"Madam Julii, a situation is developing on L22Z2. We have a breach party. Do you have that White's shuttle on your scopes? Nothing else? Definitely not Vox. Maybe Core deeplabs. Sending visual. No suits. Perforated the hull without tripping thermal sensors. That's right. Vacuum with no suits. Breach is somehow pressure sealed—a membrane. I recommend you perform a hull integrity test. Might not be isolated." A beat. "Copy." Fig shuts off her com. "You two." She points at me and Volga. "I'm not getting paid enough for this. On me. You boys got the ball. She's sending a squad of Peerless."

A low, horrible sound comes from the corpse of the smaller intruder.

Fig turns. It isn't dead after all. It is laughing. A deep laugh, like the one you'd hear from a monster in the deeptunnels of Lagalos. Like the laugh of a nightmare.

But the nightmare just deepens.

The creature pulls itself up, entrails hanging from its open gut. It licks its lips, its eyes like that of a waiting crocodile.

The Julii Sol Guards aren't slagging with this.

"Medici can inspect the pieces," the officer drones. "Put them down."

Then the lights go out.

"Null G's!" Paxton shouts.

I feel it myself. A slow lightness as gravity disappears and I drift upward. But there is no upward in the shower block. I feel like I'm floating in an endless gulf, in a darkness so deep even my cave-born eyes can't see my hands in front of my face.

A deep, manly voice bellows, *"Nag ag ak, berserker!"*

Light erupts from Sol Guard weapons, showing the horror in stuttered frames.

The small intruder scuttles along the floor like a demon crab as the soldiers float upward.

Fig zips away from them as if by magic.

The six larger intruders lunge from the ground toward the floating soldiers.

Bloody mouths.

Black eyes.

Huge metal weapons with runes painted upon them are pulled from their bags. Guns puke fire. I pinwheel aimlessly in the drift as carnage swirls around me.

The Sol Guard captain fires, the force sending him into a backward spin across my path. A crooked spear tipped in something shimmering whizzes past my ears through his low back, out his belly, and into his forearm, hurling him out of sight. I hear a metal *thunk* as he's stapled to the wall, screaming.

Spent cartridges float past.

An arm.

Globules of blood.

Shards of tile.

Then a big intruder.

He cruises past me, naked and bleeding, carrying horrible, jagged weapons. Both covered in gore. His feverish eyes meet mine. There is a manic joy there. He is at peace in the zero gravity, coasting toward his next target. To strike me is to ruin the pattern of his hunt. But his eyes say: *soon.*

Darkness. No guns fire. There's a wet hacking sound.

Then a screech.

A blaring gun illuminates the room as it fires a stream of energy at the wall. The metal glows molten. The man's arm is pinned by a spear to the floor or the ceiling or the wall, I can't tell. It's Paxton, I realize just as the smallest intruder embraces him like a child hugging its father.

"It's eating me . . ." Paxton screams. "It's eating . . ."

His voice gurgles away as the intruder gnaws into his throat and it goes black again.

I gotta get out of here.

My heart hammers in my chest so hard I can barely breathe. My mine-born eyes and my weeks in unreliable gravity save me this time from rebounding poorly off the wall. I push off with intent toward the hallway behind me, away from the slaughter block. I drift on my course, everything black, hearing only gnawing sounds, gurgles, whimpering, and shearing metal.

I slam into the wall and scramble to hold on.

I can't find anything in the darkness. Then I grab at a shape, encircle my hands around it, and feel a foot. Then another leg encircles me, bringing me close.

"It's me," Volga says. Her voice is husky and even. "Quiet. I need you to get me out of these cuffs. Tap my leg if you understand."

A man screams nearby.

I tap Volga's leg.

"Climb up me." I climb and with shaking hands listen to Volga's instructions. "There is a knife in my thigh."

"Which pocket?"

"In my thigh."

I search blindly for it and find a cold hilt. I hesitate to pull it out until Volga wrenches her leg away herself. Warm blood spills over my fingers as I slide the thick blade out. Volga doesn't make a sound. I feel the weapon's edge. It cuts my finger. *Gods, it's sharp.* Following her instructions, I manage to remove the finger cuffs one by one.

By the time I cut through the cable around her waist, someone is laughing in the darkness. Blue light emanating from her tattoos reveals Fig cornered on the wall opposite the breach by five of the laughing intruders. Slaughtered Sol Guards float around them. The smallest intruder uses the bodies to navigate the null G. Looks like Fig has killed one of them. His body floats above her, missing its head.

If anything, the intruders look intrigued by her, and eager to test Fig themselves. They line up one by one. The little one gets to go first. His knotted arms pick up two axes. He sticks out a tongue implanted with a circle divider and hisses through the hole in the center.

Fig just sneers.

"Night vision. Berserker psychoactives and pressure-sealed skin.

Someone had a fun time making you ugly fucks." Fig smiles. "How's it work in vacuum if you got a wound?"

Something blinks on the wall behind the monsters.

"Bihd am'drah zürk Fá!" the smallest says, lifting both axes above his head and closing his eyes. The others echo the call and lift their weapons.

Volga shoves me hard out of the shower block and into the hall.

Something inhales. Then a flash.

A force slams me into the opposite wall of the hall hard enough for me to bloody my tongue and dent my skull. I drift senseless, wailing in my ears.

Everything aches.

When I open my eyes, the hall is filled with broken tiles. Volga blinks, dazed from a wound on her forehead. Spheres of fire writhe in the null gravity behind us in the shower block. One of the intruders floats in the middle of the fire, wheeling its arms in vain to escape.

Then there's a secondary explosion from Fig's bomb and the sound of warping metal.

The wall of the shower block caves outward. A window opens to space.

Time stands still.

Colossal metal towers with glowing windows whip past. Inside the windows, tiny forms stare out at us, so close we can almost see the color of their eyes as the *Pandora* races along the shoulder of Phobos. The city moon glows in the darkness, and then she is gone.

Time resumes.

The shower block becomes a drain out into space.

The intruders are whipped out of sight.

We're pushed down the hall by the decompressing ship.

I ricochet against the wall. My head slams into something rigid. My ribs bend around metal, pushing the air from my lungs. The whole world is spinning.

I grab for anything. Nails shearing off until I find a jagged lip of metal to grip my fingers around at the inner edge of the breach. My legs dangle down a funnel of bent metal leading to empty space. Cold grips my bones. The water on my tongue boils off.

I feel more than see something white drifting to my left. I snatch at it and look back as my shoulder joint pops. Pain stabs through the rotator cuff. I've got a handful of Volga's hair in my hand. Is it my hand? It's *expanding*. Volga stares up at me, her eyes beginning to swell in her head. My grip is all that's keeping her and us from spinning into the void. She uses me as a ladder to climb back into the ship. Hand over hand.

Bitch is going to leave me. I consider letting go, but I'm distracted by a glowing shape in the ruins of the shower block.

Figment.

Somehow she survived the blast to crawl on the wall like a salamander. Her fingers secure her to the metal. I shout at her, but nothing comes out. She glances over her shoulder at us, and then continues along the ceiling into the hallway to make her own escape. Eager to catch her, Volga crawls more quickly. I lose my grip, and we lurch toward space before she somehow stops herself and grabs me by my hair this time.

My vision warps. Blood boils in my eyeballs. Intense pressure pushes at everything. But I can see the outside of the ship. The hull stretches for kilometers.

There's more of *them*.

Shadows float against the *Pandora*'s jade-green hull, attached by cables, sawing their way in. They look like insects from the distance. They have no ships, no metal space suits. There's hundreds. Maybe more. One by one they disappear into the *Pandora*.

I'm going to die.

I don't want to die.

I can't leave Liam without anyone.

Has it been ten seconds or thirty? Pressure pushes my urine out. Bile rushes up my esophagus and gushes out my mouth. Something moves outside the hull, large panels of metal moving like puzzle pieces to cover the breach. Volga sees them and jerks on my arm, pulling me forward. The flow of pressure from the ship has stopped, it seems. And I fly back in through the hole just before the scale armor seals the breach. Volga flies in just behind me.

Thunkathunkathunka.

The breach seals.

Emergency lights bathe us red. There's still no pressure, still no oxygen. Darkness is melting the world away. Volga gestures at one of the Sol Guards. The captain still impaled on the wall—the only one not to get sucked out. She pushes her way to him, and then goes limp before she reaches him. She collides violently with the hull, unconscious.

I wait for her to wake up.
She's not going to.
If we die, it's on me.
If Liam is an orphan, it's on me.
I kick off the wall for the corpse and feel the world dimming.

49

LYRIA

Run

V OLGA PANTS LIKE A bear in the null G. Oxygen finally fills the room. There in the emergency lighting of the destroyed locker room, she looks almost as monstrous as the intruders did. Her pale calves are thicker than my thighs and corded with muscle and thin white hair. They flex as she pushes herself up to the level of the impaled captain. His limbs float around him like a child making a dust angel.

Volga is not as gentle as in her letters as she scavenges weapons from the dead.

I flex my hands around the breath mask I hold. I don't remember how I kept us alive until the oxygen came back in. Volga says she woke up with me pressing the oxygen mask to her face. I must have taken it from one of the corpses. It must be the lack of oxygen or the vacuum slagging with my memory. Maybe that's a side effect.

Whatever happened, I did it. *Me.*

I feel numb from the killing I just saw. Body trembling from adrenaline, from the boiling blood. I dry-heave, sending me into a spinning motion that I only stop by catching a locker.

My head is all a-jumble. My hands are not much better off. Several fingernails are missing at the root. The fingers of both hands are torn to the bone between the first and the second joints. My skin feels sunburnt.

"That was scary," Volga says.

Words come out slowly. "Do you know what those—"

"They looked like . . ." Was she about to say Obsidian? She blinks. "Whatever they are, they must have hit the AGG first."

It takes me a moment. "AGG?"

"Sorry. Artificial gravity generator. Fig just left us," she says, breaking the fingers of the dead captain to loosen his grip on his rifle. How is she not fazed by this? "Did you see?"

"I saw."

"She's such a bastard."

"Personally, I'm a mite more worried about the monsters."

She looks at me over her shoulder. "If Ephraim taught me one thing, it is not to stick your nose in other people's business. They are here for Julii. Not us."

Finally managing to free the rifle, she does a series of technical motions followed by the clicking of the weapon and a *whaaaamp* sound as green lights flicker on its screen. She grins and pets it. She grimaces as she catches me watching her. "Guns like me. But I do not like the Julii. She has been cruel." She looks at the walls. The blood boiled off in the vacuum has left brownish stains. "Time to go."

"No shit."

"So?" She wipes the blood from her eyes. "Where to?"

"You're the gangster, you tell me."

"Gangster, gangster, gangster. I am a—"

"Freelancer. Yeah, whatever. I'm neither, so . . ."

She tilts her head at me and her entire body begins to rotate. Stupid null G. "Yes. You would be a worthless judge of this situation. Sorry." She hesitates. "I will lead." She starts pushing her way toward the hall.

"Where are you going? Do you even have a plan?"

She catches herself on a bent locker. "This is not our war. We must find the hangar."

"You can fly?"

"Sometimes."

She pushes off down the hall without me. I glance back at the dead captain. His pistol is still in his holster. I take it and follow Volga, not at all reassured.

The ship is quiet as we float through the pulsing corridors. Sirens wail as a calm voice instructs all Sol Guards to meet at their rally points, and all support to report to their safe rooms. An enemy is aboard. Code Black, whatever that means.

More sounds of gunfire and close-quarters combat echo down hallways the farther we go. Bodies of men in robotic armor strew the floor.

Few if any are burned. Most were victims of spears and axes. The monsters didn't seem to bring a single gun aboard, but with the way they moved in the zero G, I don't think they need any.

I can't shake the feeling more will appear from the shadows.

Or from around the corner.

My heart won't stop throbbing.

"Where are we going?" I ask Volga as we float in the center of an intersection. I feel as though someone is watching us. The bodies of murdered Yellow civilians float far behind us. She squints at the air, incredibly calm.

"Can you see blood?" she whispers. "I lost Fig's trail. My eyes are not good in low light. Sorry."

Have we been following her trail the whole time? I thought we were just going at random. Volga might look stupid, but she's done this before. Well, maybe not fight monsters from space, but the other stuff. Seeing how comfortable she looks with the rifle in her hands, I remember what she did to Kavax. How many people *has* she killed?

"Why are we following Fig?" I ask.

"She knows her way better. She'll be going for a ship too."

"Not to kill her . . ."

She looks over at my pistol. "Do you want to kill her?"

"Yeah," I say, surprised at how natural it feels. "Yeah, I wouldn't mind."

Volga glances at me before going back to her search, her face unreadable.

I squint and search lower than Volga. Sure enough, I find blood droplets floating just over the floor, seeming to head off to the right. We set off in pursuit.

The ship grows eerily quiet except for the blaring alarms. It worries me how silent our movement is without gravity. Anything could be waiting for us around any corner.

A mechanical roar greets us at the next intersection. We scramble to reverse as a big Gold in gravBoots and a nightgown tears down the hall toward us with a bloody razor.

He locks eyes with Volga as he passes.

His voice trails down the hall. "Run . . ."

We look at what lies in his wake. The hallway stretches like a pulsing red throat, bending a hundred meters down. Shadows move.

"Oh shit . . ." I mutter, and push off the wall after the Gold faster than Volga. I'm numb. Vision constricted. Don't even know if I *should* follow. But Volga is right behind me. And that gives me some comfort. Still, we're not going fast enough, but we can't look back without throwing our forward motion off. Volga shouts for me to grab her. My instinct is to trust her. I snag her leg and she fires behind us with the pulseRifle. We accelerate with its recoil just as the hall stutters black again. A mournful horn echoes down the hall like a whale song.

"Catch 'em!" someone shouts.

Two armored men in gravBoots zip forward to collect us. They bring us to a cluster of heavily armored Sol Guards led by two Golds. They form a defensive circle around the hall where it meets a gravLift station fed by multiple levels.

Blue light from the lift illuminates the soldiers. There're more than thirty, not all armored, about a dozen sailors amongst them. Some look like they've just woken up. Though they know who we are, they make no effort to take our weapons.

Not reassuring.

The leader, a huge Gold man, hangs upside down looking at a Gray's datapad. "Thermal is bunk. Go motion." A heartbeat comes from the device as white waves ripple over the image in a circle. He moves a wand about. "They've stopped."

"What's—" I begin.

"Silence," the Gold snaps. Aside from his nightgown, he wears only gravBoots. His eyes flick to Volga. "Might need your help, Obsidian. I hear you know how to use that." He looks at her rifle. She nods and he motions everyone to be quiet. "I hear them down the hall. Lucia . . . secure our flank in case they come from the vents. If they reach the central gravLift, they can spread through the ship. We hold them here." Lucia watches him evenly, speaking in a private, silent language I don't understand. "Backup is imminent." Lucia nods and departs.

I try to get the Gold's attention again. "Sir—"

"Shut up, girl," he snaps. "Germanicus, I need you to take the hostages to Madam Julii in the—"

"Listen to me!" I shout. The Gold wheels, dark with anger. "They're already in the rest of the bloodydamn ship," I say.

His eyelids flutter. He knows what I mean.

"How do you know this?" he whispers.

"I saw them from outside. There were hundreds all over the ship."

"It is true," Volga says. "She was far enough out."

"Tongue," the Gold commands. I stick mine out. "Boil burns," he says, and goes still. He knows I've been in vacuum.

"Expect hostiles," he tells the group.

Ping . . .

The motion sensor displays a single dot traveling down the hall toward us. A Gray shoots a flare. The red light illuminates a single warrior. He swims down the hall like a shark, using what looks like a grapple gun to build velocity. "Germanicus, at one hundred meters, bring him down."

But the alien warrior stops. He swims back and forth between the walls. *"Naka, rheket zü Fá!"* he bellows. A stunted metal crown seems to be fused to his naked head. *"Naké, rheket zï Uud."*

A low groan rolls down the throat of the hall from his fellows.

"Fáaaaaaaaaa."

Ping . . . Ping . . . Ping. Pingpingpingpingpingping.

Dots swarm the motion sensor, coming from all directions. "The ducts!" a wolfguard grunts. They shift their defensive position.

"They're too big," the Gold corrects. "They'd never fit."

"They have small ones," Volga says.

Even in panic, the Gold is impressive. He wheels, face absolutely still. "How small?"

Volga puts a flat hand above my head, and lowers it to my clavicles.

The Gold's lips tighten and he draws his razor and pushes toward the ducts. Then blue light bathes us as the gravLift doors open from behind. No lift presents itself from inside the shaft. Only a single warrior floating in the blue dark.

He is the biggest human I've ever seen.

A long white tail of hair writhes like a pale snake over his head in the null G. His armor looks too heavy for any man to use in gravity, even him. It is weightless now—thick, rough, and jagged, festooned all over with spikes that are almost as long as those that make the crown atop his skull helmet.

"He's real," Volga whispers, gripped with awe. The dark fairy tale of her letters appears. "Volsung Fá."

His voice is a deep vibration. He's looking right at me. No. Through me to Volga.

"Volga. I offer you these Stains."

He springs through the gunfire into the Gold leader. He bats aside the Gold's razor with a long spear. Then they collide. Four of the spikes of his helmet pop through the Gold's head like needles skewering a strawberry. Two from his shoulder punch out the man's lower back. He slashes at the Gold's neck with a crescent fist-blade, half severing the strong bone of the Gold's spine. Using the man's body as a shield, he pushes off the floor to find his next prey, his helmet spikes crowned now with the decapitated head of the Gold.

The giant kills everyone.

Some with his spear, some with his fist-blade, others with the spikes of his armor. And those he kills or wounds on his armor, he carries with him like a screaming crab shell made of the dying.

Volga fires her pulseRifle in quick bursts. The pulseblasts that find him sizzle on the armor, and send him ricocheting to kill more. The gun isn't powerful enough. The monsters swim now down the main hall coming not to help the spiked man, but to watch him kill and drone that horrible sound. Volga shoots three in the head with blinding speed, but more are coming.

"Fáaaaaa."

Volga and I run as soon as the second Gold is killed. Fá tries to come after us, but his own slaughtered victims weigh his spiked armor down as gravity returns to the ship with a downward jerk. Julii's men restored it.

Not just Martian standard, but something far surpassing Earth's gravity.

Clever.

It's agonizing to run. I feel leaden. Volga stumbles with me, tearing through the maintenance corridors, until we reach a manual transit chute that runs between decks.

Volga grabs me before I slide down it. Her eyes survey the level-map beside the entrance. We've lost Fig's trail. We'll have to find our own way. Gods, she's cool as ice. "Those are Ascomanni," she says as she studies the map.

"Ascomanni are just pirates."

"These are real Ascomanni. Far Ink," she says. "What else could they be?"

"Could we talk about this later?"

She nods and jams a finger on the map. "Pilot ready room. Ten down."

I go first down the chute. Gunfire and explosions echo as we descend between levels. Or ascend. I'm not sure which way's up in space. Is there even an up? The more I think about it, the more disoriented I get. The *Pandora* is a floating city. With districts, maybe a dozen fire departments. How many others will be rushing to the hangars?

There's no time to think about it.

We blur past little worlds of slaughter. Julii soldiers kneeling and firing out of a communications room. A scalped Silver sitting very still at a doorway holding his intestines as shadows make grunting sounds inside. Two Golds in business apparel being hacked to death by blood-covered maniacs. The maniacs won't stop laughing. They're massacring a ship, and they act like they're at a fucking party.

I pinch my legs on the ladder to slow above the ready room. I come to an easy stop. Volga bowls into me from above, kicking my face and sending me sprawling. "Sorry. Weird gravity."

The ready room is quiet. Lockers opened, gear missing. Pilots must have been fast to the hangars. "How did he know you?" I snap at Volga as she peers back up the chute, wondering if we were followed.

"I don't know," she says, looking back with wide eyes.

Not so calm now, eh? Her monster knew her.

"How the bloodyhell did he know your name? Why does he want you?"

She shakes her head, at a loss. I leave her, whatever she's hiding will have to wait. I'm not going to die like those soldiers. I head to the pilot chute to take it down to the hangars. Volga stops me.

Her eyebrows crawl upward. "What?" I ask.

"I dropped . . . something." She acts with incredible conviction as if she's searching the ground for something. Her path takes her to a metal EVA suit locker. Volga steps back and then lunges forward to kick it. The metal crumples inward. I hear a grunt and a familiar gunshot. The top of the locker divides. Light bends in the room. A half meter of bulkhead parts like butter pushed apart by two fingers.

Volga kicks the door until it falls off its hinges and crumples into the person hiding inside. Volga shoves her hand in and wrenches out a translucent ghost. The translucence ripples over Volga's arm until the arm itself disappears. Volga grabs something with her other arm and the ghost materializes, revealing Fig dangling from her throat at the end of Volga's outstretched arm.

"Figment!" Volga growls. "We meet again!"

"*Ogre*. Broke . . . my . . . ribs . . ." Fig tries to bring her gun up, but Volga grabs it and tears it from her hands, almost taking her fingers with it. It drops to the floor. I reach for it.

"Don't! Coded for her." I pull my hand back, and use a towel from the broken locker to wrap it up.

"You left us to die!" Volga slams Fig against the wall hard enough to dent it. "You shot at Ephraim at the Adonis Casino!" She slams her again. "You stole the Crown of Cortada! You stuck a needle in my chest!"

"And mine," I add.

"And Lyria too!" Volga slams her the hardest for that one. "I'll pop you like a zit. Justice for both of us."

Fig clenches her jaw. Something pops. She spits it at Volga. Volga twitches to the side. A stream of green spit slashes across the floor and melts through it. Volga laughs. "I know your tricks, Fig! No calibrated acid this time."

Apparently, she doesn't know all of Fig's tricks. The white lines on Fig's skin throb. Volga starts to convulse. Her hair stands on end. Miraculously, she holds on. Then Fig presses down on her middle finger's nail with her thumb and a long needle jumps out from her middle knuckle. I press my own pistol straight against Fig's head just before she plunges the needle into Volga's shoulder.

Maybe it's the soldier gore on my face. Maybe it's my race's habit for bad tempers. Maybe it's the muzzle digging into her skull, but Figment freezes. "Soft head, hard bullet. Bad combination, bitch." I twist the muzzle. "Drop it."

"I . . . can't," is all she manages with Volga squeezing her neck. Her face purples. "Fused . . . onto . . . metacarpal."

"Drop the hand then, ya dumb slant. And stop . . . whatever you're doing to Volga."

Fig's hand drops to her side, and whatever her skin was doing stops. Volga whimpers a little in pain, then snaps the needle off with a grunt.

"What was that?" she asks, relaxing her hand on Fig's throat.

"Nerve agent."

"With the skin."

"NEDS."

Volga's eyes narrow. "What is this NEDS?"

"Nanotech emergency defense system."

"Really?" Volga's eyebrows do a little dance. "*Slick.*"

"I know, right? I had it installed in—"

"Quiet." Volga squeezes her throat tight as the public address system crackles to life.

Lady Barca's voice comes over the coms.

"All factors and clients of House Julii-Barca, this is your patronus, we have been boarded by an unidentified enemy force of unknown strength. While they share traits with Obsidians, their skin appears to be polyextremophilic: resistant to vacuum, radiation, low-velocity rounds, and thermal imaging. They are also under heavy psychotropic influence. Pain does not register, but headshots do. They have penetrated the core lifts. We have zero containment. They are climatized to null G, so I have retaken the gravity generator personally. We cannot hold it, but the gravity will give you a chance."

She takes a deep breath.

"The enemy appears to have limited working knowledge of our systems. Thus, I am ordering total evacuation of the Pandora, *to be followed by a purge protocol. In ten minutes achlys-9 nerve agent will be dispersed. You have until then to get to your pods. Victra out."*

The *Pandora* is a legend. The Julii twice as famous. She doesn't just abandon her family flagship.

It feels like the world is upside down.

Volga looks bewildered. "What do we do?"

"Still looking for orders," Fig says with a laugh. "Poor puppy needs a—*ack.*" Volga squeezes her throat.

"Should we find the pods?" she asks me.

"You gonna kill her or not?" I ask.

"To be determined."

"Well, if you're not, I reckon she's our best chance of getting out of here. Maybe put her down?"

"Why not. I will kill her if she is shifty." Volga releases Fig. The small woman falls to the floor hacking for air. "Without her pistol. It is much easier."

"I can help you . . ." Fig says, massaging her throat.

"Can you fly a ship?" I ask.

"Of course I can fly a ship." I raise an eyebrow at Volga. "But you do not want to go to the hangars," Fig says. "I just came from there. It's a slaughterhouse. Trust me."

Volga and I both laugh.

"You two are part of my contract. I don't get paid my second half till I hand you over to Sefi." Her eyes flick to Volga. "What did the monkey mean when she said one of them knew your name?"

Volga shakes her head.

"You don't know? Of course you don't know. I fucking hate Mars," Fig mutters. "All the weird shit happens here. *Makes no sense.*" She makes that same distant expression she made in my cell, almost like taking a step out of the physical world. When she reverts, she says one word. *"Xenophon."*

"What's a Xenophon?" I ask.

She ignores me to wipe blood from the needle hole in her hand.

"Where are the escape pods?" Volga asks.

"You want to die? The pods will become murder pens." Fig sighs, irritated she has to explain to us idiots. "The small ones are moving through the maintenance tunnels like they built them. Big ones prefer the halls. They're not driving *to* objectives. They're *hunting*. What do you want to bet they know where the prey will go? It'll be a massacre."

"Then you have a backup plan," Volga says.

"Doll, I'm a freelancer. I always got a backup plan. There's an emergency escape craft beneath the bridge level. Which is *not* in the schematics. If our luck holds, the freaks won't know it's there. I'm headed there myself, after a little detour." She grins at us. "So, ladies. Whaddya say?"

50

LYRIA

Parasite

THE *PANDORA* IS A HIVE of corridor fighting. A mass exodus flows through the ship. It isn't just Julii's soldiers on the *Pandora*. It is her entire household from Luna, which she was moving back to Mars. A miniature civilization of cooks, academics, researchers, accountants, and horse trainers floods to the escape-pod levels. I watch in wonder as a dozen of the beasts are herded through the corridors by old Obsidian women.

Fig's detour took us to her stateroom, where she grabbed a backpack and a more peculiar item, a glossy black globe that contorts over the back of her neck to attach somewhat like a tick or a parasite. I've no idea what it is, but it makes her look like a hunchback. Volga stares at it in awe. Obviously she's given up the pretense of Fig being our captive if she let her have that.

"Can I have my pistol back now?" Fig asks as we float upward toward the bridge through a maintenance corridor.

"No," Volga says. "It is ours, for damages."

"Takers keepers," Fig says, giving the pistol a longing glance.

The closer we get to the bridge, the more sounds we hear. Twice, Fig saves us from running straight into one of the roving Ascomanni or whatever they are. We wait in the shadows of an armory amongst dead Grays as a pack passes.

When we hear them call to each other in joy, we know they've found their next victim. Fig motions us into the hall. It is empty. The gravity reverses as we run, growing lighter and lighter until we reach a security door marked with radioactive symbols. Fig reaches for something on her belt and pulls out a thin plastic container. Inside is a small gelatin disk. She inserts it into her eye. It expands and turns her irises Gold. A scanner appears in the door. Blue light flickers over her eye. The door opens.

"Retinal forger," Volga mutters. "This is Julii's personal escape craft?"

"Does it matter whose it is? Woman's gonna pop with a baby yesterday and she's off fighting. The maniac."

Volga takes hold of her collar and pushes her through the opening door. It dead-ends in a maintenance closet filled with cleaning robots.

"Welcome, Madam Barca," a nasty, manly voice says as Sevro au Barca's face appears in a hologram. A reinforced door shields above us. Weapons appear on the walls. Expensive weapons. The Julii's personal stash. Volga looks like she's gonna faint from joy. *"I don't want an escape craft, she says. Ha! I told you you'd need one. Now scurry home and we'll hunt whomever you pissed off together."* He waves and disappears. The panel on the far side of the room slides back to reveal a dark tube. I shove Volga to make her stop drooling after the guns.

"No, no, no," Volga says as Fig heads to the tube. "I go first."

"What if the ship is already gone? And this leads out into space?" I say. "Let her go first."

"Or she could get in and shut us out," Volga says, thinking.

"Slag it." I dive into the tube.

Its gravity seizes me immediately, hurling me up the chute. It twirls a dozen times. My breath seizes in my chest. Metal whips past. My head grows heavy. Then gravity slows. My stomach whirls at the new sensations. The chute's circular door opens and I fall into a plush leather chair, safe and sound. That was one hell of a slide.

I give a little whoop.

I find myself in a lounge, and it is already occupied. More than a dozen heavily armed Sol Guards and several bloodied Golds carrying heavy rifles turn to stare at me. And sitting directly across from me in a leather chair, in green metal armor with a weeping sun on the swollen abdomen, is Victra au Barca.

She tilts her beautiful head at me in amusement and then punches me in the face.

Reality returns in stuttering frames.

Not again. Not again.

The cabin is spinning. My stomach lurches. Sunlight rushes through a hole in the hull. Victra stands there holding on to the wall, firing out of the ship with a huge gun. Something punches two hundred miniature holes in the hull. People around me disappear in a red mist. Two tubes shoot out of my chair and jam into my nostrils. Volga wails somewhere behind me. Wind and light. A great huge roar. Victra is gone. Whipped out the hole in the hull. Trees through the windows. Then a hiss as my chair swallows me up in a cocoon of darkness.

THUUUUUUUMM.

We hit the ground. Rolling. Rolling. Rolling. A metal spear pierces through the dark cocoon. It stops an eyelash away from puncturing my eyeball.

Silence.

Oxygen comes through the tubes into my nose.

"Volga!" I murmur. "Volga . . ."

My arms are pinned to my body by the cocoon. My legs won't budge. I feel some sort of knob by my right hand. I jiggle it to see what it does. A great farting sound releases the liquid from the crash pod and the darkness around me sags. Light pours in and I forget to breathe.

I'm dangling over the edge of a Martian fjord.

The front of the ship is completely gone. In the day's last light, shards of it glint in the water hundreds of meters beneath. The rest of the ship is suspended above me at a straight vertical. It sways with the wind. Bits of body parts and fine china sprinkle down.

Bloodydamn.

The cocoon that saved me was some sort of black gel insulation from the chair itself. The outside of the cocoon looks like a pincushion. It is studded with three shards of metal the size of my legs. One missed piercing my heart by only a centimeter of insulation. A crash harness secures me to the seat, and keeps me from falling into the fjord. I can't imagine Julii putting it on me.

I reach over the crashpod and grip the armrest before unbuckling the harness. I lurch downward, but manage to pull myself up over the seat. The ship sighs on its rocky perch. The movement upsets a half-pulverized corpse and it slides from the back of the ship toward me. I duck. It clips my shoulder and nearly takes me down with it.

I wince from the pain in my mangled hands and move as carefully as I can. Remains of what were once humans litter the compartment. "Volga? Volga!"

I feel like I'm looking for my sister amongst the corpses again. Looking for those blue shoes. Most of the crashpods are eviscerated by metal. Strangers fill them. I'm relieved to not find Victra's other daughters here. Were they on the *Pandora*? Is their mother now just a wreck of bones on the ground?

I've no love for the Julii, but I grow nauseous all the same.

I flinch as another crashpod deflates with a hiss. Rigid gel becomes elastic, like a stick of black butter melting, and my friend's face emerges from it. Her eyes wide and terrified as she sees the fjord beneath. She jerks sideways, causing the ship to rock.

"Volga, don't move."

We both freeze until the ship grows still again. Carefully, I pull my way over to her and help her with the crash harness. It takes us nearly five minutes to climb up out of the cabin toward the hole in the end of the ship. Once we reach daylight, we're able to slide down the broken wing to the rocky ground below. Volga falls to her knees and kisses the frosted earth.

"No more ships," she stammers. "No more ships."

"Agreed," I mutter.

The top of the fjord is littered with ship parts, and not just ours. The remains of several ripWings burn amongst coarse grass and frozen ponds. A fighter's cockpit has part of an armored man hanging out. How did he get there? On a hill at the edge of a forest, another section of our ship smolders. Huge clouds consume most of the twilight sky. There's flashes in orbit that I see between their gaps.

"Where are we?" Volga asks.

The sun sets behind mountains to the west. An expanse of fjords stretches to the east and north out to sea. "I don't know," I say. "Maybe the Daedalus Mountains. Or . . ." I search the mountains to the west and see the triple peaks of the Hydra's Neck. I laugh in dismay. "We're in the Cimmerian Highlands. Far north. These must be the Pyrrian Fjords." I look south. A forest stretches across a misty land riddled with more fjords and jagged mounds of rock. Thousands of kilometers from here, the highlands taper away into endless plains and jungle belts.

"Cimmeria! You are home," Volga says.

Home?

I shiver as frigid wind sweeps down from the north and cuts through my thin jacket easy as a knife. It *is* my planet. Yet I've never even seen snow before. And not a single person I love breathes its air—they are scattered across the system or buried beneath its dirt. It is a lonely feeling.

Mars does not feel like home.

"You need something to wear," Volga says, taking a step toward our ship. Her foot dislodges a rock, which rolls and clicks against another, which rolls against the ship's hull. There's a sigh of metal and the ship tilts forward, losing its battle against gravity. With a groan, it slips over the edge of the fjord. Volga and I watch it crash into the water far below.

"Scary," she mutters, and points toward the hillside where the back third of the ship lies in ruins. "We will go over there. There may be supplies and people who need help."

I follow, but only because I don't have a better idea.

By the time we make it to the second crash site, night has come in full, and my Julii-given shoes slosh with freezing water.

I can see better in the gloom than Volga, so I lead. The inside of the ship is a slaughterhouse. Dozens of crashpods were skewered with hunks of bent metal. Blood leaks from them to form a soup on the floor that thickens as it cools. There's about squat-all chance anyone lived through this. Still, seems the human thing to look for survivors.

I check the back as Volga checks the front of the ship. Each pod I open reveals a new scene to fill my nightmares. By the sixth corpse, I'm right numb, and starting to wonder how the hell civilization plods on with all this going on behind the scenes.

Is this what war is? It's so bloody . . . *jarring.* I always thought by watching the holos and the parades that it was more sophisticated, organized. But it's just so . . . blunt, clumsy even. Is this what my brothers see every day? Even if they come back, is this what's behind their eyes?

I keep looking despite the dread and find a treasure trove of emergency supplies: medkits, thermals, water packs, survival boxes with a thermal stove, and protein cubes. I stack these outside the ship after giving up on finding anyone alive.

Then, toward the back of the wreckage, something moves.

At first I think it's a rat. Then I see fingers and realize they belong to someone in a half-deflated crashpod. I pull it open. The woman's face is pale. She is unwounded—except for the shard of metal that has nearly sliced her body in two. "Fig." Her eyes flutter open. The tracework of her white tattoos is queerly bright in the darkness. She doesn't recognize me. "Fig," I say quietly. I touch her hand. It's cold. "Oy, freelancer."

"Psappha?" she says. "Thought I'd . . . have more time. It's not fair. I had more . . . to do."

"Fig, can you hear me?" Might hate her, but hard to hold on to hate for someone who's in two pieces. "Fig, it's Lyria. The Red."

"The Red." Her eyes come into focus. "Oh," she says in disappointment. "You? 'Course I don't get a better heir." She snorts. "It should have been someone with *some* skill. A freelancer." Her eyes close. "Get the Obsidian." Blood bubbles on her lips. "Get the . . . crow." Frowning, I call for Volga. She doesn't answer. "I feel it unsyncing. Moisture wicking off the tendril root. Just like she said."

She's babbling. Seen it before when people go.

"Figment said," she says, talking in third person now. "Where is the bloody crow? She can use it. With that blue blood, she'll carve an empire."

"Just hang on. Help's coming."

"Idiot. I escaped. Was gonna be the greatest freelancer who ever lived. Still had that bitch Bonerider to . . ."

Her mouth contorts. Eyes go all crazy. She screams into my face. I rear back, but her hands dig into my wrists with insane strength. She makes a hacking, vomiting sound, like an old engine dying. Her eyes strain from her head. Her body starts to seize and her mouth froths. A lump moves along her face, like a snail trapped beneath the surface. It goes from the top of her nose, swells a nostril, and then it bursts forth.

It looks like a tiny metal squid with hundreds of hairlike arms tipped with little fibers. I scream as it springs at my face. But her hands won't. Let. *Go.* I thrash as the squid thing crawls over my eyes. Intense pressure in my nostril. *It's cramming its way into my nasal passage.* I struggle to breathe. Then there's pain unlike anything I've ever felt. A hundred needles between my brain and my nostril. A cascade of fire on every nerve ending. Raw pain down my spine. Spasms of light explode. Fig becomes a pulsing red thermal monster. Then she goes shock white. I see her bones. Her organs. Her blood moving through the network of vessels like the map of Hyperion's tram lines. Even the food in her belly. A pulse thunders in my brain. Still Fig has not let me go. The pain comes again like a huge tidal wave, and then it rolls back, leaving my brain leeched of sense. When it subsides I shake in stupid horror.

Fig's eyes roll back into her head. A voice comes from her mouth that belongs to no human.

> *"O my mountain hyacinth,*
> *what shepherds trod upon you*
> *with clumsy, rustic foot?*
> *Now you are a broken seal:*
> *a scarlet stain upon the earth.*
> *Figmentum es*
> *Figmentum es Figmentum es*
> FIGMENTUM ES FIGMENTUM ES FIGMENTUM ES"

Accolades, sister. You have killed Figment. You are Figment. Do not report for duty, a soft female voice says within my head. *My wrath be thine.*

Then it is quiet and Fig is dead.

51

LYRIA

Jade Witch

VOLGA CROUCHES OVER A man in the gloom, pumping at his chest. She gives up, sits back on her heels, and looks at me in weariness. "Lyria, what is it?"

"I . . . I don't know." I shake my head, unable to find the words. Did it really happen? I'd think myself mad if my nostril wasn't all cut up and bloody. Is the squid thing in my brain? What does it mean that I'm the Figment? What duty am I not to report for? How do I explain that a little monster just exploded out of Fig into my nostril? It's inside me. Whatever it is. It spoke to me. It's silent now. There's no pain. Just the sound of the wind and the creaking of metal and huge trees all around us. The world itself feels evil.

"Fig's dead," I finally say.

"Impossible."

I take her to Fig. Volga hunches over her body, feeling for the woman's pulse. She puts her ear to her heart. Flicks her nose. Pulls up her eyelids. Slaps her. "She *is* dead."

"Yeah, good thing you checked."

"Nothing is obvious with Fig." Before I can say anything, Volga takes a knife she must have found in the wreckage and sticks it into Fig's eye.

"What are you doing? Stop that." I say, shoving at her. Volga looks offended.

"Quicksilver put a huge bounty on Fig," she says, going back to her grisly work. "She stole something from him. But the contract is Amani. It requires ocular proof." She digs out the eyeball and sets to work on the other. "Have you seen the orb she had or the bag?" I shake my head. "Her pistol?"

I don't reply.

Sickened, I leave the ship and stand outside, touching the small gash Fig's metal squid thing opened under my nostril when it went into my nose. Quicksilver was hunting Fig. Why? Is it in the bag, the case? Or inside me? Would Volga cut it out of me if she knew I had it? Does she even know it exists?

A dangerous customer. That's what Fig called Volga. She wasn't lying. Just because Volga helped me escape doesn't mean she's a friend. All those letters were just a way for her to pass the time. She's a right savage when there's money lying on the ground, or in someone's eye sockets.

Volga soon joins me with Fig's bag over her shoulder, carrying Fig's black orb. "It is just business," she says, not understanding my mood. "She was already dead."

I don't say anything as she tries to open the case. Finding the effort futile, she finds a pistol on one of the bodies and shoots the orb. The metal is left without a scratch. Volga frowns. But an unusual ringing fills the air, morphing over time until it seems the orb whispers to me.

"What's in there?" I ask.

"I do not know. Maybe what she stole. It might be very valuable."

Dozens are dead around us, and she's after something valuable. I have to get away from her. I have to get away from this crash, from these people. I have to get back to Liam.

There's a high-pitched humming sound in my head that I can't shake. Not the whispering of the orb. Something else. At first I thought it was hearing damage. I dig a finger in my ear to clear it. If anything, the humming grows louder. It's not coming from my head. It's coming from the forest.

"You hear that?" I ask. Volga shakes her head. "You're supposed to have predator ears. You don't hear that at all?"

She pries at the case with her knife. "Maybe you hit your head?"

I wander toward the treeline. The sound is coming from the forest. Volga calls after me, and jogs to keep up as I start to follow it.

The humming grows louder the deeper I go, and I can see a faint rippling in the air. Sort of like hot air above a stove. There's broken branches now. Trees shattered high above our heads. A ripWing must have crashed here. Entering a shadowy thicket, where the trees have exploded from impact, I find a fallen tree trunk with a pair of green metal feet sticking out from under it. The humming is so loud I have to plug my ears.

"Fig?" a woman calls. The humming dies. "Took you long enough. Been calling for half a gory hour."

On the other side of the tree, Victra lies on her back pushing at the tree trunk with both hands. It's trapped both her legs under it. Had it fallen just a quarter meter higher, it would have crushed the baby in her belly.

The trapped Gold glares up at us from under a mess of short golden hair. Her eyes flash with anger. I jump back in fright so hard I smash into Volga and fall to the ground. When I scramble up, Victra is laughing.

"Just my gory luck. Sevro's right. Cockroaches will inherit the worlds."

"Julii!" Volga exclaims.

"It's Barca! Gods, can no one get it right? It makes him so sensitive. Where's Fig? Where are my men?"

I grab a tree branch from the ground as if I'm going to hit her on the head with it. Then I see Victra's pulseFist a ways off in the snow. I rush to it and insert my hand into the huge metal glove. *Vwoooooon.* It powers on and I point it at her head. The energy it holds shakes my arm. Gods, its heavy.

"Go on, little girl. Vox, Syndicate, Atalantia, those freaks. Everyone wants a piece of me. Take a bite. See if you don't choke."

"Lyria, don't," Volga says, stepping in my path. "You can't shoot her."

"Move."

"This is not you."

"How the hell would you know? Because of a few letters?"

"Lyria, I know. You do not want to shoot her."

My arm is aching from holding the heavy pulseFist. "She tortured you and me, put us in a dungeon, right? Let's make sure—"

Victra laughs from the ground. "Dungeon? You mean Electra's *playroom*?" We're just under one millimeter tall to her. "I gave those rooms to Electra when she turned four. She said our sophists were boring, and *my* mother did it to me, and look how *I* turned out." She makes a small face. "Though there was Antonia, wasn't there? But we sorted that." Her smile is one part satisfaction, another part pride. "Electra solved the puzzle in thirteen days. Slower than me, of course, but far faster than her father, and, a little secret between us girls, part of me thinks she liked that a bit. The little harpy. Anyway, if I were *really* torturing you, you'd go mad. Just ask my husband."

A playroom? Now Fig's display makes sense. I *feel* about one millimeter tall.

"You saw what it did to us . . ." Volga says.

"Yes, well, a little friction never hurt anyone's character. Seemed to do you wonders. If you were this bloodthirsty last year, your family might still be—"

A surge of anger goes through me and I fire the pulseFist at the ground near Victra's head. I'm thrown backward by the recoil and almost drop the weapon. Victra didn't even flinch. She yawns as steam from the melted snow clouds around her. "Gods, you Reds are dramatic."

Volga takes the weapon from me.

"She is pregnant! I will not be evil."

"Evil?" I snap. "You just plucked out Fig's eyeballs."

"She was already dead. She did not need them."

"Figment's dead?" Victra says. "Shit. Well, there's thirty million credits wasted. I'll miss her sparkling personality." A thought comes to her. "Who was with her when she died?" Volga nods to me. Victra's eyes fixate.

Does she know about the parasite?

"Thanks," I say to Volga.

"You were, though."

"Why would you tell her anything?"

"Not to be rude, but would you two mind bickering some other time and help me get this colossal tree off of my legs? My men will be homing on our signal, but it's hardly dignified to be found lying on my back like a beached whale. I'll never hear the end of it."

"We're not helping you," I say.

Volga looks like she wants to. "Where are your other daughters?" she asks.

"Safe."

"You're not helping her," I say.

Volga turns on me, a low growl in her voice. "You do not control me. I will do what I think is right."

"And you're going to help this bitch? What happened to it not being our battle?"

Volga says nothing.

"Darling, don't be such a mule. I understand you are *so* oppressed," Victra says. "But let's not be sanctimonious. *You* stole my daughter. Both of you. And I was decent enough to arrange a transfer to that Gray friend of yours when he didn't even stipulate you needed to be in one piece. By any measure, I'm positively benevolent. You were both on your way to being Obsidian pets until those . . . things took *my* ship."

"Ascomanni," Volga corrects.

"Maybe," Victra says.

"It was them," Volga insists. Victra's eyes suggest she agrees. "They knew my name." Victra frowns, not completely surprised. What does she know?

"My point is, the least you could do is help me preserve some vestige of reputation by getting this gorydamn tree off my gorydamn legs," she says. "If you want money for it, that's no problem. What's your price?"

"Money can't solve everything," I tell her.

"Wrong, but whatever."

I bend down close as I dare to her. "It won't help you here. Try some dignity. In the end it's all you have."

Her smile for me is cold. "I do love circularity. But when my men get here maybe we just leave you."

"I don't need your help, and I don't need Ephraim to trade for me," I tell her, and stalk back to the ship. Volga catches up with me.

"Where are you going, Lyria?" she asks.

"Not your problem."

"Her men are coming. If we wait here, we will be safe."

How can she say that when Victra's men couldn't even protect us from the Ascomanni in the heart of her flagship? If they come here . . . I shake my head.

"We owe her a debt," Volga presses.

"I paid mine in that cell. So did you. You think she's helpless because she's packing a baby? She's a Peerless Scarred, you idiot."

"I am not an idiot," Volga says, offended.

"You really want to get tangled with them? Is that what Ephraim would want you to do?"

"Ephraim is broken. I could run from that up there. But if I run from this . . ." She shakes her head, then raises it high. "My debt will be paid when I return her child to her." She sets a hand on my shoulder. "Do it with me."

I look at Volga's knife tucked into her waistband. The blood from Fig's eyes seeps through their hiding place in her shirt. She thinks she'll get rich off this. Fool. "Hope she gives you all the money you ever wanted. Unlike you, I'm not for sale."

I leave her.

Soon I've packed half the supplies I found in the wreckage and donned a set of gray thermal pants from a supply locker. With my feet slipping around in the too-large boots of some dead Gray, I start walking south, away from the crash site. Part of me waits for Volga to catch up with me.

She doesn't.

All that lies before me is stone and icy sludge. A vast landscape that would swallow me without anyone noticing. This isn't home. This is the first time I've felt truly alone since replying to Volga's note. How does that already seem a lifetime ago?

I look back at the ship. It's little more than a dot now. I don't have a plan, but I don't want to be saved by Victra's men. I don't want to be traded back to Ephraim and owe him for the favor. I'd rather freeze to death trying to go it on my own.

Walking along the fjord, I see several ships skimming just over the dark water down below as they head for the crash site. They're little more than dots at this distance. That'll be Victra's men. Takes me almost a minute to figure how to turn on the oculars I foraged. When I've got them working, I focus on the lead ship. I roll the magnifier. Ship looks like a pelican, one of those old transports with those round bodies and slightly curved wings. A bit less stately than I'd expect for a Gold's rescue party. No Julii or Barca insignia either. I switch to the next one. Another pelican, older. On its side is painted the face of a Pink model drinking a bottle of Ambrosia. I pause. Its lights blaze just as they did that day when my family was butchered.

I turn and run back across the plateau. I'm dizzy from exhaustion by the time I find Volga near the crash site, helping Victra out of her battered armor. Volga smiles at me.

"I knew you would come back."

"Red Hand." I gasp for air. "Red Hand is coming."

Volga slings forward a scavenged rifle. "Red Hand? Are you certain?"

"It's a day for vultures," Victra mutters. She scans the sky, and I think she finally understands that, for some reason, her men aren't coming.

"They'll kill me and the coldie." She glances at me. "Might be worse for you, Gamma."

I look at her belly. It's about ready to burst. "Can you . . ."

She bolts, already ten meters away and moving fast. Volga's on her tail. Shit.

I struggle after them in the deep snow. They're incredibly fast. Victra's legs drive her like pistons through the forest and straight up a huge hill as she cradles her stomach. Volga ambles along behind her, struggling to keep up. Soon they're out of sight, and I follow only by their tracks. But soon those disappear as well. I search the ground, and something glows on a branch. A fading yellow handprint. There's more on the tree limbs heading right. Thermal ghosts.

My hand drifts to my head.

What is inside me?

I climb up the tree and shimmy along its branches, hurling myself along them to follow until they drop down and the tracks continue through the snow. A stitch has made its way into my side by the time I catch up to them atop the hill. Volga's lying on her belly wheezing for air. Victra's squatting behind a rock, peering down at the crash site.

"Bloodydamn," I mutter as I fall into the snow beside them.

"Told you she'd spot the tracks," Victra says to Volga.

Volga looks at me in confusion, then points at Victra's belly. "How fast are you without that?"

"It would be rude to brag."

Still heaving for air, I pull myself up on a rock to look over. The shuttles are just setting down. No thermal readouts come this time. Several dozen shouting Reds pour out the back. I hand Victra my oculars. She pushes them away as if I insulted her. I pull them up to look through them, but Volga takes them away to use for herself. Muttering, I watch with my naked eyes as the Reds search the interior of the crash site. A lone figure stands apart from the rest of them.

"Well, damn my eyes," Victra says with narrowing eyes. "The chief bitch herself. What in Jove's name is she doing here?"

"Who?" I ask.

Victra considers, then refuses to answer. Volga's gone stiff. I reach to take my oculars back. Volga surrenders them reluctantly. Victra snatches them away. "Doesn't matter," she says.

"Let her see," Volga says. "She has a right."

"See what?"

"Time to go," Victra says.

"Give me the oculars." I snatch at them, but she pushes me off like a child. Simmering, I glare back over the rock at the lone figure. There's an ache at the base of my skull. Slowly the blurry figure begins to sharpen. Not magnify exactly, but become substantial, recognizable to my brain even though she is little more than a pinprick.

When she turns, I go very still. Her face is as I remember it. Half beauty. Half horrible scar. It was stained green by the gunfire that killed my brother when she pulled the trigger.

"I know that woman," I whisper.

Volga frowns. "How can you—"

"Her name is Harmony," Victra says, watching me with curiosity. "The bad seed of Ares. And the leader of the Red Hand. I see you remember her."

"She attacked 121," I murmur. Heat radiates down my spine, deepening until a pinching sensation grips the back of my skull. Pixels flash across my vision. My heart begins to race as my limbs prick with sensation. It's like I can hear everything around me. The gurgling of gastric fluids in Volga's empty stomach. The sound of each flake of snow falling. The purr of the distant ship. Even the movement of Victra's baby in her womb. Then the orb whispers again from Volga's side.

Victra frowns at me, noting a change. "So your file reads. Kavax let her slither away."

"She killed your brother," Volga asks. "Scars, yes?" I told her that in the notes.

My hearing reverts to normal. I nod my head, torn between confusion and rage. "And my father, and my sister, and her children. Why is she here?"

"Her husband and children died in a mine my family owned," Victra says. "That woman is why Sevro's father ended up with his head in a box. Couldn't stand that Ares was a Gold. As for how she knew I was here . . ." She chews her lip in thought.

"Do you want me to kill her?" Volga asks, shifting her rifle.

"No," Victra says.

"I was not asking you."

I stare at Harmony. She's clearer even than before. She's lighting a burner as two men with long metal sniffer modjobs instead of noses begin sniffing the snow. "Could you hit her from here?"

"Probably."

"Don't mock the poor girl," Victra says. "It's one point two kilometers. You'd need a drift scope in this wind. With that pulseRifle's muzzle-flash, you'll bring those shuttles down on our heads."

"This does not concern you," Volga tells the Gold.

"That woman has declared a blood war on my family," she says. "It concerns me. And when they pick us off from those shuttles because you couldn't delay revenge, it'll concern all of us. Including my baby."

Volga ignores her. "Lyria, do you want me to kill her?"

I see Harmony's head crack like an egg. I see blood smear on the snow. I see her gurgling through a hole in her throat. Maybe one in her belly. But one look at Victra's belly and her knuckles going white as she grips her razor convinces me otherwise. Would Victra kill us even before Volga fired?

"No," I say. "She's not worth it."

Is it for the sake of the baby or Volga's life that I say that?

Either way, it's not the response Victra expected. Her hand leaves the hilt of her razor. Volga breathes in relief and sets her rifle on her knees. I feel a strange comfort knowing what she was ready to do for me despite the risk.

"They'll find our tracks soon," Victra says. There are booms high overhead. The night sky spasms with light. "Those . . . Ascomanni, for lack of better classification, hacked the computer. I didn't think they could. They took control of the guns. They shredded the escape pods when you two were passed out." She grimaces. "Had to turn off our beacon, so the *Pandora* couldn't home in on an orbital strike. With all that debris . . . My men aren't coming. Not soon enough at least. We're on our own."

She squints south toward the dark forest. It stretches as far as the eye can see. Her hand drifts to her belly, her only concession to fear. I find myself admiring her coolness even as I hate her. But in the presence of Harmony, that hate suddenly feels so very small. "We need to find a com array or get a boat that can take us south across the sound," she says. "And we need to go now."

52

EPHRAIM

Pale Rain

S NOW NO LONGER FALLS over Olympia. The morning is bright as I walk the fluffy white streets. I needed to be away from Eagle Rest. It's been four hours since I descended the stairs and I still can't walk off the meaty scent of blood and manure from Valdir's murder of Godeater.

It does not take long for passing machines to ruin the snow. Sounds of industry clatter through the city. Reds who once languished in assimilation camps work on floating construction skiffs, repairing the city in Sefi's bid to restore Olympia's grandeur. They're doing a hell of a job. While Quicksilver pocketed the money from his helium, Sefi pours it into Cimmeria. Their rule is absolute. Their executions of Red Hand terrorists public and brutal. But they're spreading the wealth around.

Lines of Reds and lowColors fresh from the countryside snake out from labor registration facilities. Each is given lodging, a fair salary, and a sense of purpose they've not had in years. Many midColors now work for Sefi as administrators. Others are left alone to make money however they see fit, so long as the Obsidians get a piece. The city is coming back to life. I don't feel that same optimism. Sefi may be good for Mars, for Lyria's people, but not for Volga.

Or is it not my choice to make?

Markets which were home to vagrants and bonfires when I arrived now bustle with new shops full of produce from southern Cimmeria, fish from the Thermic, textiles from Agea, exotic wares from the Core. Obsidians walk alongside Silvers and Browns and Coppers and Reds. It isn't utopia, but it isn't war either. Sefi's dream is coming alive. It's been weeks since the last Red Hand bombing. Before his breakdown, Valdir had steadily been chasing them from their strongholds up to the highlands. Some say even across the sound.

It will all break apart when Sefi dies.

I can't let her bring Volga into this, but so long as the Julii still has her, I have to play along with Sefi's game. She knows she has me on a leash.

A Red boy tries to pickpocket me near a gambling den. I clout him on the ears and then show him proper technique by stealing the chronometer of a passing Silver. I flip it to the boy, and tell him to make his hands move smooth as the chronometer if he wants to keep them.

He stares at me after I tousle his hair. "You're Ephraim ti Horn," he says.

"Am I?" I look instinctively for Syndicate thorns and laugh when he spits on my jacket. "Hail Reaper!" he cries, and tries to punch me. I yelp and backpedal when I see more Reds coming to investigate.

I lose them by ducking into a brothel. My nose curls at the familiar smells, and I fend off the madam until the Reds pass. I think it was a bloody lynch mob. Reaper's people are damn mad. Having lost my taste for a walk, I make for the long climb up the Bellona Stairs back to Eagle Rest.

I'm almost trampled by two Reds running past. No manners at all. Am I back in Hyperion? Then I notice a change in the foot traffic. Those with datapads or optic implants stand fixated on their internal and external screens. Others rush for bars or the Alltribe's new multimedia stations. Even a uniformed Obsidian Watchman and his Red partner let a shoplifter loose to drift toward a window. I fall in behind them.

Light from a hologram of a space battle splashes through the window. It's the *Pandora*. She's under attack. I sprint back to the stairs.

The *Pandora* fell to ships bearing Alltribe colors at 0930 Olympia Time.

The sky rained bodies not long after.

I caught the battle in flashes through windows as I raced home. I watched the bodies on my datapad after I passed Eagle Rest security.

The bodies were stripped naked and dumped over Agea at high altitude. In the sunlight, the pale rain of corpses looked almost elegant, like human-shaped feathers twirling through the air. Their fall could almost be mistaken for flight until they collided with Agea's skyhooks and sky-scrapers and parks and paved boulevards and white stone plazas and the roof of Lighthold like a hundred thousand bugs on a windshield.

The corpses were dropped by four Alltribe troop carriers. Two are shot down by the time I make it to the skuggi training armory. By the time I'm kitted up in scarabSkin and skipBoots, belted with gear, and laden down with a huge insulated carry box for the neodymium magnet, new drones have caught footage of an Obsidian brave in an Alltribe uniform being dragged out of the third ship by aerial commandos. They'll think Sefi ordered the attack.

But why in Jove's name would Sefi attack Victra?

She wouldn't.

It had to be Volsung Fá. He's got Sefi's number, setting up a war. Volga was likely one of those bodies dropped over Agea. The thought almost sends me into a downward spiral. But I can't let it distract me. Without Volga, Sefi has no leash on me. She'll freeze my movement. She'll trap me in the sinking ship. Worse. She'll trap the kids. And from what I've seen of Volsung Fá, he has a plan, and its escalation. With the tensions between the Republic as they are, this will be war if they buy that the Alltribe was in on this.

That means the kids become real hostages.

So I gotta get them out, and my window for exit is quickly closing.

That kid better be wearing his harness under his clothing. I didn't get him that garage just to tinker with gravBikes.

I take care to choose spider-paralytic from the designer rounds and fit a magazine into my pistol, then throw on my jacket, loop a pack of explosives under my arm, and run to the *Snowball* to attach the hook Pax made in the garage to the back of the landing ramp. *Oh, this will be nasty.* I pick my gear back up.

"Grarnir?" a man says from behind. I turn. Gudkind, Freihild's replacement as *vynKjr* of the skuggi, stands in the doorway of the hangar. Two of my cleverer skuggi flank him. "Grarnir!" he calls without aggression. "The Queen commands your presence. You're to join her in the western bunker."

There it is. Sefi's soldiers won't mean me harm, but she'll never let me go out of her sight with the kids again. I have to act now, while I still have access to my ship.

When Gudkind sees my scarabSkin, the neodymium carry case, and the bag of explosives, his hand drifts toward his poison-edged throwing knives. The other two skuggi frown and turn the safeties off their pulse-Rifles. They're confused. They just wanted to bring me to their queen.

"Sorry lads. It's not personal."

I get the drop on them, but damn they're fast.

In one fluid motion, I grab my pistol in its holster, fall flat on my back to minimize my exposure, and push my toes down on the pressure pads. The skipBoots release an impulse that shoves me into a ten-meter backward slide. I fire three times through the holster. Gudkind's knives skim centimeters above my nose. Their pulseRifle rounds pound into the hangar walls behind me. I stand up. All three skuggi are rigid as boards from the paralytic slugs embedded in their foreheads. And then they teeter over, drooling foam.

I strip their coms and as I bound on the skipBoots like a grasshopper, I apologize. "I know you're just following your Queen's orders. But this boat's going down."

As I plant the explosives on the southern landing pad, I watch Mars go mad. The Republic news channels froth with anger and racial vitriol at the attack on the *Pandora*. They claim it was Sefi's version of poetic irony. The rain on Mercury claimed one million Obsidians. Here is Sefi's rain, on the home of Lionheart and the Reaper, on the capital of the Rising. The revenge of the coldbloods. The inevitable pestilence of their nature.

The world outside churns by the time I make it to an overlook of the training *ludus*. The children are not at their lessons. I don't have access to their safety protocols for obvious reasons, but if Sefi is in the west bunker, they will be headed there too. Going aerial is dangerous with soft targets, so they would have taken the tunnels that emerge in the western statue park just near the bunker. I can beat them there if I fly.

Oh Hades, I'm going to die.

My mind races as I bound up marble steps and across snowy courtyards. It wasn't the Alltribe in those ships. It had to have been Ascomanni. They're trying to start a war. Volga was in a cell. If they boarded, there is almost no chance she escaped. I see her falling in that rain over Agea. Her bones turning to splinters on the concrete roads.

This is the worst time for the insurance plan. I thought I'd have more warning when things started going south. Maybe I should have left the second Fá showed up, or when Valdir went berserk. I waited too long.

There will be too many of them. I holster my guns and clutch the neo-dymium box tighter. Against a pack of armored Obsidian, a pistol won't do much.

The exponential escalation has begun between the Republic and All-tribe.

Seems the Republic is eager to blame the Obsidians for the attack.

I hear it in the ripWing engines lifting off from high-mountain han-gars. In the thunder of metal boots. In the drums beating in the army camps west of the city. I see it in the throngs of mid- and lowColors the Obsidians herd away from sensitive areas. And in the metal glinting in the sky as orbital fleets prepare for a Republic response. Dammit, Sefi. Don't strike first at them. This is what Fá wants.

Volsung Fá isn't a barbarian like I initially thought. If he organized the attack on the *Pandora,* he's trained in regime destabilization. It's text-book.

Sooner or later, some nervous finger will twitch.

Or Fá will play another card.

Then the dominoes fall. And the nukes go off.

This is how a world ends.

I won't sit here and wait for it.

I'm too late to set up the neodymium magnet. I spot the children in the center of a cluster of Valkyrie making their way across a statue park toward the western bunker. The female warriors each wear sixty kilograms of pulseArmor, gravBoots, and full complements of weapons. Their hel-mets are up. Shit, there goes any chance at sonics. In battle, they could take a whole century of Gray legionnaires. But this isn't a battle, and the last thing I want is to kill them.

My legs burn as I close the distance to the Valkyrie. I shift to ghost-Cloak, and activate the bombs on the southern landing pad. They're just big enough to break windows and make huge mushrooms of smoke. Sirens wail. The tactical response teams on deck in the heights of Griffin-hold deploy like meteors toward the pad and away from me.

I activate the *Snowball'*s autopilot and initiate its flight path. Back in the hangar, it will rumble over the paralyzed bodies of Gudkind and the two other skuggi.

The Valkyrie pick up speed, shoving the children between them. *Dammit, this box is heavy.* The Valkyrie's helmet optics will spot me now despite the ghostCloak. I'm still forty meters out. There's no trick that'll work on them. No clever lie to interrupt their orders. All they'll see is warped motion sprinting toward them.

Statues explode around me, throwing off the Valkyrie's pulseRifles as the ghostCloak distorts their readouts of the debris. Two Valkyrie pop airborne. *Oh shit shit shit shit shit.* I jump as high as I can on the skip-Boots, an ungainly ten meters. I hurl the neodymium box at them. They think it's a bomb. They shoot it midair, melting the insulation and freeing the griffin-egg-sized magnet. It bowls straight into Braga on the ground, or at least I think it's Braga in that armor. There's a tug on my belt buckle as the magnet activates. The magnetism increases. Two airborne Obsidians dip. Their gravBoots' thrust capability far exceeds the magnet's force, but the metal components inside the boots' gravity generators come apart under the shearing forces. The women fall pinwheeling out of the sky. The other Valkyrie lose their footing and weapons as they're pulled toward the high-powered magnetic field in a knotted ball of twelve confused killing machines. Tiny explosions crackle around the ball of Obsidians as gas-powered munitions rupture.

I land hard on the ground, damaging my boots' shocks, and spring one more time. The boots come apart midair from the magnetism as I land near Pax and Electra. I scream as something tears loose from inside my calf muscle and stretches my scarabSkin.

There's a second pop in my chest, a hot needle of pain. I watch in horror as a small cylinder strains against the inside of my scarabSkin like a parasitic alien seeking the magnet. *What is that?* I take a wobbly step. The world is going sideways. Pax runs to me as the magnet loses power. He catches me as I fall. This is not going according to plan. The Obsidians are lurching like gout victims away from the magnet's diminishing pull.

Pax looks at something over my head and shouts at Electra. They tear off their jackets to reveal the harnesses he built for them in the garage. The harnesses are built according to the specs I gave him—simple but sturdy, secured through the legs and around the hips. A spool of fiberwire sits like a fishing reel at their belly buttons. They link the ends of the fiberwire together and inflate the helium sack at the junction. They rise fifty meters in the air, unspooling the fiberwire as they rush to separate themselves. There's a roar overhead as the *Snowball* rumbles along its programmed course. Its catch-hook hangs from its belly and snags the joined fiberwire strands. The reels unspool. Pax runs over to me and hugs me like a koala as the fiberwire tightens and all three of us are pulled off our feet and carried after the *Snowball* as it climbs away from Eagle Rest.

It all goes woozy. Déjà vu as the mountains blur under my feet, and the Valkyrie set off in pursuit. Their boots will never catch the *Snowball*. I'm laughing and wheezing by the time the hook retracts us into the back of the ship. Pax disappears and Electra peels off my scarabSkin. Rip-Wings will be in pursuit.

Electra grabs the medkit from the wall and I watch her face as she pulls a metal cutter from the wall and lowers it with narrow eyes toward my chest. What is she doing? I feel numb vibrations. Did she give me morphone?

Is that my sternum she's cracking open?

Smoke sizzles up from my chest. She sprays a coagulant. The artificial gravity in the ship increases dramatically, sealing us to the floor as Pax puts us in a corkscrew. The ship vibrates as her twin railguns spew at something outside the hull. Time drips past as Electra works over me.

I stare at a bit of rust on the ceiling of the garage. I'll have to scrub that out. The *Snowball* is far too pretty a ship to have rust. When I look back down, Electra is gone. It is dark out. How much time has passed? I'm still numb from the morphone.

I rise unsteadily to my feet and notice the long strip of resFlesh going down my sternum. It stretches when I move too fast. I'm glued together. That'll hurt when the morphone wears off.

As I stagger through the halls of the *Snowball* to the cockpit, I remember the bodies falling over Agea. As I pass the small kitchen and dining nook, I see Volga and me bickering over Karachi as we sail between asteroid ports. I see her lying in her bunk listening to dreadful music. I see her ducking under the low doorways, whining about hitting her head. The *Snowball* hums around me, but it has no melody.

The little dream of our life on the lam erodes, leaving only a ship with nothing in it but the ghosts of what was never going to be.

I find the two Gold children in the cockpit. The *Snowball* flies dark, all her active instruments off, as she carves through a low fog layer. Only her passive sensors throb. The sea beneath is dark and choppy. They look back in shock from steaming cups of tea when I sit in the back row of the cockpit. "That was . . ."

"Lucky," Pax says.

"Terrible! It was fucking terrible." I groan and hold my chest. Feels like I've been kicked by a sunblood stallion.

Electra's face gets even uglier as she wrinkles her brow. "How are you awake? I gave you enough morphone for an Obsidian."

I thumb my chest woozily. "Addict. You didn't even give me a blanket."

"You weren't hypothermic." She pauses. "Were you awake that whole time?"

"You mean when you gleefully used a metal cutter on my sternum? Yes."

"Fuck. Me." She laughs. "That's full metal."

I moan at the dull ache building in my chest. "I might need a real hospital," I say, probing the resFlesh. "What was . . . those? *Were* those."

"Tracker in the calf," Pax says, passing back a containment jar with two metal cylinders in it.

I look at my calf. *Oh*. It's still weeping blood. "You forgot something." I extend my leg to Electra.

"*Juno's cunt*. I'm not your nursemaid. There's a staple gun in the garage. Don't be a Pixie about it."

"You're just a lovely person. What about this one?" I point to the small cylinder alongside the tracker.

"That, Tinman, was a heartspike on your aorta," Pax says. "So they could turn off your heart with the flick of a finger."

"Fuck. Me."

"I think that was the general idea."

"I can't believe Sefi didn't trust me," I say, genuinely upset. They laugh like I'm joking. "Where . . ." I forget what I was going to say. "Agea?"

"We're not going back to the Republic," Pax replies. "They'll just make us wait in the Citadel. That will not do." *Atta boy*. He looks like a man sitting there in the cockpit. Not that he's grown. But he's definitely changed. The surety in his eyes, the set of his jaw—when did it happen, when he stopped letting others choose for him?

I admire the change even as I feel it's a loss to the world that he's no longer a boy. The world has enough men. But maybe he can be a different kind of man. Probably not. But maybe is enough.

Dammit, my chest hurts. There's a tube in my arm. I pull on it until

I see I've been trailing a blood bag. *Oh.* I reel it in as he continues. "If Aunt Victra managed to get to an escape pod, she'll have fallen in the northern hemisphere."

"Very specific," Electra mutters.

"Shut up. With all the debris, the telemetry was—"

"You shut up. You almost didn't wear your harness."

Pax looks back at me. "That's not true. I had to twist her ear to get her to wear hers."

"Teacher's pet."

"Troglodyte."

"Omniprick."

"Hatchetface."

Electra gasps. They pout at each other in silence. I chuckle. "I knew that got under your skin."

"Shut up," they say in unison.

I just grin.

"If they're alive, we're going to find them," Pax says after a long silence.

"Them?"

"Our people, and yours, Tinman. Like it or not, you're with us now. And we're done watching everyone else slag everything up. It's our turn."

Electra gives me the fakest smile I've ever seen and sneaks me the crux when Pax isn't looking. I close my eyes, feeling a weird warmth in my chest as I sigh. "What could go wrong?"

53

VIRGINIA

Pandemonium

AFTER MY MOTHER THREW HERSELF off the cliffs of our Martian estate, my father came to me. It was one of the few audiences with him in which I was not summoned to stand sweaty-palmed before his desk next to that bloodstain in the carpet. He found me in the stables sitting in the sawdust. He was a giant to me in those days. He stroked the muzzle of my favorite horse and said:

"Self-pity is the plebeian's luxury. All that occurs is either endurable or unendurable. If it is endurable, endure it. If it is unendurable, follow your mother."

For once, I am thankful for the lesson.

"Kavax au Telemanus."

A thousand reveries dance in the air. Memories drawn from the activity of my brain's neurons by means of the Pandemonium Chair. Free associations for the Vox to pick apart and glean and use to hunt down the remnants of my family. The Greens on the other side of the shaded glass catch these images in a net and move along to the next, cataloguing and sifting.

Hiding place.

Secret base.

Fleet orders.

Active Howlers: Locations. Orders. Rendezvous coordinates. Rescue routes.

Sevro au Barca.

Black Cathedral. What is Black Cathedral?

Doomsday protocols.

Skyhall nuclear launch codes.

Relevant faces and words speed in the air in front of me. It is a linear assault meant to bypass my brain's security conditioning. The words are an attempt to stimulate the visual word-form area; the faces, to stimulate the fusiform face area. This causes neuron activity in the prefrontal cortex and temporal lobes, which Octavia's Pandemonium Chair then converts to visual and auditory replications.

I am no easy victim.

As part of the conditioning designed by Daxo's psychotechs, every night I digested false memories, which I signified by populating the scenes with private totems—Spanish Renaissance paintings, off-colored birds, certain songs or low-frequency hums, the smell of a gauche perfume—so that I can distinguish the false from the real. The information they are gathering is a soup of false positives, incorrect data, passwords that trigger auto-destruct and locking mechanisms, and general incoherence that would take a thousand psychotechs ten years to sort. Fortunately there are not a thousand psychotechs in existence. And those my enemies use are no match for me.

At times they try to use my own technology against me; they embed small silver psychoSpikes in my forehead in an attempt to force-hack their way through. This is much more painful.

Time dilates, distends, slows, stops, disappears.

I may be in Publius's clutches, but it is Lilath who did this.

Lilath went after my child.

Lilath butchered Daxo.

Lilath toyed with me.

The *Lion of Mars* was shot down over Hyperion ten years ago to stop her from fulfilling my brother's last wish: for Luna to burn. But somehow, some way, she survived. I don't understand. Lilath isn't clever enough to do all this. She is a killer, not an architect. Did Atalantia plan it? Atlas?

When I am not in the chair, my senses are robbed from me by the psychoSpike. I cannot tell where I am imprisoned. If I even ever leave the chair.

I float in nothingness. No sight. No smell. No taste. No hearing. I am only consciousness in a void. It is my fear of what the afterlife truly holds for us.

In that void, I float alone with my private fears. What my husband will do when he discovers my fate. What devious designs my enemies have for my child. What evil has befallen Sevro and our Republic.

The despair is total and unyielding.

I continue to exist, only because with existence there is still hope.

Though it feels so very far away. Daxo is dead.

Twice they try to link psychotechs directly to my brain as I did with the Duke of Hands. My security packet activates. I unleash neurological attacks. The first man dies of a seizure. The second blocks that attack but suffers a headache and then kills himself the next day because of the insidious memories of trauma I planted in his head.

What does Lilath want? To rule behind Publius? To avenge my dead brother? To atomize Luna and fulfill his dying wish after all these years?

Whatever she wants, I cannot open my mind to her.

In time they will break through, and my self-destruct protocol will go into effect, leading to a medulla cataclysm that will deactivate my breathing and turn off my heart.

It is only a matter of time.

Then one day, I appear out of the void in the center of an empty Moonhall court.

I am delighted, but do not know why.

I sit in the accursed chair dead center before a plinth upon which Adjudicators once heard cases from behind an emblem of the Society. The emblem is gone. Instead of the Adjudicator's single chair, there are now seven. A rotating moon hangs over my head. Wardens comprise my only company.

I smile, realizing I am physically unbound, yet I cannot move more than my head. The psychoSpike has disabled the nerve reflexes of my body beneath my sixth vertebra. Quadriplegic then. How amusing and clever of Lilath. I never thought to use the spike quite like this.

A sudden feeling of amazement fills me.

Let's analyze.

I try to speak to the Wardens, who are standing in small groups along the sides of the room, talking amongst themselves. A cowlike moo comes out of my mouth. Hilarious. The psychotechs have hijacked the Broca's area of my brain, disabling my language abilities even though I maintain the motor skills to form sounds.

Lilath, you clever girl.

"Sorry, lass. Say again?" a Gray Warden says, laughing. So my angular gyrus and Wernicke's area are intact. I can understand words and concepts. He was being an asshole. That Warden is really quite handsome. I would kill him if I could, naturally, yet I still wonder if his manhood is sufficient to please me. Probably not. I have high standards.

No. Don't be distracted. My supposition was correct.

I will sit in silence as they accuse me of heinous crimes before billions of confused, frightened citizens who will be waiting for some clarity on the dreadfully violent massacre. They will have been waiting for days, perhaps weeks, for my account, and I will sit in silence as they accuse me of murdering Dancer.

In my silence, my people will proscribe condescension and guilt. If this were a time of peace, there would be a rebellion and anarchy, but in a time of war, they will swallow it just to have a leader, and I will be executed. My son will watch. Atalantia will lift the communication blockade on Mercury and let Darrow watch. And Lilath will rule through Publius.

It's masterful.

I'm distracted. That Gray warden really does have fine . . .

Oh no.

I can feel the scores of wounds the crowd gave me during the massacre, but not well. They are dull, distant, and deep beneath the pleasure. They've hijacked the dopamine and oxytocin levels of my brain. I'm happy when I should be furious. I can process and understand, but feel nothing but amplified postcoital joy.

Lilath, that bitch.

A hologram appears before me. It grows from a small blue embryo to consume half the room.

The daylight hologram of a funeral procession enters the Moonhall courtyard, the one outside the building in which I currently sit. It is led by blue-cloaked Wardens on white horses. Blackchains walk with heavy guns. Skiffs follow, the same that are used in the washing of highrise windows, now laden with victims of Publius's purge: members of my Lionguard and my household, senators, Skyhall officers, businessmen, and politicos of the required hue.

And on the front of the skiff, sitting with rigid dignity, is Theodora.

The poor woman. I was nothing but hard on her. I should have brought her closer. The distrust created gaps, and now she will die. What a horrible world, I think with a smile.

Publius stands with the leaders of the Vox's radical wing on the steps of the Moonhall. They wear their unwashed senatorial robes stained with old blood. Ashes mark his face for mourning.

How dramatic.

The crowd teems against barricades and soldiers, jeering as the procession draws to a halt before the Obelisk of Ares. It floats ten meters above the ground. Commissioned by Victra to commemorate Sevro's father, it bears images of the birth of the Sons of Ares along its one-hundred-meter length. Darrow's image, which by tradition always faces north, has been turned south. The hallowed sight of his first wife now holds the place of honor. Eo of Lykos sings in stone before the gallows that would claim her life.

I always felt jealousy toward the dead girl. She knew Darrow back when all he wanted was to love and be loved. Darrow has loved me. Truly loved me in a way that cannot exist outside of wartime, yet that love reflects a Gold love, not the Red love that consumes the self, a love I could never feel. My brain has always been too far ahead of my heart. But even then, I cannot help but think that Eo loved him less than he deserved.

Will he watch me die from Mercury as the enemy engines of doom stalk ever closer?

The procession has come to a stop.

How did it work? Did Atalantia sponsor Lilath? She must have.

Soldiers unload the prisoners at the tip of the Obelisk's shadow and lead them along its path to the base of the Obelisk. There is no struggle. Many walk with a determined step. Some few dance a little jig. Theodora lifts her eyes to behold the last rays of the sun as light glints off the bronze dome of the Moonhall, where blindfolded Liberty stands with her scales. Pigeons watch from her bronze shoulders.

When the victims all have been brought to the base of the Obelisk, Publius recites the charges of which Theodora has been found guilty by the new power of the land—the People's Tribunal.

". . . conspiracy to commit murder, conspiracy to wrest legal authority from the Senate, conspiracy to commit treason against the Republic . . ."

Each charge is met with a jeer from the crowd. The transparent partitions are lowered around the base of the Obelisk and Theodora is taken under and secured to a hook of metal set in the stone. The Vox have made their mark. Grooves have been lasered into the stone for liquid to run into troughs beyond the partitions.

Publius completes the reading of the charges.

Theodora lifts her chin and stares straight ahead, a woman of worth underneath the shadow of ten thousand tons of stone. A woman who was grown in a tank, who was raised with Cupid's Kiss to understand that pain is relieved only by sexual obedience, who was made to learn the art of pleasing the men who would one day rape her body, a woman who survived decades of sexual humiliation to become a glorified maid, and then chose to follow a young man at war with the world, not because she believed he would win, but because he was the first man to fight for her.

She fought for him, and as the stone comes down she is flattened by a marble monument dedicated to the dream she lived for.

I close my eyes.

Did she think of him in her last moments, or some childhood love? The tragedy of death is that I cannot ask, and her secret dies with her.

Theodora is dead.

The Obelisk rises, stained red all along the bottom. Blood runs through the grooves. People from the crowd rush forward to dip their kerchiefs and banners in the blood troughs. They wave them around as Servilla au Arcos, Alexandar's mother, watches them with a look of beleaguered contempt. Then the remains are hosed away and Servilla is secured to the grisly hook. She shouts something. Then the stone comes down again.

Does Alexandar feel it on Mercury?

When all have been executed, the image disappears.

I hear voices moments later as the circus comes to the courtroom. A dozen aides swirl around Publius, exultant with their newfound power. What dreams these Vox must have. What fools to think it comes for free. ArchImperator Zan, surrounded by her own staff, walks with Publius.

"Your agents missed their opportunity," Zan says to Publius. The Blue looks at me, makes a small sound of distaste, and glares back at the Copper. "I advised you to use Dunhul instead of your mercenaries."

"If you weren't so paranoid of Mars, we wouldn't be in this position."

Zan sneers. "The Reaper's brother runs two-thirds of Mars, the Obsidian bitch runs the other third, and you say I am paranoid?"

"He only runs Mars because your men put a bullet through ArchGovernor O'Sicyon. As for the Obsidian, we know whom to blame."

They look at me.

"We have more than enough helium to act before we take the mines back," Publius says. "The Telemanus and Augustus armada is on its way here. Turn your eyes to that, Zan. I will deal with Mars."

After Zan departs, Publius dismisses his staff to the far wall and looks at me. I search his face for some sign of evil. Even now it is a pleasant face. A small chin and delicate facial bones, with only a long nose to add drama. But those eyes, for so long cold and distant, flicker with excitement.

"Apologies, Virginia," the Incorruptible says. "I am sorry it came to this. If your child had only been delivered to me as requested, we could have spared you this trauma. But change is not always pretty."

An "honorable" man like the Incorruptible could harness the Wardens. They were poised for defection after Wulfgar's death. But it must have been Lilath who poisoned the togas, and destroyed the barrier to let the mob in. Publius isn't an operator. But how did he know about my agreement with Dancer? The question is driving me mad.

"I looked up to you once, you know. I truly did." Lilath's puppet smiles sadly to himself and leans against the dais. He doesn't know he's a puppet. He thinks he is in control. And here comes his gorydamn speech.

"I thought you were our great hope. After the Fall, I sung your praises. I debated radicals in our political halls. I preached an even middle ground. I thought the Vox misguided in their fervor.

"You were not perfect, far from it, but you were the best we could hope for. 'Let us be sensible,' I said to those radicals. 'Let us understand we cannot make a new world in a day.' But I was naïve. Our whole political discourse was like a great infant. None of us knew our business or how big our feet were. There was no culture to build upon. Politics was new to us, but not to you.

"I watched you dismiss the voiceless majority. I watched you accrete power even as you spouted demokratic platitudes. I watched you lead us rung by rung back into the old world. Soon I knew there was no middle ground. Only the past and the future. The poor and the rich. Us and you. It was then I realized sensibility is torpor by a more palatable name.

"Since the first ape pulled himself out of the mire to fashion an axe from stone, the meek have served the strong. We learned to content ourselves with crumbs. We allowed ourselves to be placated by religion. A promise of something after all this horror. We allowed ourselves to be enfeebled by poverty. We learned to be scolded whenever we raised our voice. Lasting change must be slow and steady and civil, we were told. That civility neutered us. But tell me, Virginia, was Gold civil when they conquered Earth? Did they assemble in peaceful protests? Or did they come with terror?"

He paces before me, waxing grandiloquent.

"If the basis of popular government in peacetime is virtue, the basis of popular government during revolution must be virtue and terror. Virtue without terror is helpless—as I have learned after ten years of being 'the voice of reason.' Terror without virtue is evil—as Gold has taught. My terror is nothing more than speedy, severe, and inflexible justice. It is an emanation of virtue, a vehicle for it.

"I know. I know. You think I allied with a monster." He picks lint from his toga, not knowing the strings his monster has put in him. "But the child was meant to be returned to you after you stepped down. You have done far worse. You allied with the Moon Lords. Fascist slavers." He looks direly offended. "Using a criminal organization is hardly comparable. And now that you have removed them for me, hardly problematic. Your attacks on their facilities were nearly without flaw.

"I know you look down on me for this monologue, but after so many years of biting my tongue, it feels good to have a voice. I wanted you to see the executions because you will be found guilty today and die tomorrow, since my techs tell me you have a self-destruct protocol in your brain.

"Before you do—die, that is—I wanted you to understand that I am different from you. What remains of the Syndicate is already being destroyed. I do not abide criminality. Quicksilver has deserted Luna, but he will be hunted down and put to the Obelisk like your spymaster. I do not allow allies to escape justice when they are villains just because they have utility. I am going to remake the world, Virginia. It will be as it should. One without hierarchy. Without economic class distinctions. One in which it will be criminal to own excess wealth. Where the loftiest goal of a human being is to serve the People. No corporations. No private citizens. All serve one another for dignity and protection of the common good. All men were created equal, and I will make them so." He claps his hands together. "Now, are you ready for the justice of the meek?"

54

VIRGINIA

Justice of the Meek

W<small>E ARE JOINED BY SIX</small> radical Vox senators who survived the massacre to comprise the People's Tribunal. Several dozen others join, but it will not be a public monstrosity. Likely Publius wanted to limit the possibility of my allies rescuing me. Whichever of them is alive. Even through the muddle of serotonin I feel the fear of the final tally. Will I ever see anyone I love again?

That's the loneliest thought.

Not my husband. Not my son. Not Kavax or Niobe or Sevro or Leanna or even Victra. No one but these fools.

They dither first with proclamations of the day's importance. Of the seriousness of my ridiculous crimes to impose my will on humanity. Then Publius reads the charges as the robotic cameras zip around for dramatic angles. With one twenty centimeters from my face, I listen and try not to smile from the chemicals racing in my brain.

"You are brought here today before the People's Tribunal so we may adjudicate your guilt or innocence as to the charges of: high treason, assassination of Dancer O'Faran and loyal senators of the people, election fraud, bribery, conspiracy to install despotism, embezzlement, and fornication with a known collaborator of the Core Golds, Daxo au Telemanus. How do you plead?"

I stare at them, finding it difficult to frown. They hold themselves with such ludicrous self-importance. Canaries pretending to be eagles. No, not canaries. Canaries can smell death coming. They're dodo birds.

"Silence will not save you from these charges, citizen," Publius says, frowning as an aide walks up and pours him a glass of water. Something moves in the glass. The robotic cameras go dead and drop to the floor, hacked. There's a noise in the back of the court.

Something resembling a scream.

Publius shouts for the Wardens to investigate. Half of the two dozen make for the door, calling for backup as if their coms weren't dead. I stare straight at Publius as the weapons fire outside and grow silent.

"Publius, what's happening?" a Red senator asks.

"It's Sevro!" one of them cries.

But Publius knows. He knows all too well, because moving in his glass is a squid. The remaining Wardens take defensive positions around the entrance and the senators. I look up at the ceiling as three transparent shapes drop from it.

They land beside the Wardens guarding Publius and tear off their heads.

Blood fountains onto the ghostCloaks. They deactivate to reveal three tall Golds in black armor embedded with the bones of complete skeletons.

I know their blood-spattered faces.

Each one was from House Pluto, the dark brotherhood my brother formed during our year at the Institute. They shared the hunting grounds with me as children and human flesh with my brother. Each was there at Darrow's Triumph, and survived ten years in isolation. They are pale and mad from their time in our aquatic prison, and laugh as the Vox senators scream. The Wardens at the door are already dead. I tilt my head back just enough to see the rest of the psychopaths enter.

Seventeen remain of the blood-soaked Martian savages that my brother collected for his own personal quest to depose Octavia and reach the highest office in the worlds. Not a one of them is out of their thirties, and it seems a hilarious realization to think that perhaps their time in defeat will be but the footnote of their saga.

Lilath, Queen of the Syndicate, walks at the head of the pack.

She pulls off the Red face, wig, and contacts she wore at the Forum, and takes a black iron crown from one of her men and sets it on her head. She walks toward me carrying a Warden's head. She rolls it like a playing ball toward the speechless senators. They murmur her name in terror. Several try to flee.

She runs a hand along the back of my head as she comes to a stop.

"Publius, you've been very naughty." Her voice is dead and empty of humor. "I gave you that seat and you try to kill me. This is not the behavior of a pet." She produces a studded dog collar and a leash. "Come."

Publius does not move. The Vox senators stare at him. "You're in league with Boneriders?" a Red cries. "Have you gone mad!"

Publius has lost his voice. Lilath's becomes a whip. "Publius, come."

"You're not a Red?" he murmurs.

Lilath tilts her head. "The right hand of the Emperor, a Red? Disgusting."

"Begone, slaver!" a Blue shouts at her. "We are free men and women here! We wear your chains no more. We would rather die than—"

Lilath lunges in a way the Blue probably never thought possible. One moment she is beside me, the next, she has tackled the Blue and is hacking her face apart with an iron hatchet. When the Blue's head is a ruin, Lilath walks back to me and holds out the collar, motioning, "Publius, come."

Publius quivers and I feel sorry for him. How this all must have started as a distant fantasy when Lilath came to offer him her services. Closer and closer he drew to his prize, a year away, a week away, a day away, and finally he had power.

Now this.

That would test any soul.

His crumbles. He lowers himself to his knees and crawls to Lilath. She fits the collar around his neck very gently and strokes his face. "You will be a good dog, won't you?" She stays face-to-face with him. "Won't you?"

"Yes." He lowers his head.

"Yes what?"

"Yes . . . *domina*."

Lilath produces collars for the rest of the tribunal. Her men pull them down to fix them tight. Two protest and are killed. After the survivors are fitted, Lilath tilts her head to the door behind me.

"My Emperor. Your slaves await."

Small hands applaud from behind me and the Boneriders bend in amorous supplication, even Lilath.

"Well done, my Queen. Well done, my friends."

That voice.

Its accent is Lunese, but I know it to my bones.

Fear eclipses all rational thought. Little footsteps make their way to the front of the court. An abomination wears the face of a small boy around ten years old. Its hair is flaxen. Its face narrow. Its eyes reptilian in their cold curiosity. It stands before the enslaved Vox carrying several simple plates.

"I know this emotion," the Abomination says sweetly. "This reminds me of a novel I've read about a shoemaker in old Russia. It's this moment, isn't it? This moment where you breathe on all fours, your heads privately tucked to your own chins, where the personal myth which you shrouded around your hearts collapses under its own weight, and you realize what you actually are. Not weak—that would still give you a victim narrative with enough tragic romance upon which to nurse yourselves. Not average—you are all clever in a rudimentary way. Just smart enough to rise above the sea of human meat to comprehend how insignificant you really are." The Abomination touches Publius's head. "We all want to be special. It must ache to discover you are not."

He goes to the Blue Lilath slaughtered and picks out handfuls of her brains and deposits them upon the plates before setting each one in front of the Vox. Lilath falls to her knee and unveils a small box. From the box, the Abomination draws an antique razor.

The Sword of Silenius.

He cracks the whip.

"The natural order has resumed," he says to the Vox.

"Hic sunt leones!" say his men.

"The son of Augustus rules the Republic. But what is a world with only lions? Do my bidding and you will be rich and mighty. Slave Kings of the Emperor." He points the Sword of Silenius at them. "Now eat your supper."

Publius is the first to eat. As they cry and chew, the Abomination watches and turns to me with familial affection. "Hello, sister. So nice to finally meet you."

55

VIRGINIA

The Wolf and the Mother

"APPARENTLY HOWLERS DO KNEEL," Lilath says.

I am in a nightmare.

The clone of my brother stands before the Morning Chair running his hand along the smooth wood as if it held an electric current. Still wearing his collar, Publius sits on the floor staring at nothing. Gorgo, the Obsidian enforcer with gold teeth, watches the clone with deep respect.

Sevro, Pebble, and Clown are driven to their knees beside me before the Morning Chair. They have been beaten to a pulp. Which means they look quite like I did after the mob did its work. Even my hair is missing chunks. My forearms are covered with poorly sutured wounds.

"You untidy abortion," Sevro hisses at Lilath through mashed lips. "How the hell are you still sucking oxygen?" He glares at the clone. "And what the fucking fuck is that?"

Lilath smiles idly and sits at the foot of the clone's chair. Boneriders rove about. Made all the more mad by their isolation in Deepgrave, they have decorated the room with the corpses of Republic Wardens.

"Mustang, what is this?" Sevro asks. "Who's the beady-eyed rodent?"

"That is a clone of my brother," I reply. The spike has not been removed, but no longer plays with my serotonin levels. Instead, my legs are paralyzed. I barely notice.

"The Jackal?" Pebble whispers.

"Bullshit," Sevro says. "Bullshit." He tries to stand, but receives a kick from a Bonerider to his stomach. He falls gasping. Gorgo walks up to him and kicks him again for good measure before returning to the clone. "How . . ."

"The Emperor is a master strategist," Lilath proclaims. "He sees all."

"He sees all," Gorgo echoes.

"I was not certain my plan to wrest control of the Sovereigncy from Octavia would work," the Abomination says, still examining the chair. "So I left dear Lilath instructions and samples of my DNA in case my life was spent in the effort. I left messages and instructions to myself. One can never be too careful." He walks around the chair, eyes barely coming over the top. "After she recovered from her own wounds, Lilath went to Earth and found Zanzibar the Master Carver, and proved her ultimate loyalty by growing me in her own womb."

Sevro literally throws up. He spits bile on the ground. "You that desperate to get the Jackal inside you, the only way you could do it was by shitting out his clone?"

Lilath lunges forward, so close to caving in Sevro's skull with her hatchet.

The Abomination calls out her name and she stops mid-swing. The look she gives him is deep with affection, none of it motherly. No one misses it, not even the Boneriders, but they don't seem to care one lick. The joy they feel being in their armor again is almost childlike.

"That is the most bent thing I have ever heard," Clown says.

Pebble squints at Clown. "Did you give us LSD again? You know I hate LSD."

"Quality stock like Victra choosing a mongrel for a mate is far more perverse than simple cloning," the clone says. Lilath blinks unhappily at the mention of the Julii. Victra's sister, Antonia, was my brother's lover before he died. And she did not look like Lilath. "But that was the opinion of my first life. I care very little, except for the pollution of the gene pool that you and your mongrel children represent."

"My babies'd eat your heart out with a spoon," Sevro says.

"Oh please, Sevro. It wouldn't do to make me fret." He taps his finger on his chin. "I have learned something watching this Republic. People only obey when it costs them something to disobey. So. The next time you threaten me, Sevro, I will teach you how much it costs, and we'll see if it happens again. Prime?"

"Don't talk to me like you know me. I don't know you. You little . . . freak. You're not a real person. You're just an afterbirth. Mustang, how have you not vomited all over yourself?"

I stay silent, unable to put my cluttered thoughts to words. Daxo, Dancer, Theodora dead. Who else? Holiday? Darrow's mother? Kavax? Who else because of my monstrous bloodline?

Daxo was my best friend.

And this . . . this is what killed him?

I feel shattered. If this creature got ahold of Pax . . .

Thank Jove for Victra. Keep him safe. Keep Electra safe.

"Mustang . . ." Sevro says. "Can you hear me?"

"Her name is Virginia," the clone says to Sevro. "The same blood runs through her veins as in mine. I am Adrius, and I am not Adrius. In some ways I am less. In some I am more. I have learned from my first life, studied the archival recordings of the Institute, and the lives of my enemies."

He sits down in the Morning Chair.

"Pulling apart your Republic was so easy a child could do it." He smiles. "I cannot rule publicly, of course. In time, perhaps. But until then, my socialist dog will do." He strokes Publius's head. The disgraced senator flinches. "I did intend for Pax to be my Passage so I could earn my scar. But Sefi interfered, and Atlas insisted Lilath not pursue."

I finally speak. "The Fear Knight would never ally with you. You nuked Luna."

"He doesn't know I exist, of course. This was my design, my Day of Red Doves, my little birds sang such sweet songs to me."

He gestures to the high windows where the pachelbel sing. There were pachelbel in the window when Dancer and I met. There were pachelbel in the gardens where I had so many conversations. But we checked them for hardware when Sophocles kept eating them. It must be something more sophisticated than that.

"Atlas and Atalantia merely liaised with Lilath in the end," the clone continues. "We were going to sell Electra to Julia au Bellona. Old debts and all." He smiles at Lilath. She looks pleased to be out of her Red disguise and back in her Bonerider armor. "The fools think they have a puppet on Luna, a Red Queen. What a hollow farce." He taps his finger to his lips. He is identical to Adrius. Even in his tics, if not in his memories.

"I'm going to kill you," Sevro says. "Didn't get the pleasure last time. And it will be slow."

The clone watches him without emotion. "I told you the next threat would cost you. This is your fault. Gorgo, please bring in the wolf and the prisoners."

The Obsidian disappears out a side passage.

A moment later, the great Sun Doors at the far end of the hall open. Syndicate thorns guide in a cargo skiff loaded with a giant iron statue of a howling wolf. It thumps against the ground as it sets down behind us. Sounds come from inside. A voice calls out through the iron.

"Min-Min?" Pebble whispers beside me.

"No. No. No. No. No," Clown murmurs.

Sevro just watches as the iron wolf begins to glow with heat. The iron thumps as the Howlers inside try to kick their way out. Smoke slithers through the wolf's nostrils. Then the trapped men and women inside begin to scream. As they melt in its belly, their cries of agony funnel through the chamber of the wolf's throat to ululate into a howl.

When no more howls escape the wolf, and the smell of roasted meat fills the room, the clone speaks. "Did you learn your lesson, Sevro?" Sevro does not reply. He's not inside his body at all. Neither are Clown and Pebble. Their eyes are glassy, their shoulders slumped. Sevro's eyes are dry and dead.

"I hope you have, Sevro. Because I have great plans for you. My sister has uncovered ways to play with the mind. I am going to play with yours. So the next time you see your wife, your daughters, you will not even know who they are. I will strip you of all you wanted, as you and your pack stripped me of all I wanted." He strokes the chair. "Then we will be even."

I have never seen Sevro afraid like this. He glances at me, knowing full well what we did to the Duke of Hands. And now that it is his turn, all the blood rushes from his face. His hands tremble at his sides as if he had been electrocuted. His girls are his everything. With an animal scream, he lunges for Adrius, and gets just far enough for Lilath to personally beat him to the ground. He gets up, and she nails him in the head with the hilt of her hatchet. He stands again, bleeding everywhere, and another Bonerider kicks him in the kidneys. Time and again, he stands up and takes a step toward the clone until Lilath kicks him in the head two steps short.

Sevro goes limp on the ground.

And I can do nothing.

My confidence, my proud intellect, are dormant in the face of this. I am paralyzed inside and out with horror.

"Just kill us and end this ridiculous show," I snap. The clone's face is blank for me as Boneriders drag Sevro away. "You are not Adrius. You're just playing the role she taught you." I point at Lilath.

The clone walks down from his perch to cup my face.

"The blood that runs through your veins runs through mine. You are my sister, Virginia. My only blood. How could I ever kill you?" He strokes my hair. "You are family. Too long you have been weighed down by fools and insects. You deserve a second chance." Behind him, Lilath sucks on her teeth. "You deserve true dominion over the sheep."

56

VIRGINIA

A Maze with No Center

I AM THE GUEST OF HONOR at a banquet for jackals. My brother's creatures could never have been accused of sanity before their imprisonment, but after so long robbed of power, they have become mad with the taste of it. As night sets, Sunhall turns to orgiastic bedlam. Niobe's fleet has arrived with the ships of my house, House Telemanus, House Arcos, and almost all the lesser Gold houses of the Republic. The Vox fleet over Luna gathers in formation to block their way to the planet. The hologram of the pending space battle floats over the room.

While the Republic eats itself, the Boneriders party.

Safe behind Citadel walls and puppet legions, they indulge in yellow and green mountain ranges of narcotics. They have emptied the Citadel cellars of my husband's whiskey and chug down bottles of wine that have been in my family for generations. Their Syndicate servants ferry them supplies of Pinks and political enemies. On them, they indulge their most depraved appetites. Some poor souls are fetched from the deep cells to be used for fencing practice, or made to fight each other naked in gladiatorial bouts to the death. The bodies fall to the floor to die, and thorns drag them out and bring new ones in. The prisons, brimming as they are with the Vox's enemies, have an unlimited supply. When I have to watch the Silver senator Britannia ag Krieg face down an unarmed, drunk Bonerider, I turn away. She no longer seems an adversary, or even a rich woman. To them, she's just the lower species.

Britannia dies with the sound of wet towels slapping stone.

I have seen almost all there is to see, so it is not the barbarity that irks me. It is the shallowness of their cause. There is no cause. There is no religion, no delusion of honor, only some vague notion of retribution and domination, which means little more to them than the degradation of their enemies. To me, these ten years have felt like a hundred, full of texture and trials and triumphs. But these savages were frozen in time in Deepgrave. They did not evolve. They only want to live in the past. In that fleeting moment of youth, where even the Sovereign feared the House Pluto of Mars's Institute. They were barely past twenty years old and all worlds were laid out before them. Now in their ecstasy, they don't realize how far behind everyone else they are. Or maybe that is the reason for the ecstasy. Maybe they all know they are doomed because of their own nature, and they want to live in the sun while it shines.

How long can this ruse really last?

I stayed quiet to assess the situation well after my initial shock wore off. I have learned much. My real brother loathed the Boneriders. He mocked them behind their backs. But the best soldiers are often the hollow ones, whom you can fill with your own purpose. This clone doesn't know he's supposed to hate the Boneriders. He was raised by a woman who worshipped the Jackal and the Boneriders, and thought the two inseparable. How disappointed the clone must be in the legends he was raised on.

I sit at his left hand, a place of secondary honor. Lilath eats her hummingbird eggs across the table from me. She feeds like a pelican, head down, eyes up, *slurp, slurp, slurp.*

Like clockwork, her eyes flick to the clone to make sure he has everything he needs. When he stops drawing with his stylus on a datapad after a Pink screams from a Bonerider arrow, Lilath bolts to attention. It is almost grotesque to see how quickly the dead-eyed killer melts into suffocating sycophant. "What is it, my Emperor? Do you possess everything you need?"

Lilath loved my brother. I've always known it. But now that love is something wrong. She would have been his lover, but he liked pretty harpies like Antonia. So instead, Lilath gave birth to his clone. I do not believe I understand psychology enough to try to unravel that.

But I wager the clone has.

And that is the vulnerability of this little cabal. I glance up at the arrayed fleets.

In reply to Lilath's query, the clone forms a simple three-dimensional puzzle on his datapad and flicks the floating image to her off his datapad. "Can you solve that?" Sitting up straighter, she peers at it. Slowly her eyes lose their gleam as she realizes she doesn't even know there is a puzzle. He looks at me to make a joke of her. I never thought I'd see Lilath squirm from shame.

Her influence is slipping. She did fail him with the abduction of Pax and Electra. Now she is frightened I will steal him away. And he is afraid that I will let him down like these Boneriders have. How long did it take for his mind to be useful to her, I wonder. Has it been four years, five? She did much on her own. But how long will he need her now that he has his other Boneriders? Now that he has the Vox legions through his puppets? She must wonder. She must be afraid. And he must be annoyed that he is still so small.

I know where to drive the wedge.

"If he had all he needed, Lilath, I would already be a blank slate, wouldn't I?" She says nothing. The clone watches intently as I solve the puzzle, add two new polygons, and spin it back to him. He looks at it for a moment and then smiles in delight. He adds a fresh twist to the puzzle and hurls it back. This volley lasts the better part of thirty excruciating minutes as the fleets probe one another over our heads.

I have a strange feeling inside as he pauses the game to spend several minutes on a separate datapad making adjustments to his battleplan. The ships above move according to his wishes after a slight delay.

His last volley was an oddity. He did not try to beat me with it. In fact, he seemed surprised and then delighted to see I could solve his puzzles. After that, he was just having fun. By the third puzzle, so was I. I would have given fingers off my hand for my twin to sigh like that when we were children. All my life, I thought my brother was born broken. He wasn't. Perhaps he was just born with an incompatible father.

"Do you remember our puzzles?" I probe the clone as he watches two destroyers test the Telemanus flank. He frowns as they are repelled.

"I know they occurred," he says, giving new orders through his datapad. "Evidence here and there."

I glance at Lilath with a smile. The puzzles defined my relationship with my brother. I don't know how many he gave me over the years, but I know how many I kept. I solved each one, and he'd smile and congratulate me. But sometimes I would follow him, and see him slapping himself and gouging his skin, screaming, "Stupid, stupid, stupid."

If this was his insurance plan, he'd have given his clone all the information he needed to become himself again. The puzzles were a key component of a rivalry that shapes his psyche. He would have included the puzzles. And if he'd included them, he wouldn't have been surprised I could solve the ones during our volley. The fact that he was surprised is the loose thread I've been looking for. I glance up at the fleets as he lures a Telemanus corvette into a trap, and pull on the thread as quickly as I dare.

"I'm surprised you enjoyed me solving these," I say.

"What do you mean?"

"It used to anger you so."

He stares at me. "Did it?"

"Don't you remember? Sometimes you would hit yourself and call yourself stupid for failing to fool me."

"Did I ever?"

"No."

He puzzles over that for a moment, then looks at Lilath. Is it possible that she redacted some of the information Adrius passed down to his clone? By the look on his face, it isn't the first time he's wondered it.

"She's lying," Lilath says, seeing the wedge but not knowing how to blunt it. Killing is more her game. "You are the brightest mind in this Solar System." Ah, so there's the difference. This clone has been raised to believe he is a god. My brother was kicked and beaten and left on a rock to die more than once. One earned his victories. The other feels entitled to them.

"Are you doing this for Lilath?" I ask the clone. "Or is it for Adrius?"

"I am Adrius," he says.

"Do you want to be?"

He tilts his head to examine me as the Martian fleet withdraws to reassess their strategy after losing two more corvettes.

"Don't let her pour poison in your ear, my Emperor. She always thought you were a monster," Lilath says to him. Turning to me, she says, "You betrayed him to slaves. You abandoned your own brother. You hung him from the gallows yourself. He should have been worshipped by the world. But you just stepped all over him. You hated him. You called him a monster."

"If I hated him, why did I pull his feet?" I ask. "If I didn't love him, why would I keep those puzzles?"

Lilath goes still. Eat that, bitch. The clone activates, leaning forward. I suspected artifacts from Adrius's life would be of almost religious importance to him. Practically feeling the evil vibrations from the clone, the Boneriders stop their play and watch in silence.

Gods, they could just snap him in half, but they're afraid of him. Not just that. They respect him, worship him. It really runs that deep. I had no idea. I thought it was just Lilath. Did my brother tell them if they lost, he would free them in ten years' time? Is he a leader? Or a prophet?

"Where are those puzzles?" the clone asks.

"My private office."

"On Mars?"

"Here."

He remains perfectly still. "Lilath." She swallows. "Did I not tell you to leave my sister's quarters as they were?" He waits. And waits. The Boneriders watch with smiles as the ten-year-old spanks maybe the hardest woman on all of Luna, and she just takes it. They all want to be number two. So there's this pack's dynamic. "Answer, Lilath."

"You did."

"So why did you disobey me?" He leans forward. "Did you plan the Day of Red Doves? Did you use the White Guilds to start a war?" What does he mean by that? "You are a blunt instrument, Lilath. You know this. I treat you with respect. And you dare meddle with my designs?"

"I thought they would prove a distraction, sir."

"I pray for your sake they have not been destroyed."

"No!" she says. "You made them."

"Where are they?" I ask, hoping I'm right.

The clone stands up. "You heard my sister, Lilath. She may not be our ally, but she is of better blood than you. Answer her with due respect."

Lilath looks at me with abject hatred. "In my quarters."

The clone looks disgusted, as if he'd found her going through his drawers to smell his underwear. "Have them restored to their original locations. I will view them at once."

"But the battle . . ."

He glances at the Telemanus fleet, which makes no new movements toward the planet. "They have little appetite for blood. They're trying to break through our jammers to broadcast to the people. We have time."

The clone stands in my private office staring at the puzzles Lilath took from the room to hide for herself. He has not spoken for five minutes. I am surprised Lilath found the hidden vestibule behind the wall. It seems, however, she did not find the hidden passage within it.

"Must that low blood watch us like this?" I ask him. "She looks like a jealous vulture."

"Leave us," he says almost in a whisper. Lilath's cold eyes dart to me.

"My Emperor . . . it would not be wise." I flop down in a chair near a coffee table covered with books and a vase of night lilies.

"Paralyze my legs if you're so afraid."

The clone eyes the table behind me with suspicion. "There were defense-related systems located in the table," Lilath reports. "We deactivated them, my Emperor."

"And the dining table?"

"Deactivated as well." The clone points to a different chair at the small dining table and another vase of assorted flowers, almost all of which are dead. I sit in the chair and he paralyzes my legs via the psychoSpike.

"See, that wasn't so hard," I say.

He turns to Lilath. "If she kills me, she kills Sevro and the others. If she'll pay that price, she's earned it."

Lilath lowers herself into a wary bow, and backs with our two sober Bonerider escorts toward the door. The clone looks back at the puzzles. I was hoping it wouldn't be paralysis, but nothing is easy.

"I know you are playing a game," the clone says as the door closes. "But I don't fault you for it. This all started as a game. It wasn't until four years ago I heard my recording to myself. Lilath had instructions to follow, a psychological profile of the proper puppet to sponsor for a Senate run. Publius fit my specifications perfectly. She did take control of the Syndicate on her own, but the underworld wasn't prepared for her level of violence. She is possibly one of the most effective soldiers I have ever seen. That's both of me talking. But she only goes in one direction at a time."

He walks down the line of puzzles, passing very near to the idle night lilies. The flowers, uncared for, droop in their vases. Many are dead.

"She would tell it to me all like a story at first. Then presented it to me as a problem set. Given the variables, which gang to kill, which product to sell. I liked it better when it was stories. I was a hero in them, or he was." He stops in front of a maze. "But we're not. And I know why. Lilath took me to a slaughterhouse on Earth when I was young. And I saw how they would kill the cows and then make them into food for us to eat. Tell me: why are cows different from people? Cows have dreams. Cows have affection for their friends and family. If you are going to say it is because cows are less intelligent than people, it is acceptable to slaughter them, why is not acceptable for me to slaughter people who are proportionately less intelligent to me than cows are to them? And if you say it is because people feel more, then I invite you to stab a cow and a human in the throat and see how very similar they are."

As he speaks, my eyes search the vase of flowers, looking for a live one.

"That's false equivalency. Logical fallacies are beneath you," I say.

"You know it's true," he replies. I look back to him from the flowers just before he glances back. "Deep down. That's what I care about. Because I can talk to you and I know you hear me. I was promised that with the Boneriders. But they are . . . aberrant monkeys. From Lilath's lips you would have believed they were Seraphs."

"You hated them before too," I say.

"Did I?" he asks, sounding almost relieved.

"You thought them ridiculous."

"They are venal. And did I hate Father?"

"No."

"I shot him in the head."

"You loved Father as a father should be loved, but he didn't love you back. That was the problem. You thought it was your fault. There were many things that were your fault. But not that. I think . . . I think what I've realized is that every father makes a mess of things. It's just a matter of if he cared when he did it. Our father didn't, and I think you spotted that."

"Then why are you . . . you, and why am I me?" he asks, turning around completely.

"Because I gave up trying to please him, and you never did. I honestly don't think you ever cared about any of this." I wave to the walls around us. "With every new endeavor, there's always the hope that you will find happiness, be less lonely. Let me tell you what I've learned: the moment you become Sovereign, you become loneliest person in all the worlds, because there is no new endeavor, no new height to which you can ascend. Whatever loneliness is already inside you is magnified, because if you were lucky enough to have anyone understand you before, they won't understand you after you sit in the Morning Chair. Only one person alive at a time knows what it means to be Sovereign."

He traces the lines in the marble floor with his toe as if it were a puzzle. I glance back at the flowers. There could be one alive on the other side of the vase.

"Do you know why I did this?" he asks. "I did it because Lilath told me it was the only way I could see you. You would kill me if you were not at my mercy, I know. You think I am a freak. And I am. But thank you for speaking to me as if I weren't. I recognize the gesture, even if it isn't a kindness."

"Do you hate her?" I ask him. "Lilath."

He replies with a slight pause and no inflection in his voice. "On the day she took me to see the cows die, I had a thought. I asked Lilath to build me an iron cow. She built me the iron wolf instead, as I knew she would. One day soon, I will melt her inside it."

I forget the flowers and stare at him. "Why?"

"Because she doesn't understand irony."

He means it, and he doesn't sound upset, proud, or even excited about it. "And doing that would make you feel happy?" I ask.

"It doesn't make me feel anything. It is just an opportunity for novelty."

To do that to Lilath, who gave birth to him, who breastfed him, and woke in the middle of the night when he cried as a baby, who trained him to walk, to speak, to read, seems in the moment to be the cruelest act I have ever heard. My brother was many things, but even his evil led with the heart. This thing is just bored.

"Just like making the Republic eat itself?" I ask.

"Indeed." He smiles, pleased. "I knew if anyone could understand me, it would be you. I only wish Father were here. Cruel though he may have been. So I could see this cruelness. Look in the eye. Smell its ugly breath. To see if I felt it."

"Felt what?"

"Evil. What precipice of the mind could conjure anything more terrifying than a cruel father?"

"I think," I say slowly, "perhaps you have spent too much childhood indoors, young man."

He reels back, annoyed that I dare try to pull out of the discussion with affected rhetoric. In his mind it is disrespectful. "You don't think I'm Adrius at all, do you?" he asks. His mood darkens. "I suppose to you this must all feel as if you are with a voyeur." He gestures to the puzzles. "I am not real to you. I am an interruption. At very best, an imposter." His lips pull upward as his eyes narrow. "Am I wrong?"

"Naw, kid, you're not wrong. If Adrius were here, he would be eating lobster as he gave this lecture on a table containing the body of a conquered foe. If Adrius were here, he'd have sex slaves brought to him after the battle and fuck them on Octavia au Lune's bed. And it would make him so very happy to dilute the most expensive liquor bottles with piss and then give them to his Boneriders to share. And then, after all that, he'd tell it all to no one. His war on the world was a joke built around a central need to prove he didn't yearn for the approval from the only man who wouldn't give it. You, on the other hand, are just a joke built around me. A visitor to this world who doesn't belong. A ghost." He looks stricken. I finish it. "And what Father was to Adrius, I am now to you."

He steps closer as if to confess. "It would appear so." Emotion leaks into his voice. "It must end in your death then, I suppose."

I spot the flower I need. It's moments like this I sympathize with Darrow.

There is a patient, longer scheme available, where I earn the clone's trust over days, even weeks. I could fix more things then, perhaps. I could ensure the rescue of Sevro, Pebble, and Clown. But if I wait so long, how much of the Republic will be left by the time I am in a position to save it? The fleets will be at it again soon if they aren't already. Both navies were built to protect us from the Golds. The prospect of their destruction at the hands of each other is more urgent a calamity than the safety of my friends.

I make the same choice my husband had to make.

"It doesn't have to be that way," I say to the clone. "I am not like Father, because I do care about you. Even if I don't love you. You killed my friends when you didn't have to. Lilath put that in you. What I said, it was in reaction to that. I don't want to be your enemy. There are things Lilath is wrong about. Things that will jeopardize your life. For instance, the Pandemonium Chair. Did you know Octavia only used it twice? It is dangerous."

"Are you trying to tempt me into asking for the codes to the Crescent Vault?" he asks.

"No," I say. "I'm trying to tempt you into asking about my research with the Pandemonium Chair. How the psychoSpike functions . . ."

He lifts his datapad and sends tendrils of pain racing along my spine. "I think I have discovered it for myself."

"Of course, but you haven't cracked how to actually erase the memories, have you? They're quite different functions, viewing and destroying, and more than twenty-four steps to the latter." I lean forward with a smile. He couldn't figure out the puzzle. "I'm sorry, rude of me to not put in an easy little button for idiots." He wants to know how to do it so he can do it to me, and make me his companion. What sort of companion, I can only guess.

He looks scolded, but walks closer. "And you would just tell me?"

"In time, all things are possible, brother." I pick the night lily out from amongst the dead flowers in the vase. And hand it out to him the way Bellona knights did as they returned to loved ones from war.

His response is a basic human response. When you're caught off guard and someone reaches to shake your hand in a comfortable setting, you usually shake it. When someone displays a deep and respectful flash of cultural esoterica that you value as well, you respond. He does both. If he had had proper kinesthetic training by a razormaster, he wouldn't. After all, genius or not, he is still only ten years old. He takes the flower. But he doesn't take it the way I would, or the way Adrius would. He takes it like an entitled child who spends too much time indoors. Violently.

57

VIRGINIA

Black Cathedral

NIGHT LILIES RESPOND WELL to a gentle touch. They do not abide rough handling. That's when their necrotic spines come out to play. I had them made that way as my last in a long line of redundant defenses, all of which have either been deactivated or removed, except my bloodydamn flowers. Precisely because it is more in line with something Atalantia would have lying around than Virginia au Augustus.

The clone flinches as several sets of glistening needles burst from the flower to pierce his thumb. He screams at the sudden, blinding pain. The shaded toxins of the lily trickle slowly down the tip of his thumb, spreading toward his hand. He falls backward, staggered by the intensity of the poison. I feel the agony as well. It seeps from my right index finger up my arm straight to my spinal column. I almost throw up, but I must move. I throw my body forward off the chair to the floor near the clone's datapad. He dropped it the second after the needles went in. The flower's spines have retracted. I pick it up very gently. Flower in one hand, pad in the other, I crawl to the puzzle wall trying to turn off the psychoSpike without getting another dose of the spreading poison. The third puzzle at the bottom on the left is a transponder to the escape door. This puzzle had to be on the door for it to open and not hidden in Lilath's creepy suite. If I press my hand to the wall when the puzzle is present, the door will slide up, and I can escape. If I can just get to it.

The door to the hall explodes inward as Lilath responds to her Emperor's cries. She's carrying two hatchets. She runs toward me. I find the right function on the datapad and return sensation to my legs. I scramble upward and lunge to touch the wall behind the pictures without disturbing the flower in my hands.

A jarring force hits my back. It almost feels like a punch compared with the searing pain in my index finger. The necrotic poison is spreading for the hand. If it gets to the torso, I'm dead. But by the wrist I'll be in such agony I won't be able to move. I slam my other hand into the wall. The wall shoots straight upward to reveal a metal chute at waist height. I duck and drop the flower just as Lilath tries to chop my head off from behind. I try to spin-kick her legs, but she steps over the kick and delivers a slash downward. I catch it on my left forearm. The bone breaks so abruptly that it pierces the skin. I stumble back into the wall beside the chute and reach for the flower with my poisoned hand. Lilath is brutal and effective. She chops me in the left shoulder, takes off my right ear, then buries a crushing blow in the right side of my ribcage. The bones break, and something inside me ruptures. I crumple downward just close enough to the flower. Lilath glances back at her Emperor, knowing I'm mortally wounded, but unable to detect why he's screaming. Almost blind with pain, I fumble for the flower with my poisoned hand. Another dose of poison goes through two more of my fingers. My vision pulses and I hurl the flower up at Lilath's face. It's the only part of her not covered with armor.

I don't see where it hits her. I just hear her screaming. She stumbles away, almost dropping her hatchet. Something clanks on the wall behind where I stand. It's connected to me. I reach backward and find metal. I pull on it till I feel pressure release in my back. It's one of Lilath's hatchets. I look at her, and I stumble from the pain and loss of blood as I wind up to throw it at her. She's hunched beside the clone. There's a ripping sound. And she stands up with a shudder. It was her nose the needles got. And she didn't take any chances with how much of her nose she cut off. She turns back to me and pulls another hatchet from the sheath on her thigh to join the bloody one she already has.

I throw my hatchet at her.

She doesn't bother dodging. It just sparks off her armor. I lose faith in the fight and I dive into the escape hole to plunge downward. The ride is a minute almost straight down through darkness. The tunnels go almost as deep as the Dragonmaw bunker. The tube levels off and deposits me on a soft landing pad, in a small room. It is one of the Citadel's secondary fallback bunkers. There are four tubes that can access it. I pull a lever to close all four.

They might have found everything else in my office, but not this. I'm going to pass out from blood loss soon. I rush past the weapons cases to the medical station. Arm broken, I clumsily grab the laser saw first. The blue line of energy comes to life. Without hesitating, I slice off my index finger at the bottom joint. The pain of the amputation and cauterization are meager compared with that of the lily's toxins. I leave the gouge where my ear used to be weeping blood. The flow has already diminished, and will stop soon from coagulation. I take off the middle finger at the top joint, and just the tip of the ring finger. I discard the laser cutter and reach for the cauterizing gun. No time for anything pretty. Even with it my internal organs will likely keep bleeding in a rupture. I moan over the medical table in pain as the gun melts closed the wound on my right side. Then I seal the other ones I can reach.

I thought I would face a dire choice. To save Sevro and my friends, or to save myself. Now I realize, there is no choice. If I don't get out, I will die, and so will the fleet in orbit. I have to get out.

I take three shots of stims to stay awake, then pump blood from the med station's supply into myself as I sit woozily in front of the communications terminal. It is located beside the ejection chute. The terminal is already in Black Cathedral protocol. Someone else must've called it. Kavax? Holiday?

The hidden network immediately connects me to the bridge of the *Reynard,* Kavax's flagship. He turns to see me on his displays. Sophocles tilts his head toward the camera. "Kavax. I am in the small chapel." The man's eyes widen. Flashes from battle wash over his face. "I have internal bleeding in the kidneys and likely the liver. Left arm is broken, right hand losing function. Sevro, Clown, and Pebble are also prisoners in the Sunhall. How many clergy in the building?"

"Four, but they are in Moonhall and connecting tunnels are compromised."

"I won't be able to go to them," I say looking down at my wound.

"Do you know where the prisoners are located?"

"No."

"Can you find out?" he asks.

"Giving you access to internal cameras still connected to the systems,"

I say. "Kavax, make the call. I'll go back for them if you think I can make it." He and his techs sort the feeds for a few moments to find the ones I sent. As they do I examine the defense systems I had installed in the Citadel. Nearly all of them are dark. Lilath and the clone peeled my fortress apart well. Oddly, the escape and transit systems are the only systems running. Likely so the clone and the Boneriders could move about behind the scenes while they pulled the strings of their puppet government. Kavax is done appraising the information I sent.

"Where are they?" I ask.

"Let me see your wounds."

I turn them toward the camera. "Eject," he says. "We have teams on the ground, ready to move at exit." *Eject.* My heart wants to be the person who risks it for Sevro in the face of certain death. My head can't decide. But in this situation, the person on his end of the line is the boss. Kavax has operational control. I look emptily at the ejection tube.

Is this what it comes down to? Leaving the best of my friends in the clutches of a ghost from my past? I suppose so. Sevro was right. I am not Mustang any longer. I am the Sovereign.

I crank open the ejection hatch, crying out from the pain as I use my broken arm. I feel very selfish as I crawl through the aperture into a small padded compartment large enough to fit ten.

I close the hatch behind me and the lights in the compartment and in the concrete tunnel glow. Electricity channels through the two metal rails on either side of the tunnel, and the compartment shoots forward.

It carries me away from not only Sevro, Clown, and Pebble. It carries me away from the place Daxo died and the people who killed him. It takes me away from ten years of work in a place I had always feared. I had dreamed of one day leaving the Citadel of Light behind, perhaps ousted from office in a hard-fought election against a worthy successor, or after my relevance had worn out. I once hoped it would be Dancer who took it on next. Never did I imagine my last time leaving the Citadel would be like this. As the compartment races along the forty-kilometer tunnel, I make myself a promise that this will be the second-to-last time I leave the Citadel. I will return to finish this, and then I will never see this place again.

It feels like a dream when the compartment slows to a stop. The hatch pops open above my head and I emerge. Large men in armor stand waiting for me. But then their rifles rise, and I see the Vox upside-down pyramid on their armor.

I stand there with my hands in the air, feeling myself fading.

Gunfire comes from the hall, and before the men can turn around, the wall behind them erupts. High-powered rounds mow them down in seconds. A team of heavily armed Lionguard and Pegasus Legion soldiers burst in from the hall hunched over their weapons. The battered helmet of a Pegasus centurion retracts to reveal Holiday ti Nakamura.

"Lie down, ma'am," she barks. Two of her men expand a peculiar stretcher with two large pods on each end. Holiday forces me down onto it. I make no arguments. I can barely walk. "*Reynard,* this is Gray Rock. I have Gold Horse. We are on the move." The stretcher locks me in place. I see what the pods are for when an intense pulseField throbs between them with a *thrmmmm.*

Two soldiers carry the stretcher as Holiday leads the squad out of the room. Gunfire echoes through the halls. Gunship engines roar outside as we ascend the bunker via the stairs. Dozens of Vox legionnaires lie dead. More of Holiday's lurcher squads join us. They look like a troop of evil gargoyles as they push from the bunker in force out into the light of day.

We're in one of my brother's craters. Now I see why Kavax didn't send in men through the tunnel earlier. It's in the center of a Vox mobile infantry legion headquarters. Lionguard and Pegasus Legion gunships lay waste to the camp. Holiday leads the special forces troopers straight into the back of a waiting assault transport. Its guns rattle as we lift off as soon as I'm aboard. Fifty Pegasus troopers activate their boots and fly close behind the transport as the door seals.

The war becomes a distant rumble.

A medical team waiting in the assault shuttle rushes to me. Before I can object, they sedate me. I feel our escape from atmosphere distantly through the bumps that resonate through the deck. When I go weightless, I know we have made it to space. When the shuttle wheezes to a stop and clunks down on a deck, I know I have made it to the *Reynard.* I close my eyes and succumb to the loss of blood.

I wake to find Darrow's mother asleep at my bedside with Sophocles in her arms. The ship is quiet. It seems they disengaged with the Vox fleet.

Monitors above me track my vitals. I am in the *Reynard*'s medical bay. Sophocles wakes up first and gives a little yip and jumps on my bed. I wince as pain races through my right side from my wound.

"Stupid animal!" Deanna says, swatting it away. She wipes sleep from her eyes and looks down on me with such protective love that I start to cry. Not for myself. But for her, for the pain I see in her eyes, and all the pain she must have felt these last days for her son, for her grandson, for Sevro, for me. And then I cry for Daxo and Theodora, and the friends I left behind with the monster. She cradles me as I do, humming in my ear as I have always wished my mother had done for me.

Hours later, when I've worked up the strength, Kavax and Niobe come to see me. I worry for a moment that Nakamura was too ashamed to come, but then Deanna drags her inside. Holiday can barely meet my eyes for the shame of letting me be captured. It wasn't her fault. I was thoroughly undone. I'd weep again to Kavax and Niobe for Daxo, but all that needs to wait.

"Has Heliopolis fallen?" I ask.

"Not yet," Kavax says. "But our agents say it only has days left."

"Darrow?" I ask.

"We don't know," Niobe says.

"Pax?"

Kavax can't answer, so Niobe does. "Ephraim ti Horn abducted them from the Obsidian. Their whereabouts are currently unknown."

"Abducted them? *Again?*"

"We don't know why. But it occurred immediately after the *Pandora* was hit. Victra is missing. Her escape shuttle was found, but the first rescue team was shot down crossing Obsidian airspace. Her legions were grounded on the orders of the ArchGovernor, for fear they would initiate a war with Sefi's Obsidian."

I lean forward in hope. "Rollo survived then." He's a good man. Stalwart. Tough. Loyal. And he was a Son of Ares.

"No," Holiday says. "They assassinated him in Agea." I sink into the bed. "Then it's Vorol?" They shake their heads. "They got him too? Then who took the post?"

"Some idiot," Deanna says.

"Kieran," Kavax answers heavily. "Temporary appointment by Mars's regional governors."

Darrow's brother. I sent him to Mars with Niobe to negotiate with the Obsidian. I'm hopelessly behind. Wait, no, Publius and Zan mentioned this.

"Who assaulted the ship?"

"It looks like Sefi," Kavax says. I just blink at him. "I never thought we should have trusted that mongrel breed. First the Coppers, then the crows." Looking up at them, I just realize they think Publius did *all* this. I don't have time to explain. Calming her husband, Niobe shows me the current disposition of ships in the system. Atalantia is still massed at Mercury, with a smaller fleet at Venus. Most of the Republic battleships are here around Luna, while the Ecliptic Guard gathers over Mars.

"Is this fleet strong enough to break through Ash Armada over Mercury?" I ask Kavax.

"Yes," Kavax says.

"No," Niobe corrects. "We cannot defeat them without Ecliptic Guard or the Vox fleet joining us. We might be able to break through as is, but to land and load under fire . . ." She stiffens. "A miracle could occur, or it could be the greatest disaster of the war."

"We have to try," Kavax says. "Darrow would for us."

Deanna heads to the door. "Deanna, stay," I say.

"No," she says gruffly. "Maybe I can one day forgive you for doin' what needs doin'. But I can't give you permission to abandon my boy." She steps out. Holiday still has not weighed in.

"Virginia, there's something else you need to know," Niobe says. "The Rim has made a secret alliance with the Core." It can't get any worse. Fresh ships, fresh legions of enemies, thrown into the fray at the exact moment they could break our backs. "They are currently unaware we have this intel. We don't know where they will strike, but we can assume it will be decisive." She looks at her husband. "Mercury is in far orbit. I think they will hit us as we cross near the sun, when our sensors are distorted."

"No," Kavax says, disagreeing again. "They will hit Mars. Take out the Phobos Dockyards. Eye for an eye."

"And that is why we should return to Mars," Niobe says. "Kavax knows better the Rim, and I know better Atalantia. Mars cannot fall."

"No one has suggested rescuing Sevro," I say.

"We sent three teams in through the tunnel after we evacked you. We lost contact with them ten minutes later." Niobe steps toward the bed.

"Virginia, we have four operatives still in the building under Moonhall. They are Sevro's best chance. But if we try to hammer our way in now—"

Massacre, and the clone kills my friends.

"We can't stay here," Niobe says. "The Vox fleet wants a fight. They're still pursuing and we're a million klicks away from Luna."

"Surely Publius can be reasoned with," Kavax says to me. "To do all this he might have used the mob, but he can be rational. If we fight his fleet, no matter who loses, Gold wins."

It's almost too much to bear. "What do you think, Holiday?" I ask.

Finally, she meets my eyes. "Retreat is the only option, ma'am. We must regroup on Mars." If we go, that leaves Earth alone with the Vox, and the swelling Gold host. It will fall unless the clone sees it is in his interest to try to defend it with his Lunese fleet. But Mars can be defended, without help from Luna. Earth cannot.

"Then we go to Mars," I say.

Though I promised my husband I would come for him, I cannot. It is a betrayal that will haunt me to the grave.

Kavax sags in exhaustion. He sees me notice and finally seems to see the scores of wounds the mob gave me on my exposed arms, neck, and legs. I had forgotten them. The tears gather in his eyes as he leans over the bed. "All hope is not lost," he whispers to me. I fail to see how he can believe that. He kisses my forehead. "I sent a man to Mercury to bring Darrow home if Heliopolis falls."

"Who?" I ask.

"The same man who told us the Rim was coming."

58

DARROW

Sevro's Palace

G LIRASTES THE MASTER MAKER stands before his crudest creation.

The starboard hangar of the *Morning Star* no longer exists. Harnassus's engineering corps have carved through the midsection of the ship
to create enough room to house the *Spirit of Faran,* our fastest and
youngest torchShip. The insides of the *Faran* have been almost entirely
gutted to make room for the most powerful electromagnetic pulse weapon
assembled in all the campaigns of the war. It is not a new device on the
surface, but it is the nature of war to inspire evolution.

In his purple robes, Glirastes resembles an evil necromancer from one
of Pax's storybooks. His hands labor with some Byzantine contraption
designed for his fourteen fingers. It measures arcane readouts, the meaning of which only my wife and Harnassus's astrophysicists could ever
hope to understand. Old researchers with large rheumy eyes check their
own notations and murmur to one another, while the younger breed
crouch in isolation, their cranial implants flickering as they attempt to
keep pace with the Orange idol.

As the EMP finishes its eighteenth preliminary test, I survey the
length of the device, its nest of wave-shaped coils, each three times as
thick around as a man, its blue lights and vacuum tubes. A steady
whoomph, whoomph comes from the oversized helium reactor at the aft
of the ship.

The lights dim.

Glirastes clicks his tongue at his servant, who bends to scratch his inner calf. Mid-scratch, he screams at a welder for silence. The thickset Red spits tobacco juice into the can tied to his neck by a string, turns off his torch, and hangs from the ceiling on his line. The engineers and construction teams hold their collective breath, not so much in anticipation of the result, but for fear of the Maker's monstrous temper.

Green integers dance across his face as his eyes dart through the report, punctuating it with murmurs of "interesting," "perfidious instantaneous amplitude," "shit shit indecorous shit," and more esoteric Mercurian profanities.

"Do we have a problem, Glirastes?" I ask. Glirastes sighs as if in prayer to give himself patience.

"Problem? You ask if we have a problem?" The folds of his neck twist red as he cranes his head to glare at me like a frazzled yet contemptuous owl. "Young man, you bamboozled me into helping you activate the Storm Gods under the pretense that you would use them only in a limited capacity, and instead turned a city I love into a coral reef. Any compassion I had for your cause has been drowned by the encroaching sea. Yet if I do not help you again, as you so eloquently and brutally elucidated when you browbeat me into helping you on this fool's errand to rid you from my planet, the city of my birth will resemble little else in the known universe except the center of a G-type main-sequence star. The fact that I find catharsis in profanity while endeavoring to fit three years' worth of research into three weeks of practical application does not reflect upon my enthusiasm for the work, which is little, nor the necessity, which is great. So, yes, we have a problem, but the particular nature of my frustration is isolated to a conundrum which you have neither the patience nor the temperament nor cognitive ability to understand." He turns the data on its side, scrolls through it again. "Ah," he says. "Never mind. I solved it." He twirls his finger. "You, why did you stop welding? Get back to work! Must I do everything?"

Glirastes stalks out of the *Spirit* and heads for his makeshift office on the floor of the hangar. "You're all bloody saints," I say to the welders.

"Aww, sir!" one croons.

"Can I have a kiss?" asks another.

"Back to work!" Harnassus shouts. "We're not payin' by the hour."

We find Glirastes sighing as he slumps into his Thinking Chair, a queer perch made from a single flowing branch of a sunblossom tree.

"I know it is beneath you," Harnassus says as Glirastes's servant pours his master a glass of port. "But would you mind explaining the device to the infantry, Master Maker? It would do them some comfort to know they're not trusting their lives to magic."

Glirastes surveys the commanders I brought with me.

"No. That sounds tiresome."

He puts his feet on a silk stool and sighs as his servant removes his purple slippers and massages his heels with rose oil. Harnassus looks six seconds away from clouting Glirastes on the ears. He has little patience for snobs. I've more experience with the breed.

"It's just an EMP. What's so complicated about scaling it up?" I say, and wait for the explosion.

"Just an EMP?" Glirastes repeats as if reading his own obituary aloud. "Am I just an ambulating mammal?" His eyes scour me. "Did you not retain anything of your curriculum from the Academy aside from astral belligerency?"

"I retained enough, apparently."

The infantry commanders chuckle.

Glirastes sighs in annoyance and regards Thraxa and my infantry commanders with distaste, offended by the sunburnt visages and thick chests of hardier mammals than he, and retreats to intellectual bullying. I track what he says, because I'm married to a woman who'd be insulted if I couldn't.

"Weaponized transient electromagnetic disturbances have tenaciously sharp leading wave edges, escalating precipitously to their maximum level before decaying slowly. Imagine a double exponential curve. Problematically, the shielding made by the Venusian Dockyards is designed to recognize this sort of blunt belligerency"—he fixes me with a glare—"and provide countermeasures for Atalantia's fleet. Consequently, I have decided to use a benign damped sine wave to create a coupling between the source and the victim equipment. Usually this is a by-product of a weaponized EMP, but the genius here is that instead of diminishing within the double exponential envelope, the sine wave wavelengths will increase. However, considering the distance required, the energy demand will be staggering. Creating a more efficient and staggered energy ignition is profoundly difficult absent a nuclear explosion, and if I do not perfect it you will all die in the sky." He eyes me again. "Now that I have satisfied the curiosity of your apes, the zoo is closed." He closes his eyes. "Begone lest you have an advanced degree or care to replace Exeter in massaging my feet."

"I'll take his spot if you like, Master Maker," Thraxa says with a smile. She holds up her hands. "I know they look like elephant feet, but they're tender to the right sort."

Glirastes makes a face of distaste. "Such a bloodline, squandered on martial absurdity. You've genius in your line, woman. Your brother was the mind of a generation, and your father . . ." He sighs. "You waste your time playing soldier."

"So that's a pass?"

"Pfah." He shoots Harnassus a look. "Don't forget my breakfast to-morrow. I can't work without sardines; tomorrow is a Tuesday, after all."

As my infantry commanders file out muttering their concerns to one another, Harnassus follows me and Thraxa out of the *Star*'s hangar. "What do you think?" I ask him.

"He's pigheaded, cruel, eccentric, fickle, and ten times as demanding as my first wife. But he's a genius."

"Was," Thraxa says. "Riches made him slow." She glares back at the man. "Little more than a lapdog to whoever holds Mercury."

"You thinking he'll betray us?" I ask.

"I'm thinking we should endeavor to remind him Atalantia is scared of us."

"What do you have against him?" I ask.

"First off, his designs are rubbish. Robbing the Egyptians blind. And the bastard cozied up to the slavers, then to us. He's a bloodfly. Inverte-brate. Permission to pop him when we evac."

"Denied, psycho," Harnassus says.

"Wasn't asking you."

"He's my second-in-command, Thraxa. When I don't speak, he speaks for me," I remind her.

"Uh-huh. But you're speaking."

"You're not killing the Master Maker."

She shrugs. "Sure."

"Where were we?" I ask Harnassus. "Can we even tell if he's full of shit? If he leaves us hanging up there, we're all dead."

"He's spineless," Thraxa moans. "He wouldn't dare cross us."

"Probably right." Harnassus grimaces. "See, I'm not the sharpest on magnetism or waveform theory. My focus was practical mechanics. But I've got two hundred brains with a thousand degrees between them going step for step with him. He's smarter than each of them in theory, but not all of them together. If he's playing games, they'll red-flag it. Long as we keep him happy, seems he'll do what we need him to do."

"That's the trick, isn't it?" I say.

"You want the genius happy, we need sardines," Harnassus says.

"Sardines?"

"He says he gets headaches without sardines for breakfast on Tuesdays. Tomorrow is Tuesday and he's fresh out."

"You have to be joking," I say for Thraxa.

"I don't damn well know. This man's been pissing into crystal decanters since he was a teenager. So far, no luck. If the Heliopolitan Silvers here have sardines, they're denying it. We could raid their kitchens, but we're on unsteady footing as it is."

"Where's Sevro when you need him?" I mutter. Harnassus raises an eyebrow in query.

"What? You think he just always smells like fish?" Thraxa asks.

"I think he smells like wet dog, personally," I reply.

"Well, it depends if it's raining or not."

"Gods, the jungles were rough. You remember that trench foot he had?"

"Thought we'd have to amputate," Thraxa says.

"Yeah, you tried."

"Then he woke up. *Heh*. That was funny."

Harnassus shakes his head. "This is not the conversation I thought I would have when the Reaper of Mars came to North Africa to make me a Praetor. I thought it'd be all fire and guts and devilish mayhem. Not prepubescent humor. You should check Sevro's pantry. All sorts of illicit goods there, so I hear."

"Why don't you check it?" I ask.

"I won't send any of my men in there."

I sigh and motion Rhonna over from my bodyguards. "Go see if there's any sardines in Imperator Barca's stateroom."

She goes white as a corpse. "Uh, isn't that a task for support?"

"Not you too."

"It's just . . . well, there's booby traps, ain't there? Alexandar once tried to steal whiskey. Came back shaking like a softfoot on their first aerial drop."

"Fine." My bodyguards all find something very interesting in the contours of the deck. "Superstitious idiots. I'll get the bloodydamn sardines."

Ten minutes later I'm shrieking like a goat on the floor just inside Sevro's room as a medicus pulls needles from my face, chest, and ass. Incredible pain races through my body as my hands and feet turn purple and start to swell uncontrollably.

A flat voice drawls from a hologram of Sevro's face.

"Don't touch my shit. Don't touch my shit. Don't touch my shit."

"It's prime, sir," the Yellow says to me as she injects me with antivenom. "It's prime. The pain will subside in a minute. Swelling should start to go down now. Sadly, the color will remain." She looks up at Sevro's hologram. "I'll . . . um . . . wait outside . . . in case you need me."

"Told you," Rhonna says from the door.

"Slag off." When my hands have almost returned to their normal size and feeling has returned to my feet, I stagger up and turn off the hologram. A hidden needle pricks my finger. Shit.

"Badass-class DNA detected," a sexy voice says. Nothing leaps at me from the darkness. *"Profile match for: Darrow of Lykos. Best Friend. Also known as: Reaper, Boss, Howler One, Apex Asshole, Brother, Mustang's Bitch. Second-class clearance granted. Welcome. I apologize for warning shots. Master has been notified of your skulking. Stickyfinger traps deactivated. Help yourself to a glass of scotch, Best Friend. Take in some music, Reaper. Admire the trophies from the decimated enemies of the noble Howlers, Boss. Enjoy the extensive pornography library, Howler One. Relax in the sauna, Apex Asshole. It has no traps. But above all else, steal nothing, and enjoy your stay in . . ."*

"Sevro's Palace," Sevro's voice adds very seriously.

"Second class?" I ask.

"Yes. Master says you know why."

I look back to Rhonna at the door. "Nope," Rhonna says, and bugs out. Screwface makes a motion of standing guard and ducks into the hall. "Pixie," I mutter, and shut the door.

The suite is large, comprised of half a dozen rooms filled with his prizes. I've avoided this place since arriving on Mercury. To be here is to be reminded of how we parted. The place is too much like my friend. Mugs of evaporated whiskey sit in ranks atop banners of fallen warlords he's trampled. Candy wrappers fill the eyeholes of solid gold skulls taken from Magnus's floating palace in Africa. The scepter I gave Adrius in Attica sits on the couch for Sevro to use as a back-scratcher. Only one place is spared the chaos strewn throughout the suite.

My wife once told me a man's soul can be seen in the room he keeps the cleanest. I asked her what room is my soul. She tapped my razor.

Sevro's soul is his armory, but for a different reason.

One wall is for use. Three suits of Sevro's wolf armor hang central on the longest wall, surrounded by a shrine of knives. Tickler, his favorite, is missing. Replacement razors gleam with oil. Several from the gens Falthe are there, as is the Minotaur's with its horned pommel. I gave it to Sevro as a gift when his youngest was born. He always coveted it, especially after Sefi won Aja's off him in a game of "who gets the most kills." PulseFists and more esoteric weapons fill the rest of the shelves.

One wall is for memories. One of Ragnar's razors. Weed's old pipe. Quinn's Howler cloak. The bloody cape Octavia au Lune wore the day I killed her. Highest on the wall, in a place of honor, is the slingBlade I used at the Institute. I look at it for a long time before I take it down. It is far heavier than my razor and far smaller than I remember. I swing it till it makes a *swish swish*. I laughed at him when I saw it there the first time, laughed even harder when I found out how much trouble he went through to track it down. But I think I skipped past the part that mattered—how much the blade meant to him. With his father always away, always secretive and frightened to show his love, that blade gave Sevro something to follow. Something to dedicate his life to. Until he found something else.

The last wall is for his family. Holos of his girls float above coin-sized projectors, so that it seems like a hundred reveries fill the shelves. They've danced here in the darkness without anyone to see them for months. There are little bracelets and tokens, ink footprints and palm paintings. An emerald cape Victra gave to him when we sailed for Earth. A golden unicorn figurine. And in the center of it all: his father's blood-red Ares armor with its spiked crescent helmet.

The bench where he would dress for battle faces this wall.

The armor looks so odd surrounded by the domesticity. But it is easy for me to forget that Sevro's life was always war, because his father waged it instead of raising him.

After I saw how Lorn's sons were consumed by his vocation, and theirs continue to be consumed, I tried to separate war and family, like Fitchner. I thought they were two worlds that should never meet. Sevro knew what I did not. What it is like to be raised by a warlord, by a distracted man. And he knew that our world is one where everything collides. He didn't close his mind to his family before battle, because he knew they did not make him weaker, they made him stronger than he was by himself. I feel the key underneath my jacket.

Even though I will never be able to agree with his decision to return to Luna instead of Mercury, I understand it. He even said it to me, though I did not want to hear it at the time. He would not make the same mistakes as his father. If I ever see him again, I will ask that he forgive me asking him to make that impossible choice. And if I see my boy again, if I see my wife, I will not close myself off to them. I will be the father and husband they deserve.

59

LYSANDER

The Impaler

I AM ONE OF THE TORTURED.

The Gorgons, a handsome Gold woman with a pert nose and a gecko of a Gray, pour alcohol over my burn on the first day. *Just getting acquainted,* they say as I scream. They inject something into my neck, and time does indeed slow down. The agony sustains itself for what feels like a week. Then it is gone, and the pain of my burn is omnipotent once more.

The Gorgons ask about the Bellona blade they found on me, about my name, but if I give it to them, then what will they do with it? The Fear Knight is away, so it seems. Would they contact the *Annihilo*? Would Ajax intercept it and send a killsquad here to finish what he started and Seneca left incomplete?

I need the Fear Knight to return. I need his direct authority.

My stomach feels inside out it's so hungry. My hair has begun to fall out from radiation sickness. Soon all of us are bald. All of us are nauseous. Our bodies are naturally resistant to radiation, but with it floating in continuously from the Ladon, our DNA unwinds bit by bit. Soon the symptoms will worsen, the Elysian Knights and I talk intermittently as the days ebb and flow. I look for some sign of insanity in them to explain their allegiance to Darrow and the betrayal of their own Color, but I detect none except for the zealotry in Alexandar and Drusilla. The rest seem only to be here because House Arcos, their patron, joined years ago. Drusilla speaks of the Dream of Persephone. Of helping the people, as if all lowColors were paupers and slaves before the Rising.

It's a laugh. I've met Reds and Browns happier than most Golds I know, and all of them with better lives than the Grays who fed our military machine. But Grays never broke under the hardship. Of all the Colors, they've remained the most loyal to the Society.

Some time in the morning, on what may be my fourth day with them, Ignacius and Drusilla are taken away. Ignacius is returned first, sheet white and holding three stumps where there used to be fingers. When Drusilla returns, she says nothing as she sobs into the stone.

Any belief that I am a plant amongst the Arcosians disappears. The torture binds me to their pack, as I supposed it would. Conversation becomes scarce. Slowly, Alexandar draws in on himself, becoming dour and hopeless. It is all Drusilla can do to keep him drinking water and eating their gruel.

My scheme begins to seem so foolish. There is nothing to be gained out of the misunderstanding that brought me here. I will die here, or I will risk telling my captors who I am, and wait at their mercy for my enemies to decide my fate.

I've resolved to tell them when I am strung up on the chains for the fifth time. The time-dilation drug is too much to bear, and even the Mind's Eye cannot spare me from its rigors. But Pert and Gecko, as I've taken to calling my torturers, disappear once I'm hoisted up. The cavern is dim and unadorned. Stalactites drip water into a shallow pool. Beside that is a chest full of torture devices. I hear footsteps behind me. A man breathing. "Can you walk?" he asks, his accent more Lunese than Ionian. I nod. A magkey unlatches the lock on my manacles. "Follow me."

I follow the man out of the cavern to a main tunnel. To the left, past the prisoners' cavern, come the faint sounds of laughter and cooking. He leads me right into deeper tunnels until we come to a small cavern.

It is his personal chamber. A thin thermafoam mattress with a field blanket serves as his bed. A small solar stove sits in a nook carved into the wall along with several weapons and a long-range com. A thin black hasta hangs on the wall beside a filthy wolfpelt. A second nook is home to several dozen figurines carved from disparate stones. Beside it is a map of what looks like a cave system. I join him to sit on two small pads facing each other.

Atlas au Raa is a vaguely alien man. It has been years since I've seen him in the flesh. After the death of my parents, he was sent to the Rim to harry the Ascomanni in the Kuiper. Whatever he did to displease my grandmother must have been grave. In his absence, she gifted his office to another.

I am struck by how soulful he now seems. Was it the distant dark that did it? Or was it the war he returned to find raging in his absence?

Behind the sunburnt eyelids lurks an intense intellectual presence. He is masculine like his son Ajax, but nowhere near as thick. He is taller and leaner than his brother, Romulus, but less dramatic in posture. His eyes are wider and a clearer gold. A scar encircles his neck where his throat was once cut ear to ear. His long hair is black shot with gold and held back in a ponytail.

I probe deeper with the Mind's Eye.

Forty-nine years of age. Left-handed. Limp originating from the left knee. Multiple hidden knives in his moth-colored light armor. Lack of ego projection, indicating absence of insecurity in body and deeds. Sociopathy? Delusions of heroism? No. That's usually supported by zeal. Why so distant? Extremely lonely? Tired? Bored? Distracted? Absent in his personal presentation is the theatricality of his public work. Which suggests a sophisticated system of operation, likely supported by the books in his library, and perhaps a personal philosophical treatise. This is a philosopher-torturer with the practical detachment of a pig butcher.

"Stop that," he says. "Unless you want me to do it back."

I go still.

Grandmother said I was her only pupil. Could this be why Apollonius wants it so bad? He knows Atlas is yet beyond him?

The man's cold eyes search the burn on my face and continue to assess without yet coming to a conclusion. So he is humble too, or at least experienced enough to have been wrong more than once before. "*Salve, au Lune,*" he says in formal highLingo.

"*Salve, au Raa,*" I reply.

"How did my brother die?" he asks, abandoning the argot before it becomes laborious. "Of course I have been told, but I hear you saw it with your own eyes."

"He walked to the Dragon Tomb. He died several steps short."

He is quiet for a full minute.

"All men who live for their ancestors do. How long did he talk before he walked?"

"Too long."

He chuckles. "Romulus to the end. I hear my niece and nephew are on the *Annihilo* to talk alliance."

"Diomedes is. Seraphina is in the desert."

He doesn't flinch. "Dead?"

"Yes. Atalantia demanded a Raa participate."

"Did you see her corpse?"

"I saw her ripped in half by a rail slug. What remained was buried in the sand."

"Shadows and dust," he murmurs without irony.

"No grief? No laugh for the dead traitor?"

"She did not betray the Society. My father and brother did. I held no malice for Seraphina. I would have liked to have known my kin." He sighs and takes the Bellona razor from a pouch on his thigh and lays it between us. "This, on the other hand, is filthy with the blood of Aja and Octavia."

"I do not believe a man like you should ask anyone to explain themselves."

"Ah. That's right. You've seen one of my forests. I'm sure you have an opinion. The Two Hundred had many at first. None to my face, of course. They prefer smiles and innuendo."

"I remember you used to make my father laugh," I say.

His eyes soften. "Do you?"

"I wonder if he would laugh at your forests."

"No," he surprises me by saying. "Brutus would call me a human stain. Anastasia would use far gentler a vocabulary. I'm sure you remember her bleeding heart."

"No, as a matter of fact."

He searches my face, as if trying to detect a lie. "She would say I am making more enemies with every man I impale. That is why I impale Martians, not Mercurians."

"To create dissonance and demarcation between interloper and loyal subject?" I reply pedantically.

"So we've read some of the same books, I see. You want to play this game? Very well. I've only barbarians for company out here. How many lives did you end in the Iron Rain? Don't you have a killcount to mark on your breastplate?"

"It is impossible to reckon. Between ten and a hundred."

"Do you feel their deaths acutely?"

"Vaguely."

"There it is." He leans back. "Distance has sanitized war nearly as much as Stoneside's fucking ramblings. It has made it easy . . . romantic. I have no interest in sanitization nor romance. I apply scientific methods to produce psychological trauma in our enemies in order to create psychological casualties. To end their willingness to fight and shorten this war. That is my purpose."

There's a resentment in him, a hostility that seems intensely personal.

I don't recall knowing him well enough to wound him. Or does he already know of Ajax's betrayal?

"Enough digression. Why would you tell my men you are this Cato au Vitruvius? Did it amuse you?"

"Amuse me? What sort of nature do you think I possess?"

"A nature which is the product of your grandmother. The same nature she imparted to all her students. Answer the question."

So that's who the anger is for. The woman who gave him this role?

"I didn't trust your men," I say. "Ajax tried to assassinate me . . . twice." By his expression, I see this is not news. "I could not risk revealing my identity to anyone but you, for fear of him completing the task."

"And you think I am trustworthy?" he asks.

"You were my father's best friend."

"I am also Ajax's father." He picks at his cuticles. "Do you mean to kill my son?"

"No."

He doesn't believe me. "Do you even know why Ajax tried to kill you?"

"It goes back to childhood—"

He laughs. "It does indeed. She used to groom the both of you." He leans forward. "Ajax is fucking Atalantia." At first I thought I misheard. But it begins to makes sense. Ajax's quiet when Atalantia kissed me. His territorial marking. His fear that I would replace him at his aunt's side. "You didn't know. Few do. She took my son as a . . . paramour before he turned sixteen. She would reward him for the heads of Gold blood traitors with sexual favors."

"Did Magnus know?"

"Of his daughter's depravity? Yes. Of its deeper depths and my son's sexual enslavement to his remaining daughter?" He shrugs. "Magnus always had a selective conscience, especially with precious Atalantia."

"And you just . . . let it happen?"

"Ajax may have my DNA, but I was off fighting for my Sovereign for half his life. When I returned . . . well, that boy is her creature to the bone now. Just as she intended. She and Aja always detested each other, you know. That Aja's boy is now her personal killing machine is her ultimate revenge."

"Did Atalantia give the order to kill me?"

"I doubt it. To do so would be to admit to herself that she cannot tame you," he says. "She would not lose such a prize as you lightly. But if she did give the order, she would not tell me." He pulls a fig from a bag and pops it into his mouth, offering me one. I take three. "So long as Ajax is ruled by his heart and cock, there will be no place for the boy who used to make him feel small. Knowing this, you still claim no intent on his life?"

"It changes nothing," I reply. "I am here for the people of the Society, for Kalindora, for my Praetorians. I will not let them burn as hostages of the enemy. I know an assault is pending on Heliopolis. I assume Darrow is besieged there?"

He watches me without speaking for some time.

"You look very much like your mother when you feign nobility, you know." He ponders over a fig. "It won't be an assault. I have recently concluded field testing of a new chemical weapon. Atalantia is intent on releasing it, so she does not destroy Heliopolis's wealth before taking it as her own. The Master Maker will watch as his city eats itself."

"What does the chemical do?"

"Omnicide."

I see it already.

A catalogue of horrors wracks Kalindora's face. I see her convulsing and vomiting blood. I see buboes bubbling on her skin. I see the skin melting away. I did not know until this moment how much I would do to stop that. She is a killer. But the weariness I saw in her eyes, the way she looked at me when the Praetorians came down . . . It was something close to pride. I can't let her die, or Rhone or my Praetorians, or any of the loyal subjects caught between two giants. Too many lives have already been spent too easily by people who should know better.

"Did you learn omnicide in the Kuiper?" I ask.

"No. I learned to outsource."

Cryptic. "You mentioned a Master Maker . . ."

"Ah, yes. Your old friend Glirastes. He's no longer just an artificer. He's proven himself a traitor. He abetted the enemy's use of the Storm Gods."

"I don't believe it."

"Trust me when I say men do strange things out of fear. Now he will die with them. And his precious city." He does not sound happy about the last part. "Now, where are my manners? Are you hungry for a real meal? In the morning we'll be departing for the *Annihilo,* but I'm sure Atalantia will cause a fuss if I haven't fed you." He fetches a bowl of fresh bread and two boiled pieces of meat.

"What is this?" I ask as I chew.

"What does it taste like?"

"Bat."

"Well, there you have it."

He watches with a strange expression as I eat. It is oddly civilized, this conversation, considering his men only just tortured me. He still has not tendered an apology, nor do I expect he ever will.

"You do not seem to advocate for Atalantia's plan," I test.

"I have no tolerance for rebels. But this planet did not rebel. It was conquered. I think you would agree it is a strategic mistake to confuse the two, and to cede the moral high ground to the enemy when we've only just reclaimed it. If we kill twenty million, will anyone remember the Reaper's Storm?"

"Yet you do not contradict Atalantia . . ."

He laughs. "I am a soldier. Soldiers follow orders."

"She gives you autonomy. Can't you infiltrate the city? Bring down their shields from the inside?"

"No. My men inside are dead. The Howlers know counter-espionage all too well. And the loyalists are as neutered as a *logos.*"

That puts me in a unique position as I ponder playing yet another stupid game.

He grows suspicious. If anything, undermining Atalantia's plan puts him on guard. I want him at ease. Get him talking about himself. About something he likes. I try his mother, Gaia, and tell him of my time with her, but he replies very little, and grows somewhat defensive. The figurines—they're the only thing here without utility. I stand and approach them. The detailing is impressive, as is the variety of subject. There are a few Golds, but most are lowColor. I pick up one of a Red woman.

"That one is called Daedre," he explains. "We became familiar on the outskirts of Olympia. Tough woman."

"For a Red?"

"Tough woman."

"Are they trophies?"

He looks insulted as he joins me. "They are meditation totems. Each is for a human who preyed upon my prejudices. Daedra seemed harmless, kind, stupid. She brought my men figs and bread every day for a week, until her figs were laced with a nerve agent. A hundred and four men died because I could not see her for what she was."

"A zealot?"

"A soldier," he corrects.

I'm still in his peripheral vision.

I take a step back and look at the figures with a frown. "Where's Darrow? Surely he's fooled you a few times."

"It's a work in progress. I did the legs before I met him, but how can you understand a man at war with himself?" He turns his back to me to reach toward the far end of the nook. Clenching Daedra in my hand, I ready to swing at the nerve packet located behind his left ear. "If you strike me, I suggest you have a plan." He doesn't turn around to defend himself. It throws me off guard. "I assume you saw my escape map? The tunnels can be tricky, and memory for us mere mortals is fleeting." He turns around and leans against the wall. "It won't work, you know. Me as your Trojan horse."

"It might."

"Let's say you did manage to subdue me. Possible, given your youth, but not probable, given your state and my vocation. You would then have to free the Arcosians, use my escape map to that blasted labyrinth, evade my men, flee across the desert, pray Darrow lets you inside Heliopolis, gamble that your thin ruse of Cato au Vitruvius holds, and then kill the most dangerous man alive."

"I don't intend on killing him."

"And the rest?"

"Prescient."

"Is it for *auctoritas*? Glory? To prove you are the heir?"

"No."

"Revenge then?"

"No."

"Humanitarian concern for your men? Or maybe you fancy the Love Knight," he mocks. "Men will do strange things out of fear, but for love . . . well, death is hardly the limit."

"Who are we if we kill a city that did not rebel?" I ask.

"Interesting. An idealist. Don't fret, it's a temporary condition." He actually smiles. "They're guarding the wall and the shield generator with an army of veterans, you know. Howlers abound."

"Predictable targets."

"What is your target then?"

"Glirastes."

"He is a traitor."

"I can turn him back."

He goes quiet, thinking.

"Why are you not calling your men?" I ask.

"Because I have lived off the contributions of this planet. They have sheltered me and my men. They have fed us. They have informed for us. They have spied and died for us. Not the highColors. They turned their backs like craven. But the low, the mid, those with barely anything to their name, because this is not Mars. This is Mercury. If we just let them burn, what is the point of this?" He thrusts a finger to his scar. "Furthermore, for two weeks my men have failed to get me inside Heliopolis. What will you do with Glirastes?"

"I will know once I see the tools available. But I imagine Darrow knows an attack is coming, and so it likely will be necessary to hoist him on his own petard."

"The chances of it working are . . ."

"Minute."

He nods to himself. "Obviously, my men can't know. Make it look real. Kill them if you must. They know their duty." He waits for me to hit him. "Well? Let's see how good the pupil of Bellona, Octavia, and Aja really is."

Is Atlas really going to be a willing participant after what he's done to Darrow's men?

"You know Darrow will kill you."

"*Pulvis et umbra sumus.* One servant for twenty million citizens is easy math. You have five days until the chemical attack. Though that may change with my capture." His conviction makes me doubt myself. "Don't balk now." He punches me in the nose, breaking it. Blood spurts out. *"Do it."* He hits me again, and I charge him. He ducks under me and tries to strip my left leg to take me to the floor in a kravat central pivot. Cassius loved that one. I counter by leaving my feet and rolling over his back, looping one arm under his right armpit as I go, and wrapping my other arm around his neck as I use my central rotation to roll onto my back with his spine against my stomach. He has a small window to reach his bootknife, but he lets it pass.

I loop my arms over his left shoulder and under his right armpit, pinning his right arm up in a salute. I pin his left arm to his side by wrapping both my legs around it and his rib cage and interlocking my ankles. He grunts there, pinned in a brachial choke. His legs kick as I constrict the blood flow to his head, but not even an Obsidian could muscle his way out of this.

I stare at the doorway as his feet scrabble against the floor. No Gorgons come to check on their leader. There is never any need.

When he is unconscious, I release my hold and stand over him, perplexed.

I haven't time to understand it. Every moment wasted will make discovery surer.

I take the tacNet from his weapons nook and shoot it at his body. It ensnares him. I take his hasta from the wall. My Bellona blade lies in the dirt. I almost convince myself that I can bring it with me, but where I'm going I might as well wear my mother's ring. I jump and hide the razor in a cleft in the rock, and use his bootknife to give myself a shallow wound just above my heart. I smear the blood all over my face and neck.

The tunnel is dark and empty. Fear's men are still busy with their meal. I move as fast as I can back to the prisoners' room, my bare feet silent on the stone. Two of the Gorgons sit on the floor playing dice when I round the corner. From his place on the wall, Alexandar sees me fill the tunnel.

"I want to see the Fear Knight. . . ." he cries to the Gorgons. The guards turn to look at him. I sprint toward them. Aja's lessons guide me. Against a single individual, you can make a nonlethal takedown with relative consistency. But two individuals, even of a lower genus, reduce your chances by seventy percent.

I could kill the two Gorgons with two neat thrusts, but I make it sloppy. As if I've never held a razor. As they turn back at the sound of my feet, I slash half the head off the first man like I'm felling a tree. The blade passes through him as if he weren't even there and carries on into the second man's throat—one of Cassius's favorite moves against the shoddy armor common in the Belt. Then clumsily the razor goes into the cave wall.

Flopping to the ground, the second man stares up with wide eyes, trying to talk, but I made sure my clumsiness severed his windpipe. I hack at him a second time. A third. Then I give a quiet sob and fall to my knees, covered in blood.

"Gorydamn," Alexandar breathes. He kicks the other knights awake. "Cato. Cato. Look at me." I look up at him, wide-eyed. "Did anyone see you come in here?"

I shake my head.

"There's keys on their bodies. Unlatch us and we can help you. Front chest pocket. That's it." With shaking hands, I free them. "Cato, have you ever used a razor before?" Alexandar watches the bloody blade in my shaking hands. I pretend not to be able to think. Finally I shake my head and give him the blade. Practiced hands strip the bodies of their night optics, their sidearms, two grenades, and the single long rifle.

"Tell me what happened. Where is the Fear Knight?"

I show them. The professional soldiers miss nothing. In thirty seconds, we have the map, the go-bag, a glowlamp, and the Fear Knight's datapad. For a moment, I think they'll discover Cassius's razor too, but Drusilla only takes a wolfpelt from the wall. She hands it to Alexandar.

"You've a promise to keep," she tells him. He holds the pelt for a quiet moment and looks as if he is going to weep. Then he throws it over his shoulders and binds it to his tattered shirt.

Ignacius grins as he finds stims in the Fear Knight's go-bag a moment later. They each shoot a vial into their necks. The zeal of the drug gives their tortured bodies new life, but it won't last long. Correctly deducing that our breakout will be soon noticed, Alexandar dispatches Drusilla and Crastus to delay the pursuit.

"How did you get back here?" Ignacius asks. "Why were you in his room?"

"He was being kind to me," I say. "He wanted me to trick you into . . . into . . ."

"Doesn't matter, Ignacius," Alexandar says. "We have to move."

"We're trapped," I fret. "They're going to impale us."

"No." He holds up the map. "This is a back door. We knew he had to have one. We can escape. We are trained for this, Cato. I know you're not, but if you keep up with us, we will keep you alive."

"Alexandar, we can't afford to be slowed down," Ignacius says. "He's a loyalist anyway. He can't—"

"If we get Atlas to the Sovereign, what he has in his head will save millions," Alexandar snaps. "This *loyalist* could have just won the war, and you want to leave him?"

"He won't talk."

"He doesn't need to."

What does he mean by that?

Ignacius isn't convinced. "I don't trust him."

"Darrow will question him later," Alexandar says. Ignacius nods. "You ever seen one of these?" Alexandar asks me, holding up a stim vial and looking at my burn.

"What is it?" I ask.

"It'll make you fly, goodman." He tilts my neck and injects it. "How do you feel?"

The military-grade neurotransmitter races through my veins like a galloping destrier, filling me with manic energy, and dulling the communication of pain receptors in my brain. For the first time in weeks my face doesn't feel like it's falling apart. There's a rumbling groan from up the tunnel. Drusilla and Crastus return, stone-faced. "Armory was too well guarded, so we hit the commissary. They'll be coming soon as they clear the rubble. We have thirty seconds at best."

Alexandar smiles. "Then we have a head start, goodmen." He slaps my shoulder and shoves one of the scorchers into my hands. "On me."

60

LYSANDER

Pup One

W E FLEE INTO THE LABYRINTH. Alexandar sprints ahead as the stims lend his ravaged body fresh impetus. Buoyed by Mercury's light gravity, Drusilla carries the Fear Knight over her shoulders. The other knights bring up our rear. The detonation of one of our stolen concussion grenades rumbles through the tunnel not far behind. Dust shakes free from the ceiling, clouding the glowlamp Alexandar uses to light our way.

The tunnel leads us into a convoluted maze cave, where a network of connecting cave passages forms a three-dimensional puzzle. Some asshole terraformer had a gory field day.

Alexandar guides us well with the map, but I hide my frustration by panting down at the ground when he needs to pause to reference it again and again. Small beeps sound from the walls as the Fear Knight's datapad deactivates booby traps along the way.

After half a dozen turns, our tunnel tapers to a keyhole where only two can pass at a time. Drusilla shoves the Fear Knight through to Alexandar as one of their compatriots lays a laser trip mine at the keyhole, hoping to collapse it shut. Down a winding slope we go until we reach a fork of three routes lit by green *Mycena chlorophos* on the ceiling and floor. Bioluminescent juice squishes from the spores as we trod them underfoot to coat our bare feet a ghostly green.

Our mines do not detonate. The Gorgons are no amateurs. And they are gaining ground.

Right, left, down we go, against all instincts, deeper into the mountain, over a natural bridge that spans an underground river, through a chamber so filled with spores it seems nearly daylight, passing gloomy grottoes and opaque pools. Down and down. Somewhere through the walls rushes that underground river. It dwindles and for several minutes the only sound is the labored breathing of the Golds. My fear is as real as theirs. If Atlas's men catch us, they will not talk to me. They will butcher me with Alexandar and his kin, and the Fear Knight will apologize to Atalantia as he delivers my mutilated corpse.

I feel that fear vibrating like a dark river, but I leech its power, and use the adrenaline for my muscles, to narrow my vision, to calibrate my senses to absorb the slightest change in stimuli.

Soon the stench of ammonia fills my nose. I hear a chittering. The air thickens and warms as we enter a microclimate and the mouth of the tunnel expands to a great cathedral, the floor and walls undercut and eroded by what I presume to be carbonic acid. I grab Alexandar to stop him just before he spills over the edge. His men almost bowl us over.

"By Jove," he whispers at the dramatic drop.

He shines his light upward. In the vaulted reaches of the cathedral roost legions of bats. Their ranks cover the ceiling and disappear up into apse flutes where unseen millions must sleep.

"Milkbats," Alexandar whispers. They paralyze their victims with spines on the insides of their wings. Then they feed on the helpless victim's bone marrow. So Atlas did feed me bat.

Damn the blackmarket carvers. This is why the Board of Quality Control regulated them so assiduously. Men just want to create apex predators because it delights them, but then those predators kill off everything else, overpopulate, and break the ecosystem.

I almost laugh at the irony.

Beneath the sleeping horde lies a sea of guano. It stretches the entire length of the cavern, its surface writhing with millions of mothroaches and albino centipedes.

"How deep you think it is?" Drusilla whispers.

"Immaterial," Alexandar snaps. "It's just shit. Let's go."

"Those are milkbats."

"I told *you* that."

"Their guano can stretch as deep as thirty meters," I say. "And there's withertails in there."

Drusilla tenses, staring at the albino centipedes. "What's a withertail?"

"Worse than the bats," I say.

"They're coming," Ignacius says with a growl. He squares his big shoulders to the tunnel behind us.

"It must be passable." Alexandar scans the cathedral. *"There."*

In the gloom he spots a narrow shelf of stone leading along right, around the guano sea. We rush along it as fast as we dare. Alexandar drags the Fear Knight awkwardly, and almost loses him off the edge of the shelf. "Six o'clock!" Drusilla shouts. One of the knights fires at the Gorgon coming out the tunnel. He misses. The Gorgons do not. A projectile hits the knight. His right leg disconnects from his body at the hip joint. He screams as he loses his balance and topples down into the guano. It absorbs him like quicksand. He tries to claw his way to the surface, but missing a leg, he can't stay atop the sludge. Then he screams as the withertails find him.

Drusilla and the Gorgons exchange fire. High-velocity rounds hiss through the air.

"Crastus!" Alexandar shouts. He's about to jump down to try to rescue his friend. If he dies, this is all for nothing. I grab him and shoot at the ceiling.

A million bats explode in a fury. Let their thermal optics deal with that.

I drag Alexandar and we make our way along the narrow shelf and out the cathedral, harried by bats the entire way. One's attached itself to Drusilla. Alexandar cuts its head off with his razor and peels out its bristles. Drusilla sicks up on the floor, but stumbles after us, eyes dazed. Ignacius has to take the Fear Knight's body. After a series of turns, we find ourselves near the end of the Fear Knight's map. It is a limestone chamber filled with pools of dark water and stalactites dripping from the ceiling. I stop, searching the bioluminescent-lit walls, and feel panic rising in me. "What is it?" Drusilla asks Alexandar. "Are we lost?"

"This isn't on the map," he says.

"What do you mean it isn't on the map?" she asks. Instead of two tunnels, there are seven.

Ignacius hurls the Fear Knight to the ground. "I knew this was a fool's errand. Looks like it's a fight after all."

Drusilla slumps on a knee, breathing heavily from the milkbat venom. "We're almost out of ammunition. Which way is it?"

"I don't know," Alexandar says. He pockets the map and slaps the Fear Knight's face. "Wake up. Wake up, damn you!" He doesn't. "Shit. We make our stand here. Hit them as they come in. Make this a melee affair."

"They have Golds too," I say.

"Not like us."

"A lovely sentiment, but untrue," Drusilla says. "There's at least fifteen Scars. But it'll be Berserks they send in first."

"Then we die with glory," Ignacius mutters.

Alexandar searches the tunnels. The wrong one will lead us off the map and we might starve to death before we find a way out. He'd rather fight than trust his chances with that.

The Arcosian Knights follow Alexandar's commands and take up positions around the room to ambush our pursuers, as if you can ambush anyone with thermal optics in a cold cave. If we wanted to fight, it should have been in the guano grotto. Positively criminal how quickly razors reduce genius IQs to simple grunt logic.

I face the tunnels.

There is no reason the Fear Knight would have a fake map in his private quarters. Therefore, the map must be real and cannot be wrong. If it is not wrong, then it is shorthand. Two tunnels were supposed to be here, yet there are seven. I search for a pattern of two. *Ah, the pools.*

"I found the way," I whisper.

"Shut up. I hear something," Ignacius says. Alexandar hides behind a stalactite, waiting for the Gorgons to come from the darkness of the bat cathedral.

"The pools!" I hiss at the fools. Alexandar turns to me. "The pools lead to a tunnel." I shine the glowlamp down. Sure enough, a tunnel large enough for three men to swim abreast is faintly visible beneath the surface.

"You clever bastard!" Alexandar slaps me on the back.

We dive into the pool. The water is hot and bubbles from cracks in the stone. The glowlamp splashes pale light on the slick tunnels beneath the surface. Alexandar covers the Fear Knight's nose and mouth to stop him from inhaling water.

When we emerge in a small grotto, I gasp for air and pull myself onto the slick stone. Alexandar and the others breach the water and I help them lever the Fear Knight out of the pool.

We find the escape gravBikes underneath a camouflage tarp on the far side of the grotto. Concussion and gas traps deactivate from the passive signal in the Fear Knight's datapad. We take a bike each, slash the fuel cells of the rest with our razors, and tie the Fear Knight onto the hauling rack of Drusilla's under a portion of the camo tarp. Alexandar cuts the camo tarp into several more pieces and secures one on the hauling racks of each bike. Clever thinking.

I nod when he asks me if I know how to drive one of the bikes. "Not much to do in Erebos except daylight fancies."

"Do not stop for anyone," Alexandar tells us. He inserts the bike's wired com into his ear and motions me to do the same. "Coms in. We're playing clamshells, Goblin style. Head straight south for Heliopolis. Drusilla will have the Fear Knight. Everyone else, we're only here to buy her time. They can't use orbit support while we have Fear. So don't shy off. Let's get this bastard back to the boss." He gives them a firm smile, forgetting me completely. "Hail libertas."

"Hail Reaper," they echo.

The engines scream like crying babies as we tear off down the tunnel toward daylight. The sunlight blinds, even this late in the afternoon. We take a thin track down the mountain. The gravBike sighs up and down on its gravity cushion, very similar to the bikes Cassius and I used in Darentan Station when running from Syndicate clone traders.

The controls are touchy, especially to motor reflexes under the influence of stims, but they're far simpler machines than starShells. A powerful engine provides thrust from behind, as low-powered gravity thrusters beneath create half a meter of floating clearance from the ground. The seat is curved to angle the rider forward, with a rear seat for the gunner. Soon I've the hang of it, though I'm by far the worst pilot.

"Pup One to Howler One . . ." Alexandar announces over the com, using our transponders to boost his signal in a desperate bid to reach Heliopolis. It just might. The Society won't be jamming its own frequencies. But if Heliopolis hears it, every Gold in a thousand kilometers will.

I thought this would be a clandestine engagement.

He just put it on the big stage.

"Pup One to Howler One. Handshake: 2345209. We have Anteater. I repeat, we have Anteater. Sliders in pursuit. Are bearing south at 53.48, 113.41, requesting LongMalice support. I repeat . . ."

The track spits us out into a salt flat. The knights push the bikes for all they're worth. Alexandar's wolfpelt streams behind. They start weaving in and out of one another to confuse enemy targeting. Seems unnecessary. Didn't we destroy the other bikes? I start weaving with them, just a moment before Ignacius banks in front of me, then swerves back without the top half of his muscular body. His gravBike drifts sideways, losing speed.

Snipers.

I glance back. The cave is barely a dot. We must be five kilometers away, an impossible shot, even for lurchers . . . Something whips past and a huge crater opens up just left of my bike's nose. I send my bike into frantic contortions, and soon it seems we're out of range, but Alexandar has not let up. He hunches grim-faced over his handlebars, looking left and right and repeating his message to his master.

Ah, of course.

A swarm of hooded Gorgons on gravBikes flow down the nearly vertical face of a sandstone butte to our left. Another swarm pours out of a mountain valley to the right, racing to cut us off before we can get free of the mountains. All over the mountain range, the acolytes of the Fear Knight emerge from subterranean bunkers like hornets from a kicked nest.

RADTATATATATATAT

The ground in front of us ruptures with railgun fire, not to kill us, but to drive us west back into the mountains. We call the bluff and drive through it. Debris rips into my burn at two hundred kilometers an hour. A rock almost takes my head off. Then we're through, pushing for the open desert, the pursuing bikes still kilometers off. Three hundred kilometers an hour. The world is a blur, but the Mind's Eye makes everything feel languorous as I bob and weave around boulders and debris.

A vertical silver slash comes down from the sky.

WAAAAAAAAAOOOO

A beam of white light obliterates the horizon, leaving a gash of light across my vision. The sand of the desert pulses deep red as it's turned to glass in a twenty-kilometer swath. *"Idle banter!"* Alexandar crows. *"We've got your dog, Grimmus. We've got your dog!"* I can't help thinking of Cassius and Darrow riding over the Martian highlands of the Institute crowing nearly the same thing.

We careen over the molten desert. The heat radiates upward. My bare feet begin to blister. I pull them up to rest on the chassis. Through the warped air, another squadron of Gorgons appears. *"Split 'em. Cato, follow me."*

Hadrian banks left with Drusilla. I follow Alexandar right. The Gorgons divide to follow us, not knowing which has the Fear Knight. More orbital strikes come down to hem us in, but Alexandar is a god on a bike. He leads a whole squadron of Gorgons into a particle beam. They disappear like mist as we bank into a canyon, then spit out the other side. I stick on his tail as we head to the open desert.

I glance back.

Two kilometers behind, an army pursues. We'll never make it.

"Pup One to Howler One. Do you read me?"

No answer but static. Soon Society air support will come. They'll be scrambling ripWings. Aerial infantry will block our path.

We continue our course. With no way to down us without killing the Fear Knight, it becomes an endurance race. The gravBikes holding steady behind us in the open desert, suggesting a trap up ahead. The giant sun begins to set and stain the horizon the color of hot metal. The stims have faded. The agony of the burn returns, and I see Alexandar slumping in his saddle. Drusilla has linked up with us again, though there is no sign of Hadrian. Only three bikes remain. Debris from the Battle of Heliopolis begins to litter the sand with shriveled remains of war machines.

Soon we can see the storm wall of Heliopolis as a thin metal line in the far distance. But setting down between us and it is a line of mechanized Grimmus troopers. They'll have electrical cannons to fry our bikes' electronics. RipWings buzz overhead suddenly. The Society trap closes. *"We have to run it,"* Alexandar says. I see no way through. The pursuing Gorgons creep closer. *"Pup One to Howler One,"* Alexandar calls, panic finally making its way into his voice. *"Our path is blocked. Pup One to Howler—"*

A voice unlike any other comes over the com.

"Howler One to Pup One. Continue course. LongMalice deployed at danger close. Midnight inbound."

"Stick tight to me!" Alexandar says. *"Cato, Drusilla! Stick tight!"*

Thooom. Thooom. Thooom.

Huge explosions break the face of the desert. They blossom into acrid clouds of smoke and sand in the center of the Grimmus troopers. Darrow's artillery guns send another salvo arching from the city through the air in the thin gap between the storm wall and the dome shield of Heliopolis. They decimate everything in their path. Huge holes are blown in the pursuing squadrons of gravBikes as artillery shells scream over our heads.

It is all absurd sound and fury. Individual patterns in the metal and noise show the intelligent hands at work—move and countermove, measure and countermeasure—and how together they make insanity.

All this for the thin man attached to the back of Drusilla's bike. Neither alliance fighting for love or hate, only the utility that one life will provide them. And when I think of that distant look in Atlas's eyes as I choked him out, that look that reminded me of Cassius when he went to face the Raa, I understand what they both knew—how foolish all this rage is.

Before I plunge into the smoke of the artillery bombardment, the last thing I see is a ripWing squadron streaking out from under Heliopolis's shield with guns ablaze.

Blinded by dust and smoke, I hug my bike and close my eye. Debris pings off the metal chassis like hailstones and bites at my legs and face. The air is hot and ghastly. I want to sob in terror. I focus my Mind's Eye, and it all quiets.

I weave around a man-sized chunk of starShell, almost in slow motion. Nothing hurts me. Nothing exists but the mind.

Then I burst out of the smoke.

A wash of clean air as I tear out the other side of the cloud to see a heavy shuttle unlike any other ever built hovering a meter above the ground. Alexandar drives into it, his bike smashing and sparking as it hits the ramp and careens into the cargo bay. I goose the thruster and nearly fall off my bike as Drusilla's slams into me from the left and locks together with mine, driving me off course. A ragged chunk of metal impales her through the chest. I crank my bike left and skid sideways, dragging hers into the transport. I feel myself sailing through the air. I collide with something unmovable. My shoulder is pulled from its socket. The engines rumble beneath. I feel us rising. And I lie there feeling very calm and present, because standing over me, roaring for retreat, is the Reaper himself.

61

DARROW

Hero of Tyche

THE AIR HEAVES WITH SHOCKWAVES as the shuttle shoots through the aerial gate in the storm wall, and back to the safety of Heliopolis's shield. Remains of bikes litter the shuttle's cargo bay. Drusilla, one of Alexandar's cousins, shakes on the floor, a piece of metal through her chest. The medici swarm over her. A second Gold groans at my boots. Lean and caked in so much desert chalk it shudders off him as he coughs. I search him for weapons. His face is mangled and melted on one side.

"Get us to the *Star*," I shout at our pilot.

Thraxa jerks a tarpaulin off the back of a crashed bike to reveal a body. She yanks on the man's dark blond hair so I can see his face. "Look what the pup dragged in!" She spits on his unconscious face and puts all her substantial weight and strength behind her knee to break his sword arm, then she breaks the right for good measure, before manhandling him into more secure cuffs. "We're going to have some fun, impaler."

I heave a bike out of the way to reveal the last body. Alexandar. He's nearly unrecognizable. His ears and several fingers have been cut away and large strips of skin eaten off. I throw myself over him and check his pulse. It is faint. When I tear open his coat, I find two exit wounds in his chest. "Alexandar!" I say, shaking him. "Alexandar!"

His eyes crack open and he manages a smile. His teeth are missing, I realize in horror. His hands pull dumbly at something as he pushes a chalky pelt into my hand. "Told you . . . I'd bring it back."

Blood bubbles out his mouth and his eyes roll back.

"Faster!" I shout at the pilot.

I cradle Alexandar in my arms and jump out the back of the transport before it even makes its emergency landing. The medici are waiting for us, but their gurney will be too slow. I sprint past them carrying the man, scattering deckhands, not stopping until I lay him down in the medBay. He's barely breathing. Rhonna rushes into the room behind me, her eyes wild. "Alexandar!" She pushes to his side as the medici prep him for transport to the surgery ward. "Alexandar . . ." Her eyes search the horror of his face. His missing ears, the strips of stolen flesh, the toothless mouth as his lips part to murmur something. "What did they do to him!" she screams. "What did they do? Alexandar."

The medici pull her away and rush with him toward the surgery ward. I follow. A chief medicus pushes at me, her feet sliding on the floor.

"Sir!"

"We're going with him," I snarl.

"Then you're going to contaminate the room and terrify my surgeons," the medicus says. "Wait here."

"Do not let that boy die," I say to her. "Do you understand me?"

"We'll do what is medically possible, sir."

Rhonna and I are left in the silence of the intake room listening to machines beep. A ragged breath escapes her and her skeleton seems to fold in on itself as she hunches in a corner. She was furious when I left her behind to get Alexandar, but she's still in no shape for combat. I thought deep down that this had to be some trick. Some trap of the Fear Knight's. It seemed impossible to hope yet I took the risk. And now that Alexandar is alive, somehow despite everything, he may yet be taken. It all seems so unfair.

"Fear butchered him," Rhonna says, too numb to cry. "He cut him to pieces."

"Do you have coagulant?" I ask a medical officer. The officer disappears through a door and comes back with an injector. "I'll be right back," I tell Rhonna.

"Don't," she says as I reach the door. "Just don't."

I make no promises as I leave.

I stalk through the brig. Saud and Carthii prisoners idle about in their cells to either side. Soldiers mill outside an open high-security cell. They press to the walls, clearing the way when they see me charging with a full head of steam.

"Darrow . . ." Thraxa warns, blocking the door into the cell and holding up her hands.

"Move."

"I know how you feel. If it were up to me, I'd beat him to death with a teakettle. But we need information from him." I take a step close enough to her that I can see the clogged pores of her broad nose.

"Move."

She moves. Inside the cell, the Fear Knight is being woken up by a medicus and scanned by a team of techs.

"Get out," I tell the medicus. "But don't go far. He'll need you soon."

The Fear Knight sits up on the foam mattress and looks at me with a start as the vebrine they've given him kicks in. I inject his neck with the coagulant and take the cuffs off his hands. His arms bend unnaturally from Thraxa's rough handling. I survey the monster. The Rim Gold is skinny from his time in the desert, like a piece of dehydrated beef. Pensive, intelligent eyes stare back at me from under the chalk without even a trace of fear. It isn't like the Jackal, whose eyes were like empty bowls. Neither are they animalistic like Atalantia's. These are soulful eyes of a man who knows he's chewing on human flesh and swallows because he can.

I lean forward. "If I came to you laid out like a suckling pig, would you accept the boon without suspicion?"

"Highly doubtful."

I look at his hands. "How many of my men have those hands impaled?"

"Enough, so it seems."

"Did those hands cut my Howler's ears off?"

"They did."

I pull my razor off my arm and let it hang loose. "Do you think you deserve to keep them?" My slingBlade forms slowly at my side.

He turns his hands over as if viewing them for the first time and speaks to me in Latin before translating to Common. "Caesar was a clod. But he got one thing right: war gives the right to the conquerors to impose any condition they please upon the vanquished." He presents his hands to me.

I prepare to cut them off.

Yet my hand stays still at my side. A week ago, I would have. Throughout the war, I've done worse. But it would not be for my army. It would be for me. Was this the compromise that poisoned our Republic? Was this rage what made us forget that our hope is founded in our virtue? Virtue that has been sorely lacking, and which led to Orion's genocide?

"All of a man's affairs become diseased when he wishes to cure evils by evils," Atlas recites. "For order, I impaled soldiers. For liberty, you drowned cities. The victor writes history with the blood of the vanquished. I wonder, in the end, which of us will turn out the hero? Don't you?"

I leave the Fear Knight without a word. Outside, I find Thraxa waiting for me with several dozen of Rat Legion. "Get information from him," I order.

"I'll lead the torture personally," Thraxa says.

I look back at the man. I know better than most how any man will cave to torture in the end, but I also fear false information. "He'll just lead us astray. My wife will crack him."

Thraxa looks concerned. "Darrow, Virginia is—"

"And so was Alexandar until today." I survey the legionnaires with Thraxa, and make it a moral victory. "Use all means within the bounds of the New Compact. If the Vox won't obey it, we will. The information he has in his head could win this war. The men will want to cut that head off. If he dies, I will hold Rat Legion accountable."

They salute.

"What about Cato?" Thraxa asks.

"Who?"

"The fourth Gold. He says he helped them escape. No confirmation yet from Alexandar."

I look back at the Fear Knight. He's a man of too many layers. Was this planned to get him inside? Cato inside? Would Atlas risk that? "I don't need another variable here. If Alexandar survives, we'll ask him ourselves about this Cato. Until then, isolate him, check his story, and order a full analysis."

A vigil waits outside the medical bay. Alexandar's cult of young Gold acolytes has swollen to include men and women from all branches. Colloway exits as I reach the door. I frown, wondering if I have the wrong room. He holds little love for Alex but now he just shrugs at my expression and claps my shoulder. "Chin up. Your boy's a Stoneside, ain't he?"

I join Rhonna and sit in the chair beside her. She looks at my razor for traces of blood. I shake my head. With a nod for herself, she puts her small hand over mine and together we wait.

We're woken some time in the night by the medicus. The cold woman has not even the faint trace of a smile as she tells us that Alexandar survived and we can see him in the morning.

When the medicus returns I let Rhonna go in first. After several minutes she reappears with red-rimmed eyes. She smiles. "He's asking for the boss."

Alexandar lies shirtless in the bed, perforated with IVs. His face is still swollen, and bandages cover the empty ear sockets. He reaches a hand out to clasp Rhonna's as I loom over him. "'Lo, boss," he says with a childish smile.

"Hey, kid. Thanks for bringing back my cloak."

Glirastes is snorting drugs as Harnassus paces a hole in the briefing room carpet. A silver chimera drug dispenser full of sol dust slips out from the Master Maker's voluminous sleeve. I pull up a chair and sit across from him.

He admires his chimera. "When I had my first bite of sol dust, I thought I had arrived. I was a young man, of course. And once you've had stallions galloping through your veins, well . . ." He dabs the golden powder that rims his nostril and looks at it. "Very nearly cost my career. It was a long time before I realized one doesn't have to drink the whole glass in one gulp."

Pulling back his upper eyelid, he works the powder into his eye and sighs.

"I'm told you've stopped working," I say. "Sardines again?"

"Gods no, it's a Thursday," Glirastes says. "I'm sure you would agree certain standards must be maintained in a professional relationship between patron and artist. For instance, I would never deem it appropriate to imprison any of your friends and expect felicitations from you. It would simply compromise the relationship."

"Harnassus says you're close with this Cato au Vitruvius."

"You sound tired, Darrow."

"It's been a long week."

"Then don't make it longer on yourself. Cato is, in many ways, my only pupil."

"That callow boy?"

"That callow boy did what all your men could not. I know. When I first met him, I was as dubious as you are now. Just another fawning sycophant relying upon the wealth of his parents for access to me. Disgusting. But he has depth to him. He appreciates the grand without sacrificing the minute.

"You drowned half of Helios. I mourned for the dead. And now that one of them, a boy who is like a son to me, has come back, you think you can keep him from me?" Glirastes shakes his head. "I have done all you asked. I am your gateway out of hell." He leans back and rests his hands on his tummy. "It is your army. So do what you will. But if Cato is not out of your prison and sharing a toast to life with me over a glass of shiraz by tonight, then you will have to find yourself another Master Maker to build your gateway."

Through the video feed I watch Cato au Vitruvius admit that he is a libertine to our lie detector.

"Science?" I ask my Yellow science officer. Harnassus has assembled the team I put on Cato to deliver me their full analysis.

"We ran his DNA against the active Society military database and Gorgon NOC list with no matches. He is not a member, nor does he have relations in their military. Of course, without connection to Skyhall, we don't have access to the census records."

Screwface nods from his darkened corner. He brought us the military database information. "Ain't laid eyes on that sorry Pixie before. If he's a Gorgon, he's young, deep, and out on a limb."

"Linguistics?"

"His dialect is rare," a Pink says. "It has inflections of Western Ladonese, which is the predominant accent of Erebos and its surrounding municipalities, but it is primarily Heliopolitan Aureate."

"So he's lying about his origins."

"No," the slender Pink says. "On the contrary, patrician families of Erebos consider Western Ladonese to be a plebeian tongue. Most embrace the Tychian accent, but a minority of ancient families consider that to be . . . inelegant, and so train their children against the grain in the affectation of Old Heliopolitan. It's a nuance so particular the notion that he would think to imitate it beggars belief."

"Why?" I ask.

"I can speak Common in ninety-eight dialects, and even I have not thought it practical to master Old Heliopolitan. No one speaks it except maybe two hundred families of Erebos."

"Medical?"

A Yellow pipes up from behind his optical display. "He has no signs of military-grade implantation. No foreign elements in his person, nor radiation marking except minor radiation poisoning. His blood pressure is low. Heart is abnormally powerful: twenty-five beats per minute, and shows significant signs of Mithridatism, a practice common in secondary Aureate families as emulation of the more significant families."

"Maniacs," Harnassus mutters. "Poisoning yourself is now fashion?"

"Been hot on the Palatine and Venus for years," Screwface says. "I slipped Atalantia a full dose of methracene, and all she got was a brief bout of bloody emesis."

The Yellow plods on. "While we cannot divine if he has razor-pattern calluses owing to the burns on his hands, he has never borne a Peerless Scar. There is no sign of facial skin grafting or bone reconstruction to cover an existent one. His wounds are consistent with his story. His brain scans do not show signs of Securitas conditioning; however, his limbic system has some unusual synaptic activity which may be signs of childhood trauma and memory repression but would require additional analysis to render conclusive. Overall, he is an extremely healthy adult Aureate between eighteen and twenty-three years old."

"So what you are all saying is that he is telling the truth. Or lying very well," I say. "Let's find out which. Screw, I want your eyes on this."

62

LYSANDER

The Warlord and the Libertine

ALTERATION IN VOCAL PATTERNS, unnatural stillness, timing lag between verbal statements and physical expression, distancing language, linear left eye drift, abnormal gesticulation, extraneous over-explanation, pupil dilation, swallowing, grooming gestures, head canting, pulse rapidity, irregular blinking.

These are some of the most obvious symptoms of lying that are drilled into Securitas agents in order to drill them out. To become a full-fledged Venator or frumentarius, one must have a ninety percent success rate in telling a lie to an instructor. Of course, I passed Grandmother's exam when I was six.

So it is with droll amusement that I stare down the optic reader of their robotic lie detector and think nothing much of it. It is profoundly large, almost the size of a small man, chrome, spherical, floating, with a hulking red eye. It is grandiosely named BloodHound XTC-1400, a product of Sun Industries, which no doubt cost Skyhall billions in research and development money to old Regulus. I can understand the investment. In a war where each side wields hundreds of thousands of informants and covert agents, it is as good as a guillotine.

But for all this new civilization's love affair with technology, they've been seduced by their own cleverness and fail to understand the simple truth: lying is not a science, it is an art. And art will always be a human language.

I was under observation when we rose over the city wall under heavy fire; when Darrow jumped out with Alexandar bleeding everywhere;

when they took me on a stretcher to their medBay; when they treated my burns and wounds; when they asked me questions while I was drugged with narcotics; when I showered; when I ate steak, potatoes, and greens laced with some mild inhibition inhibitor in my saferoom; when armed guards escorted me to be interviewed casually; when I gave a formal interview to two ethereal Pinks; when a handsome Gold Howler interrogated me; when I used the restroom; and when I walked through the hall to sit in this white room for two hours as their little toy investigated my story.

They are not measuring lies now. They are cross-referencing current patterns with "normal" patterns from their recordings by asking a mix of old and new questions. It is a fruitless endeavor.

"How did you come to be captured by the Gorgons?"

"I stepped on a landmine while trying to put your men out of their misery."

"You killed them?"

"One. Have you ever seen a man impaled?"

"You did not try to save their lives?"

"Have you ever seen a man impaled?"

"How did you kill them?"

"With a scorcher."

"What type?"

"I don't know."

"Where did you get it?"

"It was my father's."

"And you do not know the type?"

"It was a pistol."

"What are the names of your parents?" the machine asks in the fifteenth line of inquiry about my parents. It is the first time it has asked for their names.

"Actus au Salan and Leticia au Vitruvius." Real people. Real family. Paid off upon the three visits I made to Mercury to substantiate my identity. Thank Jove Grandmother was paranoid of assassination.

I would be concerned if I didn't know that years ago, when my grandmother died, my godfather activated a protocol which erased the census records of all Golds, fearing the Rising would use the list as an assassination tool. Their sole verifier for my tale is a man wildly popular with the lowColors of Mercury and invaluable to their cause, who is no doubt being questioned in another room in a much less menacing fashion as to whether he knows Cato au Vitruvius.

Glirastes will be shocked to hear the name. But when he does, he will know I am alive. And that man has never wished harm upon me. Even if they press him, a partial truth is hard to detect as a lie, because it comes from memory instead of the creative center of the brain. An entirely different physiological reaction. In any case, artists are fantastic liars.

"When did you first meet Glirastes?"

"In Tyche at his offices."

"Did you seek the meeting?"

"Yes."

"How old were you?"

"Six? Seven?"

"Why did you seek the meeting?"

"He built the Water Gardens. The Library of Erebos. The Water Colossus. The Ocular Sphere. He's a god here, as Oranges go."

"Why were you in Tyche?"

"My parents were doing something. I don't remember what. They liked parties. I know that."

"Why Vitruvius?" the machine asks instead of the perfectly functional Green and Pink humans sitting behind it. These people. First the mines, now interrogations. They're literally roboticizing themselves to death.

"My mother was . . . well, it's embarrassing." The machine doesn't care. It just watches. "She made a bit of a cuckold out of my father from the start, metaphorically, then literally. Her family was older. So . . ."

"How did you overpower the Fear Knight?"

"Overpower? I didn't."

"Rephrasing: how did you come to render him unconscious?"

"I hit him on the head with a figurine and then I choked him. He makes figurines. He is an absurd man."

"Why was he showing you figurines?"

"I don't know."

"Did you view his interest in you to be sexual in nature?"

"Sexual?"

"Did he attempt to have intercourse with you?"

"You've seen my face. I look like ground hummingbird tongue. Would you fornicate with me?"

"I ask the questions here," the machine replies.

The door slams open and over two meters of terror walks in as if it intends to stomp the room in half. The techs behind the machine scramble to salute as Darrow pushes the machine to the side. "Can it work in the corner?" he asks.

"Yes, Imperator."

"Then why is it jammed up to his face?"

"It's on intimidation setting, sir."

"Bloodydamn toaster." Darrow pushes the billion-credit machine into the corner like he's setting a rotund child in timeout. "Stay," he says to it, pointing a finger. He looks around for a chair. One appears at the door, carried by a tiny Red girl with Drachenjäger bolts. They're using children in their armies now.

Did she help kill my men?

"Uncle." She gestures to the chair.

Interesting. Kieran's eldest then, Rhonna. A lancer now, like Alexandar. She looks excited. She smiles at me. I return it in blithe fashion.

"Thank you." Darrow sighs down into the chair as if he had the weight of twenty million people on his shoulders, which may be an understatement. "Get out of here, Rhonna. I know you're dying to see the hero."

She blushes. "I am not."

"LYING," the machine bleats from the corner.

Darrow smirks. "Get."

The Red child scampers to the door, turns in a very military-like fashion and salutes, not Darrow but me. "Alexandar sends his gratitude. Be nice to him, Uncle. He looks about to piss himself." She shuts the door and the killer of Octavia, Aja, and my godfather turns his eyes on me. He wields them like sledgehammers. Yet there is some relatable quality there in those carved organics. Some weariness that lacks pretension and would make you think he's an everyman instead of a warlord who has started a crusade that has claimed two hundred fifty million lives and counting.

"Long day," he says.

"It would seem."

I look down to signify submission. Then up to signal bravery. Then down, as Cato realizes he can't match a legend's gaze. Darrow is used to this, and I make sure my hands play their proper role, knowing very well how the Jackal lost his hand. That was always my favorite scene from the recordings. But unlike the Jackal, I won't taunt him or try to appear anything other than what he wants me to be, and I dare not risk sticking my head in a meatgrinder by attempting to extract information from Darrow.

"May I just say it is an honor to meet you," I say.

"Is it?"

"I've watched all your holos. My favorite is still when you took the *Vanguard*."

"The *Pax*," he corrects.

"Of course. Not necessarily a fan of *all* your work, but you have *style*."

He grimaces. "Those holos are illegal on Mercury."

"So are Storm Gods, my goodman! Sorry. Too soon?"

"Millions died in that hypercane, and you jest."

"To be fair, you did it. But what is the north coast to me? Tyche, the Children, it's all for new-money arrogants."

He looks about to say something, but bites it back. "You don't strike me as our usual recruit."

"Recruit? No. Gods, me, a soldier? Don't be ridiculous, my goodman. I'm not nearly Martian enough for all that terror."

"No?" He already wants to be rid of me, a thousand things on his mind. Good. I'll fit into his gestalt. "You brought something dear back to me, Cato. In a way . . . *you* gave my army hope again. Alexandar saved eighty-three thousand four hundred and twenty-six souls in Tyche."

"Did he? He never mentioned it."

"No?" Darrow smiles at that, almost as a father would. "Throw in the sadist knight and it's the best bloodydamn present I've been given since my wife gave me this beauty." He sets his hand on the famous white blade. It is inert and coiled around his arm like a snake. "So you can understand if I'm a little suspicious how a self-confessed libertine from . . . was it Erebos, brought me all these presents when ten million professional soldiers and my Howlers could not."

"Maybe you should ask them that question," I say.

He laughs. "You're funny, but not very likable, are you? I can see why you're Glirastes's type."

"May I ask what you plan to do for me?"

"For you?"

"Yes, I assume I'm entitled to some sort of reward. I mean, you did say I did what ten million men could not." I give my most self-satisfied smile.

"You want a reward? Have you looked outside, man?"

"No. I don't have windows in my cell."

I think he wants to punch my head off my neck. "Gods, I hate you people," he says. His patience is thinner than usual. "If it were up to me, I would lock you away, humanely, until this is all over. I am short on time and the last thing I need is another spice in the pot. But as it is, you happen to be friends with a very . . . *temperamental* Master Maker whose services I require. And he has argued for your release due to your actions. Let's set that straight. I have no intention of releasing you. The streets of Heliopolis are no place for . . ."

"Gold libertines?"

"More like Gold corpses." He lets that sit. "My men lost a good deal of friends, and the impalement has . . . made them reflexive. But I also don't want you here in my headquarters. Friend of Glirastes or not, I don't know you, and I've taken enough risks. So I will give you to him on several conditions: you do not leave the grounds of his estate and you submit to inspections whenever my guards at his villa ask you to."

"That's acceptable to me. He has a fine villa. Have you ever walked through the orchard there? He has the most lovely orchid gazebo at the center."

He stares at me. "Right. Well, take care, Cato au Vitruvian."

"Vitruvius. No reward then?" I ask as he reaches the door.

He sighs. "What do you want?"

"Several Pinks would do right prime. Come now, my goodman, surely you don't abstain completely. What man could!"

"Say that again." He takes a step back toward me. I look at the ground. "That's what I thought."

Accompanied by Republic legionnaires and a fleet of aides, Glirastes waits for me beside a large fountain of Laocoön and his sons in the foyer of the Mound. I can scarcely believe it is him. The bald Master Maker has always been slender, but now his aspect borders on cadaverous. Amongst the slurry of modern uniforms, his crimson linen robe with silver brocade makes him seem an out-of-place actor from a vulgar Plautusian play. When he sees me, those narrow Orange eyes ignite.

"Cato au Vitruvius, my lad, my heart!" he cries, and I am swallowed in crimson linen. I feel like I am hugging a skeleton. He pulls back to look up at me. The last time we met, he was a half meter taller than me. Now it is the reverse. "Your face . . ."

"A mere souvenir of a ghastly affair," I reply. "Perish the memories."

"Yes, let them perish indeed. You have quite the adventure to share. Let us away."

63

DARROW

Unremarkable

Thraxa watches Cato and Glirastes board the flier.

"You saw how he knocked Drusilla's bike into the hold," she says. "That's some damn fine flying from a Pixie." She turns back to me. "If you gave me two minutes with Glirastes he'd have been begging to get back to work."

"You didn't see the man," Harnassus says. "It's like his prodigal son has returned. He was catatonic at the idea Cato might be a spy. Thinks we'll torture him or put him in a hole. If we didn't give him to the old cretin, who'd finish the project?"

"You," Thraxa says.

"I wish I could," he replies.

I watch Cato as the door shuts. "What do you think?" I ask Screw.

"Nothing remarkable there. Just a Pixie twit. Still . . ."

"Agreed."

One thing troubles me. Alexandar took me through their escape. If Cato is so unremarkable, how is it that he survived and soldiers like Crastus and Drusilla did not? Luck only goes so far. "Screw put a monitor spike in him when loading him with anti-rads," I tell Thraxa and Harnassus. "You're both right. We need our Master Maker. But more important, we need to know if he is *our* Master Maker. We'll watch and listen. Whether he's Atalantia's spy or just a provincial asshole, if Glirastes has gone sour we'll find out through that Pixie right there."

64

LYSANDER

To Master a Maker

Lady Beatrice, the home of Glirastes, is a wonder. Perched several hundred meters up the face of a mountain cliff overlooking the sea, the marble and glass monument to the bizarre would often be seen floating over the Bay of Sirens during the gentle spring months alongside the pleasure craft of the rich and famous. Now, with fuel monopolized by the Rising military, its womanly shape rests on its landing foundations.

It is colder than I remember. The little details have been forgotten. Flowers rot in vases, scum floats in shallow fountains, rooms are dusty and unlit, apples rot on the orchard grass. Much of Glirastes's staff, I learn, have been pressed or have volunteered for service with the Rising. Many more were lost in his offices in Tyche or excused for security concerns.

Glirastes himself mirrors the house. He is guarded and faded.

He would not speak to me in the shuttle except to extend the ruse. I took his lead, understanding that they likely fixed me with a monitor spike.

"You remember Exeter, of course," he says to me as we are greeted at the landing pad by his valet. Exeter is a spindly, bone-pale man with a cadaverous face as emotive as concrete. Few know he is the administrative genius behind Glirastes's architectural empire. In the three springs I spent with Glirastes, I've only seen the eerie Brown smile once. It was early spring and the apple blossoms were in bloom and a mother bluebell was building a nest.

"Of course, always a pleasure. Are you still collecting those queer insects?" I ask.

"I fear I haven't the time for passions these last years, *dominus*," Exeter says. "However, my collection has grown since—"

"He doesn't want to hear about your eerie collection, Exeter. It is immensely creepy," Glirastes says. Republic guards loiter in the foyer. "Exeter will see you to your room, Cato."

"I rather hoped to have a discussion with you."

"I have work to do. I will see you at supper, if I have time."

"It is important . . ."

"I said if I have time."

Knowing the spike will record all conversation via vocal vibrations, and cameras will record all the rest, I play the part of a libertine and treat myself to a long bath in the guest suite.

Inside, my clock is ticking. Four days before the strike. Four days and I sit in a bath of lavender oil. It takes me back to the horror of the impalement, and I puzzle over the enigma that is the Fear Knight. He is likely being tortured at this very moment. Why would he trust me with his life on so thin a plan? Could he possibly care so much for the people of Heliopolis? Do true servants of the Society exist now only in the most deplorable form?

After the bath, I stare at my face in the bathroom mirror. I do not recognize myself. The desert has weathered my visage and stripped away much of its youth. My right cheek is sunken and peeling from sunburn. Carefully, I take the resFlesh off my left cheek. The burn is livid. Drained of fluid, it gives the appearance of melted pink wax. It is not as grotesque as it must have been in the desert, but chunks of metal are still embedded too deeply in the drooping skin to be removed by anyone but an expensive surgeon or carver. The eye has gone smoky white. I am not repulsed. I always thought Golds who kept their scars to be a bit vain. But I understand it now. Too much has always been made of my looks, as if I earned them by virtue of being born.

This I earned. This is mine.

That night, Glirastes's rose quartz table is set for one. I eat in silence, catered to by three servants. If they remember me, they do not show it. My old friend never comes.

The next morning, I learn he has not returned from his labor in the city. I spend my time in leisure, walking the orchard, swimming in his pool, conversing with the Rising guards, as much as they will talk to a Gold. Most want to kill me on sight. But I learn their patterns, and I yearn to investigate Glirastes's domed workshop, but I dare not.

After lunch, I walk the house, bouncing a rubber ball as I go, careful to remain frivolous. I let it bounce awkwardly off a step and chase the ball down a hallway into his library. There, I thumb through his dusty books and play games on a hologrid, and when I tire of them, I make my way up the spiral staircase of the tower, poking around until I stumble upon his old golden telescope that looks down at the city.

With a yawn, I look through, and make my first surveillance.

Stretching north nearly as far as the eye can see sprawls an architect's delight of basilicas, temples, forums, triumphal arches, historical columns, amphitheaters, and the great Hippodrome. Only the distant storm wall does not shine white in the sun. In the western city, Corinthian-inspired office spires, broken only by parks, viaducts, and amphitheaters, stretch all the way to the Bay of Sirens. The mountains cup the fabled city in their loving palms. Their craggy summits are tipped white with snow and festooned with gun batteries. Their ranges stretch hundreds of kilometers, impassable by any land army.

To take the city by conventional means, Atalantia would lose millions of men she needs for her campaign. Her chemical option is not so insensible strategically, considering her losses in the battle on the Ladon.

But it is shortsighted and immoral.

When last I was here, the air above Heliopolis was clear but for the sparkling of an occasional yacht or policing units. Now it is mobbed by an ugly flood of heterogenous military vessels, haulers, and civilian rickshaws. The boulevards beneath teem with even more traffic and pedestrians. The city is near bursting with wounded and refugees. Military camps and field hospitals cover the parks and fill amphitheaters where low and high alike once gathered with chilled wine to watch Sophocles's tragedies free of charge. Troops jog through the Via Triumphia where victorious charioteers would parade their steeds to the wild acclaim of the crowds.

To the southwest, on the outer limits of the sprawling city, I see Heliopolis's spaceport. Beyond the smaller torchShips and destroyers, dwarfing even the mountains, lies a mound of metal.

The *Morning Star.*

Thousands of engineers work to repair her hull. Flights of haulers ferry fresh armaments from the southern missile factories to the space-port. They unload the missile boxes on skiffs suspended on gravity cushions to funnel into the ship's port side.

Heliopolis is much as one would imagine it to be: preparing for a siege.

However . . . Darrow knows he would never survive one.

So I pay close attention to the spaceport. There is an aberration in the pattern that sticks out like a loose thread.

I look back at the skiffs unloading the missiles, use the telescope's relative positional measuring system on all forty of the unloading skiffs, yawn, and abandon the telescope tower for a book of poetry. My mind whirs as I stare at the words on the page. Those skiff models have a de-fault 0.7-meter gravity cushion from the ground. More than half were at 0.4 meters according to the telescope. I calculate the volume of the mis-sile boxes, and the mass that the *pilum* missiles should make. It does not account for the 0.3-meter sag. Not even close. Something else is in them, something at least five times as heavy. But what? Full to the brim, it would take something with a density of at least twenty grams per cubic centimeter.

There are only a few relevant elements with military application that are dense enough to fit in the volume of those missile boxes and have enough mass to account for the substantial sag in the gravity cushion. Osmium is too rare here, and to account for the high mass, it would need to be in its pure state, which would be ridiculous because it is nearly impossible to machine-form in that state. There's plutonium, of course, which could be part of the puzzle, but why hide plutonium? Why the deception?

I lean toward iridium.

Iridium is a hard transition metal three times as dense as iron. It is often used in X-ray optics and as a contact metal because of its resistance to arc erosion. More importantly, it is used in radioisotope thermoelec-tric generators because it can withstand operating temperatures up to 2,000 Celsius. Unless they've nonsensically changed the default gravity cushions on only half the skiffs, or unless Darrow is making substantial repairs to the *Morning Star*'s reactors, which I can assume he is not be-cause that does not explain the deception, he is either building a massive secondary generator or a sustained EMP device of unprecedented scale.

I close the poetry book.

That night, Glirastes is absent again. A Thessalonican Chianti is served with lamb drizzled with rosemary-infused olive oil. The wine is rancid. I spit it across the table after my first sip. Exeter appears from nowhere. "Is the wine not to the *dominus*'s satisfaction?"

"No," I say, "it is detestable."

"It is our finest vintage, *dominus*. Thessalonica '35."

"How embarrassing for your taste buds. Is the cellar in the same place? I'll pick my own wine, since you seem incapable of basic competency."

I stalk past him and throw open the cellar door, which is located in the mouth of a freestanding merman statue.

Rounding the corner at the cellar's bottom stair, I follow a light to the back and find Glirastes waiting for me amongst dusty wine racks with a bottle of champagne. He pops it as I enter. "I believe champagne is in order when one returns from the grave," he says. His hug is more sincere this time. He clings to me. "My old young friend, you're a sight for weary eyes. Don't make that face, these walls down here are quite impenetrable to that little spy trinket. Quicksilver is such an idiot. Mass-produces everything, no individual artistry. Very gauche in his spirit selection as well. We haven't much time, so let us be quick."

I sit and share the champagne and answer his barrage of questions. When I have finished, he leans back and traces the rim of his champagne flute with his pinky. "That is quite a tale. All that to come here. All that to confront your nemesis? Didn't you read the Tragedians, boy? Don't you know how this quest for revenge will end? What if he recognized you!"

"Wrecking balls seldom stop for conversations," I say.

"Yes. You can practically see that Red girl hanging in his eyes, can't you? Gorydamn Nero. Couldn't just slap her on the wrist. I blame him for all this. Him and that idiot Fabii. And that idiot Bellona. Frankly, your ranks are replete with idiots. So many in fact, one might suspect if they were a little poorer, a little more victimized, a little more burdened with trial, they might have had the common sense to band together instead of sniping each other in an operatic game of emotional suicide chess. To make matters worse, it hasn't changed. Not a bit. They still bicker. Carthii and Saud. Votum and everyone. And you expect them to hold hands with the Rim!" He laughs. "You've always been a romantic."

"I thought it was a fellowship of two," I reply.

"Oh, shut up. You could have contacted me," he says, thinly trying to hide his grief. "You could have let me know you weren't dead."

"You have to understand what I saw." He raises an eyebrow, always curious about Palatine gossip, especially the firsthand sort. It's not his most noble quality. "I saw Aja hacked to ribbons and Octavia ripped here to here." I trace the path Darrow's blade made. "I saw the Jackal's bombs detonating, and watched as Darrow pulled his tongue out. I saw my godfather ally with Darrow for the briefest flicker to down Lilath au Faran's ships before they destroyed my home."

He shudders.

"I saw all those people with all their plans strangled by the webs they wove. I wanted out. To his credit, Darrow spared me, and sent me away with Cassius."

"All this time, I thought he might have," Glirastes says. "I would not have helped him if I really thought he murdered you."

I'm not sure if I believe that, but he does. "So I disappeared," I say.

"And did you find what you were looking for? Did you find peace?"

"It's not out there. At least not for me. Some men can stare at their feet and pretend the world isn't falling apart. I cannot."

"And behind the Grimmus banner, you rally? Atalantia is your savior?" he sneers. "She is a monster. A woman with a cape of cadavers as long as the Via Gloria. You know that or you wouldn't be here." He squints at me. "She's going to use atomics, isn't she?"

"Chemicals," I admit.

He grows terribly quiet. "If that is the woman you follow, then the worlds are already lost."

"There are certain realities—" I begin.

He interrupts. "Stop. I've heard that all before."

"From yourself?" I ask. "Is that why you helped Darrow?"

"Yes!" he snaps, slamming his glass down so hard on the table it shatters and opens a gash on his hand. He stares at the blood seeping out. "Yes. It wasn't supposed to be that way. Gold became . . . cruel after the Fall. Beyond cruel. As if it was their laxity that led to rebellion. Darrow is right in some things, you know. The metal miners here barely live past thirty. And the slaves . . . they actually call them that now. Not contractors or pioneers. *Slaves*." He shakes his head. "I just didn't realize the price my planet . . . my home would have to pay for my spasm of hope."

"Is it worth the price?" I ask.

"What's the alternative? Atalantia? Purges and camps? No. I'd rather we all burn nice and quick than line up for her pleasure." He stands, ending the conversation. "I know you mean well. But if I've learned anything, meaning well isn't enough. Whatever you thought I could do for you, I can't do it. I won't. Nothing good comes of good intentions."

He puts a hand on my shoulder as he departs.

I tried to let it be his choice to help me, but in the end he leaves me no alternative but to force him as my grandmother taught.

"I was there in Tyche when the water came in," I lie. He quarter-turns to me. "Thousands poured to the Water Colossus to seek its heights for shelter, knowing the work of Glirastes would give them safety. Glirastes's genius would give them shelter. When the wave came in, it swamped the Colossus. For a moment, I thought it would pull even it out to sea. But those people were right to believe in your work. As the waves rolled back, your Colossus endured, but of the people . . . nothing remained. Why do you think Atalantia is using chemicals instead of nukes? She couldn't buy you all those years ago. So now she'll take all your precious works for herself."

I return upstairs to finish my dinner without appetite. My words will worm their way into Glirastes's brain. When I am finished with the meal, Exeter comes to the table. He looks at the bottle I brought up. "I trust your choice in wine was satisfactory?"

"It's a stubborn vintage."

"I have faith in it, *dominus*. And in your discerning taste. Perhaps a nightcap, of the fortifying variety?"

I wake in the night to hear the expected sound of bare feet in the hallway. There's a peculiar wheezing sound from my arm where they injected me with anti-rads. My door opens and Glirastes stands in the doorway illuminated by the shadowy light of a green glowlamp. "The spike is frozen. To them, you'll appear to be sleeping through the night. I want to show you something."

The green light casts eerie shadows on the artifacts along the walls as Glirastes leads me down a dark hallway. Rain lashes the windows. Low thunder groans.

Glirastes stops at the end of a hall near a large wooden door with an old-fashioned lock. He searches a huge ring for the right key and unlocks it with a satisfying *clunk*. Lights blossom in the darkness, and I smile. The room is as delightful as in memory. Domed with a rendering of deep space. Books lining every wall. I remember the first he gave me: Silenius's *Meditations*. Antiquated machines of distant ages stand covered in dust. He fusses over the dozen teacups scattered about the room. "Really should let the servants in here. But they may twist the wrong knob, then *boom*." He slams a hand on the table. "All dead. Now, where did I put it? Ah. This way." Behind a 3-D marble printer and a statue of himself with an absurdly generous phallus, he pulls back a canvas covering, unsettling a cloud of dust, to reveal a model of a sphere city as big as the two of us put together. Intricate parks and public buildings wind together, defying gravity as the surface of the city bends upside down on itself to create the spiral impression of a human eye. He waves his hand over the pupil, and the city begins to turn clockwise. He sits in a drawing chair to watch me walk around the model.

"It is . . ." I begin, and pretend I cannot find the right words. Of course I remember his favorite poems.

"It is what?" he asks in trepidation.

"Without flaw."

"Use more sophisticated language."

I reply:

> *"Cities and Thrones and Powers*
> *Stand in Time's eye,*
> *Almost as long as flowers,*
> *Which daily die:*
> *But, as new buds put forth*
> *To glad new men,*
> *Out of the spent and unconsidered Earth,*
> *The Cities rise again."*

"I missed you, lad." He sighs back in his chair. "I haven't had a good critic in years."

"What is your city called?"

"Oculus."

I circle the model. "I imagine it's meant to be in orbit?"

"Yes! Or deep space. I knew you would understand." He runs a finger down a central aerial boulevard. "It was my last commission before the

Fall. Needless to say, there was not much demand for cities with personality after that."

"Who commissioned it?"

"Regulus ag Sun, old uppity Quick himself. I sent him a finished model just like this one, but we never broke ground. It was to be my greatest work. One I'll never see completed now. You might have noticed there is something whimsical about it." He smiles. "He asked me to build a city for a child who had never seen anything else. Of course it was just an expression, but I took it to heart. I based it off of your eye, in fact. The only child to seldom annoy me. Of course I never had children. Didn't have the time or the inclination, but I always assumed, vainly, that mine would be as curious as you were."

He must be shaken deeply to presume to say that aloud to me.

It really is one of the most marvelous of his creations, this oculus. For all its grace, it speaks of wild, hopeful ambition.

"Darrow didn't even look twice at it when he came here," Glirastes murmurs. "He sees me as nothing more than a tool. I suppose it is human nature. Golds saw me as a novelty to flaunt. Mids let their jealousy label me a social climber. The lows loved me, then hated me, then loved me. All of them thought they understood my work. And maybe they did. But only you really ever understood me."

"You were the one who told me a great artist can never be fully understood," I reply. "Even you must suffer the tedium of a medium."

"Did I ever tell you the story of the blind Copper?"

"I don't believe so." Of course, I know the story. It was in his Securitas file, gleaned from his own journals, and was the key to my story of the waves and the Colossus. I forgo a stool and sit on the floor, just as I did as a child. He wants to see me as a curious boy, not a scarred, cunning judge.

"When I was a young apprentice, my Master Maker told me of a Copper with a disease of the eye. One which surpassed even our civilization's ingenuity to cure. When he felt his vision finally fading, he went to a bench and sat before the Library of Heliopolis. Each day he went, and his world grew smaller and darker until one day his sight was gone entirely. For years afterward he would go to that bench and sit, and in the darkness he could still see the green copper dome, the Philosopher Kings in all their marbled glory, the Water Gardens and the Orbital Torch. Of all the things he wanted to remember, it was the beauty of architecture." He sighs. "My master told me the story to impress the importance of our craft.

"I was a busy mind. Busier still when I found my first taste of celebrity. Twice a week, I would attend the dinner parties of Aureate. It might seem common to you," he says with small embarrassment. "But imagine what it meant to me. An Orange from the Sledge. A guest of Votum and Augustans and even Lunes. I was treated with dignity by the finest company in the worlds. The Sovereign herself called me a genius. In their names, I built monuments, libraries, cities.

"Yet at the unveiling of my greatest work . . ."

"The Water Colossus."

"Correct." He continues. "I felt empty standing there listening to the rich tell me what beauty I had made. I could see it. But I could not feel it. I don't know why, but I remembered the story of that Copper. I sought out my master, and discovered after many weeks of searching that the blind Copper still lived.

"I went to visit him. He was a ward of the state by then, living to die in a government Loyalty Ward. I asked him about the story, and he laughed. 'I didn't go for the building,' he said, 'I went to feed the pigeons, and watch the children play in the water, and the families line up for sweets, and to see boys flirt with girls.'"

Glirastes says nothing, and for a long time, we listen to the rain on the windows.

"He went to see life," Glirastes says at last. "From that moment to this, that is why I make—to see the life that grows around the dead stone I stack. For what is a building without its audience? What is a city without its people? Now . . ." He traces the veins in his hands. "Now that life disappears. Those people become dust. Soon there will be nothing left but my stone and the bones of my city." His glassy eyes find mine. "I'm not a traitor, no matter what you think. No matter what Atalantia calls me. I thought Darrow's crusade impractical, but inevitable. When he took the planet, I helped him, because I thought I could protect life. I failed. *I failed.* So terribly. He told me he would only use the Storm Gods for electrical interference and cloud cover, but he lied and now Tyche is gone."

His eyes follow motes of dust floating through the light. His robes make soft sounds as he leans forward and runs his hands over his head.

"I've been building something with his engineers. Something that will help his army escape the planet they broke. But even if he does escape before Atalantia attacks, what will become of us? Are the buildings to be saved, because they are rare and beautiful, and the people put upon the pale because they are common?" His hands drop from his head and he looks up at me like a drowning old man. "I don't know what to do, Lysander. Tell me. What am I to do?"

"You can trust in me," I reply.

"The last time I trusted a man, Tyche was swallowed by the sea."

"Then trust the boy you knew."

His eyes are forlorn as they search mine. "Is he still alive, after all this horror?"

"Yes," I say, reaching up to fold his thin hands in mine. "And he needs your help. The people must show Atalantia that they did not abet the enemy. That they did not simply wait to be saved. They saved themselves. I promise she will see that. I promise we will show that to the worlds with spectacle they have never before seen."

There's a knock at the door. "Begone, Exeter!"

Exeter enters anyway. "Apologies, sir, but the *dominus* requested a nightcap of the fortifying variety." He strides into the room, followed by the entirety of Glirastes's remaining staff.

"What is the meaning of this?" Glirastes shouts. "Can't you see we are—"

Exeter goes swiftly to a knee and bends his head to me. The lowColor staff join him. "The Heir of Silenius has returned," Exeter proclaims. "The loyal stand ready, my Sovereign."

I take Glirastes's hands in mine. "There are more men and women in this city who believe in the order of the Society more than the empty promises of the Rising. I do not know them. But you know them, and they know you. Pick the most loyal and the most influential of each Color, and tell them the Heir of Silenius has returned. He has not forgotten them, and he asks them to join him in taking back their rightful home from the Martian marauders. Not for Votum. Not for Atalantia. But for Heliopolis and the Society."

65

LYRIA

Ulysses

"**W**HAT DO YOU THINK?" Volga asks me. Sleet rolls in from the sea to pour down on us. We crouch low behind a jagged scree of rocks, peering through scavenged oculars at a small fishing town. Several hundred homes lie scattered on the coastline like raisins in crumbling pastry. The weathered buildings are made from local rock and domed with metal roofs capped with winter sludge. Warm light glows from slits in their shutters. I scan the air for the Vox patrols that have been looking for us over the past weeks. The sea bucks and heaves, rocking the few small boats left in the harbor. Nothing rides the wind but sea hawks and gulls. I imagine them rushing home, just like the villagers, before the squall comes in full.

I wish we were in one of those little houses, maybe sitting by the fire with big blankets and socks. Not the thin polymer socks they gave out at the camp. The wool ones they gave us in the Telemanus household, so thick you can curl your toes in them.

"Look at that, the Red was right," Victra says. She jabs her finger at three long metal poles rising up from a gray building hunched along the promontory north of the town. It looks like some old military installation. Several old fliers are parked in front of it, and from the snow piling up, they look like they haven't been moved in days. "There is a radio tower here."

I could feel its vibrations through the parasite. Growing in intensity as we crept nearer across the highlands. Aside from those vibrations, the parasite has been quiet since I saw Harmony. But by the fact that Victra even listened to me, I know she knows what's in my skull.

"All this trepidation is giving me cankers," she says. "Much as I'd like to give birth in a freezing glen like a sow, it would be a dreary inconvenience if wolves ate my little girl before she could even walk. We use the array to boost our signal, we're in my fortresses at Hippolyte or Attica by tomorrow morning."

As if to taunt her, the highland wolves howl in the distance. Or is it just the wind? She looks more annoyed than afraid. To be fair, I'd pity the wolves that tried to make a meal out of this woman. She's tougher than nature itself. Nine months pregnant, she's set a pace I can barely match.

"I was not asking you," Volga says in exhaustion.

"Of course, why ask the Peerless Scarred who has led two Iron Rains when there's a perfectly ignorant mine lass to consult for strategic advice?"

"Because you are reckless!" Volga says. "You act like you carry an army everywhere. You would not make it two days as a freelancer. Now be quiet! Lyria found this place, so Lyria's opinion matters more than yours right now."

Victra sulks back against the rocks, disturbing the snow in a black-berry shrub above her. Even after two weeks of plodding through rain and snow and sleeping under the shelter of trees, she manages to look glamorous. Her jade earrings, which she refuses to remove, blaze against the snow. Meanwhile, I think I've somehow got fleas.

By her count, Victra should have had the baby weeks ago, though how many she doesn't say. I'd pull it out of her myself if I were sure her private bits wouldn't bite my hand off at the elbow. "I nearly wish you'd let the Red Hand find me. Would have been preferable to watching you two bumble about like drunk mummers as I starve to death."

"You ate all the rations," I snap, scratching my head in irritation.

"I'm eating for two. You're barely one."

"And you're the one the Red Hand wants," I reply. "How many of their mines did you own again?"

"Not enough apparently."

"We are all hungry and frustrated . . ." Volga tries. Fig's black orb is nestled under one of her big arms. Though she lost the pack of money in a river crossing, she hasn't let the orb out of her sight since she stole it from the wreckage.

"You should have let me try to kill that deer," Victra sneers at Volga. "Even carrying around this gorydamn asteroid in my stomach, I could have stalked it better than you. Can't hunt. Can't start a fire. Can't navigate by starlight. I swear, you are by far the worst Obsidian I have ever had the displeasure of laying eyes upon. Have you two never been outside before?"

"You told us we couldn't have a fire," I say. "Because of the trackers."

"Immaterial. It's your rank ignorance that matters."

Volga considers making a comment, but somehow her patience prevails. "I will go down and talk to them," she says. Victra and I laugh, then glare at each other. Volga looks offended. "I will call Ephraim. He will come for me."

"You might not give the best first impression," I say gently.

Victra snorts. "She means you look like an electrocuted rock monster."

Volga touches her huge head of hair. "It is the humidity . . ."

"And there is no way I let you call Ephraim fucking Horn. I will go and call my legions in Attica and Hippolyte," Victra says.

"They'll recognize you! You're one of the most famous people in the worlds."

"Yes, I am, aren't I? They'll know I can pay."

"What if there's Red Hand there?" I ask.

"We've watched for three hours."

"Well, they don't exactly wave flags, do they?"

"We lost those trackers days ago. Lost the appetite after I visited their camp." She did, killing four of the ones with nose mods before running back to us cackling. "For all they know, we're forty klicks west of here. I don't see any materiel or transports. If there's any here, we kill them." She fondles the hilt of her razor under her coat like it's a bloodydamn baby itself. "It's not like we need to hold a town council. We just need that transmitter. You're being entirely overcautious."

The fact that she's even letting us have a voice shows how far her pregnancy has progressed. It'll come any moment.

I look down at her belly. "You sure you're up to that sort of thing . . ."

"I'm pregnant, not an invalid."

"You just don't like people being decent to you, do you?"

"Blister. That's what you are. Red, puffy, and irritating. I'm going to go piss, then I'm going to go down there and use that transmitter to call my men. Can't reach my main force in Hippolyte, by the look of that army. But I've a full legion at my fortress in Attica. Fifty thousand of my house troops. If they were doing their jobs, they'd be scouring this countryside by now. But I'll roust those lazy piglets, and we'll be having baths by tomorrow morning, ladies. Then supper till you're both fat as hens. Then back to the kidnapper you go. And I get my loves. And gear up for war."

I glare after her as she stumbles away across the rocks.

"A bath does sound nice," I say.

"Ephraim would come for me," Volga repeats. I remember Ephraim's face when he heard the Sovereign had Volga. But would he try for her twice? I give up guessing and glare at Victra.

"You are doing a good thing," Volga says. "Just think about having that bath and a real meal."

"Oh, leave off. How do you not choke her to death?"

Sleet gathers on her eyebrows as she considers it. "Two nights ago, I thought about it after she called me a geriatric walrus. But I do not think it would work. She fought beside Sefi herself. And Darrow. No, she is too much for me, even now. Unless I was able to shoot her from afar."

"That was a joke."

"Oh." Her eyes flick left. "As was mine."

"Right." I glance back at the village. There's little movement. Likely all huddled inside eating dinner what with this weather. "I don't like it."

There's the sounds of rocks moving behind us. We turn to see Victra stumbling back, fresh annoyance on her face. "Of all the gory inconveniences . . ." She looks up at the weather. With the sleet gathering on her cheeks, and her hair matted back, she makes me think of a statue I saw in Hyperion. Lady Victory, the wife of Silenius the Lightbringer. "Sorry, ladies," she says with a wry grin. She holds up glistening fingers. "Little monster's coming. Looks like she's a mover."

"That settles it," I say, knowing we can't risk going into the old installation. But we need shelter. Me probably even more than Victra's newborn will. Thing will probably come out with fangs and a silk cloak.

I rush down the scree. At the edge of the village, a stooped old Red chisels ice off the roof of his stone house. I don't see anyone else out, and his house looks large enough and far off enough from the others to not draw too many eyes. "'Lo," I call. He doesn't hear me over the howl of the wind. "'Lo!" He turns to squint down at me through a snow mask. Then he sees the pistol in my hand. "I need your help, brother."

"You askin' or tellin', lass?"

"Tellin', I suppose."

He awkwardly climbs off the roof. "You been out in that?"

"Who's in the house?" I ask.

"None your." He looks to the hills.

"Scorcher says it is my."

"Me kids," he says. He nods to the sky. "Saw the firefight. Who else you got out there?"

I wave Volga and Victra down the hill. They slump forward in the gloom, sticking behind shrubs to keep out of sight of the rest of the town. Volga is less than polite. She lifts the man by his collar and breaches the house holding her rifle like a pistol in one hand and the man dangling in her other. Victra and I follow.

A young girl, maybe twelve, and a boy of sixteen stare at us as we come in, wet and armed. The boy bolts upright from the table and grabs a heavy mug, nearly spilling his soup. The girl stares at us from the kitchen, trembling. Her hands knot the corners of her grease-stained apron.

"Alred, Brea, all's well!" the man says. "All's well. These are . . . new friends."

The boy holds his mug tight, looking between his father and the huge women who've got his father at gunpoint. I kick the door shut and start drawing the curtains.

"Volga, set him down," Victra says.

"We do not know him."

"You're in his home. Be polite. They're just Reds, no offense."

Volga warily sets the Red man down. He smiles nervously. "Strong lass there."

"How quaint," Victra says magnanimously of the small home. She has to bend to not hit her head on the timber crossbeams. "Apologies for the intrusion. I desire hot water, clean cloth, soap, pen, paper, and the hardest liquor you can provide. Fear not, this won't be a hostile interaction unless your manners become as dreadful as the ones to which we've been reduced. By tomorrow morning, you will be one million credits richer, and we will be gone." Volga's already searching the house for weapons and coms. "Take off that absurd domino. Your mask, man. And your name."

Volga finds two old rifles in the cupboard as well as a pistol. She disassembles them in three easy movements and takes small pieces from each for her pockets.

"Cormac O'Vadros." The man pulls off his snow-crusted mask. Despite his shock of white hair, he's not quite so old as I thought. But he is stooped, and his right leg seems janky. Maybe artificial. Deep lines groove his bearded face. He takes in Victra, her bulging waistline, and nods. "'Course. Alred, boil water. Brea, be a good lass and get the linens from your room." Volga follows the girl into the other room as if she were going to get rocket launchers. Cormac gestures to my gun with a twinkle in his eye. "Big gun for a little lass. Think you need it?"

"Depends on you."

"Not what I meant." He nods to Volga and Victra. "You got them. Whatchu need that for?"

I keep the pistol anyway. "Bedroom?"

"Thought you'd never ask." He leads me across the small common room to one of the home's two bedrooms as Volga, finished with her search for now, tries to help Victra out of her wet clothing. Victra slaps her hands away. "Just mind our hosts." She follows us into the bedroom and starts undressing. Cormac watches without expression. Volga comes in, picks him up with one hand and shoves him out the door, back into the common room.

"You expecting visitors?" she asks.

"In this squall?" he says, laughing, but his eyes dart to his children in worry. "Naw. No visitors."

"Good, we will be cozy then."

The sound of their voices muffle as I close the door to a crack. The bedroom is small and simple. A narrow bed with heavy quilts lies in the corner next to a coil heater. A pair of old miner boots like my pa's hang on the wall along with a rusted slingBlade. There's a small crochet on one of the bedside stools and a little glass filled with holly and red winter berries. Must be his wife left it there.

"Where's your wife?" I ask Cormac, opening the door halfway.

"She's out to sea till week's end with the rest o' my kin. Not much for boats meself. I tend the homestead."

Volga takes over the questioning as I shut the door again.

Victra tosses her clothes into the corner. I am startled by the sight of her body. Her back is heavily muscled and broad. It's a history of scars, including two bullet holes along her spine. More scars cover her arms, her buttocks, her powerful thighs. More old wounds than a whole drill-team. Respect.

"Have the contractions started?" I ask, handing her pen and paper I found on the counter.

"You japing?" She grins. "Lost my mucus plug days back. Been having contractions the last thirty klicks."

"You didn't say anything."

"You two worry like hens. Thought I could hold it till we got to the transmitter, but you two are right. Big building. Anything could be in there." She starts writing on the paper, whistling as she does. "You ever been pregnant?" she asks.

"I'm shy nineteen."

"Well, you are Red, anyway. . . ."

"It's like getting punched by a Telemanus. Got a real world breaker in here." She leans naked against the wall, not a lick given for modesty. I strip off the top quilt and make up the bed. She looks up from her writing in amused contempt. "What in Jove's name are you doing?"

"Makin' up the bed for you."

She goes back to writing. "Why?"

"Thought you might want to lay down?"

"I am daughter of Julii," she says without looking up from the paper. "Not some mine wench who gives birth on her back. I stand when I deliver. All I need from you is silence and absence and that water and alcohol to wash my hands. Be polite to our hosts, please."

Chuffed, I slam the door behind me.

In the common room, the water is beginning to boil on the thermal stove. Alred, the boy, glares at me as I ask him to take it into the bedroom. He's a gangly one with a temper. Reminds me of my own brother Dagan. His sister brings her linens out of her room. Small and elfin-faced, she wears the skirts of a woman and a thick shawl. She shuffles nervously as I smile at her.

"What's your name?" I ask her. "Was it Brea?"

She nods.

"Sorry if we're giving you a fright. Promise we're good folk. Just a little lost is all. Where's your ma?"

She looks at the ground.

"She's mute," her father says from the table, where he leans back sipping ale from his mug. "Brea, come here, love." The girl goes and stands next to him. He kisses the back of her head and gives me a grimace. "Been that way for years. Ever since her ma . . ." He squeezes her. She looks anything but comfortable.

There's shouting as Alred delivers the water and booze. He comes back from Julii's tirade flushed red, with a note from Victra. It's just fifty lines of numbers.

"What's this?" I call.

"Cryptogram," she shouts. "Best I could come up with on short notice. Give it to Volga. She can use the array's main uplink to send it. But not while I'm in labor. I need a bodyguard."

"I could take it," I say, peeking through the door.

"Do you know how to force link to the holoNet and send a private encoded message?" I say nothing. "No, so stop trying to prove yourself and let the freelancer earn her keep."

I mutter curses as I cross the room to give Volga her instructions and the cryptogram. "Ah, a cryptogram," she says, one eye on the Reds. I don't like the look of Cormac much either. "Oh, fifty lines. She did this in her head?"

"Apparently."

"Wow."

"Yeah, she knows."

Volga tucks it away and I schlep over to the table to twiddle my thumbs. "Said your name is Cormac?" Volga asks the man from the door. She leans against it like a sentry on duty.

"That's right, love. You got some good Common on you."

"Why shouldn't I?" she asks.

"Didn't mean nothin' by it. Sorry. Always runnin' me gob." He winces and sips from his mug.

He's far younger than I thought he was even on second inspection. Not an old man at all. Maybe thirty. Why's his hair so white? His hands are heavy and scarred. Eyes blood-red and set in a passive, kind face with a natural frown. I tap my foot in agitation. I don't like him one bit.

"I am Volga, this is Lyria," Volga says neutrally. "We're not going to hurt you. I promise. We only need a place for the night. She's in labor."

"Thought Golds hatched out of big metal eggs."

"They do not."

He smiles. "Joke. You could have asked nicely. Woulda put you up. Be criminal to turn out a full-on woman in this." His eyes dart to the drapes over the windows.

"Well, you see . . ." Volga begins.

I interrupt her. "Where you from, Cormac?"

He sighs. "Can me kids go to their room? They don't need to be around women like you." He nods to our guns. Volga looks ashamed.

"Just the little one," she says. "The boy stays where we can see him."

Cormac's son drags a chair close to the fire and sits staring at it with his arms crossed. Brea looks at us, to her father. "Go on," he says with a little smile. "Brea. Go." She looks at the ground and slips away to the room, closing the door with barely a sound.

Cormac sighs. "Addled girl, but sweet. Appreciate the kindness." His chair creaks as he leans back in it. "There was some men lookin' for you. But I reckon you know that. Bad sort."

"Red Hand?" I ask.

"That's right," he says with a solemn face. "Lookin' for a Gold, they said. Victra au Julii. Didn't say anything about the two of you." Volga meets my eyes. "That's her, ain't it? The Julii? They showed us a holo. If they find out you were here . . ."

"They won't," Volga says. "We will not endanger your family."

"We already have," I say. Cormac and I know the rules.

"What's done's done," Cormac says. "Red Hand don't trouble us much, being as we're clan of the Reaper, but since the Alltribe started kicking in their teeth, they come down the coast more often. They'll butcher the village for this. Anyone else see you come in?"

I shake my head, watching him very carefully. "We just need to use your transmitter. Reach Julii's people and it's like we were never here. Can you help us with that?"

"Yut," he says. "Got the code to the building, I do. You wanna go now?"

Seeing something I don't, Volga lets her finger click the safety off her rifle. Her voice goes deep and husky. "You legion?"

He chuckles. "Fourth. Formerly."

"Why formerly? War's still on."

He pulls up his right leg and sets it on the table, jerking his pants up to show a clunky artificial limb. "Got this baby in the Rat War. Now I'm just a fisherman. Speakin' o' which, we got some extra stew and bread if you're hungry."

My stomach growls, but it doesn't seem smart to take food from someone we don't know. Not with the Red Hand crawlin' about. "You think I poisoned me stew before you came in here?" he asks. "That's some swell foresight I got. Go on. I'll sit here, hands where you can see 'em. Even if I was the Fury herself, doubt I'd try much with an Obsidian and a Peerless under me roof with me children."

Warm and filled with soup and fresh bread, I watch Cormac flirt with Volga. He's tied her about his finger with Rat War stories. He seems nice as they come, but so was Ephraim. Volga peeks in periodically on Victra like a worrying maid, and paces as if it was her baby about to be delivered. She only sits back at the table with Cormac and me when Victra yells something with a lot of syllables at her.

Victra's second stage of labor is not long in lasting. The storm comes in full outside as I bring her a glass of water. She chugs it down in one gulp. Sleet clatters its claws against the window. "How are our hosts?"

"I think the girl's sleeping. Boy's just stewin', and Cormac's spinning stories to Volga now."

"You trust him?" Victra asks.

"No. Don't know him. I say we tie him up."

"This is my planet," she says. "I don't fear a man and two children."

"But you got a blood war on you. You know well as I do what that means." She doesn't dismiss me this time.

"If only the world still had manners." She sighs longingly. "That'll be all, thank you."

I don't leave.

"You know, I'm not an idiot," I say. "I've seen more babies born than you have. Delivered half a dozen myself."

She crosses her arms and leans against the wall. Still naked. Her skin lit ruby by the heater's glowing coils. "Let me guess, it's a tribal tradition."

"That's right." I cross my arms. "Me ma taught me, and her ma taught her."

"My mother taught me how to blockade a planet with nothing but asteroids and gravity haulers," she replies.

"And how useful is that now?"

"I'm in labor. Please spare me the recitation of your culture's antiquated but treasured ways. Shut the door behind you. Volga is like a wounded puppy."

I set my shoulders square up with her. "All's I'm saying is it's at least several . . . or more weeks late . . . right? You said that yourself. You might need help."

"All my babies are fashionably late," she replies. She sighs when she sees I'm not leaving. "You deliver that blind one? The one in the Citadel?"

"His name's Liam."

"Was he blind at birth or did you boggle it up?"

"Tryin' to make me cry and run away?" I ask. She was. Words don't stab so deep as they used to. "He was premature. And yeah. I was there. I cut the lifestring with my own hands."

"Lifestring? Quaint. Your sister didn't cut it herself?" she asks in surprise.

"You lot do that?"

She frowns. "Why wouldn't we?"

"I just thought you had doctors. Morphone. Crystal glasses to sip from."

"Please. Only Pixies use morphone and the only person I had in my room when I gave birth to my three girls is the man that put them inside me." She softens and laughs. Maybe she realizes we've got something in common after all. "Hilarious really. I've seen that man pull a knife out of his own eye and keep running. I've seen him face down a Stained and smile. But he was shaking like a leaf soon as he saw me dilate. Like he's never been down *there* before. Men. If I asked him to cut the cord, he'd probably faint. It's the mother's job. You should know that."

"My sister chose who got to cut it," I say. "It's an honor."

"Oh please. It may seem insignificant, but it's enfeebling. It's saying she's too weak to do it herself. It's important to finish the things you start, Blister. Remember that when you have a little squirt. What statement does it make to your baby if you let someone else do it? Lying there with women sopping your brow with wet cloths and preening over you like you're a plague victim?" She wrinkles her nose and juts her jaw upward. "Tigresses don't need nursemaids. Neither should we."

"My sister wasn't weak."

"Maybe not. But she let others convince her she was."

"You do realize we're not all you."

"I'm dreadfully aware of that."

"Act all high and mighty. Fact is you can afford to be brave. If that's what you wanna call it. Bet you had doctors on standby. A whole team, right? It was bloody scary seeing my sister screamin' like that, not knowing if she would die. No blood bags, no plasma."

"Did she hemorrhage?" Victra asks.

I nod. "I didn't know someone had that much blood." Victra says nothing. "I loved her so much. You know? I was afraid. My hands were shakin' on the scissors so bad I thought I'd take out my own eye. Sister's bleedin' there, I thought they'd shoo me out. But all those women were looking at me, waiting for me to do *my* part. And she was smiling, pale as milk. Of all those women, she chose me. *Me*." I shake my head. "It doesn't mean you're weak to ask for help. But we'll do it your way."

I head to the door.

"Harmony has reason to hate me, and you," she says. I stop and turn slightly. "My mother knew of a radiation leak in her clan's mine. Deeming it advantageous from a tax perspective, she chose not to make immediate repairs. Radiation medication *was* distributed to the Gammas via the Laureltide boxes. As I understood it, the intent was for them to sell it to the other clans. Instead, the Gammas hoarded it while the others died due to tribal grudges. I thought my mother's plans derailed. Then she told me that their greed was exactly according to plan. I remember her words to this day. 'They'll be too busy hating each other to ever hate us.' She came down to distribute medicine herself a month later. Benificent."

"And you just let it happen?" I ask, unsurprised by the cruelty of the logic.

"I wasn't who I am now. Why didn't you tell Volga to shoot Harmony? She killed your family. Was it because you thought I would kill Volga before she could pull the trigger?"

"Would you have?"

"Yes. I protect mine above all else, because no one else ever does. So?"

I discovered the truth to her words in my cell.

I've chewed on the question she asks for days as we scrambled across the highlands. I didn't know at the time why I told Volga not to shoot.

There was too much anger and confusion to really suss it. But it wasn't fear. "Harmony will pay the debt she owes me," I say. "Not your baby."

She measures me a long time before speaking. "Revenge is best dealt with a patient hand. With what Fig gave you when she died, you won't have to wait long."

"What is it?" I ask.

"I don't know, not entirely. But it was what made Fig . . . different. *I* am different. I know that. I had things you didn't. But I saw evil too. Only difference is you saw the bottom, I saw the top. I wasn't born the woman I am. *I* made me. That's the problem with your people. You're arrogant. So busy preaching you need a clan to do everything. But you take the clan away, and you fall apart. Like you did in that cell. So easy to blame others for failing you, for leaving you, for mistreating you." She sets her hands on her belly, grimacing at the pain as a spasm flickers across it. "Some things are about the power of one. With what you have in your head, you need to know that. Now, *if* you can exist without tormenting me with sympathy, I'll show you what a woman can do by herself. But first, be a dear, and tell Volga to tie up our hosts." She smiles nastily. "As an unctuous girl once said: we don't know them."

Victra hunches over as the storm rattles the windows, consumed with and by her labor so that nothing exists in the world except the life inside her. Her triceps flex as her hands grip her muscled thighs. Her feet are planted on the stone floor over a thin layer of linens, like she's about to take flight. Her razor waits by her foot.

She is not invulnerable like I thought. She feels the pain. Sweat beads on her upper lip and dangles there, dropping only when a low moan escapes her. It melts into the sound of the storm as it howls through the chimney in the common room. She rolls her head like a fever victim, breathing heavily, scraping her feet on the ground. Muscles spasm in her lower back and around her taut belly. A huge contraction racks her, forcing her to a quarter squat. She tenses there, exhaling a low, primal moan that lasts and lasts until a gush of liquid ruptures out from between her legs and becomes a slow dribble. A tuft of matted hair peeks out. She brings her right hand back behind and between her legs, her left to the front to spread herself as she continues to push. The crown of the baby's head juts through, trickling liquid onto the floor.

Then she brings both hands back around onto her thighs and crouches a little lower for the final effort. The baby's whole head is hanging out. With another sustained push, its shoulders slip through and a purple mass of flesh spurts out.

She brings her arms down and catches the baby at the base of its skull, supporting it as she sweeps it upright while falling to her knees in a motion both complex and instinctive. She sorts the lifestring from the baby's neck as it begins to gurgle, and then cups it in her arms. Victra brings her mouth to her baby's face, sucks to clear the mouth and nose, and then spits on the floor. The baby is blotched and viscous and alive. Its eyes are clamped shut against the dim light of the room. It cries until it finds her nipple, then takes it in its mouth and, cocooned in the arms of its wet, scared mother, grows still.

Victra sways there, in a world of two, rocking the baby so tenderly, so intimately, with such encompassing love that I am unable to look away. They begin to pulse, to throb with color, the warmth inside them or maybe the emotions in me triggering the parasite so that their thermal heat glows in the coolness of the room.

"It's a boy, Sevro," Victra's glowing mouth whispers. "You guessed right."

And for a moment, as I watch, as I see the heat that makes their bodies, the vibrations that form her words, I believe the hero of my brothers can hear his wife, wherever he might be. Just as I believe deep down I could feel the death of Aengus and Dagan and Liam, the last of my family. Neither time nor space can sever the strands of life between those we love, not really. It is not the parasite telling me this. It is my heart. In the room, I feel my father and mother, my sister and my brothers. The joy we had is no lesser for having ended in horror. It is not gone, as I thought it was. It is here. In these moments that are larger than the world itself. They were alive. They lived. They were loved.

"Come say hello," Victra says.

I am startled back into the room. "Me?"

"I thought you weren't an idiot."

She leans the baby close to me as he snuffles at her breast. I take his little hand and smile as his fingers curl around mine. He is slightly larger than my brothers were, but those eyes that will mark him different from them are closed. The winged sigils on his hands are bone, not yet coated with gold. He is just a child.

"Hello, little haemanthus," I say, just as I once said to my sister's children as they took their first breaths, "welcome to the worlds."

I leave Victra alone. The door bumps against Volga, who waits outside with a blank look on her face. I close the door behind me and nod. She breaks into a smile, as confused as I am to find herself celebrating the birth of Julii's child.

Through the cracked door I hear Victra whisper a benediction to her child: *"My son . . ."* Her voice falters. *"My son, you are of the gens Julii. Your ancestors looked to the night sky when there was nothing but drips of light in the darkness. Roads they built to stitch that light together. You are also of the gens Barca, guardians of the human race. You will be hated and you will hate. You will love and be loved. You will fall and you will rise. Never will you know peace, but you will know joy. You may even sail the dark seas in ships and lie beside nymphs in alien woods. You are your father's son. Forever my boy. Forever our Ulysses."*

66

LYRIA

The Julii's Bill

V ICTRA EATS WHAT'S LEFT of the soup and bread at the kitchen table. Ulysses is swaddled in her arms. The storm's still howling outside, having lasted through the night. In a few hours it'll be daylight. Volga and I stay awake on coffee. We all know we can't stay here long. If we keep Cormac and his family inside after the storm dies, it'll arouse suspicion from the townfolk, and there's no telling which of them will call the Red Hand. We have to be gone as soon as possible.

Volga and I want to wait, fearing Victra isn't strong enough. She looks paler than I've ever seen her, and even if Golds are Golds, they're still human. She needs to rest. We manage to convince her to let Volga go to the transmitter now. Cormac offers to take her, but Victra doesn't want the man out in the village. His son volunteers. But that's just the same. Volga can find it on her own. Better they stay tied at the table.

I stand with her in the open doorway. Volga squints into the swirl-ing snow, then back at Ulysses in the crook of Victra's arm as his mother finishes off a heel of bread. Volga's left Fig's black orb by the fire. "I wish I could have watched," she says, mildly jealous. "Why did she let you?"

"Think she wanted to teach me a lesson."

"I've never seen a baby born."

"Never?"

She shakes her head.

I pat her arm. "You'll get your chance one day if you like. It is some-thing."

"No," Volga says. "They made me without a womb." She sets her hand on her rifle.

"You know with enough money, bet they can change that now."

"Twenty million," Volga says. "Twenty million is what it takes." I tilt my head. Is that why she's been doing all this? Is that what Fig's bounty means to her? I feel a sudden heaviness in my heart for the big woman. Not just because of the confession, but because she chose to trust me with it. She smiles and pats my shoulder, closer than we were even the night before. "I will be back soon. Guard them well."

I watch Volga disappear into the snow and close the door.

She is a good person. Well, maybe not good. But what is good? She was raised by a bastard, but my father was a bastard too. Not always, and not to me, but I know how he hoarded our Laureltide boxes. How other families perished while ours grew strong. All my family's joy grew in the shadow of that truth, whether I want to admit it or not.

Maybe it wasn't my mother's death that broke the man. Maybe it was his conscience.

Victra tries her best to stay awake after Volga leaves, but after the pace she set through the highlands, and the labor, it seems even a Gold has limits. She keeps falling asleep at the table. I convince her to go rest with Ulysses, telling her I'll keep watch. By the time she wakes, her men will be on their way here. She smiles at that, no doubt thinking of her daughters, her husband.

I sit at the table with my gun in my lap and glance sideways at the orb. The flames from the hearth fire bend along its glossy surface. I pick it up and run my hands over the smooth metal. Its whispers tickle the back of my mind. *What's inside you?*

Across the table, Cormac yawns, tied to his chair by Volga's knots. His son, Alred, sleeps on a blanket by the fire, his hands bound in front of him.

Maybe I was too hard on them. Maybe we shouldn't have tied them up. But with Volga gone, I sure as hell am not going to have a crisis of conscience. I may have a gun, but I'm no Obsidian. And Victra looks worn through.

"Sorry if we gave your girl a fright," I say, setting the orb back down. "Considerin' how she is. And about the binds."

Cormac looks up in surprise. "Oh, nothin' to be done, lass. If there's ever a reason to hold a gun to someone's head, it's a baby. Can't say I ever heard a quieter birth than that one. She's one tough Peerless."

I look to the cracked door. "I've never met anyone like her."

"They make them that way," he says. "Tough. Less nerves than we got."

"That ain't true," I reply. "It wasn't easy for her."

"Seem to know a fine bit about them," he says. "Been wonderin' meself how a Martian mine lass ended up with one of them. Your lilt. Ain't never heard a highRed with one like that. And your eyes are too muddy for a city shade."

"True enough. I'm from Cimmeria."

"Which mine?"

"Casseda," I lie.

"Casseda." He frowns. "You don't sound like you're from Casseda."

"Know many Cassedans?" I ask.

"Can't say I do."

"Solves that. How'd you end up here? You're southern too."

"Our clan settled here to fish early on in the war," Cormac explains. "We was one of the first mines freed. It isn't easy, but labor's a fine thing if it's for yourself. We sell most of our haul to suppliers in Attica. Goes to Olympia, Agea. Even as far as Luna. Imagine that. Came back here after I lost my leg. Figured I'd like to spend more time with my kin than lose the rest of me."

I hear Victra call my name from the other room. I glance at Cormac. "Ain't goin' anywhere, lass," he says.

I get up from the table. Peeking through the doorway, I see Victra half asleep with Ulysses cradled in her arms. "You mind fetching me some snow? Aches like a broken tooth down there."

I shut the door and take stock of our hosts. Alred's still asleep by the fire, and Cormac's yawning and resting his head on the chair's back. "Don't move," I tell him. "Just grabbing her some ice." I prop open the door, making sure I can keep an eye on them as I fill a cloth with ice from outside. Volga's footprints are already being filled in by the snow. They lead around the right of the house toward the old base. Something ticks around the corner. Glancing back inside, I see Cormac with his eyes closed. I leave the doorway to check on the sound.

It's coming from a frosted window set in the stone. I clear away some of the snow with my pistol. Cormac's mute daughter looks out from her dark bedroom. Most of her is in shadow, but her pale face looks like a ghost's. She taps on the window with her fingers. When she sees me, her eyes implore me. She points back into the house, then lifts a hand and presses it to the window. It is covered in blood from a gash she made down the center.

A chill that has nothing to do with the wind goes through me.

A shadow moves behind her. Her face tilts down and her head slams forward into the heavy glass, shattering it into large, jagged shards. I drop the ice and run back to the door with my gun. Cormac is no longer at the table. Alred's place by the fire is empty. His severed bindings lie on the floor. I shout for Victra and slip on a patch of ice as I try to run through the doorway.

I fall forward and something passes over my head and goes *thunk* into the wooden doorframe. I hit the floorboards hard and turn to see Alred struggling to pull a slingBlade out of the doorframe. He jerks it out and turns to chop me in the belly, only to stare down the barrel of my gun. He puts a hand out. "Please . . ." I fire and his arm becomes a spray of red. He looks quizzically at it. Shattered bones peek through the skin as it hangs from his shoulder socket like a wet rag.

He screams.

My second round takes off his head from the chin up. He's thrown halfway out the door. I scramble to my feet. The world tight and vivid. Something bright screams past and burns a hole through the wall behind me. I drop to my belly as more particle beams lance out from Brea's bedroom, filling the air with the scent of ozone. I shoot back through the wall. The fire now consumes a corner of the room, spreading from the blanket to the table and the kitchen. Smoke clouds the room and stings my eyes. Victra's door bursts open and she storms out with her razor, sees me on the floor, Alred dead in the doorway, and the holes from the firefight.

"Red Hand," I rasp.

"Did you get him?"

"Don't know."

"Stay down." She slinks through the smoke and puts her ear next to one of the holes. Then she bursts through the door. I follow her and find Cormac on the ground holding in his guts. His gun lies across the room.

Victra kneels on Cormac's chest and stabs her razor through his hand. He grunts in pain.

"How many are in the village?" she asks. She puts a thumb in his eye. "How many!"

"Hundreds." He laughs. "In the old base. You're dead, Gold. They'll have heard the shots. They'll have your Obsidian. You're worm food, slaver. You and your spawn."

"Do you have a vehicle?"

He just laughs. She digs her finger into his eye, but he won't say any more. She kills him with a punch that crumples the right side of his skull. I hear a gurgling from behind a dresser and find Brea there. The crochet in his bedroom was hers. She's not his daughter. His wife isn't out on the boats. This child is his wife. A piece of glass is embedded in her neck. Blood gurgles from the wound and out her mouth as she stares up at me.

Victra's no longer in the room. I hear her coming back. She appears at the bedroom doorway with Ulysses wrapped in a quilt. She's barefoot and dizzy from the smoke. "Lyria, on me."

I look down at the bleeding girl. "We can't leave her!"

Victra looks down at the girl, up at me, and gives a look of apology before tucking Ulysses tight, wheeling away, and disappearing out the door. I gasp for air as I drag Brea out of the burning house and lay her down in the snow.

"It's all right, lass," I say between coughs. "I've got you now. It's just a scratch. I've got you." Her blood slicks my hands and stains the snow. There's so much of it. She can't die here. Not this poor girl. Not after surviving that man, if it's what I think. Not like this. She can't die.

I press my hands against the wound to try and stop the bleeding, but the glass cut so deep, all I can do is watch her until she becomes as pale as the snow and her eyes stare up at me with the flames of the burning house reflected in them. I didn't know her, but I felt she could be me, or my sister.

There's shouts from the village. Having heard the gunfire from their own homes, Red men rush toward the burning house. There's twenty, fifty coming. Could all be the Red Hand? A woman in the doorway of a nearby house waves for me to run from them. Victra's already gone, her tracks leading back into the highlands. I chase after her, away from the shouting men.

I lose the tracks twice in the storm. Try as I might, I cannot summon the parasite at will. Wind bites my face and my fingers are already numb. I don't think I'll catch Victra. Her strides are easily twice the length of mine. But I keep running. My side's got a stitch. My lungs ache from the cold. Something roars in the sky, deeper than the sound of the wind. Several ships glow through the swirling snow as they pass overhead. I trudge through frozen creek beds, through a wood of lonely aspen, and into an evergreen forest before I'm hopelessly lost. I run in circles trying to find Victra's tracks, but they've disappeared, as if she suddenly grew wings. She must have taken to the trees. I search them before realizing I might be leading them to her. What could I even do to help her? I'd slow her down. Part of me knows this is my fault, but she wanted ice. Volga needed to go to the old base. None of them thought Cormac was Red Hand. None of them saw through him. I suspected. I kept close watch, until I didn't.

How did they cut through the ropes?

The wind dies down not long after morning comes. Snow falls in large flakes. The world takes on the color of gunmetal. I've carried my pistol with me, but it's got only three rounds left. I stay in the forest not knowing what to do, listening for sounds of hunting men, dogs, or ships. I hear nothing. Just the silence of a world turning.

Knowing I can't go anywhere without finding out what happened to Volga, I make my way back to the town, sticking to ravines when possible and running quick as I can through open fields. Climbing over a fence, I see a splash of color amidst another copse of trees.

On the edge of the treeline, blood paints snow churned by boots. It splashes the white bark of the trees, many of which are fallen or shattered from a gunfight. A few are cut cleanly, probably from Victra's razor. Something lies in the snow. As I bend to pick it up, I flinch away. It's a hand with Red sigils on it. More than a dozen trails of blood lead to a patch of earth where the snow melted away. Must be where their shuttle landed. I don't see any tracks leading off.

They've got her. They've got her and Ulysses.

A stone lodges in my throat.

Then I see crows fluttering around an odd-shaped tree.

Something is wrong with that tree.

I stumble toward it, my heart knowing before my head, pulled along by the dread weaving its fingers through me. The crows scatter away. My shadow darkens the tree. My legs tremble. My knees buckle. I fall to the ground, unable to accept it, unable to look away from the small trickles of blood that wind down the bark, unable to understand why they nailed the baby upside down to the trunk of the tree.

67

LYRIA

Numb

ULYSSES IS DEAD.

I sit watching the snow fall and feel nothing.

I see but don't feel myself moving as I take Ulysses down and wrap him in my coat. It is not easy or clean.

I try to dig a grave with my hands, but the earth is frozen. I don't realize it is too hard to dig through until I notice my fingers bleeding.

When I look back at the lifeless infant in my jacket, I break down.

I don't know what to do with him. I can't bury him here in the dirt as if he's a part of this world. He didn't even get to spend a day in it. I won't leave him here to be eaten by scavengers. Scavengers have done enough to him already.

All I can do is take him with me.

I shake as I walk. I'll die if I don't put my jacket on. But I can't let him be cold. His newborn flesh is so thin. So very thin. I walk. I'm not sure where, or why, but I find myself back at the edge of the village, looking down at it. There's a commotion outside the base. Half a dozen new ships sit there, including the one with the Ambrosia advert. More than fifty men with guns mill about. How many helped kill my family? How many of them raped my sister before they cut her throat to the bone? How many nailed this baby to the tree after smashing its skull?

They're surrounding something, kicking it.

I feel my legs carrying me down the hill. My hand on the cold grip of the pistol. Three shots left. Three left for Harmony. At the edge of the town as I'm waylaid by a thicket of dead brush, I see the crowd part and

Harmony giving orders to her men. She looks the same as she did two weeks before. The same as when she killed my brother, except now she's wearing a winter coat and carrying Victra's bloody razor. Her men follow her orders and drag what they were kicking onto their ships. It's Victra, and Volga.

I break into a jog. I reach the burned-out house where we thought to find shelter. Go past it through narrow lanes leading between several other houses. I'm still a hundred meters off by the time the ship lifts off, some Red Hand men on the ground, cheering them. The ships head north and I stand there with my jacket around Ulysses. My pistol useless in my hand.

"Girl," someone whispers. "Girl." A woman stares at me from a cracked door. She opens it more. And I see it was the woman who watched me run from the burning house. She motions me toward her. I'm not sure why or how, but I find myself inside her house. I pull out my gun and point it at her. She flinches away. A man on the far side of the room looks away from his HC to see me. Then looks back as it shows bodies falling over a city. Brea lies on their kitchen table. Her blood has been cleaned away, and she's wearing a dress, her face surrounded by winter berries. It looks as if she is asleep.

She is their daughter.

"Red Hand came a year ago," Brea's mother says as I warm myself by their fire. Her name is Maeve. A young boy watches from a back room. "Moved into the mine north of town. Started using the old base for transmissions and the mine up the coast as a redoubt. It was fine at first. Our Gammas had already fled. But then the Obsidians came and things got bad. More Hands started showing up as the Obsidians chased them north. So many hangin' on by the thread of their bones.

"They've got a field outside the mine where they've done and buried thousands. Their men started fightin'. Started killin' each other. Guess they thought they had nothin' to live for. So then we was told they'd be takin' wives of our clan." She stifles a sob. "They took me baby. She was not on thirteen. Too shy of wedAge, but they took her still. Said Mora was too young yet. But . . ." Her lips quiver. "But they took her to the base anyway. They'll take her away."

I sit in the chair feeling exhausted as Maeve tells me her tragedy. The rag I used to clean the blood from my arms languishes in a tepid bowl of water. The old soup she gave me doesn't steam anymore. I've not even lifted the spoon. Outside, there's occasional gunfire or shouts. I cradle Ulysses in my arms.

"Mora?" I ask. "Who is she?"

"Me youngest daughter. Not yet twelve." She sobs.

"And you just let them take her," I say, watching Ulysses' dead face. "After you knew what they did to Brea?"

"What were we to do?" the woman says. "They'd kill us. There's hundreds up there in that mine. That man Cormac . . . he's a beast. Killed a boy who tried to . . ." She shakes her head.

"He's dead now. My friend made sure of that."

"He ain't the worst of them. There's Picker—man that chooses the wives. He chose Brea and now . . ." She can't even say her youngest daughter's name. "And there's the woman."

"Harmony."

The woman nods and looks at Brea. "They're roundin' up new girls at the base. Gonna take them to the mine to be wives after they been inspected. Said we helped the Gold."

"And no one has tried stop them," I say. "You just watched."

She convulses sobbing. She tries to speak. To give another excuse. But then she looks at her girl and just runs back to the bedroom to her other children. Fear lurks over this village.

Maeve's husband looks at me now. The light from the HC bathes him sickly green. The color is the only life in his eyes. "You Gamma?"

"Why? Did Gamma rape your daughter?" I snap.

His jaw flexes. "Talk about my girl again, I drag you to the Hand meself."

"How you gonna do that from your knees?" I ask. He looks back at the HC, swallowing. "Your last daughter ain't there, old man." I point out the window to the squat base on promontory. "She's over there."

"You can stay till dark," he says quietly. "Then you go."

In the dim light of the fire, I watch Ulysses's cold face as I watched that of my sister and her children. I pull the jacket over his face. I'm tired of watching.

Through the walls I can hear the whispers of the orb.

That night, I dig through the rubble of Cormac's house as the snow comes down. The north wall has crumbled inward from the heat and the metal roof has warped. Coughing from the soot, I pull blackened timbers off the remains of the kitchen table. There sitting by the stone frame of the hearth lies Fig's black orb. Wrapping my hands in my sleeves, I pull it out and crouch in the remains of the house.

Despite the heat of the fire, the orb is undamaged, as I suspected it would be. There is no lock. No hinges or any gaps in the metal to show where it opens. I tap it with a naked finger. It's cool to the touch. Like river stone. I hold the orb in both hands, turning it over to figure out how to open it. Maybe it doesn't open. I rap it with my knuckles. Whatever is inside was worth Fig risking her life to get. It must contain something that can help me.

If it's hollow, I can't tell. But if it's not, it should be heavier. I saw Volga break rocks on it, and Victra's razor slide off without leaving much more than a scratch. Fig seemed to be able to call it with the implants in her fingers. Maybe I need those to open it. But if I need those, why would it call to me? I lower my head to it, hoping the proximity to the parasite in my head will open it. Nothing happens except the blood in my brain thumps louder.

I lower the orb in frustration and lean back. Flakes of snow flutter down from the sky and gather on my face. I suck on the opened scabs on my hands and think. What do I do? What can I do? There isn't salvation in this orb. Even if there was, Volga and Victra are already dead.

I drop my hands to the orb and consider defeat.

The pressure in my head releases, like a popping bubble. A low hum comes from my lap and I look down to see an emerald-green light appearing underneath a faint blood smear my thumb left on the orb. I sit up and wipe the soot from my eyes. The green light ripples in the black metal, becoming a swirl of tiny arcane mathematical symbols that coalesce into the shape of a woman atop a bull. The image is no larger than my thumb.

DNA sampling complete, new protocols implemented for Énatos Figment, a soft female voice says in my head, or was it from the orb? *Sfaíra access granted.* My heart thuds as the orb purrs and its surface begins to unscrew till a thousand millimeter-wide strips around its meridian are turning in alternating clockwise and counterclockwise rotations. They fold in on one another until the orb divides in two and folds over on itself, revealing an interior the color of baby teeth pulsing with soft light. Built into the orb are several hundred small compartments marked with obscure symbols.

A central device made from the same material as the inside of the orb is embedded in the bottom of the orb. It is the size of my thumb. A green light glows inside it and I sense frequencies flowing between it and the parasite in my head the same way I found Victra in the woods.

Cortical implant diagnostic complete.

A long list of green characters appears in the air in front of me. I reach out to touch them. But they aren't there. I swipe at them with my hand and they scroll downward. The list goes on and on, none of it making any sense to me.

Figment functionality impaired. Seek repairs at the Womb upon soonest convenience.

Seek repairs? To a parasitic implant in my brain? Where the hell would I do that?

Geolocation function unavailable. Mobile uplink unavailable.

The parasite is reading my mind. What is the implant?

A gift from Astarte.

Who the hell is Astarte?

She was you.

What does that mean? No response. What is Figment? How do I get repairs? No response except a reminder to seek repairs. *Bloodyhell.* Was the Brown woman Figment, or is Figment the parasite? Was she being controlled by it? Am I? Could I be if I got repairs? If I can get repairs, someone out there must know. Does that someone control the parasite? Would they control me?

Volga seemed to think Figment was just a woman, but Victra knew better. It doesn't make any sense, and right now I don't really give a shit. Apparently I expected the orb to contain a rocket launcher or something.

I prod through the supplies. Nothing is labeled in a language I understand. And each device is as inert and bizarre as the next. There are small blue disks set in gel. A black nasal inhaler with assorted cartridges. A silver device that looks like it goes around an eye, with a tiny needle injector. A credit ring with Republic markings. A credit ring with Society markings. A credit implant with peculiar winged symbols. A case of a hundred pebble-sized balls in different colors. A selection of iris implants, in all fourteen colors. A titanium sphere. Vials of clear liquid. An armory of colored needles. A miniature pharmacy—of life takers or life givers, take your gamble. Passport implants, which sprout eerie holos of my face when I touch them. And a hundred other items I can't begin to suss out the function for. But no bloodydamn gun. No magical broomstick. No teleportation device, unless it's in one of the pills. No body armor. No universal com. No grenades. No damn manual. Not one thing I could use to somehow become a hero.

"What does this shit do!" I beg. "Help me. Please." The parasite does not reply. I hit my head, trying to jar its loose circuits. "Come on!"

Implant functionality impaired. Seek repairs at soonest convenience.

Fucker.

Name-calling is a waste of neurons.

Stupid parasite. Useless treasure. That's what Figment meant when she said Volga could use it. That I didn't deserve it. Tough shit. I'm all that's here.

I rifle through the rest of the contents, determined to find something that will help me. I frown when I open a long compartment around the bottom ring of storage. I pull out a small flexible magazine that looks like it would hold bullets or pills. But neither bullets nor pills fill the gel magazine.

It is full of *teeth.*

I start to laugh.

I storm back into Maeve's home. She's lying in her daughter's bed, crying. She doesn't even bother to turn till I slam the door behind me. My eyes are bloodshot from smoke. My hair's a rat's nest. My pants are torn. I'm covered in soot and blood and carrying Figment's orb in a half-burned blanket, and I'm in no mood for the drunk bastard in front of his little HC, or for the mother who hovered by the window chewing her nails like a frightened dumb goat as her daughter was raped across the street day after day.

"How long those bastards gonna be before they take the girls back to the mine?" I ask.

"Told you to get," the husband says.

I point my gun at his head. "Shut your copper gob. I got business with your wife."

He moves his mouth like a dumb mule and turns back to his HC, pretending to find the news program showing Republic ships gathering to fight the Obsidians for some reason or another to be more interesting than the muzzle of my gun. His wife stares at the wall as if trying to become it. *"Maeve."* She doesn't reply. She smells like she hasn't washed in years when I crouch by her. "Maeve." She won't turn till I pull her ear. "You wanna see your Mora again?" I ask. "Do you want to see your baby girl?"

She looks up and nods.

"When do those bastards take the girls back to the mine?"

"In the morning," she says. "Inspection don't last that long. And they don't fly when the satellites are overhead. They'll keep . . ." Her lips quiver like salted slugs. "They keep the wives in the base until they pass. Be on ten usually."

"Then you got till daybreak to make me look pretty enough to drop a drillboy's jaw," I say. "Can you do that? Gimme a little blush, curl this nest?"

She smiles. Finally this is something she knows.

"Little oil and an iron. I got one just behind the cupboard."

"Good, Maeve. Good. And I'm gonna need a pair of pliers. Small as you got."

68

LYRIA

Shh

By morning, I'm schlepping over the frosted snow toward the base, trying not to limp for the pliers in my shoe. It's bright and blue out and pretty enough for me to be pissed at the world for putting such a lovely face on such a shit-infested day.

The sea lolls against the coast like a dancing gray lover. It spits little bursts of salt that coast up in the air and then drizzle down on my shiny curled hair. Maeve might be all closed up to a world that's beaten the hell out of whatever pretty dream she had for herself when she was freed from the mines. But she knows how to make an escapee from a genocide look like a dumb mine lass with rosy cheeks and flailing skirts and nothin' to her knowin' except how to coax fatass spiders into puking silk and how to get rustblood drillboys spitting seed enough to populate a township.

I stride down what counts as the main road for this whipped town, tucking my head like I've got something to hide. I got a bundle under my arm. It ain't the orb. I left that buried in the cinders, and Ulysses with Maeve. All I got is a bucket of salted fish from Maeve's pitiable larder and enough ankle showing for the Red Hand butcherboys smoking burners in front of the old base to forget about their morning snort of grayline. They make like bees to me. No manners. They're conquerors. What they see is theirs. And they're wondering how the Picker didn't already take his wife tax of me.

They pester about, asking questions. I act all domestic and frazzled, careening about like I'm a drunk sparrow trying to find gaps in the trees. They pull my hands, to see if I've a ring on. They hem me in and coax me into a smoke. I take a burner between my lips as one rests his hand on my ass, cupping inside the cheek, nearly where the magazine of teeth are secured by epoxy to my deeper parts. I act timid, like I can't resist the absolute magnetism of his hand halfway up my ass. The other boys get jealous, and the biggest shoulders the other aside.

"Never had a burner," I say dozily to Biggest.

"We got 'em by the carton back at the fortress," he brags. I try not to tongue my aching gums. A good part of my gray matter wants to melt his face right there, or maybe aim a little lower. Another part feels bad for the stupid bastard. He's pimply, not even in his twenties. He thinks he's something because he's got a gun and big hands and big shoulders. But the dumb fuck's never seen a Telemanus in wargear or the Sovereign sitting there with a cup of tea and the weight of ten billion on her. He's never seen Victra standing there like a god giving life to a baby that'd change the world if he ever got the chance to grow. If the dumb bastard did have a notion of his true size, he'd crumple up and die for understanding how petrifyingly small he actually is.

I know how small I am. But I also know how small they are.

The last part of my gray matter, the most important part, is occupied with the idea of melting the guts out of Harmony, sawing her head off, and feeding the rest of her to a fire. I'd have done it for Tiran alone, and maybe felt guilty. But then her stimmed-up rapists had to ruin my sister too. Had to butcher her children. Cut them with slingBlades like they were onions. Then they had to kill my pa when he couldn't even walk. Then they had to nail a baby to a tree. I don't give a piss if they're human. If they got problems. If they got drugs in 'em. If they had hard lives. If they got *reasons*. All I know is one has his hand digging into my backside, and I'm smiling, bearing it because I know I'm gonna die. But I'm gonna take as many of them with me as I can, and maybe, just maybe, find out if my friends are still alive.

The big one leads me toward the old base. Takes me around the shoulders, whispering so close I can smell the morning eggs and tobacco on his breath. His fingers graze my right tit. His boys saunter behind, half ripe jealous, half puffed up by his conquest. He steers me past the louses at the door, and tries to pull me sidelong into some room where he'll rape me first, and then share me like a half-done burner.

"Never been inside here!" I coo loudly in my best approximation of Maeve's accent. "This is what it looks like! Sure there were Grays about once. Maybe Golds! Bellonas, weren't they? I've always wanted to go to Olympia."

"Never mind about Olympia," he says. "It's a crow shithole now. In here's where the fun is."

But the noise has perked the ears of bigger dogs, and before he can pull me into the room, one of the Picker's boys comes around the corner. He's got a metal arm, kind eyes, and a beautiful head of rusty hair. "What you got there, Torrow?"

"Oh, just a friend," big Torrow says, all meek-like. "None yours, Duncan."

"You know the fish are under Harmony's hand," the handsome man says. He sips his coffee and those bright eyes of his look me over. He seems in his mid-twenties. Cocky, but a kindness to him.

"Picker already got the tax," my idiot says, tilting me away protectively. "This one's an old maid. Prolly already got a canyon from three, four?"

"You had little ones, miss?" Duncan asks me polite-like.

"Not a one," I say.

"Husband?"

"Gone and died," I say.

"Clan you?"

"Beta."

"Omicron here." He squints at me and smiles awkwardly. "How many years?"

"Not but twenty," I say.

He snorts. "More like twenty-four." He tosses the dregs of his coffee on the floor and takes one step toward Torrow, flicks his robot fingers, and the arm around my shoulders disappears. Torrow gives me a good push. "Take the slut," he mutters. "Prolly got a dead cave anyhow."

Duncan politely tells me he's gonna frisk me. He ain't nearly thorough enough. When he's done he wipes the snow off my face like he's bringing me to shelter. He leads me on into a bigger room that's got live computers and a few boys hunched over them. The Picker's having breakfast of eggs and fish and pudding. "What's what?" he asks when Duncan brings me in. Picker is lean and fox-like. Clever behind the eyes, and sinister as all hell.

"Fresh catch," Duncan says.

"Fresh? She's a relic."

"Might be, but seedless, so seems. And it's better than babies."

"Already got the tax. Toss her back."

"Them's kids," Duncan says. "You know it ain't right."

Picker eats his eggs and stares at him. "You said you didn't need a wife."

"She ain't *for* me. Some them girls ain't even bled yet."

"So?"

"So it ain't right," Duncan says, setting his hands on his belt. Whoever he is, he's got some pull. Picker doesn't take it as a challenge, but the other boys are watching.

Picker pushes his eggs away and lights a burner. Through the smoke, he appraises me. "Spin her." I get spun. Do my best to show as much ankle as my sister did when she danced. I laugh lightly, as if I'm dizzy from it.

"You wanna husband?" Picker asks me. He's got the bad eyes of a cave fish. He has to squint to see me right. I look down, all shy.

"Long as he's a good one," I say. "I get to pick?"

The men laugh.

"No, lass," Picker says. "You don't get to bloody pick. HeadTalk does that. Best blood gets top mare. And you ain't top mare. So you get what you get. Still want a husband?"

I nod. "Better than smellin' like fish day in day out."

A great show is made of giving me a little plate of dry eggs as they discuss what to do with me. The eggs are tasteless like everything else I've eaten since my spit boiled off my tongue. When I've scraped the last bit from my plate, Duncan leads me away to a room guarded by a couple lads. The smell of clustered bodies washes out as the door swings open. Near on twenty girls are nestled on old mattresses with dirty sheets, huddled together for fear.

"Which of you's the youngest?" Duncan asks.

A girl who couldn't be more than eleven points to a girl even smaller than her. "Lea is."

A look of pain goes across Duncan's face as he kneels and motions her over. "You want to go home to your family, little one?" She nods, terrified. He extends a hand. She doesn't take it until the other girls prod her forward. Duncan guides me into the room and takes Lea out.

The door slams shut behind me.

Half the girls dead silent, staring at the stained sheets like they're reading palms. Others huddle together. With the boys gone, I look around in case there are plants, but if there are, they're good enough actors to be in the Hyperion Opera. The room stinks of fear. Not one of them older than me, and to scared girls that means something.

I cross my arms and say in a low whisper: "They're going to rape all of us until we have brood." They stare at me. "Then they'll do it again, and again and again till your belly's like an empty waterskin. Some o' you will quit and take it. Rest of you they'll hook on grayline and you'll beg for prick just to get a high. They'll prolly share those ones." I look around at the wide eyes. Some of the girls have started to bawl. "How many of you have husbands?" I ask. A freckle-faced girl in her early twenties raises her hand. She nudges another girl, a little younger with long pigtails, until the girl raises her hand too. "How many of you are aged north of sixteen?" About half raise their hands. "How many of you had brothers or pas killed?" They all raise their hands. "How many had brothers or pas cry like babies as you were dragged away, but didn't lift a bloodydamn finger?" They stare at me, all too ashamed to raise their hands. The dead are honored. The cowards are hidden. It's all the answer I needed. This is right. "Any of you rats?" I glare around at them. "Good. 'Cause where I'm from, rats get their eyes stabbed out."

Some of the girls flinch. Freckles crosses her arms as if she'd like to see me try. The smallest of the girls, one with skin almost as dark as mine and a shaggy mane of hair, glares around at the other girls, daring them to be rats. Tails, the one with a husband, looks down.

I reach back down my skirts and find the head of the strip of teeth. I jerk, wincing as the epoxy pulls off half my skin with it. Holding the strip in my hands, I pull the pliers from my shoe.

With all of them watching, I stick the pliers in my mouth, secure the iron bits to my second back molar, and jerk *hard*. The tooth doesn't come out straight, but I saw Victra plop out a baby standing up without a single yelp. I rock twice and jerk again, using both my arms. The blood pours down the back of my throat as the tooth and root burst out. I hold up the pliers, open my mouth so they all see, and then I swallow the blood. I take another one of Fig's teeth from my strip and shove it against the wound. There's a sizzle, a pain that shoots through the root, through my nostril, into my eyes and brain. It's the second I've put in. I wipe the blood from my lips and smile.

Tails gives a little gasp. The rest of the girls look terrified except Freckles, who tilts her head, and the little one with the mane. We'll call her Lion. She claps her hands together until Freckles shushes her.

"I ain't from here. Where I'm from, these fucks killed me whole clan," I say. "I ain't here to be no brood sow. I ain't here to be no grayline whore. I ain't here to be saved. I'm here to kill those bastards. Any of you sisters got similar intentions, you better speak up, or you're gonna be a slag toy till you see the Vale." I hold up the pliers. "So, who wants to save themselves?"

Little Lion bounds forward.

We swallow our pulled teeth so they don't find them hidden under the mattresses. After I explained what Fig's teeth do, Freckles got all but two of the girls to get in line. She held them down when I pulled the teeth, and made sure they were quiet. One wailed so hard the guards outside beat the door with their rifles. After their teeth were stripped, I secured each of Fig's devices myself and Freckles helped Lion clean up their blood. I find out from the others that Lion is Mora—Brea's sister. Only Tails and another smaller girl refused my offer.

I sit down next to Tails as Freckles cleans up the last girl. She's murmuring under her breath how we shouldn't do this. How they'll hurt us. I put an arm around her. "Listen, you don't have to join in. All I need is you to be quiet, right? We'll get you home."

"Y-you're gonna get us all killed," she says. "You're crazy."

"Yeah," I say, realizing nice isn't gonna work. "Yeah, but you remember what I do to rats?"

"She stabs their eyes out," Lion says from behind me. Her hands are balled into tiny fists as she glares at Tails.

"She stabs their eyes out," Freckles adds. Several of the girls repeat it around Tails until she covers her ears. I lean in front of her. "Remember." I bring my finger to my lips. "Shh." I leave as dramatically as I can, but a thought catches me. "Can you read?" I ask her.

She shakes her head.

And now I've got a backup plan.

They collect us midmorning when a rumble comes through the walls. A transport waits outside. Some of the relatives of the girls come to see them off, the rest hide from their own shame in their chores, making up the boats and chiseling snow off the roofs. Some of the girls cry as we're pushed onto the transport, but none as loud as poor Tails. Others tongue their gums till I shoulder them. Lion and Freckles glare at the Red Hand militia as we board up. I slump forward and sit on the freezing metal bucket seat, keeping my eyes down as the door clamps shut. The guards don't chat much to us. They just smoke their burners. Some few women are with them. They think they're men, or at least they think they're better than us dumb sows because they've got guns and knives and pants, and we're in skirts.

A few of the girls are nauseous by the time the shuttle sets down. Freckles pukes a little in the corner. There aren't any windows, so the first time we get fresh air is in some cavern hangar that was carved ages back by clawDrills.

This is their fortress? After seeing the Citadel of Light, I almost laugh.

Ambient light dies as we're led away into the main of the mine. Maybe I thought the Red Hand was something big back when I was in 121, but next to the Citadel Lionguards or Barca Sols and especially the Ascomanni, these louts are a joke. We spot maybe a couple hundred as we are led down an ancient gravLift into the township. A few boys whistle at us as we go. A few run up and pinch our cheeks before getting clouted by Picker and Duncan, who smiles at us as if being nice will save him from bad dreams.

They dump us in some old barracks for Grays. Everything's rusted except the small sad affectations they added for the sake of us womenfolk. There're beer bottles with wildflowers. HCs playing old comedies. And a couple old hens who introduce themselves and inspect our armpits. They check our teeth for cavities, and when they see our irritated gums they murmur to themselves about gum disease. Then they bring in an old Yellow man with a limp to check between our legs for lice and other maladies, as if *we're* the ones who'll have them.

It's all I can do not to crumple the Yellow's skull with a beer bottle when the cold forceps spread me so he can look inside. He pats me gently on the knee and looks at me in sorrow. When we're done and I'm confirmed not-diseased, they let us alone with the other newcomers from other towns along the coast. No one mingles. Freckles eyes the other girls like intruders. I see Tails taking a step toward them and click my tongue. She stops and stares at the ground.

They give us a precious pack of burners for being "honorable lasses" and treat it like it's Venusian chocolate. The girls look like idiots smoking them down. Most have never even had tobacco. A few puke. I take the burner from Lion's fingers and tear it apart.

"How old are you, even?" I ask.

"Eleven."

"Going on forty," Freckles says. "She's crazy, that one."

"I ain't crazy," Lion protests. "You's the one in love with a Gray." Of the other girls, she seems to respect only Freckles's opinions. I raise an eyebrow at Freckles.

"Grays are risky business."

"So mind your own. When we gonna do it?" she asks.

"Like I said, when they pair us off. We'll be alone then and able to get their guns. Make sure the other girls remember."

"We gotta wait that long?" She glances back at Tails. "Known her since I was five. She's gonna tell them soon as we split up. Soon as we can't see her rat."

"You know that for a certain fact?" I ask.

"Well as I know anything."

I glance at Tails, who sits in the corner by herself. Freckles is right. She watches the two hens chatting with each other on the far side of the room.

"Make a distraction for me," I tell Freckles.

"What you gonna do?"

"Fix it."

She's about to press for particulars, when Lion, who was eavesdropping, screams at the top of her lungs and runs for the hallway. The hens curse and pursue. I bolt up, only the girls in the room now. I slip toward Tails. She looks up as I approach. I kick her hard as I can in the jaw. Something pops. She sprawls sideways with a cry. I can't take chances, so I pull back the hands covering her face and try to stomp on her jaw. Finally my heel gets through and her hands go a little slack. I stomp again until I hear the bone crack like wet wood. I wheel back around locking eyes with the staring girls. "I don't like rats," I say. The newcomers look away. My girls are horrified. I return to Freckles and sit back down, throbbing all over. Tails sobs through her broken jaw like she's dying.

"Shit," Freckles mutters. "What you got against rats?" Her smile sours till her face mirrors mine as we listen to Tails's moan until the hens come back. They drag a crying Lion by her ears. No one sits within ten meters of Tails. The hens demand to know what happened. After seeing what I did to Tails, the girls greet the question with ominous silence. Tails's explanation comes out as a pathetic moo. She'll live, but she won't be talking for a while.

Stupidity is not a victimless crime.

I won't let these girls pay for her big mouth.

The hens feed us after the burners and make us each drink a cup of bitter wine, making sure it all goes down. It's got something in it. I feel the buzz right off, a slow warmth and wooziness. The whole time they're talking about what an honor we're about to receive. Freckles glowers as they feed Lion the same size of cup they gave us.

They line us up in a big room like dolls. I think it's around nighttime. Hard to tell because the mine's shut off from light. Didn't feel this as a girl. Days had rhythm in Lagalos. Could tick the clock on paper by the measure of my mother's sounds and smells. Door creak. Five in the morning. Coffee smell, five-twenty. Click of tin breakfast plates. Five-thirty.

Here there's no rhythm, because there's no life.

Just like the cell.

Can already tell there's too many young men, and not enough to distract them or keep 'em loyal. If the Obsidians are tearing them apart bad as everyone says, then they must be wondering why they're fighting, why they're not trying to make it in the city like sane people.

This ain't the Red Hand we feared. I don't need the parasite to smell the decay. Is it right to risk these girls? Is it better if they just take it and survive? If I can't find Volga and Victra, if they can't somehow help us, I think I just signed the death notes for nearly twenty girls.

But it's too late to go back.

We wait in the lines in a big cold room where mine tinpots used to practice their shooting. The burning of candles and the carpets they've put down on the floor can't obscure the old purpose of the room or the holes bullets chewed in the far wall. We wait till my lower back starts to ache and Lion starts to whistle, to the annoyance of the hens. One smacks her ear. Lion just grins up at her.

Then Picker comes in with Duncan trailing behind him and tells us to mind our manners. To be polite. To curtsy because we're about to meet the Red Mother herself. Maker of the Red Hand. Sister of Ares, Narol O'Lykos. But the Reaper's uncle wasn't Ares, and all the girls know it. Another ten minutes. Then some mean, mean bastards come in and face us down like a firing squad, but they don't have that many guns. Most are men, a few women. Not boys like the others, but hard and rangy and evil, with eyes like Picker's and a quietness about them that's so inhuman I think all the girls will shit themselves and spill our plans. Good thing I took out the rat.

Then She comes in.

The woman has filled my nightmares from the bunks of the Telemanus estate to the freezing holes I slept in next to Volga and Victra. The woman who made red butter of Tiran's head. Who I remembered ruining my family every time Volga taught me to strip down her rifle. My fingers would shake from the cold, from the fear of the pursuing hunters, but all I had to do was picture her face to remember why I wanted to learn Volga's weapons.

Harmony's face is half hell, half faded beauty. And she was a beauty. There's lines there now, sour crow's-feet. But in her time, she woulda outstripped my sister by a kilometer. She woulda made the boys beg for a twirl of the skirts.

Harmony stalks forward now with a weird, lazy carelessness that I've only seen in soldiers. No preening. No boasting. Just a slump of the soldiers and a forward trajectory.

She looks at us.

Then she smiles with her eyes. A brilliant, incandescent loveliness that makes me tilt my head wondering if I got it all wrong. Or am I that drunk?

"Sisters," Harmony says before rushing forward to greet us, going down the line, cupping our faces, kissing us on the foreheads, on the mouths, on the eyes. "Sisters," she says. "Sisters. Tonight you receive an honor most Red women only dream of. Tonight you will be chosen as wives by heroes of the Red People.

"How fearful you must be, standing here on the precipice of a life more glorious than you could know. There was life before this. The life you thought you had, that they trained you to be accustomed to. The life you thought was your destiny. That life was a lie. The life of a slave is no life.

"And there is this life. The true life. The second life of liberation. The life not of clan, but of the People. One People united against oppression. United against the cruelty of the slavers who once called us by numbers, and those who still seek to shackle us." She sees a girl crying, not one of mine. "I know you're fearful. I feared once. I feared when my children were dying of a cancer of the lung. I prayed to the Reaper for them. The real Reaper who guards the Vale, not the man who turned his back on his people. I prayed to the Reaper to judge them innocent and lovely and keep them in this world. But the Reaper sorts only the just and the pure in the *next* life. I prayed and prayed, but who was there to answer my prayers in this life? Who was there to save my children? No one. They died."

She scoops a handful of dirt and lets it trickle out her clenched fist. "I watched them wither. I watched my husband wither after them. I watched the Sons of Ares wither, not to death, but to the temptations of this world." She discards the dirt. "When I was afraid, I always prayed, as you pray. But no one is there to answer. Our salvation comes in the next world. We must make our own in this one. That is why the Red Hand fights."

She looks at each one of us, eyes lingering on Lion. She smiles down at her.

Lion does not smile back.

"You are the bravest of our people. You do not hold weapons. You do not fight. But you carry the banner of liberty." She looks at Freckles. The girl can't meet her gaze. "You carry the bloodline of our people. Without women, without wives, what are a people but a doomed matchstick? To blaze and glare light, and then to die." She looks at me. It is the hardest thing I have ever done to hold her gaze and nod, but I do. "But you are the wildfire. The fire that spreads. Without guns, without ships, you are the soldiers that bring us the future. You are the wives of Red! I envy you." She nods so convincingly. "*I envy you.* If I could still bring life into this world, I would not need this." She rests her hand on her pistol. "But we all have our duty. Mine is to protect you. If your husband beats you. If he is cruel to you . . . come to me, or any of the women you see here today. And we will sort it."

Duncan takes a swig from his flask and stares at the ground in the line of Red Hand militia. But the Red Hand women with Harmony nod, brainwashed, pathetic, or evil. I hate them so much more than the men.

Many of the girls, especially the newcomers, find themselves nodding too. Either they buy the bullshit or are drunk, or afraid, or wanting the approval of the older women. Most of my lot stand rigid or shake with fear, not because they're smarter than the other girls, but because we have a plan. And once they've grasped the wheel, tiny as it may be, they feel they have control. They have a chance.

I know because it wasn't Victra who saved me from the Ascomanni or from getting sucked out her ship. Volga and I did that. It made me feel alive in a way I never had.

"One day you may hold a weapon," Harmony promises, "but today, your duty to your people is to bear the seed of your husband to fruition. To grow our union with new blood and foster boys that will become warriors, girls that will become wives and one day warriors as well. I salute you. You are the best of our kind. May the Vale wait for you, and may the blood of our people flow strong!"

69

LYRIA

The Childwives

T HE SOUND OF ZITHERS wails through the concrete halls as we're
led in a line down to the township common, where several hundred bearded men and boys with smears for whiskers laugh and drink at
long tables.

Some few fighter women join them, hair done short like the men. Oil
fires burn in metal barrels. Boys race men to see the bottom of their
mugs. The stolen wealth of other races decorates their coats. Gold sigils
clatter as they laugh. Obsidian arm torcs encircle the necks of their
childwives. The richer they are, the less the women can move. They look
like birds sitting at their tables set back from the fighters, gossiping or
staring at the cups before them, wishing what's inside would numb them
faster.

The men cheer as we're brought in, but it's short-lived. It all becomes
solemn as we're lined up in another row of dolls. Girls stare at their feet.
Some brave ones like Freckles look on ahead like they're at the gallows.
Harmony takes her place of honor at the head table. Mugs are slammed
in unison making a mockery of the Fading Dirge until she raises her
hands and quiets all.

I scan the township levels, trying to piece it all together and figure
where they keep Victra and Volga.

"Hail the children!" she says. "Hail the wives. But above all, hail the
fighters!" Harmony calls. "Coran O'Boetia!" The men roar and slam
their mugs. "For the killing of five Obsidian barbarians, and the taking

of forty torcs in the highlands, you are a boy no more. It's time a wife made a man of you! The prime pick is yours."

A drunken man-boy, uncommonly tall and handsome except for the case of childhood pox, manages to stand straight under a barrage of backslaps and jeering. With a shy grin, he makes his way down the line, glancing at each of our faces, passing mine without pausing until he comes to Freckles. She almost cracks her tooth then and there. He bows unsteadily and extends a crumpled haemanthus. I wince as she glances back at me.

One of the hens comes behind her and, pinching the small of her back so the men can't see, whispers in her ear. Freckles takes the haemanthus, hands shaking so bad she nearly drops it. The fighters roar in approval as Coran takes her hand and they walk to an empty table and sit. He pours her ale and downs half a mug himself.

Sixteen times the choosing ritual is repeated, until Duncan tucks a flask away and whispers to Picker. Picker cackles and shoves him forward.

"Duncan O'Cyros has finally dropped his balls! He wants a lass! What do you say, Mother?"

Harmony snorts. "He waited long enough. Go on, lad."

Only three of us remain—old hag me, Lion, and a plump newcomer. Duncan takes a haemanthus from the barrel, walks straight up to me, and offers it. I almost forget to take it.

Lion is picked last by a man of fifty. Even some of the Red Hands watch him with disdain as he leads his childwife away.

The farce of a ceremony is a blur. Whatever they gave us in the wine took a bit to start. It numbed me at first, but now it creeps up on little cat feet as we stand together between the braziers and some man babbles on about duty or somesuch. Many of the words are the same I heard when my sister married. Feel a little sick hearing them now. My hand's clutching dirt with Duncan's, both wrapped together by a bloodstained cloth woven by the wifeslaves. He's shifting nervously foot to foot, his early confidence in shambles for some reason. I watch the acrid black smoke from the braziers weave upward to the roof of the mine. All this is a lie. All this pretending the world ain't changing. I was jealous of my sister, but I never wanted a husband, not me. Maybe I thought I wanted one. But that was just because it said something that I didn't have one. That I got skipped over at wedAge.

I feel sick inside that it happens like this.

I repeat some words that I can't remember even as my mouth's saying them. That wine's something fierce. The other girls are like warm dolls. Wavering there with all the steadiness of riverside cattails. I'm wondering if it was a good idea to give them the teeth. How many will yellow out? How many will rat on me soon as they get their wits? Tails can't be the only coward. Maybe the wine's good. Makes them slow and easy, instead of twitchy and fearful.

I still gotta find the big girls.

Fortunately, the men are nearly as drunk as we are, especially Duncan. For courage? For fear? For weakness? Fuck knows. Maybe they're just tired of getting butchered by Obsidians. Some swill and new cunny must be the Vale itself after fighting Sefi's beasts. The few amongst the Hand who ain't drunk are the old boys. Grizzly lechers who are corner-looking out their eyes at their wives. I want to retch knowing what Lion's old man is thinking. Did any of them rape my sister? Did Duncan? I look over at him. He's so young. So handsome. So vile.

I know the marriage is done when there's a cheer. For all his smiles and earlier politeness, Duncan gives me about two seconds before I feel his cold tongue probing between my clamped lips. I let him in and he sticks it almost to the back of my throat, cupping my ass with his hands. He smells of shit tobacco and bitter swill and body odor and mint. He sighs into me, hungry.

That was quick.

Then it's celebration. Women hug me. Men hug me. I'm passed about like one of the clan. Like I'm not a sow whore they stole from her people. Then there's dancing. Duncan is popular with the men. He twirls me and probes my body like he owns it. Nausea comes in a tide. Fearing I'll retch, I pat Duncan on the chest and stumble over to a table and sit hunched and feeling the world swooping around me. A blur of faces flicker past. All laughing and gay. I want to crawl under the table. I want to hide until the world doesn't feel like some spinning kaleidoscope of horror. But a stone-cold realization sets on me that if I do that, if I curl up, if I stay seated, I'll end up waking in a tangle of sheets in a stone home like the one I grew tall in, except I won't be hearing my mother in the morning. I'll be hearing Duncan snoring drunkenly and feeling the taste of stale liquor in my mouth like old plums and the sore ache of my maidenhead split.

It ain't the parasite telling me I gotta move. I gotta be smart. I gotta find Volga and Victra. The parasite is quiet, though no longer contained to just my head. I feel its tendrils inside me, like roots along my bones. What does it want? If it weren't damaged, what could it do?

Wondering that won't save me here.

What would Ephraim do? How would he find the big girls?

I force myself to stand. Am I standing? I'm numb, but my feet are on the ground. Duncan's on his knees taking swill from a big gourd as men chant. I stumble to him. He coughs liquor as I pull at him and he puts his hands on my ass. "Dance with me," I think I say. Soon we're dancing, so I must have said it. Colors and hair and tassels flicker past. Amongst the laughing faces, I see a girl, is it Freckles? She stares at the ground as her husband twirls her and laughs.

Duncan's hot against me. I feel his rank breath on my neck. The sweat from his forehead against mine. He grinds against me, and I feel his manhood hard against my thigh. "It ain't that big a wedding," I say.

"What you mean?" he asks. "My darlin' disappointed?"

"I thought the Red Hand was an army."

"It *is* an army!" he cries. "Legions deep. We're all over Cimmeria, doncha know? No war talk for my wife's lips. Dance with me." I let him twirl me and I hold back a surge of vomit that squirrels up my throat. He pins me against him as the music slows.

"It's not an army," I say all spoiled-like. "Just a gaggle."

"A gaggle!" he crows. "We's been hard hit, sure, but there's more brothers deep here and two more mines."

"Doing what? Drinking?"

"Naw, some's mining. Some's training. Some's guarding the prisoners. You know the Gold hiding in your village?"

"I thought there was an Obsidian too."

"Huge one! Wouldn't believe your eyes. Big as the Reaper himself." She's not. "Got her with the others." I prod him a little. "Caught some coldies in the plains. Harmony put them to work in the deeptunnels clearing pitvipers and hauling ore."

"Tamed Obsidians. I heard it all now. I don't believe you."

"It's true."

"Prove it then." He's drunk enough to consider it. I grind my hips against his manhood. "I'll let you show me something else if you show me the coldies. Never seen one before." I play with the whiskers of his beard. "I thought you'd show me a whole new life . . ."

That does it.

Duncan steers me through the throng and grabs a growler of swill for the trip. I paw at him, a new notion coming to me. "Shouldn't we bring the lads some?"

"What lads?"

"The lads guarding the coldies."

He grins. "That's a fine consideration." Grabbing a couple growlers of swill, we stumble away from the party.

I'm glad I asked for the tour, despite the toll. The trip is not short, nor is it innocent. Duncan paws me drunkenly and pins me twice against a tunnel wall as we go down. Each time, I roll the back of my knuckles against his manhood and say, "Soon, my love." I make sure to remember each of the turns. Twenty steps down the third tunnel, first right. A hundred steps, down the ladder.

Gods, the drug they put in the wine is strong.

I feel like I'm wading through melting butter by the time we hit the gravLift down to the mines. Duncan pukes in the corner and wipes his lips, laughing as he washes his mouth out with swill from the growler. As he retches again, I quickly strip the haemanthus he pinned to my dress and grind it into the mouths of the open growlers we carry for the boys. By the time he's wiping his mouth, I've put the corks back in. I don't think he saw.

The gravLift spits us out into a dark cavern lit by glowlamps. The grinding racket of drills mauls my ears as we stumble together toward the mining teams.

When I visited my father's drillteam, I remember feeling wonder as I saw how important he was. A provider. A real man that I got to bring lunch to. It seemed so exciting back then. But this pit is infernal. Wet heat suffocates everything. The noise is unbearable. Men mill about the top of a tunnel where down deep a clawDrill burrows into Mars. Red, evil light glows up from the pit. HaulBacks dump hissing haultubes of helium-3 on the lip of the mine and rappel back down. Chain gangs of slaves heft the loads in metal backpacks and take them down another tunnel. There must be hundreds of them. Red Hand men rove along the chain gang lines with scorchers and pikes that glisten with electricity at the tips.

"Darran!" my husband calls to a sweating Red man with a gut the size of Cimmeria. The man shoves a boy with a hairless face out of the way and comes to give Duncan a hug.

"A man now, I hear!" Darran rumbles. "Is this the wee lass who's done the deed?"

"I scored well!" Duncan mumbles. "All the other blossoms are stumbling drunk, and me sweetheart here wanted to bring you poor nightshifters some evening swill!" He leans in. "And get a look at the coldies."

"That's a lass!" Darran says. "You did well." He thumps him on the shoulder and we hand over our growlers. I hope they can't taste the haemanthus. With the heat down here, I doubt they'll gainsay anything cold. Darran asks me a question. I mumble a sweet reply and curtsy. I tip over and the men help me up, laughing.

Dusting my skirts, I pout and scan the line of slaves. There's Oranges, Reds, Browns, a half-dead Blue, Grays, but no Obsidians. "Duncan promised me coldies."

"Can't let Duncan fall flat already," Darran says. He bellows at his men to bring up one of the ice bitch teams. Several minutes pass. Then I hear a clattering. A team of twelve Obsidians locked together with heavy iron chains shuffles forward, driven by several men with stunpikes.

"Warrior race, my ass," Darran says. "They even got a queen now. But who's your king, bitch?" He pokes one of the Obsidians with his pike. The tall woman grunts and glares at him. Her body is covered with winged symbols. "Duncan, there's the one you got yourself." Darran points to a hunched woman covered in grime and stunpike burns.

Volga. It's barely been two days since I've seen her. But she looks as if it's been five years. Her bare feet are bloody and shaking against the cavern floor. Her face is obscured by her hair, but her eyes stare distantly at the feet of Darran.

"Oh, they're so dreadful, like idiot bears," I say. At the sound of my voice, Volga looks up. She allows only a bare glimmer of recognition. I touch my head as though faint. "Oh, there's evil in those bottles, Duncan." Volga's eyes dart to the growlers Darran has passed to his men. "I feel faint, take me out of this heat."

"All right, coldies, back to work. Zoo's over." Darran shouts at her and sticks her in the side with his pike. She grunts and trudges on. One foot after the other. Before she disappears back into the mouth of the tunnel, she glances back at me and gives the barest of nods.

The party is still in full swing by the time Duncan and I stumble back. Some hard-eyed Reds loiter around the fringes. They've got pistols on their hips. That's not good. I smile at one, and he doesn't smile back. Soon they'll start taking the girls back. I wanna be first, else I might not get as free a roam of the place. I still have to find Victra.

"I don't want to dance anymore," I say to Duncan.

"But the lads will wonder where I've gone!" he says. "Did I marry a dead stone?"

I reach my hand to his manhood and feel a minor swell. "I don't want to dance anymore."

Duncan's home is not grand. I might have thought it so had I not seen Hyperion, and he thinks it so because he hasn't. He proudly shows it off, like it wasn't abandoned by the people that did live here. It's big enough for a family of six. A small kitchen with trophies on the wall—which he boasts on about until I pull him toward a bedroom. He sits on the edge of the bed and looks at me nervously. The music from the party is a whisper through the stone. "It's too dark," I say. So he searches for a glowlamp. When he finally finds it, he turns back, nervous, and pats the bed beside him. I sit.

Maybe I can talk with him. Maybe he can help us. He knows this is wrong. "This ain't your home," I say, regarding his search for the lamp. He shakes his head. "Where is your home?"

"Don't have one anymore. Rat War made sure of that." He plays with the edge of my skirt. "And you? You ain't one of the fish."

"Lagalos." I wait for a sense of recognition. But there ain't one. "How long you been with the Hand?"

He rubs his neck, reminded of something he'd rather forget. "Three years, I'd reckon. Take off your dress." It sounds almost like I have a choice. "Please."

I stand up and I go to move the shoulders of my dress. "Three years, eh?"

I run my tongue against Fig's molar as he frowns at me.

"Take it off," he says more aggressively.

"Why?"

"Because you're my wife."

"Why?"

"Because I . . ." He drunkenly searches for an answer. "I picked you. Listen, I want to be kind about this. But . . ."

"Makes two of us." I sigh. "Sometimes kind just ain't in the cards."

He rises from the bed, quicker than he looks, and grabs the back of my head to stick his tongue in my mouth. I let it worm there until he's distracted by his own pawing of my body. He looks down at my skirts so he can lift them, and his fingers are trying to find my insides between my legs when I pop the molar. There's a flood of liquid into my mouth. It is hot at first, but then grows cold as ice.

DNA calibration complete. V-7 antipersonnel system ready for deployment, the parasite says from within. I wondered how Fig kept it from melting her own flesh.

I think one thing as I stroke Duncan's face and he looks up at me, mouth open, eyes closed, tongue wet and probing. *This will be loud.*

I shove him in the chest. He stumbles over the edge of the bed and half-falls. I grab a pillow and spit the acid from my mouth, taking care to only get his stomach and legs. It splashes over him. Nothing happens. He frowns in confusion, lunges upward knowing something is wrong, grabs my throat with his metal arm.

Then the acid activates.

First go his clothes. He smells the smoke, glances down, and screams bloody murder as the acid eats into his skin. His fingers bruise the muscles of my neck, but I don't bother trying to breathe. He'll let go soon enough. I shove the pillow against his face as he goes on screaming. The sound muffles and I push at him to keep the acid from spreading from his gut and legs to me.

Sure enough, he lets go my throat and scrambles back from me, thrashing as the acid eats into his intestines and thighs. Pools of red muscle bubble and soon I see bone. I keep after him, rushing around him to keep the pillow over his face as he tangles himself in the sheets from his thrashing.

"There's a neutralizing agent," I hiss into his ear. "Tell me where the Gold is, and I'll use it." I pull the pillow from his face. He tries to scream out for help, but I shove it back down before he can. "How are they gonna treat you if you got no legs? They don't got replacements, I wager.

You'll be a freak. A crawling, leaking freak. Talk fast or you'll have nubs, oldboy."

I pull back the pillow.

"Can. F-f-f-fourth l-l-evel. W-we sealed her in the old jail. M-m-make it stop. Make it STOP. . . ."

I pat my dress. "Sorry. Musta left it in my pants." I push the pillow over Duncan's mouth as the acid eats on. I don't know why, but I leave his eyes uncovered so he can watch me watch him die. Just feels right.

The acid is something mean. In less than a minute, it eats through his intestines, then his spinal column as well as his legs.

Soon he's dead.

I've got one tooth left.

I stand over his corpse slapping myself, trying to shake off the stupor of that damn wine. There's no shaking it off, it seems. They drugged us good. I hope I got the Reds in the mines just as bad. How long will it take for them to start teetering? For Volga to get ahold of one of their pikes? How many of the girls will have had the guts to use the teeth? That's the real concern. Freckles and Lion, sure. But the rest? I didn't think of the timing. With as many Red Hand men as I've seen around here, they'll be butchered unless I free Victra.

I gotta move.

I search Duncan's body and strip his pistol, making sure the railgun's magazine is fitted right. Scouring the house, I find a well-worn pulse-Rifle and an Obsidian axe. I leave the axe, and try to recall how Volga taught me to prep a rifle as we schlepped through the highlands. I get it wrong twice before relaxing and letting my hands remember on their own. The rifle makes a droning sound as it signals it is ready. Lovely.

Rifle shouldered, pistol tucked into my skirts, I head out the front door.

Six Red Hands stand waiting for me on the walkway outside. Tails shivers amidst them. She points at me with a finger, mumbling something inaudible.

Shit.

70

LYRIA

Thunder Bottle

I STRAIN AGAINST THE ROPE that ties me to the mess hall table as the blood-crusted hammer hits my pinky. Pain explodes in my head. My stupor shatters into a thousand pixels. I reel back, gasping for air. The bone's busted. The skin's swelling and trickles of blood are leaking around the dent the hammer made. Harmony twirls the hammer and leans back. Several more of her boys prowl around the old Gray mess hall. They don't seem to mind Duncan's dead.

I could spit the last tooth in her face right now, but it's not just my life I'd be trading.

"I'm waiting for your answer, girl," she says. "You got nine more fingers. Ten toes. Two tits. One cunny. And then we get creative. How'd you kill Duncan?"

I do nothing, because I've been prisoner enough times to know doing something gets you hit again. "I hid a flask of acid in my shoe. Your boys didn't check my shoes."

"Why not?"

"You tell me. They're your idiots."

"And you just happened to have acid on you?"

"It's war, ain't it? Fun things floatin' around."

"Why'd you kill him?"

The woman seems to be expecting me to spout some ideology, or whimper about how unfair it is. Harmony's evil creeps along my spine as I meet eyes with her and shrug. Figure she only likes one kind of person. "Don't need a husband."

She surprises her men with a laugh. A door creaks and she looks up. "Picker," she says. "Just the man I wanted to see."

He goes rigid, glancing at the other men, at the hammer. "What's what, boss?"

"What's what is that upstairs, poor Duncan's guts are melted through." She looks at me with a little smirk. "Marriage ain't for everyone. But when I ask for breeders, it ain't so I can lose fighters, is it, Picker?"

"No."

"No, what?"

"No, Mother. I'll kill her right—"

"Picker. You owe me one breathin' fighter, not a dead breeder." She twirls her hammer. "Doncha?" He eyes the hammer and nods. "I got this stomach thing, right? This ulcer that just burns all through the night. Hard enough to keep sleep with it gnawing into me. Now I gotta try and sleep fearful my men can't even sniff out a Gamma." Her eyes flick to me. So this is it, then. My tongue finds the molar. "I can smell a pet rat through water. The stink . . ." She breathes deep. "So many old memories. But watch her lie through those rat teeth, boys. Watch her try to slink in with us." She taps the table with her hammer. "What clan are you, lass?"

I look her in those eyes, with plans to melt them out of her skull.

"My name is Lyria. I am the last Gamma of Lagalos."

"Lagalos," Harmony replies, searching for the memory. "Camp 121. It was an easy cleanse. Almost got a Telemanus for the effort."

"You killed my family. Their names were—"

Before I can finish, she slams the hammer down on my left index finger. I see flashes of white from the sudden pain, and hear a scream. But it ain't mine.

Harmony looks over my shoulder. I twist my head around. One of her men wobbles in through the open door, half-melted neck and torso leaking blood. He pitches forward onto the other man at the door. The man catches him and then starts to scream, holding up his hand as the acid begins to eat it too.

"How many of you are there?" Harmony shouts at me. She slaps me so hard I lose track of my efforts to open the molar. By the time I collect myself, she's up and out of her chair. I missed my chance. Harmony unbuckles her pistol as she hears more screaming from the township. She tosses her hammer to Picker. "Find out how many others there are. Rest of you, with me."

Picker stares at the door as it slams behind them, muffling the distant screams. Then he turns with a hateful look twisting his face. "Ya dumb slant. Throwing me under to the boss . . ." He gets real close to my ear and runs the hammer over my lips. "That's a bad lass."

He sits on the edge of the table. "Now, I'm not sayin' I was fond of Duncan. Fact is, this job's got me a little pinned, and he was making some moves, you know. But . . ." He taps the table with the hammer. "Man's got his orders." He leers in my face. The broken veins of his nose look like Hyperion traffic arteries this close. "You weren't exactly a looker before, but if you don't tell me how many girls you got pissin' acid, well, not even the dead'd kiss you."

I don't want to waste my tooth on him.

And I don't have to.

Behind Picker, a Red girl opens the door and slips through. It is Freckles. One hand rubs at a dark stain on the right side of her dress. She did it then. The other hand is hidden in its right pocket. Her hair is tangled, and her face maintains its dazed expression when she sees what's happening. She draws her right hand out from her pocket to reveal a tarnished pistol.

"Shoot him," I say.

The color drains from Picker's face as he turns to see the young woman he collected not a day ago now holding a gun on him from five paces. His hand reaches out. "Careful with that big iron, lass. You could hurt someone." He takes a step forward. "Just set it down, right?"

The pistol shakes in her hand.

"Shoot him!" I shout.

Picker takes another step forward, hesitating when he sees her finger stiffen on the trigger. "Think of all the times Gamma did your blood wrong," he says. "All the times your sibs were sick. How fat they got getting those boxes. While you sat with a bowl of sludge. That's a Gamma right there." Freckles blinks as he gestures to me. " 'Course she wants to get your hands dirty for her. But you ain't bad blood. Just set—"

The gun flashes. It's a small caliber, so his head only seems to lose its regular dimensions when the bullet goes into it. Picker doesn't fall. He seizes, gasping like a driller with rust lung. She shoots him again, this time in the chest. He flops down and lies twitching with his eyes open.

"Is he dead?" she asks.

"Well, he ain't talkin'," I say. She shudders in horror. "Freckles. Hey, lass. I never asked. What's your name?"

"Vanna."

"Vanna, I'm Lyria. Do me a kindness and untie me?"

"You're really a Gamma?" Vanna says, and the barrel of the gun drifts toward me. I go dead still.

"Yeah. That a problem?"

"You're not fat enough to be a Gamma."

I laugh. Of all things.

The gun goes off, slamming a round into the rope on the table and ricocheting past my ear. I jerk my head away, flooding with adrenaline.

"Sorry!" Freckles cries. "I thought that would work!" She tried to shoot the rope in half.

"You crazy? Just use a bloody knife. He's probably got one in his pocket!"

Picker is still twitching when Freckles searches his pockets and stands back up with a vibroKnife. She mutters apologies as she cuts me free.

Wincing from the two mangled fingers, I pull my hand from the ropes and bolt to my feet. Blood rushes to my head. When I blink the spots away, Freckles stands shivering over Picker. I pull the gun from her loose fingers. She looks over at me as I check the magazine. Twelve rounds left.

"Where are the other girls?" I ask.

She blinks as if coming back to herself. "Don't know. I saw them take you, out the window." Her hand rubs at the blood on her dress again. "Came soon as I could. W-what do we do?"

There's no right answer. Who knows if enough guards drank the swill in the mines? If the girls hid well enough? If I put enough haemanthus in there to do the trick? Or if Volga could convince the others to help her overpower those guards left standing? What should I do?

Even with a pistol, I'm no freelancer. Hell, I'm not even a Red Hand soldier. I can't help the girls. I need someone built for war.

The township is in turmoil as Freckles and I slip out onto the walkway. Up the town's tiered stone levels, melting men are stumbling onto walkways and bridges outside their homes. Their friends, many drunk, run to help them, but then push them back in fear that the acid will spread to them. The acid eats through a cable of a bridge and sends six men spiraling through the air to land five levels down on the mine floor. One splits his head open on a table. Several others lie calling for help, unable to move. Drunk men rush to help them.

Several childwives I know are running up the levels toward the mine's entrance. Red Hand men run to cut them off. I see Lion leading a couple of girls into a tunnel several levels up. Is she carrying a pistol?

Harmony's two levels above, shoving a man without a face off her and charging into a home. There's gunshots from inside. Knowing that a girl just died because of me woulda once put me on my heels, but all it does now is make me focus on the Can, the fortress the Grays would have used as barracks back when the mine was operating.

Its metal walls squat over the mine, and it's connected to the township by cable ladders hammered into the stone four levels up. Freckles and I rush to the ladder and begin to climb. We abandon it on the next level as we see men coming down. I hiss at Freckles to follow me into a house as a man leaves it. His wife stumbles back from the door, clutching a newborn as we shove in. I make a quiet motion, and she doesn't scream when she sees my pistol. In fact, her whole face changes.

"We gotta get to the next level," I say.

She leads us to the second floor of the home and gestures out the window to a cable. "Connects with the one above." She glances at my two mangled fingers. "Can you climb it?"

"We'll find out."

"What are you doing?" she asks.

"You should probably stay inside," I reply before swinging out.

It isn't easy, but tucking the pistol into my pocket, I scale the cable hand over hand. Aengus would smile to see all that exploring wasn't in vain. Freckles manages to follow me, a bit slower until she starts using her legs to push off the wall.

"Psst," a voice whispers as Freckles crawls up to the sixth level. I turn to see Lion's dark face staring out from a tunnel between two houses. "Is it safe?" A dozen other girls peer out from behind her.

"Not yet," I say. "Wait here, and we'll tell you when to come."

Freckles and I use a stone stairwell to make the seventh level. From there, we cross the cable bridge to the Can. I pull Freckles behind some crates as the door bursts open and a dozen men pour out past the crate and over the sky bridge to help their fellows below.

Seems most of the boys were drawn below by the screams. How do I know that? They're moving down different stairwells than I am. On opposite sides of the Can. I lean to get a view off the edge and see them going across different sky bridges.

How did I know they were there?

Or that the men were coming through the door?

Or that Freckles is just off my right hip?

It's not sight or sound, it's just a sense. A low-frequency humming in my head. A sort of texture of movement. *The parasite.* Not broken completely after all. I don't know what it's doing, but I like it.

The door to the Can is little more than a sheet of plastic. It covers a hole they must have welded into the Can to give it access from the sky bridges. It leads to a dark hall stocked with Republic rations. We pass storerooms filled with boxed electronics, foodstuffs, stolen fur jackets, and helium-3 canisters.

Finally near a stairwell, I see the level signifier. Level seven. We're three floors down from where Duncan claimed Victra is being kept. About to rush up the stairs, I push Freckles into a room and close the door at the feeling of soldiers coming up.

We wait with our backs pressed against the wall as their boots clatter the metal hall outside. Beside the door, I aim my pistol where the first man will come in. None does. Freckles looks at me after. "How did you know?"

"I heard them," I lie.

She's about to answer when I nod to the room.

It's someone's quarters. Across from a rumpled bed lies a mound of Gold sigils nearly half a meter high. I approach and see several carved figures sitting on a shelf, almost as if the sigils are an offering for them. A sacrifice. A military jacket hangs from a chair set in front of a table with organized rows of weapon parts and maintenance kits. The glass floor is covered with rugs. I lift one and see the township through the glass.

This musta been the room of the Mine Magistrate.

Ain't hard to guess who lives here now.

I unbutton my pants and take a squat. "What are you doing?" Freckles says, wide-eyed.

"Had to piss. Seems like the best place. Look for a map."

I search the room with Freckles when I've finished and we find a paper map taped to the wall above a communications console. I trace our route to the jail cells and then look down at the coms equipment.

It's all alien to me.

I fiddle with the buttons, but only get bursts of static and the internal coms of the Red Hand. I stop on one when I hear a man shouting: *"She got Darran, they're coming . . . they're—"*

Something cuts the signal short. I hammer at a few more buttons.

"Do you know what you're doing?" Freckles asks.

"What does it look like?"

"Well, what are you tryin' to do?"

"I'm trying to get a signal out."

"Me pa was the radio signal operator in my camp. Let me try." She edges me out of the chair. I breathe over her shoulder watching her work. "It might take a second."

"We don't have a second."

She shrugs and goes back to working. Unable to just wait, I scour Harmony's room for anything we can use. I find two razors in a box, and a heavy breastplate of a Gold's pulseArmor sitting on a rack at the foot of the bed. I can't tell if the battery works or not.

I try to concentrate to get some help from the parasite, but it is dormant. Freckles gives a little cheer and motions me over. "It's only a broad transmission. I don't know how to call anyone. Or if this thing even can."

"How far will it go?" I ask, taking over the chair. She shakes her head. I look back at the microphone. If I broadcast Victra's name, then her enemies will come here, and she seems to have a lot of those. Can this signal even reach Republic territory? They won't beat the Ascomanni if they're nearby, and may not be able to reach Victra if this *is* Obsidian territory. So who's left?

With a smile, I lean toward the microphone.

71

EPHRAIM

From the Static

TWO WEEKS OF SEARCHING in vain has netted us little but debris and close shaves with both Republic and Alltribe air forces. Electra and I have given up hope, and were it not for Pax, and had we someplace to go, we would have given up the search yesterday.

I drew the night shift today. As the kids grab a few hours' sleep, I hunch over the controls and watch the fjords below. Our passive sensors throb, detecting no emergency transponders. Volga is dead. I run a finger along the scar forming over Electra's incision. The heartspike the Alltribe put inside me jiggles within its container. Every day that passes makes my heart feel more and more like that spike, artificial and one big joke.

A weak signal crackles through the static. *"Red . . . base at coordinates."* I frown and adjust the sensors. *"Repeat, the whole bloodydamn . . . at 46 degrees . . . we . . . under siege. All . . . and enemies of Red Hand . . . call for your aid. Repeat . . ."*

I know that voice as it rattles off the coordinates.

It comes from a ghost.

I trigger the ship's internal alert systems at maximum volume. Half a minute later, Electra and Pax are stumbling through the hall rubbing sleep from their eyes. "If it's another false alarm, I'm going to hack off your—"

I interrupt Electra and play the recording. The two kids hunker down in the seats and help me compile the message from the scattered fragments until it's as clear as we can make it. Lyria is under siege at what she claims is the Red Hand headquarters. Her hail is for any and all enemies of the Red Hand to come to her aid. Lyria was likely kept in a cell near Volga. If she is alive, then Volga might be with her. I dare not even hope.

Pax immediately begins setting course for the coordinates. I slap his hand away. "If that's the Red Hand headquarters, we're gonna need more men."

"Obsidian are scratched," Electra says. "They'll just capture us. Republic?"

"They won't pay any attention to our hail," Pax says. "We have emergency codes, but if there were Howlers on Mars, they would have answered our earlier broadcasts. Even if we can get the message to Uncle Kieran, it'll be too late."

"Republic and Alltribe are a finger's twitch from all-out war," I say. "They'll both think this is some sort of trap. Not to mention if they find out you two are on my ship, then we're in the crosshairs of every mercenary band looking for a payday."

"Then who's left?" Electra asks.

"Mars," Pax says. Electra and I look at him for some semblance of clarification. "We need to boost Lyria's signal."

72

LYRIA

One Last Tooth

Freckles staggers under the enormous weight of the Gold breastplate as we make our way down the hall toward the jail. I lead with my pistol out, trying to make the parasite work again. I can't tell where anyone is.

Everything echoes in the metal halls. Men shout in the distance. Boots hammer stairs. Doors slam. Freckles and I creep behind three men who stand inside some sort of transparent coms room, washed pale by the light of holograms. Maybe they didn't notice my signal go out. Maybe it didn't go out. Most of the security globes are dark, but enough are alive to show the slaves unlocking themselves in the mines around the bodies of their overlords. A group of them gather around Volga. Blood drips from her head as she cradles a rifle and shouts at them.

There you go, big girl.

Then one of the men leans over his screen and goes stiff. My voice fills their room. We're stuck halfway down the hall. They know. Freckles looks at me in fear and I shove her into a maintenance closet. "Wait here for me."

"Where are you going?"

"Just wait here with the weapons. I'll be right back. Do not come out if you hear me scream." I shut the door as she nods. I grip my pistol. Men are coming from both directions. I drop my pistol and get on my knees.

"There's the bitch."

They bowl around the corner with rifles drawn, and I say the only thing I can think up with enraged psychos running toward me: "I'm with the Gold. I have information to sell Harmony."

I barely duck a boot aimed at my mouth. I catch it on the head instead and tip sideways. Someone's grabbing my hair. "What information?"

"I know where Julii's other daughters are."

The day my clan saw the sky for the first time, we toured the Can. Pa saw how unimpressive I found its jail. He told me it's a little jail for little crimes; anyone guilty of a big crime got the lash or the gallows. The jail was meant for loudmouth drunks, disobedient miners to cool their heads, and sometimes rats to spill their clan's secrets for a little cheese.

I don't know why, but I asked him if he ever turned rat, and he just grew quiet.

This mine's jail is as small as ours was. But instead of drunks or miners, it is stuffed a dozen to a cell with starving Obsidians and Reds. The smell as they throw me into a cell is tremendous.

Like I hoped they would, they'll lock me up until Harmony can come up from the chaos below. Things sound like they're settling down. I hope Lion is still hidden.

There is only one other prisoner in my cell, but her long legs take up most of it. Victra sits hunched on the floor. She doesn't move as I sit up from where the guards threw me. She wears tattered pants that barely reach her calves. Her shirt is torn and bloodied over her muscular shoulders. A wound oozes blood from her head.

She doesn't even look at me. I can't imagine the pain inside.

"Victra . . ." I say. She doesn't reply. "Victra, I'm here to—"

The jail door slams open. A dozen sets of boots come our way. Harmony leads a pack of her nastiest-looking men. "I thought I left you downstairs. Does anyone have my saw?"

A man pales. "I thought you wanted to use the hammer."

"Yes, but I also left my *hammer* downstairs."

Another man darts behind the corner and comes back with a saw crusted in old blood. Harmony smiles at him, glares at the first man, and kicks the cell door. "What's this bullshit about her other girls?" She spits. "Like the Julii would risk telling someone like you. How did you get the acid in?" She kicks the door again. "Where is it hidden?"

"Up your cootch," I say.

She points the saw at me. Then there's a shout. "Got one of them."

They drag a dead girl in. Harmony pushes through her men as they lay her out on a table at the far side of the room. Their backs are turned. I snap my fingers at Victra until she looks at me.

I pop the tooth.

Without changing her broken expression, Victra coils her legs under her. The acid releases into my mouth. She thrusts her manacles at me. When the acid goes cool, aligning itself to recognize my DNA, I dribble a line of it at the bridge between her cuffs. Then I spit the rest at the lock of the cell. It begins to smoke as it eats through the casing.

"It's in their teeth," Harmony murmurs after inspecting the dead girl. She wheels around. "It's in their teeth!" Before the men can turn back to the cell, the lock makes a satisfying *clonk*.

I've never been to Mercury or its Hippodrome. But I've seen videos of old chariot races. When the horn sounds, there is a rippling of muscle, a stir of dust, and everything becomes . . . heightened.

Victra bursts from the cell.

Wounded, tired, spent from labor, she isn't what she should be. But by killing her baby, these men get the Victra they made.

She kills the first man by breaking his back with a kick to his lower spine. The second, she kills so she can use him and his thick blast vest as a shield. His body erupts when his boys fire on them. And then Victra is amongst them, not blocking their attacks as they come one by one, but pouncing on them, breaking them as she pivots to break the next. Those she doesn't kill are mown down by their friends. Bullets and pulseblasts ricochet around the prison. I lie flat and two pulseblasts almost take off my feet.

Harmony gets one look at this, aims down her rifle, and shoots one of her own soldiers in the back of the neck as Victra throws him through the air between them. He knocks Harmony down, and when she gets up, shaking her head from the collision, she sees Victra covered in gore, crushing men in her rampage forward.

Like a good cockroach, Harmony bolts.

Victra tries to give chase, but the Red Hands throw themselves like madmen in her path, eager to let Harmony escape even if it costs them their lives. Victra takes them up on that offer.

When she takes her foot from the shattered back of her last victim, the room is still but for moaning prisoners. Victra hunches, breathing heavily, bullet through her shoulder, gashes around her legs, something red pulsing from her right buttock.

Then she walks out of the room. I glance at the prisoners, who are just starting to look up from their bullet-riddled cells. They won't be any use out there. They're so thin. I run to catch up with Victra, calling her name in the hall. She's already gone. Bloody footprints lead left. I follow them to the sound of wet thumps, and find Victra in the communications terminal I crept past earlier. Blood gathers around her bare feet as she absorbs the hologram feeds. One shows Volga and several dozen slaves firing up a tunnel at Red Hands. Several hundred more huddle behind them, ready to pick up a weapon if another drops. They're outmatched by the Hand men pouring from the township down to meet them at the main tunnel.

"You did this?" she asks without turning.

"Yeah. But I think I need some help now."

She looks over, then back at the screens. Harmony is running up a stairwell.

"She's getting away," I say.

"I am aware." She squints at the holograms, then sits at the console to take its controls. "What you are not aware of is that you have signed everyone's death warrant. They have an army camped around the perimeter of the mine's aperture. We'll never get out."

"I called for backup," I say.

"Metaphorically or physically?"

"Uh, physically."

She turns. "Howlers?"

"Like I have their number. I did something called broad spectrum."

Her body tenses. "Did you use my name?"

"I'm not an idiot."

"So you said," she says, turning back to her task.

Harmony runs from a stairwell into a large chamber with an open roof to the sky. Fifty men slide down the ladders dangling from the rim of the roof. Harmony shouts at a pilot and loads up into a shuttle. They're airborne a moment later, rising slowly out of the mine. Victra's fingers move over the keys and the camera shakes. The men who just slid down the ladders point upward. Then I see why. The sky is becoming smaller as the roof closes. It slams shut before Harmony's shuttle can escape. The top wings of her shuttle snap in half as her ship collides with the closed ceiling and spins on sputtering engines to crash back down to the floor.

Victra stands up.

"Where are you going?" I ask, throwing an arm toward Volga's holo.

"To pay a debt."

"Volga needs your help. We all do!" I shout as she walks away. "She's got dozens of men up there. If you die there, you can't help anyone."

"And why would I help you?" she asks at the door with a turn. On the holo, Harmony is crawling free from the crippled shuttle. Her men drag her along to a gravity lift.

"Because I helped you. So did Volga. And someone once told me revenge is patient."

She stares at me and tilts her head.

"We can get her after. There's girls down there. Girls that risked their lives because they couldn't take it anymore. Are you just going to let them die like Ulysses?"

She stiffens. Her eyes glare at me, then she looks at her bleeding wounds. "I will need proper armor."

I call out into the hall. "Vanna, it's Lyria. You can come out now."

A maintenance closet door opens behind Victra, making her jump. Mops spill out onto the floor as Freckles stumbles out. Picking herself up, she looks sheepishly at the Gold and pulls the breastplate forward. "Ma'am. I brought you some armor." She pulls out the razors. "And these."

Victra almost smiles.

Victra, Freckles, and I look over the bridge down into the Common. Victra made us hide for ten minutes, though she refused to say why. Down below, the Red Hand has managed to gain order. While they haven't found all the girls, they've found some. Dozens are gathered in the center of the township and under guard as most of the men pour toward the main tunnel to fight Volga's fellow slaves. Then I see why Victra delayed. Unable to escape from the top, Harmony's going out the bottom. She moves across the Common floor directing her men at the girls, and taking a group of more than forty down into the tunnels to link up with her larger force.

"She means to hunt me now," Victra says. "Fair enough." Victra hands me and Freckles the grenades she scavenged from the men she killed. "Bring these to me at the bottom."

And then she jumps off.

I thought Figment and Volga were top of the food chain until I see Victra descend into the township. While Freckles and I clamber down ladders, Victra vaults from level to level, sometimes two down, sometimes one up, killing men as she goes. She lands amongst three Red Hand men on a bridge and throws them off. She jumps a level up and destroys a portable gun turret before it's brought online. Bullets eat into the stone around her as she jumps down two levels, dragging her razor through a dozen men as they descend a single ladder to the second level. She kills the rest that gather at the base, and then, almost for fun, takes the rifles of the dead and begins popping in and out of cover, two quick shots, duck, move, two quick shots, duck, move. Soon all the men guarding the girls in the center of the township are on their backs or crawling away with holes in them.

We slide off the last ladder and rush up to Victra as she crouches behind cover, scanning for threats. Five rail slugs are flattened against the ill-fitted armor. I can see through a hole in her right biceps.

"Took you long enough," she says, taking the grenades.

Her left ear hangs on by a strip of flesh. I motion to it.

"Stop being distracted." She tears it off and puts it under her breastplate, wheeling as a gun goes off. Little Lion, who'd been caught by the Hand men, now has one of their pistols and fires it at a man limping away until he goes down. It becomes less funny when she runs up to him and fires at his thrashing body until her magazine is empty. She looks up, spattered with blood, not a single emotion on her face. Victra looks to me. "One of yours?"

"More or less."

She grunts. "Be right back."

"I'll come—"

"No." She kicks my thigh so hard it goes numb, and then silently bolts toward the tunnels, killing two men who come from the main force engaged with the slaves. Then she disappears. A cramp grips my leg. I stumble up and hobble after her as Freckles pulls the girls away to find a place to hide. I follow Victra's wake of dead men until the tunnel widens and I come out to maybe two hundred Red Hand men firing down the tunnel at Volga and her men. The sound is enormous. Victra is crouched behind where they've gathered their wounded. She finishes throwing something and turns to sprint up the tunnel. She catches sight of me and motions me back.

Thoom. Thoom. Thoothoom.

The grenades begin going off behind the Red Hand soldiers, tearing holes in their ranks until the whole tunnel is filled with dust. The explosions echo away, replaced by a growing roar down the throat of the tunnel. The slaves rush up into the dust.

I fall down behind a boulder with Victra, laughing as the Red Hand disintegrates in front of my eyes. "Don't just sit there, you idiot," Victra says from a knee, and picks off a Hand man as he runs half blind out of the dust. "Shoot something."

I join her on a knee, steady my arms on the boulder, and take aim. I fire until I see a woman pushing her way through the dust, shoving the bodies of her own men into the path of the freed slaves.

Harmony is trying to escape. I point her out, but Victra is already on the hunt.

73

LYRIA

At Last, She Screams

I'VE LOST SIGHT OF VICTRA in the tunnel. When her men's fortune finally turned, Harmony left them to die and made her escape through a side tunnel. Victra and I gave pursuit, but Victra's long legs outraced mine, and left me behind. The gloom of the tunnel is nearly complete, but I can see my breath blooming in front of my face as I walk the steep path of a clawDrill.

I stop suddenly, hearing a whisper, and go very still. Long shadows ripple on the ceiling of the tunnel, not twenty paces overhead. So that's why she chose this tunnel. I take a step, and the shadows stop. Watching me.

There's gunshots ahead, past where the tunnel bends downward.

I bolt, no time to see if the shadows are following.

I scramble down the steep tunnel, sliding half the way in my haste, and find Victra crouched behind a rock. She darts to the next. A pulse-blast turns the floor behind her molten.

"You left your men to die," Victra says. She moves to the next boulder. Two shots sizzle past her before she takes cover.

"I'll find more," Harmony says from deeper in the tunnel, where it widens to form a chamber with slick, dark walls and no source of light but the acid green spasms of her firearm. She must be wearing optics to see down here. Wait, how can I see? The figures are murky, like shadows over ink, but I can make out Harmony as she peers down her rifle's sights.

"You murdered your own people." Victra fakes a dodge to the next rock. Harmony sends a stream of shots along the path. Victra goes the other way, disappearing into a caved-in section of the tunnel. "You killed Ares."

"Because he was one of you!" Harmony shoots into the shadows. "Come out and fight me, bitch."

I lie in the shadows and take careful aim with my pistol.

"You killed Lyria's family."

"Who cares?" Harmony sneers. She checks her rifle's ammunition gauge just as Victra swings down from above.

Harmony pulls the trigger.

Click.

She exhales and then throws the gun at Victra and reaches for her bootknife. Victra catches the gun in one hand and smacks Harmony's hand. Harmony stumbles back, fingers broken. The knife clatters to the ground. She swings at Victra with her other hand. Victra punches the balled fist, shattering it. I tuck my pistol away and walk after them.

"You killed her child," I say to Harmony. Victra cracks a flare and tosses it at Harmony's feet. She rips off Harmony's night optics.

"She killed mine," she snarls, tracking my arrival with almost as much hate as she does Victra. "They rotted from a disease we cured six hundred years ago. Why? For what?" She spits. "For this." As I watch her froth with hate, she isn't the monster I remember. The powerful force that ate up my brother and family out of this world. She's just a woman enraged. It makes her so small to me, I can barely understand it myself. I pity her smallness, but not enough to scourge the hate from me.

I hear something behind her. A deep whispering. I edge forward as she glares out at the world.

"You'll all burn," Harmony promises. "I've got a torchShip. Gave the order if I don't say otherwise, it'll lay into this mine with everything it's got. What it don't burn to cinders, it'll pinch in here under two hundred meters of stone. You're trapped in here with me. But if I call in . . . we can play another day."

Victra raises her razor. "I'll permit you what I permitted the poet. Choose your last words."

I creep closer to the whispering.

"I'm valuable to the Republic."

"Nah." Victra is about to stab Harmony through the heart when I grasp Victra's thick wrist. She frowns at me.

"Trust me. Not like this."

I walk up to Harmony and rip a flare off her belt. Cracking it open, I throw it toward the whispering. In its light I can see that not far from where she made her stand against Victra, the floor gives way. A narrow cleft of rock leads across a chasm, no doubt where Harmony was trying to lure Victra to her death.

I kick the flare down the chasm as Victra drags Harmony forward. The flare lands amongst a pool of pitvipers gathered near the heat of a hot spring. Warm, clammy air oozes up.

I turn to Harmony and see her looking down, childish with fear. She thought they were her salvation.

"Those are adults," I tell her. "They won't kill you. They'll give you enough poison to paralyze you, and then they'll burrow their eggs inside. Few days' time, you'll be gobbled up from inside out."

"Poetry in motion. Bye, bitch," Victra says and then grabs Harmony's belt and collar and hurls her into the pit.

Harmony's arms windmill as she falls amongst the pitvipers. A nasty bitch thicker than both my thighs claims her first, striking before she even lands. The fangs make a meaty punching sound as they enter. Harmony grabs another knife from her waist, but the pitviper is already coiling around her arms and legs, immobilizing her with soft rustling sounds as it burrows its head into her lower stomach to implant its eggs out the womb sack in its neck.

Harmony's mouth opens in silent pain.

Then, at last, she screams.

I've never heard anything like it. Not when I look at her. Not when I reach the end of the tunnel with Victra and hear her pain echoing after us. It is the scream of a woman who lost everything far too long ago. Victra and I hear it, but we do not turn back.

Harmony lived on pain. She'll get it to the end. I don't miss the lesson.

The slaves have left the Red Hand soldiers dying on the ground in their quest for the surface. We find them gathered with nearly a hundred Red Hand prisoners in the center of the Common. Volga is giving orders to a group of bloody men and women, telling them to search for an exit. Six are Obsidian, the rest Red with crooked Gamma sigils branded onto their foreheads.

I thought I was numb until I see my girls have come out of hiding. Lion sits with Freckles on the far wall. The older girl is crying and holding on to Lion. Lion squirms to escape and waves to me, her pistol tight in her hand.

Some of the other girls kick downed Hand men. More women descend from the township, many those who were already dwelling here. The wives. Some of the slaves watch warily as the wives pick up rifles only to point them at other wives and push them in with the men. Some throw stones at their tormentors or pull their hair or try to brain them with rocks, shrieking with a rage beyond words.

It isn't my place to stop them.

"Door out is shut," Victra says.

Volga wheels from her planning to find us coming toward her. She looks like hell, but drops her pulseRifle to wrap me in a hug. She spares a nod for Victra.

"How did you—" Volga begins.

"Later," Victra snaps. She picks a piece of metal out of her bare foot. "Harmony's . . . dealt with, but she said they have a torchShip. If that's true, we have a problem."

We do have a problem. While Victra may have sealed the doors, the camp outside the mine's entrance is evacuating in clumsy fashion. Soon we see why. Via the cameras outside the mine, we watch the highland trees shiver as something rises out of sight. Soon a shadow stretches across them as a metal ship maybe six hundred meters long rises from the sea.

The chair creaks as Victra leans back. "Well, girls, it was a nice run."

"Lyria says she got the signal out," Volga says.

"Scopes are clear," Victra says. "No one listened." She taps the instruments. "Who'd you call, anyway?" A dot appears on the scanner. Victra frowns and leans forward.

I swallow as more dots appear. "Mars," I whisper.

74

EPHRAIM

Son of the Rising

Two of the *Snowball*'s javelin missiles streak toward the horizon. Thirty more missiles join them, dropped by the few ships in our ragtag fleet that possess the capability. They soar ahead in a thin line toward the monstrous six-hundred-meter torchShip and her iridescent shield that blocks our path to our girls and the last remnants of the Red Hand.

When we received Lyria's signal after two weeks of searching, we boosted it so half the continent of Cimmeria could hear. I did not expect a reply. Pax did. By the time we reached the North Thermic, our instruments looked like paint spatter from the incoming signatures. With the two juggernauts of Mars, the Obsidians and the Republic, busy assembling Armageddon, the people of Mars woke up.

More than three hundred ships arrived—dated ripWings flown by Red militia from Acaron, sleek gunboats from patriotic Silvers of Nike and Attica, war-tested fighter ships from renegade Republic pilots, civilian cargo-haulers, fishing fliers, passenger shuttles, most weaponless, with open decks loaded to capacity with Gammas hastily assembled from mines, villages, and assimilation camps all across the north of Cimmeria. All streaking low enough to sea for their bellies to glimmer with water and salt. All come to give the Red Hand the ass-kicking they've been begging for. Mars was the first planet enslaved by the Golds. She became the cradle of liberty, and her children watched as the Reds who started it all were squashed by what came after. Now they shout: "Blood Red! Blood Red!" as they tear across the sea.

Only to find a fucking torchShip blocking our path.

Pax theorized it would be understaffed, with poor discipline. He was right.

No flak shield devours our missiles. Without Blue allies to neural-link to the ship or sophisticated AI to control it, the Red Hand has to go manual. Men will be sprinting through corridors, barreling down gravity slides to reach the starboard cannons. It takes them just long enough for us to draw first blood.

Our missiles detonate in a crackling line. Their shields flash and buckle under the kinetic impact. "Alpha Squadron: Stage Two," I intone into the com. "Beta Squadron: Stage One."

With the *Snowball* responsible for boosting the signal, Pax urged me to seize authority, ordering the other ships to rendezvous with us over the sea south of the distress signal. The scattermash of ship captains bickered so much as they gathered that I took command more out of frustration than ambition. My extensive vocabulary of profanity and my badass ship certainly helped establish dominance over the pack.

According to my plan, the armed ships burst upward as the torchShip opens up a wall of fire. Meanwhile the unarmored civilian ships sweep in west and east behind the shelter of the mountains, skirting the torchShip's line of sight to make landfall near the mine to rescue the besieged.

Hold on, Volga, baby. If you're there.

Railgun rounds whistle past the *Snowball*. Half a dozen of our ships become debris. Even if the Red Hand torchShip is understaffed and a hundred years old, we're outgunned. "Alpha: Stage Three." A kilometer out from the torchShip, we dive hard at a sixty-degree angle. Screaming tendrils of turret fire lick out at us. Pax takes us into a mind-bending corkscrew and then cracks a shot on a whim.

Hot damn, he can fly.

Our railguns pour a quarter of their magazines into the starboard fuselage of the torchShip, taking out three rail batteries. Two mysterious black gunboats from Nike with twice our firepower unload their main particle cannons. Fissures of white light divide the world. When they fade, ten banks of the torchShip's turrets have been replaced by a gash of molten metal.

Using the opening, a flight of three rickety ripWings with Gamma militia sigils swoop into the gap and drop their payloads before nose-diving between the ship and the sea. The bombs rupture gaping holes ten levels deep in the decks. Seawater presses downward from the shock-waves. Men on fire jump to tumble like embers into the sea.

The *Snowball* jolts. Our shields collapse as the torchShip's particle beam lashes into our port side and overloads the secondary reactor. Warning lights throb.

"Please silence that," Pax murmurs. Sweat drips down his brow. I silence the alarms. I was hesitant to let him fly, but truth be told he's better than I ever was or could be. I don't have the reflexes his DNA gives him on the stick, and I can't even consider syncing. Electra waits behind us, a compact rifle across her lap and Braga's stolen razor wrapped around her waist.

"Fat bitch is rolling," she says.

"Yes, but slowly," Pax drones. "Told you they're understaffed."

Out the viewport, the torchShip begins a slow rotation so that its flaming starboard side will face the sea, minimizing its exposed profile as it shreds us with the unharmed topside. The com fills with mayday calls as the fresh guns of the torchShip open up. Fireballs bloom. The air shudders. "Clever bastards," I mutter. They lower their elevation as they turn, leaving no more than ten meters' room between their burning hull and the waves. "That's a narrow slip."

Pax tries a run, but is headed off by cannon fire. He banks around. "Gunboat One, Gunboat Two, I need a path."

"Is that a child?" one of the captains asks.

Pax gestures to me impatiently. I clear my throat. "Gunboat One, Gunboat Two, are you going to give me a slagging path or am I going to have to carve it my damn self?"

"They're too low to the deck."

"Not for my pilot." I set a hand on Pax's shoulder. Electra swats it away.

"Register. Form in our shadow."

"Ephraim, get a sick bag ready," Pax says.

"I can handle a few G's."

"Not these." Pax banks the *Snowball* at a sickening angle to take it low and behind the two gunboats as they sweep in a parabolic arc back toward the torchShip. Blood thunders in my head. My stomach reels at the aerial acrobatics.

Our ragtag fleet is being slowly swatted from the sky. The *Snowball* rumbles as we fall into a dive with the black gunboats and level out to skim the water, driving for the torchShip. Water is caught in our gravity cushion. Spheres of it float around us as we rocket toward the torchShip.

I hold on to the crash padding of my seat. The chop kicks our belly, heaving us upward. The gunboats unload the last of their hi-tech javelin and open up with their particle cannons. Fire laces the torchShip. Something punches a hole in the fuselage of the left gunboat, sending it skipping into the water. Its particle beam continues firing as it tumbles, superheating strips of water. Sheets of vapor erupt upward. The second gunboat is hit and peels off.

The torchShip looms before us. The gap between water and hull barely thicker than a razor. Acceleration pins me to my seat. The sea is less than two meters below. If we so much as nick it, it'll ricochet us up into the hull of the torchShip at just under the speed of sound.

The cannon on the lateral-facing topside pours fire at us. Water vaporizes all around. The gap grows, still so terribly small. We slide between the cannon's firing solutions, and I close my eyes. When I open them, we're into the gap. Something breaks off the top of the *Snowball*. The sun disappears, replaced by the smoldering underside of the torch-Ship. Pax shunts our gravity field, forcing us into a gut-wrenching spin and my organs to thump into my ribs. He unloads the last of our railgun magazine into the exposed underbelly. Debris rains down on us. I cover my head, waiting for the whole ship to fall as the world blurs past.

Then sunlight.

We spin out the other side and, with a burst of acceleration, flip upside down and shoot landward. "You forgot the missiles!" I shout.

Pax smiles.

Thunder claps behind us. I watch through the rear display as the torchShip heaves upward along her midline, like a bucking horse, and then succumbs to gravity, breaking in two down the center. As if a spell's been broken, her gravity engines fail and she plummets into the sea.

I grab the sick bag just in time to hurl up my breakfast into it.

Electra cackles and pets my head like I'm a puppy.

The unarmed civilian ships landed ahead of us on the outskirts of the mine to unload their cargo. Thousands of armed miners, fishermen, old soldiers, men, women, and teenagers roll through the Red Hand, disarming them and taking prisoners by the hundreds in the camp around the mine entrance. Since they all saw my green ship delivering the killing blow to the torchShip, they raise their fists as we pass over them to land.

"What are they singing?" I ask, still a bit woozy from the G's that the kids seem barely to have noticed. Pax amplifies the ship's external ears.

"The Song of Persephone," he says, and takes us down.

As we watch from the ramp, there is no hysteria in the victory. No rampant revenge or the beheading of kneeled enemies. Only a sweeping sense of fraternity and weary justice that even an outsider could sense. After the brutality of the Obsidians, it is beautiful.

I spot flags and armbands with the Gamma crest. And then other crests, other tribes: Lambda, Beta, Alpha, Omicron, Silver trade icons, Gray mercenary bands, and more. Already hundreds of Red Hand soldiers have been gathered on an empty airpad.

These are the demons of Mars. The butchers of Lyria's family.

More than half of them couldn't have been more than ten years old when the Rising began. Stripped of their weapons and coats, they look sickly, and they shiver in fear as they are surrounded by the people they tortured for so many years. Do they even know why they did it? In defeat, they've abandoned any creed. They huddle not together in a band, but each isolated and alone in their misery.

I'd pity them if I didn't loathe them so much.

A crowd of Gammas and their new allies rush toward the *Snowball* to celebrate the pilot and his prophetic maneuver against the torchShip. From a distance, they think it was me and not the small human by my side. As they see our faces, they slow and then stop, gathering in a sort of wary perimeter. Their faces are young and old, all sunburnt. They hold antique rifles, household pistols, even slingBlades. A ripple of recognition goes through them when they spot Pax and Electra. Then understanding as they see the pilot halo Pax wears. It isn't disbelief on their faces when he takes it off. It is fulfillment. As if they believed in something once, grew to laugh at the naïveté of their own conviction, only to see that they were right all along.

I sense the weight of the moment, and it chills me.

This is how a legend begins. The First Boy. The Son of the Rising, fulfilling his parents' promise. He looks afraid to step into his new world, as if he feared this moment but knew it would come. I wait for him to look at me to give him a nod of encouragement. This time, he needs none. With Electra at his side, he steps past me and into the crowd, which parts and raises their clenched fists in salute as they chant his father's name.

I follow at a distance.

The heavy mine doors dilate open with a groan. The first up the maintenance stairs is a young girl jabbering a woman's name. A man shoves his way through the crowd and scoops the young girl up. They're hit from the side by a woman who wraps them in a wild embrace till they are huddled together crying in a mess of limbs and red hair. This scene repeats itself until I stand stock-still, dreading my own reunion with Volga.

I wait with Pax and Electra in the shadow of this communion. Each of us heavy with dread, fearing we won't get to share the joy of the others. Each grime-spattered face, each weary set of shoulders that comes up the mine stairs, brings fresh hope and then disappointment. *Where is Volga?*

A scrawny Red wearing a tattered, ridiculous dress and carrying a big rifle comes up the stairs. She's functioning as a crutch for a huge Gold woman who looks fresh out of a ten-year stay in hell, stomach still swollen from pregnancy, but no child in her arms. Victra au Julii. In the flesh. I take an involuntary step back as Pax and Electra rush to the woman. She scoops them up at the same time, and holds them a meter off the ground in absolute silence. The Red watches with a faint smile.

"Rabbit," I call. The Red turns. She's barely recognizable in all the dirt and blood and in that stupid dress. When she sees me, she breaks into a high laugh. She drops her rifle and sits on the ground, laughing so hard I can't tell when she begins to weep.

"*You* brought the army." She laughs. "*You.*"

"Where's Volga?"

"You were right," she says, looking over my shoulder. "He did come."

"Ephraim." I don't turn, afraid my eyes will make my ears liars. Afraid now in the moment. Terrified that while I remember the good in our past, she will remember how we parted. What I made her do. What I said. "Ephraim." I turn and see her. She has lost at least twenty kilos. Her face is drawn and tired. Her pants tattered and bloody. Her arm in a makeshift sling. But she is alive.

"Hello, Snowball."

"Are you wounded?" Volga asks. "You are shaking."

I tilt my head. "No. I— Yes, but no."

She squints. "You came for me."

"Are you stupid? Of course I—"

Before I can finish the sentence, her arms are around me. For once I don't hold back. I sink into the embrace. She is my home. She has been since I found her on Echo City. What a pity I only just realized it.

"Victra, don't!" Pax shouts.

Volga and I part to see Victra au Julii storming toward me with a heavy pulseRifle held like a pistol. Volga pushes me to the side. "Victra. Enough." I can't believe my eyes when the oligarch stops dead in her tracks and Volga sets a hand on her shoulder. "Enough."

The Julii stares at Volga, her face coated with blood and dirt, her eyes gleaming from dark sockets, and it is as if all her hate turns to anguish. She heaves a horrible sob and turns away to stumble toward the treeline as if it held something that was hers.

I lean against the wall of the shower, sinking into the heat. The scar on my chest is mostly healed thanks to the Julii's medici. I've spent more time with them in her estate than with Volga. She said she had something to do. I exit the shower and dress in the clothes the Julii provided. I keep waiting for the trap to close, but it seems even a Gold can learn to forgive. Or become too tired for revenge.

A holoCan plays in the living room. I find Volga there, back from her mysterious errand. She sits surrounded by half-repaired Olympian towers and a sea of chanting Reds and lowColor, each with a fist clenched in the air as they chant for the Reaper. Beyond the holoCan's prism a city of mountain peaks glows. Attica.

After all this time, it must be fate to end up here after all.

The Reds go silent as Volga mutes the feed. "You're awake," she says.

"Did you complete your mysterious mission?"

Her face falls. "I wanted to see Ulysses. What they did to him."

"Oh," I say awkwardly. She stares at a spot on the floor, then wordlessly speeds through the channels faster than I can follow.

"How can you even follow that?" Undisturbed by the chaingun of information, she shrugs. "Stop. You're giving me a . . ." I don't finish. My train of thought has been hijacked by the silent stream of faces that flows through the living room. Volga never settles for long. Five seconds at a protest in Nike. Two seconds at a strike in a new Red mine city. Fifteen at two dead Obsidians carried by a mob through Olympia. Ten at All-tribe Obsidians landing to retrieve their brethren as pain tanks disperse the crowd with microwaves. Five of braves knocking down doors searching for terrorists.

This isn't what Sefi wanted. This isn't the world she tried to make. It's not fair for others to come in and cock it all up.

"Sefi bit off more than she could chew. Typical Martian," Volga mutters.

"Hyperionin ain't much better, love. We don't even chew."

"They must have been high on God's Bread," she says in contempt of her own people. "As if Mars would want to be ruled by savages instead of the Reaper." She whispers his name. A new reverence.

"Sefi isn't a savage."

Volga squints at me. "Concussion?"

"Just getting old. I dunno." I take the controls from Volga and turn off the holos. "I think it's time you finally tell me where you've been. Hardly had a moment with you."

"I'll tell you," she says, heading to the kitchen. "But first we will need coffee."

"Make mine with whiskey."

She brings me coffee made of coffee. Passive-aggressive little shit.

Over the pot, we share our stories as the sun sets over Attica. I go first. She grins when I tell her about fetching Pax and Electra from the Syndicate. And listens breathless to the dragon hunt and my stories of Valdir and Sefi. I do not speak of Fá. My heart breaks when I hear her tale, and at the end of it, I can only hunch forward and stare at a small crack in the table.

"I'm sorry." I meet her eyes. "I'm so sorry . . ."

She crosses her arms. "For?"

"Everything."

"Be specific."

"Julii rub off on you much?" She waits expectantly with a new air of confidence. "For, you know, trying to make you be like me." I sigh, feeling exposed. "Without me—" The words just don't come.

"Without you, I would be nothing. Still working the docks at Echo City. Or dead on a stupid battlefield. Or dead a dozen times before." She puts a hand over mine. "You taught me how to survive. I am lucky. Not all girls have a father."

That one sucker-punches me.

"Whatever you do, wherever you go . . ." She pokes my chest, then her own. "There is no distance between. Do you understand?" A snort escapes me. She reels back, insulted. "I am very serious—"

"Sorry," I say between fits of laughter. "That's just so . . . dripping in syrup. That's gotta be from Lyria." She draws in on herself and I pat her knee. "Hey, hey. I know what you meant. Me too. Verbatim." She relents and gives me a sideways grin.

There's a knock at the door. Volga rushes to open it. Pax walks in with a small box. I've seen little of him since we landed in Attica. He wears the crest of a lion on his right shoulder, and that of a pegasus on his left. He looks as if he has aged two years. "Your parents?" I ask.

"They say my mother is alive. In captivity, but alive."

"Oh, kid." I feel tears welling up and I grip his shoulder. "Your father?"

He nods. "Alive. But the Golds are preparing a final assault on Heliopolis, and Luna is a mess. No fleet will come. It's only a matter of time."

"I'm sorry."

He nods and pushes the box into my hands. "Victra wanted me to give this to you."

"What is it?"

"Why don't you just open it?" I sit down. He turns to Volga and says, "Volga, we haven't had a chance to meet. I am—"

"I know," she says, wide-eyed.

He doesn't blush away from the recognition. By the way he looks at her, I know he sees his father's old friend. Julii told him. "You should know, Tin—Ephraim spoke very highly of you."

She blushes and makes a show of going to make more coffee.

I open the box. Inside is a slim metal disk and a holodrop.

"Victra is proud," Pax says. "Obnoxiously so. And hasn't spoken much since . . ." He glances at Volga and leaves it unspoken. "But she owed a debt to Trigg. Without him, she would have died in the Jackal's prison ten years ago. She will forgive your trespass." He gestures to the disk. "A one-way signal pass to get you past Republic patrols and off Mars."

I play the holodrop. A recording of a ship-to-ship transmission appears. Xenophon's face fills the frame as he requests approach clearance to the *Pandora* for a shuttle bearing Pax and Electra. It is dated the day of the attack on the *Pandora*.

I look up at Pax.

"It was Xenophon all along, not Ozgard," he says. "He was the intermediary. Victra thought we were making the exchange. The first shuttle destroyed their main sensors, and allowed the rest of the Ascomanni to approach and board. He is Fá's inside man. Ozgard, Amel, both framed."

I set the holodrop down. "What do you want me to do with it?"

"Tell Sefi."

"You tell her. You have the coms."

He shakes his head. "We can't reach Olympia. Alltribe has gone paranoid. They think every communiqué carries a virus. To be fair, the Republic did launch one that took down a quarter of their ships. Even so, everything goes through Xenophon. We have no allies left. He's isolated her."

"You want me to go back."

"Who else could get in there? They're on war-watch."

"This is getting ridiculous."

"I know." He glances at Volga in the kitchen as the coffee machine somehow overflows. Some things never change. "The older I get, the more I feel for my parents. Especially my father. Hate him or not. There's never a right call, just people who make the hard ones." He stands. "I have to go now. If you do not have breakfast plans, I would love you to join me. I have invited Lyria as well."

"Depends on the lass here," I say. Volga nods enthusiastically from the coffee mess.

I walk Pax into the hall. "Are you going to tell her?" he asks. When I don't answer, he takes the chain from his neck and presses Trigg's ring into my hands. I'd nearly forgotten about it. "You're a good man," he says. I laugh. "Stop. Whatever you decide, you've earned the right to be called that."

I mess up his hair and he takes that for answer enough.

"I like him," Volga says when the door closes. She hides the coffee she made for him behind the bar. "Did he really fly that ship?"

"Like a Blue."

I put the chain around my neck and I look down at the holodrop playing in the box. I have to tell her now. How does one say something like this?

I know you have always felt apprehensive about your own race. One part yearns to be one of them, so it idolizes their virtues and mystery. Another part fears their rejection, and so demonizes their savagery. With that said, old girl, it has recently come to my attention that your seed donor is the most famous person of your race who has ever lived. Congratulations, you are the daughter of a god. If his people accept you—which is a dubious proposition— and if they don't think you're an abomination that must be cleansed, you get to deal with Volsung Fá. A man who eats hearts for supper. Enjoy your new life.

So I say nothing. Because the world outside doesn't need another sacrifice. Not this angel. Not my Volga. I put my hand on hers. "There's someone I want you to meet."

The bridge that connects the landing pad to the mountain tower is lined with trees. Nervous, Volga waits behind as I take a step onto the bridge. I motion her to join me.

Trigg's monument is made of marble, like so many of the rest. They captured a fair likeness of him, yet somehow made him look more noble, which means more Gold. Guess that's the way of statues. Sell the myth, forget the man.

Trigg's jaw is set in determination. His eyes fierce. The anachronistic shield he holds over a fallen Darrow cracked and chewed by bullets. Candles from visitors flicker in the wind. Fresh flowers and baubles are stacked about his feet. Most are from Reds by the look of the flowers and offerings, but the rest are seashells and totems from his home in South Pacifica. Some made the pilgrimage to see the resting place of the Pacific's most famous martyr. I wonder if Holiday is responsible for some of those shells. But no one is here now.

"They say many people come here," Volga murmurs.

"Well, they're idiots. He didn't have a shield. And he died down there."

I forget the monument and look down into the shadows. From the lights of passing ships, I can just make out the ledge on which his head split open. It's a cold, empty place, not like the monument where the orange light of the candles bathe Trigg in warmth. But he isn't in either place. His body was never recovered. He is dust.

"Better he lives up here," Volga says, and I see the respect in her eyes for the myth of my husband. It does so much more for me than words ever could. I don't really understand why I wanted her to come. Maybe it's because I buried him so deep, and felt that if I could keep her from knowing too much about him, she would never matter as much as he did. But she does. Oh, she does.

And maybe Trigg deserves to be this myth. If not for himself, for others, like Volga, or young sons of South Pacifica who yearn to be brave like he was. Could that be what the world needs? Not dirty truths, not romantic paragons, but stubborn bastards who refuse to move?

Like Holiday? Like the great Red prick? Like Sefi?

Little cracks already web the feet of the statue. My eyes don't linger there. I'm tired of looking for the cracks in everything. Tired of running. Here with Volga, I should feel complete. But looking up at Trigg, and remembering the sense of purpose that gripped Olympia only two weeks ago, I know I am in the wrong city.

Maybe the world needs another stubborn bastard.

"I have to go back," I say to her. "I have to tell Sefi that it's Xenophon. I can't let her get undone by that little bastard. It isn't right."

She stares at the statue. "You stole from them. Iceborn do not forgive. They will murder you."

"Naw. Sefi's . . . different."

"Then I will go with you." It takes real courage for her to offer that.

"Sorry, old girl. That ain't happening. They know me. They don't know you. I won't be gone long. Hell, I might even be back for breakfast."

"Ephraim, you do not owe them anything. We don't owe any of these people anything."

"I'm not sure that's true."

"I just found you again," she protests, but the fight has left her. Tears well up in her eyes. I could have left in the night, but she would have followed, and she doesn't deserve that from me. "You need me."

"You're right about that," I say. "Damn right." I stroke her hair. "You know your people have a word, something deeper than family: *aeta*."

"Tribe," she says, as if the word was sacred to her, looking away in embarrassment. I tilt her chin back so she looks at me.

"You're my tribe, Snowball. I'll be back for breakfast. That's a promise."

She smiles hopefully, then bursts into tears. I wrap her in an embrace, and I know I'd do anything to keep her safe, and do anything to be with her. But as Freihild said by that fire, *some things are more important.*

The servants bring me to Pax as he pores over battlemaps in Victra's library. I stand behind a bookcase and remove the necklace to put Trigg's ring on my finger. When I turn the corner, he stands without a word and guides me to a gravLift and then to the armory, where I pull out the old heartspike, and ask if he can do me one last bit of magic.

75

EPHRAIM

Grarnir

I CRAWL ALONG THE WEST wall of Griffinhold, sticking to the shadows godtrees cast in the brazier light. The night guardsmen on the ice-slick cobbles below are easy to avoid with my spider gloves and thermal dampening suit. More difficult were the enhanced radar drones and motion sensors Sefi had installed per my advice. *Why'd I have to be so damn thorough?* They nearly ruined my drop from the Alltribe flier I hitched a ride on from the coastal city of Nike. Luckily, I followed a murder of crows in.

I reach the pulseShield that encloses my target's window in one of the six western towers of Griffinhold, and disrupt the field with diamond refractors, creating a slip narrow enough for me to shimmy through. The room is dark, tall, and more choked with incense than a fifty-credit Lunese brothel. *Lovely.* It also looks as if a hurricane had come through it. Priceless urns and bits of shattered wood are strewn about the carpet. Oldboy had a tantrum after his fall from grace. Good. The big lads outside will be used to noise.

I slip toward the large four-post bed where a giant shadow snores. I nearly choke from the alcohol on his breath. Feeling a bit sinister, I take the wine bottle from his bedside and crawl onto the ceiling to take a swig and upend the bottle. Dreadfully expensive wine pours down over the shaman's face. He wakes to see a black shadow on the ceiling above him.

He screams and falls off the bed.

Laughing my ass off, I release my gloves and land in his place on the bed. From the floor, Ozgard peers up at me. "Grarnir?"

"Stop shouting, you idiot." I prop myself on an elbow. "Those big bastards outside the door will hear if you talk particulars." I run a hand up my leg. "Would hate to think I'm the first whore who's landed in your bed."

"Grarnir," he whispers, and pulls himself upright-ish. "I thought you were Ascomanni." His wounded eye is covered in a patch, his mangled hand in splints. Looks like a giant baby, an effect enhanced by the dewy tears in his remaining eye. "I knew you would return. I knew—"

"Shut up." I sniff him. "You drunken lout. Knew you'd be soused."

His eyes narrow in suspicion. "Why have you returned?"

"Well, oldboy. I'm here to sort out a particularly sinister case of milk worm. That's right." I pop the datadrop into my hand and let it roll. "We got ourselves a parasite."

His eye widens in horror as the drop plays its little bit of incriminating evidence. "That scheming little maggot. The two-faced malefactor—"

"He outplayed you, medicine man. No need for bluster."

"We must tell the Queen."

"Naw. I was thinking we sit on it. Let Volsung eat her heart, or whatever else that albino golem has in store, then make off with a load of helium and become emperors of the asteroids." He stares at me in horror. "Fuckin' hell. It's a joke. We're gonna blood eagle that big puke. But we gotta do it right and good, you hear?" I lean forward and tap his nose. "Problem is, Queen listened to Old Eph, and's got her sanctum as tight as Publius cu Caraval's sphincter. I almost got pinned twice trying to slip in there. But you, dear charlatan, can get it to her."

He shakes his head. "The Queen is possessed of an evil spirit. She went into a fury when you took children. Trusts no one but Xenophon, suspects a coup to take her throne. She even thinks Volsung Fá is not real."

"Damn."

"I am still forbidden from her sight, as are all but those Xenophon permits. Her Valkyrie have closed their ears to me."

"Figured you'd have wormed your way back in. Shit."

"Indeed. Shit." Big shaman looks all dour. Scheming leech or not, he's wounded by Sefi's dismissal. He's drunk, sure; but functioning alcoholics are a gift from the gods. They're never *quite* out of the game.

"So, we got a problem then." I wag the datadrop. "This here is a nail in the coffin for that little puke. How do we get it to her? Who can play messenger?"

"A jarl," he says. "She is set to speak before them tomorrow morning. They slumber in Eagle Rest."

"Thought security was a little weird. Braves I didn't recognize. What's her speech for?"

"An ambassador from the Republic is on his way. Xenophon has arranged a peace summit."

"Uh-huh." I raise an eyebrow. "Having just been with the Republic, I very much doubt that. They don't buy this Fá story. Think Sefi's lost her bleedin' mind. No jarls. Xenophon's got the playing field stacked."

"The skuggi," he says in sudden epiphany. I knew he'd get there. "They bear Freihild's death as grievously as Valdir. They can be trusted." He sighs. "But they cannot gain audience. Her Valkyrie are loyal, and will never turn against her word. I could not put skuggi against Valkyrie. Only evil grows of that."

"Agreed. I was thinking they could help us liberate an old bloodstained friend."

"Unshorn . . ." he murmurs in obvious fear.

"Now you're catchin' on, oldboy."

Ozgard waits for me in the same hangar where I trained the skuggi and later shot three of them in the face. He wears his crow-feather cloak, his dragonbone staff, his red scale boots, and his great fourteen-point elk horn headdress, tips crusted in the blood of his people's enemies. It was a mighty fine sight seeing him try to squeak out that perforation in the pulseShield outside his window with all that luggage in tow. But what Ozgard might lack in finesse, he more than compensates for in loyalty. He does not wait alone.

Fetched from their barracks by Ozgard, eighty of my skuggi spirit warriors surround the rotund shaman. Gudkind stands as their leader. They eye me with no small amount of distrust and wariness, especially the ones I shot, but Ozgard called them here, so they listen.

"Hello, you ugly sods, my name is Ephraim ti Horn," I drawl as I waltz before them in my scarabSkin. "I was once the greatest freelancer in all Hyperion, which means I am the greatest freelancer who ever lived. But then I met you pukes. You dogged, creepy assassins of the icy poles have warmed the cockles of my reptilian heart. I ain't your people. You ain't mine. Let's get that out of the way. In fact, I think you're damn weird, and you think I'm a money slut. Fine. I could give a tick's dick what you think of me. But your Queen." I pause. "*Our* Queen needs our help."

The prison of the Alltribe was inherited from the Bellona. It stands lonely and arcane on the far eastern fringe of Eagle Rest, connected to the great citadel by means of an anorexic little bridge with room for no more than two Obsidians to stand abreast. With thousands of Obsidian bloodbraves asleep in their barracks, Ozgard waltzes through the fog that grips the bridge toward six armored Valkyrie guards. One is Braga, Pax's bodyguard.

"Shaman!" Braga shouts. "You are not free to roam. Where are Ulfred and Ulra?" Or something like that in Nagal. He presses forward. "Shaman! Halt."

"Braga!" he calls in a voice that is not frail Ozgard's but possessed with the myth of the shaman he built to rise nearly to the top of the matriarchy. "I knew thee as a child. Did you not listen as you sat upon my knee? Doom visits those who shed the blood of the servants to the gods."

"We are in service of the Queen," Braga rumbles in irritation.

"And even she serves the gods," he replies, continuing forward. "It is not the duty of a servant to blind themselves to truth. It is the duty of a servant to understand the will of the master, especially when the master does not. Our Queen has been deceived—"

"Hollow words. Perhaps they always were," Braga calls, lowering her pulseRifle. Her sisters do the same. "Our Queen believes Valdir covets her throne."

"Bah! He covets only war trophies and a warm cunny. You know this!" The Valkyrie flinch when Ozgard lifts his dragonbone staff. "Strike me, and you will summon the shadows of the mist." The Valkyrie look back to Braga, seized with apprehension.

"Idiots. He is only a storyteller. A drunk storyteller." Braga holsters her rifle and pulls out her axe, stalking forward to take Ozgard into custody. Standing before the armored warrior, cloaked in frail feathers, Ozgard waves his staff with dramatic flourishes. I begin to laugh. The mist flashes and Braga stumbles back, her breastplate smoking. For the smallest moment, she thinks magic has been conjured. Then experience takes over. Too late. She looks out over the bridge, not expecting an enemy here in the heart of their power. "In the mist—" she shouts as her helmet slithers over her head. The mist stutters with color. Half the Valkyrie go down before they can activate their pulseShields.

As the skuggi emerge from the mist to overwhelm the guards and enter the prison to free Valdir, their jammers go active and I lose the signal. My turn.

I activate a jamField and drop from the ceiling to land in front of the two muscular guards outside Xenophon's room. To their credit, the sleepy Obsidians do not flinch, and run straight into the gravity mine I toss in front of me. They invert and shoot upward, crunching into the ceiling. I lower the intensity and let them float, unconscious. Wait, one's not unconscious. *Crunch* a second time into the ceiling.

"Hang tight, ladies."

I reach for the door latch to enter Xenophon's room, when instinct saves me. The latch is charged with enough power to melt my brain. *That little shit.* I strip my spider gloves, take a canister from my belt and rubberize the scarabSkin gauntlets. As the spray sets, I set a tripwire at the far end of the hall, two more gravity mines along the walls, and a gas trap above the door just to be safe. Then, with the resin set, I disarm the laser alarm inside the lock, then the secondary trigger—*someone's* paranoid—and then the mechanism itself.

The door clicks open, the sound contained inside my jamField.

Xenophon's room is spartan. Except for the size, it is suitable for a servant. The White sits facing the fireplace watching a hologram. The sound is mute outside the perimeter of my jamField. Wary of pressure traps in the threshold, I don my spider gloves again and reach inside the doorframe to crawl up the wall, then the ceiling, until I'm suspended above him in the shadow of the vaulted ceiling. I turn off my jamField.

The White is watching a recorded hologram of a severe man nearly Sefi's height, but much thinner and full of that tensile Gold terror. His face is thin, his eyes perfect crystals behind slanted lids. There's a man who knows pain. Atlas au Raa. My heart drop-kicks a beat.

"Salve, Xenophon, the product of all your toil amongst the flea-bitten is nearly at hand. The asset is hidden within the crags at the coordinates you

detailed. He will act only upon your signal, which is to be given only if the greater sum of Obsidian warbands are upon Mars. If they are not, postpone incitement. Our window is narrowing, but he will listen. He knows you are my hand. Follow my design and soon you will be home on the Palatine. In a world of protean hearts, your steadfastness does not go unnoticed. When you return to the fold, you will be honored by the Dictator with the Iron Pyramid. It will be much deserved. Destroy this message upon receipt. Per aspera ad astra."

"Per aspera ad astra," Xenophon echoes, and then plays the message again. I watch it twice from above. I pieced it together the first time, but it beggars belief. I drop in front of Xenophon, and stand amidst the hologram. Those pale eyes go wide and I pistol-whip the White in the face.

Xenophon sprawls backward. I kick them between the legs, forgetting nothing's there but a tiny aperture for piss. The slender creature stumbles back, not calling out in pain, not showing a lick of anger upon their face.

"Mr. Horn. I did not expect you to return. I knew I was missing a crucial factor." With a glance to the door, Xenophon knows the guards have been dispatched.

I flick the disabled tracker into their chest. "You little rat. You're a fucking Gorgon."

"The proper term is *Pavor Nocturnus,* a night terror. But colloquialisms do rule the day." The White folds their hands over their tummy and stands erect and pacific as a priest. "Xenophon, First Frumentarius, Legio Zero Pavor Nocturnus, at your service."

"And a frumentarius? I should have guessed it was one of you psychos." Special forces spy. The kind that could end even a centurion's career with a keystroke. I'd put a canyon in their face if I didn't want to watch Sefi do it herself. "Sefi will love tearing you to ribbons."

"I imagine she would. Ever has she feared the Gold masters. She was wise to fear them. They know all. Of course, I knew it was a risk to keep the message. In sixty years, it is the only order I have ever refused. But even I grow weary in the cold isolation of my duty." Xenophon gestures to my gun. "Must you threaten? A little redundant, considering your skill set. I've little chance against you. Though, if I call the guard, they would pull you apart like cake." My eyes dart to the door. "You're wondering what to do. This evidence is incriminating, I agree, but two death sentences are hardly worse than one. And I hear you already have mine in your belt pouch. A holo of the incriminating variety."

I shove the gun against the White's forehead. "How do you know that?"

"It is my purpose to know."

It's a bluff. The skuggi hate the creep, they'd never rat me out. They need time, and I need answers. I jerk my head at the hologram. "You been that bastard's mole for years? Since Sefi brought you in?"

"Yes."

"Then it wasn't that poor Pink who was supposed to kill her."

"Oh, no, Amel certainly was an assassin. The peril of current affairs, I fear. Many Golds pulling strings against one another, causing all to fray. I detected him quite early, but when Atalantia activated him, it was necessary to expose him."

"The hell are you doing here if not to kill Sefi then?"

"Death is sloppy. And my *dominus* does not abide *sloppy*. With a dead queen, the Obsidians would seek the strongest to lead them. Who is stronger to them than the Morning Star? Valdir? He loves Darrow. It would do little good to the Society for the Slave King to be bestowed with such a gift. Sefi must die the proper way, at the proper time, on the proper planet, with her people along the proper trajectory. For that, only a frumentarius would suffice."

"And Volsung Fá . . ."

"But another piece of the puzzle." Xenophon considers, enjoying this little bout of honesty. "Perhaps more. *Dominus* au Raa learned much in his banishment to the Kuiper Belt after his . . . indiscretions. Not the least of which was the impossibility of his task in subduing the Ascomanni there. Octavia sent him to die, he soon realized. A fact I witnessed firsthand. I remained behind as his factor, and saw her appoint another Fear Knight in his absence—one Darrow easily dispatched of. The second thing my master learned was that the Ascomanni could not be conquered from without, only from within. Ironic enough. So he left his most cherished Gorgon amongst them, not to destroy them, but to rise amongst them."

Keep him talking, let Ozgard get Valdir. They may already be en route to Sefi. Keep the little bastard's mouth here, where it can't do any talking in Sefi's ear.

"He Who Walks the Void was a Gorgon?" I ask.

"Is a Gorgon. The master called him the most talented of that martial breed. Grimmus was good to loan him to us." The White's lips make a thin line as it attempts a smile. "You are a clever *Homo bellicus,* Mr. Horn, as I am an efficient *Homo logicus.* But do not compare yourself with the best of the *Homo aureate.* My *dominus's* designs are painted on a horizon we will only see in time. My science is logic, his is illogic—humanity.

"The Raa are in motion, you see. They come for the Republic to repay old debts. But there is hubris in their blood. Thinking themselves fresh to the tired fray, they will find themselves undone. With one stroke, my master fells three."

I check my six. No one is behind me. Yet Xenophon's bragging like the gun's to my head. Maybe it is. Maybe all I've felt, all I've seen, is part of this little game the White and his master cooked up. Sefi, the skuggi, Valdir, Freihild, Ozgard, are all just wriggling as the snake chokes the life from us. I want to scream in frustration. I thought I was being the hero. I'm just the fool in their game. But maybe I can stop it. Tell Sefi. Find a way to unwind all this, and let her dream continue on its course.

"Why did you come back?" Xenophon asks.

"Couldn't stand to see a little shit ruin something good," I say. "Been there. Done that. World's better off without the likes of you and me."

"I understand the conflict you feel."

"Nah, you really don't."

Xenophon thinks for a moment. "You cannot stop this. The reason I tell you all this is to disabuse you of that delusion of grandeur. You are small, as am I. But you can be a part of something, Mr. Horn. A part of the solution to this dark age." The White's voice quickens. "When you first arrived, I thought you were a liability. And you were, thanks to that meddling shaman. The conquest of Cimmeria was meant to be a massacre led by Valdir. Millions of Reds were to die. They were to flock to the Red Hand, which was to carve Volkland from the inside, and pit the Obsidians against the people and each other. So that when Fá came, it would be as savior. Instead, he must come as terror."

"Let me guess, you needed the children on Luna, not here. Poor Fear Knight. His Syndicate stooges didn't get to play with their toys."

"They were upset. Baying for your blood—as those cretins would. I could have killed you with a nerve agent in your wine, in your food, as you slept at any time. But *I* saved you. *I* convinced my master of your utility. You more than any other jeopardized his plans. On accident, of course. Still, he knows this. He *respects* this. He desires you in Zero Legion."

"Me? A Gorgon? Don't make me laugh. This dog don't collar."

"He does not wish to give you a collar. He offers you opportunity. The Obsidians never knew how to use your skills. Never respected what you are: the greatest infiltrator of an age. Yet you came here to save them. You *crave* something that will be loyal to you, so you can be loyal to it. Join us, and help us bring order back to mankind. Is humanity better off than it was ten years ago? The irrevocable answer is no. Become a shepherd. Become a savior."

"Humanity isn't an it."

Xenophon sighs. "You stall for time because you are recording me, and think I don't know about your prison break." I go cold. My finger grazes the trigger. "You mock me, because I am different. But I have always respected you—I see the rigors of your training, the loss of your husband, how you float adrift and search for meaning. These savages only respect you for what you have given them—skillgift, the mines, amusement. Do you so easily forget the violations they have reaped upon your race? How they conspired to use Volga? They are monsters."

"Sefi is not a monster," I say. "She wants something different for her people. It ain't a clean world, but she's trying to do right by them, by Mars. You, you greasy little larva, are trying to rob that from them."

"No. They will rob themselves. You will see. It is in their nature. As duty is in ours." Xenophon's eyes flick over my head. "*Nakata.* Hold."

I turn to see three lanky monsters, with crowns equal parts metal, asteroid, and diamond fused to their skulls, perched on a windowsill. Two more, barely taller than children, with huge skulls, thick, long, apelike arms, and stunted legs, swing through a second window.

Ascomanni. Not the rabid offshoots of the Iceborn. But aliens five hundred years separated from the human genome and mutated by radiation. Their eyes are huge and black as their hair, their foreheads pronounced like proto-humans. Their noses little more than nostrils. They hold weird, twisted weapons. Their skin, thick as hide and ribbed with ritual scarring and metal implants, is the deep red of a Bordeaux-fortified sangria.

"What. The. Fuck."

"Mr. Horn, they will not attack you unless I command them—" Xenophon steps back from me, fingering something concealed in a sleeve.

My reaction is all instinct. I snap the gun up and shoot the closest stubby one in the face, then shoot at the largest of the three at the window. I miss as they vault to the ceiling like gymnasts. I point the gun at Xenophon. I can't win this fight. No matter how much I want to shoot Xenophon in the head. The long play is the only way.

Xenophon pulls a controller from his sleeve and twists a dial.

That must be for the heartspike. I play along, spasming and falling to my knees as if suffering a heart attack. Xenophon spins the dial more, likely to render me unconscious. I play dead. But, shittily, one of the Ascomanni decides to kick me in the head for his dead friend and everything goes dim.

I wake on stone amidst a distant roar of voices. A newly carved stone griffin glares down at me from the ceiling hundreds of meters overhead. I am in the private chamber off Sefi's newly appointed throne room, my hands bound behind my back by magnetic cuffs. Still in my scarabSkin, though stripped of all my gear. Ozgard blinks beside me.

Sefi stands above me. "Xenophon—" is all I manage, still woozy from the blow to the head.

"Why?" she asks, her face cold to me. "I welcomed you when the world wanted you dead. I gave you *aeta*. Why try to install Valdir in a coup?"

"I—didn't." Speaking is like trying to form castles out of dry sand. I want to tell her I respect her. That I came back to help. That I may not be *aeta,* but I believe in her. In what she stands for. But all that trickles out is: "Volsung Fá . . . the Fear Knight . . ."

Come on brain, work!

"His master," Xenophon says from her side, concealed hands twisting the dial on my heartspike. I try to fake a spasm, but I feel like I'm going to puke from the concussion anyway. "After delivering the children to the Fear Knight, his orders were to create chaos. I warned you about him."

"Yes. You did, Xenophon. You did." She looks on me in sorrow and then spits in my face. "We are not monsters, Mr. Horn. But our mercy is not infinite. Skin him and the fraud and hang them from the tower."

"Ascomanni . . ." I grunt.

"If I may suggest he witness your speech, so as he hangs, he can know the unity of Obsidians in the face of his schemes?"

"Very well," she says and walks off.

I am dragged by my hair with a bloody Ozgard into Griffinhold.

Morning sunlight filters through high windows. Nearly six hundred warjarls, all the chieftains of the tribes Sefi united into one, cluster before the giant Ice Throne. I've never seen them fully assembled, and until now did not realize how even Valdir showed signs of the encroachment of modernity. More than half of the leaders are stark savages. They wear bones in their hair and hilarious ostentatious signs of wealth pillaged from planets—gold chains, ruby-hilted axes, breastplates studded with diamonds. They have tattooed faces, fur cloaks, trophies of war brought out from the pristine confines of their bounty chests to flash their tail feathers to the other warjarls. Most are women, though a minority of taller men knot together. Alone, the six hundred fill barely a fraction of the cavernous chamber.

Two thick columns of Obsidian honor guard, mostly high-ranking men from the tribes, stretch all the way to the Bellona Doors. There must be thousands. Silence falls on the jarls as Sefi stalks up to her throne where two dozen of Sefi's Valkyrie women form wings to either side. I'm tossed with Ozgard on the floor at the far wing of the dais.

"Ozgard . . ." I mutter, managing to crawl to my knees. He's flat on the floor, his broken hands bound behind him. His lone eye blinks at me. "Oldboy, the skuggi . . ."

"Dead . . . most. They were waiting for us as we left. Valdir broke through . . ."

"Escaped?"

"I know not . . ." His mouth twists in despair. "I know nothing." His eye turns to Sefi, who stands before her throne. I reach for my right heel with my hand and find the sealant there intact. I still have my last play.

"They're here," I murmur. "The Ascomanni."

A Valkyrie hits my ear to silence me.

"Your hearts beat for war," Sefi bellows to her chieftains in Nagal. The acoustics of the room work in her favor. The jarls pound their axe hafts on the ground. "War is what you desire. But against who? The Republic? The Golds? This Volsung Fá? Ourselves?

"Are we savages who bay for war like dogs?" She glares at them. "Ragnar did not die for war. He died for the future of the Volk! Many of you cannot see past your axes. War is our blood, yes. But no people can war against *all*. You know of the treason that bathed these halls last night in blood. My own mate, whose name is forgotten to us, thought I was too weak to face our enemies. Behold his conspirators . . ." At her order, the Valkyrie drag the skinned bodies of the skuggi and throw them down the stairs of the dais to splay like grisly, giant fetuses. I choke down vomit. I can't even recognize any of them. First Freihild, now everyone else. Here I am again. The teacher of corpses. *I never should have left you, Volga. I never should have left.*

"Am I weak?" Sefi whispers. I see the hatred in her eyes for herself, for caving in the end to the cruel ways of her people. So much for progress. So much for the future. The jarls eat up the violence. They slam their axes and laugh. I work my hand on the heel, trying to break the sealant.

"This Volsung Fá, this barbarian king, put fear into Valdir's heart. But not mine! I know what he is. A vulture. He came to our land thinking it his. But he is no more one of us than we are Gold. This land belongs to the Volk! We purchased it with our blood! While he lurked in the asteroids beyond the Rim, we broke the might of Gold, the machines of Silver! Now he comes a thief in the night, to murder Freihild, may she feast in Valhalla, to claim with heretical tongue there is no Allmother, only an Allfather." She spits the word, and the jarls stomp their axes in fury. "He is our enemy. A heretic! I will drink from his skull before the moons grow full."

They roar.

"All know the wisdom of Baldur. It is not wise to fight an enemy with another at your back. This heretic king has poisoned the blood between our Republic brothers and sisters. Today we cleanse that blood; tomorrow, we turn our axes on him."

She lifts the razor of Aja and points it to the Bellona Doors, sparing a nod for Xenophon, who must have arranged this. I know in my belly what's coming. Xenophon stares at the doors with intense contentment.

They say the Hall of Eagles wasn't built to reach the heavens, but to fit its doors. The famed Bellona Doors, the last great treasure of House Bellona not sold off by looters or sculpted by the Obsidians in their own image, begin to open. Formed from the trunks of two of the tallest god-trees ever grown, the interlocking wooden wings that close off the eastern façade of the hall are pulled open by infernal machines. Raw rusted iron clatters and rattles now, as it used to for the damn Bellona family so that they could sit in their pretty armor and remember the horrors of war. As if it wasn't the definition of their own name.

The chanting of the crowd gathered in the city to protest the Alltribe's looming war with the Republic flows in. They chant for their Reaper. How far away he must seem.

On the floor, a long needle of daylight splits the Obsidian jarls and stabs toward Sefi's throne, dividing the shadows of the room before widening to melt the shadows away. All except one. As the Republic diplomatic shuttle taxis for landing, it casts a stain on the floor the shape of a bird.

"The raven shadow," Ozgard murmurs.

I've seen men snap during bombardments. It's like a physical switch has been thrown, and they go manic as an addict. Ozgard's switch goes. He bolts to his feet. Rushes for Sefi, frothing for her to shoot down the ship. To not let it spew out its evil. He is knocked windless on the ground before he can even make it four steps. The sealant on my heel won't come off. *Dammit.*

Blood leaks out Ozgard's mouth and pools on the floor like cherry syrup as he's dragged back to me. He stares at his reflection. I whisper his name. He's straight gone. Snapped at the mental waist. He doesn't even look up as the ramp of the Republic shuttle bangs down at the far end of the room.

I wait for a bomb to go off in the shuttle. For some horrible weapon to evaporate the gathered host of Obsidians. But the Fear Knight has something more intricate in store.

His slave, Xenophon, walks from the place of honor at Sefi's side down the stairs of her throne dais, nearly to the end of the ranks of Obsidian warjarls.

"Sefi Volarus, are you a god?" Xenophon asks. Her brows knit together in confusion. "Are you a god?" Sefi's taken aback by the impertinence of her only "loyal" servant.

Her voice comes out in an annoyed growl. "Xenophon, return to your place."

"No."

The jarls murmur in discontent. Sefi stands. "Servant, obey."

"I obey only one, and you are not him," Xenophon replies. The Valkyrie bodyguards take a predatory step forward. Even Sefi's competitors amongst the warjarls seem on the verge of breaking the uppity White's neck. Faced with something she doesn't understand, Sefi reverts to what she knows.

"The blood of Ragnar Volarus runs through these veins," she says to the question. "Kneel ~~on~~ your knees, or on stumps. I care not."

"The blood of Ragnar Volarus," Xenophon crows. "The blood of a god. Alia was no god. She let the Children of the Spires languish in chains. She sold her sons to the stars for her own gain. From what well-spring then does Ragnar derive his divinity? If not from his mother, then it must be from his father."

The room goes still in bafflement. Xenophon raises that crystal-clear voice and suddenly lurches, as if possessed by an evil spirit like a shaman, to sing in flawless Nagal.

> *"There was one mightier 'fore Allmother's reign*
> *Allfather, King of Stains, was his name.*
> *For him, Old Kuthul rose against Sunborn*
> *Till in Ladon was he felled, for kin to mourn*
> *To the fires his people and the Volk were sent*
> *But not all to ash and bone must we lament*
>
> *From sun to dust did the moons and dragons chase*
> *The brood of Kuthul, who hid in darkest space,*
>
> *Five ages passed of shadow and ice*
> *Entombed in floating caverns, hunted like rabid mice*
>
> *Blossoms of blood and thrones of flesh were grown*
> *As brother ate brother; sister ate sister*
> *for a savior, Allfather groaned*
>
> *Then came the Outlander to answer his plea*
> *Mighty were the Lords of Ink, mightier was He.*
> *Whores of their children, shards of their thrones*
> *Made He, who crowned Himself with their bones*
> *And fashioned Dark Wind of those not destroyed*
> *To serve, to anoint, to proclaim:*
> *He Who Walks the Void.*

"May I present to the Volk of the heatlands: the Breaker of the Black Thrones of Ultima Thule, Master of the Fleshchain, Bonemaker of

Charon, Overlord of the Kuiper Belt and Oort Cloud, Terror of Codovan and Raa, Taker of Makemake, Haumea, Xena, Eris. Volsung Great Fá of the Ascomanni, Emperor of the Obsidian, and Broodfather of Ragnar Volarus!"

Silence.

And then *He* comes.

76

EPHRAIM

He Who Walks the Void

THE FIRST SOUND IS three thousand Obsidian honor guards raising their ceremonial axes and taking the fighting stance to a warcry. The warjarls turn to see the threat. Behind their turned heads, Sefi looks no taller, no stronger, no more confident than a five-year-old child. Horror, hope, fear, and confusion all muddle together in a grotesque expression, then vanish, leaving only the icy, intelligent mask of Sefi the Quiet.

I just don't think Sefi the Quiet will be enough.

The second sound is metal on stone. Two armored boots stomp down the corridor. Even from the side of the dais, I can see his huge helmet over the tallest guards. It is made of the skull of some exotic beast, triple-horned, fused with asteroid metal, and sparkling with diamonds, rubies, and emeralds.

The third sound is the scraping of a long metal chain that he drags in one hand. Dozens of abnormally large skulls hang from the metal—Ascomanni kings. In the other he hefts a bizarre spear-saw over his shoulder. Two dozen male jarls of the Alltribe follow him out of the shuttle, instead of the true face of the beastly horde he leads.

The fourth sound is an ululation from his metal throat, like the wail tin makes when it warps in windstorms. The song carries him to the end of the guard corridor, where a wall of Valkyrie bodyguards stand at the base of Sefi's dais.

Whoever this man is, he could not be the father of Ragnar. It's a lie. A Fear Knight trick. *Kill him. Slag tradition. Slag what the warjarls think.* "Ozgard. Ozgard, I need your help," I whisper. He stares at Volsung in terror. "Ozgard, my heel. I need your hand." Even the rootlike fingers of his right hand hold more strength than do mine. He does not listen. "Ozgard!"

Volsung's entourage stops well shy of the throne, but Volsung carries on until Valkyrie block his way. He points his spear at Sefi's throne. **"Mine."** He points at her crown. **"Mine."** He points at the Obsidian jarls. **"Mine."** He waves his spear around to encompass Mars. **"Mine."**

His spear's spiked haft stomps into the stone, breaking Sefi from her trance. She signals her Valkyrie to take him. He rattles the long chain behind him like a snake.

"My father, Vagnar, is dead," she says. "Cut off this imposter's hands and feet, save his liver for the buzzards and his cock for the dogs." I cheer inside as three women slip forward in a V to do the dirty work with their axes.

Volsung moves like a whip.

His spear separates. Its tip lurches forward and pierces through the face of the leftmost woman, coming out the back of her skull. Still connected to the haft by some sort of metal wire. Volsung leaves it in, and brings the back three-quarters of the spear around to smash into the axe-guard of the rightmost woman. Something in her shoulder breaks and she's almost lifted off her feet as she stumbles into the woman in the middle. Bellowing like a maniac, Volsung overwhelms them with savagery. Small teeth on the spear's length begin to saw, and he brings the huge spear down like a hammer in colossal overhand strikes, beating them to their knees, sawing through their armor, and then staving in their skulls in a traumatic display of brute strength. In ten seconds, the three women make a meat salad on the floor.

Oh, fuck.

The whole Valkyrie bodyguard raises their rifles to fire on the man.

More than sixty of Sefi's warjarls, all men, step forward and make a human wall around Volsung. An ominous silence grips the room as all realize this was planned. Volsung is no stranger to these male chieftains.

He must have come to them in secret. When? Before Mars? When they landed? When Valdir, their idol, was arrested? Still, they pretend, and shout for him to prove his identity.

"I have lived three lives," Volsung rumbles through that titanic helmet. **"The last is that of Volsung Fá. The second that of Pale Horse, slaveknight to the Warlord of Ash. The first that of Vagnar Hefga,**

first broodmate to Alia Volarus, the Snowsparrow, Queen of the Valkyrie, broodfather to the god Ragnar Volarus and greedy little Sefi."

He removes his helmet. A long tail of hair tumbles from his shaved skull, falling all the way to his heels. The male warjarls thrust up their chins and bare their throats in submission, proclaiming him Ragnar's father. The others stare at the length of his valor tail. Even Unshorn is a boy to this man.

Volsung looks to Sefi, black eyes glittering from eyeholes of the tattooed skull of a Stained.

"Have I so changed beyond the sun, child? Or are you now just a liar like your mother?" He tosses his helmet to the floor. It makes a seismic thump. **"Look upon this face, and say you know it not."**

Sefi is shocked dumb.

The father of Ragnar would be over eighty. Yet this man covered with the blood spatter of her Valkyrie looks barely fifty, and moves smooth as any gladiator of the Hyperion Premiere Circuit. In the light, he is more than the pale nightmare I saw in the darkness of the ice. His throat must have been ripped out years ago. The front third is metal, the trachea ribbed gray. His arms are bare and obscenely muscular. The left forearm is metal with a metal hand and dagger-sharp fingernails that look like they extend on sliders. A horrible scar claims half his nose. Blue worm veins of age rejuvenation therapy web the sides of his skull—the first I've ever seen on an Obsidian. Even Julii would flinch at the cost.

"My father is dead," Sefi repeats like a mantra.

Volsung reaches under his vest to produce a broken amulet of a griffin.

"You will remember this, if not the man who taught you to hunt." He throws it at her. **"Your mother broke it in half the day I was taken back to the stars. To be whole again when I returned. Fifty years it took. Fifty years to hear there was no sky burial for the mother of my pride, Alia. No high mountain tomb for her bones amongst ancient kin. Only a lonely cairn of shattered stone, with half of me lost beneath it."**

"*You* desecrated our Sky Temple. *You* slew Freihild. You spit on the Allmother? You attacked the Republic?" Sefi says, her rage playing tug-of-war with her confusion. "*Why?*"

"To free you from your chains," he says. **"Alia was desecrated.**

Why? Because in your hearts you hold the truth. What good is a mother who sells her children? What good is a mother who harvests her young? What good is a mother who is a liar? No better than the frothing rot of a dead seal."

His voice is clever and evocative, and he mutates its tone like an amused mummer. He's no barbarian browbeating them with strength. He's trained in elocution. Far better trained than I managed to make the skuggi. I recognize the triple-beat pivot of the Palatine's politico school. This is the Fear Knight's asset, his super weapon.

"Under the Allmother, we were slaves, brothers . . ." He smiles. ". . . sisters. Under the rule of women, our men were sent to the stars to die, while queens sat on thrones and knew the joy of the hunt on the ice." He wheels around, speaking to the honor guard as much as the female-dominated jarls. "We died in Sunborn wars, in their fencing practices, ridden down by horseback or gravBoot for sport. In their gambling pits we were forced to kill our brothers, but never our sisters." He thrusts his huge hands into the air. "These hands have slain seas." He looks down. "Seas of brothers. Seas of kin."

Sefi has lost control. Volsung conducts like a master.

He slowly opens his vest to reveal a body of muscles and scars and metal plates. A thick pattern of identical scars on his back and chest stand out from the rest. Their shape is unmistakably the slave brand of House Grimmus. "This flesh has known slavery." He points a finger at Sefi. "What do you know, *girl*?" He smiles. "Only how to be quiet, it seems."

It isn't only the male jarls who laugh. While the Valkyrie stare in horror, the more numerous honor guard is intrigued. And why not? What he says is true. Most of the men were in the Gold legions. Most of them were slaves. Sefi was not. What would she know of their horror?

Even I note how small she looks. How timid her fierce veteran Valkyrie are to this lone terror. Yet she draws confidence from the movement of the women jarls. Alienated by this man, they drift to make a thick wall of protection for the Queen, each representing thousands of braves in the camps around Cimmeria. Yet Sefi is blind. She does not see how the words seep into the ears of the three thousand honor guard. How the men in the room looked at the skinned skuggi—all of which were conveniently male and castrated—or how Valdir, champion of the male braves, is now branded traitor.

It was never about old ways and new. It was always about gender. How could she be so *fucking* blind? How could I not see it festering? Volsung bares his mangled teeth.

"While you were silent, girl, I was a slave. While you struck down your unarmed mother, I conquered the tribes of the Far Ink." He waves a hand back to the skulls on the chain. **"These were their kings. While you let the heatlanders infect you with weakness, I slew with my warsaw those who would not bow. I made cups of their skulls, slaves of their children, and whores of their wives."**

He brandishes his spear. The way it glimmers . . . it must be made of a metal I've never seen.

"All I have, I have taken from the deathgrip of my foes. All you have, you have stolen. From the head of a murdered mother, from the pockets of your noble ally, Tyr Morga"—he taps his forehead in respect—**"from the legacy of your god brother, from the strength of your mate.**

"You cannot even kill a drake without your servants. Without others, you are nothing. Just a cow who bleats she is Queen." He addresses the Obsidians. **"Obsidian follows strength. I see strength here. With weakness held up by her crown. I issued your queen a challenge. But she hid from me behind you. Brothers, sisters! Look upon her! Your queen is an ass, for she leads from the back!"** The image of Sefi behind the wall of Obsidian jarls now becomes an indictment, a mockery. Fá laughs and speaks directly to the honor guard behind him. **"She would have you give up war. She would have you forsake the Wind for roofs. Your stone and bone heritage for the soft silk of heatlanders. She would let their cities suck you dry. She would have you live in their world. I would have them live in ours.**

"From the diamond mines of Quaor, to the Boneyard of Charon, to the Black Thrones of Ultima Thule, the Dark Wind of the Allfather gathers to fall on the heatlands to claim all for Volkland. Gold had its time in the day. Red faltered but now *we* rise." He turns to Sefi. **"But only one can rule. Moooooo."** He walks back and forth mooing at her like a cow in mockery.

"Bardahgi! Bardahgi! Bardahgi!" the male warjarls begin to chant. *Fight. Fight. Fight.* Many of the honor guard join them. Ozgard weeps on the floor. I sag in exhaustion. Sefi should shoot him. I would shoot him if I had a gun. But she is a woman trapped by the ways of her own

people. If she shoots Ragnar's father, the Alltribe will shatter apart. If she turns down a challenger with a claim, she is not strength, and they will turn on her. If only Valdir were here, she must be thinking. Valdir would wrangle the fools in line.

The Queen of the Obsidians looks at Xenophon in betrayal. Then to me and Ozgard and taps her forehead in respect and apology. She peels Aja's razor from her arm, draws her war axe, and steps down from her throne.

The Obsidians watch father and daughter strip themselves of armor and circle one another barefoot in the center of the hall. Volsung is bare-chested, though his muscles themselves look like armor. He wields his warsaw with both hands. Sefi wears a sleeveless vest of Valkyrie blue. In her left hand spins the razor of Aja, and in her right a great axe.

No more words are shared. They meet in a sudden flurry of violence that rattles my bones. Sefi bounds backward, more agile than the huge man, but not by much. She hops foot to foot, probing, sliding, and lashing forward. She is a spirit of the ice, nearly Valdir's match by the reckoning of the dozens of Golds she's sent to the Void.

But Volsung ignores the blades and recklessly thrusts at her heart with his warsaw, forcing her to turn her attack into a defense. He is old, and has maybe lost a step, but he is cunning, and Sefi knows it. The recklessness was a trap to lure her into baiting him, and Sefi barely twists her heart out of the way as his blade scrapes along her rib cage.

She spins back, but smelling blood, Volsung comes on like a bloody storm. Screaming at the top of his lungs, he goes berserker, hammering at the razor and axe as if he intends to chop them to splinters. He uppercuts with the hooked piercing end of his warsaw. Sefi deflects with her razor, lifts her left leg, and sidesteps to her right. He pivots his spear, and brings the saw half crashing down. She catches it with her axe. Veins bulge in his trunk of a neck. Muscles twist in his core and he pushes down, down, down. Sefi brings the razor around underneath from her left to cut him in half. He pivots the bottom end of the spear diagonal, blocks the razor outward. The metal of both instruments warps as they rebound, hers outward, his inward. He uses the momentum, driving with his legs as he uppercuts with the piercing end toward her opposite leg, ripping a canyon from her mid-calf, through the inside tendons of her knee, all the way up her inner thigh to her pelvis.

Sefi stumbles back, and in six compact thrusts, he punctures both her ankles, her kneecaps, and both her rotator cuffs. She falls like a slack puppet. Her axe and razor clattering to the ground.

It took less than a minute.

Dead silence. I grow nauseous in it. I should have shot Xenophon and died in that room. This can't be happening. Some of the female jarls bolt for the exits. The Valkyrie go berserk. But they are outnumbered and slaughtered. As pulseRifles whine and axes rise and fall in the periphery, Volsung watches his daughter crawl away from him toward her axe, leaving smears of blood on the stone. He stalks after her and stomps on the back of her head until she goes still. He places the axe in her hand, and crouches with a knee on her spine to say: **"Valhalla bears only the brave. Will you remain quiet in the end, my child?"**

Volsung straddles his daughter, putting his weight on her tailbone, and sets to grim work. With the knife from his waist, he cuts open her vest to reveal Sefi's tattooed back. In a tender sawing motion, he carves off two long flaps of flesh from the shoulder blades to the tailbone, exposing her rib cage. She flails like a punctured fish. Then with a small axe from his hip, Volsung hacks at the ribs on either side of her spine. She jerks in agony, but no sound escapes her. He discards the hatchet and pries open her rib cage from behind to expose her lungs. Tears leak from her eyes. She gasps for air.

As peaceful as a man cleaning a fish, Volsung takes a handful of salt from a pouch and throws it on the wounds. Sefi spasms, the muscles of her limbs balling up in cramps. Not one of her warjarls comes to her aid. They watch the Valkyrie being slaughtered without drawing their axes. I grow sick with hate for them, for the betrayal and horror in Sefi's eyes. When Volsung realizes she will not scream, he nods with pride and kneels to dry the tears from her face.

"Valhalla will welcome you, child. Go to our Fallen who feast, go to your brother in the Skyhall, you are freed on Allfather's wings."

"Tyr Morga will eat your heart," she rasps.

"Perhaps," Volsung whispers. **"My god is fickle with his favor."**

He reaches into her opened back with both hands, and knowing the end is here, Sefi shouts with her last breath: *"Hyrg la Rag—"* Her words turn to a gurgle as Volsung tears out her lungs and hurls them on the ground. She blinks at them. Her eyes drift closed, and only the tattooed spirit eyes look on.

I shut my eyes and hear the crunch and hack of steel on flesh as Volsung continues his work. When I open them again, he has taken her heart. He holds it above him to show the warjarls. Blood sluices down his biceps into the white hair of his armpits.

"**Allfather!**" he cries out. "**Allfather! I offer you these stains!**" It takes him two minutes to eat her heart. When he is finished, he shudders in satiation. "**Worthy.**" Then he grabs Sefi by the ankle, forming a red trail as he drags her up the stairs to the Griffin Throne and takes his seat.

I seize the moment to crawl toward a fallen Valkyrie. With the angle, I can't free myself from the cuffs, but with her blade I'm able to pry open the heel of my boot and palm the heartspike Pax altered for me.

All kneel for their king except for Ozgard, who is allowed to stumble toward the remains of Sefi. He looks at her and finally screams. It's more than a scream. It's a soul dying. He falls to his knees in horror at the sight of his Queen's ribs splayed out like bloody wings. Volsung tosses him the knife he used on Sefi. It skitters across the floor to slide to a stop in front of Ozgard. But he's no longer Ozgard. Spit drips down his lips. His remaining eye is glazed.

"**A red griffin, wasn't it, shaman? I have fulfilled your prophecy. Fulfill mine.**"

As if under a spell, the shaman picks up the blade, turns it around, and buries it into his remaining eye. As what was Ozgard weeps on the ground, Volsung takes the razor of Aja into his hand.

"**Seven hundred years of slavery. Seven hundred years of war. Seven hundred years of anguish for them.**" Seated on Sefi's throne, he closes his eyes and the distant roar of the crowd, ignorant of the horror coming for them, laps through the defiled building.

"Reaper. Reaper. Reaper," they chant.

Fá opens his eyes. "**Sack the city. Take their treasures. Rape their men, their women, their children. Remind them the Allfather's truth: the world is yours, *if* you can take it.**"

77

EPHRAIM

Worthy

THE BIRDS CHIRP. Early beams of sunlight warm the frosted stone of the plaza at the top of the Bellona Stairs. The scent of bonfires and crackling boar meat thickens the air. Two thousand Ascomanni feast beside their king as the city trembles with screams. I should be sitting across from Volga watching her try to impress Pax. I should be with my friends. With my *aeta*. Instead, I suffer the banquet of a beast.

I have never been more disgusted with our bipedal species.

Was Sefi all that held the monster inside at bay?

In the shadow of Griffinhold, airborne Obsidians rove in packs, lighting fires with phosphorus bombs, savaging citizens who thought the roofs shelter from the marauding hordes below. Not Ascomanni, but the very Obsidians who drank and sang in the streets at Winter Solstice, who shopped in the markets and waved at the Reds who rebuilt their city.

I've seen genocide. I saw the Jackal's bombs go off. The ghost of the flash stayed burned in my eyes for two years. But this is not a flash. It is . . . more human, and worse for it.

I understand us now. How easy it is to follow a pointing finger.

"Have you thought about my offer, Mr. Horn?" Xenophon asks. The White watches the burning city with zero connection. A line of slaves in chains five kilometers long stretches toward the former Julii flagship parked south of the city. Will the Republic just watch the rape of Olympia?

"I have thought about your offer. At the right price, it could be interesting."

The White doesn't believe me as I watch the slaves load into the starship. "Are you aware there is a species of bat on Mercury that begins life as mammalian larva?"

I ignore the fool and turn away to look at Fá. The odious shit reclines on his throne as braves from the city bring him women one by one to add to his harem. Sefi had more dignity in her little toenail.

Xenophon prattles on.

"In order for the larva to mature to its destined form, it must find a host to grow inside and then consume when it is ready to fly. Fá was a catalyst. But a rich, haughty city fallen from grace was the necessary chrysalis for this transformation of the Obsidians to their former selves. Where else could a tribal people be nurtured with such discontent? Olympia had every opportunity to spare itself this fate. But without a shepherd, mankind cannot help but succumb to its own greed."

The White surveys my face.

"You are in pain. How could you of all people look down and wonder how they can do this to a city they uplifted? Fear made Olympia polite, Mr. Horn. But when they realized there was nothing to fear due to Sefi's manners, they partook in incremental predation on the Obsidians. A Hyperionin should know: a city is a thief. Designed in every facet to part coin from purse. The only difference is it smiles when it does it. Did Olympians thank the Obsidians for ten years of frontline horror? For their generosity in pouring capital into the rebuilding of their city? No. No, they gouged them in shops, cheated them in casinos, mocked their race, and then, after all that, turned on them in an instant and chose the Republic that could not even put food in their mouths, and a hero who abandoned them for the Core. What greater insult is there? The question is not, how could they do this? It is, why did they not do it sooner?"

"Because Sefi was a decent woman."

"No, she was remarkable, as are you. But she was crushed under the guilt of being seen as the voice of the man she admired, when really she barely knew him much at all. She let her past overrule her nature. As do you. Why?" I ignore the White until those pale hands grab my scarabSkin. "Why?"

"Because we're something you'll never be, shithead: human." The reply breaks something inside the White. Xenophon turns away, wounded. I activate the power switch Pax put in the heartspike. "I want to speak to Fá."

"Why?"

"That, dear asshole, is between me and the ogre."

"Very well." Taking his heart controller in hand, Xenophon brushes past me. I turn at the last second and release the heartspike into his pocket. He leads me past Fá's guards. We wait for the man to finish picking a Pink for his harem. He waves us forward in amusement as the terrified girl is dragged away.

"*Salve,* Xenophon," he says with a smile. "**I see my heir's guardian returned.**" He notices the cuffs. "**Not as friend, it seems. Still. He protected her from the savagery of the heatlands. It is no good for him to be on a leash.**" He motions for his men to remove the cuffs.

"He is a substantially dangerous man," Xenophon warns. "Despite his size."

Volsung considers me. "**So I have heard.**" His men unshackle me.

"Cheers, oldboy," I say to Fá with a wide smile. I rub my raw wrists and eye the weapons on the Ascomanni. I wouldn't make it halfway through a lunge. There is no other way. It is not a great decision, not the sum of my life, as I thought of Trigg's death. It is a small choice to simply say: *Fuck you.*

"**Is my heir alive?**"

I frown. "Didn't you kill her?"

"**I had no chance to mold Sefi. She is not my daughter. When you have so many, they matter very little. Ragnar was my first. I taught him to hunt before I was taken back to the stars. Volga will be my second. She will be like clay. I will make her in my image, so that when the time comes, she will inherit the worlds.**"

"Pity she sunk to the bottom of the sea then," I reply. "Sloppy work, that. Should have hired me. I'm the tits, didn't you hear?"

"**Bottom of the sea, you say?**" He comes down from his throne and sniffs me like a dog. "**Then you must be a nøkken. For I smell her upon you.**" He runs a nail along the scarabSkin, leaving flakes of Sefi's blood. "**She dressed you in this very armor.**" His whiskers scratch my chin. "**She kissed you upon the cheek.**" He draws back and looks at Xenophon, lowering his voice. "**Does our master still wish to tame this dog?**"

"He would prove an asset. But his nature makes it decidedly unlikely, regardless the collar. The master trusts my discretion."

His nature. I chuckle. Validation after all.

"He is not worthy for me. Xenophon, kill him without marks. We will make it look as if his heart gave in to his depredations. When Volga comes for him, she will weep, but not hate." He cups his hand. **"And she will be like clay."** He gives me a mocking smile. **"Thank you for your service, Gray."**

He climbs back on his throne to continue filling his harem as Xenophon readies the controller for my heart. Fá's beasts grip my shoulders to drag me away. "Well, aren't you a cockless little yeti," I say to Fá. His big head turns toward me. "At least have the testicular fortitude to look me in the eye as I die."

Volsung grants me that honor. His men back away as Xenophon thumbs the control and activates the kill switch. I glance over at the White. Xenophon frowns when I don't fall to the ground from heart failure. "Hey, milky. You like riddles. What do you call a piece of shit with a bomb in his pocket?" I unzip the front of my scarabSkin to show the scar Electra left. "Oops."

Xenophon frowns and looks down a sleeve. "Oh . . ." Xenophon disintegrates as the signal to the heartspike in his pocket activates the explosives Pax wrapped around it. The heat hits me before the roar.

The world turns over as I'm thrown like a rag doll.

I can hear nothing. My whole body is cold. My right eye sees washed-out images. My left eye nothing. Half-melted men stumble around me, screaming soundlessly. Smoke twirls up into the blue sky. My spine is broken. My legs do not work. My right arm gone. I am cold but afraid. But not as afraid as the first day at the *ludus*.

The most afraid I have been in all my life was seeing those cold halls and colder boys and lying down to bunk. I don't have to go back there ever again. I feel the metal of Trigg's ring on my finger. The warmth of warm water. The sound of it lapping against a raft. Soon it will be the starry sky. And we will lie beside each other forever. Fá is dead. Volga is safe. Good luck, Snowball.

I stare up at the sun and wait for it to darken.

Then a shadow eclipses it.

No.

No.

No.

Half the monster's face is melted to the bone, baring his bottom teeth. His nose is gone. The iron crown melted to ruin and steaming, fused with his hairless skull. He looks into my eyes, and I see the abyss in his as he laughs at the pain. I moan something in fear. There's a lurch. A sudden pressure in my chest. He pulls away, his hand holding something red as he mouths a word dead to my ears.

"Worthy."

Then he takes a bite of my heart.

PART IV

PRIDE

The world is a maze without a center.
Become it, or be forever lost.

—Silenius au Lune,
Silenius's *Meditations*, 25 PCE

78

LYSANDER

A Visitor

I T IS TIME. After days of waiting for others to enact my will, the hour fast approaches for my own flesh to enter the fray. Glirastes has informed me that Darrow's departure is imminent, as is Atalantia's attack. Somewhere out beyond the mountains, her bombers fuel to deliver their payloads.

It is now or doomsday.

"The dinner is prepared, *dominus*," Exeter says to me as I close the book of Shelley's poems and rise from the orchard bench. It is late afternoon and the songbirds have begun to croon for night. Rising guards patrol the fringes of the estate, looking at the sky, not knowing that the attack will come from within.

I smile at a mismatched pair of guards as I fall in step with Exeter along the gravel path back to the house's southern portico. The pale man gives no sign of his week's labor. He has been busy on my behalf.

While it would have been easier to negotiate the compliance of Glirastes's wary loyalists in person instead of through a proxy, it would have exposed us to dangerous levels of scrutiny. I dare not tempt fate by playing more games than necessary with Darrow.

Soon, I'll be rid of the spike. Until then, the perfect libertine I have remained.

The dining table is set for two. Glirastes and I make idle banter of the predictable sort, but it is peculiar seeing him smiling across from me when inside I know he is churning with fear and doubt.

Neither my friend nor I have much appetite. So it is a relief when the servants take away the barely touched remains of our dinner. Glirastes stands. "I must return to the spaceport. Be a good boy and see me off."

At the boarding stairs to his shuttle, I smile at the old man. "You know what they say about you?" I ask.

"My boy, you should know I haven't the faintest care."

"You found Heliopolis a city for men, and made it a city for gods."

He snorts. "If there are gods, they are in brighter worlds than these."

He has little appetite for banter. He knows the dangers of the path I have chosen to walk, and he doubts me because the old do not remember the necessities of youth. They see only the years on our horizon to which they think we are entitled. But we are entitled only to the moment, and owe nothing to the future except that we follow our convictions.

I am finally following mine.

The desert taught me that the only path is forward.

"I left you a gift in your room," Glirastes says. "Something for the occasion." He lingers on the shuttle steps, unwilling to say farewell.

He nods, sets a hand on my shoulder, contemplates a parting word, and then enters the shuttle.

Night comes not soon enough.

At seven o'clock, Exeter's ship takes him down to the city, along with most of the servants, who are concealed in the cargo hold for their rendezvous with our loyalists. A skeleton crew remains behind. The guards are none the wiser. They watch me.

At eight o'clock, the clone program Glirastes's loyalist Greens cooked up hijacks the feed from my security spike and transmits falsified data back to them, showing that I am in the library reading. I cut it out of my shoulder with a small knife from the dresser.

Then I sit on the edge of the bed and take the card off the smoked-glass box that Glirastes left for me. The note is simple: *This summons legions.*

Inside the box is a silver horn inlaid with gods and goddesses and racing chariots with wild steeds pulling the sun. The Horn of Helios, which has begun every race in the Hippodrome since it was built. It is a priceless relic. I set it on the bed as I open a second, far larger container that conceals the gravBoots, razor, and military hardware provided by the loyalists. I'm about to slip the gravBoots on when a knock comes at the door. I frown as a servant's voice comes through the oak.

"You have a visitor, my liege."

I open the door. "A visitor? What the devil do you mean?"

"Alexandar au Arcos and his maidservant are in the atrium demanding to see you, *dominus.*"

Alexandar? The timing could not be worse. I don't have time to wag jaws at the crown prince of the Free Legions as he thanks me for his deliverance.

"Tell him I am indisposed."

"He knows you are on house arrest. He can see you're in the library, *dominus.*" He looks at the equipment laid out on the bed. "He will be suspicious if I send him away."

That suspicion will lead to a cascade of consequences that may upturn the entire venture. I am supposed to be at the Hippodrome in ten minutes. With Glirastes in motion, there is no secure way to alter the timetable.

Dammit.

"Admit him into the library in two minutes. Tell him I am finishing a chapter." I shut the door. There's absolutely nothing to be done about the spike. I have no way of contacting the Greens.

I hide the loyalist razor in my boot and race to the library.

I'm sweating by the time the door to the library bursts open, and Alexandar waltzes in as if he owns the place. Behind him trails the child soldier Rhonna. Darrow's niece gapes at all the books. I find her particularly offensive today. She wears her arms bare to show off the unnatural bolts that permit lowColors to parody the Blue mind-sync with their vehicles. This condition, compounded by her Color's adverse disposition to disciplined warfare, creates anarchy in a single individual. A sort of dissociative mania, which I can see behind her eyes.

A zealot, this one. I must tread carefully.

"This is where they keep the renegade libertines, in the library?" Alexandar asks, running his tongue along his new teeth. "I hope it was an interesting chapter to keep us waiting, you tart."

He greets me like a brother, wrapping me in a hug and slapping my back in a sort of thuggish display of camaraderie.

"You may have heard," he goes on. "Departure is imminent, and I told Rhonna it would be a crime against culture to depart without a tour of the *Lady Beatrice*. It will likely be months before we're back again." Even the thought of the Rising returning to claim Mercury sets my blood to a boil.

"What a splendid idea," I say before making an apologetic face. "But I fear I am rather indisposed at the moment."

"Told you we should have called ahead," Rhonna says. She smiles apologetically at me. "Sorry, lad, entitlement is one habit the man can't break."

"A book is hardly as interesting company as are we!" Alexandar says. He grins with his new teeth. "Fear not, goodman. I know better than to insult local customs. I brought a bribe." He tosses me a bottle and winks. "I hear Erebians simply adore Venusian brandy."

79

DARROW

Bad Blood

FEAR STARES AT ME through the glass. It does not seem as if he has moved since I resisted cutting off his hands. "Hasn't talked a lick, despite the cocktails," Screwface says from beside me.

"Neurological conditioning?" I ask.

"If it is, it ain't like any I've ever seen."

Atlas's side of the wall is blank, but I feel his eyes on me. I move left, and they follow. "He can sense us."

Screwface believes it. "I noticed that too. Should we up the dosage?"

"No."

"Darrow, we need to know when Atalantia will attack."

"She's in no hurry," I say. "But if we kill him before we get him to my wife—" I stop as I realize what I'm doing. It's always easier to plan on hope. "If she's alive, she can crack him. When we get what's in there, we'll have a chance. Till then, let's not push our luck by melting his cerebellum."

We're about to leave the cell behind when Atlas speaks.

> *"Pedicabere, fur, semel; sed idem*
> *si deprensus eris bis, irrumabo.*
> *quod si tertia furta molieris,*
> *ut poenam patiare et hanc et illam,*
> *pedicaberis irrumaberisque."*

"What does it mean?" Screwface asks.

"Fear is on the job."

"Come on. My family was full of Pixies. Didn't ever bother with Latin."

I sigh, and translate:

> *"Thief, for first thieving shalt be swived, but an*
> *Again arrested shalt be irrumate;*
> *And, shouldst attempt to plunder time the third,*
> *This and that penalty thou shalt endure,*
> *Being both pedicate and irrumate."*

"I am going to kill that man," Screw says quietly.

"Get in line."

Back in the Mound, the final preparations for departure are under way. Despite Screwface's effective efforts against Atalantia's spy rings, it is best to assume she still has agents within the city. Tomorrow's evacuation to the ships will come as a surprise to all but those within my inner circle. Until then, my army plays the part of occupying force. Patrols continue. Garages rattle with industry. Barracks swell with music and snoring and gambling.

Yet something feels wrong. The Fear Knight's poem has haunted me. Did I miss something?

To allay my concerns, I took a tour of the mountain fortifications for signs of Atalantia's forward elements after visiting Atlas. All was still. Too still. Thraxa and Harnassus think my ill-ease to be general paranoia. Glirastes's work is completed. The *Morning Star* and the remaining ships are repaired for combat. Morale is high. My confidants dwell on the coming fray, and debate our chances of slipping the noose. But in my quarters inside the Mound, my mind roves restlessly as I inspect data-packets from Atlas's interrogation, surveillance of known loyalists, and Glirastes's charge, Cato.

The five-minute gap from his detour to the wine cellar is explainable yet cloying. In secret, my men bugged the cellar after that surveillance failure, and faulted it on interference from the *Lady Beatrice*'s reactor. Harnassus himself has vouched for the integrity of Glirastes's EMP. So why do I linger over this insubstantial creature's idle days?

Is it simply the seeds of Fear?

He has done nothing suspicious, not even left the *Lady Beatrice,* yet something is off about Cato au Vitruvius's nature, if not his actions.

Perhaps it is latent sociopathic tendencies that set the hairs on my back standing on end. I watch him sit in the library reading his book, and shift back through the moments where my Greens flagged peculiar activity. Much is class-based misunderstanding. They divine malign intent from his reading selections and his ambivalence toward the names of the servants. False positives perfectly in keeping with his nature.

I should let it alone and not squander my time, but I find myself idiosyncratically flipping through his hours, unwilling to get out of my chair. I watch him walk the garden, laugh at old vids, converse with the guards, sketch idly the shadows of a lone flower, eat breakfast, yawn over evening drinks with Glirastes, retire to bed at a drunkard's hour.

A knock comes at the door. I let the video continue playing and answer.

Thraxa stands there with her hands behind her back. "Did you eat dinner? Ration bars don't count." She produces two fish pies.

"Come on in."

She tosses them on the table and looks around for plates. "We're both just going to eat them all anyway," I say. She shrugs and plops down in a chair, digging into hers with a utility knife. She waves the knife at the holo.

"That's a little creepy. Watching the Pixie sleep. If you're so fond of him, you should have gone with the kids."

"The kids?"

"Alexandar and Rhonna went up to the *Beatrice* not long ago."

"Why?"

"Something about a gift." That troubles me. I wouldn't have stopped it. I have no valid reason. Yet Thraxa senses my unease. "What's wrong?" she asks.

"Something's not been sitting right," I say. "There's something about him . . ."

"Then let's bring him in."

"Harnassus says the EMP is flawless, and we're jamming any signal that leaves the peninsula just as much as Atalantia is. If he's a spy, I don't know what the hell he's doing."

She forks a piece of fish into her mouth. "You want to talk about it?"

"It?"

"Your wife. My brother. Maybe the rest of my family."

"No." I watch her. "Do you want to talk about it?"

"Naw. Not my bag. But it ain't fun. Is it?"

"No. It ain't fun." There's an indistinct murmur from the holo. Wait. I fix on the holo as Thraxa frowns.

"What's the matter?"

"Quiet."

I amplify the sound and replay the murmur Cato made as he slept. "Did you hear that?" I ask.

"Sounds like 'something over all.'"

"'Truth over all,'" I say. I've heard that before. But when. When? I can't pin my finger on it until a slippery sensation works its way up my arm. I bolt upright and run to the door.

"Your pie!" Thraxa calls after me.

I stand over the science team as they shake their heads at my request for a DNA check. "We've been under constant attack since we got to Mercury, sir. There's no DNA census without a re-upload from Skyhall. And we ran him against all the Gold POWs."

"Run it against this." I thrust Sevro's trophy at them. The tech looks down at the bloody robes in confusion. *"Now."* I pace behind the techs as they work. It does not take long. The computer beeps and before I look up, I know.

The DNA is related.

"Oh shit," I hear the techs say as I bolt out of the room so fast I send Thraxa tumbling over a chair. I call Screwface at full sprint. He answers, covering his yawn with his Heliopolitan scarf, having just returned from a patrol in the mountains. "Iron up. Full pack."

His face falls as he knows he failed. "They're coming."

"They're coming." Next I call Harnassus. He answers peevishly from the *Morning Star.* "Are you with Glirastes?"

His weariness vanishes. "No. His shuttle is having maintenance difficulties."

"Tell him I want to speak with him in the hangar. Once he's away from the machine, stun him, strip him naked, scan him for embeds, and put him in a cell with a full century standing guard. No one is to speak with him until I get there. If he tries to touch anything unusual between this moment and then, shoot him in the head. Then order an evacuation of all support personnel to the ships. I want everyone except combat ready to go." I take a breath. "Then get a particle beam pointed at the *Spirit of Faran* and blow that EMP to hell."

There's a pause.

"Copy that. What's what?"

"Patching a pool." I use my master controls over my Howlers' network as I run, cutting out Alexandar and Rhonna. Colloway joins from the confines of his isolation chamber. Thraxa storms down the hall to link up with me. Harnassus joins as he walks a complaining Glirastes out to the hangar. When the rest of the pool has joined from all across Heliopolis, I inform them and my private horror becomes real: "An omega-level enemy asset has been discovered inside the city. Glirastes has flipped. That EMP is for us. I've ordered its destruction. But it will be coordinated with an outside assault. Prepare for heavy enemy contact. Attack is imminent."

Should I call Rhonna and Alexandar? Will it tip my enemy off? If I don't, he could take either of them hostage, or kill them if he hears us coming. I have to risk it and trust their discretion. Even then, if anyone could take down a single man, it's Alexandar. I use my master command to turn on both of their cochlear implants. Rhonna is laughing and admiring the Water Colossus. "Do not react. A Howler strike team is on its way to your location. The man you are sitting across from is not named Cato au Vitruvius. He is Lysander au Lune. Wait for us. Do not engage him on your own."

80

LYSANDER

Heir of Arcos

"WHEN I FIRST SAW the Water Colossus, I thought nothing could be that big." Rhonna admires the ten-meter-tall model inside Glirastes's museum to himself. "But then I thought I'd never seen anything as big as Tinos, or the Citadel of Light, or the *Morning Star.* That shit nearly dropped my jaw. There's always something bigger, ain't there?" She is much like her name, which means "rough island" in ancient Gaelic. I doubt she knows how apt a name it is. The young Red wants to be inviting, but just can't help being jagged around the edges.

Alexandar does not notice the jaggedness one bit.

Starlight filters through the glass dome, the light of certain stars amplified to cast columns of light over the models. From his recline on a bench, Alexandar sips his sherry and gazes at the rough island as if she were the monument itself.

Their unspoken tenderness seems already so frail to me.

Before the Ash Rain, it wouldn't have.

"Nothing is as big as the *Morning Star,* my goodlady, except the ego of a Valii-Rath," Alexandar says, enjoying his role as tour guide. It seems his education stumbled during his house's sojourn from Mars to Io to Luna to rebels. Even in my anxiousness to depart, I remind myself to be civil and correct none of his errors. "It took seven years to build. Dozens of asteroids. But most of its metal came from the mines of Mercury."

Wrong.

Gods, how long do they intend to loiter? I hide my vexation. My men will already be in motion. Glirastes preparing his program. I must get to the Hippodrome. But most galling of all, my two guests are becoming rude in their lingering. If this is what passes for Martian manners, I shudder to think of what Virginia has done to the Palatine.

My cousin's enthusiasm for seeing me again has made it impossible to extract myself from their company. Something must be done. And soon. Yet a fresh variable rears its ugly head. I've unfortunately noticed Alexandar no longer tongues his new teeth as he did when he arrived.

"From the mines here? No shit. Shipping fees must have put Octavia in her early grave," Rhonna says with a folksy whistle. "Costs me half a month's pay just to send a kilogram of loot back to Mars. How'm I supposed to get my cigars home?" She glances at me with a grin. "Raided the Votum vault, I did. You're looking at the only purveyor of Heliopolitan cigars in all Agea. Well, soon as we skip this rock and make like pups for home, that is."

She downs her glass, leaving fingerprints all over the bulb. Darrow's stock, indeed. Her other hand hangs idle at her side, no longer exhibiting the tic of playing with the leather thong of her sidearm's holster. This, along with Alexandar's diminished self-dentistry, has turned me cold. I probe with the Mind's Eye.

"Octavia made the people of Mars subsidize it," Alexandar explains. "She wanted the Rim to build a flagship paid for by Mars just to mock us. Especially after Darrow purloined the *Pax*."

"Not exactly true," I say. "Octavia commissioned it four years before the *Vanguard* was stolen. She paid the Julii trading company the shipping fees using the tariff revenues levied on Nero au Augustus's helium exports from his mines, which your grandfather, Alexandar, watched him steal from his sworn ArchGovernor. The Rising plutocrats were willing beneficiaries of the Society before they tired of it. In fact." I look at Rhonna. "How many mines did your family own, Alexandar?"

He smiles pleasantly back. "Oh, far fewer than yours, I assume."

I affect a yawn, and then resort to violence.

I seize Rhonna's left wrist and jerk her toward me, so that my tight jab shatters her jaw. In the same movement, I pull her slack body to me, strip her sidearm, and put it to her temple. The tip of Alexandar's whip stops taut less than a centimeter from my right eye.

He recalls it in a beautiful maneuver that has him poised for the Falling Leaf, a winding corkscrew of a downward slash. He shows remarkable mastery of one of the Willow Way's more complicated strikes by freezing halfway into the third motion.

His eyes stare at the gun I hold to Rhonna's head.

In the moment, there is no rage for me in my cousin's eyes. Only fear for her.

I do not want to shoot Alexandar. I found no fault with him in the mountains. Nor with his valor in the chase, nor his humble heroism at Tyche. But the man he serves is a plague. And he is just a noble symptom far too loyal for his own good.

I point the gun at him and let Rhonna fall unconscious to the floor.

"Lune," he says.

"Arcos. I see Lorn gifted you the Willow after all."

"Bold of you to say my grandfather's name after what Octavia did to him. You recall, yes? How she had Lilath au Faran saw through his spine? From behind, like this . . ." He slowly moves his blade back and forth. "All my life I was compared to you. Cousin Lysander. Perfect Lysander." He looks me up and down. "You must be more than meets the eye."

"Put down the blade and get on your knees," I say.

"Perish the thought." He levels his blade at me. "How about you pull that big iron from your boot, and we settle who's the Heir of Arcos."

"Who is your favorite poet?" When he does not answer, I choose for him:

> *"Ye labour for your fall*
> *With your own hands! Not by surprise*
> *Nor yet by stealth, but with clear eyes,*
> *Knowing the thing ye do."*

He sneers at the gun. "No honor."

"No time."

I shoot Alexandar in the head.

81

DARROW

Dark Age

THE *LADY BEATRICE* LIES in darkness except for the faint twin-
kling of lights through the windows of her west wing. My Howlers
land in force, Screwface taking a platoon through the top windows, as I
shoot a hole through the front door and thunder in with Thraxa and her
warhammer.

"Lune!" I shout.

"Come out, come out, you dumb little cur." Thraxa slams her hammer through a pillar. "Come out and face the Wee Lass!"

There is no answer. No sound except the stomping of my Howlers
upstairs and the faint warbling from the rotating crystal orb in the foyer.
Its fractal light casts white snowflakes on the stone floor as we rush into
the home. There's a shout from the west wing.

"Goryhell," Thraxa mutters as we enter Glirastes's museum.

I feel a tremor inside.

There is a body on the floor.

I stare down at it, and a maw of grief opens inside. The boy who entered my life as an arrogant lancer and through hardship became hero to
an army lies in a pool of his own blood. He has been mutilated. Half his
head is missing. Sightless eyes stare at the ceiling. Mouth half open in
surprise, as if he were wondering, *Really? Like this?* There's a low moan.
Rhonna limps from behind a model of the Water Colossus. Her face is
nearly unrecognizable, her jaw shattered. She falls to her knees in Alexandar's blood. Her scream tears me to tatters. How many years did they
stand apart from each other behind me? How many precious few mo-

ments were they honest with each other? They were robbed of so much joy, promised it, then robbed again.

"Rhonna, where is he?" I whisper. *"Rhonna, where is Lune?"*

She looks up at me with empty eyes and points up.

I motion a Howler forward. "Get her to the *Morning Star.*"

Rhonna thrashes as the Howler manhandles her off Alexandar and drags her to the door. The house rumbles. Weapons fire upstairs from Screwface's platoon.

His voice crackles through: *"Eyes on—"*

"—shit."

"—slagger dodged a bullet . . ."

"Shoot—"

"—homing mines on our six."

Something detonates.

We leap to the second level, bypassing the stairs. Screwface and his men fire down a hallway. Two Howlers are down. There's a sucking sound. Screwface's platoon scatters, taking cover as a quarter of the house disintegrates. My armor absorbs the shockwave, but the wall does not. I stand as debris and dust swirl around me. A shape moves through a distant room and then disappears upward. Thraxa bursts after him.

"He's got boots!" Screwface shouts.

The pack follows. Clearing the debris cloud, my optics pick up a tiny shape racing for the city at incredible velocity. New boots. His lead is already half a kilometer. We rocket off in pursuit. I radio other elements held back from the evacuation to cut him off. Response teams rise from distant skyscrapers. RipWings drop from the flier layer. My army constricts around him. He banks left to avoid running into a Rat Legion squad from the Mound. Mini-missiles streak after him and detonate against the sides of skyscrapers as he threads his way through the business district. Glass rains on us as we follow in his wake. We bank left to cut him off when he passes through the eye of a circular tower. He sees our intent, and shoots straight upward, firing a hole through the glass side of the building. He disappears inside. We hover around the building, forming a perimeter. I send four Howlers in after him. Then I understand as Screwface banks down.

"Ground floor," I bark. Thraxa and sixteen others rip downward with me just as glass explodes outward from the second floor. He took a gravLift shaft down. I fire my pulseFist on full auto. Screwface flies underneath, taking slow aim. Chunks of concrete erupt as Lune weaves through our fire and takes off through a canyon of mercantile buildings, heading north.

"Damn, kid can fly," Thraxa mutters.

"Thank Cassius, the pretty bastard," Screwface curses.

Is he here too? I pray not. If he's gone over . . .

As Lysander gains altitude, I spare a look south of the city to the spaceport. The torchShip I ordered to destroy the *Spirit* lowers itself midway up the *Morning Star*'s hull to gain a firing solution. Too slow. Too damn slow. Just blow that EMP to hell. I radio them to shoot through the *Morning Star.*

Lune's lead has diminished. We're barely two hundred meters behind him, close enough to see him looking back over his shoulder at us with the naked eye. He wears light armor and a heavy old helmet.

"What the . . ." Screwface mutters. *"Boss, nine o'clock."*

Lysander's face blooms in the skyline, a broadcast to all the holo-screens. Not just that. Inside a passing skyscraper, the rooms fill with sudden illumination. The whole city glows with his message. Somehow he hardhacked the feed.

I don't listen to his words. He'll be exhorting them to arms, as he watched me do on Phobos so many years ago. The attack will come from the inside first. He's heading for the prisoner camp in the shadow of the Hippodrome.

Fireballs bloom around the prison camp. Not at the guard towers with their antipersonnel cannons or at the tank garages, but along the walls. Through the billowing smoke, men on fire flail in chaotic dances. From the sky they look like lightning bugs in fog. More explosions go off across the city. Not one near the heavily defended shield generator.

My targeting system registers a lock on Lune's gravBoots' thermal signature and I fire my six mini-missiles. Vapor trails scar the air between us as they reel him in. Then he seems to divide, impossibly.

"Bailed out!" Screwface calls.

Lysander's gravBoots carry on without him as he falls barefoot from the sky. The missiles streak after the boots and detonate with a white flash. Lysander plummets downward end over end before crashing into the central pool of the Water Gardens. We overshoot him and by the time we bank around it is too late. Warning lights appear on my holo-Display indicating rapidly changing electric and magnetic fields. A black pupil spawns at the center of the *Morning Star* as the lights of the ships wink out.

Dark is the tide that rolls over the spaceport and the city, swallowing the phalanxes of tanks and Drachenjägers upon the Field of Phaethon. It plunges the office spires, the Hippodrome, the Mound, and the great shield generators into darkness. Above, the iridescent shield that protected us against Atalantia flickers, and then goes off. The glittering cloak of fliers that drifted over the city glitters no more, and the ships become indistinct shadows as they plummet from the sky.

We fall with them.

82

LYSANDER

This Summons Legions

HELIOPOLIS, CITY OF THE SUN, lies in darkness. Darrow and his Howlers disappear from the sky as their gravBoots fail and they plummet down into shadows. Ships crash across the skyline without the dignity of balls of fire or white flashes from overloading reactors.

I swim to the edge of the pool and jump down to the next level of the fountain, nearly losing hold of the Horn of Helios as I drop down. There's a terrific crash from above as a troop carrier collides with the head of Poseidon, breaking off his right ear and tearing the carrier in two. One piece slams down into the topmost pool plate. The second spins through the air, passing less than ten meters over my head. Half a hundred men are still strapped into their seats. Their faces pass close enough I can see the acne on a Brown's forehead before they smash into a building below.

Water rains down on me.

I look up. Over my head, the topmost plate of the Gardens is cracking under the weight of the larger half of the carrier. I jump from the pool to the one beneath just as the topmost plate gives way and a hundred tons of marble and ship smash down on the pool beneath. It becomes an avalanche of stone and water and ship collapsing each plate, gaining on me as I jump frantically down the monument.

I hit the ground level of the plaza and roll, barely outracing the debris that crashes down behind me. Chunks of rock the size of horses roll across the plaza, crumpling the bodies of bystanders and splintering trees. Something hits me hard in the back of the skull and I go sprawling.

Blood leaks down my back when I regain my feet. Dust billows all around. I search until I find the horn. Then I run.

Somehow, running in the darkness through the bedlam, I find the Via Triumphia. Rising legionnaires shout to one another in the black streets. I jump, grab the lip of a low wall, and scramble up till I'm on the rooftops. There I strip open my rucksack and change into lightweight boots. I wrap the loyalist razor around my left arm, and try Alexandar's bettercrafted blade. Its response to my touch is exemplary. The whip cracks as it lashes out to wrap around the metal support of an overhead solar array. I swing out across the gaps between the roofs and toggle the razor into a blade. It releases as it cuts through the array and I land on the other side. More arrays fall behind me as I swing north over the dark streets with the Horn of Helios.

The mayhem of the prison break is illuminated in stuttered flashes of gunfire. With electricity flowing, those prisoners taken in the Battle of the Ladon were at the mercy of the Rising. Now Gold and Obsidian athletes scale the walls and tear their lowColor guards to ribbons with their bare hands.

I keep well clear. I can't mobilize them in the chaos on foot. Exeter and Glirastes's servants will have laid the charges on the pen housing my Praetorians. They may already be under way. I'm the laggard here.

I vault another roof, almost impaling myself on a clothesline pole as I head breakneck for the Hippodrome. I was meant to land in the center of the arena, where loyalists would be waiting. But Alexandar ruined my timing and jeopardized my initiative.

Darrow was in pulseArmor. The lack of electrical assistance will paralyze the weaker Howlers under the armor's weight, but not soldiers like Darrow or Thraxa. He'll wake in some arcade, or upon some roof, surrounded by chaos from which no man could possibly salvage a victory. But Darrow built his legend on such moments. The EMP wave went farther than expected. I can't see the lights of Atalantia's ships in orbit. How far did it go on the ground? How long till she moves more elements in? Given time, Darrow will summon some martial necromancy. So when I come south for his army, it must be with shock and awe.

I use a market stall awning to slow my descent as I swing from the rooftops down to ground level and weave through dead automobiles outside the Hippodrome. "Lune!" I shout as I approach the main pedestrian entry arch at a run.

"Invictus!" someone replies. A dozen midColor loyalists with gas-powered rifles step out of the shadows. They wave me to the left into the arcade beneath the stadium seats where concessions are sold and bets made on race day. Gunpowder weapons crackle in the distance. I find the door to the subterranean stables unlocked. Two Rising sentries lie outside it with holes in their heads. A wall of horse stench hits my nose as I burst from the stairwell into the stables.

Lit by the eerie flames of torches, one of Glirastes's servants waits for me with a dozen Obsidian stablehands in the proud race-day livery of House Votum. "Hail Lune!" they say, falling to their knees on the straw-strewn floor.

They rise again, staring at me in the low light to tend the anxious herd of saddled sunbloods. None but Obsidians could wrangle such intrepid beasts. I search their eyes. They are barely kin with those who follow Sefi. They know no other life but Mercury. No life but these horses. No life but service. I salute them as they fulfill their noble task and extend my arms for the loyalists to buckle the waiting suit of armor to me. It is old gear. Circuits long dead. Bone white with a crude crescent welded onto the front and back.

Glirastes is incorrigible.

"So you're Cicero's Blood of Empire," I say to the horse set out before the rest. For once, Cicero was not hyperbolic. It is as if every horse I have seen before this day, even Atalantia's prized creatures, were nothing more than early drafts of this ultimate creation. He towers over me, clearing twenty-five hands at the withers with still more muscled shoulder to measure. His hooves are the size of dinner plates, his mane as brilliant an orange as his irises. His white coat dappled steel gray. Haughty eyes watch me. He bucks his head as I approach, lifting the two Obsidian stablehands off their feet.

When they wrangle him back down, I cut my hand and wave the blood over his nose so he can smell it. He tilts his head, his eyes searching mine. I bring my nose to his, as is the dangerous custom with sunbloods. He could snap off my face with ease, but I keep my voice soothing and he lets me stroke his muzzle. With a snort, he bends his front legs in obeisance.

The Obsidians cheer. They had wondered if the horse would find me worthy. "Blood knows blood, my liege," their old stablemaster rumbles. "He will bear you over a sea of slaves."

The ramp used by charioteers to enter the Hippodrome slams down in a cloud of dust. Blood of Empire has been here before even if I have not. His hooves paw the sand, impatient for the glory to which he has become entitled. It has been years since I've ridden a horse, and in all of human history, how many have graced the back of such a terrible prize as this? I fear disgracing this king of horses more than I do the coming violence. With an intake of breath, I grip the Horn of Helios and dig my heels into his sides.

It is like riding lightning.

The ramp blurs past underneath. Suddenly we are upon the surface of the Hippodrome. No sea of faces awaits us. No adulation. Only a black sky, the empty stadium, and a ragged band of men jogging across the sand in tattered uniforms, Rhone and Kalindora at their lead. The loyalists who led the attack on the Republic prison led them here for me.

The Praetorians and Kalindora are shocked to find me alive.

I spare no time for pleasantries as I circle them atop Blood of Empire. "Upon Luna, upon Earth, upon Mars, they say that the Praetorian Guard is dead!" I shout. "That they have faded into the maw of history like morning fog over the sea! That nothing remains but the memory of the giants that once walked the worlds! Rhone ti Flavinius!" I cry. "Before all things, what are the Praetorian Guard?"

"Equestrians!" he bellows.

"And what is your duty?"

"To protect the blood of Lune!"

"Will you ride with me today, Rhone ti Flavinius?"

"With honor, my liege!"

"Are you a memory?" I ask the Praetorians as Blood continues to canter around them.

"No!"

"Are you giants!"

"Yes!"

"Will you ride with me today? For the glory of your forebearers. For the resurrection of the Society. For the honor of the guard! Will you ride with me?"

"Yes!" they roar. Only Kalindora remains silent.

I take the Horn of Helios from the saddle and blow a sonorous note. And from the belly of the Hippodrome, the herd of Votum, pride of Heliopolis, stampedes upward under a black sky. The stablehands bear up crates of weapons provided by the loyalists, and when my Praetorians are mounted, Kalindora walks up beside me with a look of disapproval. The left sleeve of her prisoner jumpsuit hangs slack, the arm Darrow cut off rotting in the desert. But her sword arm looks restless.

"What a hunger for blood you have acquired in the desert," she says. "Did you survive that sandstorm just to die in these streets? If we wait for Atalantia—"

"We will be at her mercy. Is that why you brought me the Praetorians?" She does not reply. "*He will win whose army is animated by the same spirit throughout its ranks.* The Society needs victory. Not a slaughter. Too long have the rabble had a monopoly on glory. Today we reclaim it. I would have the Love Knight at my side as we do." I extend the loyalist razor to her. With a growing smile, she reaches forward.

83

DARROW

Hazard Bedlam

THUMP. *THUMP.* DISTANT SCREAMS AND RAGE. The shrieking of metal on metal. In the darkness, flashes of flailing limbs, gnashing teeth, screaming mouths. I watch the violence painted in fragmented impressionist brushstrokes.

My armor is dead. My helmet's internal screen black, vision now constricted to the narrow duroglass emergency slits in the helmet's eyes. Beyond my helmet is frenzy. They beat on my armor with fists, hammers, blocks of masonry, fence poles, and all manner of improvised urban weaponry.

They fell on me after I crashed through a storefront and struggled up from the debris, my legs snared by electrical wire. First it was two, then two became a mob. Now I cannot move for the mound of humanity atop me. They besiege the Sciantus-made armor with anything they can find. A Brown street cleaner sits on my chest hammering a long piece of rebar into the joints with a chunk of masonry, desperate for my blood. A Silver kicks at my groin till his foot breaks and he hobbles away. A Gray sits on my arm, trying to pry open my balled gauntlets so he can break my fingers one by one. Two old Red women pin my head between them and start hammering at the eyeholes with improvised chisels as they fumble for the emergency switch. They find it, but I've already locked it.

Fortunately, the armor is a tough nut to crack.

I can only imagine they're doing the same to my downed men all over Heliopolis. Lysander has woken the sleeping giant that we kept alive with our meds. But beyond the screaming mob, the sky is black and empty of Atalantia's ships. Did the EMP reach all the way to orbit? I see no dreadnought lights above.

My ships will be dead at the spaceport. Our shield down.

This is the end, but I refuse to let the mob swallow me like it did my wife.

The mob clears except for those holding me down while several low-Colors stagger over with a block of masonry the size of a man. They hold it over my head and drop it. A ringing fills my ears from the internal concussion. The reinforced warhelm dents but does not break. They get clever and drag me toward the local park, making a hideous parade, where they hold me down before a tall headless statue of a Votum ancestor. They tie electrical cables around my arms and legs, and four teams pull my body taut as the rest of them loop the cable around the neck of the statue and begin to heave. It rocks on its pedestal, each heave bringing it closer and closer to its tipping point, after which several tons of marble will fall and test the metalworking of Martian forges. I wait as the four teams on my limbs strain and sweat, pulling against what they think is my strength, but is actually the reinforced skeleton of the armor. They waste their effort. I save mine for one desperate gambit.

When the statue finally tips forward with a cheer from the mob, I roar and jerk as hard as I can with my right leg and right arm. The sudden force sends the teams of men stumbling forward, impossibly off balance. Then I see why. Several young Heliopolitan Reds smash into them from behind, knocking them off their feet. Still they don't let go of the line. In a sudden explosion of pure force, the muscles of my right leg and right arm pull for everything they're worth against their teams. They're jolted forward, even as the men on the left keep pulling, helping me drag them into the path of the teetering statue.

The timing is almost comedic.

Several tons of stone make wet boneless sacks of men. The teams on the left stop pulling, suddenly appalled by the sight of pulverized men and the bath of gore it entails. It is nothing to me. I unravel myself and stand in the dead heavy armor.

That they are not the same mob that butchered Daxo and mutilated my wife does not matter. I kill them all.

The Brown street cleaner rushes for me with his piece of rebar. My punch is slowed by the weight of my unpowered armor, but not by much, and I am still the war god Mickey carved using all his infernal devices. I need no razor for this mindless dreck. This man is tiny. My metal fist collapses the side of his skull and shatters vertebrae. I lift the Silver who kicked my groin by his throat and squeeze until I feel spine. I shatter a man's femur with a stomp, and collapse his sternum into his heart as I march over him to break a woman's jaw. Rib cages crackle under armored boots like twigs as I tread through them in systematic slaughter.

As a mob they were a single organism. In fear, they divide. In death, they become lonely as I weave them into my twitching meat carpet.

When all have fled or died, there is no one left to kill but a convulsing Silver boy who huddles by what remains of his father underneath the statue. One sight of his wide eyes and slack jaw and desperate begging stops me like a wall. Seeing myself through his eyes, I am disgusted. So I wheel away back into my world.

The Reds who came to my aid stand watching me. There are six of the sunbaked laborers. Not a one older than twenty. They stand with their fists in a salute. I open an external pouch manually and find the helm key. I insert it into the collar until a latch pops. I roll back the wolf's head helm and suck down the fresh air. The young Reds stare up at me. They might have thought they recognized my armor before, but now they see my face, and they take a step back in fear.

"I lost my razor on the rooftops. Find it."

By the time the skinniest of them returns with my slingBlade in his trembling hands, another crowd has formed down the street. They're trying to decide whether it's worth rushing me. I take the blade from the boy. They see its shape. They run.

I nod to the Red and, weighed down by forty kilos of dead armor, rush to find my men.

My miracle has turned into bedlam.

Heliopolis is in chaos. Screams drift over the city. The streets are pitch dark. Gunshots crackle from conventional arms. Downed ships smolder and send black clouds of smoke twirling up into the darkness. Bands of citizens armed with improvised weapons answer Lune's call and begin to rove the streets, dragging sympathizers from their doorways to stab metal in their guts or cave their heads in with rocks. A band of rubble-armed Heliopolitan highColors eyes me down a boulevard before carrying on, looking for easier kills. Each street is a new horror. I watch from a stone balcony looking down into an arcade as one of my citizen outreach patrols is cornered by a mob. With their pulseRifles dead, they have only their long utility knives to protect them. The mob keeps their distance and stones them to death before I can find a way down.

I encounter bands of my men and frantic stragglers in the streets. Six have conventional weapons. By the empty magazine pouches, I see they've been using them. Most stragglers come from downed ships or local strongpoints. Panic grips the army. When they hold their ground, armies suffer, but when they retreat hysterically they die. We can't all retreat at the same time. Guessing Lysander's force, when it comes, will cut off my two million support troopers billeted in the city, I order a Red centurion to send runners to the other strongpoints and tell them to marshal at the Water Plaza.

I follow the directions of a medicus who says he saw the Howlers forming up in a square nearby. Before I make it there, I'm drawn by the glow of a fire in the mouth of an alleyway.

Turning the corner, I find a gang of highColor youths standing over someone in armor, dumping mechanical oil on the blaze they've set. They take off running when they see me. I look around the alley for something to put out the blaze. Shouting comes from the street. Three White Fleet pilots, bleeding from a crash landing, tear around the corner, chased by a dozen men with clubs and a young Gold with his heirloom family razor. They skid to a stop as they see me standing there covered in blood. I pull my razor and they run.

They'll find more of my men, so I hunt them down. In the armor, I'm too slow to catch the Gold and a Red, but I kill the rest from behind.

The pilots have put out the blaze by the time I return. I brush the sand they piled on Thraxa's armor and twist the hidden emergency release. She's not breathing. The flames would have prevented oxygen from entering her helmet. I perform mouth-to-mouth until she gasps against me.

"I'm prime," she says, eyes still wild. "I'm prime. Get off." She sits up in a daze and looks around at the darkness in ill temper. "That little odious shit. The ships?"

"Dead. Seems the EMP hit orbit too. No telling the range."

"I'll wring that overbred prat's neck!"

"We got to find him first."

I help her to her feet and she staggers with the pilots and me to the square. We find Screwface and most of the other Howlers giving orders to several thousand infantry from a dozen different legions.

"Boss!" Screwface shouts over the chaos. He rushes to me.

"What's what?" I ask as Thraxa helps me roll open my helmet.

"Hazard bedlam," he says. "Whole city, looks like. Ships too. Strongpoints are solid, but there's shuttles down all over the city. We got half the pack looking for you. Been sending out teams for them and bringing the wounded back here." He nods to the wounded at the far side of the market as the rest of the Howlers form a semicircle around me. For a moment, I feel as if I am back at the Institute, though of their number only Screwface still has the stink of dead horse about him. Not for the first time, I'm thankful for my peculiar education. I know what to do when the lights go out.

"The city is lost. But looks like the EMP hit orbit too," I tell them. "It'll be hours before those dreadnoughts are back online. The fact that the skies are empty means her ground forces got hit—given the range. She'll have to bring her other ships from picket or far-side to send armor, but once it comes she'll have two thousand years of tech on us. Then it's game over. We have to get as many men out of the city and into the mountains as we can before Atalantia brings those ships around. We have far less than an hour."

I sketch a quick map of the city in the dirt with my slingBlade, making triangles for armories holding conventional weapons. They crouch to see it better in the gloom. I draw a circle for the Hippodrome to the northeast.

"Lysander knew the EMP range. If he were practical, he'd hold for reinforcements. But he's going for glory. He'll try to take the city while Atalantia is knocked out. He landed here." I draw a rectangle to the south for the Water Plaza. "The POWs were held here." I draw an *X* west of the Hippodrome, north of us. "Soon we'll have several hundred thousand veteran troops pouring south with unknown armaments." I mark several circles five kilometers south of the Hippodrome, two south of us. "These are our support barracks and administrative offices. They have not yet been evacuated. I've sent runners to tell them to move south en masse. The fleet is dead, so they'll be heading for the mountain tunnels. They are hackers, medici, clerks, engineers, orderlies. Those prisoners are Iron Leopards and XX Fulminata, some of the toughest sons of bitches in the Core. With no tech, those Obsidians and Golds will be murder machines. We will not let them catch our friends. They've held us up, now we get their backs.

"Six main boulevards lead south. We will barricade them and hold the line here." I draw a line across the sand south of the Water Plaza. *X*. On that line, what remains of my infantry in the city will die to buy the rest time. "The strongpoints have gunpowder weapons and grenades, but only enough for one man in ten. Give them to the Gray and Red snipers. All guns should be on the rooftops—expect the Golds to be running the roofs, so fortify your men the best you can between the plazas, and give them melee support. Remember they can jump streets. Use your dark-age training. This isn't the first time gear's been down. You fight a Gold alone, you die. Fight together."

I give a boulevard apiece to four different Howlers, putting Screwface on the right flank, nearest the tunnels and farthest from the Mound.

"And what about you, boss?" he asks.

I put my finger in the center of the map at the Water Gardens.

"Thraxa and I will hold the Via Triumphia. Lysander is too young to go anywhere else. If he wants to make a name for himself slaughtering my men, he has to go through me. If your line breaks, do not head for the tunnels. It's too far. Their Golds will run you down. Retreat to the Mound. We'll make our stand there." I look into their faces. Not a man or woman amongst them expects to survive the hour. But as the waiting has ended, so too has the fear. Not one quibbles or shies from duty. I could not be prouder. "If I do not see you at the Mound, I will meet you in the Vale. Goodspeed." I grab Screwface as the rest disperse. "Be safe."

He just laughs.

"Legion!" Thraxa roars.

All across the market, the infantry slam their heels together and raise their fists as we jog past. "Hail libertas! Hail Reaper!"

84

DARROW

Meat Straw

FRAGMENTS OF SCATTERED LEGIONS join my procession as we rush to secure the Via Triumphia, swelling our numbers to upwards of twenty thousand if I had to guess. Five thousand join us from the district's strongpoint bearing crates of gunpowder weapons, which are disbursed to our snipers and riflemen. We have six hundred working guns in total, fifteen gas-powered grenade launchers. Though they are little more than clubs now, many cling to the energy weapons that never made them equal to Golds on the killing field, but at least gave them a chance. Conventional rounds just don't pack the same punch.

To give our men polearms, we hew down fences and signposts with our razors as we pass. Another swell of men come from the now-useless artillery batteries. Thraxa waves to a little Pink girl who fogs her apartment's window as she watches us. We have failed her like we failed those Red boys who came to my aid. Soon they will know the mines and she will be returned to the Gardens where she will know only the pleasure of others, and one day think of her childhood when the Rising came as little more than a fantasy.

We make it to the choke point just as scouts from Lysander's force reach the rooftops on the other side of the Water Plaza. Through the legs of the mighty statue of Poseidon, I see them moving roof to roof. The fastest have already summited the stone wreckage of Poseidon's fallen plates. They double back to report our movements as our snipers start picking them off.

"So he is pushing," Thraxa says. "That unctuous twat. Why wouldn't he just wait for armor?"

"He wants to make a name for himself in slaughter," I say. "I thought better of that boy."

"Of course you did. Sevro was right. Should have ended the line in the Maw."

Together, we look north. The cityscape lies in darkness. The Hippodrome like the bent head of a shadowy giant. Through the roots of those buildings, Lysander's army will be moving south. The Golds rushing ahead for glory and revenge. No doubt thinking our humane treatment of their radiation sickness to be some kind of genetic moral weakness on our part. The Obsidians won't be far behind. And then a sea of veteran Gray killers from the shores of Venus, the furnace of Mercury, the old lands of Earth, the megahoods of Luna, and even the highlands of my home.

All coming to kill my men.

Should we not have fed them? Should we not have healed them?

The Water Plaza itself is a kilometer-by-kilometer square of white marble, in the center of which Poseidon stands over whitewashed sandstone and flowering sunblossom trees. The fallen plates make a stack of rubble to the north, but between Poseidon's legs the plaza is flat and open. The Via Triumphia encircles the Water Gardens in a roundabout littered with dead vehicles. I send snipers into the buildings on the southern edge of the plaza and on the rooftops, putting my Howler snipers in two stone bell towers and atop a triumphal arch. Gunshots crackle as they continue picking off Lune's scouts. I see the men of our adjacent force climbing the rooftops to the east.

A thin line of resistance forms across Heliopolis.

Far to the west, gunfire echoes. "Screwface is already under assault," Thraxa says. "If Lune masses there, we'll be flanked."

"He won't. I want you on the roof."

She looks at our few Golds and Obsidians. "You need me as a bulwark. To hold the line."

"We're not going to be able to hold it," I say. "But that boy out there can rally the whole bloodydamn system behind him if we let him become a hero. We're here to kill him." I shout at a group of three Rat Legion snipers. The Reds bob up to me like jackrabbits. "You any good?" I ask them. The dourest of them answers first.

"It's our calling, sir."

I take the gas rifles I reserved in case we ran into more Howler snipers. The three men drop their improvised weapons and cradle the guns like diamonds. I toss them the armor-piercing magazines.

"There are sixty-six bullets in these magazines. All sixty-six are for Lune." I point to three windows. "I want you there, there, and there. Expect snipers. Do not reveal your position, not for any reason, until you have him in your sights. Do you understand?"

"Do you know what he looks like?" Thraxa asks.

They nod. "His face was on a broadcast before the EMP," the handsome one says in the same accent. Two of them even look alike.

"You all brothers?" I ask.

"Yessir."

"If this goes tits-up, use the roofs to get to the Mound. Bag me a Lune."

They take off. Thraxa stares across the plaza. I put a hand on her shoulder. "If they don't drop him, crush his skull on the way down."

"Got it."

She jogs off. Blood sprinkles down from above. I look up and see a man falling from a rooftop. A centurion shouts a warning for enemy snipers. "Where the hell did they get gunpowder?" someone shouts. Where else but from the Heliopolitans. Muzzles flash on northern rooftops.

As the sniper duel rages, the Golds and Obsidians help me drag abandoned ground transports and civilian hovercraft just shy of the southern mouth of the Triumphia where it exits the plaza. We've blocked only half of the fifty-meter-wide artery when a spotter calls to Thraxa on a rooftop and she calls down to me: "Enemy cavalry spotted!"

I look to the air instinctively. It is empty. And then I hear the thunder on the ground. My insides twist. He's emptied the stables. The last time I heard hoofbeats and felt anxiety was nearly sixteen years ago.

The oceanic sound of an army shouting with one voice drifts from the northern city. I can barely make out the words.

". . . *Invictus! Per ordo* . . ."

"Form up!" I bellow. "Form up! To me! To me! Reds to the roofs! Reds to the roofs! Thraxa!" As the Reds rush up stairwells along the Triumphia, Thraxa peers down at me. "Let them hit, then fall on: red rain!"

She understands what I mean and ducks as a fusillade of enemy fire chews into the façades of the buildings. The Howlers in the bell tower are gone, killed already. Long shadows sprint along the rooftops west and east of the plaza, hurtling six-meter-wide streets as easy as children hop over brooks. Some are shot mid-leap and spin down between the buildings, but in a world without electricity, the Peerless Scarred are kings. They clash into my rooftop elements along our flanks.

The sea of voices is a creeping tide.

"Lune! Invictus! Lune! Invictus! Per ordo. Per ordo . . ."

I roll up my helmet.

On the ground, every legionnaire without gunpowder rushes for the meager security of our barricade. They look to each other, mouthing the dreaded word: "Lune." I stand in the empty center around a lone family hovercraft. My thirteen Golds and forty Obsidians cluster around me in their dead armor to make a hedgehog of bristling razors. I wish Alexandar were with me. I wish Sevro had my back. I wish Ragnar were here, and Orion in the sky. But these are my brothers and sisters too.

We toggle the razors so they take on their leanest and longest form, nearly a meter and a half. Not nearly long enough. The lowColors gather on our wings, sixty men deep behind the vehicles, some few holding polearms of metal fence posts or signs, and they shiver in dread as they see what's coming. Even the droning death chant of the Obsidians stutters when they hear the sonorous lament of the *initium* horn.

Once, on a mission for Nero, I had the privilege of witnessing something no lowRed of Mars had ever seen before: a race in the Hippodrome of Heliopolis. The sun was bright, the streets filled with music, honey wine, and the smell of spiced ginger locust sweets. Out of respect for my patron, the Votum allowed me backstage before the *initium* horn to see the riders preparing. In the shadowy recesses of the underground stables, I saw sunblood stallions for the first time. Until then, I'd only known the horses of the Institute, animals of sixteen hands. They were terrifying enough to my mine eyes. But they are little more than donkeys compared to sunbloods. Weighing nearly one ton and twenty-three hands tall, with bone-pale coats and fiery manes, capable of speeds up to eighty kilometers per hour at full gallop, the beasts I saw race were barely horses at all. Monsters, I thought, feeling a kinship with that unnatural bloodline. Beautiful monsters made for one purpose.

The race I watched ended in catastrophe, with the winner's prize stallion biting off the head of a competitor when he came at the winner waving a whip. The Gold owners were horrified, but how the crowd cheered.

How did I ever think these people would embrace liberty?

Now two, three, four hundred, maybe more, of the most powerful chariot horses that have ever lived have come to war. They rumble into the northern mouth of the Via Triumphia in an avalanche of white muscle and fiery manes and multihued festival saddles, ridden with terrible grace by the equestrians amongst the prisoners of war—Grays and Golds. They'll go through us like an anvil through glass.

But glass can cut. And if we run, it'll be massacre.

"Stand fast!" I roar at my veterans, conjuring the only trick I have left. Bullets smack into our armor, sending some stumbling. Grenades detonate amongst the horses, sending some screaming. "When I give the command 'Line,' form a line three deep! When I give the command 'Flat,' go flat and hold your razor like this! Trust your weapon. Trust your armor! Stand fast!"

Gunshots rattle through the plaza. Ours and theirs. Men are kicked back from windows and duck on the rooftops from precision shots by Lysander's escorts, dying as they desperately fire down at the horses. Riders spill from saddles. Horses go down with shattered fetlocks and inhuman screams. One takes more than a dozen shots to the neck before it falls full speed into a transport, crumpling the hull and throwing its rider dozens of meters through the air for him to land in a human smear. But the tide does not break. It quickens. The sound of thunder is all. Rattling my eardrums, filling my gut with dread.

"LINE!"

My cluster of armored men unfolds to stand in a thin line at the center of the formation.

Then I see him amongst them, riding at the fore of the charge in white armor, the reins in one hand, a razor in the other. The boy whose grandmother I killed in front of him. The boy I spared for the sake of decency. The boy Aja trained and Cassius raised, who looked me in the eye and mocked me with lies before returning here like a demon to haunt those foolish enough to practice mercy. Frozen in time atop a monstrous steed, bald from radiation, face set not with vanity but grim determination, leaning forward in a saddle that flutters with ribbons of a hundred colors, he looks magnificent.

His head snaps back. For an exultant moment, I think my snipers have put one through his brain. But then his head comes forward, scarlet along the side, his mouth a wild rictus as he lowers himself to his horse and it explodes forward, faster than all the rest. Two more rounds spark off his armor.

I tremble in fear as my horizon becomes one of flaring nostrils, frothing muzzles, and trampling hooves. A dozen horses fill my field. Lysander weaves right, around my hedgehog and toward the frailer wings.

In the age of starships, you forget what animals can do to men. Lysander reminds me as he plunges forty thousand kilograms of horsepower through the wings of my line. The sudden acceleration of horseflesh into human bodies creates shearing forces as the momentum of the charge meets the inertia of the internal organs. Men are literally pulverized from the inside out. Organs tear. Brains hemorrhage. Blood vessels rupture. Spines collapse backward.

Even as the friction of the corpses slows the horses, they do not stop their killing. Hooves flatten skulls. Teeth of racehorses trained for the conflict of the Hippodrome snap off faces. Screams turn to gurgles as men are spun through the blender of hooves, manage to crawl free, only to have their backs broken by the next steed.

The horses bear down on the center of my line.

"Flat!"

I fall backward before the onrushing wave, razor held in both hands, its pommel at my belly button, with the blade that can cut through ten centimeters of starShell armor sticking a meter and a half into the air. Fifty-three other armored men do the same a bare second before the horses trample us.

Incandescent explosions of lights in my head.

Unreal weight and sound. Hooves slamming into my armor, my helmet. Underbellies, tails, bottoms of bare feet, of boots as I'm kicked and trampled in an unending stampede. But even horses made of one ton of muscle and bone and blood cannot stomp through armor meant to withstand pulseFire or run through a field of razor blades undaunted. We shred them.

Gore like I've never seen pours down on us. The screams of dying horses are worse by far than those of men. Yet the herd animals keep coming, running straight over the blades so thin that in the darkness they cannot see them as they sever bones in half and open bellies and muscled chests so cleanly that the horses' momentum carries them like cannonballs past us to spill shrieking and dying into the back of their fellows who crushed our wings.

Any Roman ground commander worth his salt would tell you that robbing the velocity from a cavalry charge is the first step to killing it.

With the Via Triumphia turned into a charnel house of dying horses and dying men, I stumble to my feet. Blood obscures my eye slits. A horse on its side with its guts spilling out kicks me so hard in the helmet that my duroglass eyeholes finally crack and I go down. Try to stand. My neck is sprained. Maybe fractured. Something hits me from behind, and I fall. Through the fragmented vision of my cracked visor I see a horse coming at me at full gallop. I throw myself to the side just as a Gold rider leans sideways off her saddle, nearly parallel with the ground, and swings her razor down. The blade peels a chunk of metal from the back of my thigh, then skips sideways, and she's past. I hack blindly at the back legs of the horse but don't see if I connect.

That was Kalindora. The Love Knight herself. Out of respect for her treatment of our prisoners, I kept her with her men. Now I pay for it.

Someone hauls me up. A horse chest hits me from the side and I'm lifted off my feet, kicked under several others and spun around and around until I crawl free and find a wall to guard my back. On my feet, but unable to see, I press my emergency release and rip off my helmet.

The sound is unreal. Indescribable. Like an animal caught in a blender. Except it's thousands of us in here. Horses shattering men as they kick in their death throes. Riders crushed underneath or thrown clean, to be swallowed by my men. Horses whinnying in the plaza, terrified at the sight.

For all we killed, more than two hundred sunbloods wheel about in the swirling mass of bodies, their riders slashing down, the horses stomping on the unlucky fallen, or breaking through the lines to encircle my other elements even as their infantry advances through the plaza to pound more meat into the straw.

The world takes on a slow, soupy feel. Only a fraction of my force is Gold and Obsidian. Without armor, without technology, the vast gulf that separates the races becomes measured in the carnage an individual Gold can wreak against lesser creatures. Their skin is tougher. Their bones and thick skulls like armor. I see one of my Grays hit a Gold thrown from his horse full on in the back of the head with his rifle, only for the Gold to wheel around and with a single punch break the neck of a man who survived ten years of war. Two Reds fire full clips into a Gold in a prisoner jumpsuit. He closes in and kills them before stumbling on to kill four more before finally expiring.

In my pocket of peace amidst the battle, I feel the coolness of Pax's key on my chest. The weight of my wife's gift in my hand. The memory of all the goodness my men have inside them. How they laugh over cards. How they smile when entering a liberated city for the first time. How they hustle when beside a Gold comrade to show they are his equal. How they weep when they see their families at the spaceports.

And I watch as they are butchered by the score, and their conviction that all men are created equal is made into a mockery by the physical absurdity of the Golds atop their monsters. There is a glee in their killing. A horrid joy teaching this chattel, this jabbering mass of uppity slaves, who their masters are.

Bend. Bow. Break.

I see Lysander amidst the fray, blood-spattered atop that monstrous horse, youthful and killing with uncommon grace. His bodyguards mill around him, cutting down any who rush his flanks. I see it so clearly. All his life before him. All the worlds on their knees, rejoicing their returned supplication as they embrace their chains so long as pretty, manicured hands hold the lead. His rise will summon a hideous tide of renewed romantic vigor that will not stop until my people, my wife, my child, are swallowed whole. And then he will smile from the humble throne war built and say he is their good shepherd.

I gave him a choice long ago, a chance to live in peace, but he has returned to war. To see the boy become man scours the empathy in me.

Ten years too late, he must die.

My snipers no longer fire. Thraxa waits for my signal on the roof. I shape my razor from its long form to the slingBlade. The dread monster rises in the belly of me. Laughter spews from between my teeth. I would die for the truth that all men are created equal. But in the kingdom of death, amidst ramparts of bodies and wind all of screams, there is a king, and his name is not Lune. It is Reaper.

"For the Republic!" I scream as I enter the fray.

85

LYSANDER

Lune Invictus

I HAVE NEVER FOUGHT lowColors hand to hand.
I annihilate them.

Faces and arms and skulls scalped by the teeth of sunbloods swirl around me like so much grotesque confetti. Weapons spark off my greaves. Men fall over themselves to avoid the teeth of my steed only to be trampled by his hooves. It is all frenzied blur, which I approach with systematic detachment.

I would fear losing track of the battle in the strict focus of the Mind's Eye. So I float along the edges of its shores.

Breathe, stab, turn. Breathe, stab, turn.

Rhone and the Praetorians swirl around Kalindora and me. Our force is irresistible. Kalindora an animating spirit atop her mount. The ranks of the enemy are shattered, but their will is not. It was Kalindora who introduced me to the term *Blood Red* for the battle frenzy of the Red clansmen. I believe I see it now.

They refuse to yield the boulevard. They heave their bodies against it, forming bulwarks of the dead and living. They slash at our horses' bellies. Or fire down from rooftops, but when our attention bears down on them for a single moment, they become mincemeat.

My rooftop elements will be pressing forward. My infantry advances at a run through the plaza to support our charge. Soon the enemy will be routed, and we will sweep south to run down their support legions and force those at the spaceport and Mound to surrender.

As I try to free my horse from a tangle of bodies, I spot a Red sniper taking aim from a window above. Rhone fires over my shoulder, nailing three rounds into the sniper's center mass. More snipers provide cover for us from the rubble of the Water Gardens.

"Where is he?" I shout to Rhone. My Praetorians cluster around me, hacking and shooting anyone who comes near. "He knew I'd expect him on Triumphia." Without Darrow in captivity, my victory will be incomplete.

Rhone's flinty eyes search the milling mob. From the horses, we can see nothing but the churn of battle. Then I spot the signs of his advance from the far side of the Triumphia. It is like the coming of a tiger through tall grass. First a rippling in the distance that seems like the wind. Then a tunneling force. An outward swaying of riders. The starting of horses. Men disappear from saddles. Sunbloods collapse sideways with horrible wounds. And then, like the tiger's tail, the curved slingBlade rises above the stalks as he threshes all in his path.

He kills with impossible aggression.

I will not repeat past mistakes and rush to meet him.

"Rhone! Bring him down!" I shout. The Praetorians follow my blade and shoulder their rifles as they stand in the stirrups. Tracer rounds scream into the mob as Darrow disappears behind a horse. Then a raw-throated cry roars up from Darrow's men.

"Red Rain! Red Rain!"

I look up just as the stars are obscured by shadows. Reds rain from the sky. They fling themselves off the rooftops that line the Via Triumphia and fall three stories to land amongst us. Our fireteam becomes chaos. I slash upward at a shadow, dividing it in two. Not an arm's length away, a Praetorian gurgles and jerks his arms as a Red man lands on the saddle behind him and saws through his throat. He throws the knife at me. I backhand it away and I stab my razor through the Praetorian into the Red.

A man crashes into me, holding on to my side by the lip of my breast-plate. His knife flashes at my face. I duck my head. The knife stabs several times into the crown of my skull but fails to break the bone. I bring my razor into his gut and open his right side. He spills off just as gore squirts into my face as a woman comes down with a block of masonry atop the head of a Praetorian.

Kalindora cuts her clean in half and then looks over my head with wide eyes. "Tele—"

An immense force lands on me.

Whatever it is, it is heavy enough to make Blood of Empire reel sideways. I'm flung from my saddle. As I stand, a blur comes at my head from the side. I twist away and a tremendous impact lifts me clean off my knees and throws me through a window into an apartment atrium.

I slide across the floor until the marble stairway jars me to a halt.

The wind is knocked from me. I gasp for air, and when I sit up, I am shocked to find that my spine is not broken. A dent the circumference of a grapefruit has been made in the side of my breastplate. By the time I stumble to my feet, the doorknob is turning. A hulking shadow steps into the atrium carrying a huge warhammer.

I don't even have to look at her face. "Telemanus."

I bring my razor up with both hands over my head in Aja's favorite form for Obsidians. Bough Splitter. It is an easy transition into the Branch Which Cannot Snap, the maneuver that killed Ragnar Volarus.

"You killed a pup," she growls. "Let's see you handle me." She rushes forward, bellowing her family's name.

Without the weight of armor, I'd be faster than that hammer, and might be induced to accept her invitation. But she is stronger, more experienced, and better designed for close-quarters brutality. I could pick her apart, but one loose stone, one slip of the foot, and she'd maul me to death.

I make it a running engagement and bolt up the stairs. "Little bitch," she screams as she pursues.

At the top of the stairwell, I kick through an apartment door and wait for her thundering steps to come up the stairs. When she reaches the landing, I plunge the razor through the wall. It meets the resistance of armor, and pushes through. She roars in surprise. The razor comes back bloody. Her warhammer chases it through the wall.

But I'm already in flight. I run through the apartment, past a shrieking Silver as Thraxa trundles after me. I push a bookshelf down to block her. She shatters through it as I dive through a window back down to the melee on the street. I land on my feet.

"TELEMANUS!"

The window frame shatters as her broad shoulders knock it free of the plaster. And from the debris jumps a demigod and her hammer.

Rhone leans backward from his saddle and fires a burst at Thraxa as she passes overhead. Three bullets impact in a triangle shape under her armpit, punching through the armor into her rib cage. She lands just as I dive between the legs of a horse. Her huge hammer crumples the rider and breaks the horse almost clean in half. She teeters over the screaming animal like a weary blacksmith. I thrust my razor over the dying horse at Thraxa's heart.

She catches the blade flat between her huge gauntlets and manages to divert it into her belly. She reels me in by pulling the blade deeper. Her mouth opens in a mad laugh and she lunges to bite off my nose.

Then a horse hits us and we go sprawling over corpses. I manage to keep ahold of my razor. By the time I find Thraxa limping to her feet, two Reds drop from a fourth-story ledge to drag her toward a horse.

Rhone jumps from his own to stand over me with Praetorians. They're in a panic, hauling at me, screaming to get behind them as they shoot. Then I see why.

Darrow bulldozes toward me.

His army in tatters around him, he breaks through behind a wedge of three armored Obsidians. Rhone's men shoot the Obsidians. But they stumble into the line and Darrow explodes out from behind them. His razor passes through a man's teeth and jaw. He looks left, then disappears in a blur.

He threw his body back just as Kalindora galloped past on her horse. Still, he's clipped hard enough to spin like a top. But as he falls, his Red acrobatics shine. No one falls like the Reaper.

His whip snakes out and snaps hold of the back fetlock of Kalindora's horse. He's ripped down the boulevard before the Grays can shoot him. The horse tramples through a wall of men and clears the other side. Then it goes down. Kalindora disappears. Through the mill of bodies, I see her gain her feet as Darrow charges her. Their blades spark in an incredible display of fatigued swordsmanship. And then she falls. He hacks down at her four times before turning back to me.

A roar comes from behind me.

Back where Triumphia meets the plaza. The infantry pour in and the spirit that anchored the Rising soldiers to this plot of land finally shatters. In a weird, instantaneous snap, their dogged last stand morphs into mindless hysteria. They flee through the back alleys and down the Triumphia, flowing past Darrow, who stands there watching me. Many drop their weapons or discard their armor to run faster. As happens in all retreats, men are shot through the back, cleaved down from behind, losing far more with their backs turned than when they stood their ground.

It is a rout.

A trio of horses speeds through the broken army. Thraxa slumps in one saddle. One of the Reds who dragged her to safety holds the reins of the third horse as the other sits backward and fires with his rifle. Two shots whiz past my head close enough to flay open the skin of my scalp. Darrow mounts one of the horses as they pass. He looks back at me as my infantry pours through the plaza down the boulevard, and kicks his horse away.

I rush to Kalindora as my men push forward. A Gold says something braggadocious to me, and I shove past him to find her crawling toward a lamppost so as not to be trampled underfoot. She leaks blood from a long gash down her left side. Her remaining arm is hacked to several pieces. She tries to say something to me. I call for medici. Several Praetorians rush my way to help stanch the bleeding.

I look down the dark boulevard after Darrow. "Let him . . . run," Kalindora says. "You're no . . . equal."

I grip a Praetorian. They all have field medical training. "Keep her alive."

I grab Kalindora's loyalist razor from the ground and sprint back to Blood of Empire and jump into his saddle to pursue. Rhone shouts after me, but I know if I let Darrow slip through my fingers, he will disappear into the city like smoke.

The Praetorians try to keep up, but Blood outpaces their tired steeds. Buildings whip past. Retreating men scatter. Mobs with torches cheer. Then I catch sight of the trio galloping south on a quiet stretch of the Via Triumphia just past the Bank of Heliopolis.

"Reaper!" He does not turn. "Slave!" Somehow through the clatter of hooves, he hears me and wheels his horse around. Thraxa reaches for him and misses. Her horse carries her past. Covered in gore, his sling-Blade held at his right side, he looks a devil atop the blood-frothed steed. Darrow brings his slingBlade around to point at me. Drawn by my shout, shadowed faces fill the windows that line the street.

With a groaning howl, Darrow accepts my challenge. He kicks his horse's flanks. It springs forward. Blood of Empire needs no encouraging. He sees a horse that is less than him, and surges to meet the challenger.

For a moment there is nothing in the world but my enemy and me and the bobbing of the starlit street and the cacophony of horse hooves on stone. It forms a tunnel of concentrated destiny.

I bring my borrowed razor up like a lance in my left hand. In the mill of battle, I am not his equal. Nor am I in the dueling ring. But aristocrats have always held a monopoly on horsemanship.

Darrow jerks on his reins, angling to his left as if to pass on my right. Predictable. I anticipate he will swerve to my left at the last moment and toss his slingBlade to the other hand to turn my lance and decapitate me with a passing backhand. Or he'll crash our horses together to maim us both.

But he does not see that I brought Kalindora's razor as well as Alexandar's. I clutch Kalindora's out of sight behind Blood's neck instead of the reins. I steer with my knees as Atalantia taught me to as a boy. As I saw my father ride when I was not even as tall as his knees.

At ten meters, just as Darrow swerves to my left, I swerve right and take my shot. I flick Kalindora's razor in an underhand toss. It carries forward and disappears into Darrow's chest. Just as the horses draw even, I swing Alexandar's razor with my left arm, digging my toes into the stirrups and driving with my legs to meet his slingBlade as we pass.

Metal cracks.

The world upturns.

My arm goes numb. The razor shatters and flies out of my grip. My head slams against the ground as I skid across the street. I stumble up and fall, concussed. The world tips back and forth as I pick up the hilt of my shattered razor and look for Darrow. Somehow, impossibly, he was not unseated. He slumps from his horse, Kalindora's razor protruding through his chest and out his back.

Praetorians are galloping toward him down the street. His left arm flops unnaturally at his side as he pulls the horse around and kicks it down an alley to disappear into the city.

Rhone and the Praetorians rein the horses in as they reach me. A dozen set off after Darrow.

"My liege, are you wounded?" Rhone cries. I stare after Darrow.

"He got him through the chest," a Praetorian says. "Razor straight through the heart."

"He's dead. He has to be."

"It was his lung," I say.

"My liege, are you prime?"

I only just realize my teeth are chattering. Needles of pain shoot up my left arm. Beneath the armor, the bones must be shattered from the force of the collision. But lying between the hooves of the Praetorians' horses is a blood-smeared object. I pick it up with my good hand and hold it close to see it better as the street fills with my advancing army.

It is the hilt of Darrow's slingBlade, and its killing edge lies in shattered pieces upon the stone.

86

DARROW

Legion's End

I'M IN A NIGHTMARE.

Lysander's riders hound me through the labyrinth of dark streets. Searing pain digs deep into my chest. I did not see the hidden blade until it was inside me. My teeth chatter together. Each breath froths with blood. I have no weapon. Only my right arm works. My left is shattered along with the slingBlade. The gift my wife gave me almost twelve years ago lies upon the ground to be a trophy for Lysander's mantel. One day, he will tell his son how he took it, as I told Pax of how I took Octavia's.

The city itself becomes a devil and the prisoners surge south. Lysander's sunbloods have broken the other strongpoints. They trample men in the wide boulevards as his Golds flow across the roofs. Few escape the nocturnal predators. His infantry is comprised of all those prisoners we took in the Battle of the Ladon. Over a million join with Heliopolitan mobs to butcher survivors in sunless gardens, underneath the striped awnings of abandoned markets, and on the steps of old amphitheaters littered with refugee trash. The Heliopolitans seem to be killing Tychians as well.

I escape back to the Mound only by virtue of the chaos.

My horse's hooves clomp over cobbles deep with blood. Ragged survivors from the other strongpoints pour across the mall toward the steps of our last refuge. There are so few. There is no way to tell if the sacrifice was worth it. If the quarter hour we bought saved any lives at all. The city is lost. Lights glimmer in orbit from Atalantia's arriving ships. My men are fractured. Did Rhonna make it back to the *Morning Star*? It will be a tomb. Those at the ships will never reach the tunnels. And on foot, how far could they go? It's up to Colloway to lead them. But lead them to what? It's all ruins, and Atalantia will be coming with real weapons very soon.

Thraxa and Red Sniper wait for me at the bottom of the Mound steps. Thraxa looks nearly dead herself. "Did you get him?" she asks.

"No."

The strength holding her up evaporates. She slumps in the saddle and barely manages to follow me up the Mound's steps. I dismount inside the atrium, where Harnassus is organizing the survivors. Legionnaires rush to help Thraxa down from her horse. It takes four of them. Harnassus rushes to me, slowing when he sees the razor sticking through my chest.

"Are you—"

"Screwface," I demand.

"He hasn't returned."

I say nothing.

"They broke through his lines. Only four men have come back. They say they saw him fall to a Gold."

"They were going wild trying to get him," a man adds. "They were Fulminata."

Fulminata. The legion in which he embedded himself at my command.

I hang my head, dazed from my wounds and exhaustion. I don't know if I can move another muscle. My hamstrings and lower back are cramping so bad I have to have men help me out of my armor. I almost pass out as they take the vambrace off my shattered arm. They leave the breastplate on, for fear of disturbing the razor in my chest.

There's a commotion as they take off my dead boots. I stand barefoot in blood to see men stumbling in carrying Screwface. A shout goes up when the men see him pass. He's missing his right leg from the knee down, and the skin above his hairline. He's been scalped by a Fulminata Obsidian. As the medici tie off the wound, Screw stares at the murals on the ceiling of the antechamber and moans. His eyes are wild and distant. "I'm sorry. I'm sorry," he murmurs. "We tried to hold. We did. They had horses. It was a bloodydamn cavalry charge. Mowed us down like wheat. They'll catch the support. Some of them. Horses! Horses!"

"He's in shock," one of the medici says and then sees the razor in my chest. "Sir . . ."

"No time. It's just a lung."

Screwface grabs my good arm. "Clown. Pebble. Are they safe?"

"Aye," I say. "They're safe. They're with Sevro."

"If anyone could make it out, it's that ugly bastard."

I whisper to the medicus, "Will he live?"

"Hopefully not," Thraxa says. She's slumped on the statue's pedestal as Reds help her out of her armor. She's bleeding badly from the hole Lysander and his men put in her belly. "It's over. Here. Back home. No shame in it. We gave it a rugged shot." Her hammer is gone. Her reserve razor sits in her lap. "But I won't be tortured by that creature. Atalantia will vivisect us. There's only one honorable end to this."

I walk over and take her razor.

"It is not over," I snap. Several hundred weary faces look at me. "It is *not* over!" I shout to them. "If you can fight, assemble at center." The few able-bodied men assemble.

"Darrow." Thraxa reaches out her hand for her blade. "I'll die my way. You die yours."

For loyalty to the end, it is the least I can do. I give the razor back.

Tired beyond words, I arrange the able bodies with what remains of our guns to constitute a defense for the Mound. As if it will matter when Atalantia comes. A hand settles on my shoulder as I send snipers to the gallery. I wheel around to kill the man, but find Harnassus standing there, shrunken and tired, arms caked to the elbow in blood from the wounded. "Darrow. Enough. There's nothing more to do."

I say nothing because I know he is right.

One of the Red snipers I sent after Lune joins us, a nasty wound on the side of his head. "Might be able to get you out underground, sir." Alone amongst my men, he seems to think there's still hope. I disabuse him of it.

"The tunnel entrances are collapsed. The ships are dead. There's nowhere to go." Hearing a noise, I look back to Harnassus. "Did you hear that?"

"What?"

"A ship engine."

"Where are you going? Darrow!"

It takes me a full two minutes to climb the stairs to the Mound's tower. I throw up halfway to the top. The sick is dark with blood. My limbs are cold and trembling. The razor in my chest hurts so bad it's all I can do to focus on breathing as I look out over the city. There is nothing to see in the darkness. No lights break the spell Lysander has summoned. Only the soft, ocean-like sounds of screams. No lights illuminate the sea. No ships over the water. It was my imagination. A phantom hope. Harnassus mutters a curse for his aching joints as he joins me, breathing heavily.

"I'm sorry," he says after a moment.

I say nothing.

"Glirastes did something to the EMP. Built in a back door. We should have seen it. We should have stopped it. I told you we could. I thought we could keep up with him . . ." I look over at him at the very moment where the stalwart commander breaks. It is a single shudder, one that comes from the hidden, substantial depths of the man, and reveals for just a moment the insecure child within as he realizes what he always suspected is true: he treads in waters far too deep.

All this time, I shied from his disapproval. In the absence of Dancer, he became my father figure, in a way. I didn't even know it until now, because there is nothing like seeing a father shudder. And then he buries the child and is Harnassus again, Hero of the Vox, scowling leader of men.

"You know the curse of this world?" I ask, looking at the body the Carver made for me. "The greatest gifts were given to the worst of us."

"Not realizing they are gifts is what makes them the worst," he replies as the first of Lysander's legions begin to fill the mall below. My men die as they scramble up the steps, as if there were any safety inside with us. "You know I envied you." I look over at him. "Why him? I asked. Why did Ares choose an arrogant pisspot miner and not me? It was pettiness. Pettiness that made the Vox. Pettiness that brought us to this. But your wife believed in the Republic, didn't she?"

I nod.

"You didn't. I saw you lose faith one step at a time. Looking to solve it all yourself. That's why I stood in your way. I thought this was what you wanted. A glorious end. Now that it's here . . ." He searches my eyes. "If not for the Republic, if not for a hero's end, why . . . why keep going?"

Sometimes a simple question wakes a sleeping answer.

"I had this picture in my head where I would wake beside Virginia.

I'd let her sleep and rise to make coffee, breakfast. And when they woke, my wife and son would find me reading at the kitchen table, or maybe making something out back."

"That's it?" he says.

"That's it."

He bellows a laugh.

As insult, the sky begins to glow. Individual friction flames from descending starShells coalesce into a throbbing furnace of light. "Well . . . I imagine one of those friction trails is Atalantia or Ajax. They'll want us alive." He nods. "I won't risk being taken in a last charge. It will smell like cloves and melting rubber as the celtex comes in. We'll pass out. Then we'll wake up in hell."

The reflected light from the friction trails carves across Harnassus's eyes. "I'll be damned if I let this be the last thing I see. You shouldn't either." He pauses. "I don't think any of my men will be taken prisoner. It would mean something to them if you were with them in the end." When I do not reply, he goes back down the stairs.

"Harnassus." He pauses and turns. "Thank you."

"For what?"

"Being my conscience." I smile at him. "My wife says I sometimes need that. I know it isn't an easy role."

"But what a role." He laughs before he departs. "What a role."

I stand alone in the tower watching the friction trails glow over the city, and wonder if this was not inevitable. If all our hope was nothing more than a feeble religion that could not stand the test of time. I sigh onto the railing and work my good hand through my hair. A tinkle comes from inside my armor. I pull my son's key from within and look down at it and feel an ache. How can something so small mean so much? Even now, when I know I will never see my boy again, I feel as if he were here with me. As if my wife were by my side in these last moments. The world was too cruel to them. I was too cruel, in my own way. But there was beauty. For a moment, there was real beauty.

I look down at the lost city and feel small comfort.

I kept looking for hope in the world. Expecting the world to supply deliverance if I plucked the right chords. Demanding that it supply validation to my labor if I just gave enough effort. But that is not the nature of the world. Its nature is to consume. In time, it will consume us all, and the spheres will spin until they too are consumed when our sun dies.

Maybe that is the point of it. Knowing that though one day darkness will cover all, at least your eyes were open to see moments of light.

I pry open my thigh pack and pull out a canister. I pour Dago's Lykos soil into my hands. I would have liked to see home once more before the end.

There is a gust of air behind me.

"Oh gods. Brooding again? Some things never change," a voice says.

I turn to see a vision from the past. "Cassius?"

"Hello, goodman. Kavax said you might need a hand."

87

LYSANDER

Ghost

THE STREETS RUN RED with blood and echo with screams.
Darrow's army is in full rout. Mechanized soldiers from Atalantia's orbital forces leave vapor contrails in the air. Along the Bay of Sirens there is a great slaughter as men flee the city on foot or swim out into the bay only to be microwaved by dropships buzzing over the water. Torch-Ships descend on the dark spaceport. And in the courtyard before the Mound of Votum, thousands upon thousands of freed prisoners of war and mechanized legionnaires fresh to the fray congregate.

I watch after Kalindora as she is lifted away by Ash Legion medici. The wounds Darrow left her with are gruesome, but not beyond the ability of the trauma wards to mend. She will survive. But I feel a sense of guilt for how I left her there to chase Darrow. I could no more have stopped the bleeding than the Praetorians I left her with, but leave her I did, and there is little nobility in that. There is little nobility to any of this.

There is a thump behind me. Rhone's hand drifts to his rifle. I turn to see Ajax landing with a cadre of Ash Guard.

The irony of his leopard helmet slithering back into its collar when his own Iron Leopards flow past, bloody and triumphant, my name on their lips, is lost to no one. Least of all the insecure boy inside the dreaded man.

He abandoned his men before the storm wall of Heliopolis.

Only to find me here, alive.

Devilish in fifty kilograms of advanced armor and weapons, he looks up as I sit tattered and filthy upon Blood of Empire as the courtyard swarms with ragged legionnaires and hi-tech soldiers. He takes in my melted face, the steed, the chanting of his own Leopards. Whatever he planned to say is concealed within the tight formality: "*Salve*, Lysander."

But it is hate in his eyes. As if I did all this to mock and spite him and steal his place in Atalantia's bed. For a flicker of a moment, he considers whether gunning me down before the army may be worth the cost in the long run, but the arrival of the Votum Peerless stays his hand.

I salute his rank. "Praetor Grimmus, the enemy is split into four groups. The most numerous gather within the *Morning Star,* where Atlas au Raa is being held. I recommend sending a party immediately before they execute him, if they have not already. The next most numerous have taken to the mountains, where they have constructed tunnels. Others hide within the city and sewers. But Darrow is in the Mound. He is grievously wounded."

"By whose hand?" Ajax asks.

"Mine." I pull Darrow's hilt from my saddle and toss it to him. He blinks, unable to comprehend. The officers around him mirror his disquiet.

"How?" Ajax asks.

I lean forward. "Which part?"

"Who are you, boy?" a Falthe Praetor demands.

"He is the blood of Silenius," Cicero says from behind him. The Votum heir is alive and covered with grime from his exploits in the prison break. He stalks up surrounded by a dozen soldiers in tattered prison regalia. His sister is at his side with a flock of glittering knights. As Atalantia's legions take their city, they see another play at hand.

"The heir returned from the maw of chaos," Cicero says. His knights stiffen to attention and salute me. "*Hail* Lune!"

The hate in Ajax's eyes darkens and he shouts for his Peerless to assemble. They form a glittering knot and make for the Mound.

"They're trying to seize your glory, Lune," Cicero says. "Shall we join them?"

I look at the dangerous knights around Ajax, likely friends of those I killed in the desert. In the chaos, it would be only too easy for one to slash my spine as they flew past. "I think not."

Four hundred Peerless Scarred of the Votum and Ash Legions move on the Mound. I sit with my Praetorians in the middle of the square as the doors evaporate.

Rhone sulks beside me, ignoring the sweet wine throngs of Heliopolitans bring the soldiers. A party one-half celebration, one-half slaughter rages through the city as it seeks catharsis on the invaders after the long weeks of siege. I imagine the wine will flow alongside the blood for many days yet.

"Something wrong, Legate?" I ask.

"You should be the one to take the Slave King."

The soldiers flood into the Mound.

"We have had our glory today, Praetorian. Let us not drown ourselves in gluttony. The legions know who opened the gates," I say loud enough for the other Praetorians to hear. They tip their cups of wine and pass burners through the ranks. One thousand Gray shock troopers came to me in the desert. Barely three hundred remain. Not one is unwounded.

There is a sudden flurry of firing in the Mound. I had no doubt Darrow would make a last stand. But with the introduction of advanced weapons to the battle, it is a certain affair. One knight kitted by our age is worth a thousand on horse. Perhaps more.

I run my hands along the hilt of his broken blade and feel confused by what it elicits. He threw me down in the desert. I broke him here. But neither was a true test against the other. The fate of each battle was decided before we met. Mine by the broken chaos of the Rain. His by a series of calamities which put him in a corner. I did not beat the Reaper. I simply hit him when he was down. I hold no illusions of martial supremacy, my victory was against a broken host and a bedraggled man. The legends of our age die one by one, like autumn leaves; and when they are gone, will we be lesser for their absence?

It seems cheap.

With his death imminent, the worlds feel emptier. Almost as cavernous as they did when Cassius fell. One by one, the titans of my youth disappear, and freed from their shadow, I do not feel liberated. I feel bereft.

Nothing is permanent. No one escapes.

"The bill comes at the end," I whisper.

Rhone asks what I said, but I grow distracted when gunfire crackles on the Mound. Something has happened. I frown and stand up. The milling ranks in the courtyard point upward as ripWings dive from the sky.

Bwaaaowwww.

We take cover. The light is tremendous as a particle beam sheaves through the legs of the god Helios, who towers over the Mound. With a groan, he teeters over and crashes down into the sea. By Jove . . . How does Darrow have electronics? Anything within the city was fried. Unless we weren't the only ones to have reinforcements.

Sure enough, Gold knights tear from the Mound in pursuit of a lean, battered ship that emerges from the debris. It rockets low over the ranks of soldiers filling the courtyard.

I know that ship.

A knight fills the open garage bay. It is not Darrow. His armor is brilliant white. His helmet like that of a rising sun. It retracts to reveal his face, and for a moment our eyes meet.

Cassius . . .

The door closes. The *Archimedes* ripples translucent from a cloaking device far more advanced than any technology she possessed when I called her home. She ruptures the air with a sonic boom and races toward the sky, pursued by the Ash Legions.

Diomedes lied. Cassius is alive. And Darrow has slipped the noose.

My true heart is laid bare, awash with exultation, clouded with confusion, pure with purpose. The war goes on.

88

LYRIA

Mercury Has Fallen

Ulysses is buried on Mars in a rose garden between Victra's ancestral home and the sea. Across the water, the Julii city of Hippolyte splashes out into the emerald archipelagos. Victra stands just across the grave from me, but looks as distant as her city. She wears only green. I like it far better than mourning black. It reminds me of the emerald hills they say wait for us in the Vale.

I wish I could take away her pain, but all I can do is stand here and watch her suffer behind that stony face. I know the teeth of this pain wound not with their sharp bite, but with their slow grinding. Her fearsome daughter bends over the grave, whispers something to her brother, and then stands protectively at her mother's side. She knows best. There are no words to soothe the wounded heart of a Julii.

Only five attend the funeral. The two Julii, the Reaper's son, Volga, and me. Our retinue feels pitifully small next to the void his loss has carved. And still I cannot help but feel I do not belong.

After Ephraim came, Victra and I went to the fishing village to retrieve her son's body from Maeve's house. Victra washed him herself in Attica, but refused to bury him there. "He'll sleep at home," was all she said to me before boarding her ship.

"And now you sleep," Victra whispers to the grave, and then turns away to walk to the coast. Pax moves to follow. Electra grabs him and he stops to watch Victra's shoulders shake as she wades into the water and swims out to sea toward the setting sun.

When she is almost out of sight, Electra jerks her head for us to follow her down to the coast. We help her make a fire from a pile of driftwood. Everything inside feels very still as Volga and I sit beside the children in the sand. As soon as the sun is gone, Electra speaks.

"I am equal parts of my father and mother. But we Julii have a tradition. If family blood spills by your debt, you swim to the sun. You may look back when it is gone. If no light appears onshore to welcome you home, you swim on." She's quiet for a moment. "Some never turn to look back."

Though Volga weeps soundlessly beside me for Ulysses, in a way she buries two today. She still has not forgiven Pax for asking Ephraim to go back to Sefi. She waited at the landing pads for twelve hours before somehow duping the Julii guards and stealing a ship. I tried to follow, but Victra herself intervened.

Julii military and aid ships were the first to descend on Olympia three days later when Fá and the Obsidians left it in a heap of rubble and corpses. Even my camp's destruction couldn't prepare me for Olympia. I've never seen so many crows or wild dogs before in all my life. I thought the stench was more than I could bear, but then we found Volga sitting on the steps of the high city, cradling Ephraim. She tried holding him together, but his body fell apart when she stood up. I will never forget the look on her face. It has chiseled away the stone of my heart, leaving a wound of empathy I haven't the ken to mend.

There were no witnesses to tell us what happened to that doomed city save a mad Obsidian with both his eyes gouged out. We found him at the base of a throne swatting at the crows that came too close to a body covered with a cape. Pax and Electra knew the mad Obsidian, and the body he protected.

He somehow fled the Sol Guard who were to take him back to a medical shuttle, and disappeared into the dead city, never to be found. Pax couldn't say who killed Ephraim, but we know who killed Sefi and sacked the city. The same monster who attacked the *Pandora*.

Volsung Fá.

The name is like a curse to us. A curse that deepens the more Pax explains just what his control of the Obsidians might mean for Mars. What city will they sack next? Could the Republic survive the man who took down Julii, Sefi, Valdir, and the Valkyrie in just two weeks?

I fear Volga's name will soon be added to that list.

She wants revenge for Ephraim. It will bring her nothing but more heartache. Though my vengeance on Harmony is sated, I feel no more whole. What peace will I find if even that cannot mend me?

I did not like Ephraim but he was like a father to Volga. I saw how she looked at Victra. The slow smiles when Victra would fire a particularly clever insult her way. Her eyes focus on the dark water as she prays under her breath to the Allmother for Victra to return. She loves far too easily.

But her prayers are answered.

Six hours after Victra set out, she returns. Her dress was lost in the sea. Her legs fail her as she stumbles up the beach like a scarred ghost and sits amongst us by the fire. She ignores Pax's offer of his cloak and sits naked until finally taking Electra's riding cape. When her teeth stop their chattering, she looks around at us.

"One bill is paid. Debts are due." She looks at Electra and Pax. "I swore a life oath to both of you the first time I saw you. I renew that oath here and now." Her eyes flick to me and Volga. "To you two, I swear it for the first time. Let your enemies be my enemies. Let your errors be my errors. Let your life be my life. I do not tell lies. If ever you call, House Barca will answer."

"Me too, for you," Volga says.

"I agree," I say.

Pax leans forward. "Technically you're to say, 'You are never in my debt,' and she will say—" Electra hits him in the side of the head. He shuts his gob.

"What will you do now?" I ask Victra. "Go to your daughters?" She still hasn't said where they are.

"No, I will go to war," she replies. "The *Pandora* may be taken, but the rest of my fleet is intact. Luna has my husband. Mercury my friend. And then I will vanquish the woman who sought my family's demise."

"Atalantia," Electra murmurs in solidarity.

"My brothers are on Mercury," I say.

"You require a ride?" Victra asks.

"No. I'm going to Earth with Volga." Volga looks over in surprise. It hasn't been discussed, but I know where she wants to bury him. "Ephraim wouldn't want you getting killed going after them that did him."

"Say his name," she says.

"You don't know who did it."

"Say his name."

"Fá," Electra answers for me.

"Ephraim wouldn't want you dyin' on his accord," I say. "You know that. I'm gonna go find my nephew, and you're gonna bury Ephraim in South Pacifica like you said he'd want." She does not reply. "Victra, I'll need a ship."

"Can you fly?" Victra asks skeptically.

I look at Volga. "I hope so."

In the morning Volga and I load the coffin containing Ephraim's remains onto a Julii racing ship that Victra has given us for the journey. Victra watches Volga secure the coffin inside. "It isn't proper," Victra says. "Keeping her from her revenge when you have had your own."

"Haven't you seen enough of that?" I ask.

"Not while Atalantia breathes. Not while Fá breathes. They cost me my son."

"You wanna lose the rest of your children?"

Her eyes swivel down to me, and in a second I'm reminded of who she is, and who I am. "Careful, Blister."

This woman owns cities and fleets, but I let her alone out of respect for her loss more than fear of all her legions' and ships' might. When it came down to it, she was just a mother on her own.

A Sol Guard rushes up to Victra and whispers something I can't hear. She frowns. "Let them in."

"All of them?"

"It's the Reaper's gorydamn brother. What do you think?"

Five minutes later, ten Republic shuttles crowd the landing pad, and the ArchGovernor of Mars walks out. Not Rollo. Somehow in all this mess, the Vox put him down in a firefight in the Citadel. Instead it is now Kieran O'Lykos. You wouldn't even think he was the same species as his brother. He's barely bigger than I am. And his is the kind of face meant for laughter and Laureltide dances. But he ain't laughing as he strides toward Victra with two hundred Sons of Ares at his back. He looks like he's gonna puke.

The Sol Guard nod in respect to their allies.

I haven't seen that spiked helmet painted on armor in years. It really does chill the blood. The ArchGovernor greets Victra with a hug and casts a look at Volga before swooping Pax and Electra up—as much as he can, them being as big as he is. He garlands them with kisses, and then turns back to Victra with a somber look.

"Is there someplace we could speak in private?" he asks. She motions him to the shoreline. The two groups of soldiers chat across the lines as Victra and the ArchGovernor walk along the water. Pax watches intently. "What are they saying?" Volga asks.

"My hearing isn't that good," he replies.

"Nor your judgment," she says point-blank. Pax looks up at her and is about to say something when she turns her back on him. Only eleven years old, and already sending men to their deaths. If Volga thought it didn't weigh him down, she'd be dead wrong. He is in agony.

Ephraim must've gotten under his skin.

He was good at that, wasn't he?

There's a shout from Victra at something the ArchGovernor says. She wheels away from him and stalks back to us. "Volga, get in the ship," she says. Her guards look as confused as Volga. The ArchGovernor catches up.

"It is this or another Olympia," he calls.

"Since when do we kneel to monsters?" Victra snaps, stalking back toward the tiny man. "Since when do we abandon our own?" She jams a thumb against her chest. "I am Victra au Barca. I do not *sacrifice* my friends."

The Reaper's brother does not back down. "Heliopolis has fallen." My heart sinks. My brothers . . . But he's not done. "The Free Legions were slaughtered to a man. More than two million were impaled. My brother is dead."

His brother.

It's like watching wind move meadow grass. Grown men's knees buckle across the landing pad. The Sons of Ares did not know. The Sol Guard did not know. Victra did not know. He hadn't told her yet. She looks as if she is dying as she glances at Pax. The boy watches with a tremble in his hands. Whatever anger Victra had when she stormed away from the ArchGovernor crumples.

I feel something break inside myself. I don't know what it is. I long ago gave my brothers up for dead. It's for the Reaper, this emptiness. I guess I held some weird belief he couldn't die. Some thought that as long as he lived, the Society could never come back.

But now it all seems possible. The Reaper is dead.

And they have killed something in all of us.

"By noon, all of Mars will know," the ArchGovernor says. "Victra, my brother *is* dead. I know Virginia told you she sent a man. He's been dark since he got to Mercury. Whatever happened, there were no survivors. And the Heir of Silenius has returned." Victra stiffens. "Atalantia will sail on Luna. If the Vox don't see reason . . . Earth won't be able to hold. It will just be Mars that's left. We can't afford to fight the Obsidians with what's coming. You know that." Something goes unspoken between them. Something they can't let us know. "Old debts are coming due."

Victra turns to look at Volga. "I swore an oath to her."

Volga looks around in confusion.

"What you lookin' at her for?" I snap. "What's going on? Victra?"

"You tell her, if you can stomach it," Victra says to the ArchGovernor.

The man looks tired, but his voice is almost soothing. "After Volsung Fá left Olympia with more than half its citizens in chains, he sent a deputation to us. He claims to be the father of Ragnar Volarus." Pax flinches. The ArchGovernor looks Volga sadly in the eye. "And he pledged no further acts of violence toward the Republic, and offered to give us the survivors of his massacre and depart Mars. . . ."

"Depart Mars? For what price?" I demand.

"His granddaughter," Victra says. Volga does not move a muscle.

I look back and forth between them. "Slag off."

Volga's mouth moves up and down. "But . . ."

"You were born in a Grimmus slave kennel," Victra says. "You are the product of a dead Terran gladiator named Wrothga and a man I fought beside. You *are* the daughter of Ragnar Volarus. And if this Fá is telling the truth, you are his only living heir. Just as you were Sefi's."

"What?" Electra whispers. Pax closes his eyes in thought. They open just as Volga whispers.

"No . . ." She looks at the shocked soldiers first, as if they will save her or something, and then to her own hands. "I am a freelancer." She looks up. "Did Ephraim . . ."

"No," Pax says. "He didn't know." I think he's lying.

I step in front of her, wishing I had a pistol.

"Get on the shuttle, Volga."

She doesn't move. She looks at Victra for guidance. "Get on the shuttle. They won't fire through me," Victra says.

"You're a freelancer, Volga," the ArchGovernor calls. "So let me put a price on it. If you go to Fá, he leaves this planet and you save millions of lives. We may beat him if you refuse, but when Gold comes after that, Mars will fall in a day. Volga, my brother is gone. We need heroes."

That does it.

Volga straightens to her full height. I try to push her toward the shuttle, but she settles me with one hand. "Lyria," she says. "Lyria. Promise me you will take Ephraim to South Pacifica, and that you will find your family."

"Don't do this."

"I am not a slave. It is my choice."

"You can't. You don't—"

"Ephraim would," she says. "He did not raise me to be a bad woman. But he did not raise me to be good, either. Fá will bring me close, and he will pay for his evil." She smiles down at me. "Thank you for helping me. I have never had a friend so small be so big." She kisses me on the forehead and steps forward.

I watch from a tower on Victra's estate as the Obsidian ships disappear into the evening sky. They are said to be bound for the asteroid belt, but who can be certain? Pax joins me from below. I'm too disgusted with his Republic to look at him. Mars rose up for us against the Red Hand. Gamma rose up. At just the moment when I was beginning to believe in people, they sent Volga to hell.

"I remember the first time we met," Pax says after a while. "I was presumptuous and wounded you. I would like to ask your forgiveness, because I've done it again." He waits for me to turn. I don't.

"What did you do?"

"Victra came to me and asked some rather peculiar questions. Innocently, of course. What she asked, however, led me to believe you may have a . . . parasite . . . So, I hacked and read the doctors' reports on your physical."

"Your father just died, and you're going through my physical? What? Never seen a pair of tits before?"

He goes quiet. "I recently learned my mother has come back to life."

I glance at him. "The Sovereign's alive?"

He nods. "She's coming here and has ordered the Republic to summon its strength to Mars. So I believe I should be very industrious until she arrives. Especially in matters as curious as this."

"If you read the report, you know." I knock on my head. "Poor thing went and broke on me. Done's done. Her people can't figure anything, and don't know how to extract it without killing me. Still got the orb, though, and that's mine."

"Why would you want it extracted when all it wants is to be repaired?" he asks. "Isn't it giving you instructions?"

I don't answer. Even now, I feel the urges of the parasite. They heightened near the city. Maybe it's the communication towers. I feel an emotional ache to return home to someplace I've never been. But I know that's not me talking, because I don't have a home, and the feeling seems to be coming from a great distance. Then Pax says something I didn't include on the report.

"*O my mountain hyacinth, what shepherds trod upon you with clumsy, rustic foot? Now you are a broken seal: a scarlet stain upon the earth. Figmentum es.*"

I blink at him. "How did you—"

"So I was right." He smiles to himself. "I read everything and cross-reference latently. Including files only ten people have access to. My mother wanted me to be prepared, and I think I know how to help you. Her spymaster had . . . relevant information. Wouldn't you like to be someone who could make a difference, Lyria of Lagalos?" He looks up after the Obsidian fleet.

"Did Victra send you?"

"No. She wants to protect you from what you could be. But she only knows that Figment inherited the parasite, and gained . . . advantages from it. She has no idea what it really is, or where it comes from."

"And you do?"

"I have my suspicions."

I don't take the bait. "My brothers were in Heliopolis. Liam's the only family I have left."

"Family is more than just blood."

I look up after the ships. I helped those girls save themselves. I helped Victra. I helped Volga. The little man is right. I do want to make a difference.

"What if I told you that I could find Liam easier than you could, without leaving a computer? Would you do something for me?"

I squint at him. "Be more specific."

He pulls out a thin holoMap of the inner asteroid belt and hands it to me. "Have you ever heard of a city called Oculus?"

89

LYSANDER

Triumph of the Long Night

I STAND LOOKING OUT AT HELIOPOLIS from the *Lady Beatrice*. Cassius is alive. I do not know how, or why. But somehow he survived the Rim's perversion of justice. Diomedes must have had a hand in it. Was it for honor that he was spared? Or some nefarious purpose I cannot yet divine? I would ask the man, but he departed Mercury to prepare the Rim's entrance into the war long before Heliopolis's liberation. Pytha told me he searched the Ladon for ten days for his sister before departing with a heavy heart.

There is a war inside me. I would have given nearly anything to bring Cassius back from death. Anything except this. He died for the Rising. Now he fights with them.

He is my enemy. I cannot come to terms with it.

I believe I am the only one who knows Cassius's hand in the fiasco at the Mound. If Atalantia found out, the ramifications for me, for the Rim, would be calamitous.

Whatever pact Cassius made with the Rising earned the *Archimedes* a boon. Her new engines were faster than any the Core ships possessed. Her hull cloaked even more thoroughly than Atalantia's hunting corvettes. I sense Quicksilver's hand at work. Because of my old friend, Darrow, Harnassus, Telemanus, and the core of the Howlers managed to either hide on Mercury or slip out of its orbit.

Their army was not so fortunate.

Those who survived the Long Night, as they now call it, languish in camps south of the spaceport, pressed into labor to rebuild the planet they helped break. After seeing the ruins of Tyche and northern Helios, I know it will be no short affair.

Today is the first day since recapturing Heliopolis that the city does not rattle with sounds of construction. The cranes are quiet in the city sky today, but the streets bubble with noise. Rooftops along the Via Triumphia writhe with color and jubilation. Mercury has turned out for my Triumph.

"Are you there?" I ask the air. "Apollonius?"

No one replies.

"Whomever are you talking to?" Glirastes crows from the doorway.

"Just phantoms." Did he ever really exist in the desert? Did he follow me, or was it the imaginings of a sun-leached brain?

"You look as if you were bound for your own funeral," Glirastes says. My old friend sways up behind me to look out at the city.

"It may yet be."

"Oh, please."

"Do you have it?" He hands me the Dux pendant I had made for Rhone. "I am told there are crescents painted upon every street corner from the Hippodrome to the spaceport. You go too far."

Glirastes shrugs. Today he wears silver and white, the colors of my house. On his neck is a gold chain with a great pendant of an eye with a ruby iris. The Eye of the Society, the greatest award any civilian can receive. Octavia gave it to him long ago at the unveiling of the Water Colossus of Tyche.

Though Atalantia has not executed him as a traitor yet, neither has she gifted him with a pardon.

"You're projecting frustration, dear boy. Desist. *I* am the artist. If it is to be a diva duel, I'll match you cry for cry and then piss on your pillow and blame it on my dead ocelot, and you'll wonder if I'm insane, and I'll cackle, because *yes*. Yes, I am. And I can get away with anything."

"Atalantia still may kill you," I say. "Don't forget."

"If I were a betting man . . ."

"Which you are."

"Then I would wager all on the proposition that my head is more secure than yours, young Lune. After all, I am the best kind of hero— harmless. And you are the worst—young with a name."

I sigh and lean on the railing with him. "I suppose I did ask for theatrics."

"Yes, dear boy. And right now they're the only thing keeping you alive." That, and the furor for the Heir Returned that sweeps through Mercury and the legions.

I really don't mind it much at all, but I fear Grandmother's wisdom. Will Atalantia break me if she thinks I eclipse her in the mirror?

Ajax already tried. With my polite imprisonment in the *Lady Beatrice,* and Atalantia spurning my requests for an audience, I fear he is pouring poison in his aunt's ear. She will think I did this for my own glory, to supplant her. Did I?

Glirastes searches my face. "Kalindora was asking for you."

"I know."

"She said it was important."

I say nothing. Kalindora's wounds were mended by the medici, but not the poison Darrow's blade slipped into her bloodstream. She is dying. And I do not think I could do what I must were I to look her in the eye before the Triumph.

"Do you love her?" Glirastes asks.

I look at him. I left her on the ground to chase Darrow. What a hideous thing to do. "I never had the chance, but I believe I would."

"Then I will find a cure."

"You're not a medicus."

"No, but I am a genius."

Heavy boots clomp the tile. Rhone stands in the entry. I am appalled by his armor. It is as black as the space between stars. Purple bands cover the joints, and on the chest plate is a silver crescent moon inside the pyramid of the Society. "*Dominus,* the shuttle has arrived."

"Where did you get that uniform?" I ask. Rhone looks suddenly embarrassed.

"Their old gear is on Venus," Glirastes explains. "I had new uniforms made in Naran and shipped here for the occasion."

"You have to stop. The provocation . . ."

"Exists regardless of the accoutrement. I know. I know. You are not the Sovereign, nor do you campaign to be. But you are the last blood of Silenius. If Atalantia wants to kill you, she must kill your destiny before the eyes of the worlds."

Atlas au Raa waits at the Grimmus shuttle eyeing the ceremonial dress of my guards. It is a product of chance that he survived the Long Night.

When the power died, his cell went into lockdown. I hear the queue to kill him was a thousand men deep. How he must have smiled at them as they beat at the doors. Rhone says it took the man's Gorgons four hours to drill into the cell to free him.

He looks peculiar groomed and without his desert gear. His Fear Knight ceremonial armor is bone white and perversely etched with screaming children. Unlike most, he does not hide his true vocation behind gilded heraldic symbols. Yet there's an anxiousness to him here in civilization which I did not see in the desert, a sort of alienation from the very thing he sought to protect.

"Aren't you minorly overqualified for an escort?" I ask.

He eyes the Praetorians. "Aren't they minorly overdressed?"

"For a funeral?" I ask.

"Kalindora has several days yet," he says without pleasure. It says something about Kalindora that even a man like Atlas would look at his toes considering her death. "I know the poison. It is favored by the skuggi. Slow but thorough."

"We both know I wasn't speaking of Kalindora."

He eyes me with amusement. "Well, Lune, I suppose that depends entirely upon you."

Our shuttle arrives at the staging area outside the storm wall of Heliopolis. The triumphal arch that was commissioned in haste by Glirastes stands before the open gates. It is the most heterogenous gathering of any Triumph I can remember. Glirastes's servants mill together, gawping at the spectacle as they share cups of wine and receive instructions from the Copper planners. Hundreds of the loyalists who answered my call and risked their lives to save their city are here. Most are midColor, though many low are amongst them. I could not have designed a better message to the people gathered here. *You* saved your city. *You* walk with me. Behind them, sprawling out into the desert, are the hundreds of thousands of soldiers captured in Ajax's failed assault on Heliopolis. Their line snakes four kilometers long. Gold, Gray, Obsidian, and Blue drink down spirits passed out by Reds and Browns. Together they sing the ancient hymn Battlecry of the Lightbringer.

If only Aja could see this. If only my parents could.

A buzz goes through the assembly as I walk to my place at the honored fore with Glirastes and Rhone. The drunkest of the loyalists shout my name or begin to applaud. A Copper *actarius* bustles over to me with a huge datapad and a gaggle of assistants. She greets me with alacrity and guides me to my chariot. "It is made of the finest Mercurian onyx, *dominus*. A gift from the Dictator herself. It is incredibly light compared to most triumphal chariots, and with four of the Dictator's bucephelon geldings to pull, your charioteer will be—" I raise a hand. She stops mid-sentence.

"Of course she favors geldings," Rhone whispers.

I hide a smile.

"You expect a self-respecting Lunese Gold to ride in onyx like a Venusian sprite?" Glirastes replies. "Au Lune has brought his own chariot." Several Praetorians wheel it forward from one of Glirastes's shuttles.

"But the color coordination!" the *actarius* squeals before my Praetorians guide her away. Rhone stays to oversee the sunbloods' transfer to the white chariot Glirastes had made specially for the event.

Pytha watches me from amidst Glirastes's servants. They lower their heads as I approach. My friend held me in her arms for three whole minutes when Atalantia's men delivered her to the estate. She tilts down her eye shades at me.

"My liege," she says with a bow. Since I told her Cassius was alive, she has been distant, spending most of her time in Glirastes's gardens. "I've decided I'll be sticking around."

I'm stunned. It is not what I expected. "May I ask why?"

"You need me more than the old boy does." Her eyes dart about at the sycophants watching us. "Be a shame to see you survive the desert only to die in your sleep." She jerks her head. "Now get. The worlds await you, *my liege*."

I return to the chariot to see the horses ready to go. Rhone pats Blood of Empire on the neck and begs a word before I mount. His eyes focus on my chest. "I merely wanted to say, formally . . . We failed your family. More than once. I . . . I never thought I would see the Praetorian Guard reclaim its honor, my liege. I never thought I could reclaim my own. But you gave us the opportunity." His eyes find mine. "We will not fail you."

There's equal parts pride and humility in this man. I wish he knew for a single moment how high the legions hold him in esteem, but if he were capable of knowing, he would not be Rhone ti Flavinius. I worry for him, for what awaits at the end of this Triumph. I have seen how easily lives are spent.

I do not wish to spend him or the three hundred who survived the Ladon.

I put a hand on his shoulder. "I believe for some reason that our fates are entwined, Flavinius. I will need you today, tomorrow, and all the days after. Within my household, I grant you the title of Dux."

He blinks at me.

"Dux, my liege?"

"Are you fit for the task?" A Dux is an appointed right hand with unlimited *imperium* within a house. His word is my word. It is usually, but not always, reserved for Golds like Aja, who was my grandmother's Dux. It will honor him as he should be honored, and at the same time show the Grays of the legions how I reward loyalty.

I have the sneaking suspicion that as go the Grays, so go the legions. After all, they do outnumber my race a thousand to one. As Glirastes would say: "Never pass up the opportunity to shore up your foundation."

I pull the warrant of Dux from my pocket. He lifts his head and I seal the metal to his forehead. The skin burns as the hawk and crescent moon meld with his flesh and bone. He salutes with tears in his eyes and mounts his horse to follow my chariot.

I join Atlas on the chariot. He rides as my daggershadow, a place of honor, and trust. Two things he has not earned in my eyes. But Kalindora is too sick to stand where she ought. "He's a good man, Flavinius," he drawls. "Be a shame to waste him."

"Is that a warning?" I ask.

"Advice, rather." He glances at Glirastes on the horse next to Rhone's. "It seems you heed the wrong men."

"I know how to handle Atalantia."

"That would make you the first."

I lean past Atlas and press a DNA scanner on the side of the chariot. There's a *thrum* as the reinforced pulseShield flickers into place, distorting the world around, and encasing the entirety of the passenger compartment with enough shielding to take a direct hit from a *pilum* missile.

Atlas chuckles. "A promising start."

Trumpets signal the beginning of the Triumph. A blind White girl walks ahead of my chariot with a flaming torch. With an old White guiding her, she finds her way to the crimson curtain that hides us from the crowd. She pushes the torch into the wool. Flames lick upward. When they have consumed all but the topmost remnants of the curtain, my charioteer snaps the reins and the chariot rolls forward.

We are swallowed by noise. A street cleared of rubble bisects a sea of humanity for four kilometers until the street bends to the right. Millions roar on the ground, on the rooftops. Trumpets blast. Bells clatter on horses. The sound washes over me as we ride forward. An honor guard lines the parade route. Not Votum or Ash Legions.

I feel the chill of the past.

The Praetorians have returned. Thousands of purple-and-black-clad men and women stand with their rifles shouldered. I glance back at Rhone. He smiles and bellows. *"Praetorians!"*

"Ad lucem!"

"Lune!"

"INVICTUS!"

They have returned from their disbandment by the thousands.

The Fear Knight's voice is barely a whisper. "Poor choice, young man. Poor choice."

I miss the desert. It was simpler there.

The route is twelve kilometers long, exactly the length of Silenius's first Triumph on the Via Triumphia from Hyperion to the Citadel. After ten minutes, I am exhausted from sensory overload. Flowers cascade, children rush from the crowd to bedeck the honored with floral wreaths of mountain flowers. The Battlecry of the Lightbringer echoes through the city. Verse after drunken verse. Military ships hover with snipers to cover the rooftops for signs of terrorists or agitators. Despite the best efforts of Society forces to round up all the enemy at the spaceport, it's inevitable that thousands more will have melted into the city.

A Triumph in this climate is as good as a death sentence. And we all remember Darrow's fated day. But how could I refuse Atalantia?

Of course, there are snipers. Shots slam into the pulseShield over us, and send response teams swarming over rooftops. I almost pity the shooters. With each shot, I wonder if it is Darrow's men or Atalantia's or someone else's. Who knows?

The procession carries through the heart of the city and comes to a halt at the Mound of Votum. The statue of Helios still lies fallow in the sea.

High upon the steps of the great palace, Atalantia waits, surrounded by the Two Hundred heads of the prominent remaining houses. The brooding Falthe killers, vile Asmodeus au Carthii, and Cicero au Votum are all there. The Carthii tap their feet in resentment, as if they have better things to do. The Votum beam at me. I saved their city from extermination. And now they see a chance to escape from under Atalantia's thumb.

"Remember you are but a mortal," Atlas whispers into my ear.

I hop down from the chariot. "As are we all."

He frowns as I ascend the steps toward Atalantia. Ajax looms behind her amongst her officers and Olympic Knights.

She smiles in lovely fashion.

Behind that smile is so much malice. She wonders, just as the crowd and the Praetorians and the soldiers wonder, when we come face-to-face, will I kneel?

When I reach the top of the stairs, the crowd goes silent. Atalantia is in pure white. Her shoulder spikes are gold, her necklace that dreadful pet Hypatia, and two ornate gauntlets of gold cover either hand. Her gold razor is at her side, but I know she looks at the broken slingBlade I wear on my right hip. It is the envy of all the legions.

"Darling, I do believe you took me far too literally," she says with a sexual sigh as she looks at the left half of my face. "I said earn a scar, not become one."

"I left room for one more."

"From boy to man, and all it took was a little friction," she replies. "If I knew it was that easy, I could have made a man of you myself." She winks and draws her razor. "Shall we make it formal?"

I can practically hear the tension coiling in the parade behind me. I expected my stomach to ravel into knots, but I feel impossibly calm. "All men are not created equal." She draws the razor along the right side of my cheekbone, cutting deeper than necessary to give me my Peerless scar. "So you have proven." She does not return her razor to her hip, but watches my blood run along its edge. Ajax stares a hole through my head from amongst her officers.

"Look how they fawn over you," she whispers of the crowd. "Ten years you abandon them, and now they *drool* like inebriated sheep. Disgusting." She tilts her head at me. "It's funny, isn't it? How some questions continue to be asked even though they've been answered in every age. My favorite is one you're probably dwelling on right now. Is it better to be feared or loved?"

"We both know the answer to that."

Her teeth flash as she glances at Atlas several steps beneath me. "Don't we just?"

"I imagine it will be a sniper?" I ask.

"Oh, you did not fence half so well as a child. It's a dreadful Red pulled from the depths of their unholy horde. I thought about doing it myself," she replies. "But we've seen the value of martyrs, haven't we? And to think, the heir had returned, only for his head to disappear with the flash of a distant muzzle." She leans forward. "Good thing he has others to carry the flame in his name."

"And it will come when I put on the laurel," I say.

She coos. "Aren't you just the most precocious of creatures. Yet you came anyway."

"Could I have refused?"

"No, not really."

"There is an alternative to nepoticide," I say.

"No, I don't think there is, and you're not technically my nephew anyway."

I glance at Ajax. "From what I hear, the position is taken."

She laughs at my boldness. "I wished you no ill. But Ajax did what he did for me. Because he guards my heart's delight. You see, I will sit on the Morning Chair. I will become Sovereign. I will establish an empire. First there was Lune. Then there was Grimmus. Much as I love you, darling, my destiny will not be denied, not by those sneaky Moonies, not by Darrow or his piglet wife, not by you. But by all means, *beg*."

"I'd rather not."

"Then shall we proceed with your assassination?"

She motions for the White. I hold up a hand for her to stop. The crowd whispers behind us. The legions shift anxiously. Ajax can barely wait another moment for my blood.

With a smile made especially for Atalantia, I bend a knee. Ajax stiffens, and takes a half step forward before remembering how many watch. "All this, I did for you," I say, playing to her vanity.

Atalantia laughs. "Oh Jove, it is begging, then." She looks away. "How vile."

"All this, I did for you," I repeat. Her eyes become interested. This fits her understanding of the world. "When you looked at me on the *Anni-hilo,* you saw the boy who used to run with Ajax through the Palatine. All I've wanted since my return is to be a man in your eyes." Her suspicion heightens. "I don't want to be the Sovereign," I say with all honesty. "I have no desire for it. No claim on it. It was never meant to be hereditary. It was meant to go to the strongest. And if I tried to take it from you, it would tear Gold apart."

Her gold gauntlets clink together. "You apart, at any rate."

"I did not beat Darrow. You did. I just pushed the blade home." I glance at the Gold families behind her, ignoring Ajax. "The carrion birds circle us both. They seek division between us because it feeds their own delusions of ascendance. We must show them unity."

Her eyes narrow. "What are you proposing?"

"That Grimmus and Lune become indivisible, once and for all."

Her lips curl into a wary smile. She doesn't even glance back at Ajax. "Formally?"

"You are feared, I am loved, what better marriage could one hope for?" I ask. To save Heliopolis, I had to undermine her. To undermine her, I made an enemy of her and validated her suspicions and the poison Ajax and the Carthii have likely been putting in her ear. I do not love her as my parents loved each other, but duty outweighs my heart.

This is why I could not look Kalindora in the eye. I knew I would remember how she brought me the Praetorians in the desert. How she helped me when my face was a tattered ruin. But as she left me to the storm to save herself, so I must leave her behind.

"Two can be a very awkward number," Atalantia says carefully.

"Not so long as all know who kneels."

"What a matchmaker you've become. Rim and Core. Lune and Grimmus." She ponders the idea. "When the old milkbat sets the crown on your head, don't take my hand."

That's my answer, and her signal to whatever sniper lurks in the buildings. Whether it is death or life, I will not know until it has happened.

There are cheers of relief as we turn together toward the crowd, but the cheers are far too premature. Neither Ajax nor Atlas know what has happened, but down below, Rhone and Glirastes wait for the answer.

The White steps forward, her dark face as ancient as her tattered robes. Milky eyes watch me with inhuman distance. Her hands hold a green laurel crown. My heart thuds in my chest, forcing my vision into a tunnel.

"Son of Luna." I barely hear her voice for the blood in my ears. "Today you wear purple, as did the Etruscan kings of old. You join them in history. You join the men who broke the Empire of the Rising Sun. The women who dashed the Atlantic Alliance into the sea. You are a Conqueror. Accept this laurel as our proclamation of your glory."

She sets the laurel on my head. Atalantia smiles beside me. I lift my right hand, open as is the way, to grip invisible destiny. Atalantia does not seize it.

"Per Aspera . . ." I say.

". . . ad Astra!" roars the human sea of Heliopolis.

No bullet finds me. "Celebrate, my love," Atalantia whispers. "For you have lived before death. In the immortal words of Plautus: 'Let us celebrate the occasion with wine and sweet words.'"

The Triumph festivities extend well into the evening. The sound of rooftop parties and the debauched celebrations of the Core Golds within the Mound itself lap at me as I stand with a cup of wine atop the stairs and watch the Brown and Red crews sweep the flowers from the Via Triumphia.

I smell roses as Atalantia joins me from behind. Her gold gauntlet squeezes my shoulder. "Bored of the sycophants already, my love?" she asks. On her neck, Hypatia stirs to eye me before returning to her slumber. My Gray Praetorians in the shadows watch her Obsidian Ash Guard with their hands on their rifles.

We have not yet shared news of our pending union. Considering how much wine Ajax has downed, it would be violent timing. "As a boy, I always wondered how you put up with them," I say.

"And as a man?"

"I wonder how you put up with them."

"You would do wise to make friends. Many have spent their years climbing the ladders to heights upon which they might share wine with a man like the Heir of Silenius. If you spurn them, they will hate you."

"Let them hate me, provided they respect my conduct."

"I want to show you something." She extends a hand. I glance at my Praetorians. "I've held your life in my palm before. I haven't squeezed yet." She smiles innocently. "Don't you trust me, my love?"

I nod to my guards. "Tell Rhone to enjoy himself. I am with the Dictator."

Atalantia's shuttle flies us over the desert. As we ascend, I catch sight of two lines of impaled bodies that lead out of the city and into the desert.

"Reds and Golds," Atalantia says. "It stretches to the sea they stirred. The others can work, or join the line."

To react would be to lose respect in her eyes. To contradict would be to make her doubt my acceptance of her supremacy. So I remain silent.

Her shuttle takes us to the *Annihilo*. The Triumph has spread to its halls. Soldiers toast one another in mess halls, and give proclamations that soon the legion eagles will fly over Luna again. Atalantia leads me along by my hand.

Her meditation chamber has changed since my arrival. Gone is the garden, replaced by sleek black walls and a white floor. The mural of our family still hangs on the wall. The viewport looks down on drowned Tyche. The waters have receded, but the city is in ruins. Only the Water Colossus stands equal to its former glory.

Atalantia brings me before the viewport. "This is our victory," she says. "Three days from now, I would like for you to break ground and lead the restoration of Tyche personally. Glirastes will be your Master Maker. You will not want for funds. I intend to deliver most of your inheritance from my own coffers." Her largesse surprises me. "All the worlds will see that what the Slave King destroys, the Heir of Silenius will rebuild greater than before."

I examine her face for some sign of deception and find none. Just a deep, feline satisfaction. "Why?" I ask.

"Because my husband must be loved." She turns her body to me.

Her gold gauntlet strokes my burn and slides to cup my head. Her eyes flutter. Her tongue wets her lips as she pulls my mouth to hers. Her teeth glide along my bottom lip, nipping tenderly. She pulls back, sees something in my eyes to her satisfaction and then crushes my mouth against hers in hunger. Her tongue probes mine, and the heat of her body presses against me as a gauntlet strokes my groin. My blood quickens in guilt. I feel light and heavy as my hands explore the taut muscles of her back, sliding down and down, and down.

I pull away. "Ajax will—"

"Ajax is a puppy." She puts a finger to my lips as I try to protest. "On your back, love." I find myself obeying, watching in lust as she removes her jacket and clothes till she wears nothing but the snake and the gold gauntlets. She cuts off my pants with a small blade that emerges from a finger of the gauntlets. She takes me in her mouth, and I shudder in pleasure as she crawls up my body to put me inside her. She gives a little gasp, her mouth hovering just above mine, and then a devilish smile grows on her lips as she begins to grind back and forth between the drowned city and the mural of our dead family.

90

LYSANDER

The Love Knight

GLIRASTES HAS GIVEN KALINDORA a villa by the sea in which to die. If any doubted the honor of the Love Knight, one need only look at the quantity and worth of those friends who gathered to see her once more before she passes from this world. Despite the Triumph, the air is somber. I have felt dirty since I awoke with Atalantia. But not too dirty to reject her morning advances.

Kalindora's room is littered with tokens of affection, including two golden gauntlets from Atalantia. The same gauntlets she wore when we had sex in her meditation room just hours before. A patio ambles down to the waterline, where blue crabs skitter in the surf. It smells not at all like death.

Kalindora lies on a humble bed. There are no servants in the room, nor any sign of the immense wealth she inherited as the last eligible member of House San. She looks up at me with a wan smile as she sees the flowers I've brought. "Where did you find haemanthus?" she whispers.

"Glirastes knew of a hothouse in Naran that carried them," I say, wondering if, even after showering, I still smell of Atalantia.

"Of course you remembered." I hold them close so she can smell them. "Like home," she says with closed eyes. "Put them by the bed for me." She nods to the door. "Are they all still swarming?"

"About a hundred or so," I say of the well-wishers in the courtyard. "There's some good ones in there. Rhone came."

"I saw him. You gave him the Dux."

"Yes."

"No one deserves it more. He will guard you well. I only wish I did not have to leave." She looks so weak. Her remaining arm is wrapped in bandages. After Darrow's savagery, it is a wonder she did not lose it. His poison has leeched the color from her face. She is so pale. To remember her in the Palatine—young and so full of promise—and to see her now . . . it is almost too much. She was the future. Now she will be the past. It isn't right that she dies and all the sycophants and monsters get to live. "Don't look at me like that," she says.

"Like what?"

Her face tightens. "I should say congratulations on your betrothal, I think."

"It is a political affair, nothing more."

"You think so?" She knows. I feel wicked looking down at her. I should have left the Triumph. Come here instead. Her eyelashes flutter in pain as a spasm racks the left side of her face. A bit of drool works its way down her chin. I dab it off with my cloak. "Has Ajax called you out?"

"Not yet."

"He will."

"He won't risk Atalantia's displeasure."

"He will. Love may give one wings, but everything burns when it flies too close to the sun." She looks down at the sheets that cover her dying body. "It's funny. You always promise yourself you won't become a cliché. You won't be the person who yammers about their school years with old friends, trying to relive the glory. Then you do. You won't be the soldier who doesn't bother learning the names of the fresh troops because they won't be there tomorrow. Then you are. You won't give last-breath confessions, then you must." Her smile disappears. "Sit down."

I take the stool at her bedside.

"There are things you must know." She looks at the door and takes a small jammer from under her sheets. Her fingers suffer nerve damage and fumble with the controls, so I must help her. The noise outside the room disappears, and the sound of the sea can be heard no more.

"I have known Atalantia all my life," she says slowly. "I've seen her as a courtier, and a soldier. She has always had . . . something missing. She was here before you." She looks at the gauntlets. "Despite what I did—bringing the Praetorians for you—she held my hand and confessed that she believes you're her missing piece."

For a moment, I don't think she'll continue. Then, with a sigh, she forges on.

"Those were the happiest days for her, you know. When Octavia would let you alone from your lessons and Atalantia would take you to Hyperion. She does love you . . . in her way. She thought you were the saddest little boy. We all did." She touches my knee. "Don't take it as a slight. You saw too much to ever truly be a child. You never had a chance to be one, not really, and neither did she. Octavia was hard on her. She was hard on us all." She coughs and blood flecks her lips. She waits as I wipe it away. "She was like a poison."

I've never heard her utter so much as a single word against my grandmother.

"Octavia was a hard woman, but she made us what we are."

"She poisoned us."

"She was our Sovereign."

"Sovereign." She spits the word. "All my life I've served. Octavia, then Magnus, then Atalantia. Everyone sits on that stool and tells me I did it with such honor. And every time I hear it, I want to tear their tongues out."

She looks out at the sunlight as if it were the enemy.

"If you regret you are evil, it is still evil. I've killed old men in their beds. Children under the feet of their own horses, mothers who begged me to spare their unborn. All because I was a stupid girl who thought her father looked beautiful in his armor. When he retired, I begged to take his oath to my Sovereign. He wept that day. I never knew why till after he died.

"I thought his oath gave him purpose. He was too honorable to say it imprisoned him. And the day he found freedom, he saw his daughter enslaved." She swallows, reliving the horrors she's done in my family's name. "I only wanted to be useful."

I don't know what to say.

Her voice softens. " 'Get them while they're young,' she told Magnus once. 'Get them while they're young, then you've got them forever.' Honor, duty: it's all a lie. By the time you know better, you're too dirty to get out. Octavia poisoned me. She made me fear to be alone so much that I believed only the darkness would want me." Her hand trembles upward to touch my face. "Somehow she didn't poison you."

Her fingers feel right against my cheek. Not electric like Atalantia's, not rank with guilt, but like they've been missing all my life. I want them to stay forever. I feel safe here. Her touch is not maternal, nor is it hungry, but at this moment, I realize she does not see me as boy any longer, but as someone who understands the world as she does.

It is already too late.

"You were always good. You still are. They all thought you were dead, but I didn't. Say what you will of Virginia, she wouldn't let Darrow kill a boy. Sometimes, when I was in a shuttle and all I could hear were the engines, I would think of you. I would see you off somewhere by the sea. Living a true life, falling in love maybe." Her fingers leave my face. "When you stepped onto the *Annihilo*, it broke my heart."

"Why should me coming home break your heart?" I ask. "This is my family."

She stares at the door, forgetting me and the sea.

"I have to tell you something. Something that will make you hate me. Something I know will make you do what has to be done. But I'm afraid . . ."

I take her hand and surprise her by kissing it.

"Nothing you can say will make me hate you."

She swallows. "Your mother . . ."

I go cold. "What about my mother?"

"She was a Reformer. Did you know that?"

"No . . ." Did I? Do I?

"No. Of course you didn't. She . . . saw what Octavia was. How her grip was squeezing tighter and tighter till it would choke our world. She thought the burning of Rhea was an abomination. And she saw how slowly her mother was trying to corrupt you. So with Romulus's father, Revus, and Nero au Augustus, she planned a coup. Lysander, it wasn't Outriders or terrorists who killed your mother. It was Octavia who gave the order."

"How do you—"

"Because Atalantia and I planted the bomb on their shuttle."

I stare at her, unable to comprehend.

"You and Atalantia."

"Yes."

"You . . . were her closest friends."

"Yes. Though it broke my heart, I did as my Sovereign commanded." My hand slips away from hers.

The world shrinks to a very small, very quiet place as memories and all their weight fall upon me. All the times I sat with my grandmother, dined with her, flew with her, tried to impress her, and she sat there, the old crone, pretending she didn't send my father and my mother smoldering into the sea. All the times Atalantia took me to Heliopolis, held my hand at the opera, squeezed me between her sweating legs . . .

A dark glass slides over the world.

I will never be the same.

"Why can I not remember my mother's face?" I ask.

"Do you remember a chair?" I say nothing. "Octavia had many monstrous machines. But none so cruel as the chair. She called it Pandemonium. With it, she could . . . pervert the mind. When she discovered Anastasia's treason, she swore she would erase her from history. She did not succeed in that. But she did steal her from you. Lysander, after your mother died, you were inconsolable. She was a good mother. She loved you more than anything in the worlds. Octavia grew jealous. After two weeks in the chair, her work was done, and you didn't cry anymore."

I wish I did not believe it, but I do. What else could erase the face of a mother from the memory of her only son? I feel myself struggling to breathe. It was not enough to rob me of my childhood, not enough to rob me of my parents. She robbed me of the one thing that is mine. The one thing that no one should ever be able to take away.

"Did Aja know?"

"Know? She nearly broke her oath to Octavia over it. Atalantia didn't bat an eye. She is a monster. Yet I swore an oath to serve Magnus, and when he found he was dying, he made me swear an oath to her." Kalindora swallows. "I am a monster. I know that. I turned my back on the covenants of the Olympics, on my own heart. But I will not die a monster. I won't let her devour you. She *cannot* sit upon the Morning Chair. She must not. She would burn the worlds so long as the ashes kneel."

I stand, unable to look at Kalindora.

"I wasn't strong enough to make a stand. But when you came back . . . I knew it was time. That is why I called the Praetorians." She reaches for my hand. "*You* are the Sovereign, the last heir of Silenius, the last hope of Gold, and you are *good*. What are the chances? You can repair what

Darrow and Octavia broke. Make all this horror be for *something*. Fix what is broken in our people, Lysander. I know it won't be easy. And I am sorry I cannot be there to help you. Keep Rhone and Atlas close. He loved your father and mother too much for Octavia to ever tell him the truth, so she sent him to the Kuiper, thinking he would never return. He will protect you with his life."

I can't take any more. I head for the door.

"Do your duty!" she says. "Do your duty or the worlds will burn."

I leave the room, a hollow avatar of myself, and find Atalantia smiling at me from amidst the Golds, waiting to say farewell to the hero. She motions me to come to her, and I do. I smile and laugh beside my lover, the killer of my mother, and later that night as I sit across from her at supper as she gloats over the wreck her creatures have made of the Republic's Senate, and Darrow's heart. We receive word that Kalindora has died.

We attend the spectacle of her sunburial on the *Annihilo*. The honor guard of Praetorians, led by White ceremonial virgins, carries her casket to a burial gun set in the main hangar, which fires her toward the sun. Rhone stands at attention, Atalantia weeps, Atlas does not speak, Ajax wavers in rage, almost too drunk to stand as he glares at me with such hatred it is a wonder he does not call me out then and there as Atalantia gives the benediction with glassy eyes.

That night, she sends for me.

I have no choice but to go.

I find her weeping in her meditation chamber. I console her, and we stare at the mural of our family, at the blurred face of my mother, as Atalantia kisses my neck and whispers in my ear for me to take her pain away and take her to bed.

When she is done with me, she turns over to sleep, and I lie there staring at the ceiling feeling dead inside.

91

VIRGINIA

Salvation or Vengeance

"*D*EJAH THORIS, THIS IS PHOBOS COMMAND. *Your approach vector is prime. Welcome home, our Sovereign.*"

There is a small vault in my heart where certain words are guarded like fragile artifacts. *Family, home, love, son, husband, brother.* My enemies have cracked the vault open, ransacked it, and defecated on its floor.

Home. I don't recognize that word anymore. It has been violated. I have been violated.

A corner of my heart was always reserved for my twin, despite all his failings. Now, the existence of Lilath's Abomination eats at me. The Abomination has Sevro, Mercury has fallen, my husband is still missing with Cassius, and I have fled to Mars. It was the only choice; our failure to come together until too late robbed us of any alternatives.

I left Sevro and Clown and Pebble.

I left my husband to die.

It was Cassius Kavax sent for him. The man was found in his deep-space corvette. The communications equipment had been destroyed and his ship barely managed to limp back to Mars. The details of his escape from his Rim imprisonment are fuzzy at best. But it seems he was spared from execution by one of Romulus's sons. He was secluded in a private estate on Europa to be released when the war ended. He broke out, and stole his ship back to escape. After delivering the news to Kavax, he offered his service to the Republic.

I never thought I'd hear that in all my life.

I watch out the viewport of the *Dejah Thoris* as forty nimble corvettes form an honor lotus before our fleet and head back to the outer picket line. I don't deserve it. While Cassius plunged into the heart of the enemy for Darrow with only a small strike team, I had an armada and I ran away. It was the right choice. But those are the ones that age you.

Ahead, the blue ion tails of our honor guard await. Thirty crimson Ecliptic Guard torchShips guide us toward Mars's defensive sphere. First through roving patrols, then a ten-thousand-meter gulf followed by thickets of minefields and light cannon array, then the hunting grounds for attack squadrons of destroyers and torchShips, and finally into the realm of the apex predators—the defense platforms, the dreadnoughts and their battle groups.

Mars has rallied for its Sovereign.

"The loyal stand ready, ma'am," Holiday says from my shoulder.

"But will they be enough, Nakamura?"

She is not used to hearing doubt in my voice. Nor do I often allow it to intrude. But I feel a kinship with the commando that has deepened these last days as our shared dream crumbles around us. She took the news of Ephraim's death stoically, but I know it eats at her. Just as I may be free from the Abomination's grasp, but I am yet enslaved by the work undone, the enemies unvanquished, the friends unsaved, and the mistakes I made.

Could I have gone for Darrow? Or was the Rim waiting to close the trap and pin me against the Ash Armada?

As ever, Holiday senses my mood. "Ma'am, I know you'll think you were only one hundred meters away. Not gonna lie. That'll haunt you sure as a fold against a single comet bluff. But they taught in the *ludus* the surest path between two points ain't always the shortest."

I turn on her. "You think there's a chance we'll get Sevro back?"

She gives me a grim smile. "It's been done before."

"Victra found my son. I lost her husband. No amount of calculus will fix that arithmetic."

"Yet Victra did not sail on Luna. She respected your orders." She gives a curt nod out the viewport where Mars's moons are coming into sight. I step forward. The full might of the Julii fleet roves around the pincushion city moon of Phobos and the battle moon of Deimos. The *Pandora's* comforting mass is sorely missed, but Victra's personal fleet is larger even than my own. With her lost child, and Sevro in captivity, I feared she would run wild. Instead, her trade armada readies for war.

Light flares on the Julii-Sun Dockyard halo as we pass. Hundreds of new ships teem with expedited industry as the workers and automatons race against the doomsday clock. And then we are past the dockyard, and the planet itself looms before us.

On Mars, I was born and rode horses at Ishtar. On Mars, my eldest brother bled to death on the Agean cobbles before Karnus au Bellona, my mother jumped off a cliff, my father and best friend were killed by my twin. On Mars, I met my husband.

But only my son waits below.

It seems a lifetime ago that Darrow led my father's Rain against our planet. I watched the friction trails bloom from this very bridge. How simple the world seemed then in the tunnel of youth. Could I have really been only nineteen? Can it be wrong to feel nostalgic for a day of blood? Or was it the innocence I miss, before we truly knew what turned the world?

The melancholy is scored away by wrath as the nightside of the planet comes into view. Cimmeria is cloaked in darkness. The Obsidian I allowed to seize the continent in hopes they would call it home and defend it with their lives have ravaged it instead. The central cities of Nike, Phoenicia, and Olympia are dark. I believed in the Obsidians. I believed in Sefi. I was too optimistic. It only took a single man to topple her reign and unleash her people.

Now, the Obsidian army and fleet are gone, having disappeared mysteriously after Kieran gave Volga over to the father of Ragnar. It seems all this Volsung Fá wanted was Sefi's army and only half her stores of helium. The rest they left abandoned in containers on the tarmacs as casually as if the containers were filled with surplus dining utensils.

"What does Mars mean to you, Nakamura?" I ask.

The Terran hesitates. "Hope. And you, my liege?"

"War." I turn on a heel for the hangar.

As pitcrews prepare *Pride Two* for disembarkation, Kavax sits on the hangar floor. He stares out at Mars floating on the other side of the pulseField. Sophocles spools in his lap, watching his master with concern. I set a hand on Kavax's shoulder as I approach. He closes his eyes in a moment of warmth, then looks back at the planet.

"Daxo loved Mars because she never pretended to be a maiden," he says.

" 'The beautiful scarred,' he called her," I reply.

"The beautiful scarred." Kavax loses himself for a moment in the echo. "He loved South Pacifica, but he was born here, in Zephyria. Where I was born. When he was as high as my knee, I took him, as my father once took me, through the heartwood, and I showed him the tree that grew from the seed of my father's heart, and his before him. I showed him where mine would be planted. Where his would be planted beside his brother's." His voice trails away. Kavax was not able to recover Daxo's body. The Vox cremated the slain senators and mixed them into the sewers so they could not be collected by their kin and brought back to Mars. "Pardon me," he says, collecting himself, "sometimes the indignity . . . is more than I can bear."

Kavax is no longer the indestructible man who helped raise me. His decline started with Volga's grievous wound to his side, then Thraxa going missing, and finally Daxo's remains floating through the sewers of a moon Kavax hated. He despairs he will lose his remaining daughters, his wife, and his planet. He looks up at me with wet eyes. "Must it be here?" he asks.

"It must."

I offer a hand to help him rise.

With a heavy sigh, the weary family man kisses his pet on the brow, takes my hand, rises, and transforms once more into my father's enforcer—the warrior giant of House Telemanus. Even I feel inclined to shiver. But it is a tragedy to see any man sacrifice his nature for his vocation, much less a man I love so much. To be what we need, what I need, he must go to war again. All his life he waited to pass the reins to his children; now so few are left.

It is not how he thought it would be, but he endures.

He puts an arm around my shoulders. "There is evil in us, as there is good. But we do not regret our good as we do our evil. So we know what we are, my daughter. We know what we are." His voice fades, his conviction exhausted. So I pull him closer.

"We know what we are," I reply.

He hears the certainty in my voice and straightens to his full height and pulls away. "When your father would return to Mars, he would run the Iron Circle to prove who owned the planet."

"I am not my father."

"Not in all ways. That's been proved. But sometimes you need to show a little fang."

The Iron Circle is an old custom popularized by Silenius. To prove the depth of his dominion over a planet or moon, he would fly his shuttle without escort in a ring around it upon arrival, no matter the political tensions or adversaries at large on it: take your shot. It was his fucking planet. The custom has gotten quite a few powerful men killed— sometimes people just can't resist tossing a stone at Goliath—and fell out of practice with most households. To do it now, in the wake of the violence Mars has seen, despite the threats at large, is saying no more and no less to the worlds than "Look how big my cock is."

With my main shuttle, *Pride One*, in the hands of the Abomination, we leave the hangar of the *Dejah Thoris* in *Pride Two*. The war shuttle bucks as it descends through atmosphere without its escort of ripWings. Niobe's *Fox One* joins us starboard. As we perform the Iron Circle, I sit rolling my fingers along the rim of my husband's ring. Cassius sent it back to him, and Darrow gave it to me. He gave everything to me he could give. I wish I could let him know it was enough. Let Cassius have found him. Let me slide into bed with him one last time. Let me feel his warmth again.

I need him more now than ever. Mars needs him.

All the ships and gun batteries in the worlds don't make Mars seem safe without the Reaper. My officers in the cabin do their best not to look nervous as we pass over the Amazonian Sea toward war-torn Cimmeria to complete the Circle.

What will I say to my son when I see him? Pax is neither stupid nor helpless, especially not with Electra at his side. He would not have woken up every day praying it would finally be the day his mother would save him and make everything right in the world again. No. He would use game theory. He would work the models in his mind until he saw the reasons, the permutations, the tectonic plates in motion. Then he would scheme a way to help me as much as he could.

I wonder if Pax realizes yet that I raised him to be as much an ally as a son, and if he understands my guilt over that? If he knows could he still grasp how losing him was like losing a limb? How my love for him goes beyond logic, beyond explanation?

"Virginia . . ." Kavax whispers at the viewport. "Look."

I can't muster the energy. "Either someone shoots at us or doesn't," I say. "The Iron Circle was your idea."

"Just look."

Holiday tries to join Kavax at the viewport. When he won't move, she takes the next viewport down and shatters my officers' grim mood with a throaty laugh. "Ma'am. You'll wanna see this."

Frowning, I slide open my viewport shade and see a line of fire racing across the dark landscape east of Nike, another flaring west of Phoenicia, and yet another southeast of Olympia itself. To be so visible at this height, the lines must be nearly a hundred kilometers long.

As I watch, the lines of fire curve into the shape of a slingBlade.

Mars endures.

Despite the recent violence, no surface-fire licks upward at my ship during its passage around the planet. Even I didn't believe we'd complete the Iron Circle without incident. The mood of the officers has changed. The holoCans in the back of the shuttle rumble with beating drums and singing crowds in cities all across Mars. In my shame, it is not the response I would have expected. Mars's zealotry has always been reserved for my husband and his first wife. Kavax sits by the door, tapping his heels, eager to set foot on his home soil again. Holiday watches the holos with a look of love for the planet as it hails Lionheart and the Republic.

Clouds embrace the shuttle, and when they pull back, we see the Valles Marineris gashing the world with its glittering towers and the glowing green parks and forests that sprawl along the cityscape and crawl up its towering walls.

Millions of civilians line the rim of the great canyon. Hundreds of thousands of new recruits pour onto the grounds outside what was once my Institute but is now the Pegasus Legion barracks. As we approach Agea, the ground becomes lost beneath the shifting tides of humanity that gather in the parks and the courtyards and main avenues. The Via Triumphia is as clogged as it was on Mars's first Liberation Day. They are all holding something red above their heads.

My shuttle sets down between the Republic's Victory Obelisks that lead to the Lion Stairs. The sounds of the sea of humanity that fill the courtyard wash against the shuttle. I see now what they hold above their heads.

Their millions of clenched fists are dipped in red.

A great murmur seeps through the crowd as I descend the plank with Kavax and Holiday at my side. They grow silent enough I can hear my boots on the metal plank and then on the marble as I cross the Courtyard of Victories to the Lion Steps. Niobe joins us along with the centurions of Pegasus Legion, loyalist Skyhall and house naval captains, and the remaining three widows of Arcos. The drums along the courtyard boom from the labor of Red tribal drummers.

I ascend the steps quickly when I see my boy waiting at the top of them. He is real. He is alive. Just ten meters away. It is as if he has walked through a doorway and come out not as a man, but finally the blueprint of the man he will one day be. He's a hand taller, his cheeks shrunken, new scars on his face. But the real change is in his eyes. The look of childish wonder is gone forever. Now they hold the dullness that marks the passage into wisdom.

I wish I could wrap my boy in my arms and hold him until he became part of me again. I would garland him with kisses and apologies and promises. But we are at war, and I am the Sovereign, and so the mother must wait her turn.

Kavax sees my distress, and breaks from the procession to scoop my son up into his arms with a madman's laugh. He perches him on his shoulder and crows about the Boy Who Killed a TorchShip.

I approach the ArchGovernor. My husband's brother smiles up at me. As charismatic as Darrow, but without even a hint of his brother's violent temperament, Kieran was always demure in private and popular with the crowds. It looks right to see him with the Sword of the Rising on his hip. Behind him stand the Praetors of the Martian Legions, the Imperators of the Ecliptic Guard, and the old Sons of Ares commanders, all battle-hardened and clever, if a far cry from those we lost on Mercury.

Kieran clears his throat.

"My Sovereign." His voice floats over the crowd. "Luna has fallen. The Senate is dissolved. The ArchGovernors hold planetary *imperium*. According to the New Compact of the Republic, in this time of peril, I exercise my power to grant total *imperium* to my Sovereign." He pulls the Sword of the Rising from its sheath. It is the battered slingBlade of the slave once known as L17L6363, his brother. The very tool Darrow used in the mine of Lykos. Kieran passes it to me. It is heavier than I expected a Red could wield. I turn to the crowd beyond the obelisks and thrust the blade in the air.

"Hail libertas!" I bellow.

"Hail Reaper," echoes the crowd.

After I have received my debrief, I find Pax sitting with Holiday in the garden where my brother killed my father twelve years before. The blood has been washed from the stone, but I still see it there. Whatever Pax has told Holiday has her in tears. He presses something into her hand, and she surprises me by kissing his forehead. She salutes as she passes me. Scampering around the edge of the garden, Sophocles salutes her departure with a bark and weaves through my son's legs in delight to see him again.

My old memories of the garden disappear as my boy spots me. I feared he would greet me as I've seen him greet his father. With that cold, scolding remove. But my fears were unfounded. All pretense fails between us and we crash together in an embrace. That hollow his absence has made in me is filled. I feel as whole, as warm, as loved and proud as I did the day I first held him in my arms. How many times did my willpower almost break? How many times did I let myself imagine what sinister designs my enemies had in store for him? He has survived. As I pull back from him, I see his father's anger in his eyes. His mother's patience. His own animated curiosity. But he has changed.

The sounds of training razors clack through the seaside courtyard at Hippolyte. Victra curses loudly, then barks, "Again!"

Pax sees me hesitate to pass through the fighter's arch. I am afraid to see my old friend. He takes my hand and steers me clear of the training yard and together we approach the burial place of Ulysses. Grass has begun to grow over the small mound. The burial stone is wet with the morning rain. This could have been my son. Pax knows my mind and steps closer to me.

"You were right about Lyria of Lagalos," he says. "She did have virtue. Without her and Volga, it seems Victra would have been lost."

"I would like to see her again. Her brother was evacuated by the—"

"He's on the *Reynard*. I know. I've sent her away."

I look at him without surprise. "Where to?"

"After Ragnar's daughter, in a manner."

I don't understand. "She's just a girl."

He pauses. "Not anymore."

We look back to the grave, guilty for speaking over it. Sevro told me he was having a girl. It seems Victra was waiting to surprise even him. A boy at last, a chance to make up for his own father's absence.

"Mother wanted to give him a sundeath," Electra says. Always fleet of foot, she has grown quieter. I didn't hear her approach. Like Pax, she's grown since I last saw her. "But she knew Father would want to visit him when he gets back."

"Electra. Thank you for taking care of my son," I say.

Her narrow eyes flick to him. "That his story? No one likes liars, Pax." They flick back to me. They were always hard, but not like they are now. I can see that now all she wants is to grow up so she can kill. It's no longer cute.

"Whatever the Obsidian were feeding you worked. Look how tall you are."

She shrugs. "Maybe you're just smaller." She bows slightly for her Sovereign, then stalks away. Pax watches her go with a worried expression.

"She doesn't like waiting," Pax says.

I glance toward the training courtyard. "That makes two of us. Wait here."

I find Victra in the center of the courtyard, facing down three of her best knights. I silence my datapad before entering. Even at her peak, three prime opponents would have been one too many. Sweat lathers muscular arms swollen with welts. She trains like a woman possessed. Already the curves of motherhood burn away.

Practice razors whisper through the air as I walk in. A clutch of sixty Peerless stiffen and bow at my arrival. I whisper hello to Victra's youngest daughter, Selene, and the middle child, Calypso. When they hug me, I see their hands are bandaged from training. Sons of Ares practice martial arts along a bluff on Victra's estate.

Both parts of House Julii and Barca are preparing for total war.

In the square, Victra eliminates one of the knights with a neat thrust to his neck, and then receives a sideways slash to her shin and another to her temple from the fastest of the three. The head strike is a killing blow. Blood trickles down Victra's face. She stumbles, growls, returns to the center of the circle and shouts for them to go again. The knights stop and bow when they see me. Victra casts me an annoyed glance and stalks over to a towel to wipe the blood off her face. I join her there.

"Does Mars ride for Luna, *my Sovereign?*" she asks.

"You know we can't yet."

"Then what do you want?"

"Just to speak with—"

"And of what would we speak? Of how they nailed my son to a tree? Of how Ascomanni came like fucking monsters out of the ether? Of how you could have saved Darrow but didn't?"

"Victra . . ."

"Or maybe of how my husband is being tortured by that Abomination while you run back home to lick your wounds?" She glares down at me. "You might think I obeyed your orders, that I . . . molder here out of fidelity to your leadership. No. I am here because without reinforcements my fleet would be massacred by the Vox, much less if we ran afoul the Core." She sticks a finger in my chest. "You abandoned my husband. Our enemies move uncontested. So unless Mars is riding for Luna right now, fuck off."

She turns back to her practice.

The knights look away as I strip off my jacket and unbutton my tunic to my compression bra. "Victra." She turns. Her eyes trace the divots Lilath's hatchet left on my stomach and neck and the several hundred punctures the mob gave me on my flanks and arms, and a tension releases from her shoulders. Her love and hate are made of the same passion. "I tried," I whisper. "Truly." Her eyes search each one of the scars. I now have more than she does. Her heavy hand reaches to clutch my shoulder, and then the bigger woman pulls our foreheads together.

"If we cannot engineer salvation for our men, then vengeance will suffice," Victra says.

I nod against her.

My husband would have it no other way. No matter what they say, Darrow is not dead. He endured for me, and I did not arrive. I will endure now until he does. Victra will have her wrath till her dying breath. I will have my hope. I will make our family whole again.

There's a stirring in the courtyard from the knights. A defense pulse-

Shield warps the air of Hippolyte, and Pax rushes into the courtyard with his datapad in hand. By the look on his face, I know what it is.

"Earth has fallen," I whisper.

"Already?" Victra snarls.

"To whom?" I ask. "Rim or—"

"Both," he whispers distantly. "Cassius was right. Lune has bridged the divide."

92

LYSANDER

Graveyard of Tyrants

"ARE YOU CERTAIN YOU want me to leave you alone out here?"
Rhone's eyes search the warped horizon of the Ladon. Pytha
stands behind him before my personal shuttle. "Until the wedding, Ajax
will look for any opportunity . . ."

"Ajax is on Earth. It must be done."

"But, *dominus* . . ." He looks again at the feast. In the middle of the
desert, upon a great dune, two broad couches of purple silk and raw
nebulawood lie on either side of a long table weighed down by a feast to
feed twenty. "Are you certain this is safe?"

"I don't believe my guest would respect *safe*."

"Are you certain he will come?"

I look out at the desert. "The better question is if he is even real."

"What do you mean?"

"Never you mind. Come back for me in two hours," I say. "If I'm in
more than one piece, collect my remains and fire them into the sun." I
hand him a datadrop. "My will. Glirastes has a copy too."

Glirastes, who took the day to scout locations for a new library in
Pan, would be furious if he knew that I was out here in the desert instead
of overseeing the rebuilding of Tyche, but despite what he thinks, he
needn't know all my affairs.

After a hesitation, Rhone salutes and enters the shuttle. Pytha remains behind. "Do you know what you are doing?" she asks. "He is not
a sane man."

"Are you afraid of him, Pytha?"

"Yes."

"So is everyone." She understands as she remembers her advice in the fitting bay of the *Annihilo*. But she does not like it.

Soon the shuttle is out of sight. I sit on one of the couches and sip chilled wine. With Kalindora's revelations, my inner world is in shambles. But the strings of oaths, fidelity, and history that conspired to strangle me are cut. I know the rules now, Grandmother.

There are none.

At last, I feel free.

Here in the aftermath of the Battle of Mercury, I sense a great horizon of opportunity. The Free Legions are broken. Darrow is in flight. Luna is run by a madman. Mars trampled by Obsidians. Earth fallen to the Rim and the Society.

That sense of insignificance and guilt I permitted Cassius to instill within me has not disappeared, but remains in the back of my mind as a reminder of the fate one can accept if he lets the mercy of others define him. Darrow's mercy all those years ago, Cassius's mercy in serving as my protector, Kalindora's last testament—all of it rooted in some vain attempt to rekindle honor they long ago sacrificed for one reason or another.

The same honor Lorn preached, after painting a legend in blood. The same selfish honor Romulus preserved before abandoning his people at their most dire hour. The same honor that led to my engagement with Atalantia, and let me delude myself into thinking that honor was about personal sacrifice.

My grandmother was the most cunning person I ever met, but still she was wrong. She thought there was no place for honor in the world. I cannot agree completely. It was her cruelty that chipped away at the foundation of her power and poisoned all who served her.

It is Atalantia's cruelty which makes me prey to people like her. Is it honorable to kill her for my mother? Honorable to thrust us into civil war? Honorable to fulfill my pledge to submit to her every whim? Honorable to be trapped between her legs night after night so that Gold might have unity?

I think not.

I think, as with all things, honor is best appreciated in moderation. As is cruelty.

After all, there is no crime with a court.

The whine of gravBoots disturbs my silence. My guest arrives. He is no figment of my imagination. He is real, and dreadful. His Martian armor radiates heat in the sun until he steps into the cool provided by the pulseBubble I have prepared. He looks over the table from beneath the horns of his helm.

"A mirage of no finer quality has ever graced this wasted tomb to ambition and martial men," he declares through his helmet. *"Libations of Elysian red, Terran Bordeaux, Mercurian soletto. With gustatio of raw oysters, wine-steamed sow's udders, candied pecans, olives, azeroles, and medlars and jucellum. A mensae primae of walnut-and-herb-stuffed thrush and pachelbel, garlic venison, honey-drizzled wild boar stuffed with dried figs, garum sauce, and, do mine eyes deceive me?"*

His giant helmet inspects the centerpiece.

"A hare decorated with the wings of a peacock—no, 'tis but a noble pegasus! And, not to be forgotten, a mensae secundae of Lunese iced frizeé, tactun, chocolate pecans, and white pudding."

He looks up at me. That metal helmet impassive and dreadful.

"Now, this is a cena! A feast fit for a conqueror, a gourmand, a student of Apicius himself, and set before such grandeur." He waves at the desert. *"Yes, yes! I at last am paid the respect I am due."*

"If I have learned anything, it is that one does not simply summon the Minotaur," I reply. "If you would please do me the honor of joining me, I believe we have common interests to discuss."

He doffs his helmet and reclines on the couch. His face is that of an evil angel. Masculine, suspicious, amused, and tan from what I assume he considers his vacation in the desert. He peers under the table with mocking eyes. "Gelding or stallion, my goodman?"

"Were you not there when I was tortured?" I ask.

"I was mocking your union with the Fury, not your time with the Gorgons," he says. "How well I know the unlimited depths of her voracious appetites. Though I hear Ajax has filled the holes my absence has left. Now you seek to do the same." He grins. "But, yes, I was outside the cave, I waited, listening via my sophisticated drone hardware to the ministrations of the Fear Knight. I confess, I considered striking when you purloined him for your own purposes. Such opportunity seldom presents itself with that most dangerous game. But the show . . . oh, the show was far too interesting to interrupt. The flight across the desert will be held forever in amber in the hollows of my mind." He leans forward, very sincere. "I do apologize for claiming you lacked theatricality. It is always a pleasure to be wrong." He strokes his purple chest plate. The grapevines of his home in Thessalonica stretch to a horizon gilded with silver sunlight. "Alas, my armor died from that infernal electromagnetic pulse. I have yet to divine why its shielding failed to that device. I have many questions for Glirastes. Many questions to which I must have answers."

"They can wait. I confess, I am surprised to find that you did not go witness the attack on Earth. Most of your quarry were in play."

"My path to my quarry runs through this moment," he says. "And after the Ash Rain?" He looks offended. "After a cup of '21 Thessalonican Chianti, one does not rinse one's mouth with sangria. I saw thirty million men in mortal conflict. *Oh,* my need for violent theater is quite sated. In any matter, it was a pathetic affair. The Vox fleet gazed lazily from their perch above Luna as Atalantia feigned a retreat and led Earth's fleet straight into a Rim attack group. The only thing of interest would have been to see the son of Romulus lead his commandos to the surface to lower the shield generators. What a specimen is he. Perhaps we have a new lead on stage."

"Well, I hope you still have room for theater of a different sort," I say.

A great mechanical groan tears the sky, frightening the dishes and the sand of the dune into frantic palpitations. The sound rushes toward us in a flood of decibels till it seems that the torrent of it will swallow the dune. And then it is overhead and Apollonius grins. A great mass blocks the sky. Slowly, a thin wedge of blue elongates in the darkness as two vast legs of stone pass through the midday heat. They are but the lowermost extremities of the ancient mass born aloft by six heavy-cargo haulers. The haulers creep across the sky, and soon begin to lower their charge.

The statue is immense. Its face, riven by the ravages of desert storms and chipped by the target practice of Rising riflemen, sneers at us as if to say, *You think yourself worthy?*

The stone lips of my first Ancestor, Silenius au Lune, curl in contempt as he resumes his rightful place under the sun. The haulers release the towing bonds. The Sovereign sways. His stone feet sink into the sand. Dust from his recent grave shudders from his shoulders, nose, and the creases of his robe to form a billowing cloak. When the dust clears, he is still and solemn amongst his mighty fellows. Two-score Sovereigns stand in the desert to form a circle ten kilometers in circumference.

It is theater fit for the Minotaur. He claps his hands like a delighted, monstrous child.

"In each individual, one might find vanity, cruelty, pride, all or any of the excesses and deficiencies of the *Homo aureate,*" I say. "But together they stand for something more than their individual parts. Each was a custodian for his or her time, forming a chain of order that guided the human spirit from the dark ages of war through seven hundred years of expansion and growth. They erred in the end. Each small corruption spawning one more evolved and potent, until the natural evolution of that corruption induced decay and torpor, and the death of all empires: *aristocracy.* In that decay, how could they not expect a new predator to rise?"

"Darrow." Apollonius smiles. "My ultimate prey."

"Indeed. I will not be like them. In their shadow, I will create something greater, something stronger, something fairer. But it seems nothing fair is made by fairness."

"I care nothing for fairness, nor any of your pretentious-minded virtues," he declares with a wave of an armored hand. "They are for simpletons. No morality constrains my limitless mind, save my word. You know what I want, little paramour."

"Atalantia, Ajax, Atlas. And then Darrow."

"And the Mind's Eye," he says with hunger.

"I can give you that, and the rest, but I need something in return."

He leans his huge mass back. "Dare I ask? What must I sacrifice upon the altar for my heart's delight?"

"Nothing." His eyes narrow. "You have been mistreated, misunderstood, and betrayed. You have watched me suffer the same. We are alike, Apollonius. It seems a pity that we should be so alone." I lean back and sip my wine. "May I ask, do you care at all for rule?"

"It bores me, as does this conversation."

"I know how you will die, Apollonius."

"Ooo, much better. How?"

"You will die the apex predator of this world, having stained it with your legend and the blood of your foes. So that when, in old age, you sit beneath the sycamores of Thessalonica to die, you know you venture into the Void not burdened by your conquests, not fettered with responsibility of rule, but light as the ether that binds the heavens as you drink your Thessalonican red and reminisce of the enemies you cut to their knees."

He is enchanted. "And with whom will I reminisce?"

"The ally who asks for nothing but your blade and cunning mind, who takes the burden of rule from your shoulders and exempts you from fealty, from all oaths, save the one where you gave your word to stand beside him against the worlds."

I extend a hand. With a smile, he seizes it in his immense gauntlet. His eyes blaze with excitement.

"To the trembling of the worlds," he whispers.

Together, we gaze at the graveyard of tyrants. In the days before the Rising, the people of Mercury would come to this place and follow the statue's extended arms, which pointed at midnight to Luna to remind them where power truly resided.

When I found the statues, they lay fallow in the dirt, covered with war machines and blood. Their arms pointing in all directions. Now, no longer a bickering mass in a shared grave, they stand together again. They point together toward a small patch of the sky where at noon a distant sphere, appearing no larger than a small grain of sand, circles the sun. They point to remind my guest and all of Mercury our task is yet unfinished.

They point toward Mars.

ACKNOWLEDGMENTS

THIS ONE WAS A MENTAL TWISTER. Frankensteinian to the highest degree, it is the jigsaw sum of many false starts and wayward narratives. It came together only with the help of the legions of support shock troops over at my publisher, Del Rey. Ever since I published *Red Rising* with them in 2014, they've had my six (that's my back, for the jargon-weary), and moved mountains to make sure my books find new eyes. Without the platform they create, and the marketing efforts of David Moench, Emily Isayeff, and Julie Leung, this series would never have found so many of you at comic-cons, or its way onto the shelves of your local bookstores. All hail the propagandists of the Reaper!

To my editor, Tricia Narwani, thank you for all you've done on this book. Your contribution and patience cannot be overstated. For countless midnight editing sessions, enduring my nonsensical Apollonius soliloquies over the phone, for indefatigable cheer, sinister notes, bloodthirsty spirit, unflagging trust, and that childlike sense of joy you exude when I finally hit the right note—thank you. But most of all, thank you for believing in my vision for the book enough to give me the time to see that vision through. Somehow, we survived the Ladon!

A hearty thanks also goes out to the Del Rey and Penguin Random House command staff—Gina Centrello, Scott Shannon, and Keith Clayton. It's a hell of a thing to push back a publishing date once, much less twice. Yet you let me do it, simply because I said it'd be a better book if I had more time. Not once did I feel pressured by you to turn in an inferior product to meet a deadline—though I'm sure your nails are rather ragged from nervous biting. You gave me the time, the space, and the trust to make this book a bloody spectacle.

Thank you as well to Dennis Ambrose, who, with his copy edits, performed a last-minute miracle Gandalf himself would be proud of. I'm sorry I made up so many words. But somehow Tim Gerard Reynolds still makes them sound bloodydamn slick. And thank you to Alex Larned, who's cheerfully done all the unglamorous day-to-day work of keeping this project rolling and who gave me all those pesky-but-necessary notes on the details.

A shout across the void for Hannah Bowman, my literary agent. Without her, *Red Rising* would never have gotten past the slush pile, and more characters would certainly be alive. Thank you also to Havis Dawson. I promise those 6166s are on the way any day now. And to Jon Cassir, Dave Feldman, and Elizabeth Newman for their continued support even when I disappear for months at a time with only an Instagram post of my dog for explanation.

A Telemanus-sized round of applause for the cartographer Joel Daniel Phillips, who dreamed up the sigils for the Society with me at his parents' house in the woods nearly eight years ago. Having an artist of his stature bless this story with his maps and house sigils is a true gift. For those of you who do not know how very special Joel's art is, I suggest you take a look at JoelDanielPhillips.com. His latest work was inspiration for the devastation of Red Reach.

Certainly we can't forget the mentors. Thank you to my personal Lorn au Arcos, Terry Brooks, who chuckled when I went radio silent, accurately diagnosed my fears that I'd created a Phrygian Knot, and who, along with Judine, gave me a blessed moment of respite along the Oregon coast during my last kamikaze writing spree. And to my mentat (yeah that's a Dune deep cut), Jake Bloom, who gave me sturdy advice and solid ground to stand on amid the shifting tectonics of the film industry, and Ruth Bloom for many happy meals and happier conversations.

Thank you to my friends for bearing with my hermit habits, irrational stress, tunnel vision, and Swiss-cheese brain. I may not be entirely sane after writing this book, but any claim to partial sanity is owed in no small measure to you, and the ministrations of Lily Robinson. Lily, you, more than any other, bore the day-in, day-out weight of this book's writing. Thank you for the countless midday teas, the psychological counseling, the accidental wisdom, the purposeful wisdom, your utter forbearance, your acceptance of my weird mania, my inability to multitask or find my keys, and my obsession with this wonky world of hi-tech Romans and space Vikings.

Thank you to my parents, who read me stories before I could read. They bought me books and books and more books, and let me play in the forest, and took me to see *Star Wars,* and went to every sporting match I ever had, and put a roof over my head when I wrote *Red Rising* and those many books that came before. It's impossible to say how grateful I am to you two for giving me a foundation, and a sister as loyal as Blair. Blair, thank you for always being the attack dog at my side, for your work with the Sons of Ares, and for the management of my website with the good folks at Marca Global. You, my goodlady, would certainly be a Peerless Scarred.

To all my friends and co-conspirators in projects not yet revealed, thank you for your encouragement and for lifting my spirits in good times and bad. JC, JP, TH, TP, MM, CY, WR, EO, DO, BP, MB, HP, world ain't much without y'all in my life. Xoxo.

And last, but certainly not least, thank you to the Howlers and more casual readers who urged me to continue playing in this sandbox. Since I can remember, I've wanted to tell stories. You folks let me do that. The debt of gratitude I feel is immense. I hope you loved and loathed this story. I hope you read into the early morning, well past any reasonable hour, and that you come along with me for the conclusion of this little tale, and many more that are yet to be written.

PHOTO: © JOAN ALLEN

PIERCE BROWN is the #1 *New York Times* bestselling author of *Red Rising, Golden Son, Morning Star, Iron Gold,* and *Dark Age*. His work has been published in thirty-three languages and thirty-five territories. He lives in Los Angeles, where he is at work on his next novel.

piercebrownbooks.com
Facebook.com/PierceBrownAuthor
Twitter: @Pierce_Brown
Instagram: @PierceBrownOfficial

To inquire about booking Pierce Brown for a speaking engagement, please contact the Penguin Random House Speakers Bureau at speakers@penguinrandomhouse.com.